'TWO-EIGHT-SIX'

Two Men against Europe
One Woman between them

Clive Ashman

Pen-name of an artist, writer and
lawyer working in the English Lake District.
After his first novel, **MOSAIC,** here is in
some ways its sequel, in others a prelude.

Clive
Ashman

'TWO-EIGHT-SIX'

CLIVE ASHMAN

VOREDA BOOKS

First published by VOREDA BOOKS - 2012
Copyright © Clive Ashman 2012
Sales address: BCM Voreda Books, London WC1N 3XX
www.voredabooks.com

The moral right of the author to be identified as the author of this work has been asserted for the purposes of the **Copyright Designs & Patents Act 1988** and all other copyright and intellectual property rights applying. A **CIP Record** for this book is available from the **British Cataloguing in Publication Data Office**

ISBN 978-0-9556398-1-4

Printed & bound in Gt. Britain by **Biddles (MPG Books Group) Kings Lynn**

Title illustration, map & photo: **'TWO-EIGHT-SIX'**   ©The author
Rear cover illustrations: **'The Carausius Milestone'** ©The author
Cover design by: **www.liquiddesignonline.co.uk**

For Marcus and Joshua

My two students of political science

*"I like the feeling of fear. After a while
a man becomes an addict and has to have it"*

Count Alfonso de Portago, sportsman and racing driver
(1928 – 1957)

The Prologue

(Approaching Bologna, Italy: Sunday, 12th May 1957, am)

That famous Spanish sportsman and racing driver, Alfonso Antonio Vicente Eduardo Angel Blas Francisco de Borja Cabeza de Vaca y Leighton; Grandee of Spain; Count of Mejorada and of Pernia; Marquis de Moratalla; Marquis of Portago and Duke of Alagon; comes from a very long line of men used to getting their own way.

'*Fon*' as his closer friends call him, is also a millionaire. One famous playboy.

All of them the factors to make him intolerant of delay.

On this day of all days. An historic occasion. The day he finds himself lying third overall in this year's running of the famous '*Coppa Franco Mazotto*'.

Its Twenty-Fourth.

Italy's legendary road race, the *Mille Miglia*, with barely a hundred Roman miles of its eponymous thousand left to cover. His greatest chance to pass into legend. Tantalisingly close to a win, dangerously close to losing any place on the podium whatever.

All to play for.

So when, on the outskirts of Bologna, the half-cut driver of an overloaded gardener's van has the nerve to lumber out onto the route of Italia's finest motorsporting occasion and right into his path, despite warnings signalled by roadside crowds, De Portago gives him both barrels. Air horns at full blast.

Serve him right!

Maybe so, but when the FIAT's befuddled steersman finally registers a rear-view mirror full of main-beam headlight and red *carosserie* so close it is almost nudging him off, our unhappy gardener panics. His little beige *giardinetta* shimmying up the minor road as it is pushed along. He gets the message though, swerving back off the highway and straight into a field entrance to let the Count go howling by, his four-cam Ferrari's astonishing acceleration fed as much by fury as *benzina*.

Idiota!

It was not as if the fool could not have known what was going on today. The crowds, the carabinieri. Flags and banners

1

everywhere. Decorated umbrellas. The unique *'freccia rossa'* red-arrow symbol of the *Mille Miglia* writ large on every one. Plastered over houses and shops. Painted across roads, even onto churches. So how could anyone Italian have been so stupid? The roads may not have been officially closed but they are lined with people. Soldiers, police and public. Every one of them knowing that while the *Mille Miglia* is running there'll be sports and racing cars coming through here at speeds which *average* one hundred miles per hour. Nearly one hundred and sixty kilometres an hour.

Yes, average!

Idiota!

Born in London, brought up in Biarritz, flat in New York; *'Fon'* could swear in any language. Including Anglo-Saxon.

"*Fon*' forget him!" shouts Nelson, the Count's co-driver, above the engine's roar. Only just audible. "He's gone, he's finished! Calm down, Alfonso, we're nearly there. Just keep her on the island. Look after the car. Hold onto our place for Christ's sake!"

Good advice from a good friend.

Edmund "*Gunner*" Nelson and the Marquis make a good team on specialist road events like this one. Unless De Portago is off doing Formula One instead, smashing up *Grands Prix* single-seaters at exotic locations around the world. Last year, if proof were needed, they'd won the automotive Tour De France together. And wasn't this 42 year-old US Air Force veteran the guy getting De Portago into motorsport in the first place? On his keen encouragement. Wasn't it friend Edmund who had ruefully admitted to *'The New York Times'* in interview how often things like this would happen? How the aluminium nose cones on De Portago's circuit racers always came into the pits a little bit crumpled, from his naughty habit of nudging the opposition out of the way.

At one hundred and thirty miles an hour.

About the speed they were doing now as it happens. No, probably a lot more.

On a public, open road.

Hang on, he'd said. Not far to go. We're on the homeward run and our open-top Ferrari is running like a Swiss watch. A beautiful car, no doubt of that, if a bit dirty and travel-stained from all those miles she's covered in the race. Right across Italy but everything aboard still working fine. Engine and transmission a mechanical symphony in perfect motion: *"Bella macchina!"* As the crowds by each Time Control always comment to her crew.

Whose Bologna checkpoint is coming up fast on the rails.

Only the wear on his *'Englebert'* tyres giving Alfonso anything to worry about on the car, but by this stage in the event that was to be expected - for every competitor. Like they said at Rome. With no question of losing time or a place by stopping and changing them at the next Control, even if the rules allow it. So we'll rush in, Edmund get the time-card stamped, some petrol sloshed in the back if need be, then on our way again.

Anyway, Linda might be there.

Tyres and the car the same, like all my women. High on maintenance, always a source of worry. Taking a hammering on a long-distance event like this one, especially the tyres. Taking more every time I unleash the power that's pent-up inside this fabulous V12 engine. Stripping the rubber. Four-point-one litres coming in like a rush.

Linda in the Hotel Medina at Modena, four days ago. Visiting the factory to finalise the car.

But why did Enzo give me this car of all cars? An out-and-out racer instead of something more refined, like that GT tourer he let me practice in? He's so greedy for success, that's why. A clean sweep for his team. Hey, that man: *il commendatore* Enzo Ferrari. A genius at building cars, a devil for exploiting human weakness. A Ferrari win at all costs, his drivers expendable. Still grieving over last year's loss to illness of his one and only son, the beloved Dino, but never less than careless over other fathers' sons. The manipulative bastard. When that's all that matters, all he cares about: an Italian car, his car, in an Italian team. His *Scuderia* winning an Italian event. OK, maybe with a Spanish driver - it'll just about do. Yes, as a Latin, suppose I'm near enough.

Gotta' be better than some German in a kraut car, one of those bloody Mercedes. Or else driven by an Englishman, some Anglo-Saxon like the year-before-last. That Stirling-Bloody-Moss and his weirdly-bearded mate, with their crazy idea for a set of pace notes that unroll like toilet roll.

All the same, Enzo must have known. Still, it's his decision, he's the boss. But letting me loose in a big car like this vee-twelve, on an open-road event like this one, is surely asking for trouble - like some folk are saying. Hell, I'd even bent one in practice, dodging all the hay carts and cyclists. What a bloody shame, a beautiful thing broken. Like my marriage to Caroll, I suppose, the American showgirl who's lost to me now. Knowing it's a shame, but that life must go on.

Such a beautiful body but what a brutal thing, this Ferrari 355S - matching those we use at Le Mans. Except that's held on a closed circuit, unlike this road route. Brutal to drive, too. Bloody hard work. A man's car if ever there was one, with enough power under the bonnet to strip tarmac off a road surface, let alone the rubber and cord carcass off our bloody Belgian crossplies. Yes, those tyres. Those bloody '*Engelberts*'. No, they'll have to last to the finish. We've no time to be fannying about tonight, chopping and changing.

Look on the bright side, '*Fon*': tomorrow it will all be over and you'll be a free man. The race and your marriage both. Divorce papers coming through tomorrow.

Freedom at last.

Married at twenty to an older woman I hardly even knew. Oh Caroll, we managed two lovely children together, but hardly knew each other. Not even furniture in our apartment, let alone time. While I was too young, too handsome, and too rich to settle down - the world too full of pretty girls. So little time, so many women.

Tomorrow, Caroll, I'll be free and so will you. Except that I won't be, because already I'm torn. Torn between two more women. Between my darling Donna - with whom I've had a young son - and dating one of the most desirable women in the world: screen-idol Tyrone Power's gorgeous ex-wife, Linda Christian.

What a choice, eh? What a chance!

Can you believe it? Me and Linda Christian, a Hollywood star in her own right.

Never mind bad thoughts about bloody Enzo or Caroll, it's the nice idea of lovely Linda waiting for me that matters. Fair, fragile and fey. If I married her now, would that make me into a proper Christian? And could she, could anyone?

4

Sinner that I am.

Loyal Linda, who was there for me at Rome and might be waiting by the Bologna control too.

If I'm lucky. And when was I ever not?

Bologna, il Grosso. Bologna, the Fat: rich and comfortable.

Linda The Legs.

We're speeding towards them through her suburbs now, Carabinieri troopers in black Alfa Romeo saloons turning out to escort us through cheering crowds lining the route. No traffic on these city roads, the local police have seen to that. Barriers and road blocks. Trains stopped, level-crossings down.

Skittering sideways across polished cobble junctions past red lights on too little tread, under Pirelli, OM and SEAT banners lining the piazzas.

Middle-aged race officials in sports jackets and ties waving us down. Enzo there with his big nose and undertaker's scowl, watching over us while they do but saying nothing yet. And good old Luigi of our race-mechanics, smiling away. Kindly, unflappable and reassuring in his greasy overalls, unfastening the alloy fuel-filler cap before competing car five-three-one has even stopped rolling, tending to his baby:

"How's she running, Fon?"

"Fine, fine, she's perfect. Just the tyres getting a bit thin, Luigi. Not much tread."

"A change?"

"No, no, she's fine. There's no time. They'll last as far as we need to go...."

And then she appears.

Linda pushing forward through a friendly mob. Yes, she's really here! Leaning over the open cockpit on my side and into the scarlet car. Finding me filthy, but at least with the foresight to have slid my goggles up and over the peak of my crash-helmet.

Ready for her.

One succulent kiss, me stinking of petrol, engine-oil and sweat. The sweetness of her scent. The Ferrari's motor still running while I hold her tight for one priceless moment.

Heat and fumes.

"I love you..." she says, and I realise how much I do her. Far more than any of the others.

I really do.

5

"Taruffi's got axle trouble…" says Enzo in his raincoat "….you could make second!"

Bastard.

Back in the car, I gun the engine and we're away.

(At an undisclosed location in Britannia Inferior - c.300 A.D.)

No sooner here, friend, dust off the road still on your clothes, than already you ask me.

Where to begin?

Let's start with a weapon.

Like so many enemies - and even we Romans do now - those sea-peoples we lump together as *Saxones* prefer a longer, slashing sword for warfare on the land. Sometimes however, especially in close-combat between ships out at sea, they will confront us with an instrument of a different colour. A pretty little short-sword of their own design and making. That sweetly-savage thing they call a *seax*.

No doubt about it. An interesting and a deadly choice.

And in the right hands and context, offering an enthusiastic collector and practitioner like me their more interesting foil for my more usual choice of weapon. That anachronistic slice of shortened Spanish steel we Romans think our own.

The classic *gladius*.

Yes, the famous *gladius*, Rome's slim stabbing-sword. Everyone knows about them. But what can I say about the *seax*? Other than to remind you, I owned - well, captured - one once. As a youngster, prized from the hands of my first kill.

A gorgeous thing she was - taken from an ordinary, ugly man.

Did I say '*she*'?

Sharp, well-balanced and wieldy, but only the one edge. A curious defect in design more than made-up for by her balance of blade, beautiful appearance.

Intricately-decorated with incredible beasts laid down in gold wire to writhe all over her hilt. Dragons and fabulous birds, patterns and knots. Her whole pommel set on fire with red garnets as if to create that sleepless eye she tracks her bearer with. Elaborate filigree work burned into roseate stone at the hands of an unknown magician beyond the German Sea. Casting a spell to capture light forever, slowly enchain a keeper.

Where northern barbarians like that found rocks like these, I simply cannot imagine. Traded from half a world away, I shouldn't wonder. From some southern, sultry island as hot and fiery as their colour.

7

Yet these Saxon blades weren't always so hot in action – not if I remember them a'right. Bending too often and blunting too soon in battle for their unfortunate owners' good.

One reason for them getting a blow in first - why their cuts should always be given early, if to count at all. Yet if there are too many iconic artefacts turning out like that – as a surprising disappointment – then I should make it clearer. For all this nature to their type, those flaws and weaknesses were never present in mine. No, not in her, that special one I won so hard, have kept so long. Back then, where my explanations to you must also begin.

Concerning those great days whose events I have from the outset aimed to set truthfully down in my journal. Record them as they happened, in what by now seems only like history. Out of a time when the memory of how I came to confiscate this sentient weapon from its dying owner; from a thick-set, ragged man staggering about in the surf like he was her discarded messenger; remains so clear he might have been yesterday. His image to the forefront of my mind's eye, even today.

Conscience catches you unaware like that, doesn't it? Even now and after all these years, but where does it spring from? From our heart or our soul? The Underworld?

Who knows - though I can still see him now: job done.

Sagging at the knees then toppling face-forward into the rising waters of a British beach, the full length of a hot-forged Spanish blade from the Léon *fabricae* forced past his collar bone. My original Roman *gladius* sliding through him like glass. Yet if his last look of hurt surprise on its receipt was something I'll never forget; and if there was once a time when that grating feel on withdrawal could leave me sick for a week; by now it's become only work.

Bothers me but little.

No, since it seems you will press me.

My answer stays 'no'.

No, I cannot say I feel anything in these situations anymore. Not really; apart from that rush of blood in my head and heart whenever action calls. But, yes, that first time was special and never to be forgotten. Like my first time with a woman.

The first time I'd killed.

It wouldn't be the last.

If I knew I'd come to love that urgent feeling so much, then hate its rapid decline afterwards as the rush subsides, it was only those who knew me well - or once had loved me - who could mark how much and how fast the Fleet had changed me.

From the harmless youth who joined.

As in so much of this, an important development where I was last to realise. That, and the growing personality of a powerful weapon. My fabulous possession.

The sword I won as a prize which grew into a curse.

'She'.

Sit down my friend, take some wine, and let me tell you how it came about. Unearth some of the earliest entries in my journal towards your very purpose. Their musty explanations of what followed. For why it is you find me, salted away up here.

Hiding from it all.

9

(S236, approaching Brescia, Italy: Sunday, 12th May 1957, pm)

Near the wayside village of Giudizzolo in the administrative province of Mantua, located half way across Lombardia between its parent city and *'The Lioness of Italy'*, there is a popular spot at which to spectate on the famous Mille Miglia. An otherwise undistinguished point on the old Roman road running between the two cities, about one hundred kilometres south west of Brescia. Located near enough to the chequered finish-line that romantics may claim you can occasionally hear a faint cheering from her Viale Venezia, wafting on the wind.

The *cognoscenti* know this spot well, so there are a great many people who come back year after year to see the final act in this annual spectacle played out before them. Here in a festival atmosphere bolstered by sunshine. People walking, people cycling. Whole families come in tiny cars laden with wicker baskets, folding chairs and blankets, wanting to see the leading drivers making one last determined effort, their final assault on the leaderboard. From a peerless vantage spot where you can see such a long way across those featureless fields and dykes - towards where the competing cars first appear. Emerging sideways and all crossed-up in a cloud of rubber, tyres squealing from a testing series of curves before their drivers open up for the long, flat-out straight that follows.

Forza! Let her rip.

Almost the last chance in the whole race for the bigger, more powerful cars to reel in some of their lesser opponents; those smaller competitors who'd set off in front, hoping a nimbler handling through the bends might keep them ahead of the leading sharks, snapping at their heels.

By Giudizzolo they're definitely caught.

On an open plain that's seen so many important battles in the history of Italy: Roman against invading Carthaginians; Gauls, Goths and Huns. The victorious blow for her independence won by Garibaldi over the Austrians at Solferino in a terrible slaughter inspiring the formation of the Red Cross. Remembered today by the hilltop monument at San Martino di Battaglio, its mound and obelisk just about visible over flatlands to the north.

The S236 counts as a provincial road, but is wide for the amount of traffic normally carried. Because of the low-lying nature of the land it crosses, a deep v-shaped drainage ditch flanks each side, crossed at intervals by the occasional culverted bridge laid for farmers to access their fields. Concrete bollards are set at regular intervals into the kerbside to remind a driver from wandering off into these ditches, while beyond them run endless lines of poplars. Trees to frame a monotonous landscape hardly changed in two thousand years. A petrified forest spearing north to Brescia like the marching columns of a lost Roman legion, frozen in time.

Today, you won't need the bollards.

An almost continuous line of humanity marks out the road-edge beyond question; spectators' excited faces leaning-in to catch the first sight of an oncoming car in its cloud of dust, narrowing the track. There is a spiritual passion in Italy for this sport that's verging on the physical. Their sensation of it surely is, for they crowd in so near the track, these men, women and children, that they must feel its shockwave through the frame when the leading cars come through. Pass them at such unbelievable speeds. Blessed Maria, these top guys are hitting well over one hundred and fifty, sixty, or seventy miles per hour on the straight. Two-fifty kilometres showing on the dial. So fast you get a visceral tug in the gut when they go by, while what it must be like for the crews inside is hard to imagine.....

Mad or brave; or maybe both.

Forza!

After some minnows, first of the leaders through is Italy's own Piero Taruffi, the *'silver fox'* himself. Driving a red Ferrari 315 Sport for the Scuderia in what is his fiftieth year of life and fifteenth attempt at a Mille Miglia win. Starting the race from Brescia at five thirty-five a.m. - hence the number *'five-three-five'* on his bonnet - this wily Grands Prix racer has decided to take advantage of a rule-change from three years ago, allowing solo drivers.

Lighter and faster as a result, and knowing the route like his own soul, he hopes that this may finally be the year. His year of victory after all those years of trying....

Neat and tidy, Taruffi keeps the car in a straight line with no timewasting-fishtailing out of the bends, then rockets away down the straight. The crowd are euphoric at the sight of an Italian leader, cheering and waving flags, hats or handerkerchiefs as the Ferrari squats down on its rear suspension in front of them. Before tyres bite into tarmac and propel it smartly away.

When he's gone there is much chatter and shaking of heads in astonishment, but their collective pleasure at the demonstrated skill of a master, his total command of the car, starts to be spoilt when some hawkeye in the crowd speaks up to claim a whiff of oil-smoke from those twin exhausts, or others report a background rumble from his axle. Groups of younger men pontificate loudly on both these symptoms' potential as omen, and soon the tragic possibilities for their leader's retirement through mechanical failure, within sight of the Brescian hills, are being hotly debated along the whole crowd.

Needless to say, they are all wrong. The 315 can be heard long after it's gone, screaming over the plains like a fighter plane. Unstoppable.

Then it's the handsome Grands Prix star, Wolfgang Von Trips, going it alone in another 315S. Another red, works-team Ferrari; car *'five-three-two'* is part of an expected four-car steamroller of this year's event by *'il commendatore'* and his scarlet *Scuderia*. Calm and assured, there's little stylistically to choose over Taruffi. Just as tidy, but seemingly with time to give the crowd a cheery wave to accompany his quick dose of air-horns. And why not? Like them, *'Taffy'* Von Trips is in buoyant mood. Last year he crashed out at Pescara in the rain, but this year the sun is shining and he's going like a train. Reeling in Taruffi faster than his rival can the finish line.

The audience loves any response from a competitor and the closeness of their contest. Even those sitting rise to their feet on his symphonic call, waving him on to go faster. Old men, mothers and aunts forgetting their dignity in the excitement of the occasion. Why, for a moment, they even forget he's a German. What a sight!

In the gap before the next competitor, people settle a little again while cigarettes are passed round, bottles uncorked. Children play; conversations are resumed: *"Going by what we've had, it's going to be a great day's viewing. Still plenty of the top cars to come through yet..."*

The sudden arrival of Olivier Gendebien in a Ferrarri 250 GT *Scaglietti*, out of order, comes as a bit of a surprise and creates much hilarity when the Belgian war-hero misjudges his exit from the curves. Playing to the crowd with a bit of sideways action in his closed *Gran Turismo* car, a *berlinetta*. Their appreciation and flag-waving is all the stronger and his acceleration down the straight all the wilder, as if he can recoup vital seconds lost at the esses by keeping his accelerator pedal pressed flat to the floor until he's almost out of sight.

Next car in is *'five-three-one'* lying third.

Even at this distance, you can read the big white numbers across the red bonnet. Those who know their list of leaders from the hourly radio bulletins shout *"De Portago...355S"* and nod wisely. Another Ferrari. The *tifosi* lean in closer.

This should be good.

'Fon' takes his approach more like the last man than the first. A little bit sideways out the esses, the balding Engleberts banging across central reflectors in the roadway, its unforgiving catseyes, while he floors the throttle and gets her set up for the straight ahead. For a moment the Ferrari settles level as all that power goes down into the road, then it rockets away with its nose lifting towards the horizon.

A flat horizon that's approaching at ever-increasing speed.

Towards a Brescia almost in sight.

Enzo? I'll show him.

Driving this ferocious Ferrari is all about strength and feel, hauling on the big, wood-rimmed steering wheel to make it turn, but using the accelerator to steer her as well.

Man's work.

Judging when is best for sliding the ball-headed gear lever in through the oiled gate. Sensing how the car responds through the seat and the floor like a living thing, her whole chassis alive beneath him. So the bang from the front as the left-hand tyre explodes is felt more than heard, though he sees that side dip slightly in answer. Feels a sudden, unexpected lightness in the car and stiffness to her controls when it does. A sickening sensation in the guts he knows full well, the call-sign of an old friend.

Fear.

Here is no time for reason and logic. His reactions must be instinctive and they certainly are. Like that powerslide in the

Nassau Grand Prix last year, where he crashed at two-fifty kilometres an hour but made sure he missed the crowd.

The power is coming in from the back OK but he needs to steer her through the front. The Marquis de Portago is a strong man and his arms and shoulders give everything he has to correcting her course, but the burst front tyre collapses into a still-spinning, wire-braced wheel. Tucking cravenly under its rim and rapidly starting to shred as rubber and canvas becomes ground between its rounded steel edge and the tarmac.

He fights to keep the steering wheel and the car pointing straight ahead but cannot prevail. The change in attitude caused by the deflated tyre instantly drags her away from him, so that the red bonnet of *'five-three-one'* is pointing towards the left-hand verge. Almost unrestrained. Wrestle her as he may, there is no power in his body that can overcome the elemental physics taking over and now he has lost her altogether.

Linda!

His car heads at unabated speed for the low parapet of a culvert crossing and the glancing blow its stones greet her with immediately bends the metal steering-arm. Launching the out-of-control car like a missile over the gap between two concrete edge-markers and down into the adjoining ditch, scything down the bodies of at least five spectators on the way. Knocking down a telegraph pole which collapses pole-axed onto the roadway in a skein of wires. So many threads of life.

Onlookers are frozen in terror but the slaughter continues, for the car's speed on entry is so high that neither the jaws of the drainage ditch nor the concrete fangs of its edge-markers can keep her penned in. The red Ferrari bounces back out, facing completely backwards, spinning free from their maw to hurl itself across the full width of the road again onto the opposite side.

Smashing down another bollard and instantly reaping the lives of as many spectators along the right hand verge as she took on the left. Rolling over and over before coming to rest upside down in the water-filled ditch, both crew pinned dead beneath her.

Those rushing to the scene find the Marquis de Portago cut in half.

Torn.

Beyond them, it is the immediate silence which feels so shocking. No moans. No cries. No engine. Just the utter silence of the fields. The mangled wreck, bodies everywhere.

A wire wheel rotating slowly, under the shroud of a shredded tyre.

The wheel of fate.

Most cursed of sabbath days.

In the aftermath, that poignant photograph of him with Linda Christian at their last checkpoint together is syndicated around the world: *"Kiss of Death"* the papers call it. Her sweet and dainty wave caught in flickering black-and-white ciné. Almost immediately mournful from the moment given, that *"Last Salute"* newspaper editors dub it.

While Caroll McDaniel is left as his grieving widow, not a divorcee.

By a day.

"La Corse Della Morte" scream the Spanish papers – *"The Race of Death"*.

"BASTA!" say their Italian equivalents: *"ENOUGH!"*

Today at Corto Colomba there are twelve names inscribed on the pure white column standing tall amongst the trees in this melancholy place. Recording the names and lives of real men, women and children. Ten in fact, plus the crew of *'five-three-one'*. From so many families, all shattered forever by this single moment .

A catastrophe serving to kill off the Mille Miglia and the insane road-race it had been allowed to become. Why, three days later, their national government finally banned it or any other form of outright racing from being held on Italian roads again.

Inevitable result of a tragedy happening so long before I was born yet arguably still the source, the germ, for what became of us.

For what I will describe.

That crucible for change born belatedly out of its dust: one notorious European tragedy leading on to another. Years later, no less a catalyst all the same. Occurring indirectly not directly, via a revival and restoration.

A nostalgic renewal of old glories which, like all such attempts, can never fully match. Unsatisfactory in outcome, never feeling quite the same. As Bill and I came to find, that year we gained our entry on its prestigious modern successor.

Along with Xenobia.

"We have a small army, dispersed all over the whole globe. We have no North Sea naval base, no North Sea fleet, and no North Sea policy. Lastly, we stand in a highly dangerous economical position."

Erskine Childers, epilogue to: *'The Riddle of the Sands'* (1903)

I never forget the first time I saw the Admiral Carausius.

He was leaning with one arm propped to support him against the rough flint wall of one of our 'Saxon Shore' forts, down there on the East Coast. Sheltered from the biting wind off the sea and supping hot soup out a soldier's skillet.

That mad look in his eye, even then.

His little flotilla had been driven inshore for shelter by the weather, respite for everyone from harrying Saxon or Frankish raiders. His warships tied up among reeds, under the lee of the new fort's lowering towers; most of his men already off down into the village to see what meagre entertainment its wooden bothies might offer their kind.

"And who the hell are you?" he'd asked straightaway. Without even pretence at courtesy. Letting soup trickle down his curly, ginger beard as the ring of captains around him closed imperceptibly.

"Left Venta Icenorum this morning, sir" I responded, dodging the question. "Governor sent me over. Check on the scale of rendition. Everyone knows you're doing a great job out here. But questions are being asked."

"Venta, eh?" he almost spat. "They've got the wind up, yet again. Has the town council no faith in the Admiral Carausius?"

"You are our island's defender, you and our great fleet. There is no Saxon lands on our shores gets back to Frisia alive. Everyone knows that. But the corridor-whisperers of Londinium still say too many raiders get inland first. Too many towns are left burning and too much loot onto the black ships for their homeward trip, before the Classis Britannica intervenes."

"And this the contemptible allegation you rode all this way to share with me?"

"I am sorry, Admiral. People are not thinking clearly. They look for blame. Since the raids increased, there is panic in the countryside. I saw yesterday how the council of Venta has torn down the houses of free men, the wharves of merchants, to make rubble and space for a city wall. All the way round a shrunken city, cowering behind ramparts. We live in dangerous times and no man can be careless."

"So they sent you. A junior tribune of infantry come to lecture its defender and look in my holds, to see what riches of Britain the Admiral Carausius has saved for its people?"

"There have been complaints, sir. Petitions in the law courts. Claims for the recovery of goods. And the little question of taxes".

"Am I to risk my life and those of my men on the high seas every day, only to be persecuted by the procurator no sooner than we make port?"

"My lord's directions to me match those of the Emperor himself. Your fame spreads more widely than your modesty imagines."

"The Emperor whose commission I bear knows me as a faithful and loyal servant - unlike those jealous serpents coiling into his ear. Who is behind all this?"

"If anything, sir, a statue. The Goddess Diana. A detailed description in this sworn affidavit: *'Lifesize in green bronze with white enamelled eyes'*, it says. Diana as huntress - *'Diana of the Downlands'*....*'a Syrian bow in hand (gold) and balanced on one leg, cloak over her shoulder'*. Has the Admiral seen anything like her? Her lovely little pert behind spoilt by a repair-patch on the left buttock, where they did not cast her properly. Stolen by criminals from the country house of a senior official with friends in high places. A man of taste, less like than others to chalk his loss down to experience, say no more about it."

"I've not even checked our haul from the last little lot intercepted. But no-one's stopping you from coming down to the riverside, tribune, seeing what we've got."

"In that case, I'll come along and have a look, Admiral, if you will allow me".

"You've got your job to do, laddie, I've got mine".

He handed the skillet wordlessly to someone from the fort then turned to go without a backward glance. I followed him and his officers in single file down a muddy pathway bordering the ravine opening-up on the southern side of the fort rampart, where a stream runs down to the fen. Nature's emphasis to the defensive ditch our people had cut there, her extra protection for our fort.

Where the land bottomed-out below the shallow cliff we descended, the cliff topped by six, catapult-crowned towers and curtain walls of our stone fortress rising above, a path of laid-wicker was made to cross a field of reeds grown higher than your head. Beyond them, moored on sagging lines to a piled jetty driven into mud beside the navigable channel, we found that ill-assorted set of warships comprising half his fleet.

If the tide seemed low already, it was still going out rapidly. Only the odd floating tree-branch or reed-stalk sliding past for clue to how fast its silt-brown waters ebb.

All the vessels tied to this jetty had dropped well below its walkways, and I saw Carausius jump down onto the forward deck of his first in line. Like each in the queue behind, it seemed a plain but sturdy tub. Painted in a flat grey-green with no scrap of ornamentation anywhere, beyond that gold name tag and red-framed 'eye' painted each side of the bowsprit.

The necessary *oculus*, by which a ship may see a way for itself.

He called out loudly in a guttural tongue. One I did not recognise, certainly not Latin. Most of the crews were ashore by now but a white-bearded man in sea-green tunic and matching trousers answered the call, popping up from a hatch-cover in the centre of its deck. Carausius joined him in the hole then bobbed quickly out of sight. High above them both, his seven captains, the *trierarchi*, stood in a huddle on the jetty. Talking in low tones and scowling across at me with ill-disguised disapproval. Determined to keep up with their commander but affecting ignorance of scrutiny, I sat carefully down on the quayside for a moment. Letting my legs and fur-lined infantry sandals dangle briefly, before sliding awkwardly forward and downwards onto the ship's deck.

All the more embarrassing then to land so heavily like the land-lubber they knew me to be; that sword-harness of scarlet leather gifted by a favourite uncle riding up to tangle with a mooring stanchion. Something snapping as a result and me lucky to catch the scabbard before it fell into the river.

Fool!

It was only while disentangling myself from this troublesome fixture that I noticed what lay across the deck. Realised what formal display its tarred planking presented – as something of a shock. It need not have done - after all, killing was their daily business.

Laid out under a green tarpaulin in a neat line crossing the full width of the foredeck was a row of human bodies. Bare legs and blue feet protruding, skin the colour of Carrera marble. Stone dead and stiff, every man-jack of them. Soldiering was new to me then and so considerable a number of dead in one place not yet something to which I could claim much exposure. Nevertheless, I was determined to keep a proper self-control. Act like a man of experience, familiar with slaughter.

Even so, it gave no sight to dwell on. So I took my eyes away and looked instead to the open hatchway, finding the face of Carausius bright in the gloom of the hold, looking steadily across at me as if appraising my reaction.

"Frisians" he said. "Caught them hiding in a creek off Branodunum Roads. Waiting on the mud for a tide to lift them up, carry them off to sea and home. Sadly for them, it never arrived in time, while we did. "

"Why keep the bodies, Admiral? Their spirits will be restless. I thought you just heave them over the side?"

"Bounty, my boy, bounty. The governor promised us a special payment of two silver *denarii* for every dead pirate we bring in, but his bean-counters always demand proof for their ledgers. Miserable buggers that they are. Either way, it gives well-deserved bonus for my men, helps keep their books straight. Even if the governor's Mint pays us out in a coinage that's as silver as anchor-chain. No matter, if it only goes to line the purses of whores and innkeepers, why should we care? Fair exchange is no robbery, and what better use for Saxons?"

"What else lies there in the hold, if I may ask you, sir?"

"Step down and see for yourself, soldier. First good chance we've had since tying-up to take a look ourselves. It's usually a mixed bag".

"I am sorry if you think me distrustful, Admiral. Or even interfering. But questions are being asked and my lord sent me here for answers."

"I have nothing to hide. From you or from him. If we can trace the people some of this stuff was robbed from, and get it back to them, then so much the better."

"And if you can't?"

"*Res derelicta* – abandoned goods. Go to the Emperor, obviously".

21

"Obviously. *Via* the taxation authorities, I presume?"

"Whatever's best. Render unto Caesar. After all, this is an expensive war we are fighting. Aren't they all? Sailors, forts and ships cost money – while the public exchequer is stretched to the limit".

"Which is why the governor sent me".

"Like I said soldier, you've got your job, I've got mine".

The first thing they threw out onto the deck from the hold was a curved piece of wood with projecting inserts. I picked it up, then threw it down in fearful disgust when I realised what it must be. Fearing the evil eye.

"Superstitious heathen!" he had said, laughing coldly as it clattered to ground from my fingers.

Just about recognisable as a model of an open boat, three stick-like figures of bleached wood fastened to it by a peg arrangement to represent its crew. Crude holes drilled for their eye sockets were filled with a black, shiny material - Whitby jet or such-like. A similarly-mounted projection for the phallic instrument. Who knows what dreadful gods or grotesque rituals it is meant to invoke?

Earthly powers are one thing but the primitivism in this votive Saxon relic spooked me more than any tax-gatherer.

"Nothing for the procurator there, their cocks have broken off!" he scoffed, and spat upon the decking where it lay abandoned.

"I wouldn't joke about that particular department, Admiral. Did not Emperor Diocletian add torture to their powers of enquiry?"

Carausius seemed unconcerned about the potential reach of government. He pointed to the relic instead:

"Human sacrifice" he said. "That's what this object is really about. Its value and its message. Let me offer you a piece of advice, young fella': don't find yourself their prisoner. One in three go over the side, sacrificed to secure a homecoming. And drowning's hardly the quickest death. Not the one I'd choose."

"And you, Admiral, can you swim?"

He laughed, probably amused by an innocent impertinence I realise probably struck him as child-like. High contrast to that fear and discipline I saw him wring later from senior subordinates in the field.

"Oh, no! Not me. There's no need. An astrologer, the Sybil in the Temple of Fortuna outside Londinium walls, reassured me on that score. Her horoscope very specific – I'll never die at sea. Born lucky. Why else do you think so many volunteer to sail with me?"

"I understand that, my lord, but may I see what other treasures you have down there?"

With hindsight, I remain amazed at how familiar he let me be that day. As if it entertained him in some fatherly way. I also think it was that sense of a kindly indulgence towards the next generation, when away from the battlefield, which made me warm to him for all his peasant ways.

"Take a look, my boy, it makes no odds to me!" He lobbed a heavy bundle wrapped in sailcloth onto the deck. It landed with a thump. I unfurled it carefully but its contents fell loose onto the deck, where some rolled away, glittering.

"Chopped-up silverware" he said. "You can still see the shape and outlines of figures."

Sorting through the pile showed he was right. Plates, goblets and trays which once took time-served craftsmen many weeks of patient skill to form into the finest dinner service, embossed with dancing fauns, were now torn into random pieces.

Carausius climbed out of the hatchway to join me. Bent down to the deck and picked up a jagged triangle from someone's erstwhile treasure. "Once this is done, you're hard put to say who it once belonged to. To the pirate, these objects mean nothing. No appreciation of art - even less than an *ignoramus* like me. Its only value to them is bullion. Melted down into ingots of silver scrap. Easier to carry back to their ships."

"And *'The Diana of the Downlands'*?"

"Hmm, yes. We'll certainly have a look. I'll check our other vessels. But don't hold your breath, my son. She probably went straight into the fire. Bronze is too valuable a metal for barbarians for them to leave a beauty like her unmolested. Why precious little statuary gets recovered intact these days, I'm afraid."

Then he was on the move again. Gone before I could even reply. Swarming surprisingly quickly for a man of advancing years and portly stature up the climbing-ropes hanging down the jetty, strolling off along the top. His captains falling-in behind him like shadows as he moves across to the next ship, a grey-green painted coaster. The humped shape of a bolt-firing catapult distinctive in her bows despite thick wrappings of greasy oilcloth to protect its mechanism against salt and spray.

By the time I caught up with him again, he was down on her main deck. Surrounded by officers and talking to a new name: a long-faced man with prominent, jutting chin. Eyebrows like caterpillars, brown hair, and a thin beard cut tight to the jawline. Wearing a cream woollen shirt over leather breeches, its shoulders embossed in blue with the lighthouse badge and abbreviated initials of our resurrected British Fleet: 'CLBR' – *Classis Britannica*.

The first time I'd seen its uniform.

His dainty shoes were those you would reserve for the cleaner streets of Londinium, not the slippery decks of a galley out on the German Ocean. Not one hobnail to scrape. If this character were armed, it was only with a short dagger in an enamelled scabbard. What I straightaway judged his sharpest weapon was that brass-bound accounts book where he wrote on wax with a bronze stylus. Spread out on sacking across the deck before him, with scales for weighing, were the seizures and prizes from their latest patrol. Hoards of weaponry, much silver scrap, and a great many pieces of lead sheet in every size.

No bronze.

At least they made a proper inventory.

He looked up at me crossly when I landed heavily on the deck, then looked quizzically across at Carausius. As if to say "*Who is this fellow, and is he trouble?*"

The Admiral grinning back at him:

"Not finished your accounts yet, Allectus? Let me introduce our young visitor – or would if I knew his name. Seems reluctant to say. A bashful boy, a tribune of flat-footed infantry sent onto the east coast by a governor more interested in our book-keeping than how we defend the Empire's seaways. For all that, I mark him down as a lad of potential, a pupil keen to learn. A student of maritime law we might transform into a proper son of the sea. If ever we took him on...."

"A son of the sea, eh?" said Allectus, his brown moustachio flaring. "What, great Neptune's child? Then I must call you '*Triton*'...." he purred across at me.

I shrank back: "Don't worry, I carry my commission with me...can identify myself."

24

"Fear not, young friend, we take the insignia on your armour as good enough proof...." said Carausius, laughing like they did not. "Besides, I imagined your boss sending someone here, days before you were sent. Get a result for *'Squint-gob'* on this job and I think you can expect a promising career in government. If that's what you really want. Until then you're still just a soldier. And while you are, let me ask: ever fought from ships before?"

I shook my head. I'd never yet fought anywhere, but would never admit that to anyone – as if it wasn't obvious anyway.

"No, didn't think so. A pity.... vital part of a military education. Never mind, my lad, I'm sure you'll learn. Knowing potential when I see it. Get chance too, sooner than you think. Like the old curse says, we live in interesting times. Modern soldiering must adapt to new enemies, and there'll soon be more than enough fighting to go round for everyone. But first, you must find your Diana. And we must help you try......"

"His Diana?" said Allectus looking up again from wax tablets, interest suddenly piqued despite himself. Putting down his pen.

"Stands on one leg, holding a golden bow and arrow. Lovely arse, done in green bronze. Check your lists again, Allectus. Have we recovered anybody like hers out the bowels of those filthy ships we captured and burnt this week? Or maybe less recently?"

"A statue?"

"Correct in one, my chancellor. Bronze, he says. Top quality. Property of a rich man. The pen-pushers sending young *'Triton'* out here seem to think we gentlemen of the Fleet can't be trusted to return stolen goods. An affront to the honour of the *Classis*. Why it would be good to produce this little madam, if only to prove them wrong."

"I'm sorry not to be more helpful, Admiral. We would certainly remember someone, or something, so unusual as her. But definitely not. Nothing like her to be found around here, free on board. The governor's boy can be sure of that."

There were seven ships of different size tied-up there under the coastal fort that wild April day on the marsh: the 'M' squadron. Absent a standing fleet, this eccentric patrol of purpose-built galleys, ropey trawlers and portly merchantmen pressed into common service together during the Emergency, probably made up half the *Classis*.

Surprisingly, Carausius and his surly captains let me go on board to inspect each and every one of them. Inch by inch, yawning holds and all. While what I found there is exactly what he and Allectus said I would, even before they completed their own inventory. Namely nothing at all, save the kind of butchered metal scrap only barbarians value.

And when I looked for myself within what narrow living-spaces were left them below; among the sea chests or food and weapon stores, the personal effects and rolled bedding; between those fighting decks and rowing benches his men sluice-down with leather bucket from all stain of Saxon blood; I arrived at the same conclusion:

That there really was nowhere left. Nowhere anyone could hide a life-sized bronze with bow and arrow: *'The Diana of the Downlands'*.

So that, when it was done, it was natural I should be left believing the pair of them; this famous fleet commander and his creepy quartermaster. When they said their little squadron had never in all its patrolling recovered anything to match the rare green beauty I'd been sent out there to find, but none of them had seen. How I knew I could promise my master with confidence that he and I were not gulled in that conclusion by anyone. And nor had anyone tried. Convincing me of this last was why, on the admiral's insistence and with his support, our grand finale was to make an equally-thorough examination of the fort itself. Of that lonely seaward garrison official Itineraries still label as *'Garrianonum'* – whatever remains of it now.

My report closing: *"He received me courteously and gave your enquiry every practical assistance. The Admiral facilitated a comprehensive tour, made together, of every wooden barrack or stable block in the fort. Where I will report his popularity and authority with the men seems high, his discipline strong. Troops of light cavalry standing quickly to attention as we passed-by; with every conceivable hiding place for a figure of this size carefully examined between us. Which is why I can reliably assert, My Lord, that had the missing statue been present there, then I am certain we would have found it."*

26

While this authentic extract from another copy, one kept back for that journal I show to you now, is useful for its illustration of another thing. Of how most people at the time thought it appropriate to refer to Carausius: as an *'Admiral.* (Whatever other titles came along later). Though nowadays it's more often the younger generation who need to ask me why.

Our response to his ingrained seafaring background the obvious answer. To where he made his name - out at sea. A man ordinary and undistinguished in appearance but whose extraordinary naval skills had prompted the emperor to make this appointment of him. To his latest operational role, one for which the questioned title provides my convenient shorthand for a wide brief and those combined forces coming with its duties. The military units he so ably deployed by land or sea that their limited number might prevail against more numerous foes.

However, and since my critics may expect a private memoir to double as reliable history, then I should still strive for accuracy over detail points like these. Why, friend, and whether it be over names, dates or formal titles, you can be sure to find this journal attempting my best; its success your own affair.

And one point I can be confident most British readers old enough to remember agreeing over, is the critical importance for their safety of this strategic command which the Admiral Carausius by our Emperor's Grace then held. More than whatever we called him. Entrusted as he was with as vital a role out at sea as any previously exercised on land, this Menapian peasant charged with our fleet became counted among the most-senior military appointments in the Western Empire.

A popular hero, in short.

And if the wild cheering charting his progress down the public street could tell you what most people felt about him, then, it did nothing to prevent those pedants staffing our Governor's Office from criticising my report for not classifying its subject as a *'General'.* No matter if, on the private remembrance of his friends, he remains to this day their fondly-remembered *'Admiral'.* (While how his enemies recall him is a separate issue we may get onto later).

And if none of these semantics matter anymore, all I can say now, and however my guide that day deserved classification, the personal tour of a remote outpost which he gave me as its commanding officer still ranks among the few - and the most remarkable – courtesies of my junior service. Why I appreciated it all the more, resolved never to forget him. Even if, behind that easy smile and rough-cast friendliness, lay a cunning, manipulative man. As needs must, to survive at his level.

Whatever his motive, this experience also gave me something else – my first whiff of power. Its unique scent. That unexpected inkling to youth of what rare glories are theirs to savour, these generals of Rome. Whole legions and fleets to command, cohorts and warships parading at their beck and call.

Like I say, if this was the flavour of his world and its responsibilities, then it left me the more impressed when nothing seemed too much trouble for an admiral aiding the minion that I was in mine. If this was the measure of his generosity, then I was schooled enough in Roman social *mores* to understand what matching courtesies it would require of me. How a favour done must be met with favour: favours and fealty. He might have been no native-born Roman, but the great Carausius wasn't stupid. An experienced operator who'd learnt the ropes of Roman political life before I was born, quite as well as coastal navigation. So yes, a clever man for all his ways, doubtless imagining already what level of reciprocation was appropriate to his indulgence. That positive report on negative discoveries he knew I would send Londinium about him, before I'd even penned it.

'Patronised' you say? Not really, not how I saw it then. Just taking this unique chance to return his elevated compliment with the generous reply it surely deserved. *"...As authorised representative to his civil 'Brother', the Governor of Upper Britain"* how I pretentiously put it.

"Clear evidence of patronage..." you comment *"...voiced by his newest client?"*

Quite possibly, but only in the public interest. Because - sad to say but true - there was then and remains now, an obvious ugly tear across the wearing weft of our fabricated state. If its rip leaves the brothers of our military and civil powers no longer seeing eye-to-eye, hardly even speaking, then I was naïve enough to imagine myself a new-and-coming man to bridge their filial gap. Unilaterally, and through no better medium than my one, ingratiating report. Where I would stress how helpful, co-operative and positively-willing this senior naval commander showed himself towards my civil master's serious mission of enquiry. (As represented through myself).

What a self-important young fool I must have presented as, to anyone who met me.

Looking back, it seems ridiculous. All those exhausted soldiers and marines out there on the coast, up to their necks in an active theatre of war. Tired and filthy, just back from patrol.

And there I was, turning-up on this mission of my distant bosses. Pompously demanding these soldiers' last remaining reserves of human effort be diverted towards a missing piece of art. Towards confirming the one recurring negative which was all we ever established.

That wherever else in the fort we and the weary men of Carausius looked and searched, or she another day appeared, the lost 'Diana' really wasn't here.

"Are Britons here? They go abroad, feel calls
To trace old battlefields and crumbling walls..."

(Character of Mephistopheles, in Goethe's '*Faust*')

- 1 -

Bill was flying straight in to the *Aeroporto di Malpensa* from Newcastle. My job was simple: to be ready, waiting, and on time when he got there. With the race car:

'*Xenobia*'.

He'd had a criminal trial running at the Crown Court, down on the Quayside. Bill for the Crown. Only the sheer bloody-minded indecision of a West Road jury reluctant on principle to convict anyone of anything that involved the former Northumbria Police, however it was re-branded, was preventing him leaving until the last minute.

Time was running out. At one point I thought we'd have to call the whole thing off. From the chaos of an Italian motorway service station outside Milan, I phoned his mobile in the barristers' robing-room at the Crown Court with that suggestion in mind:

"If they can't agree and get sent to consider their verdict in a hotel overnight, then you're sunk, Bill. Won't get another cheap flight out here at short notice. Shall we tell the organisers we're withdrawing our entry?"

"No! Bugger the jury. I'm not missing out on this..." he'd said. "Our once-a-year lad's tour. Anyway, I bet His Honour won't let them: '*Appropriate Directions*'. Knowing he'll want to be home early today. Circuit Dinner tonight and him their guest of honour, speech to prepare. Boring old brute that he is, but I'll be sorry to miss it myself."

So our trip was still on.

Me and Bill – men of a certain age. Thirty-something, still kidding ourselves we're 'young'. Off on our annual Big Adventure. Thinking ourselves some recreated version of "*The Likely Lads*". In better nick, yet still needing the rest of the year to recover.

30

I sometimes wondered what his family thought. Imagining Mrs Bill and the Little Bills, left far behind in a big stone farmhouse up in the wilds of Northumberland, miles beyond Hadrian's Wall, while he goes off on his yearly treat.

While the wife whose virtues he frequently extolled to me in lunchtime pubs off the Quayside ran her own business. Kept house, looked after the horses, and tended to the Little Bills. So what they thought, I didn't really know, since we never talked much about children. And never having actually visited the place or been invited-in, other than to drop him off at the road-ends, I couldn't rightly say. Could only guess what respite Mrs Bill got as her side of the bargain. Her payback if you like.

If she ever did.

Likeable and good company as Bill undoubtedly was, he remained a selfish man. Expert in organising life to his own convenience. And people, including his wife. This year's run a case in point. Not for Bill the long slog across the Continent. Like I told him at the time: "Hell, Bill, all you have to do is get your carcass across the city."

To Newcastle Airport, near Ponteland, to be precise.

And all I had to do to spare him any greater inconvenience was to meet and greet him over there. With Xenobia. "*Not a big ask…..*" as he'd implied himself, but since Bill was currently a disqualified driver, we had little choice in the matter. I knew this because I'd seen the recent press-cutting: '*Middlesbrough Evening Gazette*'.

Clocked averaging 97.5 miles per hour on the southbound A19 heading into Middlesbrough and Teesside Crown Court. All for the sake of a measly Case Management hearing for which he was twenty minutes late anyway and would be paid in washers. That and the '*totting-up*' provisions in the Road Traffic Act putting paid to what lingering hopes we might have had of him sharing this year's driving.

His ban shrugged off by Bill as occupational hazard of a busy barrister, its outcome left me crossing half Europe and the Alps alone in a worn-out 4x4, pulling her over on a trailer. My normal road car was an ageing Alfa Romeo coupe, high on miles but loveable still. If only for the sake of lingering sentimental associations: old girlfriends and stuff. Without a tow-bar she was completely out of the question and I certainly wasn't going

31

to the expense of vandalising my red Alfa, or its patinated memories, by fitting one just for Bill's benefit.

So the tired alternative I fielded instead was a chunky pastiche in rusty tinplate normally stored down a friend's garden. Reserved for local use in what few bad winters global warming dumps on Tyneside, but a terrible choice for trans-continental travel all the same, even solo. And once loaded-up with 'Xenobia' aboard Bill's trailer, a tow-car whose lifeless shockers and sagging springs made each corner into a challenging adventure. 'Construction & Use Regulations' eat your heart out.

"No worries..." he'd said: "Mainly tunnels and motorways, driving straight lines. A doddle, you'll be fine."

When he couldn't have been more wrong.

I know beggars can't be choosers but the old Toyota's road-manners on bends resemble an Armada galleon in heavy seas. Making my journey there to meet him memorably unpleasant, right from the off. In the only vehicle at whose wheel I ever felt car-sick, but Bill gave me no choice. Offered no alternative. Where I have to be at Malpensa on time and this the ramshackle rig I'm blessed with to get me and his car safely over there. Ready to greet him off the plane.

Factors conspiring to mean I nearly never was.

Why I was travelling so fast with a trailer behind me on that critical May afternoon. Making my ill-fated final approach-run, inbound to the target and the Milanese ring-road: il tangenziale. Heading oblivious towards whatever might happen.

While honesty dictates my account of what actually did is a bit more involved. Less-straightforward than shockers and springs; shocking enough all the same.

"We do not follow any of the restless stars which move in the sky, for they deceive poor sailors. We follow no star but the one that does not dip into the waves, the never-setting Axis, brightest star of the twin Bears. This it is that guides our ships"

(Marcus Lucanus, poet and writer, c.64 A.D)

- II -

In the endless marsh country bordering the estuaries to this Island of Britain's south-eastern coast, the light is thin and goes very suddenly. A localised phenomenon still new to me then.

One moment it is day and you can see from the wooden fighting-tops of the fort's stone bastions for miles and miles, right across the estuary and its rippling sea dykes. To the lonely cattle roaming this wilderness between scattered mounds and fences. Then the next there is a terrible, flat-grey gloom sweeping in from the sea to muffle sound just as effectively as it does the light itself. A strangely-universal human melancholy descending with it, where the odd disembodied cry might as like be the soul of a drowned sailor as any seabird.

Some say that if you stay out there alone there are other lights which appear. Flames that flare spontaneously. Spirits and wights. Wispy moving globes of plasmic blue, faint energy and sound, luring men out to a watery doom. Gone to be eaten by eels.

No wonder the local people disappear so quickly into their low huts and reed shelters at dusk. Fleeing the fog. Apart that is from the solitary, unmoving figure I saw that night from the fort ramparts. Standing alone down there in the distant reed beds. Looking east and fixedly away seawards, out into the inward-creeping mist. Whoever they were or whatever their lonely vigil. Perhaps some wildfowler waiting with weapon in hand to take a last snipe of the day, phosphorescent against the fading light.

Whatever their aim, my interest lay elsewhere. With the ships, and my hopes for another closer look. Of a renewed access onto one of these floating fighting-platforms to double my enjoyment.

As a boy from an inland farming town and till today, I'd never boarded any ocean-going vessel, let alone a warship. Why it took his galleys to impress and fascinate me most - these biremes of the fleet. That grim aura surrounding them. Those clean lines and lightweight build, unspoken hint of menace. That sense of being designed for one purpose and one alone – the taking of life on the high seas.

Form following function, like my old *gladius*.

The largest ship Carausius had lined up by the quay that night was a type even the rookie that I was knew for a 'Liburnian'. A battle-hardened veteran they named *"Medusa",* she was his flagship and location for what in my eyes was an unexpected invitation:

"Night has fallen and you won't be going anywhere till tomorrow, tribune, so let me summons you aboard. To dine among my officers...." he'd said to me, suddenly.

Only eighteen years old and green as grass, I can't tell you how delighted I was. No question I'd accept. Carausius knowing a refusal to be inconceivable, too, whatever antipathy exists between soldiery and administrators. (Though I doubt my then-master, the civil governor, would have agreed quite so readily).

When travel by night is dangerous and usually unheard-of, the admiral's invitation gave my only practical solution anyway. Arriving so late in the day made a return from this remote outpost to Venta, let alone Londinium, completely out of the question. Not an option to be attempted, whether by road or water. Making his offer of hospitality extra welcome, not just for its chance of intriguing society, but also for resolving my urgent problem. As well he knew.

Even if Carausius started off cross, and some thought me officious, it seemed no lasting grudge was held by the admiral over my mission of enquiry. Whatever the rights and wrongs of it now, that doesn't mean I don't still look back and cringe. At how gauche and impressionable I was, a 'baby' army officer flattered in self-importance at his chance to be dinner-guest of a living hero of our times.

And why not? Who in those days would not? When the governor's enquiry seemed easily over, and I could dine at an admiral's table with a clear conscience. Mindful of his recent successes in Gaul, but without letting deference descend into servility, what fair-minded person would not acknowledge those achievements or his fame? Respect the daunting task Carausius had now so cheerfully accepted for our common good. His brave defence of the home provinces.

No wonder a callow youth with military ambitions might tend to more respect for this soldier of the seas than his notorious lack of manners often won from stuffier generations. (Or in those early days, from our precious landed gentry).

But it wasn't just amongst the young that this coarse charm worked so well in his favour. That endearing impression of down-to-earth ordinariness in Carausius, so unusual in the High Command but always seen on meeting, made him as popular with the basest of men. Wherever he went. When he spoke to them as equals, stood in their dust and shared in their trouble.

A man of the people.

And nowhere was such a temperament and mien more useful than within the military. Qualities attracting the most extraordinary loyalty and devotion from our common soldiery. In the camps and entrenchments; among all the non-commissioned officers and other ranks serving under him. Yet this common touch he bore felt always natural. Not cultivated in any self-conscious way, but carried without contrivance, even if I suspect our little admiral did come to realise how to develop it for maximum effect.

In short, his gift from the Gods. Maybe also their curse and his biggest mistake. What so upset the Caesars.

To take a characteristic example, his way when discussing anything - even the least - was always to treat the whole conversation as if some private disclosure. Like he did that night with me. As if he was taking you, and you alone, into his personal confidence. A sense of trust I felt determined to honour, as does anyone treated this way.

Looking back, I can see that he was what these emerging Christians would call a *"fisher of men"*. For all his bluff and bluster, the swearing and oaths, he had an unerring instinct for people who could be useful to him. Knowing quite literally how to bring them on board. One reason why there are still those who wonder if he was a secret Christian himself. That and his obvious dislike for their persecution.

35

On the basis of my early experience, I'd identify the generosity in this spontaneous dinner invitation as defining mark of the man. Further good reasons why a junior officer barely out of school could feel so thrilled to find himself ambling casually back in the dark from fort to mooring with our commander-in-chief of naval forces. Finding in him an enthusiast disdainful of status, one more interested in explaining to his subordinate the practice of their service in deploying the *'liburnian'* class, than to retreat behind the barriers of rank.

Lessons in sea-power and personal indulgence combined, as I would never forget. Breeding a sense of gratitude never to diminish, whatever else might follow. As I suspect my heirs are sick of hearing, and why I am driven instead to set it down here, for another generation which might not be.

No, in my whole military apprenticeship, his were the longest conversations I was ever granted with any commander - and probably the only. In the grown-up world I suppose he came to represent my first, my last, and only professional mentor. When it is surely natural to harbour gratitude towards what senior figure played that formative part in your own development; once home is left behind and with it whatever thankless guidance fond parents attempt. Just as it was in my own case, and why I can still remain proud to claim mine as being the late, great Mausaeus Carausius.

(If not a fact to voice too widely nowadays).

"As a fighting ship, your standard *'liburnian'* has several uses..." he'd explained to me, as we threaded our way back in the deepening dusk to where his squadron lay at mooring: "Sailing ahead of the main fleet, they reconnoitre the coast. Not the biggest ships, I know, but as a bireme with only two banks of oars they're lighter and swifter in response - once oarsmen are called-on to act. A fantastic acceleration from rest and manoeuvrable with it. '*....off a bath-house shovel'* how their crews like to put it, with a turn of speed vital for the bays and estuaries round here. Showing more than a match for our dopy, local opponents, flailing about in some tired old tub more basket than boat, like they do."

"Ideal for Britain, sir?"

"Exactly, my son. No need for triremes out here, when these biremes do us nicely. Not usually, anyhow, though we still keep one or two. Mainly just for show, to impress the natives with on formal occasions. Because in major exercises out at sea or those set-piece battles of the old Civil Wars, Actium and such-like, it was always the liburnian we relied on. For our lines of communication, liaison between the bigger or more important ships. But out here on the German Ocean, set against smaller opposition, our priorities grow different. Why the twin-decked liburnian's is our main line of battle, the very fleet itself."

"And better-built, I guess, than might do for Mediterranean conditions, Admiral?"

"Oh, yes, you can bet on that, my boy. The ones round here are local-built. Fully-decked and higher-sided, rowers boxed-in. Leave us proof against anything the British weather can throw, howling a gale or pissing-down like it usually does. Though their rowing galleries can get a bit hot and smelly in the summer. No, I'd say our liburnians are generally just the job for normal British weather. Close pursuit of the enemy. And since the latest emergency, precisely the kind of coastal patrol and anti-piracy work we're faced with. Why I've got another six on order from the slipways of Clausentum, framed in the best Anderidan oak. Provided I can somehow conjure up the cash to pay for them, that is......"

I took his voice trailing thoughtfully away like that as chance for another question, keen to show my mettle: "*Liburnian.* It's a strange name for a ship. What does it mean, Admiral, where does it come from?"

"Don't you know? A proper book-schooled lad like you? Well, I'll never open a book in my life, but those who do say we Romans borrowed its design. Back in the days of the old Republic. Copied long ago from a sea-going people called '*Liburni*'. Bad men who had it coming, like our Saxon, Angle or Frankish friends will shortly find. A tribe of pirates, my boy. Wicked, thieving robbers and kidnappers who used fast ships shaped like these for raiding. For capturing honest Roman sailors off '*Our Sea*' then holding them and their ships hostage. Hidden in havens all along the Adriatic...."

"What happened?"

"It was a national scandal and the shame of Rome. Criminals holding her ships to ransom. Outrageous, not to be tolerated a moment longer. Something had to be done. So the Senate built a new fleet and sent it out with the sort of Consul they knew would put paid to the Liburni and their nonsense. Who immediately on arriving offers talks under a sign of truce then captures the ringleaders once they show up at his tent waving white flags. Crucifying the lot down the coast in company with their crews. Showing a single-mindedness Rome would do well to rediscover if she wants her world and its ways to survive another thousand years...."

Whenever I encounter the distinctive smell of muddy water and wet grass combined, it takes me back to that night-time talk. Walking companionably through the marsh with an undistinguished-looking man who's set to become one of the most important figures in the whole history of Britain. In my life.

On a treacherous riverbank where dark had fully fallen and the dockside path was narrowing, Carausius striding on ahead of me, gesturing with his hands and absorbed in his arguments. Talking away over his shoulder while I listen from behind in respectful silence, pausing only occasionally from the rhythm of his seaman's gait to check I'd not missed my footing, slipped quietly into the river. Where, once satisfied his young audience stays close and pays attention, the admiral continues in a heavily-burred Latin. Relaying a traditional story whose moral seems close to his heart:

"Piracy and hostage-taking? Didn't happen no more. Those Liburnian ships we didn't burn, the Republic either pressed straight into service or sent back for shipwrights to copy. There's a lesson in this my boy, direct from our Roman ancestors. That you've got to be tough to survive in this world, got to be ruthless. And my favourite part in this word-of-mouth tradition? That these Illyrian pirates we wiped-out long ago got the idea for their ships from vessels seen in Britain. During the tin-trade, from craft they saw being used by native Britons. You see those ancient navigators travelled around a lot further than we usually credit them. Just think of your Strabos or your Ptolemies. And if that old story's right, then I like even better the one saying these ancient Britons were only copying an earlier Caledonian type."

"You mean the design comes full circle?"

"Got it in one, my boy – I knew you were bright. Copied from a people whose nasty little narrow boats are raiding so much

further south nowadays than ever before: Picti and Saxonici –
the very peoples against whom we'll turn their original design.
Setting our Liburnians on them for a bloody reply I'll see to it
they damn-well never forget...."

The low-lying mist of dusk had cleared as quickly as
descended, and now we could see our way under the whole
night sky. Its blackness pierced only by the silver lights of
countless stars and seven navigation lamps from the line of
ships ahead. Ambling along beneath a starry heaven and
beside these man-made wonders, happily absorbed in an old
salt's sea stories, I realised what marvellous proof it was. Of
what I had so often been told by my teachers and tutors about
the unifying power of a great empire.

That such a man as he, born a Belgic Celt of peasant stock
below the German frontier, barely within the outermost margins
of Rome's sway and likely never to have seen the
Mediterranean, could unselfconsciously talk about *"We
Romans"* or *"Our Sea"* - *Mare Nostrum*. And never for a
moment think himself excluded.

Truly a wonder, in a time of change.

When not just that social-mix of which my guide was living-
proof but also our traditional rites and beliefs were bending to
change. The continuing decline in our Old Gods – *Di Veteres* –
their observance and respect. An emotive point my late father
was prone to pontificate about before the usual captive
audience: his long-suffering family.

As *paterfamilias* taking his proper place at the head of our
table. Below the wall-niche for our household gods, the *lares,*
after the usual sacrifice. Sitting as we always did in dutiful
attention, I can retain a mental picture of him pointing up at
them. Telling us where these new trends were bound to take us:
"To Hades in a handcart, down a cultural decline".

What pain it caused him to see the proper worship of Jupiter
and so many other Gods of our Roman state, of Fortuna and
Luck, palpably fading away. Whether at home or in public.
Translating into concepts similar but different, into a multitude of
lesser beliefs: *"More material and hard-nosed; less spiritual,
more selfish. Almost amoral, even here in Britain"*.

And it wasn't just this loss of belief which so upset him but also
those social values he felt they'd always underpinned. Popular

ideas of right and wrong "*becoming more arbitrary...*" how he described it: "*superstitious; personal and exotic. Less grounded in duty.*" Bowing to what he used to refer to as "*corrupting influences from the East....*" (He didn't just mean Christians, either, but other extreme cults too).

"*If we stop believing in the Gods who made Rome...*" he'd warn our little dinner-table: "*if we abandon the old rituals of belief and their values...*" for these perverse substitutes "*....then our world is doomed.*" And this from an ethnic Atrebatean, whose forbears once worshipped at the stones of Lughu, inside a Druidic grove.

Pointing this last out as intellectual inconsistency to my late father would have been a waste of time. Bound to be treated as cheek, lead to a clip. So far as Dad was concerned, we were Roman citizens and had been for generations. And that was that, for a man of fixed opinions whose admirable consistency I can recognise for both his greatest personal strength and at the same time the very failing which finally did for him. His views staying firm, wherever the rest of the world's might wander.

(Let alone the emperor's).

But if, as mother would gently observe, he genuinely "*....thought anyone in far-off Imperial palaces at Treverorum or Mediolanum cares a gnat's foreleg for their private moral denunciation at table by a minor official of Calleva Atrebatum, then you've got another thing coming.*" The sort of quietly-provocative remark from her which, in our little household at least and however gently delivered, we watching children knew was sure to start a major row.

About her belief that we were now so poor - by her family's former standards - precisely because of her husband's inability to adapt to new philosophies and outlooks spreading across the globe. His cussed refusal to accept those modern ways he so deplores; in a world where contacts and patronage, manners and breeding, good family or wealth, had ceased to be the arbiters of political and career preferment. Or, as he put it himself:

"*Where honest servants of the state like me go hungry. In a new meritocracy built on how many rivals – whether Rome's or your own - you can denounce or cull. Whether for Greater Rome's good, or her latest emperor's jealous self-defence.*"

Not where you were born, nor to whom.

Criteria to give us a world dynasty of butchers, of killers not conquerors.

Plus a few honest men notwithstanding.

Like this plain M.Carausius I found myself literally following for the first time that night. Where my struggle along a greasy riverbank behind him and into an adult world I still thought novel brought me to another startling realisation. Of how my new career, and this journey a civil governor despatched me on, had combined to initiate another. In discovering what dad really meant, without even wanting to. Coming face-to-face with harsh realities hidden behind those boring monologues he used to inflict. All those tedious diatribes his wife and offspring endured twice-nightly, once dinner was over.

And if this clerk of Calleva was a nobody to those powerful personalities he dared roundly despise, perhaps *pater* had not been such a fool after all. When it became increasingly likely to prove his generation's fault, once my own found itself taking a turn at confronting those outcomes he'd warned of, their inevitable consequence.

Sins of the fathers?

A thought to set me wondering if the spirit of my own could see me now, strolling along in private conversation with a famous commander. If he could, then I knew how much he would have swelled-out with pride. When it finally hit me, I suppose. That father was gone and I was left. Their only surviving son, once Flavius died. Suddenly realising the burden of family responsibility to be carried: my turn to make a go of it, be a credit to our ancestors. Carry their torch. How tonight's fateful encounter might have been meant, its starlight an omen. That today I was starting on their shadowy behalfs to go down a path towards military attainments from which father was thwarted in his lifetime. Whether by illness, politics or poverty. A thought to make me the more determined to succeed. For him, for all of them; doing justice to my beloved father's memory more important than anything.

"*Serve us right!*" he would say when news of the latest disaster arrived from the east. Defeat by the Persians, disgrace on the Danube. Implicit in his outlook that underlying point we dutiful children should all be quick to recognise. Of how different things would be were daddy put in charge. Made-up to emperor - assuming the *'Worshipful Guild of Calleva Scribes & Corn Factors'* ever declared him so; obedient armies along the Rhine or Danubian frontiers meekly assenting after.

To be fair to him, the rot set in before *pater* was even a baby. When he and the entire Empire endured those fifty years of civil anarchy following the impulsive murder of Alexander Severus by an embittered loner among his palace troops. Including that strange interregnum of a separate *'Gallic Empire'* - when northern provinces of Gaul and Britain unilaterally declared their independence from Rome, an *'Imperium Galliarium'*.

Living as Romans, but not of Rome.

A legendary time for which I realise citizens like my father secretly harboured a nostalgic fondness. Its dangerous precedents bringing us a localised safety in Britain that only emphasised increasing instability on the continent. Days mentioned wistfully, as if not only wanting to pass on family history to the next generation but also this wider concept. A state of affairs which, someday, I think he hoped might return. That I could somehow help.

"It was a good solution you know, son. If one they wouldn't let us get away with now. When my own father, your grandfather, commanded a mounted regiment of Batavians. Up there on the northern wall: The Entrenchments'. How he loved it! No trouble from the tribes and half their time spent hunting. Till they're brought down here to guard the southern coast for Postumus. A transfer to emphasise where the real threat now came from. Correctly as things turned out, but your granda' didn't care. He was young, you see, having the time of his life. A wonderful time, as much for him as the province. Peaceful too, though they knew it wouldn't last. Realised Britain would be brought into line one day. Whether she liked it or not. Brought to heel, put back in the fold, by force if necessary. And once this clique of Dalmatian peasants took over, took charge and recovered the rest of the empire, exactly what did happen. We were!"

Whatever my late father thought about this, and whatever you think of his nostalgia for British isolationism, even reactionaries like dad respected some of the men recovering Gaul and Britannia for Rome. The determination of figures like the soldier-emperor Aurelian. Or even some of those lesser men following-on after. After Aurelian was killed. Like our current Emperor Diocletian or his muscle-bound mess-mate, Maximian.

My little admiral's bosses.

Beneficiaries of that new age of social openness and "*cultural decline*" father so hated. Where anyone can succeed to high office - as long as they come from Illyria, have an army at their back. Where any citizen of ambition mistaking its novel creed of equality for an open invitation to themselves is guaranteed the chop.

"*Aren't most people the same...?*" he'd demand of our meal table during these one-sided debates. Looking round fiercely: "*Wanting fairness for themselves, denying it others. To people like us.*" While we just felt embarrassed, not knowing what to say.

And, when loudly repeated one time too often in his cramped office beside the basilica at Calleva, the typical sort of remark from dad finally bringing him to the attention of informers. What most '*upset*' our egregious local magistrates. Those shallow men as keen to show themselves publicly collaborating with Diocletian's frequent purges as they were secretly frightened for themselves.

Put him into the arena to die beside criminals and Christians. Know equality in death.

Yet until that terrible time came when the emperor sent one of his cruellest procurators into our sedate part of the world; specifically armed with a set of iron chains and an open brief to identify the more truculent local citizens fit to decorate them with; the irony is we'd always felt safe.

Until then, if there had been one thing my parents could always agree on, it was telling me and my sisters how lucky we were. Lucky to be Atrebates, lucky to be brought up in a secure place like our peaceful tribal capital. Calleva Atrebatum, the city in the woods. A quiet country town with strong walls. Far from the sea. Somewhere the endemic violence of the continent could not touch us. Here in our remote province of Britannia where life is slow and politics wisely left as the pastime of few.

Those whom the gods would destroy.

That comfortable sense of security and reassurance Calleva once offered me, that confidence gained from childhood, only started to unravel in a big way once father was taken from us.

What was left of it finally erased in the weeks following that fateful day when I chose of my own free will to walk through the gates of an army training-depot at Glevum. While by the time I found myself strolling along a darkened riverbank in conversation with a senior admiral, beside his garrison of the eastern fen, it felt like yesterday's tide.

Completely run-out.

As if this short line of fighting ships we were walking towards through the gloom suddenly became the last and only refuge left me. All that's still standing between my distant family home and those ceaseless waves of *Saxones* our intelligence reports on every tide.

Last defence to the province.

Hardly that of course and I exaggerate, too much the pessimist, but I cannot overstate how reassuring I found their sight that evening.

These spectral vessels, most of their bulk resting hidden below the jetty on an ebb tide. Strained on a mooring-rope but ready again for action once daylight and water returns.

These few our island's defenders, showing his flag against a whole world.

"And do as adversaries do in law – strive mightily but eat and drink as friends."

('Taming Of The Shrew' - Act 1: Scene 2
William Shakespeare)

- 2 -

I'd first met William Cariss years ago. Not long after he was married as it happens, although we'll get onto that later. Briefing him to prosecute in a major criminal case where I'd already done all the hard work. Assembling and improving the trial bundle from those unpromising crime-files the local police provide my service with. Witness statements with their usual, classic opener: *"I was sat in my patrol car...."*

Showing how distant it was, our first case together came not so long after the repeal of that trade-protection rule-cum-cartel which his 'senior arm' of our legal profession was once so reliant upon for a steady stream of work. Using *'Rights of Audience'* to deny public sector lawyers like myself their entitlement to present criminal matters before Her Honour in person.

An unfair bar the English Bar was long since forced to lift.

Comparable with demarcations once existing between riveters and welders in long-vanished Tyneside shipyards, this awkward rule might have disappeared altogether if my short-staffed organisation had not continued needing to brief independent lawyers like him on its behalf in the bigger Crown Court cases. However many of the lesser ones we now take-over for ourselves. You can't get the staff, you see.

And tedious technical background only mentioned now as professional explanation for how Bill and I met. As opposed to social-networking ones we're sure to get onto later.

"Hello, you must be the CPS guy. I'm Bill Cariss...." he'd said, his handshake nearly breaking every bone in my palm.

As well as being strong, Bill was unusually tall. A thick-necked tax lawyer who never let his work tax him. Partial to port, claret, and Newcastle Brown Ale - in that order. Generally larger than life even before he entered politics, his imposing frame drew stability from a relaxed attitude to most human problems and

45

two feet the width of supertankers. God knows where he got his shoes, but I can promise you there was no shipyard left on Tyneside big enough to build them. His family's nickname of *'Mouse'* their obvious in-joke.

And I suspect the reason he never got enough tax work was because businesses up in our part of the world tend to make greater call on insolvency practitioners. Result not just of the recession's *'Harrying of the North'* but also the harsh reality of how insolvency tends to reduce a bankrupt's liabilities to tax. If not wipe them out altogether.

Whatever the reason, Bill *'The Tax'* soon found himself forced - perhaps unwillingly - into less arcane fields of practice. Where he first found me and my grubby life of crime, and I'd gone looking for him.

Let's be honest, and whatever he might pretend to his chums at the Bar on Circuit Mess dinners, what Bill knew of the canons of criminal law could be written on the back of the proverbial cigarette packet. If you could find one of those rare commodities anywhere; smoking, along with sarcasm, wearing a cross at work, or allowing livestock on the public highway being added to a list of outlawed anti-social behaviours proscribed by Parliament.

I'm here to tell you about Bill, so don't get me started on our legislators. On halcyon days when I was a baby lawyer and a new Criminal Justice Act exciting. A thing of wonder in the days when not every offence was *'arrestable'*. Before passing one major piece of criminal legislation every year became insufficient to satisfy the Mother of Parliaments. The tipping point, when so many new and arrestable offences were being created by a hyperactive legislature with little else to do, that her final stroke of genius to resolve this distinction became inevitable. Their ultimate declaration: that now you can be arrested for anything: *"proportionality and the Human Rights Act permitting"*.

Leaving me among the diminishing band of public servants stuck with enforcing an ever-extending web of compliance upon a puzzled public. From out the offices of what in those days they still called the Crown Prosecution Service: the *'C-P-S'*.

Why?

Why not?

I'd qualified young as a lawyer then consciously chosen to become a full-time prosecutor. Chosen it in the sense I was an idealistic young person hating injustice who wanted to help win redress for its victims. Because I'd thought – no, believed – that there were truths to be found out there. That *jousting for justice'* in an adversarial system like ours could provide myself and the society I served with genuine means towards a worthy end.

Honest.

Whether I was right or wrong on that score doesn't matter anymore, though I don't want to come over self-righteous. While you might be interested in a background only mentioned now, insofar as it matters, because it was there this sincerely-held philosophy started causing me problems. Not to mention some of what else followed, inside a cash-strapped public organisation charged with justice and its delivery. Facing difficult times with fewer and fewer staff expected to do more and more. While I suppose most other consequences were down to my own stupid fault.

That and a private obsession.

It was Charles Dickens who long ago remarked that the only way for ordinary people to understand the labyrinth which is the English law is by realising that for lawyers it is all about the getting and keeping of work. No more or less. In Bill's case, this was not something at which he – or more accurately his barrister's clerk – was always terribly good.

Like the very first time I phoned his Clerk. Asking if they had anyone available to do a last minute return-brief, late-listed at the Crown Court the following day. While Bill admitted to me later that he'd been kicking his heels in chambers, wondering whether to go home instead and cut the top meadow, where his wife keeps those rare horses they breed.

What actors call '*resting'*. (I mean Bill, not the horses).

Kept waiting by the usual Clerk's tomfoolery about Mr Bill being just the man for the job – but he'd have to see if he could be made available, his skills being so much in demand – I could have rung off. Fortunately I didn't, so we eventually met up next day at the door of Counsel's Robing Room in Newcastle's Combined Courts Centre. At the place and on the threshold where those solicitors upon whom a barrister's entire commercial existence depends are normally kept by them at a suitably condescending arms-length.

Happily, and whatever the stuffy traditions of his profession, condescending was never Bill's style. Diffident and rather shy, yes. Strange in such a big man. Red in the face once he got going. Bull-neck, booming voice, but just the hint of a stammer. Until the heat of action, when he became a different person. No tax geek now but a raging bull among the usual herds of bovine, uninspiring cross-examiners. Not cross, but forensic.

And no stammer.

I think you can date when he first got the idea of using his new-found confidence in the political arena to this rather public piece of self-discovery.

Apart from it being some sort of long-firm-fraud, I can't remember what this first case was actually about. The important thing to note is how completely Bill surprised me; the judge, reporters from the Journal and the Evening Chronicle, detective officers in the case, and most of all himself; when he played such an absolute blinder.

Why, I think he'd even read the brief.

Perhaps the only people Bill had not surprised were the defendant and jury – which was precisely why he won. The witnesses, poor devils, with no prior inkling of what was to come. What would hit them.

After that, I briefed him in a lot more cases. With practice he just got better and better, so it became like a relay race. Where I built the prosecutor's case for the state: assessing, assembling, and then re-assembling the order of witnesses whose statements the police had gathered then supplemented on my advice. Before handing it all over to Bill, who reviewed the file again then ran with it for the Crown. Not that I could not have myself – but for that little *"rights of audience"* problem, anciently put there to keep the English Bar in work and somehow surviving in practice today, if only for *'efficiency savings'*.

How it happened later on, once I became a Crown Advocate myself with *'Higher Rights'* - turning out for the prosecution at the Crown Court before a purple judge and defence teams whose matching complexion spoke volumes for their professional view of CPS staff taking work from the Junior Bar – that Bill and I sometimes found ourselves on opposite sides.

Crossing swords as it were.

Back then it didn't seem to matter and, all credit to Bill, at least he was one barrister who never seemed to mind. Even when, occasionally, I won. While afterwards if I had, we'd still go off for an early-evening pint or two on Newcastle Quayside, just like the old days.

It was one of these occasions when he told me. One summer's night a few years or so after the London Olympics, sitting inside an old-fashioned pub on the Quayside sadly no longer there now, when he announced his intention to stand for the European Parliament.

No, since you ask, in one way it didn't surprise me a bit.

You see there's quite a tradition at the English Bar of part-time involvement in politics. Not so often found with solicitors like me, but frequently seen as natural progression for a professional type that's accustomed to standing up in public and talking at length before an audience obliged to listen.

Something we men know ourselves to be rather good at.

Prompting the toast I found myself making as I raised my near-empty beer glass to catch a reflection of the Tyne Bridges outside the pub window. A gesture only incidentally emphasising its urgent need for refill:

"An MEP eh? Let's drink to the European Union and Mr William Cariss, soon-to-be Member of the European Parliament. Our nation's representative abroad, for Tyneside. If I for one can't wait, Bill, I'm still left baffled what's involved. What you'll actually do for us once you get over there. To Brussels, I mean....."

He'd laughed sheepishly and started weakly. Embarrassed, I'd thought. Even stammering a bit, something not witnessed from him in ages. Starting his story from the wrong end so to speak. Diverted by procedural niceties like a typical lawyer. Not outcomes that matter.

His opening mistake.

Trying and failing to describe the merry-go-round in view in jokily-positive terms. As if an excuse for a 'jolly'. All those endless committees and expenses-paid, first-class flights to look forward to. Flying out from the north-east of England across to Brussels; from Brussels to Strasbourg, then Strasbourg to Luxembourg, Luxembourg to Brussels. Brussels back to Newcastle. Newcastle to London.

Journeying between a series of semi-detached European institutions, each with its own separate remit and not one of them answerable to anyone. Or each other.

Commission, Council, Court.

Divorced and dysfunctional, apparently by design.

And one he plans on joining:

Explaining to me how seven hundred and eighty-five elected MEPs in the European Parliament don't actually decide on anything, but are only 'consulted'. *"Though they might still 'influence'..."* he insists. While those lucky Commissioners in a European Commission no-one elects enjoy gold-plated salaries and live off matching pensions for ever. Rewarded for waging supra-national power over domestic policy from their own separate body. An unaccountable entity initiating and ruling on the actual changes. A burgeoning Super-state producing real laws of grinding effect to affect millions, without asking any of us.

Not even Geordies.

"The more you try and explain to me how it works, the less I understand..." I'd complained "....let alone half the laws they produce."

"Well, I....." he'd started, till I interrupt:.

"But isn't that the root problem? What's fundamentally wrong with the whole mullarky? That no-one understands it? The laws they make. On the engineering principle that if a thing looks right, then it is right? That it will work. While this thing clearly doesn't."

Maybe I'd been talking too loudly. Whether in England, Scotland or Wales, it's always unwise, positively bad manners to mention *'The Law'* in any British pub. Bound to upset someone sitting nearby who's had the rough end of it. An unhappy experience. Of a subject more guaranteed to cause offence than politics or religion, women or sex.

There was hardly anyone in the pub that night - barely tea-time after all - but a tall man silhouetted against lights by the bar obviously overheard me. Turning around and looking directly over to us as if to signal to female bar-staff his early-warning: *"What sort of law are these two in the corner shouting about? Is it trouble; are they cops?"*

"I know" said Bill, conceding an unspoken rebuke coming down the room by speaking more softly. "D-does anyone? And it's that lack of transparency showing the EU up as fundamentally undemocratic. T-too complicated, impossible to understand. Almost as if it's meant to be anti-democratic. Another reason why it's high time someone in my position, with my background, got over there. Got inside the machine, or at least tried......"

"Not forgetting the added bonus of trousering an extra four hundred pounds in daily allowance for every Friday morning? Just by signing-in at their parliament then slipping away quietly for the weekend?"

"OK, fair comment, Michael, and p-perfectly possible. See you've heard about that. Just part of what needs changing in the institution. But playing the expenses game isn't part of my battle-plan, believe me...." he'd said softly, looking nervously towards the bar as if wary of being overheard again.

Even taking Bill's sincerity and motivation for granted, which I did, the part really bugging me was his explanation for the extra travelling involved. If he got elected. Their 'carbon footprint' and its cost, all incurred for nothing. How every month about five thousand people like him must pack their bags to make a pointless three hundred-and-fifty kilometre trek by rail or air from EU HQ in Brussels, across to monthly *'plenary'* sessions held in Strasbourg. Setting up the same shop in a different place, simply for form's sake.

As if I'd somehow find it funny.

"Why?" I'd coolly asked, not thinking it was. Annoyingly, Bill didn't get chance to answer:

"To give them idle, useless burgers in Strasbourg a job to do!" shouted the same man from his barstool, one of very few customers present. A young man with short gelled hair and one earring. Wearing a blue, hooded sweatshirt, leaning back on his stool. A dude out on the town, 'earwigging' our private discussion.

I ignored his interruption and quietly pressed on, questioning Bill about his example:

"Plenary? So what happens when these hundreds of people finally get there? Arrive in Strasbourg. Is it like those *'plenary'* sessions they close training-conferences with? Some sort of closing *'wash-up'* session and *'safe journey home'*?"

Bill scowled, knowing the whole thing sounded like a wash-up. Or a washout.

"Well, go on, then, answer your mate's frigging question..." commented a familiar voice. "Explain what sort of bloody parliament needs all that backwards and forwards, can claim it's useful work?" sneered the man in the hoodie, come-in close to gate-crash our conversation uninvited, invade our social space: "What sort of bloody talking-shop is it, what frigging good does it do us? What right have we to say?"

The girl with blue, green, and pink hair serving behind the bar reaching over it to touch his sleeve approvingly. Laughing soundlessly as if to say: *'You tell them, pet!'*

"The first thing you should realise is the European Union is not a parliamentary democracy. In any traditional sense we'd understand..." boomed Bill gravely, addressing him, the peacock staff, and the rest of a near-empty bar in his best courtroom voice: "In terms of what we're used to in Britain. No proper political party-system and no cohesive 'European public', just three hundred and twenty million people affected in one way or another by what EU institutions do. Like it or not. So, no, I'd be first to admit to you it's got no real voters' mandate for anything, actually."

"Told you!" said hoodie-man, triumphantly, leering back across to the girl of variegated thatch and his night-time dreams, decorating the beer-pumps. If she was the real focus of his interest, who he's out to impress, I was too. That so unpromising a punter might even hold an opinion, take trouble to ask.

And why our new *'critical friend'* joining-in uninvited set me privately thinking more deeply about his questions myself. Was he really right? Is that all the EU amounts to?

Meetings, meetings, meetings? Travel, travel, travel? Talk, talk, talk?

If it is, surely the natural environment for that whiff of pomposity Bill unwittingly displayed. While the more he saw this mental picture grow in his audience, the harder he tried to put a better gloss on it. Defend the indefensible. As if even imagining joining the EU elite, its gravy-train, corrupts you into taking their side. Even someone like Bill. A point the younger man instinctively closed-on with more questions of his own. Gate-crashing our discussion, physically and intellectually, before Bill could come back:

"No mandate you say, like it don't matter? But we're good enough to shell out for it, aren't we? Out of our taxes, the United Kingdom as was. For people like you. Yeah, all that Brussels carry-on funded by muggins here out his own pocket. Fifty million quid a day from this poor bloody country, ain't it? What that whats-his-face said on telly last night? Never mind what we spent on the IMF bailing out the losers: effing Greece and Spain; Italy and Portugal. Not as if we can afford it either, eh? Bankrupt ourselves. Teachers, soldiers, police, and nurses out on the dole. Scotland off on its own like the EU always wanted.....breaking us up."

I didn't know about Bill but I was impressed by the vehemence. The passion, if not his delivery.

Imagining how it was for him, some random guy off Elswick Road or someplace: Newcastle's West End, its Wild West. Thinking that for the first time in his life he had someone in his sights who might be called-on to account for the whole Euro-show. Be held responsible. And even if he was completely wrong there and Bill wasn't party, not even elected, there was me - to my everlasting shame - helping gang up on my friend like he was. Interrogating poor old Bill as critically. As if my drinking companion was complicit in the whole thing and these failings of the European Union somehow his fault:

"Yes, Bill, he's right. How can the EU succeed? What's useful from all its expenditure? Apart from Stalinist buildings of no architectural merit. The only thing monumental their cost. What good has building these temples to perpetual motion done us? What outcomes result? And what are the chances of you improving anything - even if elected - alone?"

"Outcomes, chances?" he'd said unhappily. Looking up at the smoke-stained ceiling like these were questions you'd want to phone a friend over, in some TV show.

"Yes, Bill, outcomes! Plenty of words, we know: printed and electronic. Conferences and summits - seen them on the news.

Rows of shiny Merc's and Beemers lining-up outside a fancy hotel in Cannes. But what else do these eurocrats achieve? Apart from shunting other people's money around, including our own. Handing back some of what we gave them in the first place. Like they've done us one big favour. Out of what little's left us from propping up the euro. Recycling our cash in the form of EU 'grants'. Recirculating their bureaucracy and a load of hot air, is that the best they can manage?"

Bill was in retreat, almost apologetic: "Well, yes. Miles and miles of printed word, to be honest, *are* issued. Every day in twenty-three different languages. But, no, it's true. To the layman, more obvious sense of purpose does look hard to find. But don't be deceived, it's there alright. When they talk about *'fiscal union...integration'* then you're nearer the heart of it. Sounding hazy but where we're heading. Not a case of mission-creep but what they're really set on. Where we should be careful, why it's time I got......."

"Faceless technocrats. Working night and day to absorb us into legal and fiscal union. Into a new empire, their European empire?" I interrupt provocatively, towards the same ceiling. Bill didn't answer, and I knew he couldn't. Putting his empty beer glass down with elaborate precision onto the cardboard beermat he manoeuvred to receive it.

Even our interlocutor from the bar got that point: "A Roman empire?" he sniggered. "Like the one in *'Gladiator'*? Is that what we've got to look forward to? You politicians selling us off, to work for men in brass wellies?"

Rainbow-girlfriend tittering silently at his filmic paradigm: that old jibe and hackneyed parallel everyone recognises, still wonders might be true. In a conversation where suddenly nothing felt right. Like no sort of arena – whether gladiatorial or otherwise - for the sensible Bill that I knew to want to enter. For him to get enmeshed with.

Why I kept on pressing him further about his true motives. Probing like he was a reluctant witness and these two kids up at the bar our *'citizen jury'*. Trying to defuse their obvious dissatisfaction, get them on side:

"Our friend here's got a point. About how it looks. Or why a sensible man like you would want to get closer to an enterprise like that: a Man of the Bar? A successful guy with lucrative lines of work, a life to lead. Thinking what happened to the eurozone. Haven't you got enough on, Bill, better things to do?"

Barristers, like actors, always being "*busy*".

Pressing him harder on the encouragement of a stranger. Bullying Bill in public for the sin of offering such weak explanations, so oddly procedural. Unconvincing and lame, so unlike Bill. Not to his usual standard at all. All that tired talk of self-fulfilment. Of '*Making a difference*' and 'G*iving something back*'.

Yeah, yeah, yeah.

It really wound me up, I'll tell you.

Me and two love-birds at the bar unexpectedly combined into the one selection panel. Unlikely guinea pigs on which to test out all this self-deluding, self-centred, self-indulgent interviewee's jargon my mate Bill has somehow learned off-pat from somewhere. The *lingua franca* of our public appointments' circus, those dreary clones we breed to people it, audit its reach.

Modern Puritans: chameleons and quislings. Cod-faced evangelists of efficiency and logic, effectiveness and economy. Managerialists enforcing tick-box regimes so rigid that they would strangle true difference.

No, when metropolitanised jargon of this quality is spewing out the mouth of William Cariss, a decent soul whose character I respect - whatever his other failings - I can't believe a word of it. Instinctively smell a rat.

Why I bluntly tell him so, Romeo and his flaming Juliet nodding away vigorously in the background. Unlikely allies for my unfriendly challenge.

Getting on my high horse to show a side of me a friend has never seen. Telling him that if this is what it takes to get '*selected-then-elected*' in our devious modern world, then "*Good for you, Bill….*" For him and all the devils he'd surely sold his soul to.

When to me it sounds like cobblers, and not the man I knew.

Why I'm rudely demanding of him: "*But was the sacrifice worth it?*"

This questioning so unexpected and needlessly fierce, I see it make him pause.

Shamefaced and taken aback at my confrontational reaction, Bill looks down at my empty beer glass instead, talking quietly to the floor:

"Tell you what, Michael, I'll get you another p-pint. Then we can start again. Talk it through a bit more sensibly. When you know I always value your opinion.......don't want to fall out."

"To remain ignorant of what occurred before you were born is to remain always a child."

(Marcus Tullius Cicero: Roman lawyer, orator & politician)

- III -

By the time we reached *'The Medusa'* it was getting late – more a time for supper than dinner. For an uncomplicated sort of meal to complicate my life for ever.

Before we got onto the ship, a group of his men had set up an impromptu altar in the dark beside it, where one of their number who doubled as a priest led formalities of sacrifice. The scrawny goat they'd tethered there ready on the river bank might have been no cleverer than its kind, but bleated plaintively throughout the ceremony. Like it worked out already the way things would go. What its captors had in mind.

If only I'd been so bright.

Today's officiates were men of the sea fulfilling vows previously made. Pacts reached with the gods towards a safe return from operations. *"Willingly and deservedly..."* as the usual catechism has it, preamble to a kill.

Carausius and I joined them without a word, each of his seafarers acknowledging their overlord's presence with a bow from the neck. Respectful but restrained, disciplined but dignified before their *'primus inter pares'*, first among equals.

The priest continued uninterrupted with their ritual, face cowled under the hood of his robes. Lit only by a flaring yellow flame atop the centre bowl of a stone altar the sailors had dragged into position by the quay for this purpose.

So far as its limited light would allow, I studied their admiral's reaction.

A leader prone to boast how he always put to sea armed with the protection of a famous prophecy, yet someone I saw later show contempt for its forms. Happy to dismiss the taking of augury or omen as simple childish nonsense, but content to stand beside me, joining in its words.

I could imagine already how this man Carausius might prove fertile source of other contradictions, similar to compare. The hero who defends our island and its liberties against barbarians

57

come over the ocean to rob, rape and kill. An officer also bearing the sacred commission of a pair of cruel emperors who preside over murder, world-wide.

A dutiful lieutenant who finds himself defending a civil society where any citizen coveting another's possessions; whether house, wife, or silver; can have him killed through no sharper weapon than words. Upon no more onerous a motion than their denunciation before a court. Whereby once so accused - whether for the holding or the voicing of prohibited opinion, its treason to the state - then any man with lands or villa attracting the envy of neighbours may be reduced to the arena. Condemned to the mines within days. Their goods forfeit via an insatiable government machine which has created specialist career-grades to prosecute this process. Reward its informants in kind.

An institutional rapaciousness becoming as arbitrary and unjust an imposition upon the common people as any atrocity once inflicted by savages from the sea. And eventually permeating so far down the hierarchies of state that even a nonentity like my father could become its latest victim. Redefine the meaning of our 'Imperial Peace' for his sadly-grieving son.

With the tethered goat dead and its hot blood extinguishing the altar-flame, only the lantern burning at the tip of 'Medusa's sternpost remains to mark her out as that vessel we should board. For sailors this trick is routine, even in the dark, and I copy their method. Sliding vertically down a ladder onto the main deck of his liburnian. Filing respectfully next into that small cell overhanging the stern which Carausius uses for day-cabin, where we his guests would eat together. Not reclining on couches but bolt-upright on a motley collection of folding furniture and campaign stools otherwise stowed-away for action.

In a hastily-convened 'mess' whose walls stand lined with weathered waiters and orderlies only hours ago hauling on sheets or rowing up the estuary. Informal, yes, but no finer setting in which a commander-in-chief could hope to hold sway. How I like to picture him now. Squeezed behind a table laid across the back of the cabin, illuminated like a statue beneath the oil lamps which swing from chains off the ceiling while his flagship rises and falls on the swell of an outgoing river.

58

A restful, soothing motion.

On what could be seen by their guttering lights, I guessed the admiral was by then in his middle forties. Of an age in those days considered not far off old, though not sufficient for a Consulship and still young enough for fighting. A thick-set and muscular but hardly-towering frame gradually turning to fat. Standing most flattered by the drapes of that shirt of welded rings he took for daily working-gear, the crudest type of armour.

A distinctive bull-neck offers our truest hint to his essential nature - like the trunk of a mighty oak. A contented, stubborn man who never bowed to any storm. Short and stout and brown as a berry, with nothing else about his kindly, rumpled face or mariner's features to distinguish him. Holding none of that haughty, patrician dignity considered traditional in a Roman general or looking so good on a statue.

What those who met him remember most instead is his enduring cheerfulness, however trying the circumstance. A veritable Hercules of Optimism, this blessing of temperament and the gods why he kept so much hair, not losing it like lesser men. Why ginger it remained, uninvaded by grey and luxuriantly curly. The beard running unchecked down a tree-like neck as if to hide his want of a singular chin, the presence of several.

What it could never hide was his complete lack of airs and graces.

If Carausius and those pale imitators coming afterwards never overcame the stigma of lowly birth, he was that one who didn't care. He more than all the others. Those 'New Men' to whom the Roman army must become used; my father's generation laments. Well, lament away, but there is no getting round the fact we live in desperate times, these men our only hope.

Living as we do through an era where bad weather brings us floods and the failure of harvests. Monetary inflation and epidemics of unemployment lead on to civil strife. Wars between our own, political chaos and disease as side-effect from suicidal raids launched by desperate barbarians fleeing something worse. Why we felt ourselves the generation who'd copped for the lot, the whole Pandora's Box.

When the first Millennium since the founding of the City of Rome had passed-us by, and too many were left believing it the end of our allotted ration. Heard superstition clear her fevered throat to whisper in their ear: *"Rome is finished, her days are done....."*

In a febrile climate like this, no wonder frantic calls for help are met with desperate measures. So that the only criteria now mattering for any army officer wanting to fight their way to the top of the *cursus honorum,* the career-ladder, are based around a measurable ability to destroy barbarians, on an industrial scale.

And being Illyrian.

Leaving literacy or any basic grasp of Latin, never mind table manners, treated as optional extra. Major policy changes in selection-criteria coming through too late to stop a well-brought-up lad like me from joining a worsening party. Yet if I was daft enough to think myself lucky to have this exciting chance, observers and family friends more worldly-wise just wondered what I thought I was doing. Joining a profession society no longer deemed honourable, right at the point when the Emperor Diocletian's new rules on heredity made me one of the fortunate few who no longer even had to.

Reporting to the run-down depot at Glevum regardless, still brimming with misplaced hopefulness and an inherited sense of duty, I was that rarest of rare commodities for our times – a volunteer, a willing recruit.

Come from a decent background, too.

Aspects to make me the obvious target for every bullying bastard a barracks could field, during those four months of basic training no-one can avoid. The *"beasting"* they called it, insisting that even someone who planned on being an officer should not expect exemption.

Any of these realities, a deranged drill-decurion or the mindless brutalities of my training, could easily have killed me. But for an unexpected development. A few stale favours and remnants of patronage earned through my late father's contacts in the military levies section of the tax office, plus some legal training of my own, suddenly being recognised by the system. Quite out of the blue and much against its normal working, they nevertheless won me what at first I mistook for rescue. In the shape of my first junior staff post and a travel warrant up to Eboracum.

A distant, cold and stressful place where my introduction to the bleakly-conservative garrison environment of Northern Command's legionary headquarters, under the legendary tyranny of Quintus Pomponius Bassianus, gave valuable insights useful later on. A knowledge and some early operational experiences eventually to be drawn-on in ways unimaginable to my younger self.

And a very senior kicking.

As not only the commander of *Legio VI Victrix Pia Fidelis Britannicus Maximus* but also governor of *Britannia Inferior,* the province of Lower Britain, this Bassianus was a notorious martinet. He might not have known me from the cowed slaves sweeping leaves in the quadrangle outside, but when I stood smartly to attention inside the *principia* with my crested helmet tight under my arm and confidently handed him the wrong set of despatches from the wrong commander in the wrong garrison - unaware of minute differences in bright-tin seals between communications from Pennine forts like Lavatrae, Verterae, or Brocavum - here was another bad experience providing stepping-stone.

Bawled out of his office on a volcano of obscenities and abject humiliation, my abandoned helmet and free transfer following within the hour, I could still make the long journey south in philosophical mood. Not sacked but seconded, as I would later insist to my mother and she would surely tell her friends.

I was determined to treat this fresh setback as yet another great opportunity. Passing my horseback days over flooded roads in a state of growing certainty about the better career chances and weather sure to be found in my new role. Looking forward to deployment into that sophisticated hotbed of cosmopolitan intrigue I expected from the civil governor's offices in Londinium for *Britannia Superior.*

Another piece of optimism proving wildly misplaced. Truth is, I probably never even thought to wonder why the Army seemed happy to despatch such a witless child as it doubtless thought me; on a mission to provide their nominal point of contact with the officials of a civilian administration it so despised. Fact was, the modern military mind had bigger fish to fry, and could not have given one single phallus-plaque in terracotta, whether wheeled, walking or winged, for the views, news, and priorities of my civil governor boss. Neither did the latter's other responsibility, as High Priest in the Cult of the Emperors, cut any thicker ice with these glacial Army men.

They simply did not care.

And maybe they were right. For if he was fortunate to be born into the right family and a distinguished line of Imperial priests, Q.Martinus Probus - another Quintus, and my latest boss - was less so in the alignment of his eyes. How an evasive nature, astigmatic distortion, and the lasting effects from an abcess in the jaw conspired together to fix them. Looking forever at his nose. Leaving any conversationalist stuck to know which one of them to check with for some sign he spoke the truth.

When the reality proved neither, for he almost never did.

"*Squint-gob*" as office colleagues called him behind his back, turned out yet another priestly high-official more concerned with the private profit to be had from exploiting rank than the effective administration of his province. But if there was no useful guidance to be had for his staff, at least we knew the score. That he in his elevated position and we in ours were as equal passengers in the same, rudder-less boat. And while both he and his staff worked away in the same none-job, although at different levels, at least it explains why he gave me so very little attention. So little else to do.

Welcome to the club.

Our cross-eyed *Superior* governor presided over a provincial civil service where, by his active default, such complete free-range was granted to as idle or, on frequent occasion, as corrupt a band of public and taxation officials as were ever inflicted on cringing Roman province.

Left to do as they pleased, nothing could have more clearly defined this useless corps of administrators. Men reduced by sloth into such negligent complacency that they could even think of sending a credulous greenhorn like me, alone into the uncharted wastes of the eastern marshes. Armed only with their short instruction to cross-examine a great admiral upon a grotesque (and in the event unproven) allegation of petty theft.

As unequal a match as it was surely a doomed mission.

Dear Gods, did they not realise?

Maybe they did. Or perhaps they'd underrated him – and possibly even me. If they had, then they would hardly be the last. Not when official historians writing about his meteoric rise following my unedifying errand would assert this man with only two names, the simple Mausaeus Carausius as he was perfectly happy to be styled, as a person of *"villissime natus"*. The lowest possible birth.

I know Carausius would be the first to concede these retrospective dismissals of his social status as utterly fair. Probably with a great bellow of laughter to go with it, mixed with a joyous curse. Fist on the table. And, yes, in his own inimitable words, why the hell should he care? Maybe he was an outsider, but there are many mightier than he to claim no better provenance.

Like I've said, the precedents are already made. For him, for all of us - at the very highest level. Now we have enthroned as our emperor *'Diocletianus'* himself. A common man born as the son of two Dalmatian slaves, serving in a Roman senator's household. Thanks to whom the game to climb up there has been totally changed forever.

Though not for the benefit of senators.

Yet if old-fashioned folk like my parents still thought this Diocles appalling, then he was hardly the only embodiment of such new modern orthodoxies to horrify their generation. Speaking out publicly against them a rather different matter, as father fatally found. Courting public disapproval from the right-thinking classes and more covert attention from Imperial spies. Both likely to be followed by denunciation, arrest, and arraignment. Legal processes inevitably concluding with conviction; the sequestration of goods and execution of their owner. True in father's case and ruining his family, as we the survivors found.

Now that informants and self-appointed enforcers of these new norms seem everywhere, the confiscated estates of those denounced for prohibited opinion grow more important to the state. Indispensable revenue, in fact. One reason why – until it hit them personally – respectable folk like my parents only dared chunter round a provincial meal-table. Complain behind closed doors, never voice their resentments wider. While the fool that I was then dismissed these grumblings for the irrelevant carping of an out-of-touch generation. No problem for my own.

In this volatile climate, the old social classes were failing and possessing two names only gave guide towards recognising a plebeian. If in the case of Mausaeus Carausius this marker stayed reliable, his status only confirmed on meeting, the origins of our *'Admiral of the Narrow Seas'* went meaner than that. A native from beyond the frontiers, a literal outsider. This barbarian of the wetlands, this river-pilot-turned-skipper-turned-soldier, was heir to a whole litany of debased social rankings troubling him not even one jot.

As he would remark to me: "*If a freedman is good enough to be emperor, then surely a free man may serve him as admiral?*"

Sometimes I would wonder that if Carausius did not by the time I knew him deliberately cultivate the manners of a peasant, then neither would he let them be erased. As if it pleased him for some at least of Nature's chisel-marks to show.

Born on the edge of Empire in the low country of the Menapii, a coastal tribe of north-eastern Gaul whose marshes easily resemble those bleak British fens where we found ourselves that day, I learnt later how many of his formative years were spent on its seaboard. Navigating merchants' barges and freighters round the estuaries, canals, and drainage channels of his homeland at the mouth of the Rhine. Gallia Belgica. Before he joined the Roman navy in search of better prospects, a formative life-event he often mentioned. The start of his rise to the top.

Like most people, I knew more about his recent route to fame. When security failures along the Empire's Rhineland frontier, our *Limes Germanicus*, were coupled with exceptional falls in river levels, catastrophic barbarian raids from Outer Germania erupted into the adjoining province. The invaders' atrocities in Gaul were unprovoked, unreasoning and unbelievable, but for a long time went unchecked. Creating a state of emergency from which only the most exceptional could save us.

If those larger cities with the foresight to have built defences could at least hide and starve behind them, the fate of provincial Gaul's prosperous countryside held no such compensation. Undefended towns and factories, unsuspecting villas or whole country estates, were taken by surprise. Wagon-trains of barbarians descending unannounced, contemptuous of laws. Torched and burned by German warbands; their families, house slaves and farm workers butchered, violated, and carried off from field or garden into worse servitudes yet. Gangs of murderers, rapists and thieves streaming off a network of paved roads our empire had constructed as if for their assistance. That web of highways which led the enemy so unerringly like arteries into the beating heart of Gaul.

Even an amateur student of history could wonder at the wisdom of any society creating so accessible a means as this vast system represented, without pausing to think how weak it made us. When we could not have done any more to aid our illiterate enemies in Rome's destruction than offer them these waymarked routes into the centre of Empire. Short cuts to loot.

With civilised life teetering on the edge of collapse in Gaul and Germania, we could only watch these events from the relative safety of Britain. Horrified but helpless spectators. That time I remember most: vivid childhood episodes of unexpected arrivals at my father's house in Calleva Atrebatum. Uncles and aunts, family friends, refugees and fugitives, appearing in the middle of the night. Once-wealthy, now missing everything. Driven empty-handed from more comfortable homes abroad but counting themselves fortunate to have escaped with their lives before the onslaught of savages.

Shocked, shaken and shabby. Middle-aged couples owning nothing more than the clothes they stood up in. Clinging to sanity and respectability, possessions clutched in a few sacks and bringing into my parents' ordered life their shocking tales of sheer terror and utter disorder. Come in their best or warmest clothes with what money or jewellery they'd sewn into the linings to a distant province untouched by these horrors consuming Gaul and the Rhine. Come to start a new life with whatever they had salvaged, it was true these new arrivals helped bolster our prosperity, though the news they brought with them cast a cloud of uncertainty and insecurity over every city in Britain.

Cometh the hour, cometh the man.

Maximinanus, Emperor of the West, another Illyrian from Pannonia campaigning on the Rhine. First as a common soldier, then a junior Caesar; now promoted to the role of joint Augustus with our Emperor himself. An obedient general and loyal lieutenant keen to show Diocletian his mettle, he'd heard about the naval exploits of our Menapian candidate and resolved to entrust him with finding further answers. Why his appointing Carausius to the land defence of Gaul proved so inspired. For not only as a general on land did Carausius help Maximian drive these Germanic invaders back across the frontier, but next he was set towards undoing all that civil chaos erupting in their wake. Behind our broken *limes*.

Where the biggest problem of that ilk men called the *'bacaudae'*. A lawless horde whose suppression Carausius could only obtain after two solid years of fighting. Mainly against Roman citizens, and why there can be no question of a Triumph once he's finally won.

Understanding all this history, proud to be dining with its victor on a plain meal of fresh-caught estuary oysters washed down with Rhenus white, I was as glad not to be placed beside his sarcastic quartermaster. The inscrutable Allectus, angular and lean, whose mocking nickname for me I never was to shed.

My nearest neighbour introduces himself instead as Intrepidus, the sailing-master of a converted charcoal-freighter they call the *'Minerva'*, her hull as black as any Saxon barque. His crew a similar shade, stained by below-decks life on a vessel recently requisitioned from the coastal trade to an active defence of their country. A down-to-earth *navarch* I feel lucky to find as fellow-diner, this Intrepidus is pointing with the tip of his oyster knife to where Carausius sits at the other end.

"There's history in action here, my boy. Three months ago me and my lads were just another coaster. Flogging up and down with wood and charcoal for the hearths of Londinium, but all the time scared for our lives and livelihoods. Praying to Fortuna we may never meet Saxons. A fearful way to live. Then suddenly this man's sent. Transforms a province where before people only whined: *"...there's nothing we can do!"* Now attitudes are different – he's got everyone united. Reinstating a navy, sorting out the army. We're all behind him now, privileged to serve. I don't know what your orders are, my boy, nor who it was what sent you, but if you get a chance to be involved, don't hesitate. Opportunities for action, just what a young blade needs. Fighting for fame and fortune, for the safety of your kinsmen. And never forget it, my boy, that this is the very man what did for Amandus, and all those bloody bacaudae!"

A recent success which the admiral harks back to from his place at our head:

"In the days of the *bacaudae*...." he announced "...there never was in Gaul a sight so rare as an old man or a good crop. Expecting to see neither again. Fighting the rebels by land, we find them aided from the sea – those perfidious Franks. *'Free men'* they call themselves, but slavery is all Frankish men ever brought citizens in Gaul. Knowing this from my time on their rivers, soon they will be paying a higher price for my lessons."

It felt strange to hear him speak with so much hatred of the Franks or their Saxon allies. This man with only two names, both Romanised from the native. Brought up beside the Rhenus mouth so close to Frankish lands he was probably related: the typical *'poacher-turned-gamekeeper'*. However high Rome promotes them, however hard they strain for the mantle of *Romanitas*, condemned forever as barbarian stock. Even by those very citizens they must defend with their lives.

German barbarians. These are the peoples Rome has tethered, taught and trained to do her dirty work, the fighting and killing. Relies on for defence. Why Italia need no longer tremble, when no comfortable citizen will exert themself ever again. When you will not find one Italian in five thousand among those expendable armies of Germans and Goths we send out to fight our own. In a war its victor is describing:

"First they were just travelling criminals, then a few rioters. A motley collection of too many lawless gangs joined as one. A newly-created under-class of violent individuals who roam a devastated Gaulish countryside. Exploit the collapse in law and order resulting from invasion. Alienated outcasts from a broken society. Misfortune finding a focus in treasonous thoughts of disaffection for a state they claim has failed them. Banding themselves together in defiance of laws. At first into several and then the one cohesive, armed, and cunningly-directed whole."

He pauses to swig from a flagon and so we do likewise, then raises a hand for our attention:

"When autumn came and the Germans were gone, driven back by our legions into their dank forests, the *bacaudae* remained. Defiantly filling a vacuum, almost an army by now. Seamlessly-formed out of all those unemployed labourers, escaped prisoners, fugitive slaves, bankrupted taxpayers, dispossessed landowners, homeless orphans, outlawed criminals and deserting conscripts who infest a burnt-out, empty countryside."

He coughs.

"An 'insurgency' Maximianus called it, and be sure he was right. Once the insurgents' desperation had turned to arrogance, their over-confidence to wilful savagery, then social collapse looked permanent. Knowing that for as long as this situation continues there'll be no chance of people returning to the land. Of them providing the revenues and supplies our emperor needs to feed his armies on the Rhine. So, while criminals thrive, ordinary citizens stay as frightened, imprisoned and hungry inside their city gates as before the tribes withdrew."

Resting above Carausius' head on the cabin-wall that night, bulging out from where it was fastened onto end-timbers, hung a unique totem of his military success. A circular shield, convex in profile and decorated with a painted Gorgon's head of unusual realism. A trophy meant for display, too precious for battle.

Set in the centre against a green background, the monster was captured by its artist moments after her decapitation by the legendary Perseus. Such a quizzical, almost humorous aspect to her reaction. So lifelike, that combination of surprise and irritation imprinted on her face. One dark eyebrow arching with helpless displeasure below a fringe of writhing black vipers. Only a ragged edge to the creature's neck and dark, bloody drops below belie the life in her face, confirm an execution.

Powerful symbolism and so incongruous a find, to see valuable artwork concealed below decks in a naval patrol craft out here on the marsh. Hidden in that same fen country where I'd come looking for another.

For all his uneducated ways, or how often the eating of oysters made him belch, it occurred to me that our barbarian admiral hid more sparks of cultural sophistication within his soul than we Romans generally gave him credit for:

"This 'Shield of Achilles' with its portrait of the dead Medusa was given me personally on the steps of the lighthouse at Gesoriacum...." he said gravely, turning slightly to point. "A token of his Imperial commission presented on my appointment by our brother-in-arms, the Emperor Maximian. His way of showing me the vipers I must slay, if we are to restore peace to the world and protection to the provinces. His solemn promise to young and old alike of happier times restored for our Empire of the West."

After what some might think my officious enquiries of earlier in the day, I was determined to stay in the background that night. Respect the seniority of those about me, keep quiet, and only provide answer when courtesy or questions required. A private resolve leaving me listening intensely to everything Carausius says. Absorbed in his words, maybe too deeply.

The only explanation I can offer for the outburst that I made. Why hearing his last remark prompted my automatic reaction. One involuntary and conditioned, beaten into me by tutors:

"The Golden Age returned, and a new generation let down from Heaven above!" what I actually came out with.

(Vergil, of course).

I can still remember blurting this classic phrase out loud then colouring and shutting-up. If those cut-price pedagogues parents inflicted on my childhood did good after all, it didn't feel like it now. Not when it left me so embarrassed, cheeks going red.

Naturally everyone stops talking and looks across at me, something I hated. If most of his captains only glare all the harder, at least good Intrepidus claps me on the back. Whilst Carausius himself beams down from the other end of the table with a frank approval:

"What.... *'the Golden Age'*? I had you down as a book-learned boy from the start and by Jove I was right. Always saying to Allectus how we need someone like that if we are to win over the landed gentry. Those fancy folk who call the shots and we go cap-in-hand to. Whose goodwill and gold are vital if I am to payroll the troops and build the ships to beat this pirate menace. Someone who can talk to gentlefolk like that in a language they understand. Put my plans and ideas to them in a nice refined way, not annoy or offend them like these hairy-arsed captains do..."

Carausius paused and grinned at the near-soundless rumble of hurt surprise he detected from their table then continued regardless: "....and by Jupiter Best and Greatest, I really believe we've stumbled across the very answer. In you, my son, sent to us by the Fates for this exact purpose. Why I will be writing to your boss straightaway to demand it. Allectus, prepare me a note at once. Tell Squint-gob he has no choice - the boy shall be transferred!"

Of course you can guess that nobody bothered to ask my views on the matter.

Though I heard later on down the grapevine how the civil governor on receiving this letter said he couldn't understand it. Publicly stating his amazement at a direct request coming in from so high an official, about so low an officer. When cross-posting between units was in those days a rarity, especially without Imperial authority, yet this second example in my short career went through even more quickly than the first. Was equally irregular. As if everyone wanted to keep moving me on. On from my last mistake.

If I was someone whose erratic career path, let alone fate, could never be of the slightest importance, it was this request from an admiral which provoked the governor into noticing me for the first - and final - time. If only for a moment and to make the fleeting observation that I was *"...a fool to volunteer, and the fleet a ragtag of renegades - a floating refuge for buggers and criminals".*

If I have former friends among the clerks to thank for passing on his high-level put-down, they did not scruple to spare word either of how gladly their boss had signed the order for my transfer, dictated letters of agreement. But why should I care? When all I wanted from Londinium was for *'Squint-gob'* to say *'yes'*, so I could get on with this next, most-promising stage in life's big adventure.

When mother heard where I was being sent, I'm told she cried out loud, but not with tears of joy. Recognising that this wasn't the first time her son's tongue had got him into trouble, just like *pater's*, and nor would it be the last.

But, hey, what in the name of Fortune was there to be so upset about?

In this eighteenth year of my age and the space of barely three months, she had seen me grow from idle nuisance round the house and general disappointment - as much to her as those tutors she funded out what little survives from father's estate - into a military embarrassment. That gangly juvenile in an itchy new uniform of whitened wool still reeking from the fullers. Their awkward, brutalised cadet in whom a succession of infantry officers could diagnose no greater sense of purpose than his unproductive love of swordplay. And a preference eccentric in one so young for an obsolete hand-weapon our legions no longer bother with carrying:

The glorious 'gladius'.

Carried by a country youth who finds himself out on the heaving seas, soldiering for Rome. Responsible officer in the active service of a famous fleet.

This then is my journal, recorded in these parchments for my heirs, and proud I am to be reciting from it here. The story of an immature supernumary whom both Eboracum and Londinium couldn't wait to offload from their rosters, joining instead an elite cadre of naval staff officers. Bright young men of initiative and daring sent to liaise with mobile forces on land and together bring Victory to a loyal British Fleet. A fleet recently restored by its greatest-ever commander-in-chief; raised from a state of near-dereliction into the most implacable scourge of Frank or Saxon the Narrow Seas ever saw.

Waging his promise of a 'Total War'.

A fantastic soldiering opportunity and, whatever people say about him now, I will never forget that I owe it all to the Admiral Carausius.

To him, and an unusual sword.

And all because, if you believed what he said to me that damp and foggy night out there on the Wensum River, I was the only man present who could quote him any Vergil.

"Each Union republic shall retain the right freely to secede from the USSR"

(Article 72, Constitution of the former Union of Soviet Socialist Republics)

- 3 -

"*In vino veritas*" it says on foreign wine bottles, but that night in a Quayside pub it was a few pints of well-kept Scotch bitter which helped bring Bill and I closer to understanding the truth behind his decision to stand as a candidate in forthcoming European elections.

Prevent us coming to blows over the institution he intended serving.

While by the time Bill was returned from his assignation up at the bar with rainbow-girl, carrying two more pints of that excellent Scotch she pulled, it looked like he'd successfully re-ordered his thoughts and she'd found better things to talk about, with hoodie-man.

Like where to go later.

Doubtless both helped by Bill's generosity, after he'd bought them each an expensive drink and resolved on greater frankness with me. Stop me getting bitter.

"Don't get me wrong, Bill, I admire your dedication...." I'd said, reaching across to grab my new pint the moment he returned. Trying to re-start our discussion on a more positive note. My friend had looked pleased and relieved at this improved reaction, leaning forward conspiratorially and starting to open up: "Look here, I've given you the standard story and everyone's had a g-good go, but we're proper pals. '*Marras*' from wayback. Know each other better than that. Why I should fill you in on something more c-complicated..."

"Complicated?"

"A question of filling a vacuum…...."

"A vacuum?" I'd asked. "J. Edgar Hoover?"

"Don't be daft. No, a vacuum in accountability. Or maybe one of power. "

"Not just a vacuum, Bill. According to what you said earlier, it's a complete failure. Moral and philosophical. Remembering what they did to Greece, or else the poor Italians….."

"One where we're all at f-fault. For letting this happen and doing nothing to prevent it. Yes, I know everyone ignores that merry band I plan on joining - the MEPs. Dismisses our Westminster MPs for being nearly as useless. But we lawyers can't escape blame either. Brought up on the English Common Law but blinded to what's been happening in our own backyard. In our own field; hour by hour, day by day. Another unreadable regulation announced. Another impenetrable EU Directive to chew on. Another sneaky change to what we always took for granted, now find we can't do a blessed thing about. Changing what we thought we understood - our constitution, our sovereignty. Our idea of ourselves. The labels on jam. None of us lifting a finger to prevent it."

"Well, that's the British way, isn't it. Saying *'mustn't grumble'* and putting up with it. While Mordor takes over The Shire."

"Absolutely! Our undoing. Everyday life in our little bubble. The inward-looking world of Newcastle's courts. Or down in the Westminster village - self-absorbed and self-sustaining. While across the sea we overlook the EU's relentless progress. Where it's really happening, Michael, as you well know. What's really so scary. Why I've got to get there before it's too late. Join the real law-makers, now the UK Parliament's reduced to a side-show. A hollow shell left in place to distract our voters with, give MPs something to do. Why finding foreign wars to fight seems the only issue left them."

"Shall I put you down as *'Euro-sceptic'* then?" I'd asked, cocking my head on one side and hovering an invisible biro over an imaginary clipboard like a high street survey. I saw the man in the hoodie and his girl behind the bar grinning at my little cameo but they quickly went back to their own conversation when I stared so coldly back.

Bill raising a pair of bushy eyebrows then returning to his theme without hesitation:

"Whether I'm Eurosceptic or not, or you are, is neither here nor there. What matters is what enormous reach the institutions of Europe have gained over our lives. Over you and me. Over millions of people. Yet held accountable to no-one, answerable to nothing. Not even the European Court. All that power but no responsibility. A recipe for abuse if ever there was one: the hallmark of a harlot. Why I plan on heading there soon, if enough Geordie electors will grant me even half the chance."

Not an apologist now, and I knew once my friend got into the groove on a major issue there'd be no stopping him. Though if I thought the speech I'd just heard held many hallmarks of another case in point, Bill's strength of feeling was still a surprise, even to me:

"Europeans are our neighbours, Michael, should always be our friends. But never our masters. I'm all in favour of a Europe united by peace, a common trading area, but simply refuse to accept the EU as our replacement sovereign institution. The new union currently being framed to replace that British one its colourless drones work so hard to undermine. The secretive creation of bankers and civil servants, some of them British. A gravy-train for ideologues, built by a foreign elite never asking our view but working as relentlessly away to govern us as they hide away from the light....."

"Shadowy, arguably. Unaccountable, certainly, and some say corrupt. But hasn't the EU often been a force for good? " I said, attempting 'devil's advocate'.

"OK, well if you want to talk outcomes, let's start with what they publish. Apart from all those impenetrable laws, I mean. Their PR of ineffable blandness. Picture of a sunflower and dancing children here; an unelected Commissioner pointing assertively to a far horizon over there. Soporific but deliberately so. It's meant to be soothing. All of it like a ruse, a diversion. As if we didn't know we are being had, by a chaotic organisation. One whose annual accounts have never in its history satisfied their auditors, ever been approved...."

"Is that true, Bill?" I interrupted, astonished: "Never?"

"No, never! Never been able to say where all our money goes, what they do with it. For years. I find that incredible. You and I have seen some dodgy outfits in our time, the local fraud cases we've done together. That discount warehouse taking customers' deposits but never delivering. The firm of successful Northumbrian builders so busy building they never stopped-by to check on their faithful book-keeper of years, busy cleaning them out. None of them filed accounts either."

"So how does Brussels get away with its own never being approved?"

"Well might you ask – year after year. What have they got to hide, and why doesn't their so-called Court of Auditors do something about it, seeing they claim to be a court? When the EU has the nerve to lecture a basket-case like Bulgaria about public corruption; or Greece and Italy, Portugal and Spain about budget deficits. Takes over their governments. Imagine if a UK limited company tried that - failed to file accounts, I mean. Wouldn't it be closed down by the authorities overnight, its directors banned? Or maybe even jailed?"

Now I understood the mainspring to his passion. I should have remembered. Never mind the Law, Bill *'The Tax'* was a closet accountant. And if this diagnosis was right, there could be no sacrilege cutting closer to the heart of that calling than failing to maintain or file proper accounts. Devotional climax to the book-keeper's year. And in the case of a huge organisation the size of the EU, then even a cynic like me could concede it was a fairly elementary requirement. Not one to opt out of, not even if you're bigger than Enron.

"Especially when it's actually *my* money....." the man in the hood called down to us from the bar, just when I thought we'd lost them. He needn't have bothered. By now, Bill didn't need egging-on by anyone. Positively steaming with self-righteous rage and his second pint of bitter. Why I suspect both myself and our *'Citizen's Panel'* at the bar were listening to his latest outburst with collective jaws dropped. Like everyone else I was guilty - or so Bill declared. *'Hoodie' and his girl, too?* Guilty of letting our national inheritance be smuggled away in the night. Guilty of dismissing the EU and its works as simply too boring to think about, what he said.

"I tell you, it's, it's....I-like a growth. Some b-blueish mould blooming in the corner of a cold room you often notice but never get round to c-cleaning away. L-looking at more c-closely."

"*Blue mould...?*" I said. "For crying out loud, Bill. That's a bizarre metaphor coming from a politician, if ever I heard one. You're hardly going to set young voters' hearts ablaze with rhetoric like that, are you? Perhaps you need to get a better speech-writer. And when did you last clean a mouldy room, anyway?"

He grinned ruefully: "Maybe it's been a w-while, but I do know teenagers have the messiest ones. And joking apart, represent the generation who'll live with the consequences. Without what we're losing, gave away on their behalf. Are perhaps the easiest to con'. For Eurocrats to sneak past. Who don't really care, don't want to know. Lost in a world of digital, reading nothing unless it's on a screen and then only for a second. Flitting-off to whatever's next. Titbits of social gossip, who's posted what. No wonder kids seem indifferent if they can't c-concentrate on *anything* for longer than five minutes...."

"That sounds a bit harsh, a bit old fogey-ish. And mould, Bill, mould?" I gaped back.

"Yes, mould! If you insist on questioning it, a comparison I'll stand by. Forensically speaking. Starting with ancient Greek – where I read somewhere that our word for *'mould'* and the Greek one *'Europa'* share in the same etymological root....."

His face had grown sober and displayed no humour now, but surely he was kidding:

"Get away! Really?"

Bill might well be *'My Learned Friend'* in court, but I never imagined he was. Not till now.

"Honest, Mike, it's true. And while we're on words, ever heard of the *'Acquis Communitaire'*? No, well that employs the same biological principles for growth as mould. Always taking ground, never relinquishing any. An invented rule whose insidious effect ensures we're ratcheted-into Europe forever. No going back, never got rid. Forget that crap about *'Bringing Powers Home'*, Michael. Fact is, once the EU has captured a particular field of *'competence'* as they call it from our government, then we'll never get it back. Any of it."

"OK and if you're right, then how do they get away with it? Why does no-one notice?"

"Like I keep on saying, simply by being so boring. It's brilliant. The ultimate camouflage, like a Stealth Fighter. Makes them invisible. You've only got to attempt it, to start to read any official EU publication, whether on-line or in hard copy, before you're completely overcome. Dull to look at, dull to read. Gassed by Brussels sprouts. That creeping *ennui* which pervades their every, turgid announcement. Or those hard letters of power that are hidden inside the more important legislation. So clever."

"*Ennui*? A French word isn't it? No, don't worry, I won't hold it against you. And sympathise with the points you're making. Honestly I do, but let's get real, Bill. When did you last settle down beside the fire with a Jura malt and the Maastricht Treaty. Attempt to work out what it means for you and yours? The Lisbon Agreement or Schengen?"

He laughed: "No, I can't c-claim to, Michael. Though soon I'll be forced to. We lawyers are used to finding our way round their awful regulations, but hardly representative. Not the experience of ordinary folk. Precisely what's so b-blooming clever about the whole enterprise. It's inspiring public indifference lets them off the hook of public accountability."

"Because no-one understands it, no one really cares?"

"Exactly. So the eurocrats can keep on creeping forward. An empire of Sir Humphreys, lots of them French. Spending half their year away from the desk on holiday leave, the only mercy we're granted. But as someone who likes words, I can see you're still not happy. Not convinced by my choice of metaphor. OK, well if it's not to be mould, let's try another. Let's call it Japanese knotweed. Yes, why not? As valid a comparison. Green and organic. A monster that never stops growing, night and day. Swarming and plant-like, cunning and cruel. Impossible to get to grips with, what piece to hack off first?"

"I never saw you as a gardener, Bill" I laughed, leaning back against the red leather settle.

"No? Then call me Theseus. That's more like it - a champion, a hero entering the maze. That's what I'll aim to be for people if I'm elected. Get inside the beast, infiltrate its lair. Work out how far it's penetrated into ours. How deep. And how much further it plans on going - if it even knows! What it's doing with all that money we feed it. Them and the IMF."

"A god *and* a people's hero? How modest is that?"

"As honest a goal to aim for as any, Mike, my friend. When I don't think most ordinary British people have even the faintest idea what the EU's about. What damage it's done their country, using their own money to do so. Ordinary people like our young friends at the bar....."

"Don't underrate the wisdom of crowds, Bill. We both learnt that lesson long ago in jury trials. These two showed a real interest in what we were talking about. At least to start with, anyway, before the place filled-out. But most folk don't have a clue and care even less. As long as there's something good on telly, shops in the Metro Centre, petrol stays low."

"No, they don't know, do they? How much it's taken us over, changed us to the extent it has. Breaking up the old country into malcontented 'celtic' nations, mythical bloody 'regions'. Like that made-up new one they've invented, covering both sides of the Channel. Both sides, I ask you, both French and British. Brussels must be having a laugh....."

"Have you got nothing good to say about the EU, Bill? Surely it's saved us from more World Wars? Kept Germany from France's throat, everyone slaughtering each other. Three-quarters of a century of peace and a common trading area. Duty-free wine. Holiday homes in the Dordogne. Cheap air flights. Regulated pet travel. What's not to like?"

"Oh yes, I'm sure it's helped, along with democratic government, but what's been the price? Didn't our grandparents' generation pay it for us anyway? Scottish, Northumbrian, Tyne-Tees and Highland Divisions, winning half of it back on their European Tour 1944-45? Then what they thought an iron and steel confederation changes into a trading 'Community'; a community that suddenly becomes a 'Union'. Without anyone asking us....."

"They did in seventy-five..." I said, bending a beermat in half and making a glider.

"With a false question, Michael, on a false premise. When political integration was always their intention. Monet and Chirac and Kohl thinking they could do it by stealth. Financial and fiscal integration their means to an unspoken end. The current lot intending no different, whatever they say. I heard a retired eurocrat talking in a podcast the other day about what he described as the EU's tradition of "political corruptness". An entity unable to grow without systematically weakening other ties. Poisoning old loyalties, undermining old institutions. A Franco-German cartel, their dreaded 'Commission'. Another unaccountable institution where Europe's 'parliament' has no real say. But subtle and devious enough to go about exploiting and creating division under the device of *'Regionalism'*. Balkanising Britain....."

"Hell, what are you actually saying, Bill? That they want to replicate some form of Yugoslavia across Europe? With all its inherent risks. Are you serious?"

"Who knows? And maybe its consequences. Scots against English; Welsh against English; Cornish against English; Irish ditto. England against the rest. The commonwealth against a common market somehow suiting a wider purpose. Dividing to rule."

"Do you genuinely believe that? It's more than a bit drastic, a real conspiracy theory. So what are you alleging – that they have an interest in upheaval? In dismantling the Union?"

"I fervently hope not, Michael. But sadly how it feels. How it might go if we aren't careful. Playing into the hands of malcontents. Home-grown extremists seeing an opportunity to make hay at public expense, paint democracy into a corner. Fatally-blur the line between honest patriots and dangerous facists....."

"You're joking? Sounds like Armageddon to me...." I said, throwing the glider. He ducks.

"No. Believe me, I only hope I'm wrong....that we're not sleepwalking into disaster, playing into their hands. Cravenly without being asked. Thank God it's without any shots being fired, but it still feels like we've been surrendering all along what previous generations fought to defend. Why it makes no sense. Voluntarily dismantling everything good about Britain. What she once represented. Wanting to save eurocrats the trouble, meekly ending our Union and with it our liberties. Just to please them."

"I understand the point you're making, Bill, but let's hope for the best eh? I know you're sincere, accept we've probably gone too far. Selling out to the unaccountable, uncontrollable institutions you describe as determined to take Parliament's place. But if someone like me struggles for positive outcomes, perhaps it's little wonder the only thing Westminster politicians feel they have left to tinker with is foreign policy. Playing at wars."

"My fear exactly. Everything apart from that becoming devolved or surrendered to the EU. To concepts I personally consider corrosive. A corrupting entity with no democratic legitimacy. A creeping form of totalitarianism which electorates should insist on our government countering. They should actively reform."

"Or else walk away from....?" I added.

He paused, face florid like I'd noticed it go during trials:

"Maybe that's the answer, the eventual solution. Though I doubt the politicians will let us. But there it is – you've had it now, Michael. My full and frank confession. Real reasons for wanting to stand, whatever I told the selection panel. That it's out of patriotic duty!"

This last with a flourish that oddly unnerved me, swelling his chest out as if closing to a jury at the end of a case.

Blimey.

Whatever encouraging noises I'd made along the way, the fact is these were things over which to date I'd held few strong views. Knew fewer facts, gave even less thought. But Bill obviously did and now he was cooking on gas. Even so, I think it was his last comment and delivery which alarmed me the most. Coming from him, of all people.

Sounding rather less like Bill, too much like Mr Toad.

"It still makes me uneasy. You know what Doctor Johnson said about patriotism?"

"Yes, of course I do...." he scoffed "....*Last Resort of the Scoundrel.*"

"Where you know the score, especially nowadays. How when an Englishman gets patriotic he risks unattractive friends. The car parks of Essex pubs......"

"Is it a sin to love your country?"

"I'm not so sure any more. Definitely feels close. Yes, flag-waving nationalism seems OK for the Celtic nations. *'Braveheart'* and all that, a saltire on everything, no sign of the *'Jack'*. Hatred of the English permitted; generally thought amusing. Though at Murrayfield I'm always treated politely, whatever it says in *'Flower of Scotland'*. But once good old Saint George and his red cross gets onto the agenda, well, that's somehow different. Ugly undertones appear. Nearly as ugly as some of the people who turn-up with them. Neo-fascists and social inadequates; hard-core racists. The worst we can field, hard work to drive away. OK Bill, and maybe I'm teaching my grandmother to suck eggs, but I think you'll need to be super-vigilant who joins you on this journey. Who you let tag along, what company you keep...."

"Look, I know what you mean, Michael...."

"I'm sure you do. But as a longstanding friend, all I'm saying is I'd hate to see you attract unwelcome attention. From the wrongest of sorts....."

"No, of course I won't. Because I'm not stupid, not daft. But maybe if I persuaded an old mate like you to join me on the journey, then you could help to keep me right. Because, no, I don't mean England and Saint George at all..." he added "....it's like the whole of Britain. The idea of keeping Britain together I'm concerned with. In all its diversity...." he said pointedly, before a pregnant pause:

"*Britannia*...." he said.

Crikey. Maybe that's worse. For a moment it felt like a live outside-broadcast from '*Last Night of the Proms*', an event I always found toe-curling. Not some tatty Quayside pub on a wet Thursday night, with hardly any customers. At least I finally knew where Bill was coming from. Or thought I did.

While Bill went off to the toilet, he left me reflecting glumly on what he'd just said. How Doctor Johnson was fundamentally right, but sometimes even imperfect men and women are forced to stand up for their country. To risk letting it down. And that private journey Bill had set himself, his mission impossible. Rather him than me, what I thought at the time. Little realising how far what had started off as banter in a pub would eventually lead him.

Or me.

Either way, you had to hand it to him. Whatever anyone thought of his formulaic opening to our discussion earlier that night, and however much he'd climbed down later then painted-in a bolder passion, Bill was learning fast. Hearing him speak fluently of Tyneside as a "*Developing Region*" where once he'd speak of countries, of counties even. Glibly making distinctions from the old Northumberland and Durham as unfashionable examples.

A serving civil servant myself, his politics were strictly not my business - whatever my private opinions as citizen, cynical man in a pub. But Eurosceptic or otherwise, I knew the day would come when I was entitled to reach a voter's view. Just like everyone else. To decide that William Cariss was surely a sound bet in anyone's book, the ideal choice to represent Tyneside in Europe.

As he'd said himself: *"What's not to like? A practising professional and family man with a good understanding of law, tax and business. Self-employed, loyal to the area. With some inside knowledge of European defence issues as added bonus to my CV. A record of voluntary work: free legal advice at the hospice plus ten years' service in the Tyneside RNVR - Royal Naval Volunteer Reserve - to boot. Who wouldn't vote for me?"*

In the end, when European elections came along shortly after, the major problem turned out as more one of who'd actually bother to turn-out and vote for anybody.

I'd heartily assured him that night of my support and - whatever else happened or came between us - I like to keep that picture of him. Leaning cheerfully back against the torn red leather of his pub-chair and beaming. Contented and at ease. Looking for all the world as if my personal endorsement there and then was all it took to clinch it.

Happily for Bill I was not alone. It turned out there were just enough impressionable souls like me willing to turn out at a polling station on a warm summer night and cross his box with pencil, when he did stand. And even if it was on the basis of so feeble a turnout from so indifferent an electorate - well below twenty per-cent - William Cariss was duly elected.

While for all we know it might not have been me but that hooded man up at the bar and his strange girlfriend behind it who were the two floating voters finally clinching it. Every vote counting, as the democrats like to say.

However slight his mandate, I felt personally pleased for Bill, if only as a friend. A new interest for him where he could keep his legal practice on, albeit at reduced level. While I could continue to brief him for the Crown on those few criminal prosecutions where no conflict of interest with his '*Regional constituency*' duties arose, and he still had the time.

An ethical position I was surprised to find my employer accepting, although it was unfortunate if increasing commitments over in Strasbourg and Brussels left me seeing rather less of Bill in the courts as an opponent.

Leaving a shared interest in motorsport to provide what few occasions or reason - apart from Christmas, New Year, and the odd e-mail – remained for us keeping in touch.

Apart, of course, from that long-standing booking which we'd both made in our respective desk-diaries, for Brescia the following May.

For our own Italian 'job'.

"The small state exists so that there may be a spot on earth where the largest possible proportion of the inhabitants are citizens in the fullest sense of the word"

(Joseph Burckhardt, writer and explorer,
re-discoverer of the lost city of Petra)

- IV -

If they say you can taste terror, then I know I did. And never did its flavour lead me more fervently to desire death nor imagine it closer than during that terrifying first voyage along our eastern seaboard.

My opening combat patrol.

An endless journey where land lies always in sight but helmsmen won't allow it nearer. Fearing its distant promise of stability might subvert the crew, too close an approach break our vessel on its hidden rocks. Such tantalising country: one moment higher than our masthead, the next beneath the waves. Its see-saw motions echoing in a landsman's guts. Mocking my human dignity with what animal degradations I'm reduced to.

So much for the long-awaited great adventure.

Mother had been right.

If I'd thought the sea would make a man of me, all it was doing was killing me. Alone and ignored, I cling like a crab when the tide goes out to the carved railing framing the centre deck of *'Medusa'*. Wrapped in a sordid tangle once my uniform and a borrowed cloak so spattered with spittle no lender would ever reclaim it. Unfit for a shroud.

Did not Publius Vergilius Maro, Rome's greatest poet, die from a sea crossing? If he was my favourite, it hardly meant I wanted to go out the same way.

Unmarked and unwounded, uninfected with anything, it still felt like death. Numbed by the cold, the acids in a parching throat. That taste! No sooner do I try and neutralise its tang, wet my lips from a soldier's flask, than my insides are off again. Sick, frozen and scared, I could no more obey the call of duty than fly away south; reclaim our lost citadel at Dura-Europos or fend-off a Persian raid.

The rest of her crew ignore me apart from that thoughtful marine who tied a rope from around my waist onto this balustrade. Cheap insurance against a bigger wave crashing across the deck and dragging me out through an open oar-port into a raging sea. A servant of the fleet with more important business than this one seasick boy, his kindness in the thick of it welcome all the same. A business to which Great Neptune and his towering rages, out there on the German Ocean, are mere incidentals. The backdrop to routine.

In a quieter phase, I drag myself at the length of my safety-rope like a Triumphal Captive to the rail. Offer more stomach-lining in sacrifice, votive accompaniment to prayers for respite begged from implacable gods. Saliva on my lips, eyes turn from water sweeping-by to look behind. See the skein of green ships that follow ours in close pursuit dip behind a staggering wave then rise high and triumphant on a towering crest. Their pocketed leather sails billowing out like the swollen cheeks of those divine Furies who drive us on and northwards: Boreas and Aeolus.

Even an amateur like me can realise this is no weather for rowing; wind and sail our only deliverance. Begin to glean more understanding of what is really going on. The land our captain consistently kept by us at a distance, over to the left, now fading away while a new shore rises up ahead instead. Our bows heading towards it, if why I don't yet know.

Surely nothing could have been more dangerous?

The sailors start using a lead-weighted line over the bows to test for shallow water. Calling their findings aft. Everything might have been confusion, all shouting and running about, but for the hallmark of professionalism its undercurrent. That sense of something important reaching a conclusion, even before I see marines collecting weapons from their centurion. Sight of their familiar faces etched with such grim purpose galvanises me, diverting self-pity from the pressure in my ears, that rolling in my guts.

During a dash for the shore which stabilises our hull and its motion into something more regular, its rhythms more predictable, almost even bearable, I see a new flag go up on our bowsprit. Blue cloth embroidered in gold with a crescent moon: his badge of Diana, the Goddess of Hunting. And an unfamiliar dark ship some way ahead and to starboard, driving hard like us for a fast-approaching shore.

How I recognise a hot pursuit, all trim and gear of the flagship of Carausius, his famous 'Medusa', set for hunter-killer. Even a land-lubber like me feels the meaning of windpower in our sail, understands the rise in its deck. Realises where its inexhaustible breath is sending us. With no ports out here, ours and the black ship run pell-mell together for the same shore; race for the flat beach lying prone ahead as if it were a haven. Awaiting us both like a reluctant bride.

As we get inshore and cross a line of surf some nearer marines are sent below to take up oars again. Not both banks, there are too few left from the stony-faced crowd assembling on the prow with shields and swords for that, but sufficient muscle to give us extra degrees of control in shallow water. Enough to count.

The sailors using the lead line give up on that method and go over to graduated sounding-poles. Calling their measures out loud to the steersman, sung like a song. Whether this makes the difference between our running ashore smoothly or a total shipwreck I am in no position to judge, putting my trust in a great admiral and our even greater sea-gods instead.

"Pull up, my fine boys, pull up for the shore!" booms his voice from the stern.

If there is good to be had in what unfolds, it is how signs of impending action close my mind to *emesis*. Allow me to wipe bile from my face and clear a streaming nose. Re-order my appearance like a soldier's, untying the safety cord for the first time and giving more thought to what help a tyro like me could offer his new-found comrades of the Fleet.

"*Beyond just quoting Vergil....*" as wags were bound to joke.

My armour and fighting gear are stored below but as soon as I step down the ladder to retrieve them, into its mobile dark, my stomach resumes its churning. Like those madly-dangling pots and kitbags twirling from rafters. So all I can manage down there is to snatch my *gladius* in its oiled scabbard-casing before dashing back up through the hatch. To that place by the rail where I crouch again, wet-through and wretched. Waiting without helmet, armour or shield to go into action against real Saxons for the very first time. With only a short sword to save me

To think how much I'd longed for action, how useless I felt when it came.

The nearest cliffs are clearer now: low, fissured and friable. Of red-brown clay and little height, tumbling like a ruinous city wall onto smooth beaches. Remains of a British Troy?

Our quarry, that dark ship ahead, stays firmly on its bearing. Straight for their welcoming sand at unabated speed: *"Nine knots or so..."* I hear men guess, its narrow-waisted hull maintained at a steady right-angle to the shore at the hands of a committed steersman.

"Most seamanlike..." say ours in grudging admiration.

While we do just the same.

Whether those on board have seen us, I know not. Incredible they don't. Through the spray I can make out no figures, no crew, only their vessel itself. Set in silhouette against the chosen beachhead, still aimed at a shore so smooth and flat there appears little sign of wave or breaker until their furthermost reach.

I look behind me over the stern again to our other ships of the *'M'* squadron, faithfully following their leader. Straight onto the beach without one hint of hesitation. Then feel a jolt as our own trailing-oars start to bite and *'Medusa's'* mainsail shrinks, sailors releasing sheets and dropping it on our deck in piles of folded leathercloth.

Looking down over the side the water is transparent, waving strands of podded yellow and green seaweed streaming-by below. Suddenly the black ship ahead stops dead in its tracks; stopping hard and fast like it's been nailed to the sea. White water boiling up all around her, only feet from the land, and from somewhere high on the *'Medusa'* a command-trumpet blares out.

For the first time I see signs of life on the enemy vessel. A white face, waxy pale, turning to look straight back at us while his fellows pile over the side, wading chest-deep for the shore. Then he follows their example.

Running away.

The slim keel of our bireme is next to hit the beach and I fall in a heap when it does. Banging my head on the deck, stunned by the impact. Astonished what agony is contained in the noise of wood and iron hitting sand. Another sound too - of running feet on deck. Someone with hobnails stands on me then is gone, leaving their imprint on my leg as souvenir. The first marines going in, oarsmen arming and quick to follow over the side.

Leg bleeding, I get onto one knee, half-upright on her planking, to find *'Medusa'* pointing forward, bows-on to the cliffs. Most of her soldiers already launched into the water beyond, swimming and wading. Then another wave comes in, slewing her round at an angle, followed by another. Crouched by the deck-rail, I hear cursing from the rear steering-position where our commander stands. Carausius's unique tones, calling for anchors and remaining hands to go out:

"Go to it, my boys, hunt them down on the beach. Not one of them leaves it alive!"

When crouching there is probably safest, once tower-mounted *catapultae* on *'Medusa'* open up. Directing streams of flying iron over my head and into a Saxon hulk that's well and truly stuck. The crack from their mechanism when the bolts let go, the smash once they hit. While the good old *'Minerva'* grinds the matronly hips of a freighter's hull onto the beach beside us, her single catapult already firing at close range from a tower in her bows even as she does.

Into a sitting duck.

Struggling to my feet, I am alone on *'Medusa's* deck apart from the catapult crew and a few sailors, busy about what's needed. No-one to care, while of Carausius himself there's now no sign. No-one to tell me, no-one to stop me.

I step out of my borrowed cloak and unwrap the *gladius* from its oilcloth. Its scabbard is little use without a belt or buckle to hang on, but affection for my antique sword's oldest companion prompts my finding a niche on deck to hide it in. Only then can I slip away – over the side with the carved handle of an ancestral weapon tight in my hand. Looking for what? For glory, a duel? No, beyond an intention to be useful, I could not tell you now what I intended that day. All that mattered was to be counted with the lads, be part of their team.

My new mates.

Unarmoured as I was, I might well have been naked for what protection a rancid tunic gave me. What shield it was against the freezing shocks of ocean. For a moment I go under, the world disappearing beneath glassy-green prisms. Then I break surface again, splashing wildly until upright in the shallows, shaking water from my head like a shivering dog. The cold grips me like a metal vice - as if to crush my ribs, solidify my lungs. Coughing and spitting salt water. It's brackish, worse than bile, limitless in volume. Heart racing, blind eyes stinging, I try to wade forward against the weight of an outgoing tide. Struggle against Neptune's hand. Maybe he sees me and takes pity, coming to my aid with another wave to shove me shorebound. Pushed further-in and higher onto the sand by its massive force.

Into battle.

If I flatter myself only instinct or some remnant of professional rigour kept my sword in a claw-like hand, it might just have been cold. The sopping weight of my woollen tunic many times its dry, heavier than armour but far less useful. And if I can hardly stay upright for its chilly flapping, at least when the next wave knocks me onto all fours by now it is into shallow water. Hauling myself upright once again, streaming eyes can begin making out shapes and figures even if my ears are full of German Ocean. As much through stress or fear as water in my ear-canal, I stand there completely deaf. Surrounded by so many silent madmen running round me in the surf.

Soundlessly screaming and yelling in battle, these men are fighting to the death.

In, on, and around the black ship of our enemy. Knee-deep in sea, with me so perished all I can do is stand helpless amongst them. Their lone observer, drawn-up like a tottering pillar in the ruins of civilisation. Shaking violently from the cold as much as any fright, my breathing comes fast and uncontrollable. Tremors convulsing my frame while water drains away in rivulets out the weft of my uniform. The wind off the sea cooling my skin through its sodden threads, this chill the agent of an unexpected happiness, an inherited sword by my side. Useless and never to be used.

Soon I will die alone and unlooked-for on this innominate British beach and no-one will remember me. None of it matters any more. For the first time in the whole ordeal I suddenly felt glad, looking forward to an ending.

Men leave no mark on the sea, and nor would I.

That fatal point when I will swear the Gods showed me a vision of my own mother walking or maybe floating towards me from the direction of those crumbling cliffs.

Odd to find her here, I knew.

Naturally I cry out, for all the chaos around. She calls back with anxious words of warning. Gestures behind me like theatre-goers do at a farce. Turning with more speed than my poor state should allow, I find a big man standing there. A helmeted Saxon warrior as alone and wet-through as I am. Immobile too, but holding an upright sword light in his hand. Pausing for one moment as if savouring the choice of whether to split my skull in half or disembowel me first.

Thanks to a fleeting sight The Unknown God there gave me of my own dear mother, I gave him neither option. The mother to whom they say dying soldiers call out in agony on the point of death. True or not, what seems oddest to those who knew me, or bookmakers taking odds at the Games, was how little my upbringing might suggest – in so unequal a match as my youthful self, set against a large barbarian – I would not prove the likely loser.

And looking back on life, a pretty sheltered upbringing it had been.

The well-brought-up surviving son of a minor civil servant and his well-connected wife, born in a country town, I was a quiet boy. Schooled in knocks no harder than tracts by Ovid, Homer or Vergilius may fully describe, his education delivered at the point of nothing sharper than the end of a tutor's cane. Let loose later in what spare time and wildness was allowed me, my weapon-skills honed in no more dangerous, daring, nor productive ways than chasing wolf, boar or deer to little effect and even less success around the woodlands of Spinaii.

Until the army got me, there was no more useful military skill in which I was drilled nor tested - by no more rigorous an institution than commercial fencing-schools – than in how to use a short-sword. Our showy wielding of this obsolete weapon at their annual passing-out parade the traditional feature of ceremonies normally concluding with the student's demonstration to his doting parents of no higher technical proficiency than will decapitate an impaled turnip from a passing pony. At an undemanding pass-rate set by our over-generous instructors no higher than one-try-in-two.

As if it would do.

There would be no second chance this time.

If life is a journey, the recurring moral of this memoir is to show how we change. Or as Heraclitus puts it, that the man I am now is not the boy who started out. How it took the harsh benevolence of the *Classis Britannica* to stand the child I was once, just about upright, in some terrible place where all this gentle breeding and unsure background could be tested to its limits.

Once and for all, to the lofty amusement of a watching God.

The how and the why I found myself there in this position. Up to my waist and half-naked in the salty waters and freezing wastes of an uncharted British beach, out on its eastern seaboard. Staring into the uncaring eyes of my potential *nemesis*. Facing the ultimate test.

To see whether I had enough presence of mind in a chilled head to produce an unconventional street-fighting move my old fencing-teacher would have deplored in a gentleman. A quick and unsporting stroke demanding far more strength in body, mind, and purpose than I'd ever called-on in life before. Every ounce of which is needed if I am to take the white-boned handle of a Léon-forged *gladius* in both hands - not one - and plunge its blade down straight and deep like a dagger. Push it firmly past the grating collarbone of a Saxon pirate staggering around in the surf before me. A nameless person whom hunger made slow, yet would kill me if I waited.

Someone a complete stranger to myself and our Fleet, until he and his kind commit their punishable offence. Come all this way over their *'Whale Road'* into our sacred waters, borne on a black ship. Upon no kinder purposes than robbery, rapine and raiding. Come in a malign state of illegality they can only seal by stepping down on the lordly strands of our Island Province. Their absolute Act of War, deserving our hardest, most Roman reply.

This one got it.

As he slid slowly and reluctantly below the waves, his blood billowing up like clouds in the sea, he looked sadly up at me just once. As if faintly aggrieved. While I as kindly took a Frisian sword from his relaxing hand to return it only a moment. Into the receptive custody of his weakly-welling throat, blood fountaining up in a shower to drench me like the sea. Washing away bile and vomit, the baptismal sacrifice of Mithras. An act of mercy and renewal – the final end of suffering. The end of his and mine together.

Leaving me holding two swords.

In the faithful service of our Fleet, this life now taken was to prove the first of many, but I can still see his face to this day. Gently rebuking me for his departure but gifting me that proudest of proud boasts, when among the marines:

"My other sword is a seax".

A truthful claim too.

One which means that, when I make a sweep of them through the brothels and bars of Rutupiae with it strapped close to my chest, drawing the unwilling jackals of the *Classis* back to their ships and the dawn patrol, I know there will never be a marine nor man of the Fleet to dare challenge or stand against me, quoter of Vergil or no.

They know me now, not as a callow boy but a proper killer.

Respect.

"I have often remarked on the generous hearts of individual Englishmen, and at the same time the total unscrupulousness that seems to inform every action of their government."

(Auguste Gicquel des Touches:
'Souvenirs d'un marin de la républic' c.1815)

My mind often goes back to that evening's debate in a Tyneside pub when I wonder how I got myself tangled-up in Bill's political work. When what seemed like an ordinary drink after work and the current-affairs banter that lightens it, is suddenly turned with hindsight into a definable historical event.

Thinking of everything it led us into. Me included. Though never against my better judgement.

A process probably getting into gear the night I unexpectedly bumped into Bill next. Among a mixed audience of lawyers, students and academics at a Wednesday-evening law lecture held at the university. Inside a modern building resembling nothing more than an exploding towel-rail, its chrome frozen mid-blast.

At least this venue made a change from seeing him in the pub.

"What are you doing here?" he'd asked me almost crossly, while we queued in the atrium for complimentary glasses of red wine. "At a lecture on procurement law?"

Like I was invading his scene.

"Could ask you the same question. At least I try and broaden my field, insure against the next CPS redundancy-round. Keep the mind active, the knowledge-band wide, the CPD points fresh. And I'll do anything for free wine, especially red. So what about you?"

"You remember Alec?"

Oh, yes. I remembered Alec alright.

Entrepreneur extraordinaire and local celebrity, he was fellow member of a local motor club, run from its bunker-like clubhouse out on the coast. The club whose membership we shared, not for tribal reasons or geography but its distinguished history and active present as an organiser of Tyneside motorsport.

Coincidence didn't end there. I knew Alec Cadwell first became friendly with Bill through another shared hobby: the Tyne Squadron of RNVR ('*Royal Naval Volunteer Reserve*') of which both men were current members. Acting as officers, weekend sailors playing at Nelson. Messing about in boats, on a rather big one in fact, but at least it wasn't golf. Personally, I never liked the egregious Mr Cadwell.

How he kept on popping-up.

Smart Alec, the accountant-turned-businessman who'd made his pile of money in a worldwide chain of hotels, then inexplicably sunk most of it into a new shipyard at Wallsend. Fair play to Alec, it represented the most daring commercial venture Tyneside had seen in years. His personal blast, straight from a tragic local past.

Madly-courageous say some, foolhardy say others. When manufacturing experience on the Tyne seems all decline and closure, Alec took the brave step of opening his new maritime production facility on a shabby riverside site at Wallsend. Slap-bang on a location with more above-ground evidence of the ancient Roman fortress at Segedunum than now remains of the world-famous 'Swan Hunter' shipyard we only lost in living memory. And he's just built over.

Anyone providing new jobs for four hundred Geordies, especially when it's rejuvenated heavy industry, must be a local hero. A role Alec revelled in, even on days off. While Bill and I fiddle about in vintage sportsters on glorified regularity-runs, Alec would be scorching over the Army ranges out on Otterburn in a state-of-the art tarmac rally-car. The latest version *'Evolution FQ'* - sign-written with his company logo, hoovering up the silverware. Winning every big event, when *'...Quick'* is exactly what it was.

In all the papers.

"What does a man like Alec want from you, Bill?"

"He's my client, my valued client. A special *'Brief for Counsel to Advise'* just passed me by my clerk. Covering novel points of EU law, tendering procedures and the like. Alec's been doing really well, you know. Lots of orders. Fast patrol boats for the Arabs then places like Singapore. Till he hits a bit of a cash-flow problem."

"Judging by what he spends on his rally cars, I'm not surprised."

"Now be fair. Alec is a big employer with the chance of yet more jobs. No-one wants to see that threatened. Local and national government both wanting to help."

"Good of them both. Like happened with DeLorean? It's taxpayers' money, remember."

"Obviously. But there's a problem. A tricky legal issue which tonight's lovely lecturer is likely to touch on. What I'm hoping to learn more about."

"Like you've found out he's a crook?"

"Oh, come off it, Michael! You're only jealous of his cars. No, to be fair, it's nothing of the sort. No, it's the European Union's rules on State Aid. In particular, Article 107. How sad is that? You see, I can even remember its exact number."

"Which says....go, on, remind me?"

"A Member State cannot grant aid which distorts or threatens to distort competition by favouring certain undertakings or the production of certain goods. If aid from the home state has this effect, it's incompatible with the Common Market...." Bill parrots mechanically.

"Shame on them. But I didn't know they called it the *'Common Market'* anymore. I thought it was grown into a rather bigger concept than whatever our parents and grandparents thought they were joining in 1973, voted-on in '75."

"Yes, Michael, undoubtedly so. While I'm no integrationist, as you should realise. But what matters most is the fact that if government or the unitary local authority in Tyneside attempt to shore up Alec's yard with financial assistance, they breach EU law".

"Ist verboten?"

"Jawohl..."

"Deary-me. So four hundred families in Wallsend must lose a breadwinner and countless local businesses a source of local spend. Just to comply with one EU rule?"

"Unfortunately, yes. Apparently a Turkish yard does similar work. Could cry 'foul' and very probably would, now that they're in. Reason I was called on."

"Not just because you're now our local MEP?"

"Partly, of course, but also formally. As a source of professional legal advice."

"Great stuff. Your big chance to shine at last, Bill. I always wondered what you've been getting up to over there. *Sur le continent.*"

"It's not been easy, Michael."

"So what are you planning on doing about this particular issue?" I had asked him, but the answer swept in from elsewhere:

"He's going to write the definitive article on the subject, for this department's new venture. Our glossy, in-house legal journal..." breathed the slinky woman in tight-fitting black dress and killer heels suddenly appearing between us and placing her hands on his shoulders.

"...Aren't you, Mouse?"

Over-familiar, I thought it.

Diane Donington herself, the absolute siren of academic contract lawyers everywhere. This year's new editor for 'Cunningham on Contracts', her fine-boned face gracing its frontispiece.

Who says law is dull?

Bill leering openly down at her fabulous figure while I, the modern hypocrite, try pretending that I'm not. Though catching an eyeful in the valley of her cleavage. And the only rational explanation I can offer for how I ended up volunteering to help Bill write our utterly-boring article together, about Article 107 of the EU Rules on State Aid, for her fancy magazine. The one that later got me into trouble.

While the next bit of bother he caused me didn't involve Diane one bit – and maybe more's the pity. When I agreed to take a day's leave from work in order to perform an interesting but unpaid role as Bill's unofficial bag-carrier. That day he was summonsed - or invited, whichever you prefer – to London. Called down by the Home Office to attend on their open-plan premises in Marsham Street.

Called in by the Home Secretary for a quiet little chat.

Invited to discuss his group at the European Parliament's position on international criminal justice arrangements, now Bill was starting to be an international mover and shaker. In chaotic times for government where any straw was clutched, he'd really got a voice.

Me?

An impostor who simply shouldn't have been there. No right to say anything. The fact I carried a genuine electronic ID card in my pocket from a legitimate British law enforcement body was good enough to get me in, but neither here nor there.

Fact is, I simply shouldn't have gone.

On what I believe employment lawyers would call a "*Frolic of my Own*".

And if "*The Mummy*" or my other CPS bosses ever found out, I'd be walking the plank. An independent public servant finding himself slowly drawn-in to the activities of a discrete political group. Bill's in particular, the '*Carissian set*'.

Very naughty.

It made for a grand day out all the same. Great spectating.

And the first thing I noticed, if not for the first time, is another best expressed by the French. Misquoting by analogy their notorious tag about Paris - "*London and The Rest*". Acknowledging that nowhere could that schism between capital and country, government and governed, be any more apparent than here.

In a building like this.

The façade of this archetypal hymn to governance - or academy for secret policemen - is decorated with overhanging overtrays crafted in coloured perspex. Architect-designed to bestow their multi-coloured blessings in tinted light on anyone entering a temple to policy. Aids to conciliation or goodwill, their intended enlightenment of the arriving spirit about as beneficial as a cellophane sweet-wrapper before the eye. A shopping mall whose flim-flam entrance through beneficent rays only cements sarcastic responses the deeper in gruff northerners like Bill. Men unused to sunshine.

Allowed through the front door on sufferance to present ourselves before the next obstacle, a row of armoured desks. Installations manned by twelve year-olds, none of them male. Those metrocentric tyros who now struggle to classify what types we represent:

"He says he's an M.E.P." says one girl to the other, *sotto voce.*

"They all say that. What about the pale one?"

"Not sure, claim to be together. Gotta' CPS pass, presume it's OK."

"CPS what?"

"It's a prosecutor".

"Do we let them in?"

"Think so. Usually, anyhow....."

99

And then we turn to the naming of place:

If Northumberland they've not heard of, then Newcastle's little better: *"Staffordshire...?"* Cursed with no concept that's not *"...Under Lyme?"*, at least the word *"Geordie"* conjures a thin smile of comprehension. Like we wear animal fur, are entertaining savages fled Reality TV. But what else should we expect? When the origins confessed to are so far from imagining, let alone a Tube Map, no wonder our status plummets once juveniles realise. Grasp the true horror of latitudes they can imagine only in terms of *'Going outside, and being some time'*.

North of Watford, virtually polar.

After a short discussion, original "VISITOR" necktags are withdrawn. Another pause, while Reception considers how to punish our recondite whiff of Geordie, implied hint of cheek. The ideal solution soon being found in humiliating replacements, their self-explanatory "ESCORTED". Classification for the despised, that warning to colleagues about visiting provincials. Its labelling round our neck requiring adult supervision.

If truly irresponsible, fit only for 'ESCORTED', then we must wait while such an escort is found. Eventually one is: a blue-uniformed school-leaver pushed forward out the labyrinth to take on this job. Our personal guardian through the open-plan corridors and secret by-ways of one of the great Departments of State. While who it is helps him onto evening buses home, we the escorted can only but wonder.

A silent boy not returning one single word we say. Embarrassed by pleasantry and only offering the same mirthless smirk at all our feeble small-talk, His Majesty's agent sheepishly escorts us into rotating air-locks. Using no more than hand gestures, as taxy-ing aircraft are invited into hangars.

When it comes to his turn and the thing rotates, Bill gets stuck. Fortunately only briefly.

Once he's extracted it's a case of more waiting, the Minister being late.

So we descend to a ground-floor canteen where, no sooner have Bill and I bought tins of cola and opened them, than it's the Minister who's kept waiting. Rushing back to the lift and rapidly elevated several floors from the basement to a windowless conference room, we join three or four similar delegations come-up to meet him. Slugging our fizzy drinks on the way in the lift, bubbles dancing in my nose like a diver with the 'bends'.

Settled at table, I have just suppressed another gassy burp of cola when a mahogany-veneered door swings inward to admit a flock of civil-servant advisers. Along with their latest Home Secretary, a gardener with dirty fingernails. A safe pair of hands come hotfoot from a potting shed in Orpington upon his predecessor's resignation - over a parliamentary researcher, some private club in Cheshire. His replacement opening straightaway without further ceremony, not even allowing us the usual round-table introductions:

"You all know each other...."

We hesitate to disagree but recognise a politician in a hurry, red-faced from the stairs:

"I've asked you here today as identified opinion-formers. Part of a listening process. Consulting on your group's role in the current crisis, our best way forward. Not the monetary issues, when that's a job for Treasury and IMF. Government promising what's necessary. While what you're tasked-with is contributing constructively. Help restore order; aid equilibrium. Pacify the public"

"When you say 'you'....?" asks a smartly-suited man in bright blue turban, sitting nearby.

"You and the groups you represent. Groupings able to identify obstacles to a diverse range of political or community interests supporting the package of measures we adopt. What government might do to overcome those challenges. And in return I should say, we expect a constructive and co-operative attitude. 'All in this together' as it were....."

Where to begin? We knew from daily exposure the prisons were full and our courts working overtime, but Bill wasn't slow in coming forward. Kicking off for the team:

"There is one particular concern, Home Secretary, for my colleagues at Strasbourg. The groups I represent. Unfortunate side-effects from what I think a member of the Lords once called "a more expansive approach to criminal law" now evident in the European Union."

"Not suggesting something inherently wrong in that, are we?"

"So far as it threatens our traditional liberties - in what many still prefer to call the United Kingdom - then yes, I'm afraid we are, Minister. Effect on others hardly our concern - folk in Lower Saxony, say, who should look out for themselves. But for people here, their fear of these insidious effects gets exacerbated by the emergency. By what we consider an indecent rush. Government's scramble to subordinate their interests to third-rate criminal justice systems. To foreign forces alien to British policing, inimical to British law."

"Indecent, you say, inimical. What on earth do you mean, indecent?"

"Undemocratic and maybe unlawful. Processes driven by unelected civil servants. European police chiefs making-up policy on the hoof. Done without reference, meetings in Trier. International bodies and cross-border organisations newly set-up, acronyms about which we know nothing. Save that they answer to no-one; sit uneasily with Sir Robert Peel and his *Ten Points of Policing*. Concepts and protections we always took for granted."

"Relevant to today's discussion because….?"

"People feel unhappy when His Majesty's government shows subservience to legal cultures and traditions not their own. Judicial systems lacking in our checks and balances. And no, Minister, I don't just mean the United States, Third-World as their fondness for *'plea-bargaining'* or parading the unconvicted in chains so often seems by our standards. No, I mean how a slavish adherence to agreements for *'Mutual Recognition'* lets British citizens be surrendered into the clutches of foreign legal systems. Thrown into EU-member jails unfit for human habitation. Handed over without even the basics of a case. Abandoned to unreconstructed justice systems; to courts at best incompetent, at worst corrupt."

"Agreements, agreements? You refer to which ones…?"

"To Schengen and Maastricht, of course, Lisbon above all. Pre-and post-Third Pillar…."

"I've not invited you here today to discuss our European membership…" said the Minister coldly, looking down at the briefing note in front of him as if it was more interesting.

"I should think that the majority of British people who are opposed to it – and it is a majority, Minister, nearly seventy per cent, as you already know - are well aware of your government's stated position. Of the opposition's. Feeling bereft, no choice in the matter."

"Well why can't you do like they do? Just accept it for the done deal it is...." he snaps.

Bill putting hands to his shoulder to check on a gown that wasn't there, this unconscious mannerism always his prelude to demolishing a hostile witness. Only I can sense it for the humdinger coming. Hoping it won't start a fight, get us thrown onto the street:

"When the *Common Market* we joined in 1973 suddenly announced itself the *European Union* in 1997, or the Scottish Executive at Holyrood declared itself a *Scottish Government* in 2009..." asserts Bill "....we knew democracy had changed. Without anyone asking us. So who needs tanks round the radio station when bigger coups are won with a bloodless re-branding exercise? A silently-circulated press-release, round-robin e-mails?"

"A coup, Mr Cariss? That's a totally ridiculous statement!"

"Not when nations, complete sovereign states, are quietly being taken-over. Dismantled and reduced to convenient *'regions'* by bureaucrats. Like the EU did to Greece or Italy – an unelected administration parachuted-in. You know what I mean, Home Secretary. Step by step - including our own. What my group calls *'Balkanising Britain'*. Fostering division as a means to submission. No wonder we can see countries where building crises over national sovereignty translate into trouble on their streets. Why we mustn't let it happen here."

"Oh! You really believe that's the case, do you? Somehow gives you grounds to deny policing co-operation between nations? Mutual recognition of enforcement?"

"Not what I'm saying at all, Minister, no. We live in a shrinking, globalised world. Everyone becoming more interconnected. Why it would be ludicrous for me to suggest national police forces shouldn't co-operate. But co-operate, please; not collaborate like Vichy..."

"Vichy, excuse me....?" interrupts the minister, open-mouthed, but Bill presses on:

"In a nutshell, my group's position, Minister. Opposing further collaboration with EU policies we see as deliberately-divisive.

103

Anti-libertarian. Especially when it's done so secretively, unilaterally. At the whim of local police chiefs and prosecutors, not through national legislatures. Unelected officials' cosy get-togethers behind the scenes driving forward a programme none of us signed-up to. In an operational field - criminal justice - where my group's otherwise the first to accept international co-operation is vital....."

"Well if you accept it's so vital, what really is your problem...?" asks the minister, crossly.

"Limit it to co-operation, Minister, and the answer is 'nothing'. But not when it becomes a sell-out. Not if it leaves us spectator to the dismantling, to the wholesale surrendering of cultural, political traditions. Happening not just in policing but in our wider law. When regionalising and breaking-up a far older Union seems set at the heart of it. An unspoken secret mission. The dilution of precious ancient rights. Rights far more worth fighting for than peripheral stuff getting attention. Priceless concepts like our Common Law or national sovereignty. The protection of individuals from arbitrary detention through *Habeas Corpus*. Concepts which – with respect, Minister – even the most home-spun would expect His Majesty's Government to be standing up and fighting for. Upon all our behalfs....."

"Fighting, you say?" said the minister, raising one eyebrow theatrically.

"You know perfectly well what I mean, Minister, let alone the Loyal Opposition. Resisting through all lawful, democratic channels. Including in my group's case, through the European Parliament."

"Ah, yes, your group....the *'Carissian Faction'*. Isn't that what the media are calling it?"

"Journalist's hype, Minister. And we're no faction, anyway."

"But you're not a proper political party either, are you? Not properly funded....."

"No, we're not. Not in terms of new EU rules for state-funding coming-in for political parties like yours, Minister. Another one of their *'Roadmaps'* meant for ensuring compliance. Finally eliminating those pesky anti-europeans from our national discourse...."

104

The minister glowered but said nothing, the aide beside him looking up uneasily from his notebook. Shifting a sedentary rump on his leather-backed chair. They exchange meaningful glances. Speaking plainly – or indeed, extravagantly - is not the done thing. Not in these circles. The more senior civil servant who spoke up to fill the awkward void resulting was in his early fifties, smoothly-spoken and old-school:

"Colourful claims, Mr Cariss, but unfortunate for not taking us too far forward in our subject for today: *'Enhancing International Policing Co-operation in an Era of Challenges'*. Whether those challenges are social or economic, the Secretary of State is keen to receive views from a diverse spectrum. Share in community opinions for active problem-solving, not obstruction by nay-sayers. Why you were invited. On the basis international co-operation proceeds and not, if you please, to revisit that old chestnut – our EU membership."

"Yes, as I realise. When I was coming to that...." said Bill, giving him a cool look back

"Good. I do think the Minister would appreciate it if each of the groups represented here could confine themselves to offering just the one point. Ideally their best. And related to this aspect only. To international policing. One thing they can identify as their key issue of concern. In a simple form he can take away and put in front of the Prime Minister......"

"Stopping rendition...." blurts Bill, like a dog with a bone.

"Rendition, Mr Cariss?" said the minister, bending so low his chin nearly kisses the table.

"Yes, Home Secretary, rendition. And, no, I don't mean notorious post-911 scandals. Western intelligence agencies allegedly air-freighting terror suspects round the globe. From Afghanistan or Iraq, Libya or Syria. No, I mean something rather closer to home..."

"I do hope the minister will find this relevant...." groaned the '*Sir Humphrey*'-type.

"....and in its way, just as bad. The form of rendition I mention is wholly domestic. And utterly relevant to the responsibilities of His Majesty's Secretary of State for Home Affairs and Policing. If a nation state's shortlist of primary duties starts with protecting its citizens, including from foreign powers, then surely charity begins at home?"

105

"I fear we're not with you, Mr Cariss...." breathed the Orpington gardener slowly.

"The European Arrest Warrant, Minister. You should withdraw from it completely - or else re-negotiate the whole damn thing. Reverse your government's unquestioning *'rendition'* of citizens into the jails and courthouses of EU countries. Into states frankly backward, whose treatment of suspects lies far below our own. Below what normal people from this country should reasonably take for granted, feel naturally accustomed. Requiring a cowardly surrender by their own government into what's little short of a living nightmare. Whether it's Greece, Portugal or Spain, we can take our pick. Have no certainty of seeing a lawyer."

"You're not seriously suggesting we stop extraditing organised bullion-robbers from Spain, or drug-runners from Turkey.....that we declare some sort of amnesty?" sneered the minister, folding his arms. Wilfully misunderstanding Bill's point, turning questions around.

"No, Home Secretary, but I do suggest it isn't right for government to allow its own people - His Britannic Majesty's subjects as they once called us in passports – to be abducted. Lifted from the protection of a legal jurisdiction they know, whose rules they accept. Hold some basic understanding of, some confidence in. Uses a language they understand. To be handed unconditionally-over instead to an alien country where none of this applies."

"Are you saying we should never hand anyone over?"

"Not when that other country isn't required to have assembled even the basics of a case. Not when their evidence stands in such short supply – is so bloody non-existent – that our domestic police couldn't arrest on its basis. Wouldn't dare lift a suspect off our streets. Yet just because this request to do so is freighted-in from abroad, suddenly it seems that any of this can happen....on the astonishing basis of no evidence at all."

"Look here, Cariss, I appreciate the sincerity of your concerns. Why we're working hard to mitigate exactly those extremes you and your group claim to describe. A House of Lords Select Committee allocated to the issue. Changes already made, EU *'Roadmaps'* put in place, the promise of more. But look, we can't ignore the terms of previous treaties, can we? Whether they're made with Europe itself, or our transatlantic cousins....."

"What? For something a kid didn't even leave his house to do? Some teenage computer hacker whose electronic signal bounced theoretically once in America?"

"You're getting miles from Europe now...." the gardener says wearily, wafting an invisible fly: "Don't start us off down that road...."

"It's still the same point, Minister. The same core question of why can't we try them here? If it was a foreign terrorist, the European Court of Human Rights would tell us we couldn't send them home. For fear of torture, of inhuman degrading treatment. Yet our own government won't turn a hair on seeing a British citizen despatched to face cell-conditions as bad as any in the Gulf. The ordinary holiday-maker or business-traveller caught-up in bother abroad. Accident with a moped, bust-up in a bar. Shipped out on the next available flight with no questions asked. Plucked straight from the freezing streets of Newcastle, Liverpool or Barking, to find themselves banged-up inside an Athens jail. Torrid summer heat. Treated like the international criminals or terrorists this power should be kept for....."

The 'Sir Humphrey' clone spreads his hands in the air as if to calm the sea:

"Alright, Mr Cariss, all right. That's quite enough. I think the Minister's grasped your point."

"OK – I'll finish now but summarise, Home Secretary, about what we call a scandal. A state of affairs we say has been allowed to go too far. Government abandoning a primary constitutional duty to its own for the sake of international goodwill. Quietly subordinating our legal sovereignty and its citizens' safety to the greater project: completing EU integration."

Sovereignty, eh? Bill's biggest mistake - it could only have been worse if he'd mentioned 'the national interest'. Never was unhappier body-language seen in an audience - not since counsel for the defence invited a Carlisle jury to acquit the Netherby Hall burglars of shooting policemen. When both could lead to a hanging.

Bill had given an electric performance but he was no Cicero, and rhetoric would never persuade the row of statues we had before us. Nor a Home Secretary in their midst, suddenly turning puce.

Yet I bet everyone here knew that, if we'd had a mob of ordinary folk with us in the room - what politicians call 'hard-working families' - Bill by now would be shoulder-high. Though the audience we were stuck with meant he was surely wasting his breath, I knew Bill would never give up. Not in his nature and among aspects to his character most to be admired:

Bill had played a blinder but you can only push so far.

So after that we behaved ourselves. Sat quietly for the whole of the rest of the meeting. Listened politely to other delegations failing to score: their beige and fawn against Bill's purple prose. Paid-for lobbyists from sainted social orthodoxies, advocates for ambivalence. Demanding final decisions be put off until government held more data for analysis from consultative events. Impact-assessments with partners, cost-benefit reviews.

Buried it in paper. All of it pleaded with the passion of a trodden-on whiting protesting backwards to the snail.

Though while they spoke I couldn't help noticing the fourth civil servant. The burly one with large forearms and overdeveloped shoulders penned inside a straining pinstriped suit. Who sat in the corner and never said anything, looking pleasantly across at us with hints of humour in his eye. Only stopped writing once these other drones started.

Why for us, when this high-powered ordeal was over, it was surprising to find the Home Secretary all smiles again. Detaining Bill briefly by the door as if nothing had happened:

"Do give my regards to your old county, won't you, Mr Cariss. And tell me, are the rhododendrons out at Cragside yet......?"

While we just felt happy to be getting away with a handshake each, no further rebuke. Assuming for our part that this must be it. The mahogany door about as far as Bill's take on those emotive issues he dared raise with the minister would ever go.

Arguments doubtless swiftly dismissed by his entourage as OTT no sooner than it fell shut behind us.

And we step out into spring sunshine on Whitehall together, looking forward to Italy in May.

"Keep the seas we must - live if we can"

(Gnaeus Pompeius Maximus - *'Pompey The Great'*:
soldier, admiral and triumvir; 1st Century B.C.)

- V -

Rutupiae will always be important for us - militarily and symbolically. Rome's original beachhead in Britannia, right from her conquest. Where she first landed.

Sentiments holding good today, centuries later, when every grateful traveller crossing the Narrow Sea from Gaul still makes the same landfall. Beneath the huge triumphal arch towering over pantiled roofs of the town, marsh-lined estuary below. A Flavian emperor's firm reminder of historic fact. Built at the very spot where – two hundred and forty three years ago, exactly - the invading legions of that big-eared emperor, C-C-Claudius, dug their camp for Rome's opening night in Britain. Its meaning and its message to the little Brits as clear today as when those tough old legionaries of long ago carved 'V' ditches deeper than lettering into the virgin turf. As if to tell the world:

"Rome and Her Empire – here to stay."

Standing there with hands resting on hip, thumbs tucked inside my armoured belt to support the back while I crane upwards to inspect the crumbling fabric of its monolith, I couldn't help feeling what a crying shame it was.

Those overfed and aggressive herring gulls which endlessly circle its summit in mewling sympathy, night and day, seem to agree. Why indeed had we let this building of all buildings, this important symbol of Rome's eternal dominion, decline and decay? As every year yet more of its thin veneer of carved Italian marble cracks off. Attacked by piercing frosts, the cursed British climate. Piece by piece they detach, slide to the ground and shatter. Exposing the coarse core of a once-great arch. Crafted from nothing more sophisticated than millions of individually-rammed flints bound with our famous *opus signinum*, hardest mortar in the world.

These fragments of shining white debris at its foot don't stay long, Carerra marble or no. Not in a desperate world where everything has a value and a use. When it was widely known in the taverns of the town that someone came by night. Perhaps a sneaky farmer, systematically removing every last faller to burn then spread across their fields as lime.

Big bronze letters from triumphal inscriptions of Imperial success once decorating its veined expanse occasionally fall with them. Grabbed in triumph by the coin-forgers, brooch-makers or scrap-collectors who scamper away into the dark to melt them down before awkward questions are asked.

Still resenting our capture and sack of Athens, centuries ago, men from the small community of Greek merchants in the town huddle outside their dockside warehouses. Nodding sagely at a hidden meaning, muttering darkly about the just rewards of Roman *hubris*. If *Hellas* may never recover the artefacts she's lost to Rome, how satisfying to watch Rome now losing her own to that most ruthless of generals: Time himself.

As for other citizens, they appear indifferent. So much for any sense of heritage or civic pride in an ancient past among residents round here. At least the scavengers keep the site tidy, I suppose, which is more than can be said for the rest of Rutupiae. Not after the present Emergency has caused a massive fort three-times the size of Garrianonum to be built from flint at its very centre. Cutting ruthlessly through the quaint, chaotic port-town beside the river against the protestation of freeholders. Those traders whose business premises must be sacrificed on the altar of military expediency.

Located at the heart of this newly-fortified enclosure, a neglected monument reluctantly takes on a new significance, learns new purposes in a new age. Reason why a junior officer of the fleet with time on his hands finds himself standing before its mass, brooding on changes in meaning. Scratching my neck where the edge of a helmet guard always rubs when I lean backwards, then opening the wooden door to the tower stairs. Parlous our public finances might be, but I still believed something more should have been done about maintaining this marvellous arch: the *tetrapylon*.

Large enough for not one but two ceremonial roadways to intersect at ground level below its centre, you didn't have to be what Carausius calls a *"book-learned boy"* to understand how '*The Conquest Memorial*' might conceal other coded allegories about Rome. For those who can see. Including about Janus, the two-faced God of our Roman Pantheon, who like many others looks backwards with the same intensity as he also looks forward.

Why it seemed to me and plenty others I've discussed this hobby-horse of mine with, that our grip on Britannia was never so tight we can afford to be careless. Even after nigh-on three centuries. Risk what message from the state a perceived indifference to totemic structures like this gives out. Whether to Saxon and Frank offshore, or obdurate Celts in the north. People like the Brigantes, that bloody-minded tribe which still hasn't got the message, hundreds of years post-conquest. People whose loyalty can't be trusted, even this side of the Emperor's Wall and after all this time. Who don't know when they're beat.

Why the last thing Rome should do is let negative messaging like this escape in uncertain times like these. Not when the fate of Gaul makes everyone nervous, worrying what gods will do next. How easily an inattention to Their Ceremonies may become translated into misfortune in the Affairs of Men. Military disaster, the incidence of plague, an economic crisis. The rational analysis of challenges we face disintegrating into superstitious fear.

Hauling myself up the uneven stairway, this private darkness of the soul lifted by light from the occasional air-slit, gave me time to ponder on philosophy. When like this ascent, life is short, dark and full of mystery, mine grew simple. Only to be careful. Why it is better to be wholehearted about religious observance than dismissive. When a wise man is one who hedges his bets, avoids more obvious risks. Takes time to get the temple procedures right and with it the omens. Ensures each sacrifice is correctly carried out, avoids the unpredictable wrath of unknowable gods.

It is not about belief. Oh no, that part is optional, arguably unnecessary. More a question of showing respect, the proper public demonstrations of allegiance. To Gods and State alike. Above all to the emperor, most frequently for ancestors. To Gods those ancestors placated in life and are now set off to join, far beyond the Styx. Leaving me as my poor father was, ever that dutiful worshipper who *"willingly and deservedly fulfils his vow"*.

Pacifying the Gods, keeping tribal rebels down, defeating Saxones. In my book they all boil down to the same thing – how well you manage the risk. Not just a philosophy but also an insurance, like contributions to a burial fund. As father always said: *"We're standing on the shoulders of giants"*. That's why personally, and if it had been within my official responsibilities, I would have found money and labour to restore the Rutupiae Arch. Maintain some semblance of its grandeur, remind us of them. By way of a tribute to our forebears and a positive statement for future generations to come. Or else the enemy.

Too late now.

The Carausius I saw presented as unsentimental, rarely troubled by appearances. Why he'd already sealed its fate, the double-arched monument butchered on his orders. Crudely converted into nothing more prosaic than a naval observation tower, a signalling platform. The last few sheets of Italian marble chipped away in a week to save winter the trouble. Sold off in three wagon-loads to local limeburners, whether for grain or for cash.

Clambering out today onto the expansive lead of its roof, beside the iron frame of the new signal beacon, whatever respect youth retained for a glorious civic past was obliged to concede its military usefulness. The highest man-made structure along the whole western Channel coast between Rutupiae and Dubris, from whose lofty vantage a matchless panorama unfolds. A lonely location where two bored soldiers from the Second Augustan Legion whom I found on watch atop were glad of company and their chance to explain it:

"Hail and good morning, Tribune. Very pleased to see you indeed. Nice to have a visitor, if I may say so, sir. Can't say we get too many of those up here. Most probably it's the stairs that put them off. Either that or Decimus's socks. Have you been on Rutupiae Light before, may I ask you, sir?"

"No I haven't, soldier. Shame really. Anyway, here I am and it's a great view you boys enjoy up here. In every direction. So, tell me, what can we see?

"Well, there's the wine shop down there, sir – sign of *'The Grape and Sandal'*. We often get a really good view of that particular serving-girl with the dark hair Decimus has a thing about. Bending right over to pick oyster shells up from under the benches...." confided the older one, whose pock-marked face and drinker's belly imply a campaign history that's limited to bars.

"Oh, yes, I can see what you mean. Lovely. And anything else important to the Army?"

"Er, yes, obviously! We see everything, sir. Any activity – shipping, I mean, not just the local talent. Far off to our left is Regulbium fort, guarding the other end of this channel. With young eyes like yours you can probably see it now. Only a grey smudge at best but it's much easier at night when their beacon is lit. Looking west is Portus Dubris with its two lighthouses. And right opposite us are Marcae and Gesoriacum. Across the Channel in Gaul but as fleet-bases run from over here. Patrolling the seas, protecting our traders. Easier said than done, sir, as you doubtless will know. Decimus and I were thinking what a weighty thing it is the Western Caesar Maximinianus has asked of our Admiral Carausius."

"The Caesar – he's an Augustus now - has chosen well. If there is anyone who can pull it off, then Carausius is our man. Believe me, soldier."

"I never had much time for the navy beforehand, sir, I hope you don't mind me admitting. But everyone knows the answer to this one's in their hands."

"No, it lies in yours, soldier! In all our hands. We have never faced an enemy like the Saxon in our history. Same point going for their friends, the Franks. Mobile and relentless, cowardly and cunning. Gone on for years now but only getting worse. You boys will know what I mean. Slipping in the dark or rain up our estuaries and creeks in their longships for a surprise attack. Robbing, stealing and killing, then slipping away with the tide. Cowards terrified of meeting our legions in battle, these peoples are a nuisance we've tolerated too long. A different type of warfare has arrived and Rome must adapt. Fortifying ports and inlets like Rutupiae, reinstating a proper fleet, sending you two up here. It's all part of her answer. Believe me, lads, southern Britannia is no place for R&R any more, no cushy option. You're not serving in safety behind the lines now. You boys are in a frontline posting. Standing guard on our empire's newest frontier: *The Saxon Shore!*"

Their faces were a picture. Rough-hewn souls who'd taken what I said to heart all the same. At least for the moment, though the big question remained. If - as Carausius feared - the centre could not even feed them properly, let alone pay its armies what they were owed in a coinage worth something out on the markets; if it could not raise enough in grain and tax from farmers and citizens willing to shoulder the burden; then for how long could we keep a hold on the obedience of men like these?

"How often do you light the beacon?" I asked, keen to change the subject. Focus on the small, the positive and straightforward. I gestured at the neatly-piled logs beside the small treadmill crane overhanging the Monument edge.

"Every night, sir...." said the one called Decimus, finally speaking-up for himself. "We *are* Rome's light". Privately encouraged that even an ordinary soldier could see our predicament in that compelling way, I grinned and turned to go: "Yes, that's a good way of putting it, soldier. Hold fast to that idea and you won't go far wrong."

"Sir..." he said, detaining me a moment longer.

"Yes?"

"That's an interesting sword you've got across your chest."

"It's Saxon. What they call a *seax*."

"I thought so, sir. How do you come by a rare thing like that?

"More easily than you'd think. A kind man gave it me. The kind of men you boys are put up here to watch out for. Keep your eyes peeled and you might even get one of your own."

"Sir!" they said as one, standing smartly to attention on the roof.

I was encouraged by their response but drill and fine words were not the answer. Only denying the Saxon use of our rivers. Which meant Carausius building an unscaleable physical barrier along the whole southern shoreline out of threadbare men like these.

May The Immortal Gods Protect Us.

"The accusatorial system may be a civilised kind of warfare"

(Richard Du Cann QC, barrister, 1979)

- 5 -

Casting one sardonically-raised eyebrow at a World War Two steel helmet balanced precariously nearby, ready for action above a shelf bowed down with law books and case files, it was the Attorney General of a long-gone government who once stood in front of my office desk, stuck out his lantern-jaw and asked: "*I say, do you get into many good scraps?*"

In those halcyon days I did, if only confined to the courtroom. The rough and tumble of legal practice. Even if not taken out and worn, it is true that silly helmet was sometimes taken along, hidden in the bag for a trip to court. On the First of April perhaps, '*All Fools Day*', for a harmless in-joke with fellow lawyers. Symbol of an expected bad day; the likelihood of, well yes, a "*good scrap*".

But the mother of all scraps I ever got into was made for me by a sporting little minx we call "*Xenobia*'. The girl who helped put me - and a good few others - further beyond the law than any of us imagined.

A '*girl*'?

OK. A machine with personality.

Some of its finer aspects feminine. Maybe even feline.

OK, I know, it's just a car; my analogies trite.

But what a car! A dainty-looking Lancia - though Italians say '*Lancheea*'. An understated 1950s coupé, ready to pounce. Endowed with a jewel-like Fabergé egg of a V6 engine and a bodywork that's liquid in steel, coated in flawless black. Series VI, their latest model called according to the factory tradition after those Roman roads of northern Italy Lancia would test them on. Her given name: '*Aurelia*'.

A proper Roman name for a proper Roman lady, and if we were wiser we would have left it there. Hoping the odd observer might recognise the link, accept associations drawn. Harmless enough fun of the time, calling it - her - '*Xenobia*', I mean. An alternative, classical reference. One too few inheritors of a

115

dying culture would nowadays recognise, let alone crack a smile for. While you doubtless think it feeble, your proof how 'sad' we were. When humour is *"so intensely personal...."* as a former girlfriend once put it, post-one of my jokes, but sometimes all that's left us.

Like my dented dome of khaki tin, this naming of names is a matter of taste but once a common ritual. Taking the example of wartime: popular with tank-crews and aircrew, so why not for a race-car? Like I say, not her real name or correct title, but I remember taking a signwriter's brush to write it lovingly along her sinuous flanks. One unseasonably-hot April afternoon in Jesmond before our adventure together.

How *'Xenobia'* she became.

And this Xenobia when I met her had reached a dangerous age. Matching too many attractive and expensive examples of her type, she belonged to another, while I should have known better. To my mate Bill.

But what monika could have been more appropriate for an Aurelia – as one to another? A Parthian warrior-queen in what they now call the People's Republic of Syria, their region of Homs: *"Not many people know that."* A desert queen of Palmyra once running the Romans ragged, out there on their far-eastern flank in the far-off days of a mighty Empire. That proud and upright leader: Julia Aurelia Septimia Xenobia. A brave and determined woman extracting her fatal price from columns of marching men. From too many ill-judged military expeditions of Persia or Rome, they launched into her little corner of a greater East.

Before Rome and its Emperor Aurelian finally caught up with her, took their revenge.

So what better name for a car intending to do the same to Italians, at their own game?

In motorsport.

But looking back, if I'd thought it would make a difference, we might have been wiser calling her *"Boudicca"*. After Norfolk's home-grown, better-known, domestic equivalent. It might have upset fewer people: what a pity we didn't.

An alternative to do as well for joking but without the consequences, though some people never learn. Forget the danger when old-fashioned humour encounters the functionaries of our modern state. Those unsmiling individuals wielding executive power, inventing limits to discretion. Legislating for our every thought, word and deed; for what we have left undone - or sometimes even done. Their zeal extending not just to what you say but what they suspect you don't like, might decline to support. What they would threaten with a court.

Old-stagers tell me of a time, late-twentieth century, when the most mundane judge-in-chambers bail application – never mind trial – felt incomplete without classical reference. Those latin tags dropped-in as shorthand for a longer explanation: *'res ipsa loquitur', 'prima facie', 'ex turpi causa'*. Laid to pique the interest of a dormant judge, keep them entertained. Whether these old barristers' tales were true, how drastically our times and another century have changed them. Modified our language, outlawed their practice.

For the sake of modern 'correctness'.

Courts are serious places where time is money and reputations or liberty deserve more attention than indulgent wordgames imply. Where the patience of a lay jury come to do justice in their own time won't extend to watching public schoolboys swap in-jokes. No wonder a backlash rolled in from a laity for whom a dead language learnt in few schools no longer made sense – whatever lawyers thought.

And no, before you ask, I didn't go to public school either; just a failing Kentish 'Academy'. Though it doesn't mean I still don't miss the Latin. Even if the only place left to use it is signwritten down the sides of a car. And having admitted my unfashionable liking for Latin, let's go the whole hog and admit these nostalgic tastes extend also to them. To old cars.

What a case, eh? Another *"inappropriate outlook"* for public disapproval, my apologies taken as read. The first instalment of a deserved retribution arriving on the Milanese *tangenziale* that sunny afternoon. Though for me it felt like things went wrong right from the very outset. Like we were fated before either of us got over there, before we'd even started.

Bill flying out in first-class at the last minute, and me travelling over in third. Optimistically agreeing to tow Xenobia there on my trailer, to Italy by road. And what a false economy that arrangement proved to be. Once the temperature gauge on my

4x4 packed up in a queue of traffic by the 'Chunnel' mouth, stuck in a hold-up. With hindsight, another bad omen. First sign of Lady Luck's displeasure.

Another woman it all went wrong with.

I forget the reasons – for this hold-up, not the women. The latter stay etched in my brain. Maybe some terrorist alert, another French blockade. A major delay anyway, long queues of lorries lining the inside lane of the A2 right down to the Channel Tunnel itself. Police activating "*Operation Stack*". If my immediate concern was the engine overheating, truth be told there were worse things than that to worry about:

Like those ANPR ('*Automatic Number Plate Recognition*') cameras which those in the know will recognise, all down the A2. If I'd but realised it, my journey out was already being tracked - on whose behalf another issue. When the 'pinger' goes off in a police control room, alerting to the target's movements, there is little comfort to be had from that hardy perennial: "*If you've done nothing wrong, you've got nothing to hide*" (Munich Law, 1933).

The cooling problem at least I could sort, thanks to a quick fix made to some wiring on the electric fan, and once loaded onto the tunnel train we finally made good time. '*La Manche*' was crossed in minutes, not hours, then off we go down the ramp to despatch France and the Alps in a couple of days on the autoroute. Paying a king's ransom in tolls.

Confidence boosted by these achievements, I must have been pulling a steady eighty. Heading towards Milan in my old Toyota, the Italian Lakes fading away behind. Entering onto an endless plain of industrial and suburban sprawl.

Towards *Il tangenziale*.

Ahead is Milano itself, the great city growing gradually more visible in a shrouded blue haze; the Alps retreating north-westwards into ever-fainter bands.

Tutto e bene.

Xenobia sitting pretty, squatting primly on the four-wheeled trailer. Together really motoring. In the back of my mind, maybe I realised we were pushing it a bit. With unrealistic deadlines at the airport and distant Brescia to meet, there'd seemed little choice at the time.

Right way to go.

Then I saw the headlights behind. If we were shifting, then this thing was a missile.

A dark green saloon travelling in the outside lane at such a speed everyone else was diving out of their way. Provided they saw it in time, but no argument offered either-way. Against a current model Jaguar XJJ - its type a popular buy among Italian businessmen who imagine leather interiors and a walnut dashboard the epitome of Englishness.

Or in this case, impatience.

I keep to my course. No need to slow down, the lane beside me empty. Plenty of room.

He's hitting one hundred plus, I casually guess. Maybe one-twenty.

I brace my hands against the steering wheel anyway. To be on the safe side, keep my outfit steady. Just in case. Lashed down so tightly onto a twin-axled trailer, you wouldn't think Xenobia capable of anything, untoward or not.

If you did, you didn't know her.

When the Jag' shoots past us, he suddenly veers inwards towards the trailer. Deliberate or inadvertent, I couldn't say. So close when he goes by that I catch a momentary snapshot of her driver; rear three-quarter's profile. A big man, shoulders massy and hunched over the wheel. Wearing a broad-brimmed hat of yellow straw.

"Hey, steady on!" I shout, as if there is any chance he'd hear.

Then the Jag' is gone and the wash from its passing hits us like a giant wave. When I first feel that unaccustomed lightness creep into my stomach and then into the whole outfit. Am forced to acknowledge my mistake. My own complacency and speed.

Too late: she's shifted on the moment. Maybe a strap has eased, a hook moving?

Releasing Xenobia.

Either way, the trailer starts to snake.

At first, I'd thought I would be able to drive through it, until in the rear-view mirror I see a bad sign. The traffic behind starting to slow to a respectful crawl, giving me space. Italian motorists showing an unusual willingness to grant another the maximum space to perform.

It took a certain Dutchman I met later to disclose how the subsequent investigation report from their *Polizia Stradale,*

Italy's motorway police, established the precise point when I gave in and hit the brakes. Leaving lurid skid marks across all three carriageways in permanent witness. Where the Aurelia high on her trailer and me inside the Toyota began our fateful trajectory, helplessly leftwards together. West into a waiting wall.

In a Western European country and the twenty-first century from Our Lord's naissance, the material science of deformable structures is surely well-advanced. To a point where, worldwide, the eponymous trade name of 'Armco' is synonymous with sophisticated, alloy crash-barriers designed to soak up velocity. Dissipate harmful momentum.

So can someone out there tell me why - in the homeland of Galileo or Da Vinci - it is the Italians of all people who choose deliberately to line the centre of their motorways with a wall of concrete blocks?

And that Jag' was English-registered....

"Yield, ye Roman writers; yield, ye Greeks.
A greater than the Iliad is born."

(Sextus Propertius on Vergil's '*Aeneid*')

- VI -

Pitching and tossing about in the swell, pity the long-suffering passenger only able to raise their eyes from its deck once they realise their ship is finally got over the Narrow Sea and safely round the troublesome promontory of Itium. Our fortress of Gesoriacum and its immense lighthouse awaiting, below them the huddled town and harbour mole of Bononia. Arms open in shelter.

Today you will know them differently, but in the days of my youth these installations were as jewels in Carausius's crown of command. Standing out from afar in his defensive system of control and communication, spanning both sides of the Channel. Overseers to what he called his '*Litus Saxonicus*' and we our Saxon Shore.

Where tide conditions and the season allow, it is fair to say that successfully tacking-out from Rutupiae or Dubris in Britannia, then getting over here to Gaul, will take a vessel like ours the best part of a day.

If the Gods are Willing and Their Winds set Fair.

Good enough reason for any seafarer that's sensible to check out the auguries. Why there is not a bireme releases mooring-line below the white cliffs of Dubris without consulting first with Neptune and Fortuna. Taking of their auspices, seeing they are good.

Why that particular dawn in Portus Dubris felt much like any other, when operations demand our departure at first light. With legionary hosts awaiting over the water, generals none dare disappoint, no wonder our dockside ceremonies felt rushed. When delay leaves mariners vulnerable to bad weather, or those tentacled creatures which grope around in ocean like augurers will do for meaning in the bowels of fowl.

The longer I spent in his service, the more frequently we confronted these inconveniences of light and timing. So common with Carausius that Selucidus the *victimarius* - his onboard augurer - appears always compelled to devine no good reason against whatever putting-out-to-sea his commander requires: "*Every portent favourable...*"

And why should he not? In a world awash with misfortune, why should men care what the guts of pullets say? When everyone knew we sailed with a lucky admiral, the hero who brings his own answers.

If these urgent voyages and their frequency were hardly unexpected, why was I so dim? To sign-up onto the staff of a busy naval general whose headquarters lay Gaul-side of a notorious, choppy channel; then discover my surprise at dreading every crossing? If even sceptics pray at sea to any god that's going, I was more dutiful than most. Fear behind my regular entreaty of Whoever or Whatever, was out there:

"Neptune, Father of the Seas, protect me! An humble soldier whose leaders dare style him as if Your own 'Triton'. May their naming be auspicious; aid not hinder that vow I make for a sacrifice on safe return. May You, with Oceanus and Triton Himself, calm those depths only You can command. Hold back the growing storm but confound the Saxon with shipwreck and failure. That You with Fortuna Redux the Homebringer, may bring me and my shipmates to safe-arrivals back....."

Something must have worked, if not the power of prayer. For if these morning crossings were never the happiest, at least the worst enemies we encountered were those of human minds. Like my own personal nausea, our collective fear of drowning.

Whether it was indeed a god - let alone one identifiable as 'Neptune' - who brought Carausius and his fleet to safe passage, protection out at sea, we mortals never knew. And if there were cynics, including our admiral, who derided these precautions for childish superstition, then my own responses were those of a dutiful son. Holding more respect for traditional belief or spirituality than many do today. Tending to accept what's taught him by mariners about the mysteries they adopt, their pantheon of the seas. That biddable boy who always conformed; discounted alternatives and did as he's told.

Whatever the motivation, sometimes our preparations as a crew resembled the anaesthesia of incantation. Chanting as if a priesthood ourselves, novitiates of Neptune. Ritual building a team: whether to fight Saxons or just weather. Those sailors' songs and repetitious calls comforting my earliest days with the fleet, sending me slowly to sleep. Counterweights to a landsman's fear of ocean, its aweful unpredictability. Prayer our comfort against those vengeful spirits we must bargain with as men have done for centuries. Offer-up our vows for their promise of safe-return.

If most comrades accept the need for these rites instinctively, the more-educated cite that contemptuous Consul, the legendary Publius Claudius Pulcher. An arrogant man defying ancient gods. The Republican general who, moments before his fleet joined battle with Carthage off the coast of Sicily, threw his sacred chickens overboard. As if losing their weight could clinch him a contest for Rome's control of the seas. Or a battle which, as every schoolboy knows, he then as promptly lost. Where no moral could be clearer, no Roman admiral risk similar. Repeat his mistake, however great their rush.

Why I'm down on the harbour of Dubris at half-light, doing as mariners do and honouring the chickens. On no nobler impulse than a fear of the consequences, my liking for eggs. Even if it usually takes mid-crossing before I can manage one, my appetite restored. The first welcome sign that my sea-legs are growing; however much our barque may still roll in the swell, stagger over waves.

A point of personal development I particularly remember the Admiral Carausius being gracious enough to remark-upon that day I describe. Descending from his usual vantage in the captain's shelter, high on the steering deck, to join my group of junior officers gathered in the bows. Eating fresh-boiled eggs.

"If nothing pleases me more, young Triton, than to see you filling your face for a change, 'stead of emptying it into the sea...." he had said, with that easy humour uncommon in his rank ".....I think it's time you and your colleagues looked up from the trough. South together to Gesoriacum, where no finer prospect exists for your understanding of her place in our empire's scheme of things."

Of course he was right. As we rounded Itium and the sweating rowers on 'Medusa' set her bronze beak through a wall of waves towards river-mouth and harbour, we of his staff did as he said. Turned keen young eyes towards the detail of her seaward defences, mighty stone towers and crenellated walls floating-by. Realised how proud they made you of what minor part each man among us played in the glories they represent: Rome's monumental response to the crude forces of barbarism. Convinced by what their impregnability told us about the inevitability of her eventual victory.

Comforted by the solidity of architecture, it suddenly dawned with land in sight how quickly my fears on embarkation had flown. My gratitude to the gods for our safe-arrival lying overlooked. Just as the base of my stomach gave one final little lurch – '*Medusa*' tightening her turn into the river-channel, onto the rip-tide. As a gentle rebuke from the gods perhaps, their divine reminder of how human we are, how soon we forget.

"Neptune be praised…" I breathe to the rail.

"Though it's Carausius what got us here…" replies the augurer joining me beside.

"Ah, Selucidus….didn't see you."

"Oversights excusable while a ship is in motion. Though I'd not marked you down as a believer, Triton. Communing with gods…."

"Caught me out there! Maybe it depends on the danger, the worry in a moment, just how scared I feel. Though what our admiral Carausius achieves at sea is surely less divine intervention and more his reward for brilliance, not luck. Like that strategic matrix he's devised for us protecting the coasts. A fantastic web of patrols, spinning out from every single fort and port…."

"Yes, Triton, exactly. And as our great general will so often tell his staff, the more and the quicker we prepare, the luckier we get. While never did I see man in more of a hurry!"

"You can say that again, Selucidus. No wonder ordinary folk admire him just as much as we soldiers. The ingenuity and drive. Always questioning and cajoling, encouraging and motivating. Why they believe he hides some magic power, can be everywhere at once…."

Speaking as one of his staff, and for how long we spent out on the road or riding the waves beside him, I'd say the people were right. He virtually was, as Carausius knew he must be to succeed in his Imperial commission. And as he himself emphasises, once we're got onshore and into the fortress to meet with more senior officers. At an important occasion where my duties were limited to the secretarial, mere taking of notes:

"Gentlemen, we should be realistic, face up to the facts. Out at sea, our Roman galleys and requisitioned Gaulish coasters will never rule the waves. Set against seas too vast and unruly, enemies too numerous, our forces will never suffice. When out there it's hard enough work just staying afloat. Reason enough to demand an approach that's different. My ambition now to command the coastline instead. Holding fast to the land as our new priority. Cease squandering our resources on backwaters where they make no difference, risk a total loss at sea. Why from today I want an end to chasing phantoms, hunting down individual raiders. To replace that instead with a defence in depth. The regular inshore-patrolling of every estuary, river-mouth or inlet that accesses our more important towns."

A change in tactics I witnessed him organise against the backdrop of those vast coastal forts whose construction or reconstruction he oversaw both sides of the channel. A project which might not have been Carausius's original idea, but one his appointment certainly injected with renewed vigour, expanded in scope.

"Don't think I'm building these enclosures for fun. For their garrisons to sit quietly inside, sheltering from the weather. No, my order is for you to set your soldiers on the hardest training routines their centurions can devise. Forced-marches and javelin-practice daily the kindest regime we can create for any man wanting to survive what's coming. For men who'll need to be fit. Ready for that day when they're called on to deny a landing to Saxon or Frank. Defend with their lives the beaches and rivers these forts will command."

Of course he was right. With improved fitness in his troops came improved morale and sense of purpose, vital to steering young men in barracks away from other distractions. From fighting over women or gambling debts; meddling in mutiny or politics. You could sense the growing confidence abroad in our military, and every indication was that his new containment strategy really would work. The only pity its enormous cost.

Reason among others why our little admiral is banging his fist on a wooden table inside Gesoriacum fortress. A key meeting of his *consilium* held inside that white-washed hall currently

125

headquartering the Tenth Theban Legion. My *stylus* struggling to keep pace with the flood of expletives and ideas pouring out of Carausius's mouth like a torrent.

Bumps and hillocks quivering at his fist's impact on a trestle-table where beakers of watered-wine, platters of cheese and apple, lie hidden beneath campaign-maps unrolled over. Simple provisions for our conference: plain food hardly occupying high-level delegates whose courtesies and small talk of arrival are soon dispensed with. That good-natured joshing about different regiments' speed of construction; what moral frailty or vice in their commander these contests reveal.

Banter soon ended when Carausius gets them down to business. Makes each admit to disappointment and embarrassment that he, their leader, should still be receiving reports of Saxon raiding in southern Britain and northern Gaul. Let alone Gallia Belgica, our general's homeland. Accounts not making for happy reading, some of his officers visibly bracing themselves for his rage as Carausius pounds the table again with a slab-like fist:

"Enough of your handwringing, gentlemen! That these raids continue is intolerable. Things must change and make no mistake. We in this hall; you my chosen commanders; together we are the generation to stop them. Blessed by Fortuna with a fantastic opportunity, given full authority to act by Maximian. Entrusted by him for the sake of our whole Empire and those traditional Roman values which once built it; entrusted with the protection of Britain and restoration of Gaul; we are the men who will finally get a grip. And win.....!"

His face shone, no-one doubting the passion in his words. Or his determination. One by one, he looked directly at each man sitting around that table and fixed them with an unblinking eye. Inviting personal challenge.

Including even me, his humble scribe.

No-one flinched or demurred. He knew we would have crewed a ghost fleet to storm the Infernal River, the Styx itself, were he the man who led it. Only the insouciant Allectus, present in our party crossing the Channel that day and ever the soothing voice of fiscal reason, dared to bring us down to earth:

"You have the men, you have the ships. Soon you will have the forts. You already have our undying loyalty, Admiral, but how do you plan to pay for it?"

Carausius's smile never flickered: "Your loyalty or the campaign?"

Allectus smiled back undismayed, his teeth white and even under the neat moustache. I had seen this unmatched pair spar like this before and settled lightly into a chair to record for posterity with my *stylus* their latest bout:

"Both! My lord, we might as well pay the soldiery with glass beads as those ragged and degenerate – I do hesitate to call them coin – discs of copper we dish them out at present. They do love you like a father but will not work for nothing. Let alone die. When remoter garrisons already stand at risk of starving, without money to offer farmers for food. Nor can you expect the timber merchants of Anderida and leather makers of Glevum; the corn-brokers of Venta or shipwrights of Clausentum; to supply your fleet or provision whole armies out of simple charity. On the promise of good times to come - even if they believed you. No, my lord, money talks and we must find more of it, if you would succeed."

"I thought that was your job?"

"I am doing my level best, Excellency, believe me." Allectus's steady tone never rose nor fell as his words uncoiled: "It is only a shame that the great blessing of your Commission in Admiralty from Maximianus did not extend far beyond His letter and warrant of authority to command the fleet. The general's baton in solid gold and painted shield of Medusa were magnificent, but kind thoughts and artwork will never feed soldiers. Let alone pay them. I have been pressing his Treasury officials hard, but our new Augustus pleads problems of his own, all along the Rhine. They are sorry but regret, no money."

"The baton is already melted down for bullion. For you and your mint, Allectus. His other gift is different. Most sacred of objects, true emblem of a divine helpmate – Achilles' relic. His 'Shield of Medusa' priceless, authentic; meaning more to me than words. So let it be with you. Take it as inspiration for our fleet, not a negotiable instrument. When Brother Maximian can offer us little else so long as other priorities draw him, whether on Rhine or Danube. Now our Emperor Diocletian has elevated him as equal, a Hercules to His Jupiter. Entrusted with all the West, there are bigger calls on the exchequer of Maximian than we soldiers may imagine. Greater threats. No, friends, our answer is simpler. Why we in Britain and you, our comrades here in wounded Gaul, together we must look to our own defences...."

"Yes, and pay for them, too..." retorted Allectus. "Excellency, we know the situation is far from hopeless, but its solution may well boil down to how much we can squeeze from those comfortable taxpayers whose lives and security our soldiers are sent to defend."

"Ah yes, Allectus, now there are the ones. How to win over the *honestiores* – our lovely, landed gentry. As self-satisfied a class imaginable. Unwilling to spend one copper *as* on repairing a barn roof unless they're satisfied it's already falling down."

"But perhaps the class with most to lose? Who've seen friends and relatives fled to Britain. Heard what they suffered at the hands of *bacaudae* and barbarians. Stories to count their blessings by - sitting pretty in some downland villa while a colder wind blows-in from Gaul. Their Britannia has been lucky, Admiral, our job to keep it so."

"Quite right, my chancellor. You never spoke a truer word. Join Saxon and Frank with their German allies, the appalling Alemanni, and you've got a major menace. Though one I can deal with, believe me. Like I did the *bacaudae*. Both emperors know me for a lucky general, that Fortuna is kind and loves me. If only we can persuade the people to support me as strongly, to provision my fleet and feed their army, then Rome can win through."

"Through you and Quintus Bassianus....?" put in our host, Mauritius, *praefectus* of the resident legion. A thoughtful older man with dark-skinned, weather-worn features, so far sitting through Allectus's monopoly of their debate without interruption. His intervention seeming the more daring, even if everyone was thinking what only an officer of his seniority and standing could voice. Only an Egyptian broach so delicate an issue, minimise offence.

The Carausius I knew did not always smile and here was one question – or rather a name – to provoke thunder in his wings. Suddenly unrolled, like Jupiter his lightning:

"The military governor in northern Britain holds no concerns for Gaul, prefect, let me assure you on that score. Doubtless a man to be relied on to do his duty, to fulfil his distant commission as faithfully as I do mine, away up here. But how brother Bassianus deploys and provisions, let alone pays for whatever forces he commands from Eboracum, or those he has on the Wall, is no more my business than our navy's are his. No, Mauritius, we need no more trouble that busy general with the affairs of my sea-command than I him. A military convention your colleagues here should kindly observe - you need not mention him again!"

There were mumbles of agreement around the table then Allectus resumed the previous thread, rolling up his account scrolls and smiling blandly as ever:

"Excellency, we are sure to obey. Though thinking it unfortunate our population do not understand these operational distinctions. Do not love their defenders."

"No, Allectus, there you are wrong. They do not love the taxgatherers, the officials who gather the money we need to run on. When there will be no peace without warfare and no victory without an army - or a fleet – that's paid for. Why we must teach people that sacrifice is good. Not only to the Gods but also to their State, if the peace they love and security enjoyed is to continue. For the public good, their safety and protection, a little belt-tightening will be required. Are we are not all Roman citizens, embarked on this together?"

If Mauritius of the Thebans dared come back on this point, one could see how he might. Along with his lieutenants - Candidus the deputy; Hippolitus and Exuperius, their adjutants; Asclepiodotus of the camp - he and his veterans of the Tenth had crossed half an empire, obedient to an emperor's summons. Men who'd seen more than their fair share of the world. Tasted the turmoil and uncertainty consuming it, even on the way.

If word in the camp was that he was a Christian, like many of his men, you would never have guessed it from the eagles of Jupiter embossed on his breastplate. Or the figures of Mars on its shoulder plates, the sun god on his shield. And if half his whole legion was rumoured to be Christian, no one doubted their reputation for tough, disciplined fighting. Brought over on an emergency-posting to suppress the *bacaudae*, no sooner had they done the job in Gaul than some new campaign would beckon elsewhere. Waiting for fresh orders during our sailing season, squatting uncomfortably in those empty barracks at Gesoriacum normally reserved for our CLBR marines, these Thebans must have wondered if they would ever see the sunshine of Africa again.

"Belts tightened for whose sake, Excellency? Which state should we love, what really are we Romans? This thing called *'Rome'* we all fight for - is it a city, a state or an empire? Or just an idea? Creation of God or of men? When its meaning to people seems constantly to change. Too often I fear, reduced to nothing at all. Especially for the young. When no-one in Gaul or Britain under fifteen remembers direct rule from Rome. When they say neither emperor visits the place and both despise the senate - who from the current generation is left likely to care? When the army in Italy killed every emperor we had this century, whether good, bad or indifferent. And when everyone is supposed to forget how you troublesome northerners of Britannia, Germania, and Gaul once dared to stand alone. Apart for thirteen summers, for so long it almost seemed normal. Even to loyal provincials like us in Egypt. Proclaiming your so-called *'Gallic Empire'* as if the solution to it all...."

"Your points are fairly made, Mauritius, historic not disloyal. Exactly why it is Rome we must restore first. The idea of Rome: of Rome and her Republic. Starting in Britain but here in Gaul too. Perhaps one day your lads can do the same back in Egypt. Help rediscover civic values and beliefs wherever they end up. Values making Rome great and strong – courageous and determined. A Rome that makes no more demand on a man's soul than one simple oath of loyalty. Made to her emperor. Why when we falter it is my belief we stand punished by those gods - for abandoning them, abandoning Rome. And I choose to cleave to Diana, the moon goddess. Or else Medusa, wise and ferocious, the *hydra* we should emulate once Alemanni come. And if our strong renewal may make northern lands safer, imagine what it can do for the peace and security of our whole empire. If that's what young Triton here really means when he talks to us about a *'Golden Age Restored'*, then be in no doubt that we are the men and ours is the generation to do it...."

130

When he spoke like this, there was not a man in the hall who did not share in his conviction. They stood to their feet and applauded, and I put my pen down to rise with them. For me it was the most thrilling moment, one never to be forgotten so long as I live.

If Allectus and Mauritius were till now the real instigators and the rest of us mere spectators to their debate, once again I would surprise and embarrass myself. When an excited tongue suddenly broke away, inspired by his words and a gracious mention. Why I heard myself call out with more of my own:

"Then Admiral, to persuade the people you must find a common message for them to remember. A motto capturing their mood and your ideals in one ringing phrase. That form of words you choose to represent what we all stand for today. Your unique dream of Rome. An idea to cling to, come hell or high-water, and in our line of work probably both...."

There was a whisper of astonishment that grew into a welcome ripple of laughter. As it ran down the table to break the tension of the moment, I rattled on regardless, unabashed: "....words as your ultimate weapon. In their message your certainty of victory. Carried in a simple couplet our soldiers can take forward with them, through hardships on the way."

Astonishing to see and hear these hard-bitten senior officers, many twice my age, banging the table in fierce agreement. Even moreso to bask in their commander's open approval of what I'd just blurted.

"Then when I do so, be sure of one thing. That you are the officer I will ask to devise them. Your Labour of Triton, when that time of testing comes!" he had rejoined with a grin.

Me and my big mouth again, laying-up more trouble for the future.

When would I ever learn?

"It is with baubles that men are won"

(Napoleon Bonaparte, Emperor of France)

- 6 -

Mercifully, I remember the slide beginning, but not when we hit the barrier. That point where I got knocked-out. If only for a second.

Then I come to and discover - incredibly enough – that the Toyota's engine is still running. Leaving me and Xenobia slewed at an extreme angle across both outer lanes of the autostrada. Cubes of broken glass showering down over the cabin like ice, but fortunately no-one hurt - not even me.

Only shocked.

And with no one around to report this incident to - apart from the flock of anonymous motorists waiting at a safe distance, much further off - I suppose it was the shock which left me deciding the best thing to do was put the 4x4 into first gear and drag ourselves back to safety. Onto the hard shoulder for a quick inspection.

I hadn't just lost the windows. The whole front of the Toyota was badly damaged. Especially around the nearside where its grille, bumper and headlamp were shoved back into the wing. Yet amazingly it still drove, and if the trailer sat awkwardly on the road then at least its four wheels were touching, to a greater or lesser extent. So I went around tightening all the straps to be sure, then got back in the cab and took a deep breath.

Meanwhile, a stream of cars had started going past in the outside lanes, puzzled passengers carefully inspecting me and my wrecked *equipe* as if an obvious madman. Their diagnosis was not so far off but I aimed east anyway, following signs for Malpensa: to the airfield of *"bad thoughts"*. And how appropriate was that, with my nerves so frazzled? Why I soon got lost, arrival at the *aeroporto* only the startline for my next set of challenges.

Milan's airport had doubled in size since the last time I'd been. Half construction site, half city, a place where successfully bringing an ailing jeep and trailer through the gyratory and to

132

the correct terminal would be three-times more fraught. A palace of concrete and glass whose maze of car parks and one-way systems caused several unwanted tours before I finally found somewhere safe to abandon Xenobia within walking distance of Arrivals.

But not before several oncoming bus drivers had flashed me and made offensive gestures towards these blue-arrowed signs. "What are you on about?" I'd shouted angrily back at them in English through an unglazed window: "I am only going one-way!"

Parked adjacent to a Carabinieri compound and feeling calmer, here at least I figured less chance of an insecure Aurelia being abducted by an admirer from under their office windows. Foolishly not reckoning on the extra attention she draws wherever you put her. Those more material considerations to which, if thinking clearly, I should have given more thought. Like the effect of a rough-looking 4x4 and its damaged trailer abandoned so close to what's a key security installation.

At a major international airport in the Time of Terror.

With hindsight an obvious bad move, but I was harassed and not thinking straight. Rushing to the main terminal building in a lather, where I found myself hot and alone at Arrivals. Fretting about Xenobia but not the broken rig she sat astride, nor where I'd stupidly left it. How to break the news to Bill.

Bothered about how I would find him, even to confess, it was the gorgeous young woman manning their 'Welcome' counter who helped get me the chance. Her public announcement by special request: *"Attenzione, prego! Signor Guillermo Cariss de vole numero cinquecento e venti de 'Newcastle' est recommande urgenta a l'accetazione con baggaglio a mano numero nonedice!"* she told a world indifferent.

Lovely, I thought it. Another day I'd have given her more attention but this was a crisis. One where I had no time and even less Italian.

"What's the matter with you?" asked Bill on his phone, not having understood a word of her beautifully modulated announcement beyond his own name and *'Newcastle'*. At least it made him call me on my mobile, in the slack time while he waited for his suitcase to come down off the carousel: "You seem very quiet…"

As if to prove the point, I made no greater explanation: "See you in the Arrivals hall, Bill. Got something to show you.…"

Once he's through Customs and found me, I led him and his trolley out of the Terminal Building and past the hire-car lots. Trundling towards the twisted outfit I'd parked for safety beside the slumbering Carabinieri post, all blinds down like they're taking a siesta.

"Bloody hell…" Bill observes judiciously after one quiet circuit.

"We hit a concrete wall…" I say in the plural, as if complex issues of culpability and collective responsibility are still to be ironed out. As if the cause of all this white-flaked damage wasn't obvious. Or a third-party stayed missing, should be present to share in blame with me - as maybe they did. Lawyer to the last, immediately disclaiming liability.

"Someone went by me on the *autostrada* too fast, then the trailer went into a snake…" I reluctantly confess.

"Hit a snake, eh? Some sort of crazy python, answers to the name of Monty?" snarls Bill.

Then we noticed together how the pool of rusty water from its smashed radiator forming under the stricken Toyota had wasted no time in escaping from my marked parking-bay. Starting to spread further while I'd been off and finding Bill.

Perhaps it hadn't been such a bright idea to think of parking Xenobia so near that inscrutable Carabinieri barracks. No sooner had this doubt occurred than a Land Rover station-wagon arrived. Glossy in navy-blue, a light-box high on its white roof and 'CARABINIERI' emblazoned in the same colour down its doors; into the space alongside.

Parking beside our miserable assembly as if in answer to a prayer.

The armed policeman in its front passenger-seat flung his door open and stepped out without looking. Down into the orange lake beside my Toyota, rust-coloured water splashing over his polished cavalry boots and onto the blue serge of sharply pressed, red-striped jodhpurs.

"Bloody hell…" said Bill.

"Pig of the Devil…" said the policeman in Italian, or words to that effect.

134

This would cost us.

They were armed and we were in trouble. Why we would spend the next two hours as invited guests behind the blank venetian blinds of their adjoining police post. Present on military property as their warning signs make clear, because mess with the Carabinieri and you're taking on the Army.

"*A most disturbing experience, and all because of a snake...*" how Bill later described it.

Lots of official forms for them to complete with our assistance, though whether the entries they made bore any relationship to our embarrassed replies, we could only hope.

All we wanted was out.

Interminable questions from "*Pig of the Devil*" and his older superviser, framed in halting English. Polite enough for all that, I'd allow. A third officer soon turned up after we'd arrived in the interview room, then went off to search our cars; the point when I realised their supervising sergeant retained only one arm.

"*IRAK*" confirmed the embroidered badge on his pinned-up empty sleeve, and we forget. It wasn't just our lads and lasses: Carabinieri served there too. No wonder they'd kept the sergeant on. And bloody good for him too, in staying on.

They wanted proof of ownership but Bill's paperwork for Xenobia was in English and his schoolboy Italian limited to two bottles of '*Nastro Azurro*' and '*il conto, per favore*'. Mine was little better but the Toyota and its trailer interested them less.

There we were: two fully-grown, experienced criminal lawyers sitting meek as children. Willing to answer every half-understood, potentially-incriminating question they put us. Without even requesting the deployment of an independent, local lawyer. Someone who could have advised and protected us from the terrifying journey now beckoning through the arcane mysteries that are Italian legality.

Into Roman law.

'*Physician heal thyself*'.

The reason why we felt so cowed was that all we cared about was her: Xenobia. To get the Aurelia out of here intact and ourselves with her. But already my mangled Toyota and the deformed aluminium trailer she was strapped-to had been dragged painfully across the road by our inquisitors' colleague, using their Land-Rover. Into a security-spiked compound, as if to confirm how our best hopes of release had just been penned-in with hers. The 'clang' of the Italian state, its doors slamming shut behind us.

How many times had we both shrugged in disbelief at defendants in the Crown Court? Men and women swearing to a jury they'd only made those admissions, only agreed to anything, because they'd wanted an escape from the claustrophobic, windowless world of a police interview room and its glaring camera.

Now here we were, two Englishmen abroad, doing the self-same thing on unfamiliar territory. Because we knew what we wanted, all we needed. To be reunited with Xenobia before she disappeared into the underground bowels of a police car park somewhere near Milan, and the dark heart of the Italian legal system closed around her forever.

Thank goodness Bill had his brainwave.

Thought to play our ace card.

Reached into his document case and took out another one - a complete set, in fact. A line of entry forms headed with the distinctive coat of arms of the *Regilio Auto Club di Brescia* which he laid out on the table like a Royal Flush.

Why had we waited so long?

"Mille Miglia?" asked the one-armed sergeant, his face lightening and suddenly animated.

"Si."

Things happened fairly quickly after that.

It only took a couple of signatures on a couple more forms - mostly for me, as I was the relevant driver - and suddenly all five of us were standing together outside. Back in the sunlit compound, blinking like moles at the wreckage.

My smashed and windowless jeep was a goner, its aluminium trailer as bent and twisted as the Byker Strangler. Ratcheted tightly down onto it with nylon webbing straps, we feared as much for Xenobia. Only the one daintily-raised rear wheel to show her disdain for the deviance from rectitude still pinned beneath. To illustrate virtue's distaste for her carrier's weakness. The miraculous integrity of her superior monocoque - Vincenzo Lancia's posthumous triumph, May God Rest His Soul.

All disapproval seemingly fled, our interrogators and captors could not do enough as we swarmed over the broken-backed trailer together in a new camaraderie. Desperate to release Xenobia from its *rigor mortis* grip.

Laying down the trailer ramps with just one hand and a reckless disregard for knife-edged creases on his spotless shirt and blanco-ed bandolier, the Carabinieri sergeant was dexterous despite his injury. Seizing the tyre-change jack from the boot of a squad-car in the yard to support a couple of planks beneath Xenobia's utmost wheel, as Bill slid into her driver's seat and primed the carburettor.

In a moment, her V6 is alive.

The sergeant and his two colleagues wave him back and Xenobia rattles shakily down the wooden planks onto *terra firma*. Not wasting a moment of the astonishing goodwill suddenly on offer, no sooner was she back on all four wheels than Bill kept her going in reverse. A daring move, out through the open compound gates and onto the public road.

Liberty beckons.

Undismayed at his exit and not one of them having for a moment removed their black sunglasses, our new Carabinieri friends stand there showing a frank approval of our motor they would not think to hide.

"*Bella macchina!*" they breathe as one, disarmed by the noise if not the sight.

Scramble, panic, rush.

While I feverishly transfer my sparse luggage, tools and effects from the wrecked Toyota into Xenobia's boot outside, Bill is recovering a road-wheel and some other spares from the trailer locker to put behind her seats. Laying his prized analogue stop-watches out in full array across her metal dashboard.

All the while we continue with this, it feels like we are failing to capitalise on open avenues of escape. Trying to hide our tension as the sergeant gets on his radio, jabbering away.

Italian read on paper is easier; latinate and logical; but once the words are spoken live it always seems much harder. At least to slow learners like me. Where the words flow one into another, defying division inside a big country whose regions contain so many different versions of the same tongue; dialects and inflections. So while I might have caught the simpler, more obvious bits, key words like "*Brescia...Mille Miglia... Lancia Aurelia... Inglese.....*" his overall meaning was otherwise lost to us both.

For all we knew, this might have been more trouble.

Were they going to have a change of heart and "*head us off at the pass*"? Obtain a warrant from an examining magistrate and put us away for good?

The car packed, I strap myself tightly into the passenger seat beside Bill, who starts the engine again. Then the moustachioed sergeant leans the one good arm he has on my door edge and fills the open window with his tanned face. Eyes invisible behind designer shades, though radiating nothing but honest cheeriness. And all the time he rests across Xenobia's *carosserie*, Bill dare not move off.

"*Signori, uno momento, per favore!*"

Our hearts sink at liberty delayed, but we affect nonchalance and a radiant smiling back.

What now?

The answer comes in like a lion.

With impeccable timing, an almost regal majesty and delivered on a tidal-wave of power, two Carabinieri motorcycle patrolmen come sweeping onto the airport concourse.

"Richard Branson!" says Bill ".....I think they're giving us a fighter escort."

"And beyond this army that you see there is nothing to be frightened of – only forts without garrisons, colonies of greybeards, towns sick and distracted between rebel subjects and tyrant masters. Which will you choose – to follow your leader into battle or to submit to taxation, labour in the mines, and all the other burdens of slavery?"

(Calgacus, Caledonian chief, before the battle of Mons Graupius, 84 AD – *per* Cornelius Tacitus: *'The Agricola'*)

- VII -

After the meeting broke up and its delegates walked sociably together down the stone steps of the *Principia*, the old headquarters building in Gesoriacum fortress, glad to be out in the air again, it was Allectus the accountant who moved silently alongside:

"What you said in there at the *consilium*, young Triton, was very interesting. Very interesting indeed. Some sophisticated ideas - if I may say so - for a lad of your age. And I really think you're on to something....."

His acrid breath had the reek of metal but I was unused to praise and must take it brightly. Gratefully smiling and accepting his approval at face value while he continued:

"One day, when we have a coinage that's worthy of the name again, there'll be no better way to get that message out to ordinary people. No better vehicle for maximum impact. When we do win that opportunity to work for the public good, as I believe one day we will, then you can be certain that I'm the man to help yourself and our admiral achieve it."

Accepting his remarks and mysterious promise with polite mutterings of thanks, I could not help wondering how he imagined his hypothetical scenario unfolding in practice. What kind of opportunity so important figure as he could envisage for a minion as new to their great game as I was.

Meanwhile and until that moment came, Carausius the commander in Gaul was set on a full-scale tour of coastal defences to the westward end of his responsibility, this side the narrow sea. If we spent that night comfortably billeted in barracks retained for the *Classis Britannica* within Gesoriacum fort, then once again at first light his executive staff found themselves boarding yet another ship with him. This time for Marcae, in the territory of the Amoricani.

When we left port next day aboard it, I found it incredible to witness the entire Tenth Legion paraded in open order upon the grass-topped dunes which flank the entrance to the River Lianae and its harbour. The Prefect Mauritius perfectly stationary and alone on a pure white horse at their head, its mane and tail waving free in the early morning breeze. Capturing the loneliness of command.

His cohorts were lined up like blocks of iron behind him with their gilded eagle standard. Nigh-on three thousand silent soldiers come to see our admiral and his ships safely off. Drawn up on the sands beyond the fort overlooking the estuary, under the long shadow of that lighthouse at its entrance which the mad Emperor Caligula ordered be built, two-and-a-half centuries ago.

He who appointed his horse a Consul; or once set legions to collecting seashells near very this spot: *"Conquering Neptune"* how he claimed it. Mad and bad Caligula may have been, though his construction's lasting value for modern mariners preserves his memory better than he properly deserves. While who's to say how many of his successors have proved much saner? Either way, an incredible engineering achievement and one of the greatest wonders of our Western Empire. Two hundred feet, and twenty-one alternating stories of polychrome brick, orange and white.

This spontaneous parade beneath it was nearly as exceptional. Exceptional in the honour paid our commander and the spectacle it gave for everyone as we rowed out the river mouth and towards the open sea. In my short life, I had never seen anything on this scale – so many soldiers. Evidence of that peculiar loyalty our little Admiral always inspired unbidden, among his whole command. Everywhere he went.

Exceptional, but also dangerous.

I wondered privately what an Augustus might make of it, if word ever got back – as word surely would, government spies being everywhere. While our ships slipped further out to sea, mainsails unfurling, I stood at the stern rail beside a massive steering-oar, beneath the Admiral's rippling banner. His flag of Diana. Catching one final glimpse of the reddish ranks of the Tenth maintaining their disciplined patience over there on the land, their last roar of hearty farewell carrying faintly on the wind.

Never in my wildest dreams did it occur to me then to imagine that this would be the very last time that any of us would see them alive again. Including their quiet-spoken Prefect.

We sailed south-west down the coast and met no-one. No ships. No raiders. Slipping inshore again on arrival at Marcae, you could see even before tying-up the scale of major works.

141

Third Felix Legion, but nothing lucky for them about this posting.

Gangs of soldiers busy mixing lime-mortar, carrying stone, delivering bricks, cutting timber, and building sections of curtain wall. Clusters of scaffolding poles rising skyward at intervals showed where stone bastions able to withstand the recoil of roof-mounted catapults would soon be constructed.

"Soon!" was their promise too. Coming from a harassed legionary centurion in charge of one construction gang, his uniform whitened with lime, as his commander pressed him for completion dates.

"Not good enough." said Carausius. "The Emperor comes here sooner than you think. Expects more from us - now. For His sake, we must push these works forward."

"I am doing my best, General, believe me. But you should know, my men have not been paid for months. Left poor and hungry. With worse effects too - *disciplina*. I think you understand me...."

"I understand you all right. You are a diligent officer and wise to warn me. It is important. Though do not worry, soldier. Be sure it is something I will raise with the Emperor in person, when he and I meet. That this money will come, the Third will be proud again."

Another day, another fort.

This one Grannona, its mounted garrison of Moors from North Africa better-organised and motivated compared to similar units seen in Britain, as if our climate depresses their spirit. They'd served Carausius well in his suppression of the *bacaudae,* their joyous welcome on arrival wilder and more enthusiastic than anywhere. A cheering so loud and long you might have heard it across the Alps: in Rome or Mediolanum. This public affection for their old commander was sincere and obvious, but could embarrass our admiral more thoroughly than those silent ranks of the Tenth. As well it might, for these times were dangerous.

Though it was these *Mauri* who lent us some superb horses plus a large cavalry escort for our protection. Precautions to see us safely through the next part of our journey; inland and up-river into the adjoining province, Gallia Lugudensis.

We rode out early the following morning from Grannona under their pennants and lance-points into a pleasant landscape, easy

142

on the eye. Rolling green fields and lush woodlands, teeming with game. Straight, properly-maintained roads enabling good progress across it, but they were to be the only well-kept thing we ever saw.

Everything else was broken.

This whole day taken up with what I remember as a punishingly-long ride by any standards, before arriving past dusk before the gates of Rotomagus. Why we had not simply taken another boat to get us up river, I did not then understand, though it probably would have been too slow. This rush to cover terrain typifing our commander's obsession with seeing the latest situations for himself out on the ground. Out in the garrisons. If so, there certainly were things we saw out there worth noting.

Beside trips to Gesoriacum HQ or its sister forts-cum-ports, this was the first time I'd set foot in Gaul proper. If I've implied the countryside we encountered on the way was beautiful, then indeed it was. Not dramatic but quietly comforting, like the scenery I'd been brought up amongst in Britannia.

This superficial, pastoral beauty hid a disturbing aspect we saw more of the further we drove inland. Rich farming land no doubt, but too many of what had been fields were now abandoned. Given over to no better crop than fast-advancing weeds. We saw precious little livestock, even less healthy, the people themselves barely more numerous or favoured. Those few we saw had a hollow-cheeked and haunted look. Living in ruins and crude hovels beside the road or passing by us quickly as travellers, pressing on urgently with an air of urgent preoccupation. No-one acknowledged us or smiled, nobody lingered.

It felt too risky for that.

"The cruel legacies of war live on long after the gentle reign of peace returns..." said Allectus from his horse, waving his arm airily at the passing landscape in the manner of a poet.

Almost as if he cared.

Any recovery of the Gaulish provinces from Germanic invasion or the treacherous anarchy which followed them under the bacaudae, if recovery would come, seemed passing slow. Taking decades. I'd often heard about their recent plight but it still came as a shock to witness it personally. How reluctantly these slight improvements dawned.

At Rotomagus we found a walled city set like a ship among a sea of rain-flattened cornfields. Their battlements were high, the towers higher, commanding a total civic safety from long views and arrow-slits in all direction. Zig-zag patterns of alternating red and white brickwork decorating the massive walls of this impregnable stronghold, art and defence combined into one confident statement of Roman power.

Safe they may have been, but too many of those its bulwarks shield occupy shabby shelters no better than tents. Enjoy no more protection against weather than sailcloth or tarpaulin can offer. The stench of human waste what strikes us most on arrival, not the wonders of architecture, in a place where every green or cultivated space within its urban plan, the pleasant orchards or paddocks between houses, appears defiled. Almost disappeared beneath an insanitary shanty town filled-up with starving refugees from the barbarism of Germania, brutality of bacaudae. Hiding inside, not daring to take up the thread of old lives beyond the walls, even as a hero who's destroyed both threats rides triumphant through their tent-lines. Through residents too ill-disposed to notice, clustering instead around a skeletal preacher on a pillar who waves a cross of string-tied birch to rant of eternal lives hereafter. Their rescue through death from this life of misery in camps.

"Welcome, welcome, welcome to our wonderful city!" says the tattered senator in faded toga; waiting at the head of his municipal peers outside their three-storey, double-arched gatehouse in duo-chrome brick. Those middle and merchant classes with him equally effusive: "Welcome to our Lord Protector!"

'Tutela' the admiral says in reply, setting the reins down on his saddle bow and holding up his arms to them as if in blessing: 'Protection'.

Over and over, this was the word and this the concept he stressed. As if he was picking up on my ideas already. An idea and reality which, to my unquestioning eye, Carausius had undoubtedly brought them. His military achievements and positive message which, among the ruins of Gaul, her surviving citizens should surely grasp as genuine. Be willing to accept.

144

While over the sea in Britain - and as I learnt in his service - a more independent-minded population suffering less would show itself even harder to persuade.

Yet if their official reception was rapturous, there remained a nagging doubt. Even if those who ran Rotomagus seemed pleased to see him, who could tell how many of the broken folk it held once ran with the bacaudae? Mistook the arrival of barbarian chaos for a rescue from their hated taxgatherers, before a worse and bloodier harrying began? However the loyalty of the emaciated lay today, if they could not leave the safety of this city to cultivate wider lands without, then, within its circuit of walls, all they would find to eat was brick.

Sensing this renewed crisis in the city, Carausius set himself straight away to a cycle of meetings convened in its basilica. An impromptu council where civic worthies and the desperate deputations from its chaotic camps could jostle for attention.

His first announcement there was meant to win friends; the redirection of several corn ships from the many departing Britain daily for our Rhine frontier. His promise of humane relief from the grain stores of Britannia, the wheat fields of Parisi or Iceni, diverted to the hungry of Lugudensis. And their garrisons would be paid, their first meagre instalment from what he swore he'd send that centurion. The back-pay Allectus had somehow rescued from metal offcuts recycled from the floor of local Mints. Going by ship in iron chests to his lime-spattered men of *III Flavia Felix* on the scaffolds of Marcae, the black cavalry of Grannona.

Cash and grain.

"This is what we were waiting for. A general who knows how to impress, a man who gets things done!" I heard a soldier saying in the street to the owner of a bar.

Shame then that those coins these chests contained were little better than tokens. Promises only of worth, stamped out in flimsy alloy from the sheds of Rotomagus.

Mockeries of Rome's wealth begging the underlying question: where had the good times gone? If nobody knew, I suppose it was the thought that counts.

But if the senators of Rotomagus, the soldiers on her walls or the beggars in her streets, seemed gratified by Carausius's generous sincerity; even a political innocent like myself could

145

wonder what an Augustus like Maximian might make of it. Of those unilateral orders, that general joy in Gaul. Let alone the hungry tough-guys Maximian leads along the Rhine, noticing their military granaries are down a shipment or two. So that a general up from Britannia can get all the thanks, feeding soldiers' rations to the Gallic poor.

In the meantime, while Carausius fielded crowds of petitioners in the basilica, I received an unexpected invitation from Allectus: "Come along with me this afternoon, Triton, while I tour the Imperial Mint. Good for your education, show how important this inland city is to the seaboard we're tasked with defending. Money problems we face."

"What could be the harm?" I'd thought.

From a narrow side-street, part of the basilica, we entered an anonymous industrial building adjacent. If not for the soldiers making discreet guard inside the entrance arch, it could have been any sort of factory. Searched those leaving as thoroughly as arrivals, even our eminent selves, but the dark interior we entered next was like no other I have seen. Its stink of hot metal and smoking yellow fires, the constant din of tools. Hellish in scale.

The balding overseer in charge was caught by surprise by our deputation but quick to seize its opportunity for official recognition - his wife would never hear the last. An overweight man sweating anxiously in his woollen tunic and long trousers, obsequious yet proud of his responsibilities in the output of this place.

Quick to present a neat but doubtless well-rehearsed show to illustrate the reach of its production, we were jokily required to surrender British coinage from our soldiers' purses into his filthy hand. Before he picked those out stamped with an 'R'. The official mint-mark of Rotomagus circulating in number across the Narrow Sea. Encouraged by our interest and flattered by our presence he warmed to this theme, leading us into the workshop.

Where I marked when we went in how Allectus opened his nostrils and sniffed at the foul air of the foundry like a dog-fox returned to his copse. Breathed-in deeply of its metal rank.

There we heard the overseer's account of how blank patterns for coins and medallions are stamped out by heavy machines

146

driven by water. Or otherwise moulded. Saw how tiny images of the Emperor Diocletian which oil soldiers' palms in the market place are carved out by craftsmen in reverse-relief. Finely-wrought onto stamping-die or master-mould.

"This is old news to me..." yawned Allectus: "What I need to see most are the stores."

Where we finally saw what a sparse reserve of raw copper and bronze is actually held in ingot form for melting down on site. What pitiful remnants of silver are left a robbed government to bestow on its subjects. How the Imperial Mint floats a faint silver-wash little better than glaze across cheap discs whose illusion of value it bolsters through no more cunning a device. A feeble deception attempted by a cynical state, sufficient to fool none of its citizens still in possession of their own teeth or savings.

"Money made without the reserves to back it, I'm afraid. You can see how little..." began Allectus, handing me a heavy tray of fresh *antoniniani*, when suddenly there came a clatter behind us followed by the most appalling shriek. Everyone in the workshop spun around to see a moulder writhing on the floor. His opening becoming one continuous, awful scream.

My blood ran cold.

The baked clay mould he was using had suddenly burst, exploded. Its molten contents pouring down his bare leg and onto the floor like rainwater off a drain, to glow in angry red pools around him. The unique scent of burning flesh, once smelt never forgotten.

His fellows rushed forward to drag the moulder away but the damage was already done. Probably fatal. Their overseer started forward too then hesitated; torn between his duty to an important deputation and a natural concern for his staff. Even if the moulder didn't die from pain and shock, he was sure to lose a leg.

It was Allectus alone who never turned round.

Not a flicker.

As the dreadful screams continued, he barked at their overseer over the din: "Get that idiot out of here immediately, these people back to their work - before I have to do it for you! Now, where were we.....?"

147

His calm technical explanation to me of a poor quality output and its harmful effect on economic centres like this city, not to mention the tax-base, resumed as if nothing had happened. Useful learning for an ambitious junior no doubt, but I'd understood his cold indifference as clearly. It had to be confronted.

"That man in there….." I started, as we elbowed our way back towards the basilica through a muddy street blocked by yet more refugees in a crowded city, roadside beggars tugging at our military cloaks.

"What are you on about, Triton? It was only a slave. Worthless, a nothing, while the metal is not. Recovering the silver he spilt what you should worry about, what we can't replace. Not the groans of slaves."

Afterwards I used to think how strangely-appropriate a setting it was for acquiring so significant a grudge. At an impromptu lesson on the value of money, the metals that make it; received in the field from my first-ever tutor in currency economics.

Young, inexperienced, and still ignorant of state responsibilities; what perhaps I hadn't given enough credit for was the hard war Allectus was busily fighting. A different war to ours but arguably just as significant. Just as difficult. While we fought *Saxones* on the beaches and the landing grounds, his war was being waged through the army commissariat and public street markets; in the emperor's mints and weapon factories; on the slipways of shipyards and in the stinking vats of leather workers; his campaign maps the inked returns of tax gatherers.

I knew we could not succeed in ours if he did not succeed in his, but that never made him into a likeable or an easy comrade. A cold-hearted man who fought his war as hard and ruthlessly as we did ours, but with the bronze stylus of a nibbed pen his only weapon. His 'soldiers' a legion of account-clerks, of wagon-masters, scavengers and metalsmiths; their 'battlefield' a ledger.

No, our general of the balance sheets could never win us victory, but he was the only warrior among us whose personal failure would cause everyone to encounter a total and collective defeat. Immediately.

Allectus himself, the great *Rationalis*.

*"If you have ten thousand regulations,
you destroy all respect for the law"*

(Winston Spencer Churchill)

- 7 -

Thanks to certain stressful experiences at the *Aeroporto di Malpensa*, we could easily have arrived too late for scrutineering held at the Mille Miglia Museum, on the outskirts of Brescia. Late enough to be disqualified in fact, officially excluded. Fortunately, the flat-out procession two Carabinieri outriders gave us down the *autostrada* put paid to any chance of that. Even if several drivers we rocketed past on the motorway probably witnessed greater danger in the various overtaking-manoeuvres our escorts incited on the way.

To the point we felt surprised and lucky to be arriving at all, let alone intact. Scared but pleased, shaken *and* stirred. A full half-hour early for our appointment in the museum yard,   the assembly   point   for   pre-event   inspections.   For   daunting procedures competing cars and their crews undergo as a prelude to driving back into the city and receiving its confirmation through the application of an official seal. Moulded in lead, then hung on the steering wheel in a colourful ceremony to show they've truly passed.

But first we must pass.

On technicalities I find trickiest in the whole entry-process. Formalities of regulation to be complied with by competitors gathered like supplicants across the dusty yard of what was once a Benedictine monastery, is now a shrine to machinery. By which I mean the Monastery of Sant' Eufemia della Fonte, begun by the Bishop of Brescia in that Year of Grace, One Thousand and Eight.

Built for the Glory of God, not the motor car.

Dedicated to the memory of one of His Holy Saints: the innocent Eufemia. A fifteen year-old Roman girl executed for her unshakeable faith, on the personal orders of the Emperor Diocletian during one of his ferocious persecutions of Christians. One among thousands.

149

If some things, like the cruelty of tyrants, never change; that was then and this is now. Today's the day when we must get it right. *'Failure not an option'* as they like to say on management courses. Inevitably meaning more stress.

In Italy, the paperwork must be complex and time-consuming if it is to carry any weight, show serious endeavour. On the Mille Miglia Revival there are no exceptions. Not even at Monaco can their Auto Club approach the *gravitas* of a Mille Miglia entry form and, because I spoke slightly more (not better) Italian, here was another job Bill happily left to me.

"Typical barrister, delegating the paperwork to instructing solicitor...." I mutter.

A trestle table was set up near reception inside the shade of monastic cloisters, their ancient arches infilled with plate glass. Walls hung with the toothed-wheel badge of the Auto Club de Brescia and a larger version of the Mille Miglia's red arrow symbol; the famous *"freccia rossa"*.

Here the nervous competitor makes their way down a line of tables and serious-faced officials stationed behind. Getting a signature on a form here, a bag of road books and meal vouchers there. Driving licences inspected, insurance documents studied, entries checked.

Along with the elaborate records necessary to prove the expensive chunk of metal parked outside really is a genuine period piece from 1957 or earlier, when the MM was last run in anger as competitive event. That she is no latter-day replica wrought in secret by a criminal gang; by master craftsmen of wondrous skill and no ethical sense secreted inside a remote barn on the Po plain, somewhere beyond Modena.

In our case, Bill went for the full trial-bundle: typical overkill. Two A4 ring-binders of history. Xenobia's build-record from 1953, photographs of several professional restorations undergone over the years, and even a letter from the Lancia factory archive in Torino. All of them to prove she was what he claimed her to be. Not a kit of parts cobbled together on an anonymous bodyshell, under a period chassis plate preserved in a drawer then pop-riveted on as afterthought.

Processing as monks did to Stations of the Cross, and for all the charm and courtesy of every interrogator, the strain this cycle of interaction placed on my grasp of spoken Italian was draining. Its unwelcome reminder of an interrogation by Carabinieri coming at that stage in scrutineering we dreaded the most:

Technical and safety checks.

If there is one thing spoils modern motorsport, it is submitting yourself and your beloved vehicle to the whim of humourless scrutineers. Where do the organisers find them? A race of pedants, drawn towards racing and rallying for reasons unclear but causing competitors so much stress. Beyond what's already involved in getting a recalcitrant old car onto an event start-line. As a lawyer trained in statutory interpretation, I suppose it's the arbitrary and occasionally unfair way such individuals sometimes interpret our sport's book of rules that feels hardest to take. Especially when there's so much effort in just being there. When arriving is an achievement in itself.

Today the scrutineer is waiting for me outside, standing to attention by our car. *"Commissario tecnico"* - a serious-looking man in his late seventies, wearing a navy-blue '*Auto Club di Brescia'* polo shirt and white chinos under a red-badged bodywarmer in black. The top already off his marbled fountain pen, hovering over a clipboard sheathed in crocodile skin. An important man who should not be kept waiting.

"Ciao!"

He greets me warmly enough, but the corded maglite hung from his neck promises light and certainty to the darkest recess of a rusty bodyshell. His demeanour that of a man never shrinking from duty. Unflinching from robust challenge at best, declarations of unfitness to compete at worst, should monocoque or applicant seem weak.

Not me.

I was braced and ready for him. Ready to prove the red 'FIA' (*Federation Internationale de Automobile*) approved battery-switch on the dashboard could 'kill' the whole electrical system instantly - even with ignition on and engine running. Primed to insist that, yes, those bumper-mounted '*Carello*' spotlamps were period-correct. Even if the modern bulbs permitted inside produce searing beams of white wattage far beyond 1950's candle-power.

Produce labels confirming the two-year-old race harnesses holding the crew tightly onto replica seats bolted inside her cabin are still 'in-date'. Whip out of my file faster than a Western gun-slinger their manufacturer's certificate and receipts. Confidently 'twang' the bungee cord holding down the spare wheel and wheelbrace in the boot to illustrate how, no, they'll never come loose in any accident. However big the impact.

All these demonstrations I stand ready for as the scrutineer makes his preliminary circuit of inspection around Xenobia. Arriving at the front again by the shield-shaped chrome of her radiator grill, he pauses and turns to scrutinise me carefully for moral rectitude, before looking down again at the competitor's checklist on his clipboard. He has made his decision and clears his throat in prelude to an important announcement.

As it proves:

"When I was very small, still a *bambino*, my father and I would sometimes be given a lift into town from our lakeside home in Limone del Garda. In one of these cars. A beautiful silver coupé of this exact *tipo*. The very type and year. That is why I feel emotional. It belonged to... to a *Dottori Ingeniere*....Oh, let us say he was a neighbour and a great man. Yes, yes, I forget his name, even now! Though it is so well known to me. Old age, eh? *Mi dispiace!* Anyway, it was my father who told me its owner was a famous engineer at the Lancia factory in Turin. I'm sure you will find him in all the books on the marque, though now it is my turn to be old. I may have forgotten the owner's name but I will remember his car always. The smell of leather, of travelling in the back. How I used to slide across the bench seat whenever he went around the corners a little fast. *Troppo allegro! Io,* with no seat harness *di securienza* in those days!"

The scrutineer pulled out a wallet of softest Sienese leather and from it a faded black and white photograph of a little boy in baggy shorts. Standing with one foot on the bumper of an old car, holding the hand of a man with thick glasses wearing a double-breasted suit.

"It was a GT2500 version of the Aurelia B20, body by Pininfarina. A coupé just like yours, my English friend, same series. From new. How I loved riding in that car – always to remind me of my dear father. But all he could afford was a Fiat Topolino - the one you can see in my picture. You are a lucky man, *signor*, and I am very glad you have brought your black B20 back home to *Italia*, where she belongs. You are very welcome here and it will be wonderful to see her run again on our great Mille Miglia. Have a nice day!"

His Mont Blanc pen flew down the boxes in a flurry of ticks and that was it. We had the scrutineering form and everything else followed. I carried it down the line of tables in the monastery and all the officials welcomed me back like a sinner reconciled, in a shower of documents and decals.

Finally clutching all this paperwork – a roadbook showing our route across half Italy; a list of time controls along with the chip-embedded time cards which marshals running them complete but orbiting satellites monitor; some Supplementary Regulations containing last-minute changes to the roadbook resulting from floods in the mountains or road works in towns; and yet more sponsors' stickers.

Most important of all, the racing numerals we decorate Xenobia's doors and bonnet with. Big black roundels carrying our competition number under the corporate sponsors' names. Banks, yacht and watch-makers, purveyors of leather luggage. And there, underneath all their advertising, we find ourselves – as car '286'.

After ten fiddly minutes unrolling these numbers onto her doors and squeezing air bubbles out from under their vinyl, we are ready. We jump into Xenobia and I start her engine.

All we have to do now is find our way down the Viale della Bornata to the mediaeval heart of Brescia. Then have the car formally sealed at their traditional ceremony in the town. Once we drive out of the yard, past the monastic church and around the back of the museum beside open fields, the roadbook explains how there will be a complicated right turn to make to get onto the dual carriageway running back into town.

I wait patiently but it is lunchtime and everyone is either going home or restaurant-bound. The whole town flowing slowly up and down the main road with no sense of urgency. Never enough space available between each car before the next comes trundling along.

Seeing one white van travelling more quickly west than the rest, followed by a yellow Fiat hatchback that clearly isn't, I floor the accelerator and drop the clutch with less finesse than Bill normally likes; so that we shoot forward across the road with a yelp from the back tyres and a weak toot of protest from the Fiat, before slotting neatly into the townward procession.

On our way and no more harm done than that.

It is then and only then that two motorcycle policemen on pale blue Ducatis suddenly appear in ambush out of nowhere. Gesture sternly for me to pull over.

My heart sinks.

"I don't believe it..." says Bill "Not again!"

154

"Let it be clear to those who insist on admiring disobedience that even under bad emperors men can be great, and that a decent regard for authority, if backed by industry and energy, can reach that peak of distinction which most men attain only by following a perilous course, winning fame, without benefiting their country, by an ostentatious self-martyrdom."

(Cornelius Tacitus, *'The Agricola'*, 2nd Century A.D.)

155

-VIII-

Maximian is coming, and we must brace ourselves for his arrival.

No one would ever accuse Marcus Aurelius Valerianus Maximianus Herculius, as this peasant-turned-soldier-turned-emperor officially styled himself from first of April last, of being any sort of 'softy'. Too many years lived under canvas in the field in company with his old mess-mate, Diocletian, saw to that. Which is not to say the access to sumptuous Imperial facilities his role and titles now ensured, nor the grovelling of citizens to which his new status exposed him wherever he went, did not soften a craggy exterior. Help him love his comforts better.

Of the choice of residences available, our new emperor normally spends his leisure - what little he gets of that - in the Italian city of Mediolanum. Reclining at ease below snowy Alps, girded by lakes. Excepting when he finds himself engaged instead in the endless campaigning necessary to suppress those unruly Germans along the Rhenus frontier. Where his billet becomes one of many splendid palaces decorating a favoured Imperial city. That northern oasis of golden wine and matching architecture we call Augusta Treverorum.

Significantly - as it turns out - in going nowhere near Rome, the Mother City, Maximian is simply emulating the contemptuous example of his senior sponsor and co-Emperor. That Blessed Prince of Men whom Gods have chosen, the Safeguard to our Republic: Diocletian Himself. So that when Maximianus obediently does likewise, he must as openly spurn the Senate and through them the people of Rome themselves. Demonstrate our joint rulers' shared disdain for the senators; for *Senatus Populus Que Romanus* – SPQR. The very badge and embodiments of our ancient state.

So openly it rankles.

Carausius understood these sensibilities of course, and also what a long way it was from Treverorum high on the Moselle to here in northern Gaul. Though it seemed distance gave us no protection, for he had from early in our stay been given to understand, *via* a succession of official messengers arriving from Germania, that the new Emperor to whom he owes his

156

command would shortly be arriving. Wanting to see how good a fist his Menapian lieutenant had actually made of it.

Coming to Rotomagus.

Our response was frenzied. Resources pouring in to feed the homeless and hastily repair the buildings. Make good the defences, re-populate the farms and villas. Putting on the bravest of brave faces for our most important guest.

The eventual arrival of the Imperial party when it came was more stately and measured an affair than its sweaty heralds. Watching it finally approaching from our high vantage on the walls, a distant body of wagons and horses spread out over miles of road. Still only a smudge of gold and purple but unrolling slowly towards us, relentless, to the cheers of crowds ordered out for the purpose. The coming of an emperor, his *adventus*. We heard trumpets and drums, saw flags unfurled, while our stomachs clenched instinctively. In an unreasoning sense of dread.

Our visitor's bloody reputation walked ahead of him. When we saw him, we read it.

Big as befits a soldier or a breed that works the land, his wispy, straggly beard seemed more like an eastern horseman's. Almost as curious an addition and unlikely in its homely effect as that rounded soldier's headwarmer he perches carelessly on top. From beneath whose woven rim the occasional black curl escapes, flopping forward over a lined and discouragingly-shallow forehead to meet a short cliff of intellect. A crag whose lower edge is crested by the one, undivided hedge of eyebrow. That single bushy thread overshadowing a pair of deeper-set and faintly-glinting eyes. Orbs revetted so far from light and scrutiny behind those heavy lids and gathering bags which enfold them as must comprise no clearer warning to cunning than a wiser man might ever want or need.

Taking his cue from this, and that singular signage to cruelty to be gleaned from two deep and central grooves running down the emperor's forehead like scars. Down from the hairline to that nodal point above the nasal bridge where most others' eyebrows choose to part, but his only combine.

Together the clearest clues available from so many imprinted. To an unbridled vicious temperament, unpredictable but always unkind. Barely-literate and proudly contemptuous of any legal framework, all he'd ever been good for and known was fighting and soldiering.

Horses for courses.

Capricious and cruel, coarseness of speech and thought was branded into his hide. It is often said of Maximian that his lengthy train included a wagon-load of girls. Dispensable children who were barely women, carried with him everywhere to refresh his basest needs. Whether that be true I had no chance to see, but with crudity his benchmark for humour, you could see it in the attendant crowd of flatterers and courtiers he dragged along. How they calibrate their laughter to his lowest scale. Fear, sycophancy and the road together creating the largest touring assembly in our empire of servile and cowardly minds.

One of the two most powerful men in the world, indulged to the utmost degree, yet still carrying the ingrained resentments of a land-bound serf into the most glittering assemblies of his day. Hating any class higher than that one he was born to, saving this imperial caste of two he's but lately joined, even their mark or style. Quick to take offence at any imagined hint of social superiority or the faintest whiff of education, neither a slight smile nor a cultivated word could safely be aired in his presence. Not when either fuels fury.

Yet in saying warfare was his only skill, I do not do this Balkan barbarian true justice. For there was one other human quality the world knows our barrack-room emperor held in spades. If only narrow focus. When his personal loyalty to Diocletian was a real virtue and never ever wavered. You had to admire that.

Everyone else could go hang.

Knowing what he didn't like was one thing, an understanding only making it the harder to guess what he wanted from anyone, let alone the professional servants of Empire. Beyond that principle they should never for one moment eclipse his jagged sun.

"My soldiers love me, but those who are not loyal are worth nothing at all. I would rather we did not have them than tolerate insubordination, disloyalty. All that I ask...." announced our one-time Caesar, now their joint-Augustus. Holding out a huge be-jewelled paw like an oriental monarch from his gilded seat on

158

the rostrum specially constructed for him beside the monumental west gate. As if he sensed our moral dilemma.

Carausius knew his boss of old and got the message instantly, going down on one knee without hesitation and kissing it.

Yeuch.

I had never seen anything of the craven in Mausaeus Carausius, but in mind of what we knew of Maximian's unpredictable nature, it was hard to blame him. All the other officers, including myself, did likewise. Falling to their knees and holding arms aloft in a common gesture of supplication. What the Greeks call *proskinesis*.

Us, prostrate, and not even Greeks.

My, how we hated it, but we were soldiers and conditioned to obey, never asking why. That doesn't mean we didn't privately wonder:

They say our first Imperator, the original Augustus, walked unprotected amongst his fellow men and swore to restore the Republic. It couldn't happen now. If the last words of Vespasian were supposed to have been "*I think I'm turning into a God!*" then soon, certainly by the time of Trajan, people began reporting definite a religious sensation in their emperor's presence. Even while he was alive.

Our times have got stranger but emperors woefully worse since those happier days. Why it got harder to inspire a reverence in the public for that chaotic procession of rulers they suffered in recent times. Those military unknowns put up for the Purple and as quickly killed by an out-of-control soldiery. Whatever the shortcomings of recent emperors, none of them dying a natural death, that principle their office should attract reverence and respect surely remains important. Crucial to the coherence of empire, its survival.

In an empire, a super-power, whose latest rulers seem made of sterner stuff. And after what we've been through, some think it as well if Diocletian appears more durable than his predecessors. That rare thing, a stayer. Equipped with qualities necessary for survival in a world where decency or decorum count for naught, represent only weakness. Like his brother before us today, rough and tough to the core - another Illyrian got here by killing.

If Diocletian loves to play the 'Father of His Country' nowadays, it is only after too many assassinations made at his own hand - upon his own kind. Like Aper, his old boss in the Imperial bodyguard, whom he murdered before the whole army at its general council. And when he re-captured Alexandria, they say Diocletian told her population his legionaries would not stop killing till the blood in their streets had reached his horse's knees. Luckily for Alexandrians – or perhaps by design - the beast slipped and fell on the stuff. Bringing his master's measuring point and the order to stop along a little sooner.

Typifying that same flitting between vengeful slaughter and flashes of mercy experienced ever since, we in Rotomagus knew where the Maximianus met that day took his model from. Those last-minute pardons; the subordinates called-off from proscription and slaughter, that climate of constant fear; all of them earning our leader his reputation as ineffable prince. Wise and merciful, stern and benevolent. Iron and gold, night and day, our moon and sun. Unpredictable, inexplicable.

Like a God.

We Romans always hated kings. Still do, even after three hundred years of an *Imperium* whose rulers have kept up a Senate and a few other fictions from our old Republic as if to pretend things were otherwise. Why every citizen still shuddered inwardly on that watershed moment when they heard Diocletian put on a pearly diadem in the manner of the Persian. But also knew to keep quiet. Silenced by the knowledge that one price of the peace his authority has brought us is found in those opinions he proscribes. When we live in an era where so many private thoughts – whether of intellectual disapproval, religious prompting, or moral revulsion - must never be voiced or shown.

By law.

And so it goes on. Whatever was thought outlandish becomes positively prescribed. Once orthodox, illegal and proscribed. The wheel of fate turns, crushing those not fast or wise enough to adapt. As even a provincial nonentity like my father found, to his fatal cost.

Now Diocletian has split the Empire into two halves, East and West: taking the former for his own. Now there are two *Augustii*, not one, to rule over us and here before us is the latest. Their

160

asiatic rules of court following-on naturally, now we loyal folk in the West are entrusted into the tender care of this, his faithful attack-dog. That former junior *Caesar.* His bug-eyed, scar-faced creation, the great Maximianus.

Another Illyrian rustic, accompanied here to the walls by irregular German mercenaries ready with spear points to ensure we Romans show him deference. So there can be little surprise on this fine, festive day in Rotomagus, if the butcher's dog demands the same rituals of abasement from us as His Dear Father introduced.

Rites to cement him in power.

And the very reason why we military and naval officers are laying down on the ground in his presence, privately wondering if the world had gone mad.

When the answer was simple.

Of course it had.

"To finish first, first you must finish"

(Apocryphal saying in motorsport)

- 8 -

As we swept into the fifteenth-century square of the Piazza della Loggia, our latest set of Polizia Stradale friends on their two Ducatis peeled off with one final, friendly salute tipped in farewell from the brow of immaculate white helmets. Under their rocketing supervision and firm instruction we'd run countless red lights across Brescia. Covering the distance between here and the museum at three-figure speeds, urban traffic parting like the Red Sea before Moses.

Even after they're gone, I can still hear sirens in my ears. Diagnose tinnitus. What a way to make an entrance, but no-one even looked. Every other competitor enjoyed the same treatment, no big deal for anyone.

To be accurate, the square we enter is more of a narrow, rectangular box. Built from brilliant white marble and roofed with pure azure, the open sky itself. Its stone sides the Renaissance buildings today masked by long pavilions badged by the luxury and corporate sponsors who make this event tick. The different logos and emblems of watch-makers and yacht-builders; of leather goods suppliers, perfumiers and local banks; are overlooked disapprovingly from stone roundels set-in façades above. By the thick-necked busts and furrowed brows of carved Roman Emperors who knew only one:

"SPQR".

The whole piazza is swarming with officials, competitors and enthusiasts. Milling around a disorderly queue of exotic, ancient sportscars waiting their turn to get through the last formality of pre-event scrutineering.

A parade of people as much a parade of cars.

World Champion racing drivers lucky to survive from forty years ago, designers of trendy sweaters, and rock stars from bands no-one remembers; come together to defy advancing mortality and wring the last juice from celebrity in a whirl of mobile devices and air-kissing.

When someone well-known shows up in a car, photographers descend in a swarm to obliterate our view. Leaving us comforted by proximity, the satisfying certainty that *'what's-his-name'* or *'so-and-so'* is in there somewhere. Close enough to touch, even if we cannot see them. Feeling their presence like a saint's.

Contrast with special admission granted people with disabilities to enter the competitors' paddock. The powerful upper body of a young man with no legs; or the long-haired, older guy pulling at a fashionable jacket while he's pushed around by a woman whose thin frame was once her ticket to a catwalk, is now a testimony to love. Hallmarks to worry, the spin of Fortune's Wheel:

"Keep your jacket on" she says, "you might get a chill."

"Stop fussing..." he snaps: "I'm fine!"

With an event tag on an official lanyard, then you are *'in'*. Even if only to promenade up and down the paddock, see and be seen. Lacking this accessory, you are an unfortunate. Irredeemably *'out'* or else obliged to borrow one over the safety barriers from dear friends posing nearby. "*Mwah, mwah...*" the prelude to nipping past security with its one quick flash, officialdom outfoxed.

"How a few of these characters got to where they are today" observes Bill, a little sourly I thought. "Hurdling barriers and fiddling permissions. No wonder some condone it now...."

More ordinary onlookers, the tagless and other riff-raff, are corralled on the east side of the square. Behind security barriers running down to the arcaded corridor at its other end, their outlet for competing cars. Where I notice a stark memorial raised in brown marble to eight victims of the 28th May 1974 bombing, departures in innocence outlined in gold.

It seems all humanity is gathering here in the Piazza della Loggia, ninety per cent of them probably unaware of the atrocity once marring its arcade. Perhaps even the man on a bicycle who pulls up beside the memorial then unfolds a wooden trailer to reveal his instant stall. Laden with enough badges, decals, or key-rings in chrome to complete the motoring pilgrim's iconography of heraldry.

While nearby an angelic child drives an electric replica of a Porsche Spyder at ankle-level through the crowd, followed

163

discreetly by the father who creates these one-third scale marvels. Hoping for customers among the wealthy competitors owning similar who kneel down to photograph his cherub at the wheel of their ingeniously-reduced equivalent.

Around them all swirl local strollers and celebrity hangers-on, mixed up with tourists and drivers. People of every creed and race mingling together to marvel at the craftsman-made beauty of full-size cars. The swooping bodywork designed in clay then hammered out from aluminium or sheet steel over sectional 'bucks' of timber, else rolled on a wheel.

Extremes of fluidity, permanent sketches in metal.

'Retro' in motion.

Under cloudless skies and an unforgiving sun, Italian *rosso corsa* and British racing green shimmer and gleam together to reflect Renaissance rooflines that frame them. The shady colonnades of the loggia, bleached stones of the square.

Drawn into the atmosphere of a major sporting event, Bill and I forget recent unhappy experience. Careless of a wrecked Toyota and a twisted trailer that lie uneasy in a Carabinieri compound like echoing rebukes. In a country with more legislation than cats, where you're only allowed to do what the state says you can (as opposed to our fading British tradition of whatever's not prohibited) here we are. Two Common Law lawyers too ready to forget the dangerous potential in these forgotten transports for providing evidence of some infraction. Should someone have a mind.

No, our own minds were definitely elsewhere. On exulting in all the attention Xenobia was getting, even in such company. "*Lancia Aurelia....bella macchina!*" says a moustachioed gent' in his early 80s, cool in a crisp linen jacket and blue silk tie. Pronouncing it correctly, of course - "*Lancheea*".

"*Si, si!*" responds Bill, using both the Italian words he knew. His thick, Gosforth Rugby Club shirt had been a poor choice for a warm Italian day in early May, dark rings at his armpit as he returns her admirer's courtesy with magnanimous waves.

Between receiving the traditional lead seal - ceremonially applied to Xenobia's steering wheel by an official with blue-handled pliers - and the opening car setting off down the ramp on the Viale Venezia at 19:30, there were several hours left for the crew of car '*two-eight-six*' to kill. Starting as we must nearly three of them behind car '*one*', the 1927 OM 665S '*Superba*' of Capilano and Zima.

"*Viale Venezia*, eh?" I remember saying privately to myself back home in Jesmond, on reading in the organisers' regulations of their start-ramp's location. When I knew very well where it was based - every year - yet still relished seeing it written. Letting the lead consonants from its title roll down my tongue like grappa. Taking as much pleasure in their sound as if I could taste them. Loving the name, the romance in its association.

Tonight we'd actually be there. Leaving its ramp.

And if we were to be on the road the whole night, then expected to start all over again for the Bologna-to-Rome leg next morning, it seemed blindingly plain that grabbing a bit of shut-eye now should be our priority. '*Numero uno*' for both. So that when my sensible suggestion we pass on the organisers' offered afternoon tea, and head straight back to our hotel opposite the Duomo for a rest, met with resistance from my co-driver and team-owner, it came as quite a surprise.

Turns out he has a different plan.

"Don't mind me..." says Bill. "You get your head down, Mikey. We're good to go, bags and everything in the car, but I need to pop over to grab a word with someone. Thingummy and his mate.... oh, you know. The British crew of that Frazer Nash we saw in the Piazza. Little bit of networking. So if you could do the honours, make sure Xenobia's in the start queue, then I'll catch you later. On the dot, before we hit the line....."

What on earth was Bill on about? Wandering the crowded streets of Brescia on a casual errand. Looking out for two people, among eight hundred in the event and a cast of thousands come to spectate, seemed the proverbial needle in a haystack. No obvious - nor any - priority for a conscientious co-driver shortly expected to find their way through a roadbook describing in diagrammatic form one thousand Roman miles of back road. Our crossing in the next forty-eight hours of the highest, toughest, roughest, and most remote terrain northern and central Italy has to offer, with little rest between.

Why a more assertive driver would have told any 'office manager' in their spare seat who fancied wandering-off before the 'off' where proper priorities should lie. An attitude only tricky when your co-driver not only owns the car, but pays most of the rather large fee that charming organisers demand for their gracious invitation to participate in the first place. Why in all the circumstances I chose to smile amiably and say nothing.

"Don't worry, Mike, we'll be fine. We know it's no race, as the organisers insist. More of a 'regularity'. Average speed and consistency what counts. No worries, we'll do great. And you'll see me there at the start, fresh as a daisy, believe me."

I'd known Bill long enough not to quibble with his sweeping declarations of policy. Knew an acquiescent grunt would do. I also knew how much of Bill's success lay in his ability to appear bluff and straightforward when the opposite was true. A quality emerging not just in his newfound political career but observed in more than a few criminal cases we'd done together. So where was it driving him now?

I'm not a suspicious person, not unduly nosy either, but something in me sensed a colleague being less than straight. Wanted to know the real reasons behind this sudden wish of his to go off into the night.

Finding out the answer is what made me decide to make no fuss but discreetly follow him instead. To see for myself what he planned on getting-up to during the late afternoon and evening that's left us, before the main event begins.

This would not be the first time for something I'd acquired some skill in, but tailing him as a suspect that night in the Piazza proved easier said than done.

"There are only four passages which are habitually used in crossing from the mainland to the island (i.e. Britannia), those which begin at the mouth of the rivers – the Rhenus, the Sequana, the Liger and the Garumna. However, the people who put to sea from regions that are near the Rhenus make the voyage, not from the mouths themselves, but from the coast of those Morinini who have a common boundary with the Menapii. On their coast also is Itium, which the Deified (Julius) Caesar used as a naval station when he set sail for the island. He put to sea by night and landed on the following day about the fourth hour..."

(The Geography of Strabo: Book IV Chapter V
pre-conquest – late 1st Century B.C.)

167

- IX -

When the Emperor; along with all his wagons and soldiers, his trailing retinue of over-dressed courtiers and arrogant Praetorians, bullying Germans; was finally gone away to Treverorum, but only once Admiral Carausius was satisfied he'd done everything else he could for this city, its defence and provisioning; then only then was it agreed that our long overdue return from Rotomagus to Gesoriacum, then afterwards to Britannia, could resume by ship.

Sailing back as we found it, towards a rather different reception.

Not that we'd been away that long but while we were things had changed. A lot, in fact. So that when we eventually arrived and dropped anchor in the Lianae, it came as a complete shock to see this enormous, thirty-acre fort lying completely abandoned. Hearths and ovens cold, its doors swinging open on rusty hinges, and so much rubbish blowing about between the empty barrack-blocks you'd think them gone a twelve-month.

As we walked cautiously up from the harbourside past some bemused townsfolk and in through the unguarded west gate, you could have cut the sense of gloom and ill-omen that awaited us with a knife. The only living people we found on these military premises were a CLBR quartermaster and his bustling clerks. Newly-over from Portus Dubris to make their melancholy inventory of depleted storehouses and empty granaries. Much tutting, sucking of pens, and scratching of tablet-books.

All they knew was that *Legio X Thebanei* had suddenly been ordered south, taking away with them too much of our own food and stores. Why and where to were military secrets, if not a complete mystery. To these clerks as much as ourselves.

All we knew, as would be obvious to an amateur tactician, was that a major strategic hole now yawned unfilled in our defence of the Saxon Shore this side the *Fretum Gallicum*, the Narrow Sea.

I would imagine Carausius felt as dismayed by the news as any, but if he was he certainly wasn't showing it. Cheerful as ever. Neither did he waste time reacting. The biremes which brought us back were immediately sent racing off to Rutupiae with urgent orders, calling *Legio II Augusta* over to fill this breach instead. Every spare vessel that could be commandeered from either side the channel, large or small, was instructed to make themselves available for ferrying bits of the Legion across. In as many daily crossings as were necessary to put something like a proper garrison back in place, ready to guard the narrowest point between two sea-facing provinces.

He didn't want the Franks and Saxons to have even one day to take advantage of this weakness in our defences, but I feared in my heart for how many of their ships might already have got through the straits. Acting on the unique opportunity granted.

The beacon bonfire on top the great lighthouse was hurriedly relit in front of its mirror - shameful it was ever allowed to go out - and the whole place started to come to life again. Within a couple of days our first instalments of the Second started marching up from a variegated collection of ships and boats arriving in the crowded harbour. Singing and joking in good-natured fashion, but still puzzled at being roped-in to counter an unexpected emergency. Among these long files, those hundreds of armoured men weighed down with marching packs and cooking equipment that snaked up from the dunes, I spotted two familiar figures, along with one other.

Two old soldiers. Decimus and his fellow lookout off the Rutupiae arch.

There was a fine-featured, dark-haired girl walking along happily beside Decimus, smiling and laughing despite the grain sack on her shoulder. Almost half his age - that bar girl from '*The Grape & Sandal*' as I guessed it.

He caught my lingering look over her then recognised me in the same moment and winked: "Good morning, Tribune. How nice to see you again, sir. Thought I'd be needing someone to keep me warm of nights. In case our little Admiral detains us over-long, here in cold, cold Gaul."

A comforting aspect of life I'd increasingly come to realise as missing from my own.

"After federalism, we'll devolve all the ministries. They can't all be in Rome, where you find SPQR, Senatus Populusque Romanus, is written all over the place. Here in the north, they say it stands for "sono porci questi romani" – these Romans are pigs... Federalism is a done deal. It's in the bag because it.....stays in the Council of Ministers, where the Northern League counts. Then there'll be the next step, devolution."

(Umberto Bossi, leader of the Northern League)

Brescia calls herself a city but in central scale ranks more like a town. A compact centre of elegant streets, mediaeval or Renaissance alleys, white arcades and long boulevards. All of them laid out on a grid-iron pattern bequeathed by Roman veterans retiring here after twenty-five years' service with the legions. Settling in Brixia.

'*Colonia Civica Augusta Brixia*' to state her full Imperial title, as set out in the guidebook.

Today '*il centro*' retains this timeless matrix and, if Bill and I were actors in a spy film, then you would imagine its long views ideal for tailing a suspect at safe distance. And probably were if its crowded streets had not been swarming with countless dawdling spectators; plus the promenading locals on their nightly constitutional: '*la passeggiata*'. Every one of them gradually migrating towards the western side of town, to where they know the Mille Miglia start-ramp awaits us on the leafy suburban edge beyond her city walls:

Viale Venezia.

In a discreet district where modest apartment blocks and nineteenth-century mansions cluster for shelter among mature trees whose foliage won't spare its residents the annual cacophony of revving engines. And a broadcast commentary that continues all night, into the early hours. In a bosky suburb of overhanging shade and walled gardens whose lengthening shadows could as easily hide a fugitive.

Even one as big as Bill.

On the way over there through the old town, you pass hundreds of beautiful, valuable cars abandoned in the streets and squares. Every one of them donated by their owners to the care of reverent crowds. "*Jewels on four wheels*" Italians call them and, in an era which has learnt to distrust financial savings products, their prices at auction make this no exaggeration. Yet there they stand, unlocked and unattended, with ten thousand loving eyes laid upon them. Surely as safe on the streets of Brescia as in any bank vault.

It had been a sunny, late afternoon, blue skies turning to gold as evening draws on. With the light starting to fade, some of the first competing cars begin to appear on the move. Running through the town with sidelights lit, heading for the start line. Feeding in from the event's assembly paddock out at Fiera Di Brescia.

Our conversation and its temporary farewell ending at the corner of the Piazza where a few late-comers were still leaving scrutineering, I lingered there to watch Bill pass alone along the arcaded boutiques of Via X Giornate.

When Italian shops are so much smaller than the clones sapping the life and character out of English high-streets; every one of them individual. Their nearest UK comparators 'The Rows' at Chester or York's mediaeval 'Shambles', these 'negozio' resemble walk-in jewel boxes. Each one unique in style and content, what marketing types call the 'Offer'. Except Italian proprietors have neither time nor need for advice, drawing on two thousand-years' innate trading experience. Their narrow-fronts a direct continuation from Roman predecessors, only the wonders of halogen lighting and display cases, their jewellery and watches, bringing these caves of luxury-retailing into the twenty-first century.

Absent his wife and so (I assumed) immune to their temptations, 'Mille Miglia'-themed displays and all, I was by now actively following when Bill turned sharp right into the Piazza Vittoria to confront the fascist brutalism of Mussolini's pre-war Post Office. His replacement Town Hall. So different to the Renaissance centre from whose heart he tore them, yet here was the traditional start location for the real road-race, before and after World War Two.

Whatever else was wrong, it did look as if Bill was genuinely searching. Looking for someone specific. Why he didn't linger there long before cutting back. Across towards the Piazza Paolo V where hundreds of race-goers relax al fresco at the tables of establishments like the 'Café Storico'. Seated within touching distance of priceless Ferraris and Maseratis while they sip cappuccino. Whoever he sought, they weren't here either, because Bill's stride never broke once. Not in this crowd.

I already knew the original City Offices as off this square, a base for the organisers. Had seen the corporate sponsors' BMWs and Alfas slipping-in and out of its mediaeval courtyard. Through an arch straddled by a thirteenth-century Lombard tower which looks down disdainfully as they disperse through its maw. Into the teeming streets, off to deliver race officials to key locations around the route, bristling with importance.

On his current bearing, I wondered if Bill might be heading for the event press office that's inside, but just when I thought he would, he suddenly turns on his heel. Marching out and back down to the other end of the square with renewed purpose and a 'phone to his ear, while I melt into the opposite doorway of a bar.

The vantage from which I first notice another guy involved.

A muscle-bound prop-forward in purple *'Ranulph Lautrec'* polo shirt and yellow straw fedora, who also seems to follow Bill. Only closer. When I see this character stride into my vision, going past the protruding apse of Duomo Vecchio at a trot and following Bill along the pavement into the Corso Zanardelli, he too has a mobile phone pressed to his ear. As if requesting higher instructions, without the trouble of entering church.

I wouldn't have minded some myself.

The more our little crocodile zig-zagged around town, the more my curiousity was piqued. Increasingly fascinated to discover what was going on. What Bill was up to, where all his roaming-about would lead us. And who this big guy was.

Nosey? Me? Wouldn't you be?

Bill's unwittingly-shared stroll now took all three of us – separately but next - past the five-star frontage of Hotel Imperiale. Towards two English-registered Frazer Nash 'Le Mans Replicas' exhibited outside. Both cars backed up tight against a marble façade more reminiscent of banking than the hospitality trade. Intended contact with one of their crews Bill's original excuse for wandering away into the Brescian dusk.

Their back story I relish for its links with a darker side of Mille Miglia legend. Easily dismissed as an ugly open torpedo, its road wheels under cycle wings, the post-war Frazer Nash is virtually spoils of war. Copied from the pre-war BMW design (and its designer) the good guys once importing them effectively captured later for good, while on war service in 1945. Like Bristol Cars, an English road-racer unashamedly replicating and developing those pre-war German BMWs often winning this event, up to and including 1940. That darkest of dark years, when exclusion by Mussolini of our stout British crews from the last fascist Mille Miglia allowed a bespectacled

Nazi Count bearing a black 'SS' motif on his overalls to win instead.

And if Fritz Huschke von Hanstein and his aerodynamic BMW 328 help to explain the Frazer Nash-BMW's enduring mystique at market, they don't explain why my co-driver shows no interest in speaking to their modern celebrity owners. When both hold court nearby but Bill attempts an approach with neither. Striding on down the street like he'd not even seen them. When I knew he had.

Curious and curiouser.

Since the overnight bags and equipment we needed were already in the car, why was Bill carrying another? That black, branded holdall I saw hanging heavy over his shoulder. And since we were going to be together at the startline anyway, why did he need to make his journey over there separately? On such a private errand?

At least I knew Xenobia would be OK. Parked where we'd left her, reversed at forty-five degrees to a pavement kerb off Via X Giornate. Resting between her near relative, a 1954 Lancia Aurelia Spyder once Brigitte Bardot's; and a priceless two-seater Ferrari Testarossa in *rossa corsa* raced at Le Mans the same year; she looked a picture of contentment.

We'd agreed – or I'd accepted – that it was going to be my responsibility later-on to move Xenobia up the queue of starters. A few hours after 'Car One' sets off at half-past seven. In the meantime she'd have to stay here - unattended and unwrapped. Exhibited in the street.

Not an issue to me.

It says a lot about the good people of Brescia, not to mention the impeccable behaviour of the many of all nationalities who come into town to view these cars, that priceless rolling artefacts can be left out in this way. Unsupervised. As if all the Botticellis, Simones and Pierra Della Francescas in Florence were taken from the Uffizi Gallery and propped outside in the street for every tourist and passing idler to gawp at, run their finger over.

Cars worth millions that spend all year in the subterranean security of a carpeted and dehumidified garage, the hush of a Californian museum; which rest under breathable covers removed only occasionally for waxing with carnuba; are now

174

released into the world. Into the abrasive reality of mediaeval streets. An Italian road network of loose grit and apocryphal maniacs, where radar traps are suspended and speed-limits advisory.

More than anything, it seemed to me that envy was the feature most lacking from this pageant – for anyone imagining similar attempted in Britain. That and the puritanical disapproval of 'Greens'. Perhaps because the Italians see these cars as *'theirs'* – as part of their patrimony: *"We made them; they are returned to us. We rejoice in their art and engineering."* I would hope a Jaguar D-type or XK in Coventry might get similar respect parked on Browns Lane, though better not to bet. Not once pubs and clubs are closed.

My thoughts wandering in this vein while Bill and the man in the hat dawdle as vaguely along the Corso Magenta. Beside its Music School, where I nip into a corner-bar to buy what everyone else is drinking – a mix of campari, cinzano and soda. To sip an *'Americano'* as my alibi from a high stool beside a window set ideally for watching quarry, both of them lingering nearby. Even if most stays in the glass, with a night's driving ahead of me.

It is from here beside a door onto the Corso, that I suddenly see Bill enter the foyer of a small hotel: *'The Caracciola'*. The one facing onto a side-street visible across the adjacent crossroads. After a short pause, *'Fedora Fred'* looks up and down the street twice and then does the same. Goes right up to the front of the hotel and into reception.

Where Bill is presumably waiting for him already?

If they had and I was to discover what my respected team-mate was up to, then it looked like I should do the same. Stick closer to his tracks than is recommended good practice on what few TV-cop procedurals I could remember viewing.

Without falling over *'Fred'*.

This job was getting tricky but I stayed cool, didn't rush. Stayed at my place by the bar, held back from approaching the hotel. What a good thing I did.

Whew!

The right decision, because Bill suddenly slips out a side door of the *'Hotel Caracciola'* giving directly onto Corso Magenta. Moving along quickly with a strange look on his face. Like a person with local knowledge who has played this trick before - upon some woman's husband? And if this ingenious exit had successfully outwitted *'Fred'*, then Bill could as easily have caught me on the hop as well. If I'd followed everyone in, instead of walking briskly past the unlit doorway to a nearby music shop where I'd had the wit to move myself, hide in its shadows.

Though I really had to control myself in there. Regulate my breathing when it came in short gasps of fear and exertion, so he'd not hear me as they wandered by.

Fear? They?

Yes, there was someone else with him now. Latest arrival.

If you add Fred to Bill, our common target, then the guy now walking along the street with him must count as number three. Someone fresh I'd never seen before: the Third Man, let's say. I'm sure about this because, at least where it shone, the orange sodium lighting was strong. Gave me a pretty clear view of both men, even if they couldn't have spotted me.

Real cloak-and-dagger stuff. How clever I thought myself, especially on realising I was still near enough when they went by to hear what they were saying. When I did, wishing I hadn't. Catching a snatch from Bill to him: "*Just because my group in the parliament's looking for links with like-minded others, don't think it means we'll compromise on principle. Find ourselves in bed with neo-fascists. Be a stooge for Uncle Sam!*"

The other man mutters something irritable in reply but I can't catch any of it, beyond the single word '*gladio*'. My Italian the stronger for a grade 'B' GCSE in Latin, it only helps me recognise their term for '*a sword*', though little else the wiser. However, this word must mean something to a Bill I thought knew none, because he snaps back as if stung:

"*In Brescia, of all places!*"

His new friend, the Third Man, resembles a home-going businessman in a suit. A man of affairs delaying going home to wife and kids while he settles a commercial issue with colleagues. Pacing the night-time streets among the promenaders, students, and *Mille Miglia tifosi*; confident the noise of its crowds gave cover for a very private argument. While carrying himself what looks very much like the same MM briefcase I'd seen Bill with just before. As if he's handed it over.

176

With *'Fedora Fred'* presumably still lost inside the warren of ill-lit corridors that is the *'Hotel Caracciola'*, comparing notes with a crowd of angry husbands, let's give Bill's latest companion a name: *'Alfredo'*. But whoever this third man was, I felt satisfied that he represented the real point of Bill's nocturnal excursion. Not the man in the hat.

And maybe not Italian.

"What did they call it, back then.....?" Bill asks *'Alfredo'* as they stride along together:

"The *'Strategy of Tension'* wasn't it? The deliberate fostering of instability their ideal. A suggestion, a suspicion, a theory - call it what you will - that most of the urban bombings happening across Italy at that time, and we're talking a long time ago, mid-1970s, wasn't it....the *'Years of Lead'*.....?"

"Have nothing at all to do with my people. Or with us approaching you...." says *'Alfredo'*, interrupting crossly.

"Were the work of right-wing extremists, maybe even *Mafiosi*. Designed to create a public backlash against communists? Stop a left-wing landslide at the polls?"

"Ancient history! That's all that stuff is, fairy stories for old people. But I'll tell you straight, Bill. It pisses me off bigtime to hear a neo-con like you digging up these left-wing conspiracy theories. Shame on you! When all the people I act for want to do is kick-start constructive discussion. A sensible conversation with guys like you and – say - the Northern League. Identify those fields where national groups like ours could work better, to our mutual benefit. Come together and shape a modern Europe, to our common purpose....."

"Bombs planted by sleepers, didn't they suspect? Including the Brescia bomb in '74 - or so it's claimed. By trained and determined men who would have been left behind enemy lines to wreak havoc, when and if the Soviet tanks ever rolled across Europe. Except they were never activated - not that way, anyhow. So NATO's shadow plan is unleashed unauthorised on a democratic society the operation in question was originally meant to defend. Now remind me, what did they call it?"

"Look, it's not my bag, friend.. Only a throwaway comment. Not what I'm here about...."

"But that's where *'Operation Gladio'* comes in, isn't it? That phrase you just used to me as if it were funny. Like you think people round here have the memories of gnats. Or fanatics will get off on its connotations. Operation 'Gladio'. From the latin 'gladius' - noun, masculine singular - word for a sword isn't it? A short sword in fact, like the Roman legions carried. And weren't your people its paymaster, according to some versions going round the 'net?"

"Rubbish, that's outrageous! The internet is awash with nutcase theories like that one. Ten a penny. You're talking complete crap, Bill, and you know it."

"When there is a marble monument in the Piazza Loggia to the memory of eight innocent people falling victim to perverted power games like these.......while you and yours expect me to collaborate in some modern equivalent? Whatever side you're on....."

"No way! You've got it completely wrong there, pal, you're deliberately screwing-up."

"Am I? Or maybe it's your people who've screwed up?"

"You're making a big mistake here, Bill, a really big mistake. "

"Is that a threat?"

"No, just a straightforward statement of fact. About a mistake you'll regret. My people are persistent, Bill. Don't recognise a 'no', won't easily let go. Whether it's you or someone else. No one can survive alone in a globalised world. Sooner or later, you and your little country will come around. Will have to return to the fold. Come in with us....."

After hearing that last remark, I suddenly lose them in the crowd.

"Nowhere does the sea hold more sway: it carries to and fro in its motion a mass of tidal currents, and in its ebb and flow it does not stop at the coast but penetrates deep inland and winds about, pushing its way even among highlands and mountains as if in its own domain"

(Cornelius Tacitus *'The Agricola'* Ch.X, 2nd Century A.D.)

- X -

It was good to be back home, safely over the seas and away out of Gaul. Freed from the troubles of a benighted land. That day we rode fast in a jovial group along a rough country lane in the middle of nowhere. A trip-out on horseback, travelling deep into southern Britannia, the rural heart of our province.

In almost holiday mood, our eyes nearly blinded by reflecting sunshine off the road.

This dazzling metalling we rode over was formed anciently: not through human labour but long-user by traffic. From billions of bright, white stones, each one slowly crushed and compacted into a smooth, hard-packed surface by the hooves and feet of countless generations, gently passing over. Hundreds of years of unhurried usage by those lucky men who farm this hidden vale, bequeathing us their lasting consensus on the best path through it. A private road whose line meanders in constant deference to the shallow, chalky stream unwinding beside. A perfect watercourse of leaping trout and gurgling crystal that bisects the narrow valley of arable fields and water meadow we follow, its tranquil margins bounded each side by ancient broadleaf woodland venturing down from old hills.

In the fields beside our track, the occasional figure cranks a stiff back upright from tending the land. A workparty pauses from the scythe, country folk harvesting the cereal fruits of a good soil. Though farm labourer or slave, it's grown difficult to say, but perhaps doesn't matter any more. When these days you are hard put to distinguish in bondage or misery between the landed slave and a former freeman, fled to the country. That new class we call the *coloni*. The increasing number of former tenants bound by debt, the obligations of patronage, or Diocletian's laws on heredity to work another's land in feudal perpetuity.

Maybe a question not worth asking, about social distinctions no longer mattering. At least for we military men. So long as someone is found to produce sufficient crops to feed our armies, maintain that increasingly militarised and polarised state which claims to protect them.

Whatever class they were, these figures in an Elysian landscape, they were not cowed enough to prevent them stopping work long enough to watch we horsemen riding by. Followed by a cloud of Moorish cavalry, Carausius's usual armed escort. Typical, these watchers might say - in a southern backwater like this, you go a lifetime without seeing a soldier, now fifty come at once. Something big is up, that much is obvious. Where do these riders head?

To an appointment with their Master, the lordly *Dominus*?

Their peasant analysis is not wrong but why should they care, so long as field is ploughed, corn grown, and the next generation of children and bloodstock bred? While we go by in a haze of dust, fluttering white and scarlet. On our galloping way to meet a gathering or *concilium,* an informal council of *honestiores*. Of those wealthy landowners and ruling class who are the backbone to this corner of Britannia. Rich and powerful men whose private estates might exceed in acreage the largest Imperial holdings on this island, the opinionated local types we must somehow win over.

An independent-minded elite of good taste and polite discretion, every one of them burdened with unshakeable confidence in their own authority. Quietly-spoken yet arrogant at heart, these are the men whose moral and fiscal support is vital precondition to our ability to function - let alone succeed. Even for an Admiral of the combined *Classis* who can hold up the *'Shield of Achilles & Face of the Gorgon'* in proof of his Imperial Commission.

My master's power was based on force, the deployment of ships and soldiers in a *classis*. Theirs on class and soil. On the possession of land and its documented legal title. Reinforced by the social prestige coming from cultural knowledge and a good education, patronage and a loyal clientele. Patronising men - patrons who are petty, resembling local kings. Ancient tribal chiefs.

Now I was understanding rather better why an uncut agate like Carausius wanted officers more polished to be serving on his team. And if it wasn't exactly soldiering I would be learning today, it was certainly as fascinating. That point where my military apprenticeship extended to an impromptu lesson on why those wiser generals always court the approbation of rich men.

"Why should we help you?"

181

He'd barely gestured at the food spread out for our party than Gaius Flavius Justinianus cut to the chase. A wealthy man used to talking over others while they listen. The self-appointed leader of his peers, owner of this house. Where the whole of my parent's little *domus* in Calleva Atrebatum would have fitted inside the pillared reception hall he's packed out with red-faced neighbours and property-holders, all come to see us.

It grieved a young man's idealism to see that leader he most admires come to bow before the powerful once more, but today I was to be his student in a more localised politics. Carausius knowing he must cultivate these influential gentlemen, however hard the argument, however long it took. Only the first of many more missions of persuasion like this one.

"Citizens, I am here to protect you. *Tutela* - your protection. From the threat from the sea."

"From the sea? Oh, really, General, I cannot remember the last time I saw the sea. It must be two days' hard-marching from here. And these are isolated events, isolated events...."

"Senator, we face a new and implacable enemy. The sea wolves do not march, they ride. Rivers their roads, black ships their horses. Two days' march from the sea maybe, but only one hour uphill from the banks of your nearest tidal-reach. What Saxons call the '*Swan's Way*'. A rising tide that will allow their ships of little draught to float so far inland. So much further than you might imagine. Dragged and carried overland from the river if need be...."

"No, I hear what you say but that's impossible. Quite impossible! Not here. Yes, we've heard what's happening on some coasts, but no-one will find us here. Not in our lost valley. Where most farms and estates of my friends in this room lie as well-hidden as mine. The busy world goes on without us, General, as it always has. We are tired of politics - of empire trying to ruin us, taxing us to death. For what? So our crops can be taken for faraway soldiers who can't protect us anyway, garrisoning the Rhenus or that distant Northern Wall. Endless wars and emperors come and go but our countryside endures, believe me. You and they pass us by, General, simply pass us by."

"*We didn't*, did we? In Jupiter's Name wake up, gentlemen, wake up. *Saxonici* can smell your silver. They see your smoke, senator, and hear your cattle low. Their intelligences are excellent - uncanny. The number of raids increasing all the time with one gang learning from another. Who knows who aids them? Is it Gods or men? One thing's certain, treachery breeds on itself like a disease. Does your workforce love you, do your neighbours? These times are different, their dangers unique."

"You threaten us with bluster, General, nothing but bluster. A ragbag of filthy nonentities. Unknown sea-peoples from the edge of the world. Rome will smash them to pieces as she always has. Life goes on. Why should we believe your alarmist talk?"

"Because some of you have served with the army and all of you are patriots. Even if you wonder about a man like me. About why the Joint Augustus entrusts an uncouth foreigner with so significant a commission. A coastal barbarian. Oh, yes, don't worry, Senator. I saw your lip curl from my first arrival, but remain what you see. A man from the margins. Still good enough to die on your behalfs, wherever I'm from. The Emperor Maximianus has handed me your fleet and a mobile army, both sides the Narrow Sea. His orders are clear - to confront the greatest threat we've ever faced. The Gods alone know I will fulfil those orders to my very last breath. With or without you."

"You exaggerate!"

"Not a bit of it. This side of Britannia has been lucky till now, but those days are over. Ask anyone from the east coast – they'll tell you. Who has seen what these men, my diligent officers about me, are recently returned from in Gallia. Seen her charred farms, the blackened bodies of gentlefolk impaled on their boundaries. The starving cities of Gaul and her empty fields. They take my message seriously, as should everyone in this room. The Roman Peace is over, my citizens. Your whole way of life in danger. War is coming and if you will not play your part, support our army and fleet in practical ways while they defend your homes, then it shall be your turn to see. Believe me!"

"Is that another threat?"

"Not a threat – a prophecy."

"We trust in the Gods. Gifts of prophecy or our safety are for them to bestow!"

"The Gods cannot save you from the sea-wolves. Believe me. I am telling you, only my men can do that. My men and their ships. In the name of any God you care to name...."

His voice becoming hoarse and nearly breaking.

"And what is their price, these soldiers of yours?"

I looked along the stolid wall of farmers lining the back of the hall, arms sternly folded. Emboldened not moved by that unusual glimmer of emotion. That falter in his voice. So lacking in judgement that some of them might have taken it for weakness. Rather than the passion of a brave man, one who happens to care.

As Carausius himself had remarked, we are good enough to die for them yet stay a breed apart. An elite brotherhood of our own. How greatly my life had changed since I first joined it, and how well I had learnt with them to despise these cowardly civilians. No wonder there is such a gulf in experience and outlook. When we can strut through the towns in our military belts, the only men on their streets allowed to bear arms.

Them and us. Civvies and soldiers.

"Their price Senator, is my price" he continued. "And not very much at all. Only that you feed them and arm them. That you grant them the slipways and bring us the timbers we need to make you the ships that will chase down the Saxon. My men's lives on the line in your protection. Their side of the same bargain. And it is in my mind to think that you gentry in your fine houses will be having the best part of that contract."

Maybe that comment about fine houses was going a little too far. Something must have irked them because the answers he got were more sarcasm than support: "Land, timber, grain and weapons. Is that all? What else do you want from us – surely you don't expect ordinary farmers like us to have the money to fund a whole army. Or a fleet!"

I looked around at the statues, vases, mosaics and wall-paintings and wondered. The floor beneath my feet showed the legend of Europa and the bull. A beautiful goddess carried away on the long back of an enormous beast herded by Cupids. Jupiter the king of gods in a beastly disguise, decorous prelude to her brutal rape. Some lines of verse were written above but I thought instead of the words of another writer. The one who once remarked that to surround oneself with learning is not the

184

same as to be learned. When these rich men in their country bubble, comforting themselves with ostentatious display, were among the most stupid I ever met.

Carausius only smiled a little more and persevered: "No, no, gentlemen, don't worry! Money is not the whole answer – or not with what worth our official coinage is reduced to these days. But never imagine it relieves you of an obligation. Because I expect you will have heard of the special tax-raising powers delegated me under my commission......"

"What, will the emperor who sent you tax this province more? While we His loyal provincials are left with no say in the matter, no right to represent before your Senate?"

"Ours is an expensive island to defend, Senator. How else do you expect Him to pay for it; to feed and pay my soldiers? But, if you must question, also believe me when I say that I want to work with you in the just enforcement of His necessary demands. To be fair to you and your people in their exercise. Why I am come to you in brotherly solidarity, seeking help from fellow citizens at a time of need. In a national emergency. To say that if you and your estates will co-operate in their gathering, then I can commute my reasonable demands of you into military supplies or raw materials. Instead of coin and money, gold and silver, bring me corn and meat to feed my British battalions. Timber and iron to arm them. Rope for anchors and leather for sails. Every contribution helps and which is your choice. But don't imagine you may evade them. Or forget that eventually, I will also ask for help with men."

"What, will you oblige us to send our sons or labourers away as well?" asked another. "Let the fields fall into ruin like those you describe in Gaul? Where will you get your precious corn and leather then, General? Not here, that's certain! It seems to me, if these raiders ever came, then we could defend ourselves well enough hereabouts without your greedy army. Provide a local response faster than anything you or your emperor could muster. Why, between us I should say my farming friends round here could put the equivalent of half a legion onto our valley floor in the space between two sunrises."

There were nods and murmurs of agreement across the hall. After our repeated victories in the Gothic Wars, slaves were ten-a-penny. Now it seemed that every household in the Empire had a captured German standing-by. Ready to peel a grape, lift a shoe, turn a sheet or weed a field. Or maybe take up arms.

"*Equivalent*? You tease us, gentlemen? An aimless mob of untrained labourers and household slaves. Armed only with harvest scythes, meat hooks and bread knives? Back home every night, safely tucked in their truckle beds by dusk? I really don't think so Senator, with the greatest of respect. This is not cattle-raiding but large-scale warfare. No, a properly-trained, permanent force in the field, armed with the right equipment, is what you will need to beat an enemy like this one."

They didn't like his scorn for their slave-gangs either. If my lesson on cultivating the co-operation of the country gentry was starting to resemble a classic '*how-not-to*', Carausius had ceased to care. Changing tack to make men and materials his main goal instead:

"I'm sorry to alarm you gents, but must speak plainer. Now our Lord Diocletian Himself has restored the draft, I as his servant hold delegated rights to requisition more than just goods. To warn that you must co-operate whenever - or if ever - I am obliged to return here and ask it. Armed as I am with His authority to conscript your people under legal powers. If or when it proves necessary, and whether you like it or not. Presuming of course that you   finally decide you do want proper, professional soldiers rescuing your family and estates. On that day when the black ships come, there are *Saxones* in your fields......"

"What? You expect a man to pay good money for a farm-slave at auction only to end up donating him to your army? An army we know would ship him out to die on the German frontier, 'stead of guarding our lands? As we've seen repeatedly, by the way. No, General, not as far as I'm concerned. You won't be getting any of my boys, I'll tell you that. Free, *gratis* and for nothing. Anyway, whatever happened to respect for our laws of private property? For ancient Roman rights enshrined in the Twelve Tables..?"

Shrilled a fat Briton who'd never seen Italia, let alone Roma, but thought himself her citizen. A man as wide as he was tall, previously content to lean silently in the corner on one of his patron-neighbour's finest pieces, a bronze statue of Mercury, until his own selfish interests felt threatened.

This last outburst from the floor seemed to fire the senator's other clients up the most. A taller countryman in a hooded cloak fastened with trumpet brooches now pushed out to the front of the group and almost shouted: "Yes, he's right! What about the laws of private property indeed? There's some that say you are no better than these pirates yourself, General. That you deliberately let the black ships land, then confiscate their loot on their way back. Stealing plunder like you were a pirate yourself!"

I have never seen Carausius so angry, the blood gone into his neck, a blue vein pulsing on his temple. A red line across the forehead where his helmet normally sits. Obvious self-control on provocation only underlining the chill blast of his fury:

"Why, sir, I will insist you find out for yourself. At first hand - my staff will arrange it. Here we are, tribune, note down his details. A brave patriot to join our next patrol. Out from Anderida or Clausentum...whichever he chooses. Come as honoured guest for the very making of you, friend. All those stories to tell your wife and family. Of our forced march by night, the pitching dash by sea. Rushing to pre-empt whatever misery the Frank or Saxon delivers with each tide. What slaughter. Seeing what proceeds our fleets do recover - or not as *Fortuna* bestows it. Provided, of course, that you – and I – ever get back alive to tell this tale. Believe me, friend, when you see what these barbarians can do to honest citizens like yourself, then maybe you will understand what drives my men to risk their lives on the open sea. For your sake in all weathers. And maybe when you have, we'll hear no more of this slander of slaves, this tittle-tattle of women. These tall tales of stolen goods unreturned."

Our whole unhappy meeting had not occupied the space of even one hour and we hardly touched their spread left-out. The outcome peeving me most at the time, still at an age where I always felt hungry. Outside, as we turned our horses and my empty stomach for the long ride back. Carausius leaned gravely across to me from his saddle: "How would you say it went today, young Triton?"

"I'm sorry, Admiral. They've not grasped it at all, but no-one can say you didn't try."

"No, they can't. And it seems this wretched slander about unrecovered property won't go away. Though at least it brought us you, eh, Triton? These country gentlefolk are a different breed. Backwoodsmen to a man. Men who can't see beyond their own valley though they are the very belly of the province. Not only do they feed it, but every rumour running up through its guts erupts from their mouths like a belch. Why we must take what they say seriously, even if it's false. Unwitting voices to a lie. One that someone, somewhere, is busily broadcasting. Even here, in the heart of their country. Someone spreading it deliberately. And why – as a way of getting back at me for something? For whatever reason - a campaign, a fog they want to raise. Wishing to make a divide between my brave fleet and the good people who should be supporting us. That's the real question to ponder on, young Triton, what we need to know."

"Who is behind all this?" I asked.

"Yes" he said "....this *fama*. The who and the why of its making."

As we rode away at last, I saw Gaius Flavius Justinianus standing outside and apart from his milling crowd of tenantry as if to emphasise his status. Further away from them, watching us go. Stationary on the path up the terraced hillside from his elegant white villa, beside that huge mausoleum we'd noticed earlier. Dedicated to an only, grown-up son. A dead man who could never help his ageing father defend their secret house in the country against swarming barbarians.

From looters fresh in from the sea, bearing no inkling of pity.

Tutela.

188

"We are here for a good time, not for a long time."

(Colin McRae, World Champion rally driver, 1968 – 2007)

- 10 -

The start of the Mille Miglia Revival - surely one of the most atmospheric occasions in the whole world of motorsport. Or maybe the whole world (period).

It's certainly the best.

Even if you don't like old cars, the people-watching is priceless. All the more galling my focus this year should be stuck on trailing Bill. Instead of those lissome girls in tight jeans who stalk through the crowds like antelopes, handing out corporate freebies. Legs to their armpit. Antelopes loose in a city of lions, many of them starving.

Including some as bad as me.

In Mille Miglia week, Brescia, *'The Lioness of Italy'* how she became known on resisting the Austrians, comes to a complete halt for two nights. Once for the event's start and then again, forty-eight hours later, at a tumultuous finish. Casting her people out upon her to greet an entry of nearly 400 cars as they form meandering queues through her streets to drive up, over, and off a sponsor-bedecked start-ramp and into the great adventure.

If our seeding at 286 was based on Xenobia's vintage, not the skills of her crew, it left us starting well down the field. Not till the early hours. And Bill thinking it perfectly OK to go off on a private walkabout until then, me secretly trailing. Disturbed and upset at my developing suspicions but determined to discover what he was up to. Baffled when I heard.

Whether it was my business or not.

Why I ended up following him right to the Viale Venezia. To the start-line itself, where Xenobia waits and thousands of people stand crammed behind safety barriers, packing the pavements to see the festivities. Others lean from balconies to get a better view, while loudspeakers hanging from tree and lamp-post relay to sleepless suburbs the running commentary of a suave Englishman organisers enlist as compère. Who can slip

189

between his native tongue and immaculate Italian to greet and describe each entrant.

Rolling onto the top of the ramp, each car and its crew is introduced affectionately, closing with a token interview on their sporting hopes and fears. If the car is the star, its parentage or technical lineage detailed in two languages, the crews are often as celebrated. Unusual.

Many of these cars were the real deal. Genuine items competing on the original event in their pomp. Authentic period machines long outliving their original crews and now given a fresh lease of life by a new generation. Sanctified by association, akin to Holy Relics. Mobile antiquities with provenance and pedigree to triple values at auction across an international market in classic cars. Traded reverentially with the deference and cupidity once reserved for Leonardo and Raphael, as testaments to genius: *"Nuvolari sat here.... he gripped this wheel to cross Futa and the Raticosa. Remember always who made me...."*

Waiting in the start-queue at their tillers, retired F1 racing drivers or captains of industry hail each other across the street like long-lost friends. Wanting to outdo the other with the value and exoticism not only of this year's machine but also their celebrity companion. The film-star co-driver here, dewy rock-chick there. Central European royalty whose private car collection fills the courtyard of a German *schloss* compete against designer-label heirs. A 1930s BMW in silver navigated by Lady-in-Waiting in baseball cap, beside them an open Aston Martin whose 'Miss World' finalist in head-to-toe leather is already on the maps.

Whatever crew-combination it was had inspired the editorial in English language programmes given out free by the antelopes to call them an *'explosive couple'*, Bill was cute enough to turn up waving it. Hoping to ward off difficult questions over his absence with a hilarious titbit he hoped could distract me.

Returning like the prodigal son to where I'd moved Xenobia into the long queue below the castle, at that point where Via Brigida Avogadro descends towards Viale Venezia. Travelling alone now as I noticed, but looking no less sheepish.

I wasn't going to be drawn but Bill tried to break the ice by reading aloud further strange snippets from the programme.

Mentioning in passing what poor substitute I made for some of the more nubile crew-members on offer. Actresses and dancers, princesses and heiresses, gas oligarchs' daughters. Blonde and Swiss-educated. Rich, favoured and fit.

As he put it: "We're more a Walter Matthau/Jack Lemmon *'Odd Couple'* don't you think? Not incendiary. But, hey, isn't it fantastic just to be here taking part? Worth all the aggro?"

He had a point there and I nodded silently. Smiling warmly as if prepared to forgive and forget Bill's recent expedition, at least for the moment. When neither was true.

Though maybe I ought.

Parked as we were beside a monument that's dedicated to this very virtue. Near where the Via F.Turati comes downhill from the castle in its park to aim for the Viale Venezia and its crossroads, beside a white plinth supporting the bronze statue of Arnaldo of Brescia. A monk who held no grudges but was burned at the stake in the twelfth century after Christ for daring criticise His Church. Arnaldo's arms staying fixed, permanently outstretched to epitomise the forgiveness of God. In blessing of a scene where all main boulevards leading into the Viale stand closed-off below him with safety-barriers, as if to contain his grace.

Garrisoning these alloy defences is an important job entrusted to the *Polizia Municipale*, leaving car displays across town to be guarded by *Vigilante di Brescia*. Local officers whose electric buggies speak volumes for their ranking in the Italian pantheon of 'copperdom', a masculine profession replete with horses for courses and status symbols on wheels.

On a pavement opposite I check another specialised breed, a short line of *Carabinieri* riot-police standing watching us with amiable interest. Only half a dozen, so it would be a pretty small riot to require their deployment, be susceptible to so short a shield-line, but there is little chance of even one that big tonight. Their padded black battledress, shaved heads and paratroopers' boots are to mark them out as a tough elite squad, but the sensitive, thoughtful features and grey goatee beard under a black beret distinguishing an older one are complete contrast to his calling. An officer whose uncanny resemblance to one of Rembrandt's later self-portraits is closer than a knocker-in-of-heads and breaker-of-skulls should rightly

191

deserve. If he really is a painter then his easel has been left at home, while his yawning mates look equally aware there will be nothing doing tonight. Seeming content to do no more than populate the crowd with gothic uniforms, they are come along on overtime to greet old friends and acquaintances with handshakes and slaps. Decorate their town's greatest annual occasion.

See and be seen.

If it appears tonight in Brescia is *Polizia Municipale*'s show, then not all have uniforms and fewer yet have time to talk to each other. Each seeming busier with the police radio or mobile phone on which they are so engrossed. But even Italian mobiles will not pick up on hand-gestures and their most senior officer present - here in plain clothes, an expensive alpine jacket - seems a case in point. Busily clearing pedestrians from an ill-chosen viewpoint in the middle of the junction while simultaneously fielding another call.

"You're not staying here....." he tells them pleasantly but firmly: "It's dangerous."

As the line of competing cars of which we form part slowly passes the Good Friar and approaches the crossroads, it comes to a complete halt. Some hold-up on the ramp why we must spend a while here waiting. Bill and I getting the chance to observe an interesting and a growing crowd which had thought its only role tonight was in coming to watch us.

Spectators become the spectacle.

Why the inspector in his alpine jacket has called in reinforcements, a small blue and white hatchback from *Polizia Municipale* suddenly arriving with four uniformed officers squashed inside it. Three step out at once on his orders to start clearing more spectators from the middle of the crossroads, while their Fiat's driver pulls across the bottom of the main road down from castle hill to take a blocking position, racked blue lights flashing.

Overhead, a helicopter is also circling, cameraman visible at its open side-door. The noise of its rotor blades adding to the build-up, that sense of rising tension.

A mother on an upright bicycle with a toddler strapped to a seat behind pedals slowly across the crossroads, heading into town. Followed by a couple of teenagers on raspberry–powered mopeds or scooters, the police officers gesturing at them to *"make it quick"*.

The wide junction is finally cleared of people when a cream and red van suddenly comes tearing downhill towards it, blue lights going and sirens wailing. Making that curiously-weedy lament Italians reserve for their emergency two-tones:

"Knobbly knees... knobbly knees!" it calls, plaintively but unmistakably.

The *Carabinieri* on the other side of the carriageway do and say nothing but the *Polizia* are quick to react. The inspector's men rushing to drag their alloy defences out of the centre and so let it through. The grim-faced ambulance driver gives a curt nod of thanks for their rapid response to these uniformed policemen, leaning on their now-open barriers, and then he is gone. Straight across onto the Cremona road and out to the city limits.

"He'll not sell much ice cream at that speed..." says Bill watching it go.

The portable barriers are dragged back into the middle again and the very last spectators pushed out to the margins. Left standing on the grass verge of the dual-carriageway Viale, looking wistfully back across towards this top-notch vantage they've been forced to abandon. His job nearly done, the mission complete, our plainclothes inspector is about to wave through the building queue of our fellow MM competitors when yet another Fiat appears out of nowhere. This one's a private car, bang in the middle of his crossroads.

"Where in the name of Donatello did this thing come from?"

The *Polizia* are nonplussed to be encountering a gatecrasher when they thought all boulevards blocked, but step out in front of its driver anyway. Whistling vociferously and signalling her to stop. Abashed by police attention and sarcastic cheers from the crowd, she brakes to a halt in the very centre, as requested. Our plain clothes inspector gets the door open, remonstrating crossly. No explanations needed, the Fiat's interior piled high with designer carrier-bags. A motorist unaware of tonight's festivities, ignorant of road closure.

Doesn't she live here, doesn't she know this event happens every year at this time of night, the sort of questions policemen are asking, but her trenchant defence is patently clear. *"I always come this way on Thursday....."* she almost sings in soprano.

If she thought this answer would get her away with words of advice and an early release, our late-night shopper is disappointed. Directed instead, for reasons of health and safety, to position her car inside the *Polizia's* alloy stockade at the centre of the crossroads. If she obeys the senior officer's directions to do so with operatic displays of petulance, it doesn't mean their captive will enter into our carnival spirit. Their first detainee of the evening staying put inside her Fiat with the windows run-up tight. Refusing to smile for anyone, let alone speak. At least she's not alone, for already a few of the spectators previously ejected are infiltrating back to stand beside her in the middle. Anxious to show her some solidarity against these forces of the state. Resume this uniquely-ideal position from which to see MM cars going by twice – arriving once for the start, then speeding away after.

The *Polizia* do notice unofficial additions to their ranks and seem about to challenge, when there comes a familiar warbling note and the same ambulance passing through five minutes ago is travelling back towards them: *"knobbly knees... knobbly knees!"*

The barriers are dragged out of its way again, more quickly now thanks to public-spirited assistance from those returning spectators. After a short exchange of words, the ambulance crosses their line once more and accelerates away on a completely different tangent. Police eyes turning uneasily to their interlopers-cum-helpers, rethinking gratitude.

Yet no sooner are barriers successfully reinstated behind the departing ambulance than he's back from a u-turn. Obviously lost, reedy sirens still going and driving faster than ever, with the same patient-patient presumably still aboard: *"knobbly knees... knobbly knees!"*

This time it's really too much and the *Polizia* are helpless with laughter, almost bent-double. Leaving it to their good friends the spectators to do this harder work. While the barriers are scraped back over tarmac a policeman takes off his uniform peaked cap and wipes the top of his head with a handkerchief, crying and shaking with amusement.

By this stage, the backlog of competing cars overdue at the startline - including us - is reaching critical proportions, while the latest assault on the *Polizia* stockade comes in from another direction. In the shape of a whole fleet of Alfa and BMW saloons carrying MM decals and lots of concerned officials from "*il organizzazione*". Living embodiment of why there are three 'z's in the Italian word for organisation. A convoy arriving just to enquire, followed by a large Alfa Romeo four-door decked-out in the distinctive mid-blue and white-flashed livery of the *Polizia Stradale*. Our *Municipale* friends' highway-department cousins, come mob-handed in a big car decorated with a black puma set in a heraldic shield atop each wing. Ominous emblem of their squad.

At this point we have come near to collecting the complete boxed-set. Official representation from every known corps in Italian policing - apart only from Forestry and those accountants with guns in *Di Finanza*. Every one of which late arrivals at the 'Viale Ball' has to be let in through this focal, alloy lineout. So that by the time what must have been a very senior police officer indeed steps out the back of the large Alfa; also wanting to discover what is going on and dressed as he is in a sensational sky-blue uniform which even Napoleon's brother, Murat King of Naples, would have rejected as too 'showy'; the amount of barrier-shifting necessary to admit him has become entirely delegated. Entrusted by his red-eyed and weeping officers to self-appointed volunteers from the increasing number of MM *tifosi* now crowding out its centre.

Truth be told, and thanks to their undisciplined efforts, the line of safety barriers stands in a pretty sorry state. Hardly safe but hardly seeming to matter. The buoyant mood of this diverse crowd; of those police officers, race officials, promenaders, cyclists, motorcyclists, spectators, shoppers, dog-walkers, office-workers, courting couples, and MM competitors waiting on foot for their car's turn to start, now assembled inside them; at the centre of that junction between Via F.Turati and Viale Venezia; one of the happiest and friendliest collections of humanity I ever had pleasure to witness.

And if he could somehow come back, I felt sure Arnaldo of Brescia would have enjoyed this priceless atmosphere as much as anyone. While for a fig Bill and myself would have got out of the car and joined-in too. Obliged instead to keep to our seats inside Xenobia and her correct place in the queue, merely amused observers.

Another time, perhaps.

Watching all this puts me and everyone else into such a good mood, my temporary amnesia over Bill's earlier walkabout pushes it further to the back of my mind. Even the lady driver of the captive Fiat is persuaded, stepping out of her car and straight into animated conversation with another woman about the wonders contained in expensive-looking carrier-bags visible through its hatch.

As the light fades to a golden glow to match the collective mood, headlamps and streetlamps come on and we trundle slowly forward in a line of cars towards the ramp. Waiting there in the dark, a matron in thick woollen two-piece suit and pearls the size of gob-stoppers lunges over the safety barrier on my side, pointing her mobile 'phone directly at Xenobia. Her husband was working away in Arezzo, she announces, and it is her belief that his love for the Lancia Aurelia B20 GT exceeds even that she knows he holds for her. So if we could only oblige by revving the engine while she films it on her 'phone, then much matrimonial happiness will result.

Which I do, the whole crowd going wild with joy, windmilling their arms in approval.

Eventually, by the early hours, it is finally our turn to drive up onto the start-ramp, exchange cheery banter with the English master of ceremonies, then roll off and into the mysterious night. Finally fleeing the crowds and people through a mainly-sleeping city. Following the big motorway signs for "*AUTOSTRADA A4, CREMONA, MANTOVA, BERGAMO-MILANO*", Bill's nose deep in his maps as if nothing untoward had happened.

Getting into his groove.

The rain which had held off before the start now began on the autostrada, almost as soon as we get outside a darkened Brescia. Five and a half hours short of Bologna control, but hard to complain and not untypical of early May in Northern Italy.

Sheets of spray obliterating the Verona road ahead, but the few locals in their modern cars out and about at this hour go steaming past regardless into a watery oblivion at unabated speed. Bonnet-to-bumper behind the less daring, harrying them with lights and gestures to hurry up.

As in Macaulay's *"Lays of Ancient Rome"* when Horatio kept the bridge, it was an automotive case of: *"...and those behind cried 'forward', while those in front called 'back'!"*

Then overhead gantries light up with warnings to *"accendere fendinebbia..."* or suchlike.

"What does that mean?" asks Bill.

Struggling with my meagre mental dictionary of Italian, I still can't believe what I think:

"Er...well, strictly...if I'm right...'*set fire to your wardrobes!*"

"Right..?" says Bill, doubtfully.

We press on regardless, not having a wardrobe handy.

"I want the old girl back in one piece, you know" he says, sternly.

Just then a navy-blue 1950s Maserati with no roof, its crew in matching black-and-red helmets, white circles on the doors, goes screaming by in a cloud of spray, quad exhausts crackling on the overrun.

"Come on...." says Bill. "What are you waiting for? We've got to be at the next time control by one-fifteen!"

Xenobia's bonnet lifts and we chase after the Maserati.

Regularity-run, my foot.

"It is my settled practice, Sir, to refer to you in all matters where I hold doubts; for who is more capable of removing my scruples, or informing my ignorance? Hence, having never attended any trials of those who profess Christianity, I am unfamiliar not only with the nature of their crimes or the measure of their punishment, but with how far it is proper to enter into any formal examination concerning them? Whether, therefore, any difference is usually made with respect to age, or else no distinction should be observed between the young and the adult; whether repentance entitles them to a pardon or else, if a man is once a Christian, it avails him nothing to desist from his error; and whether the very profession of Christianity, unattended with any criminal act, or else only with those crimes inherent in its profession, is punishable?. Upon all these points I stand in great doubt. In the meantime, the method I have observed here towards those who have been brought before me as Christians is this: I have asked them whether they were Christians; if they admit it, I have repeated the question twice and threatened them with punishment; if they persist in it, I have ordered them to be punished at once: because I was persuaded, whatever the nature of their opinions might be, it is a contempt and an inflexible obstinacy which deserved correction."

(Letter from Pliny The Younger as Governor of Bithynia, to the Emperor Trajan, c. 112 AD)

There was an unexpected partial eclipse of the moon that evening, between the eleventh and twelfth hours, and a great many people in the town who did not go to bed but stayed up all night on rooftops to watch. The moon was made red in colour for several hours - or *'bloody'* as others wilfully put it. Frightened by this event and fearful of what it might mean, no-one could opt out of the popular contagion following.

I say 'unexpected' though it's well known the temple-seer Carausius consults keeps a machine constructed by Greeks to do this very thing. Predict an eclipse, I mean, right down to its colour. Just through turning a handle, rotating toothed wheels. If this really was the case, then I never saw this machine myself and no-one bothered to tip us off at Rutupiae. In a place where treating the movement of heavenly bodies as a branch of mathematics, eschewing superstition, offers no guarantee of protection against bad things likely to happen anyway.

As if washed in by this omen, come the following morning a strange ship had appeared in the harbour channel of Rutupiae, showing Gesoriacum colours. One not there by nightfall. A small, fast vessel with two red sails and no proper oars, of a type the army use for carrying messages between forts along a coast. Not much more than a skiff and, if I still found our regular crossings of the *Fretum Gallicum* scary by day, even in the usual bireme, then what on earth would it be like by night, on so flimsy a plank as this?

What desperate errand brought it here, or led men aboard to risk a crossing in something so insubstantial, so late in the day and our normal sailing season? What weight of message demands so urgent a delivery?

When he came unsteadily up to the fortress by the road from the quayside, its messenger was still just about recognisable as our former comrade in arms: Hippolitus, adjutant to the Theban Legion. When he came into the *principia* to be presented to Carausius, the latter saw straightaway from his face that something terrible had happened, even as he saluted.

"Hail, General, and good health!"

"Welcome, Hippolitus our brother, and thank you. *Salve!* But what makes you risk your own and chance a night crossing? What news of the Tenth?"

"You found us gone and deserve an explanation. I am here to make it and you will find my narrative simple; if harsh in scope."

"I will admit we wondered. But now you will tell me?"

"My lord, yes, and it begins with your own departure. No sooner were you gone to Rotomagus than the Emperor Maximianus issued us a movement order. Now the revolt of the *bacaudae* is crushed, we were for the Danube. Returned to her frontier with the faint hope Aegyptus might be next. So we packed up quickly and left Gesoriacum two days later. I am sorry about that. No chance to get word out or to warn you. Had to abandon the fort, simply leave it empty. I'd say you did right to fill the breach we left, and quickly, with Second Augusta. Right lads for the job, no-one else would have done. Quite a while later while we're still on the move, heading south-east for Italia, we stop to resupply at Solothum....."

His healthy olive tones were turned to grey and blue, stretched like vellum across the bones of his face, dark shadows round the eyes. It wasn't just the British cold. His speech was slow and halting. As if he couldn't bear to tell us, get to the crux.

"What is the matter, Hippolitus? You do not look like a man who has slept or eaten since."

"It was while we were waiting at Solothum that a General Order of the Day came up for the whole army to join in offering sacrifice for the Gods. For our recent success over the *bacaudae*. And of course, since his recent promotion, Maximian includes himself in that category – the gods, I mean. His deification another cause for celebration, and in his own lifetime too. Unusual by any historical standard, I think you'll agree...."

"Unusual, but not unprecedented. Unfortunate, from some of your men's particular viewpoint. That your Thebans won't have liked it, I realise."

"Excellency, we always found you a wise and tolerant general, which is why you guess what difficulties this element to his order was bound to cause the Tenth. There are a lot of Christians back home in Egypt these days, in our regular recruiting grounds around Thebes. Same reason why there are so many now among the soldiers out here. It doesn't make

200

them any lesser fighters, as you would be first to allow. Or the bacaudae too, were any left to testify. And we're well used to these ritual offerings as normal part of everyday army life. It's just they sometimes cause us....certain procedural difficulties.....little wrinkles we commanders must find our own way round. *'Ways and means'* as the old sweats put it. Until now, I flatter myself we always found a workable solution. One to satisfy everyone in the legion. Officers and men. The Christians themselves or veterans like us, loyal to the old religion. As the emperor himself did when he was a man of the camps."

"But not this time?"

"No, no. I suspect he was deliberately putting us on the spot. Testing us. Testing our loyalty. One of the few units left with serving Christians. Requiring everybody to recognise an emperor's claim to divinity with sacrifice, only this time while he's alive. Perhaps Diocletianus put him up to it. After all, they've both had their occasional bouts of Christian-hating, have they not? Then it usually goes quiet for a while.....for a little while, anyway."

"So what did you do?"

"Maximianus himself and his entourage, his court, were resting nearby on their way back from Gaul. Close to where we'd stopped ourselves. At a little place under the mountains called Octudurum, where it turned out there were some private citizens in that town who were also Christian. When these people refused to attend the public sacrifices declared, their town council told Maximian, who called in the army. Fair enough. Since we were only a few miles away up the valley, that obviously meant us. A put-up job maybe? Who knows. Anyway, when a small detachment of the Tenth duly turned up to scratch its head and see what the problem was, it was told to join in with his Praetorian Guard....."

"In doing what?"

"Killing every man, woman and child from any local family declining to worship the new emperor as a god."

"And did they?"

"No, they certainly did not! Our soldiers make a vow before God to defend Rome and her Empire. To serve their Emperor faithfully, not murder our own. But there were bodies in the

201

streets because those bastards in the Praetorians didn't hesitate. Dead civilians everywhere. Only the Theban Legion daring to refuse to comply with his insane order. We withdrew all units from Octudurum, encamped further off near Aguanum and refused to take any more part in his obscene rites."

"Our Dear Emperor will not have liked that...."

"Obviously not, but we seriously underrated how much. When he heard, he repeatedly commanded us via a procession of palace messengers to obey his ruling and orders. So Mauritius parades the legion and puts the options to the lads, who consistently and unanimously refuse. On the third day, a column of Praetorians arrives at the gates to our latest temporary camp while we are still digging-out its ditches. Most of them barbarians: Germans and Goths from the wrong side of Rhenus or Danubius, beneath their Italianate armour, fancy helmet plumage."

"This does not sound promising...."

"Their only promise was death. From an Emperor not to be outdone in obstinacy. They carried sealed orders for the Legion to be decimated according to Army Regulations governing wilful disobedience to a lawful order. And so we let them in without any resistance. This was a straightforward order we would obey. Some military hard-liners might say we had it coming, but the Emperor could still have dealt differently. We paraded in uniform but unarmed in the pouring rain coming down off the Alps. The Praetorians came in to walk the lines and every tenth man was put to death on the spot. A sword cut to the neck, according to the ancient rule. Nobody moved, not even those who knew themselves to be in the next ten. I was so proud of those boys. Their discipline never wavered and they fell where they stood. The parade ground covered with blood and bodies, and we're left with three hundred to bury that terrible night".

"And the end to it surely, as I pray?"

"No, General, no. The Praetorians return next day with orders for a second decimation to be carried out unless our men obey the original order. They wait silently outside the camp palisades whilst we inside decide what to do. Our *Praefectus,* Mauritius, standing before us in the centre of the camp on that earth tribunal we'd raised in front of his campaign tent. The way he often did when we were about to go into action against the enemy. Flanked by those senior commanders I know you will remember fondly from Gesoriacum. Brave colleagues all. Candidus, his deputy, then Felix, Regulus, and Victorinus. Orsus The Bear and good old Exuperus, the *Compidoctor*. Fine soldiers every one."

"Precious Gods, I know that they are. To a man! And my Saxon Shore would be a poorer command without officers of that calibre to serve it. Say what becomes of them – promise they survive!"

"They were, General - were! The *Praefectus Legionis* says our dead brothers are martyrs gone to heaven before us, and that the Christians in our company should stand ready to die in turn, if only for their birth-vow to worship one God. Many loud cries of support from the assembled cohorts at that – I can still hear them now. It felt wild, like a great hunger for martyrdom suddenly burned in all our hearts, whatever once we believed. I never saw a group of people so carried away by one single idea. So drawn to death, for its release from a world they'd come to despise. Like a madness. Even those of us not baptised, not Christian, were moved by the power and emotion of this occasion. By so noble a resistance shown to so wicked a tyrant. Carried away by the emotion of what we saw and heard into thinking our late comrades were not to be pitied but the most blessed of men. So when Mauritius asks us what we would do, a ringing answer echoes through the camp. One the Praetorians waiting outside can hardly help hearing. A universal declaration made in one voice, to say we will never allow ourselves to carry out so sacrilegious or unnecessary an order. The Christians among us saying that they are instructed to believe in the One Eternal God and would rather suffer the most extreme penalties man can devise than offend against their religion. While we non-believers stood right beside them, saying we would rather die with our brothers than stand by and see them march across the Styx alone."

"The Emperor was unmoved?"

"When Maximianus heard, they say he became angrier than ever. Foaming with rage. Said we were asking for it and in a way he was right. Dead right. The Praetorians were ordered to carry out the second decimation almost immediately, in the belief that whoever was left afterwards would bow at once to whatever foul work we'd till now refused. After this second decimation, there were two hundred and fifty more corpses left on the ground to punctuate the lines of the Tenth Theban Legion parading at Aguanum. Once we've buried our comrades in defensive ditches they'd only just dug round our marching camp, Maximian's palace servants came up again to warn us, his swaying remainder, that there is no mathematical safety to be had in hiding among their survivors. The sum was simple. If we persist in disobedience, then not one man among us would escape from death."

"Decimation upon decimation? Precious Gods, no one heard the like! Never in the history of Rome, never in our army's regulation. Old ways I'd thought fallen away were never on this scale. It must be unlawful, how could this be....was there no mercy shown?"

"I watched Mauritius sit calmly in his tent as if he was writing despatches from the front. Penning a letter to our supreme commander, the Emperor. I hold a copy here. He wrote of how the Theban Legion were not only Rome's soldiers but also of their One True God. Owing and giving the Emperor military service and dutiful obedience without question, they could not renounce that Creator and Master whom Maximianus rejects. So far as his orders do not offend against God's Laws, then the legion will obey. Opposing the Emperor's enemies, whoever and wherever they are.... just as we now march to the Danube at his express demand, under his eagles. Mauritius tried to be conciliatory. He used logic to explain his men's decision, like a lawyer making a case. As if that could excuse it or impress a man like Maximian. Explained on the basis of a baptismal oath to their God, taken *"...before ever that vow we made to You. Where no Emperor can have confidence in our second oath to them if we violate this first through the sin of killing our own – our fellow Christians. Where death is no discouragement, so that we do not weep for our slain comrades but rejoice at their honour. Holding weapons in our hands, we will not resist - because we would rather die innocent than live by any sin"* – how Mauritius closed it."

"Strong stuff. It didn't work, I take it?"

"No sooner had Maximianus at Octudurum snatched the dispatch from the messenger and quickly read it, than he

204

ordered the final massacre. It had become a struggle of wills you see, and we should have known how it would end. An Illyrian peasant, bred for fighting and unused to anyone saying 'no', his final decree was for us all to be rounded up and slaughtered wherever we stood. Whether based at out-stations along the road or cornered in our tented headquarters, they hunted everyone down like rats. I was still at Aguanum, where I saw whole lines of strong, experienced men put aside their weapons and offer their necks to the executioners."

"You claimed a just cause, with men and weapons enough to outnumber the Emperor's domestic force, yet never lifted one single finger in their defence?"

"They had but one thing in their minds, this angelic legion. To bear witness to Him who was led to His death without protest. Letting themselves, like true sheep in their Lord's flock, be massacred by the ravaging wolves of a savage tyrant."

"Woah! Incendiary abuse to voice in my presence - or that of my officers. Dangerous weakness - would you put us all at risk? But, of course... you are converted, I presume?"

"How could I not, surviving experiences like that?"

"And alive....which feels like something you regret?"

"Yes, General, it is true. How ashamed I feel. When the Praetorians finally found me I was hiding in a hay barn. Disguised as a labourer and lying who I was. Cowardice and dishonesty – mortal sins both. Denying Christ three times, like His Peter did. Yet knowing I would be spared to serve a higher purpose, one where someone living was needed. An unworthy like me. Surviving and able to bear witness."

"Rather than be counted among their saints?"

"The chance denied me so His Work may yet be done."

"Well, you seem to be managing that much - even if it hardly makes for happy hearing. We're not of your faith and struggle to understand some roads it leads you down. I'll tell you straight, Hippolitus. Ask why you Christians won't do as everyone else. Why you can't keep your gobs shut, but utter once a year whatever formal words of belief our rulers may demand of us. When any refusal is treated as treason, why – just that once - you can't go along with his ritual. Make your public proof of private allegiance, and then just slip away?"

"My lord, our faith would never suffer its followers to participate in a ritual of lies!"

"True or not, that's all it is, Hippolitus. Just ritual, a secular process. When a wise man can save his life in the Temple Of Jupiter at no more cost to his dignity than a few nods and the right words made in the right places, his private thoughts go free. When even emperors don't believe in their own divinity and Vespasian's dying joke about: "*I think I'm turning into a god!*" proves that none do. Even if we all go along with it, with only your bloody-minded Christians refusing. Leaving your military kin as appalled over so many valued comrades gone, our dearest brothers-in-arms dead, as we are at your incredible pig-headedness. And leaving you as our only senior survivor?"

"No, not your only. Not their last."

"Why, who else has survived?"

"Only Asclepiodotus, the apostate, who changed his mind and left the camp. The only one of our senior officers to come around. Agree to make the sacrifice. Where he is now I cannot say, but know he will have explanations to make before God in the Final Days."

"Maybe he will, yet leaves us all upset, Hippolitus. Upset and sorry. More than that, I'll admit it – enraged. Over the needless loss of one entire legion - while we in Britain scratch about for a hundred extra yokels fit to patrol our cliffs. What a bloody waste! Even if I appreciate your personal courage in coming here to tell us. Carrying news so grim it might put us all in danger. So, there we are, my brave friend, is that it? Have you done your act of witness, how your Christian friends would put it? Is your work of faith here done?"

"No, it is not. There is one further thing I must in loyalty advise you of, my General....."

"Which is....?"

"That I have not added to your danger, General, and nor are these events an end to it."

"They are not?"

"I regret to say 'No'. When the other reason for my crossing is simpler - that I came here to warn. To report what I hear privately the Emperor Maximianus Herculius is saying."

"He is saying?"

"Yes. That next he is coming after you...."

"All Roads Lead To Rome"

(Traditional, anon.)

- 11 -

Desenzano del Garda was waiting for us, its time-control located under a temporary white gazebo. Sited beside an elegant, hump-backed bridge which crosses the outlet from the old fishermen's harbour to flow into the nearby lake. Because of the event and despite its hour, the surrounding harbourside restaurants were still packed with diners, some daring to sit outside despite the threat of rain. Light dancing from busy cafes onto shimmering reflections in the harbour, their patrons cheering loudly as we pass.

Bill hands in his time card for stamping to the marshal inside his gazebo. Then we are off again, speeding along the tree-lined promenade. The lapping waters of Lake Garda close-by in the darkness, over to our left but invisible. Brightly-lit shops and eateries of the town flashing past on our right.

Here between the Ponte Veneziano and the steamboat pier are several time-trials. Technical tests where what matters most is consistency, not outright speed. With Bill and his watches governing my accelerator foot - accurate to within a hundredth of a second, so he claims - I take a few of these to brake very hard. Stopping astride the white line at the final test-finish in a cloud of smoke, while Bill gets our times through the window from a marshal and says we've done OK. Then it's back on the road again.

The smell of burning brake drums fills the cabin then dissipates with speed.

Further along the southern lake-shore to Sirmione, its thirteenth-century Castello Scaligero floodlit. Xenobia cautiously pushing her grille through an excited throng to reach another time-control sited in the car park opposite the moat. It has started raining properly now and we see the wet-through support crew for a stricken Ferrari lying beneath it. The red car is jacked up high on axle-stands like a monument, its mechanics lying miserably on a tarpaulin beneath. Vainly trying to stem a torrent of vital fluids down their upraised arms. Gearbox oil glistening darkly, life-blood on the ground.

"Casing cracked!" replies the elderly, American owner-driver when I ask. "We're through!"

He has a team of four mechanics accompanying the car but none of them can fix it. This is a job for a foundry. His round glasses are clouded with raindrops and he stands there alone, hunched in front of the castle and looking down at them like a distressed turtle.

"Bad luck, old chap!" I say, surprised despite myself to be falling into syntax of a stereotypical Englishman. Almost like it's expected. The best I can do, my involuntary cameo to amuse. As maybe that famous Roman poet, Catullus, would once himself, from his lakeside villa on the end of this penunsula.

On the flatlands below Garda we reach the mound of Solferino, scene of the battle and then its town, but in the dark and rain there is nothing to see beyond the marshals in their waterproofs. Smiling and chatty despite the weather. Headlamps picking up the shining faces of countless spectators lining the roads, equally happy. We cannot hear or understand the officials for the noise of petrol generators powering the floodlights of their time-control, but smile back and make positive gestures. Thumbs-up, to show our appreciation of this fabulous event and their sterling efforts. Thanking them for turning out in the middle of the night to make it happen. Knowing we couldn't even start without them.

Verona is next, a much bigger place, a city. Xenobia rattling over her cobbles as we approach a time-control in the very centre. Crossing a large open space between the Roman arena and the white frontage of the nineteenth-century town hall. Enormous chunks of monumental wooden scenery propped up here are intended for operas staged in the adjacent arena. Gigantic Pharaoh's heads and two-dimensional pyramids making unusual backdrop to the parked Alfas, Maseratis and Jaguars: why professional motoring journalists or the more artistic competitors take this opportunity to photograph their cars against them.

Car 286 has time allotted for a short break so I walk around in a circle for five minutes. Consciously breathing in the cool night air and finding some interesting monuments to Bersaglieri, their famous Italian mountain troops, over by the town wall.

Where Bill went I couldn't tell you. The toilet, I assume.

Back on the road again and now the main objective is Cento, which we reach on time and with no bother. It is getting on for two in the morning and Bill especially is starting to flag. I show little sympathy for a man who wouldn't rest before.

Bill is kept busy anyway with his clocks and maps, checking with the road-book we are on the right route, looking out for roadsigns. Maintaining the correct speeds and a set of averages that range between moderate and completely flat-out, I must concentrate on the road. Peering ahead through the gloom. Fending off Morpheus, my eyes gumming-up.

A Jaguar D-type in British Racing Green suddenly takes advantage, overtaking us on a short straight, the upright fin behind its driver's head the dorsal fin of a shark. One which has just gobbled us up. Then the Jaguars exhaust spits back in the dark at us like a flamethrower as he decelerates for the next corner.

"You're slowing down!" shouts Bill, sternly "Get a move on. Need to step on the gas!"

His unexpected abruptness annoys me but Xenobia's bonnet lifts and I add nothing else.

Fortunately from Cento it is not far to the rest-stop and that night's finish in the old part of Bologna. A prosperous industrialised city on the banks of the river Po where we receive a rapturous welcome from crowds who must have been standing in the Piazza Maggiore all night to greet us in the rain. The hotel is expensively impressive but I am too done-in to notice the décor. We turn-in to a high-ceilinged, twin-bedded room where Bill mumbles some perfunctory remark about a good day and then goes out like a light. Snoring away.

Downstairs, the hotel bar remains packed with a hard-core of fellow competitors. Old hands burning the candle at both ends then returning noisily to their rooms at four in the morning. Talking at the tops of their voices. Despite the row from them in the corridor and him in the adjoining bed, I sleep well enough. As Bill obviously does, because next day he is up early and full of enthusiasm for a long slog south to require all our stamina.

Joining the Adriatic coast after Ravenna, at Gambettola we glimpse a wave-tossed sea. Then it's a quick blast onto the tiny, hill-top confection which is Repubblica San Marino. To the point of our cars actually passing through the postage stamp-sized square up in the clouds, from which this Republic issues its postage stamps. Followed by a more circuitous traverse of that high and rough country between Sansepolcro and Spoleto, before the day eventually culminates in our arrival through heavy traffic at Rome itself.

Roma, the Eternal City.

What a place to enter past midnight!

It may be late but looks like everyone is still awake and outside awaiting us, the atmosphere electric. The Via Flaminia, amongst the most famous Roman roads in Italy, brings us across the Tiber by Ponte Milvio where Constantine the Great saw his fiery cross and destroyed the Praetorians. Past the white arches of the Stadio Olimpico and into another time-control. All we can see is thousands of people, crowds of flashlights going off, filling my eyes with stars. Small children demanding my autograph, as if I was one.....

From here we get another pair of those high-speed motorcycle escorts through town we'd rather got used to. Through the Piazza Navona and over to the Castell Sant'Angelo, the converted Papal fortress originally built as Emperor Hadrian's tomb. Where, after further pleasantries and banter with the usual commentator and an unexpected midnight diversion allowed with the car into the centre of a floodlit Saint Peter's Square - for me, at least, the emotional and visual highlight of our whole trip - they finally let us go.

Xenobia spending the night under armed guard in the gardens of the Villa Borghese.

But don't let me forget to tell you about the Via Aurelia. That we got to drive her at night on the very road, that old Roman highway which Sgr.Lancia himself used to use for testing his latests cars on, then duly named her after.

And so to bed.

From which, on day three, we rise bright and early to leave Rome under the fluffy white clouds of a fine sunny morning, from the Castell Sant'Angelo restart. The morning view from the Castell across the city's rooftops, its countless monuments and churches, so sublime I can hardly tear myself away. As Bill agrees:

"Yes, very nice..." he concedes. "Do you know, it quite reminds me of the view from chambers' windows. Looking across to Gateshead....." he adds wistfully.

Stretching as it did across from Saint Peter's to The Pantheon, from Victor Emmanuel monument - *'The Wedding Cake'* - to Colosseum with sacred Tiber and its bridges snaking in between, I could almost see his point. We must leave anyway. With yesterday's blustery storms no more than a memory, we head reluctantly out of Rome's sunshine on a route using Via Cassia Nuova to swing north-west again, half its total distance left to run.

At the racetrack of Vallelunga, in the welcome shade of its woods and eponymous long valley, MM entrants divert to get a few laps in. Good fun to clear the cobwebs, Bill and I taking it in turns to helm a quick blast round the circuit. Confirm Xenobia is on top form and running beautifully. This is just as well since, unlike many crews, we have no chase car or support team available to help us if anything went wrong. All we have if it did are a few tools in the boot and what basic spares we brought along in case. Plus whatever spontaneous help organisers or fellow-competitors feel moved to offer in the spirit of the event, should we strike unlucky.

So far, so good.

With me back at the wheel, Lago di Vico, Viterbo, and Radicofani are successfully despatched on time and on schedule. Bill expressing his surprise at how well this year's roadbook - subject to the organisers' last minute amendments - was doing at matching the route we are expected to follow on the ground. Roadworks and all. In fact we are apparently doing so well he asks if he can have a go at driving, the weather and visibility being so clear that even a shortsighted mole like Bill could see where to go. Ban or no ban.

"It's your car...." I say pleasantly, feeling mellow and relaxed. "Whatever you want."

So now the navigation and our pace are left to me to set. I look down at the maps and establish we're well into Tuscany. Which from a selfish point of view I'll admit was a bit of a shame. Because when you are co-driver, when you are navigating on a high-pressure event like this one, then the very last thing you ever get chance to look at is the scenery.

And if you do, you are either lost already or will shortly get lost. So I console myself by reminding myself that it was Bill's car we are in, and he's met most of the entry fee. That I am lucky to be participating in the Mille Miglia Revival at all, especially at someone else's expense. Even if it meant spending the next section looking down at my knees.

I do know we were approaching Buonconvento and still running on the Via Cassia, another Roman road. High on that twisty section which clings to the dusty hills near Quinco d'Orcia, where I begin to feel queasy on the bends, though not enough to mention, when Bill suddenly does an emergency stop.

I should have been glad but wasn't: "What the blazes do you think you're doing?" I ask, looking up in injured astonishment from my roadbook and maps as we pull up in a cloud of white dust before a pair of metal-plated gates to a private house. Yesterday's rainstorms had evaporated in this morning's sun to leave the yellow countryside around us as parched as summer, were it not for the new greenery of May.

To add to this confusion was a double dose of airhorns coming from behind. That streamlined 1950s Fiat *speciale* in scarlet with white numbers on its doors - more clockwork-mouse than competitor but doubtless thought racy in its day - we'd forced to swerve when Bill veered off at the gateway. Quite right too, he'd never even signalled.

"Sorry, just got to speak to somebody" said Bill sharply.

"For crying out loud, Bill, we're in a flipping race for goodness sake! You'll throw away our allowance for Maximum Lateness....." I say, pointing to the dashboard row of clocks.

"Sorry!" he said again but was leaving regardless, the driver's-side door already open before we'd slid to a halt. He'd dragged the handbrake up on its ratchet so the rear wheels locked solid, and the Aurelia ground to a halt with the ghastly graunch of tyres on gravel, brake shoe on drum.

Mechanical sympathy? *'Nil pointes'.*

"I knew you were up to something – asking to drive. You've never wanted to before.... should never have let you!" I shouted after his retreating form, but was wasting my breath. Bill was already crouched down at the intercom by their marble gate pillar, negotiating an entry like they expected him.

Both steel-plated gates opened quickly on motorised arms and I saw him slouching off down the drive they revealed at an ungainly cross between a run and a walk. Bill was no athlete. It was only then that I spotted another folder under his arm.

"Twenty minutes... and we're out of it. Otherwise we might as well not have come!" what I hurl at him.

He was back in ten.

I was already across the car and belted into the driver's seat by then. It might have been his motor but hanging onto our place in the Mille Miglia was vastly more important than the minor detail of whose name appeared on the entry form. Funded our fee.

As the gates opened to let him out again, and just for a moment, I caught a distant glimpse of gracious living beyond our ken. Framed in a dark-green arch of cypress trees down each side of the drive was its snapshot of a white Palladian villa. Cream umbrellas and ornamental fruit trees in giant terracotta pots shading a raft of sunloungers across its terrace. This year's model Ferrari *Scaglietti* discreet in grey metallic, resting a quiet potency and long bonnet at the foot of marble steps. Doubtless there would be a helicopter somewhere, snoozing in the orchard under a zipped cover. Waiting to be called.

Returning sheepishly to our car, Bill saw where I sat and went round to the passenger side instead, folderless now. I threw the closed roadbook and mapcase onto his knee without a word, accelerating rapidly away before he could belt up. Or dented sheeting and an automatic gatecloser block my momentary glimpse of an earthly paradise.

"Steady on, Mike!" he gasped. Struggling to make sense of the tangle of full harness straps lost beneath him as we rocketed off down the road.

"What's going on, Bill? What the hell are you playing at? Now's no time to be delivering Christmas cards!"

"Look, I'm really sorry, Michael. Just a bit of business. A c-coincidence. Realised we're passing by. Had to manage a word, face-to-face always best. But I've done it now, job done. It's over, we can get c-cracking now".

213

Thanks to me we were.

Screaming downhill on a near-vertical country track more yellow gravel than tar, straight into an innocent valley-village. A sleepy hamlet where linen-topped tables are crammed down main street onto a metre-wide pavement so their roadside diners can get the full effect. Of competing cars blatting through at full chat in a cloud of dust while they savour the *antepasti*.

I don't think they were disappointed.

Bill lost his maps in the footwell and I glimpsed a table-guest spill hot soup into his lap. Hardly surprising. I could tell my co-driver was flustered, but serve him right. What sort of business did a Geordie criminal hack with pretensions in politics need to conduct in a remote Tuscan hideaway? And with whom? What was in that folder and why hadn't he brought it back?

My irritation was fading, something unexpected and worse coming along to replace it. Unwelcome thoughts. Reinforcements for a serious unease previously pushed to the back of my mind despite that odd conversation I'd overheard on Corso Magenta.

Bill was sound, I'd stake my life on it. Honest as the day is long. But the missing folder troubled me further, revived my concerns. Signifying a second handover of some sort, like that bag he gave '*Alfredo*'? But a handover of what?

Of documents?

Or cash?

Money laundering?

I was actually getting quite annoyed. This was meant to be our Northern Lads' trip out. No hassle, just fun. But first the crash on the *autostrada*, now this.

What was going on?

Car 286 virtually had to find her own way to '*Via Primo Maggio*', where the Buonconvento time-control came and went in a glacial silence. Neither of us talking to the other. With hundreds of miles of this bad atmosphere potentially left to go, I pressed on anyway. Bill bumbling around with his clocks, muttering brief instructions.

Saying little else.

'Quis custodiet custodes'

('Who guards the guardians?')

- XII –

Up at dawn for another urgent crossing of that wretched sea. Our most critical yet. Accompanying a revered commander as he journeys over to the other side. Like to face judgement in another, under-world. Gone to confront an unwelcome rumour brought him by a hunted refugee. News of ill-fame brought by a man so ill from forbidden belief and this weighty warning he carries that he could not wait to defy an emperor's anger over either.

My tutors told me how Socrates remarked at his trial that men are judged on what people say about what they do, not what they have actually done. And my private fear, probably universal in the party, was how this little trip of ours had all the makings of another case in point.

Dashing my face in cold water from a glazed bowl before stumbling out from the unfinished barrack-room where I'd spent a short uncomfortable night, I was going anyway. Down through the muddy lanes of our admiral's half-built fort at Dubris to where a row of ships were preparing to leave at first light. Long queues of soldiers boarding.

On the quay where his squadron assembles, their mood is grave. This time more than any other, we ought to pray. To any god who'd listen – whether Neptune, Oceanus, or Jupiter Best And Greatest. For all the sea gods we knew of and any we don't, somehow to combine together. Protect and save Carausius.

Even that troublesome one who'd brought us Hippolitus.

And if any deity declined to help, then all Britannia would not.

It seemed like everyone was coming with Carausius, loyalty and solidarity tangible in the air, even affection. From an assembling force whose officers and men made it very clear, if left unspoken, how closely they intend standing by him. Including that eighteen year-old Vergil-quoting, sword-collecting, most junior of junior tribunes his admiral has made something of a mascot of.

Lingering just long enough on the quayside for that professional he called down from the Temple of Mars to snatch a quick look at scarlet entrails from two slaughtered goats. The old priest looking up from his deliberations and smiling calmly: "Go in peace, my sons, and trust in the Gods. *Bonus Eventus* - Fortuna travels with you."

As if ships could hear his encouragement, *Medusa* takes to the open sea like a salmon to the river. With her as escort the trireme *Radians,* two hundred oarsmen bending their backs aboard our biggest ship: 'The Gleaming', pride of the *Classis*. Their Admiral, Carausius, standing on *Medusa* as if for the last time. Looking back towards Dubris while his flagship and its winger battle a rising swell together. Surmounting a September sea already readying to swamp puny freeboards like ours, should the gods or fancy take it.

There is a brick-built hearth inside *Medusa*'s gilded stern-shelter which the crew use for cooking porridge and warming wine, and I appreciated his compliment in being called up from deck to join him there, Carausius spreading his hands over its glowing coals.

"Even a general should take orders, Triton, and headquarters is where he must go to await them. Why your commander is off to Gesoriacum once again, because it is his duty. Not to question the whys or the wherefores of how the world goes, nor its unfairnesses, but resume my place of station and wait. Only orders? Maybe, who knows what else may come, but I know not to guess. And if you would stay a soldier, Triton, then obedience to duty is the only rule to live by. At the mercy of gods, living and immortal, we are clay in their hands, but I never fret."

He looked back ruefully towards tall white cliffs now disappearing over the horizon.

"What Hippolitus tells us is disturbing, though that does not make it truth. My advice is - never take anything you hear for granted, and always trust no mortal. These Christians have their own agenda. If they choose to make trouble over principle where wiser men bite their lip, they should realise how it is. That the state will always prevail. And if I find Maximianus a

216

hard man to know, harder yet to please, that's the only kind of emperor we ever get nowadays. No wonder men find comfort in worship - how else to propitiate their god-like whim? Though it won't stop me believing that things will work out right. That the Augustus will accept us for what I'm sure he knows we are. Kindred spirits and honest soldiers, as once he was himself. Loyal men he can always rely on. Ready to obey orders and defend the empire without challenge – unlike those tragic Thebans...."

He paused, then looked straight across at me with a kindness in his eye I'd not seen from any man, not since my father died: "All the same, young Triton, if things do turn out for the worst, I don't want you hanging about in Gaul. Do you hear me, boy? Get yourself straight back here to Britannia, my lad. To your family on any vessel going. I tell you, they'll need you back here far more than you want a part in this escapade, believe me......"

He was wrong about that but I dare not be insubordinate enough to say so. Answer him back. Fact was, every one of his officers, high or low, thought themselves an equal partner in whatever jeopardy their charismatic admiral might come to face.

Even if, as we found things on arriving at the other side, the routines of everyday military activity were going on as if to insist that nothing untoward would ever happen. As if through embracing such an odd normality, they, and those other British detachments arriving in Gesoriacum to join us, wanted to demonstrate the same message of solidarity to their general.

Why I'll always remember this onboard conversation. Epitomising the mainspring to that loyalty we all felt in those days. Believing him that unusual type: a military leader who genuinely cared about each and every one of his soldiers. About his men and never himself, or his own aggrandisement. And because, more than anything else, we shared in what he saw as the overriding aim: protecting the home provinces of Britain from that awful, endless battering which the European continent still endures to this day.

While he was only fortunate we ever got a chance.

This being late September, our official sailing season was virtually over for another year - the bumpy crossing we survived proving sense in the rule. When so many breaking it die - those

217

that gods choose. And if that day they spared us, then perhaps it's thanks to prayer.

Sailing being seasonal, by this point in the calendar those old naval barracks inside Gesoriacum which our Theban friends of '*damnatio memoriae*' had so recently abandoned normally fill-up. Are re-occupied by their usual winter tenants from the British Fleet, obeying nature's rule. And as each bireme of the *Classis Britannica* rows up the estuary to be man-hauled out, and into covered pens for storage, so their crews of marines and sailors will come marching into the fort with songs. Reclaim winter quarters in the *navalia*.

Knowing, whatever tricks the weather plays, Gesoriacum will soon be full again. With the rest of CLBR's home-fort taken over by those vexillations from Second Augusta he shipped over to replace the Tenth. Sensible, practical men who set about the repair and maintenance of its neglected installations with disciplined enthusiasm: Decimus and his boys.

Compared with what they'd managed at Rutupiae it probably seemed easy. So that if our patrol group had left Dubris in some state of fear and loathing, all that we discovered on arrival, over on the other side, were the reassuring routines of military life. An uncanny sense of order and calm, with plenty of time to kill.

Why you will always find more people than soldiers to depend on life in forts. Merchants and traders, craftsmen and undertakers, innkeepers and whores. Now the straggling riverside township filling-in that gap between Gesoriacum's crenellated walls, up on their headland, and Bononia's port down in its estuary, appears so rejuvenated by all this revived military activity. Those busy streets I entered in the hope of finding a suitable craftsman among its bothies and sheds. Someone competent enough to fix a few odd bits of worn and broken harness-gear which stay important to me.

Ideally, for not much reward.

At the workshop of Victorinus in the Street of the Cordwainers, I found an ex-army smith who swore he could fix anything; on a bench his Altar of Vulcan. Yet if I was secretly hurt when he scoffed at the quality of my equipment, it felt even more disappointing to hear his considered solution to every breakage seemed to involve rivet and repair-plate, bolstered with further rivets. And since his estimated price for this expensive-sounding bodgery could exceed three days of my modest pay, were it ever to arrive, I saluted him smartly as befits a veteran. Said that I would reflect awhile on his generous offer, before marching quickly on.

The smoky cubicle off a side street which held the tools, anvil and furnace of one Sextus Geminus gave barely enough space in which to swing a club-hammer. Though his quietly-explained approach to my parted scabbard-frame or a broken bronze swivel felt to me ingenious; exploiting as he would the natural reduceability and reconstitution of metals, using solder and weld. So I hid my pleasure in offering him the commission and he promised its completion by tomorrow afternoon. At whatever price I might think he deserved, upon a final inspection of his fully-finished work.

When I emerged, an urchin in ragged shift and greasy hair stood on the kerb-edge outside this craftsman's smithy. Above the stink of the public roadway, mesmerised by the beat of hammers, their steady rise and fall. Patting his matted head on my way out and dropping him a coin, reminded of my own. Rat's-tails on my neck escaping a soldier's hat. If my own need for a haircut or bath was less urgent than a street-child's, it didn't mean I didn't; points of personal maintenance which the current lull up at the fort should give me time to arrange. When even a junior officer's duties include being presentable, here was another job for good craftsmen, but where would I find one?

If the barber's shop I discovered on the same street as Sextus the Smith could be trusted with the scalps of men as skilled as Geminus, then surely he's good enough for mine?

Not just for a low price either, but also to avoid that gladiator's crop my older colleagues tended to favour: maturity attempting virtue. Disguising Time's ravages, as if that hairless style could emphasise masculinity and a military aggression. Counter growing bellies and biceps gone stringy; or else symbolise their bearer's recent survival of shipwreck. None of these problems were mine and, being young, I could never imagine they would be.

Eighteen years-old with a full head of hair, and guessing the girls would prefer it that way, yet wanting better than those basin-cuts which kind friends in barracks will do you for free. So

219

getting what you pay for. Confident too in how little that slight extent of shave I needed back then should add to any professional barber's fee.

You see, I might have been an officer, but they paid so little for what few benefits my obvious immaturity brought the army, even when a pay chest did get through, that I could hardly afford any sort of cut at all.

I remember it was a broken-nosed centurion in Eboracum who once told me my main job in life was to go forward and die in front of my men. Provide encouraging example. Based on what we know of casualty-rates for centurions in action, he hadn't meant this as a joke, but it was advice like that which taught me to appreciate my peripatetic role on the Admiral Carausius's staff all the better. An exciting job where the nearest to uncertainty became when or if we'd all drown together; a pay-chest arrive.

When one did, treating it as bonus.

Today in Gesoriacum proved such a day. Special, an advantage of visiting headquarters. Today I'd been paid, the sight of soldiers staggering in and out of bars and taverns in the town a testimony to others in the same happy position. Each one as pleasantly surprised as I was - though how pleasant they'd be by nightfall stayed a question for the Watch. One I didn't envy them for finding likely answers to, when a haircut would do me.

The barber of Bononia I selected for this task had no inkling of my cash-flow. No measure of what bars I'd drained that day, how many Germans I'd killed. If he was deferential but friendly while I hung my felted helmet-comforter on a hook in his shop, you cannot blame him if he was apologetic around my chosen profession. Why I must excuse his firm requirement for receiving payment first, he said, looking with one eye out the door as if planning an escape.

In cash, if you please.

"You soldier boys, eh?" he laughed, nervously.

Sitting down where directed, I could still see him out the corner of my eye. Warily counting the worn-out brass discs just handed over. Looking disapprovingly down at the curling, greasy strands spread out across my neck, while sharpening his sprung-metal shears on a grainy whetstone. As he did so, a

220

silver-coloured cat with dark forehead came in from the street to sit down in front of us, preparing to watch.

"My Persian Queen!" he said happily, patting it on the head. Seeming straightaway calmer.

It seemed a good place to pick up on gossip of the port. When all I needed to set him going was the standard question about whether trade was busy. After that, I never got another word in.

"Oh yes, my soul. Yes, indeedy. Does hair grow? Why, only yesterday, I had the master of a Rhenus wine-barge sitting here. In your very seat. Needing a full trim and hot shave, the works. Waiting while the empty wine barrels on his vessel were filled up with meat for their return, he said. The life of a trader, eh? Up and down the rivers, up and down. Last trip home apparently, before winter sets in. Moguntacium-bound...."

"Any more off the front? Yes, of course, tribune..." he asks before resuming:

"Saying the latest word on the German frontier is a chance of seeing Constantius here. You know....that Praetorian Prefect they promoted, once Maximian stepped-up to his new job as Augustus. Likely to be visiting our coast in a few days' time, what the captain said to me. The *praefectus,* I mean, not our Augustus. Making a surprise inspection-tour of the seaward defences, what the captain thought. So if he's right, it sounds like you soldier boys had better look out!"

"And the back? Only slightly shorter? Straightaway, tribune, no problem..."

"An inspection..." he repeated. "Seems a bit damp and late in the year for all the spit-and-polish involved in an official visit like that. Don't you think? You military boys will know best of course, but tell me your opinion, tribune. Is my customer right? I should say, I find they usually are...."

"And, while you do, how's that looking? Try this polished plate. There, can you see anything? No, you don't want any more off the back than that? Quite sure? Well I know my...my more-mature customers would.....quite a lot, actually. No, you're absolutely sure? Oh, well, a young blade like you will know the fashion. Entirely as you please....."

"So back to this visit, eh? Don't know if you've heard the same story, tribune. Something big your friends up at the barracks can look forward to, eh? Just as welcome for us business folk down in the town. If it brings a last bit of extra trade in, from Constantius and his party. Provides us all with some end-of-season colour, eh, a bit of glamour and excitement to finish with. Just what we need, for the old year to go out with a bang, eh, tribune?" he laughed, nervous again while I looked in the plate.

The cut itself was fine, but for someone who was only exposed later as an Imperial informant, this barber of Bononia had an unfortunate way of describing things.

As they turned out.

Like he probably knew all along.

"There are some in this country who fear that in going into Europe we shall in some way sacrifice independence and sovereignty. These fears, I need hardly say, are completely unjustified."

(Prime Minister, The Right Honourable Edward Heath MP, on Britain entering the Common Market, January 1973)

- 12 -

Our mood of estrangement lasts till Siena. Crossing a dusty plain, Xenobia climbs its hill to enter a town from the fourteenth century that's frozen in aspic. Once Etruscan, later a Roman colony, in the Middle Ages she became a powerful city-state. Republic in her own right, but it was defeat in war at the hands of her perpetual rival, Firenza, which starved Siena of further development for ever. That fatal feud between Guelphs and Ghybellines which eventually broke her. The military disaster bequeathing us a miracle - the unspoilt wonder she is today. Saved us her for ever, ultimate triumph over over-blown Florence.

My favourite Italian town.

Driving through the brown Renaissance brickwork of Saint Mark's gate, Porta San Marco, then coming down via Casato di Sotto into the main square, Piazza il Campo, the infectious euphoria and excitement marking our passage through every town on the way felt more intense in these canyon-like streets. Locals and race-followers alike - what Italians call their *"appassionati"* - a crowd whose passionate enthusiasm carried us all the way.

I swear Xenobia almost danced as I steered her down into the Campo, finest piazza in all Italy. Site of the old Roman forum, still absolute heart of the city, stage for her greatest event. More famous than the Mille Miglia but fielding as many prancing horses, the Palio is Siena's bi-annual bareback race and, for one week, only the focus of such intense inter-parish rivalries you'd think its *contrades* could kill for them, church or no church.

223

No Palio today, but behind wooden railings its sloping oval is packed with people and parked competitors, race officials waiting at a time-control in front of the thirteenth century Palazzo Publico. The town hall whose hundred metre tower of orange brick, the Torre del Mangia, and view of the city I can remember from childhood holidays. Admiring more recently those fourteenth-century paintings by Ambrogio Lorenzetti concealed inside, his parables on 'Good and Bad Government'. Regretting we couldn't borrow them for a day: take them home on a budget airline to show a Home Secretary we knew, in want of urgent guidance.

My personal pleasure at returning to Siena and Bill's apologetic manner together help soothe the frosty atmosphere in the car. If not cure the rift. Bill's clearly trying hard and hops out promptly to get the time-card stamped early so there's chance for a breather, maybe a proper lunch. A choice between speeches of welcome from officials on stage in the hall of the Palazzo or a tremendous lunch in its courtyard for those who were hungry.

You can guess which option we went for.

It was while sitting there, sharing with other competitors a spread laid out for us by the organisers on white linen-covered tables in the Palazzo's open courtyard, that a small man wearing designer sunglasses came up to Bill:

"Signor Cariss?"

This latest stranger was nothing to do with the race, of that I'm certain. No MM lanyard or any of the other clues to automotive allegiance displayed on this event. Smart but simply dressed, in well-cut, dark blue slacks of Egyptian linen and one of those pink shirts Italian men like self-consciously to adopt in counter-intuitive assertion of a confident masculinity. Its cuffs were left unlinked and open in a mock-careless way which must take some arranging, while a folded lambswool cardigan of pale blue warmed his shoulders. No tie, surprisingly, though the pink shirt was buttoned-up tight to a taut neck whose tan he'd clearly obtained pool-side. Never on a building site.

Hard to date overall, I'd have probably put him as late-40s, the few silver threads in his glossy black hair so perfectly distributed you wondered if they were retro-fit too. Applied by aerosol and stencil in some salon off the Via Condottieri, meant for a distinguished look.

After they'd dyed it.

"Yes?" said Bill.

"My name is Michaelo Arcangeli, and I have been sent here to meet you."

"You have? Oh....and who by?"

"People like you, Signor Cariss. Patriotic people believing their country can survive alone. Retain the blessings of peace and friendship with our European brothers and sisters. Won through free trade and good relations, not tyranny by bureaucrats. People whose last straw came when that buffoon Berlusconi surrendered Italy's sovereignty to the EU. Paid the price of financial rescue by selling off our Second Republic to the highest bidder. Like Praetorians once did with Roman Empire. Delivered our government and democracy into the hands of EU bankers and technocrats, denied our people their voice."

"People?"

"Organisation."

"Can you excuse me?" Bill says to me, taking Arcangeli by the shoulder and leading him into the centre of the square. I put my fork down but continue chewing, watching them go.

This was becoming a habit.

A bad one.

While Bill talks with our latest visitor, and to stop my blood boiling, I send my eyes round the piazza. Taking-in the more unusual cars, the prettier girls. Lingering on the latter. Plenty of them local people, come for the atmosphere and sense of excitement; plus some fellow-competitors I'm starting to recognise.

Their inevitable interleaving with police and priests. And a man in a purple *'Ranulph Lautrec'* polo shirt with a straw fedora, sitting half-concealed behind a line of potted plants at a pavement café away over the Campo: *'Fedora Fred'*. Staring straight across at Bill and Arcangeli, although mercifully too far away to hear their private conversation. Provided of course that his mobile phone was not fitted with one of those new 'lip-reading' apps' that are suddenly all the rage. Popular for spying.

Eventually Bill comes back on his own, Arcangeli leaving the piazza through a street at the top. My friend is embarrassed, well aware that I was good enough to come along to the Home Office with him but not to be privy to his latest Italian discussions. I feel the contrast too and say nothing, head down and chasing pasta round my plate with the fork while he resumes his own meal, knowing it's cold.

"I'll talk to you about this later, Michael..." he says to me in a low voice: "This is no place to discuss it now."

Up at the top of the square 'Fedora Fred' stands up to leave his table in the café. Folding a newspaper with such vehemence, muscles rippling under his shirt as he does, that I'm surprised he doesn't tear it in half. Dropping some change onto the table then briskly heading off towards the same exit Arcangeli used, out of the Campo. A broad back that's probably a Full-Back's disappearing into crowds.

This is the longest look I've managed at Fred, and the first one taken in daylight. Thinking he looks familiar, but unsure from where.

Then I remember.

A conference table on the top floor in Marsham Street, Home Office; and the Secretary of State's personal minder. That bulked-out note-taker in a straining suit who always stopped noting whenever Bill stopped talking. Never stopped smiling. The home team, his faithful acolyte, following us out to Tuscany. Special Branch or MI6, seeking more insights?

I didn't know what he was, or what these disturbing discoveries were adding up to - not yet anyway - but for so long as Bill wasn't willing to share his side of the story with me, then I wasn't going to share mine with him. Not when a major personal grievance needs settling.

"I'll be five minutes...." I say coldly to Bill, as he looks up at me, surprised. Giving him a dose of his own medicine. Moving out of his sight, I go over to Xenobia's boot and remove a folding wheel-brace fastened to the spare. One that's small enough to slip up my sleeve, handy insurance against the big handy lad I intend following out of the square.

This trick becoming my habit.

At the top of Piazza il Campo, I enter its encircling alleys just in time to see Fred disappearing west. At a safe enough distance to trail without him noticing me. Jogging along through dusty lanes beneath stucco apartments, till we approach a barbican of the old city walls, where a line of parked cars is jammed between intermediate bollards to halve the width of the road. I think I know what I'm going to find next, but want to be sure.

Need to see it for myself.

The dark-green metallic Jaguar saloon with English plates he approaches to open a back door and put his newspaper in. While I press myself out of sight behind the entry pillar of an underground car park. Aim to rationalise my anger, imagine revenge.

Fred looks round, locks the car again, then saunters carelessly off. Leaving me thinking.

If I can't hit him with the wheelbrace, what else can I do? The answer is obvious.

Hit him with the wheelbrace.

Squeezing into deep shade between the nearside of his Jag' and the brick wall of an ancient palazzo he's parked up against, there is just enough space for me to get in, and out of sight.

Get to his wheels.

In no time at all, all ten studs holding his passenger-side alloys onto their two hubs are so loose in their threads that only a dozen rotations under power would spin them off completely. Wheels running after.

Job done, I wriggle back out from the wall, covered in dust, and check the street. Nobody about. For a moment, I entertain the tempting idea of doing the same to the wheels down his driver's side, facing the road, but dismiss it as too obvious. Too much risk of being caught. And Fred might notice before he gets in, while the two he's already going to lose in the shadows will be more than enough to drop his Jag' onto its floor.

Ruin his trip.

What a pity I can't hang around to watch, only imagine it happening.

Whiplash on stilts.

"It is a common belief that soldiers lack the powers of fine discrimination, because the summary proceedings of a court martial – tending as they do to be rough and ready, and often indeed, high handed - give no scope to forensic skill."

(Cornelius Tacitus, *'The Agricola' IX*, 2nd century A.D.)

- XIII -

"The Pale" they called him, and here he was before us. The very man. The general who'd successfully managed to campaign from the snows of Caledonia to the sands of Palmyra without ever acquiring even the faintest hint of tan.

A victor of Xenobia, conqueror of Germania.

One day to become junior Caesar of the West, you should remember this historic meeting at Gesoriacum I describe to you here was years before he got that far. Sorry to disappoint, although he was top brass even then.

Praetorian Prefect, to be right, which was why Carausius and his staff stayed standing. Me included. Meanwhile, the Second Legion – or what we had of it, over this side of the water – stood to as well. Lined-up in the driving rain off the sea on the parade ground outside. Completely out of sight from the meeting hall but out there all the same.

Waiting.

Detachments of the fleet in barracks called to arms beside them on that blustery afternoon. To show respect but also as insurance. When it had been their sailors on the citadel walls who first spotted six of those extra-narrow, extra-long river galleys which the *Classis Moguntaciensis* had used to bring him down the Rhine, suddenly arriving.

Tying-up unannounced inside Bononia haven.

For those of my readers familiar with his face as now shown on the coinage, you're probably expecting me to describe a physiognomy matching the brutish dynastic likeness of his Imperial patron, the Augustus Maximianus. A man whose features we're grown accustomed to in metal. As if they were poured from the same mould, Dalmatians all.

Well you'd be wrong about that. Not then, anyway.

228

Nothing like.

This *'Chlorus'*, the famous Constantius Chlorus as we knew him, showed a rangy leanness in the flesh and alert charm of manner which came as refreshing surprise. Chalk to our General's cheese, but I could immediately see why men would follow him. He leaned back, smiling equably, on a backless folding-chair in the commandant's house at Gesoriacum - the whole of which Carausius immediately surrendered to his party - to survey a captive audience. We stood obediently to hear his findings, even the Admiral.

As if on parade ourselves.

An air of gracious self-satisfaction hung around Marcus Flavius Valerius Constantius and that natural sense of superiority might be forgiven, considering his remarkable career and recent promotion. What was attractive was how it never seemed to stray into condescension. He ran long fingers thoughtfully down both sides of the neat, thin beard which graced his hawkish cheekbones and prominent, pointed chin, as if it gave him quite enough pleasure in life just to be proprietor of such fine facial decoration. This Chlorus obviously had a good barber, as good as any to be found on the Street of the Cordwainers.

"I am here on a tour of inspection" he announced, breaking not a line in a smooth face.

We junior officers winked at each other and pretended to look surprised.

Only the recurring cough marred his absolute command of the moment. I'd already clocked through an open door the unusual sight of a ring of *Protectores Augusti Nostri*, elite special forces and Imperial bodyguard, forming up at the double in the inner courtyard of our fort commander's house, the *praetorium*. Had anyone else noticed them? Praetorians, the very types who'd wiped-out *Legio X Thebanei*. As the new Prefect's primary unit, it looked like Maximian must have let his assistant borrow a few of these characters for this particular trip, for old-time's sake and his personal security.

So who was guarding whom?

A silk to the mouth and he was restored again. The easy smile remained, almost too easy, but still I found him hard to read. Anyone who lived a life as close to the dragon's breath of

Maximian as Constantius surely did, and wanted longer, had little choice but to cultivate inscrutability. Or die in the attempt.

As a student of style, I was as quick to spot how Constantius had gone for the shaven-headed option I'd yesterday declined. Maybe he should speak to my barber after all.   Either way, it had to be admitted how the style suited an unusually elegant skull, his nose long and curving like an eagle's. Aquiline, like the sacred bird of Rome and Jupiter. A flattering comparison which had probably occurred to him already, so conscious did he seem of his own self-image. As I say, the contrast with our salty admiral could not have been more acute and maybe Constantius always intended to make it:

"Delegated by His Imperial Majesty as Oversight Officer for all forces in Germania, Britannia and Gaul; I am to be based on the Rhine but will remain responsible for overseeing the valuable work you men are doing here. Dealing with Frankish, Saxon raids."

"Excellency, we are at your command. If there is any information or assistance we can offer you at any point, then tell us and it will be so."

"Admiral, your successes over the *bacaudae* are well known and earn you much deserved approval. I have heard good reports too, a few, of how you are tackling these raiders from over the sea."

"We have made a start only, Excellency. There is much left to do."

"It is a sideshow but an important one. Important done right. Britannia and Gaul are vital for feeding the garrisons of Germania but my strategic priority must remain the Rhine. And also the Danube, stopping the tribes breaking through. Though however many we kill, yet more press down on our frontiers. Where something is driving them on, making them move. Something beyond. What we must deal with nowadays. A hundred years ago in the time of the great Emperor Marcus Aurelius, there were many more tribes: Marcomanni and Cheruci, Heruli and Celti. You name it, there would be a bunch of hairy Germans answering to the name. Hating each other as much as Rome - why divide and rule was our keynote to diplomatic and military policy in the region. Tribe against tribe. The Empire could exploit that well. Making a big effort to wipe

230

out their young men too, at least once in every generation, part of a wider approach always working well for us. But suddenly it seems we in Germania hear only one name. As if these warring barbarians have somehow got together and made a confederacy amongst themselves. A completely new tribe. Can you imagine that? Now it is *Alemanni* they call themselves - '*All Men*'. How about that for a name, eh? What an impertinent conceit, one whose potential cannot augur well."

"Rome will prevail."

"Of course it will, Admiral, but only if the Augustus is satisfied of our commitment and loyalty to him."

"It is without question."

"I am afraid not, Admiral, and the reason why I am here."

A shiver went through the staff and then I suddenly saw how there were *Protectores Augusti Nostri* lining every wall of the chamber in which we had gathered.

"I am a simple soldier, Admiral, but the post of *Praefectus Praetorio* to which the Divine Augustus has in his infinite generosity and wisdom elevated me is more than military. It leaves me responsible not only for military implications from strategic and operational responses we adopt during the present emergency, but also their legal ones. It means I have had to become something of a courtroom lawyer as well."

Carausius stood there unflinching at our head, shoulders level, as we all waited for where this was going. He looked very alone, and it was this I hated most in the situation.

"I have had letters at Treverorum, and the Augustus Maximianus similarly at Mediolanum. Sent from the *honestiores* of Britannia and others elsewhere. Petitions and complaints."

"They are liars! It is a conspiracy!"

To my mind, my commander had been too quick with this denial, but who could blame him. It was an old claim in Britain and the stress of the moment was immense.

"Steady, General, steady yourself. Let me itemise their allegations first, before you rush to deny them. The petitioners of Britannia are saying that you are operating a criminal racket. That you deliberately let the raiders land and do their worst, waiting until they are making their way back to their ships with the loot before intervening. That you confiscate their stolen goods for your own benefit and do not return them to their

231

owners. That you are in league with the Saxons and the Franks. That you are a near countryman of the latter and so your loyalties lie with them, not Rome. Also, there are intelligences given to our Master which imply you are a secret sympathiser with Christians, an officer whom witnesses claim to be in league with a mutinous and traitorous legion of odious memory. A disgraced unit once unlawfully-risen against our true and lawful master, the Augustus Maximian. And that you never stand recorded in the books of His Priesthood as ever making sacrifice to the Imperial Cult. In short, a traitor, were various informants to be believed....."

"*Praefectus*, surely you realise they are not. When I have faithfully and successfully defended five hundred-odd miles of British coast with my life, one legion, and over there, little more than seven ships. Almost all remaining of CLBR, the old British fleet. Plus twenty biremes of Bononia and our few scattered garrisons hanging on over here. My total force to protect all of coastal Gaul and your own flank, while at the same time taking this war deep into your enemies' heartland on the Rhine delta. We have taken a great many enemy lives and ships but they spawn like eels and you must know how some raiders will always get through. Fewer each week, as I fervently pray, and fewer still when the new ships I am ordering can take to the sea, but occasionally they do. Excellency, you cannot believe this. It is a fix, someone who does not wish us to succeed putting my accusers up to it....."

"Your denials are noted and naturally to be expected...." Chlorus said languidly "...but these remain formal matters needing to be tested with witnesses in another place. Due process must be followed. I am here to relieve you of your command until an army tribunal has heard the proper facts. You will come with me to Moguntacium and await justice there."

The *Protectores Augusti Nostri* might well be top troops to have in a palace but - deployed in an unfamiliar little army house on the edge of Empire - they were frankly a bit slow on the uptake. Like that pivotal day in Gesoriacum where a minor officer like me, one normally kept at the back in important gatherings, could slide from his place in the shadows and out through an adjacent service-door at that point I grasped how badly things were going.

232

To be fair to them, their priority and focus was presumably on successfully making a quick arrest of this General they'd come to collect. Not some shrimp lurking at the back.

As I ran down the outer corridor beyond, heading for the next door, I do not think that at that moment I had any clearer idea of what I would do, beyond telling somebody more senior outside about what was going on inside. Beyond that simple intent, I held no greater plan; while Carausius's personal advice about my fleeing to Britain could not have been further from my mind. It was clear to me that my leader would have about as much chance of a fair hearing in Moguntacium as an African leopard in the arena at Calleva. All I cared about was his being spared the experience.

I reached the door into the courtyard, out of whose colonnaded archway I could run into the centre of the fort, and pushed for freedom. The unexpected force that returned instead threw me off-balance and I staggered backwards as it swung in at me, not outwards. Where in fell a member of the *Augusti*, all plumed helmet and one-piece cuirass like those old sculptures of Mars, to go flying right past me as he tripped over the stone lintel and went skidding on his armoured chest down the polished floorway.

The wooden door now swung back in the other direction and I dived with it. Outside in the courtyard there was another sentry from the *Augusti*, standing at ease by the archway exit with a javelin at the slope in his right hand. He put his other hand straight to the silvered bronze brow of his helmet as if momentarily perplexed by what he'd just seen, then guessed at once that trouble was up.

"Hey, you. Come here!"

When this one stood right in the arch between me and the parade ground there was no alternative to compliance, so I sauntered calmly over. Just as if the doorway from which I'd emerged had not a moment ago sucked one of his friends inside, like some scene in a Greek farce. By the time I got to where he stood he'd had time to think what to do, his colleague in the corridor dragging himself upright to put his head out the door and shout something unintelligible.

The great advantage I have found in a *seax* held close to the chest, over any sword held low to the waist and to your side in the traditional way, is how fast the blade can be out.

For some inexplicable reason, the sentry carefully put his javelin down to lean against the wall and went for his *spatha* instead. This and the time it took him was his biggest mistake.

The *seax* took the whole of the front of his throat out with one sweeping slash and the sentry went down with its flap, drowning in his own blood. Before his mate over the courtyard or any more Praetorians could get me, I turned and ran for the parade ground.

Now I'd really done it. There was no going back now. Not for any of us.

The parade ground was a sea of white faces and brick red cloaks. I couldn't make anyone out and the sky seemed to be spinning. There was blood down my tunic and a stained blade in my hand as I ran through the ranks of the Second, looking for a familiar face. Lucky they didn't kill me on the spot, mistaking my rush for an attack.

Suddenly I was lying on the floor winded, an officer in a crested helmet bending over. He was probably the one who'd tackled me.

"Triton, my lad! Whatever are you doing? What on earth's going on in there? What in Mithras' name have you been up to, my boy? Looking like you've butchered a pig!"

I hear Marcus Saturninus Lupus of the Second Augusta, at that time this legion's most senior man on the base, its toughest and most experienced. Centurion of The First Spear – *Centurio Primo Pilo* – their commander of the camp. Harsh, humourless and stern; hard as iron and probably conceived in a crucible; but one man above all others on whom I knew I could depend. His booming voice on the parade ground could wake the dead, make whole cohorts quake, but never did I hear him more soothing than that day when he lifted me from the ground with this question in his face.

"Centurion, a disaster! The *Praefectus Praetorio* is come to detain our General and strip him of his command. The *Protectores Augusti Nostri* detachment come with him have got Carausius and our general staff penned-up in an audience chamber. Right inside the commandant's house. Saying he will take our leader in chains to Moguntacium. To stand trial before an army tribunal. Charges of theft and collaboration with the enemy. And I've just killed one of their sentries, right here on army property......"

Then I'm ashamed to say that I burst into tears. Whether of distress or rage, no-one could tell. Either way, not a very soldierly reaction for an officer, I know, but you will remember I was still only eighteen. Completely overwhelmed by the sheer enormity of the situation in which I now found myself, I wept like a child.

The last time I ever did - bar one.

I don't suppose the senior centurion felt too chuffed, either. This affected everyone. He let go of my arms once he'd pulled me onto my feet, looking down at me for a moment in utter disbelief. Then M.Saturninus Lupus clamped his fists tightly-shut, breathing hard in the way he did when most annoyed, and said loudly:

"Not if we've got anything to do with it, he won't!"

The Second formed up quickly to surround the *praetorium* but Chlorus and his men had already barricaded themselves inside.

With our General.

"The key object of INDECT research project is to contribute, through innovation and technology, to the security of all in the European Union......it is important to note that a person highlighted by tools based on INDECT detection algorithms would merely be brought to the attention of the relevant authorities, so that normal lawful measures can be taken......The sentence: 'if you have done nothing wrong, you have nothing to fear' is only true if every aspect of the criminal justice system works perfectly, on every occasion. Tools based on INDECT project research outcomes will provide EU Member States with the technology to ensure that decisions around public safety are based on the maximum amount of relevant information available. Signed: INDECT RESEARCH Project Board"

(from) 'Ethical Issues – the INDECT Home Page'
http://www.indect-project.eu/approach-to-ethical-issues

- or University of York, on:
http:www.cs.york.ac.uk/aig/projects/indect/index.php

Still with a race to run, Bill's curious encounters can't be fully questioned, while Fedora Fred is soon forgotten once we're back on the road again, under a scorching sun. His wheel studs down a drain. As the land heats up, we leave burnt Siena behind to head over the rounded hills of Chiantishire by that pine-bordered route they call '*Chiantiagna*'. Out in its countryside, flowers and grass are the vivid green of early spring but our roadbook takes us riverside, to places more urban. Along the Val d'Elsa and her main road into Poggibonsi.

The gauge is dropping fast, so we fill-up with fuel there from a supermarket gas station, Xenobia suddenly old and fragile. A time-traveller fallen to earth, reported missing in the present. Vulnerable not valued. Lost among the glossy hatchbacks of sated shoppers fleeing giant shopping malls. Giving us no quarter, taking no prisoners, their mirrors canted over for checking hair and lip-gloss, not manouevre.

From San Casciano in the Val di Pesa, this year's revival heads for Firenza - how could it not? Over roads and highways each with their own stories of this race to tell if they could but speak, their own traditions following. Towards the city holding highest place in European travellers' affections; whether for the sight from its belvedere of her domes, campaniles and terracotta roofs spread out below, Ponte Vecchio spanning the Arno, or her unmatched role in western art. Florence herself, perhaps the largest open-air gallery in the world, where for one day only our cars can claim a place beside the banks of Arno in a touring exhibition.

As we get nearer the city, roads get busier. Spectator traffic provided a distinct problem for us right from the start but now these dawdling fellow-travellers are mixed-up with commuting motorists, indifferent to us both. A dangerous mix.

The *afficionados* are hanging on our tail then overtaking at the very last minute before a bend to grab some drive-by photos. Hanging-back again in front to get a few more while holding us up, back-seat passengers turning round to wave and smile as if they've just done us a favour. At first their enthusiasm for our adventure and its chosen steed is charming but soon becomes an irritation, Bill and I glaring back.

Almost as bad and nearly as dangerous are the streams of team-support vehicles. Big 4x4s and anonymous white vans single-mindedly chasing 'their' car through Tuscany, devil take the rest. This flying multitude is joined by organisers, sponsors, or media in BMWs and Alfas - glossy squadrons tending to overtake in batches. Three saloons typically forcing their way into a moving gap only large enough for one. Armed with the self-importance of officialdom and journalism, the self-righteousness of umpires. Impervious to challenge.

In the cut and thrust of city traffic, a mobile melée where we always seem to be in the wrong lane and Bill has to keep pointing me over to another, I stay in constant fear of shunts as we skip lightly from one carriageway to the next. Waving airily behind through the mirror to motorists we've forced-in on: *Peace Be With You*.

A few restrained hoots and the occasional despairing hand all the protest we ever get from the patient Florentines, their graciousness belying reputation.

And always above, to the right and in the corner of our eyes while we pass, is the towering spine of Italy. Her mighty Apennines. Looking down on us until the siren calls of tradition combine with roadbook directions to send us climbing up there, once Florence is dealt with. So up we go, circling countless bends towards the mountain passes of Futa and Raticosa, Xenobia's tyres squealing. Outside temperatures dropping rapidly, engine oil's rising.

Towards passes whose unforgiving roads so often form the backdrop to classic 1930s images in sepia from the original event. Photographs of open Alfa Romeo 6 and 8Cs with all lamps reversed in protection to their lenses from a hail of flying stones. Crews goggled likewise. Tearing round mountain hairpins in a trailing cloud of dust and the thin air of this Italian Olympus, a natural Home for Gods. Such immortal Italian winners in these cars as *The Flying Mantuan* Tazio Nuvolari; Baconin Borzacchini, Guiseppe Campari or Achille Varzi. Heroes from another world who lived in brown-and-white.

Up here, in the spring of those days, they sometimes had dust. This year there is snow.

The heater in the Aurelia is little use at the best of times and by the time Xenobia reaches the snowline we feel chilled to the bone. No hint of global warming. If constantly working the big steering wheel is what keeps me vaguely warm, Bill the navigator has no better exercise than drumming his feet on the floor to get a blood supply to his toes.

We may be high but there are no panoramic views to be had today; the low cloud, mist-draped ice, and roadside snowbanks seeing to that. Shivering inside a black car with the thermal-retentative qualities of an open fridge, we look wanly out through misted-up windows onto a monochrome world of fog. Black tarmac, brown rock, and off-white ice or frozen snow all merging with cloud and the last skeletons of trees surviving at this altitude.

Our initial excitement on tackling the legendary Raticosa is soon dulled by these conditions. Unremitting labour in an all-pervading gloom, the sheer drudgery of it. The repetitious monotony of accelerating Xenobia briefly uphill and into the murk in too low a gear for her liking, along too short a straight to matter before the next hairpin looms. Where I must brake hard, return Xenobia's 'box to her bottom gear then twirl the wheel so her bonnet points uphill again; engine revving and its exhaust's bark trailing us down the following straight. At the over-revved end of this replica to previous, the next unsatisfying sprint, we find another hairpin waiting in the fog. Followed by another and another, Xenobia howling upwards through its cloying, icy vapour like a mountain wolf in search of dying men.

By which laborious means we haul ourselves higher into the Apennines. Deeper into cloud, further away from civilisation. Nearer the cohorts of Italian car club members drawn up at their summit to greet us, their bright ski-jackets embroidered with all the heraldry of petrol-hedonism. And because this is a regularity event, Bill still busy on his watches, nagging me to slow down or speed up. Exhorting the dreary averages we are meant to maintain when any sort of progress feels hard enough to gain.

To be fair, it can't have been easy for him, finding his way over such difficult terrain with so few landmarks for reference, but my sympathies are running thin. Bill's endless fussing about regularity-timing getting on my nerves. Our experience not that flat-out rush from Brescia to Rome and back through sunlit alps which the *Coppa Mille Miglia* once evoked, and I fondly imagined. No wonder that all anyone present; whether crowds, self or *Polizia;* wanted to see was these lovely cars actually going fast.

Letting them rip, not pussyfooting about.

But since the regulations generally preclude this, I must drive at six-tenths, leaving me free in the back of my mind to wander off elsewhere. Happily imagining a gorilla like *'Fred'* as the sort of driver bound to boot his Jag' from standing starts, its wheels falling off within yards. Less so when brooding on Bill's other odd encounters – like his secret conversation with a Sienese stranger, yet another with a Yank. Wondering what each of those strange episodes meant, what they add up to. Who you can count on, where it would end.

The Mille Miglia, at least, can always be relied on to end precisely where it begins.

In suburban Brescia well-past midnight on a scaffolding ramp emblazoned with sponsors. On the Viale Venezia – no more beautiful a name for a street!

To make our triumphal return there, first we must make a complete circuit of the Old Town. Preceded by another police outrider, flashing blue light up a pylon on his 'bike. We are used to this by now and after him comes an official press car, a new Guilietta provided courtesy of the Alfa factory, then the next batch of competitors. Including ourselves in Xenobia.

As we approach the long Palladian arcade of the old Corn-Market - south side, Piazza Arnoldo - a younger crowd who seem mainly students attempt a 'Mexican Wave' against any competing car whose crew they claim to recognise. Pressing forward with excited shouts and almost falling over its bonnet. Children among them amused most by those smaller, open cars whose crew's heads project above windscreen level, are encrusted with grime. As they have for a thousand miles, catching flies and every kind of insect.

Passing the same building, other drivers entertain this crowd by opening their throttle for the long straight beside it. Accelerating away into Viale Venezia with headlights flaring and a languid backwards wave to appreciative cheers. Inside the arcade itself, restaurants stay open late. Diners pausing from animated conversation to watch with affectionate dismay local teenagers well known to them and probably related, their madcap antics on the verge.

"Together!" shouts the group when they see a competing FIAT *Topolino* puttering gingerly towards them. Nearly blocking its path as they surge suddenly in a body onto the roadway and surround the little car.

"Vi, Vi! Avante!" they shout to its driver: *"Go, go, go!"*

Another open-top version - why its crew look so nervous, fearing exposure to the crowd. They need not have worried. This gang surrounding them are utterly friendly and pull back at once to let them on their way, though the FIAT's release demands another target be found. Instantly rewarded with the sight of one of their peers, a teenage moped-rider who wobbles into their midst on a huge cheer of recognition. He waves sheepishly back but they swamp him with goodwill, running alongside and slapping him on the back with so much joy that he wobbles again and this time nearly falls off. Fortunately retaining enough of a hold on his machine to twist his throttle-grip and accelerate out of their clutches. Shouts of glee following him down the road as he rides to claim sanctuary beneath the arms of Arnaldo.

"What a good laugh we'll have about this, tomorrow morning in college!" promises one.

Next arrival is a cyclist who receives more of the same, although about as far from *Mille Miglia* competitor as could be imagined. A home-going librarian embarrassed by all their fuss but without the acceleration to get him so quickly out of it. His wobbling more critical. Bespectacled, bearded features betraying a deeper concern. And almost like they can recognise his insecurity, social and kinetic, the teenagers seem kinder. Quicker to draw back and cheer him on his way, the librarian recognising mercy when he sees it. Waving gratefully as he pedals awkwardly off at an angle into the safety of obscurity.

Yet when it comes to our turn all we get is a brief 'wash' from their Mexican Wave before they part to let us through. *"Bella macchina!"* what they shout through my open driver's window as we speed forward into the night.

Drawn-on into town beyond by the dappling reflection on cobblestones ahead of our headlights and an unusual stroboscopic effect, attractive to cameras. So that when a photographer in an expensive bomber jacket suddenly lies down prone in the gutter, to take low-level shots of our car as it passes, it is only narrowly I avoid crushing him while we do.

"*Great picture!*" I hear him shout to his companion on the pavement, the one who insists on 'high-fives' and striking palms with the co-driver of every open car coming through. Both of them as lucky not to be hit or run-over, equally unaware.

When it seems like a miracle that no one actually is. The protection of Arnaldo?

By this point in proceedings, the restaurants and pavements are so crowded that people chatting, dogs on leads, and children in pushchairs inevitably spill over onto the narrow roadways. Leaving careful drivers like me to pick our way around them, find ourselves at eye-level with a serious-faced baby or the maw of straining hounds.

The car directly in front is a black Alfa Romeo saloon from the 1950s. An official entry in the race from the *Polizia* themselves, driven by two handsome young officers in full uniform. Successfully completing the whole event, there is little doubt their progress was helped along the way by certain period equipment, including a blue light on the roof and clockwork siren on the bumper. Accessories they don't hesitate to use for clearing jaywalkers like that photographer from the gutter as we approach the Viale Venezia itself.

When our little convoy arrives there and I watch the Alfa nip smartly up the finish ramp just in front of us, tonight's master of ceremonies is alert enough to notice that they'd begun the event as a crew of two, but now there seems a third. The attractive young woman sitting happily between the pair of them.

"Oh, yes..." the officers concede vaguely when pressed: "We made an arrest."

My enduring memories of the finish are made from endearing episodes like these. Its unique atmosphere and that surprising sense of safety to be had in the dark. On foot in the middle of a European city in the early hours. Even in streets emptying so quickly once the last car is gone. When you find yourself alone and some distance from what few bars and restaurants were still open, beside the competitors' route.

But how else to capture a night-time atmosphere feeling so much more benign than any comparable British town or city? Diagnose what difference makes it so? Is it just better weather; the relaxed attitude of Italians, their greater sense of culture or that – declining - importance they attach to family life? The natural result of lives more commonly lived out on the streets by a people renting crowded apartments, usually without gardens? And by the time you've got round to reading this, will those social and behavioural differences between us have been ground-away anyway? Eroded and erased by the homogenising effects of globalisation, consumerism, legislation, the diktats of Europe?

Who knows.

All I can say is that - walking around near the finish-line, then through the darkened streets of Brescia, as Bill and I did that night for a while to unwind - we felt totally safe. If there is only the omnipresent graffiti to belie this favourable impression, I still don't believe our assessment was wrong.

Of a pleasant nocturnal atmosphere where we could gratefully accept our finishers' awards and grab a coffee at the all-night bar. Make our excuses for not attending the closing dinner. Take this final chance to exchange banter with our rivals of the last few days, those crews finishing closest to us - whether in front or behind. Exchange e-mail addresses with them and faithfully promise to send pictures of their cars, during enough of an unwind to defray all the accumulated tension and euphoria.

Before we return at last to where a grimy Xenobia waits patiently on the Viale for us to make our final journey of the night. Heading towards Garda and our lakeside motel, utterly exhausted but proud of what we'd done.

Finishing the modern Mille Miglia.

As if that were an end to it all.

Not the start.

> *"It is an instinct of human nature to hate a man
> you have wronged."*

(Cornelius Tacitus, *'The Agricola'* - 2nd Century A.D.)

- XIV -

If every door and window of the commander's house was already firmly barred with salvaged timber and rammed stone, or the sharpest weapons of the Praetorians, the rising wave of fury from our British veterans of the Second pouring in all over it must have felt like thunder to those cowering inside.

Indignant at our General's unexpected detention, every individual legionary or soldier of the Fleet in the camp had gathered up their arms and rushed to the building at its centre.

Taking immediate command of the tumult with that natural authority and severity of manner typifying his way, Saturninus Lupus at once ordered a detachment to form up with shields as the classic 'tortoise', the *testudo*. This textbook infantry formation advanced slow and insect-like under its shell of interlocking shields towards the plated doors of the archway marking the courtyard through which I was recently fled.

Waiting for them was the hail of rocks, roof tiles, javelins and burning pots of oil, hurled down onto them by its haughty defenders. As flames and spears penetrate the 'tortoise', some of its individual elements collapse. Concussed, cut, or burnt and exposing further gaps in their formation for more missiles to pierce. Trapped before the double-barred doors of the archway and pinned there under relentless fire, our poor soldiers' *testudo* began to disintegrate.

"Withdraw, withdraw!" shouted Saturninus.

Its survivors needed little encouragement to break and run but the boiling anger of their comrades was fomented by the sight. Going back-in to recover the casualties only stoking the flames of mutiny. What we realised our actions had surely become, almost in an instant.

The instant I took out that first Praetorian sentry. Our first illegal act.

Mine, to be precise.

"Wait a moment, lads. Back into line. Calm down. We need to think about this" said the *Primus Pilus*. "These guys aren't going anywhere. Let's take our time."

The senior centurion was right. We were the home team while the Praetorians were out on their own. Surrounded and far beyond rescue. The suave Constantius Chlorus had completely misjudged what obedience his high rank commanded, or the deep attachment of Gesoriacum garrison to this man who commanded them.

Saturninus set a group to breaking open the aqueduct which supplied the house with water, levering back the stone flags and diverting the culvert below, while a catapult with throwing arm was brought up to start lobbing burning torches into the courtyard atrium in the hope of starting fires.

Now it was a waiting game. No need for any of us to get hurt. The encircling shield lines stood at ease, leaning on their javelins and chatting quietly. Waiting for thirst and fire to do their dirty work.

It took most of the rest of the day before they did.

By evening I should think we'd run those inside quite ragged, what with our deliveries of various airborne, heavy objects and the regular, fiery missiles we'd sent in. Arriving by air with no stores of water left to put them out on landing. A service wing along the eastern side of the complex had acquired several holes along its tiled roof and the signs of smoke curling out around them began to be accompanied by the occasional flash of flame, darting angrily above the topmost ridge. The main house still looked more or less intact, but there were grey whisps appearing from windows and chimney-vents that had nothing to do with cooking.

Around the sixth hour, the double doors suddenly opened and a Praetorian officer slipped through before they shut close behind him again.

A filthy white rag tied to a stick in his hand.

One of ours got him in so tight a headlock his helmet fell off, and dragged him unceremoniously around the back of the nearest barrack block to where Saturninus and the centurions were waiting:

"Hallo, my lads, what message of goodwill does this sooty pigeon bring us out?"

Poor fellow. The messenger in question was probably more afraid of those that sent him than anything we would do. Affecting a show of bravado:

"The *Praefectus Praetorio* says you are mutineers who disgrace the name of your legion. If you do not want to face the usual consequence of that crime, then your only chance of mercy is to let him leave in safety. At once. Without further delay......."

When he raised his arm, I thought Saturninus was going to hit him but, instead and showing admirable self-control, he merely snarled: "You can get back inside the oven with your palace mates, my friend. You're not done yet. Tell your boss that if we do not see our Admiral and the officers of his fleet released unharmed, within the very next rotation of my water clock, then we'll be watching the *Praefectus Praetorio* and his guards baked alive before us."

"What if he did ... release him, I mean....what would happen to us?"

"I cannot say. A decision for our commander....either when you let him go, or when we've rescued him. One thing's for sure, the longer you leave it, or if there's any resistance, then all hint of kindness goes. Harm one hair of his head and we'll nail every one of you to stakes on the beach, to await the next tide. If nothing else, be certain to tell Chlorus about this, the one important promise you did wring from us."

The legionary who led him back gave the Praetorian one last, friendly boot up the backside to speed him on his way, then let him go and scuttle off inside.

A servant brought the waterclock out to Saturninus in its box, from its special place in the offices of the *Principia*, and he settled down to watch the hour.

"Let's time this meat" he laughed. "I prefer it well done!"

There was a crack from the nearest catapult as a missile went in, then a crash as it smashed through a roof. Its crew going through the process of reloading and rewinding before it would be followed by another.

By now we had a proper bonfire. If we let it go on much longer, we could lose the whole fort to its flames. Despite what puny intervention our primitive fire engine might offer *via* two adapted bilge-pumps salvaged from a galley and mounted on its cart.

246

Fortunately for everyone involved, it was at this point where the besieged inside finally lost their nerve.

The courtyard doors opened once again, and this time they didn't close. You could see right through them into an open space where numerous fires were burning widely. We saw the shape of an unarmed man walking slowly through the smoke with his hands high in the air. The easy style of one used to crossing a moving deck, distinctive.

"Stop firing!" demanded Saturninus.

He had a vivid purple bruise to his right cheekbone but otherwise looked intact. Carausius grinning broadly at us, like an experienced traveller missing in bad weather and returned home to unexpected fuss. He turned to look back the way he'd come and a file of figures followed him sheepishly out. The remaining officers of the *Classis* penned inside with him.

"All present and correct, sir" they called.

Saturninus gripped Carausius in a hug, like two bears meeting on the floor of a forest, one big, one not so. The legionaries of the Second rushed forward in a mass, cheering and punching the sky with their javelins. Four of them held a rectangular shield horizontally like a table, inviting the admiral to step onto it. Carausius hesitated, wary of its meaning, but the growing crowd of soldiers who were chanting his name louder and louder kept pointing to the shield. Demanding he go on it. Reluctantly he complied but now it took six to hold it up, and then there were eight. With this much muscle and further willing helpers, they were able to raise him higher. So that he towered over the hundreds that by now milled about on the wide, paved area in front of the burning commander's house.

It was an incredible scene, one I shall never forget.

A centurion of the Fleet shouted "Health to Carausius!" and there was a huge roar of enthusiastic agreement. The Admiral smiled and tried to say something suitably thankful, but I could not hear what it was for all the noise. Then during a sudden pause, an ordinary soldier being carried on the shoulders of a colleague came up right beside him to take his arm by the wrist and raise it in the air. Yelling "Hail to Carausius! May the Admiral live for ever! Carausius for Emperor!"

Bona Dea!

Good Goddess, *Roma Dea,* now we'd really done it.

"Hail, Caesar! Hail, Caesar! Hail, Caesar!" the whole mob went, legionaries and men of the *Classis* combined. Repeating the phrase over and over again in an ululating chant which never seemed to stop. "Hail, Caesar! Hail, Caesar!"

"My friends, my brave friends, I want to thank you......"

The chanting began again and drowned him out for a moment. As soon as it faded he held his hands out flat in front of him in a gesture for calm and tried again:

"Soldiers of Rome! Your officers of *Classis Britannica* stand beholden, owing our lives to your valiant obstinacy. Without your rescue, who knows what would have become? Gratitude is one thing, but now you demand a more dangerous road and I for one would never want to put such dear and valued friends as you are grown to me into the way of such danger. By accepting this great honour you would bestow on me. So please, no, relent! You know me unworthy and that I cannot. You, me. We are all of us foot-soldiers in the cause of *Romae Aeternae,* loyal comrades together. With soldiers like you, why need Britain and her cities fear Saxon again? When we have each sworn an oath of loyalty for the faithful protection of Britannia and Rome. Where our real duty....."

"Carausius Caesar! Emperor of all Britain, and Emperor of Rome! Hail to Carausius, hail to the Caesar. Hail to our new Augustus!"

And so it went on. There was no going back now. Carausius knew that. We all knew that. "*Alea iacta est.*" The die was cast, just as the first Caesar once put it, the Divine Julius, but Emperor of what? The Narrow Sea? Two provinces of Britannia?

What about Chlorus, too? As the cheering gradually subsided, that was the next practical question and not an easy one at that. There were different views about it emerging from factions in the crowd already:

"Let us kill him now. See, we will finish what we have started. Him and those bastard Praetorians!" shouted the men of the Second.

"Let the fire do its work" called Saturninus. "No need for casualties from us. Or action. Just keep them in. Report an unfortunate accident."

"No, no!" replied Carausius. "He set me free on my promise. I gave him my word. If they let me and my officers get out unharmed, that I would do same for them. All of them. Free passage down to the harbour and safely away on their ships. That was my promise."

"To which they are the only witnesses left. Kill them and no-one will know."

"But the all-seeing Gods will..." said Carausius. "... and I gave them my word, so that we could each return to our posts. To our places of duty. Defending the Light of Rome. No arrests, no punishments, that was the deal. Sworn on an altar of Jupiter in the courtyard of this *praetorium*...."

"For the sake of an emperor who has killed more of its defenders than the Alemanni ever managed...." put in the naval centurion whose shout for the health of Carausius had set the whole 'Imperial' thing going. The noble answer he got to this last remark was a short speech still remembered by many survivors like me. Witnesses to history who can recognise it now for setting the shape to everything that followed – for good or for ill.

"Would you have me made into a perjurer? No! My mission and the solemn promise I make to you now as your new emperor is to restore Rome. Her fortunes and her reputation. Starting over in Britain and here in northern Gaul. Reinstate a new golden age like the great Augustus did. One that can start right here and now with that ancient Roman quality of simple honesty. When there is no man, not even an emperor, capable of restoring anything worth keeping if he cannot keep his own promises. Who leaves no-one believing he will..." said the very first British emperor in our history, though sadly not the last.

"I understand your motives, my lord, but in the Holy Name of Jupiter, if you can really believe in Chlorus – let alone Maximianus - keeping their side of this bargain after what's just happened, then you are indeed the good man we take you for, but one sadly deluded" sighed Saturninus. It did him no good, for Carausius stayed adamant.

We should let them go, and the emperor's decision was final. He was the boss.

An envoy was sent into the courtyard to let them know the decision but his generous news of unconditional release met with a stony reception. The Praetorian Prefect had heard what happened out on the forecourt and his gratitude was invisible.

He and his men were allowed out all the same, on condition of having first laid their weapons down on the cobbled yard. Valuable pieces of equipment which would soon be molten scrap if we didn't do something quickly about the building.

The fire engine was connected to a stone cistern via a leather hose and its crew of sailors began pumping water onto the house. Its leaky old pumps were made of wood and carved in a spiral according to the widely-known principle of an Archimedean screw. Much like those we use in the bilges of our ships and little more efficient. At least there were plenty of teams of men available, passing buckets hand-to-hand to do more good.

When the fire was out, the armoured line of soldiers from the legion and the fleet which marked both sides of the cobbled lane running from fortress down to harbour was even longer. Watching in silence as Constantius Chlorus, *Praefectus Praetorio* of the Western Empire and his hunched band of *Protectores Augusti Nostri*, shuffled miserably downhill to where their ships waited at the quayside. Empty-handed.

Theirs were narrow, river ships, designed for use inland. An unsuitable, uncomfortable, unstable, and probably slightly-dangerous choice of transport out on the seas, but the swell was slight and they were lucky.

Lucky to be leaving with their lives.

No one saluted, no one shouted, certainly no one cheered. While the rude townsfolk looked on in utter mystification at the sight of a high Imperial official leaving like a dog in the night, his retinue stripped of weaponry. Taking their only other clue to noisy events heard from the camp above in a pall of black smoke still rising up from its centre to hang over their town like a morbid flag.

I followed the Praetorians all the way down to the quay, as aware as anyone of our guilty role but mesmerised at its course. Eyewitnesses to a history one day to become legend. Like everyone present, I knew there would be a price for this humiliating procession and feared for whenever it came to be called in. With it seeming to me that the resources available to a scorned *Praefectus Praetorio* would exceed in fury anything that either Hell or even a wronged woman could ever summon up. A strong argument in itself for not showing any of our faces, but for the grisly fascination this unprecedented humbling of an important general naturally held for everyone.

So, yes, since you have asked me, I was there too. Its witness. Standing nearby with only the cheekplates of my tightly-fastened helmet for a disguise among the dockside crowd of soldiers and civilians, jostling for a view of Carausius supervising the boarding of our opponent's sulky bully-boys. Chlorus standing there too, completely impassive. Ship-side of the rail as their ramp was pulled aboard and the mooring lines cast over.

"You'll see me here again" was all he ever said, fastidiously wiping the side of his mouth with a silk as the rowers started work and his ships began tracking towards where the estuary opens out. When he turned to face the sea and never once looked back.

Carausius, in his great magnanimity and despite this ambiguous remark, nevertheless still drew himself up and saluted. I for one knew he intended a conciliatory mark of respect, but anyone who wanted could have taken it for mockery. As Chlorus surely would. A generous gesture which also marked the point, at the very height of his astonishing success, of how our new British Emperor had already made the biggest and most fatal mistake of his life.

Such an unwise concession, so why did he let him go?

The ultimate enemy.

As so often, the answer is simple. The principled choice of an innocent man of honour. One who somehow imagined that the personal fulfilment by him of a private promise he'd made to another, would be matched by theirs of similar made to him.

A man of the world who should have known better, when the powerful, greedy or ambitious were never made like that. Precious few ordinary folk, either.

Let alone those mighty men who've done him so much wrong already.

"It is only by having a loud voice in a united Europe that we can promote the open economy that will deliver growth. Being shoved to the margins, or retreating there voluntarily, would be economic suicide."

(The Right Honourable Nick Clegg MP,
Deputy Prime Minister, 2012)

- 14 -

On the morning after the night before, Bill and I wake late from our billet near Brescia, a motel on the shores of Lake Garda, to find white clouds gathering over distant mountains. Blue skies overhead and a car park red with Ferraris. I walk among them to check on Xenobia, sprinkled with dew over her dust of passage, to discover a brown-metallic example nearby. Incongruous among serried rows of scarlet, and one white van.

I sense there's something unusual about this brown Ferrari straight away. A set of English registration plates adding to her mystique. Old-style black and silver, a 'D' reg. While I stand there inspecting curvaceous bodywork and a faultless interior in cream leather, two Englishmen carrying travel-grips emerge from the motel to approach me.

"This is nice. Yours?" I ask.

"My father-in law's - 250 GT Lusso, 1966."

"Lovely. Good of him to let you use it. Especially on a job like this."

"Absolutely. A tough event for everyone."

"Car got history?"

"Yeah, first owner a Hollywood actor. You know, that wartime escape movie: POWs, tune they whistle at football matches. Him on the motorbike - dead now, of course. But she's still in the original paint he specified from the factory. As special order from Modena."

"Wow, she's lovely. Surprising the Americans let it leave their country. And well done for getting her here in one piece. So have a safe journey home."

"Yeah, you too. Take care!"

Now the euphoria of the event and managing a finish had ebbed away, Xenobia's crew faced the same practicality as this unique Ferrari. Getting home. Emerging from a nostalgic bubble into that everyday world we'd all opted-out of for the best part of a week.

No news, no internet, and as little mobile use as we could bear.

"I don't know about you, Michael, but I don't fancy returning to that Carabinieri barracks up at the airport. Asking for your heap of Japanese scrap back..." he'd said, like it was a decision not a question.

"No, you're right. Would only cause trouble. Not as if we could move the thing anyway, even if the police agreed. Not without a low-loader or a lorry. No, let's leave it to the recovery club. Insurers have all the details, can soon sort it out. Back to England if they want it or else written off. What they're paid for, after all."

So that was it. Without my 4x4 and his trailer, the only way to get Xenobia and ourselves home was the traditional one – actually drive her. If she'd been good as gold for the last thousand miles, we faced a longer run. With the obvious risk it might be asking too much of her, after what she'd been through already.

Till Bill suggested an alternative.

Why the following Saturday we drove slowly back to Verona. Famous as the home of Shakespeare's 'Romeo & Juliet', or the operatic amphitheatre we passed only days ago, its historic core is hidden behind eighteenth-century artillery bastions and that outer ring of commercial grunge disfiguring too many modern towns. Industrial estates and roadside malls ringed with mesh fencing and advertising billboards. If the Montagues and Capulets ever saw it, I like to think of them settling their vendetta and combining to demolish these blights on their fair city without more ado.

Our reason for returning wasn't theatre, but as Two Gentlemen wanting transport out of Verona, by rail at rather short notice. The next available Deutsche Bahn car-train in fact, heading north for Dusseldorff. And, thanks to a last-minute cancellation from the Austrian owners of a Porsche 356, parked down a

253

ravine while descending a hill outside Sienna during the event, it looked like we were in luck.

Less lucky in a late-ticket price to make your eyes water, and some difficulty we had in getting the inspector's portable credit card-reader to do its stuff. An impasse only resolved by handing over instead every last bit of cash, coin, and currency Bill and I could discover between us. Find in Xenobia's ashtray.

At least we knew we had a place aboard, and to that extent were better off than many others. As we realised the more our journey wore on.

The original plan being that once we got to Germany where the car-train terminates, our next stage would be to drive across to Rotterdam then catch a direct ferry to Newcastle. With that in mind, and while we waited that evening in a queue for Xenobia to board the *'Autozug'* by its quarter-to-six deadline, Bill rang round the various providers. Expecting to get us booked onto that particular route pretty easily, this goal soon changed to any ferry going anywhere, once he discovered nothing doing.

Not Newcastle at any price - no option it seemed.

"Had to book us onto Rotterdam-to-Hull, instead" he said. "Sorry about that, Mike. All I could get. Reception playing up, total confusion the other end. Lucky I got through at all."

"No worries....." I replied.

When I couldn't have been more wrong.

Nevertheless, within an hour we were glad to be aboard the car-train with Xenobia safely-stowed, pulling out of Verona under leaden skies at bang-on ten-to-seven. Settling down in a five-berth couchette among a hardly-diverse social mix. A passenger-clientele able to afford so expensive a way of moving their private cars about, but disliking its proximity. Too snooty to chat.

"Once we've got this part under our belt and we're finally off the train, then I make it only about a hundred and sixty miles to Rotterdam..." whispered Bill, as if conversation was frowned on. "Three hours, tops, for us to reach Europoort on the autobahn, I'll bet you."

Regrettably, I didn't take his word or try and claim a wager - I could have made a packet.

While Bill thought our troubles were over. Waving an imaginary scarf over his head and chanting *"Eng-elland, Eng-*

elland!" under his breath like he was some dyed-in-the-wool supporter, not a home-sick patriot. Beige middle-aged couples in our compartment looking over their bifocals at him and each other in tetchy mystification. As if there'd been a terrible mistake at ticketing, they're shacked-up with a skinhead.

Stiff letters of complaint to the company about their experience of his company already being drafted in their minds.

We were due in at Dussledorff about half-nine the next morning but this was not to be. That leg of the journey where we first started to get a real sense of some quite serious communication and infrastructure problems which began hitting Europe during this time.

The earliest of them when our train, which was supposed to be an express, kept on slowing to a crawl during the night. Clanking and shuddering. Sometimes coming to a complete halt in the middle of nowhere for twenty or thirty minutes at a stretch.

With no explanation.

Most people peeked out of the window at a solid blackness then huddled down. Pretending to be asleep and hoping these stationary episodes would soon be over, but others called out to the guard when he passed-by on his rounds. A man who didn't seem to have much more idea than we did, just mentioning something generic about *'signalling difficulties'*.

It was early the following morning, while we were sitting in yet another siding, somewhere out in open countryside, when more and more people on the train started announcing their pads and mobile phones weren't working.

You'd have thought from their behaviour it was the end of the world.

By the time we finally crawled into Dusseldorff, a full twenty-four hours later than timetabled, some of us were definitely wondering if it might be.

*"The Golden Age is back,
now a new generation is let down from Heaven above"*

(Eclogue number IV – Vergil, first century B.C.)

- XV -

Stretching the goodwill of the weather gods to their limits, but armed with the confidence of a man living all his life with the sea who knows its unpredictable moods like a patient husband his wife, Carausius had no sooner returned to the applause of troops and citizens awaiting his arrival at Rutupiae; staged his *adventus* into Britannia then sacrificed six black bulls to Jupiter in gratitude; than he was gathering up every warship, ferry and requisitioned merchantman he could muster.

Having filled these with more soldiery, stores and horse than they should sensibly carry, he immediately sent them sailing north at whatever speed they might make when riding so dangerous low in the water.

Did I not say Carausius was a lucky admiral?

His luck was built not on daring but careful observation and long experience. Even in good weather it is three days voyage by sea up from our Gallic-facing British coast to that northern port and naval base they call Petuaria Civitas Parisorum, set on Abus River. Since a safe arrival there was what he promised every crew, and happily for everyone, his mariner's instinct for some unusually-settled sailing conditions of early Autumn proved spot-on. We did not lose a single ship.

As one of the first soldiers he sent there, I was personally glad about this. It had been an anxious voyage all the same, fearing at any moment for some taller swell coming over a   limited freeboard to send our overloaded transport to the bottom.

Whatever my nickname implied, I remained no Merman.

The political and military situation was volatile - why our rapid transit to Petuaria proved worth the risk. The target might have seemed a tiny, run-down little place, hardly deserving of our attention, but it remained an important strategic objective. Vital beachhead towards his winning total control of *Britannia Inferior*, Lower Britain.

Eboracum.

Everyone instinctively understood why our leader needed to act, and fast. If the Upper Province had already declared for the new emperor, here was the one major command left unreconciled. Perversely-loyal to Maximianus in its northern fastness. My old boss, Quintus Bassianus, holding the Sixth Victorious Legion *'Pia Fidelis'* and the Wall-garrisons above, still in his grip. So if Carausius was to consolidate and complete his mastery of both British provinces, then he must take Eboracum soon. Turn the loyalties of its resident soldiers and their brothers on the frontier before it all went up in flames.

If and when we ever got into Eboracum, I'd been warned that Carausius had another special job lined up for me there. In the meantime, on the slimy banks of Abus, mine was more mundane responsibility: as liaison officer directing bivouac for all this infantry piling up in Petuaria. Making sense out of chaos.

The new arrivals' immediate priority was to dig-in. Build a temporary encampment of bank and ditch. Laying out their tent-lines on the open fields of an undefended town where nice questions over whose land they appropriate are immaterial to these men working spades. When there was legal authority enough to be had from an acquiescent council and the supine magistracy of a *Civitas* to once-proud Parisi. Worthies immediately surrendering all jurisdiction upon our soldiers' proclamation inside the forum of Carausius's elevation to the Purple. Craven in their enthusiasm for change.

"Anything, anything the Emperor needs!" what they repeat when I enter their roofless basilica to regularise with the magistrates, via some ragged clerks, the many confiscations now proceeding. If I saw a place poor enough already without the depredation of soldiers, I could not help but despise an indecent willingness to submit their neighbours to every imposition of our regime. If it preserved their own civic titles or status, the monies going with them.

Our wonderful public representatives, eh? If I could entertain the certainty my late father would have handled things differently in Calleva, I should at least recognise the collaboration these idiots offered us as militarily useful.

Of course these councillors' meekly co-operative attitude was aided by the fact we'd long had an advance guard on their patch, anyway. In the shape of the Abus squadron and its marines, holding the harbour and their galley-pens nearby. Our friends in the north: an isolated detachment of the Fleet bold in declaring early for Carausius before anyone else had arrived. Leaving grovelling councillors with little choice in the matter, however secret loyalties might run. Their compliance clinched by our reinforcements arriving in number to disembark in the haven, casually walking down main street to claim the place as a possession of Carausius.

Nor were the town council to know his demands had only just begun. When, from what friend Allectus was telling us, in regular reports to our counsels-of-war up here in the north, those commodities we'd soon be wanting more than land were bulk-grain and precious metal. Enough to feed and pay troops. Allectus acknowledging from Londinium these latter requirements as hardest to satisfy. Silver and gold above all, and why secret orders now went out for our commanders in the field to secure any that they can.

Wherever they find it, whoever the claimant.

At least for the moment though, we enjoyed a short breathing space in Petuaria. Where we could regroup and the momentum or routines of campaign distract his soldiery from wondering when their new ruler would be providing those 'donatives' or cash bonuses traditional to a new reign's beginning. At least it had been an easy invasion for them so far, but he recognised a current state of local weakness which Carausius did not want to see the enemies of Rome or his opponents ever replaying again.

Why its remedy was obvious - Petuaria must be fortified.

If he told her wealthier residents they were funding its construction for their own civic protection – an honoured vanguard of his 'New Golden Age' and a guard against Saxons – the wiser ones at least could still privately wonder if these walls were being raised more against Chlorus and Imperial forces on the Rhine, than any foreign raider.

Whatever the true strategic imperative, our emperor's next order to every detachment arriving at this latest beach-head of his was to pass their time usefully, pending further orders. Construct these stone defences for the western half of town from any materials they could find. Like that masonry we

258

robbed from its crumbling theatre; or those cartloads of limestone blocks a reluctant villa-owner and magistrate found himself obliged to set his estate workers about cutting, from a country quarry overlooking the river.

The true shape of these projected works soon becoming clear: a fortified naval landing to leave the eastern *civitas* and its grumbling residents as blatantly exposed as ever. Their discontent shared with another undertone to unpaid soldiers' gossip about what form their next set of orders might take. A subject widely canvassed in smelly latrines or along the rows of pegged-out tents, their muddy consensus envisaging a glorious march overland. The bold rush to fill that ring of fortified positions which the brighter amateur tacticians confidently imagined Carausius would soon be establishing around Eboracum. His textbook reduction by siege and starvation of a recalcitrant legionary garrison.

Their conversations were speculation but useful for suggesting what the opposition might equally fear. When what we knew for fact was how many forces loyal to our leader's cause, not just infantry units we left behind on quaysides at Rutupiae and Dubris, were slowly making their way north by road instead. Including detachments from garrison forts all over *Superior,* coming to support the emergency battle-group our new emperor was busily assembling here.

Meanwhile, Petuaria's established status as a patrol base for units of the Fleet meant Carausius could reinforce its existing craft with transports now released. Combined, he had a major naval force available on the spot. Immediately capable of blockading the Abus estuary, every river and creek running down into it. Especially the semi-tidal Ouse, which floats supplies by boat up-river into the City of The Legion.

"This will clinch it" he had said. "Close this river down and the Eboracum garrison under Bassianus loses the bulk supply that countless lighters and sailing barges once brought them in, daily. Now I'm seizing all those as well. Plus any Rhineland-registered freighters mooring-up here. When I hear their whole fortress has gone soft, too dependent on the regular delivery of food from places down-river. Only three days away from starvation, with every eight men there needing one pound of meat and a *modius* of grain per day just to fill their empty bellies; six hundred *modii* for the legion. And, if we get our way, soon they won't be getting any."

One of Allectus's own staff-officers, Livius Gallus, chipping-in politely with an update about what stores the legion should have laid-by, their income from *annona*, but Carausius too impatient to listen: "So the informants say his procurators cream off too much for themselves. Well if that's right, tell me something new! Lax with the tax-gatherers, condoning greed and inefficiency, yet friend Bassianus is too miserly to make-up any shortfalls through the marketplace. Letting his garrison's granaries run down from that year's supply required by regulation. Now it's down to weeks. And once those stores are exhausted, his men may get by for a while on whatever might be carted-in. From, say, a twenty or thirty-mile radius, the *territorium* of their legion. But it won't be long before all the farms around and about are completely stripped bare. Soon - by the tenth month, I'd say. That will be the time, eh, Livius?"

Pity the poor civilians of the city and its *Colonia*, the veterans' settlement adjoining. Likely to end-up fending for themselves in competition with a ruthless, starving military. A potent recipe for trouble just as much as Carausius's significant other: his order that all cereal shipments going out from here to the Rhenus should cease at once.

Another decision guaranteed to up the *ante* with Maximianus and his Praetorian Prefect Chlorus over there, while we knew how much the major landowners wouldn't like it over here. And if our British and Gaulish garrisons were going to absorb their cereal output instead of Germania's, then we were going to have to find the means to pay them for it. Quickly.

"At least Chlorus always paid us regular for what he took" said those farmers we hadn't.

"In worthless counters?" said their new emperor. "Believe me, you'll get far better from us."

"I just hope you know what you are doing...." said Allectus sourly, his long, square-jawed profile looking more like an ingot every day. "Not taking on too much at once....."

Now that this one-time quartermaster of our tiny fleet was promoted to *Rationalis Summarium Rationum* for both the provinces in Britannia - including that one we hadn't yet

260

captured - his strategic approval and fiscal counsel became increasingly indispensable to effective governance of the island.

A man whose word counted: a player without peers, not one single competitor.

"There will be no battle" said Carausius. "Trust me. Not even a siege. Provided we can close the Abus and they get no more reinforcements or supplies in from the north, then the Sixth will come over to us without a fight. Believe me, provided three things are done first. One – we make sure to stop them getting those supplies, and while that bastard Bassianus is a different story, let our screw of starvation begin turning on his men. Two - before they surrender, but to ensure their obedience once they do, we must take delivery of the first batches from your Londinium Mint. Coins bearing my head. And while those two work through, the third is an important voyage I must make before autumn's weather finally closes in....."

He'd organised the trip in a day and we were gone by the next.

Three ships only in the convoy. His hunter-killer, the *'Medusa'*, because he loved her and never feared the sea from her decks; the *'Radians'* because she was the largest and most beautifully-decorated vessel we possess, on a mysterious journey whose primary aim was to impress and subdue; and last but not least, the *'Minerva'*. Because she was a tough old barge guaranteed to survive anything, whatever else happens to any of the rest.

Three ships, only.

Aboard them, beside the usual crew and marines, their roster recorded an emperor and one small vexillation of the Second Augustan Legion, supported by a dozen Nubian cavalry of exotic style. Plus that eccentric Vergil-quoting youth who always carries a *seax*, come along by special invitation. And twice the number of *catapultae*, to make up in ship-to-shore firepower what our little expedition might lack in numbers.

In case we should find ourselves in a tight spot and need to get out fast.

Behind us, M.Saturninus Lupus, now promoted to *Praefectus Legionis*, was left to begin the slow reduction of Eboracum while we were away. Now there at least was one deployment you could have an absolute confidence in.

Which is more than could be said about the trip itself.

261

"We are not an island economy. We can't turn our backs on the rest of the world."

(The Right Honourable Nicholas ('*Nick*') Clegg M.P.
U.K. Deputy Prime Minister, at Brussels, 21st July 2011)

- 15 -

Arriving eventually in Dusseldorff's central railway station at Konrad-Adenauer-Platz on the Monday morning, we were delivered into scenes of utter pandemonium. I left Bill to deal with the simpler job of unloading the car and headed off on my own for the passenger information office in the *bahnhof*. Wanting like everyone else to find out what was going on.

From the fast-moving crowds swarming across the station concourse, it looked like all Europe was on the move. Students with huge rucksacks topped with rolled camping-mats, families with small children, migrant workers from the south unable to get home, commuters in raincoats, and armed forces personnel in olive fatigues; all milling about together with no obvious sign of purpose or direction.

All of them fiddling with mobile phones and every kind of mini-computer. As if their *'No Signal'* icon would disappear, if only they switched the wretched thing off and then on again.

It didn't. I checked mine and found the same problem.

And when, if they did find a signal, it was still as if every computer and server in the world was gradually slowing down. Running out of memory. Big Data going floppy and tired. Servers stalling and crashing across continents. Everything taking longer and longer, even simple transactions like debiting stuff on your phone. Getting foreign cash out of the wall in a post-Euro Europe losing its connections: *"Please Try Again"*. Digital dying on its feet, right there in front of you.

Even my attempt to phone work and England, on the last old-fashioned landline left in a public kiosk at the main entrance into the *bahnhof*, so they would know I might be a few days' late. Proving as dismal, a complete failure, although at least I got through. Had enough credit on my card, if only to hear our standard out-of-hours recorded message - though the office wasn't out of hours. While calling my sister's private number in Kent instead obtained the *'number unobtainable'* tone, when it never was before.

Like everyone else, there seemed nothing better left to do than go off looking for more information. Find another explanation, whatever I'd do with that when I got it.

Squinting against sunlight streaming down from a huge window the width of the hall, while trying to read the electronic *"Abfahrten"* departures board conveniently mounted beneath it, a business man ahead turned round and said to me in perfect English: "No trains to Brussels for three days! No spaces left, they're all full..." before stalking off in disgust.

I gave up queuing for the *'Passenger Information'* counter shortly after. This was not the sort of information I wanted and more meaningful stuff seemed in short supply. On the way back I saw the shop selling magazines in the station had a two-day old British newspaper. It was marked-up at an exorbitant price so I didn't lift it or buy, just stood there studying its front page until the stallholder came along tidying. Trying to disrupt misers like me who treat her shop as a lending library, but I'd got the picture. Of problems in France, the headlines dramatic, photographs moreso. Burning lorries and police carrying shields.

"Just back from there myself" said a friendly man beside me, buying a copy of *'Allegemeine Zeitung'* and two American economics magazines. His home was in Tunis but he was currently working for an international agency in Sweden. Reason for his ambitious cross-continental rail journey, currently being attempted against ever-increasing odds:

"They say the French President has sent the riot police in again..." he told me. "Workers on strike in the oil refineries because they haven't been paid, including tanker drivers. Of course they haven't been paid because of this computer crash everyone's suffering, but hardly alone in that. Millions out on the streets. Taxi drivers shutting a terminal at Orly Airport in protest, while their lorry drivers threaten to block the roads. Policemen hurt. Rioters shot. No fuel, no planes, no flights. It's a nightmare you Brits would be wise not entering. Do not try to go home via France, my English friend, and don't even think of flying."

263

I grinned: "That's France for you! Just practising for their summer - *fermeture annuelle* - when all this is normal. But I do hope you get home OK yourself. Good luck!"

He smiled back: "Yes, and you too. Have a nice day!"

I called after his retreating frame: "Sorry, but I've made other arrangements...."

The road journey Bill and I endure from Germany into Holland the living proof of that.

"These remoter shores were now circumnavigated for the first time by a Roman fleet, which established as a result that Britain is in fact an island. At the same time it discovered and subjugated the Orcades islands, hitherto unknown. Thule, too was sighted, but no more was done because their orders sent them no further and winter was close at hand. But they reported this sea as sluggish and heavy on the oar, not rising in a high wind like other seas."

(Cornelius Tacitus, *'The Agricola' X,* 2nd Century A.D.)

- XVI -

We Romans have known the marine geography and topography of this area for centuries, even if it took a Greek to survey it properly for us. One of the first men to map and make the journey we embarked on, as a serious expedition.

Except Ptolemy chose to go in summer and Carausius left it till autumn.

The Abus when we returned to its embrace felt rough enough for me, churning brown and wide, but when we left the mouth of her estuary and emerged into the open ocean, the going got harder still. Nausea returning to the throat and my customary vigil by the stern rail. What the Nubians and their poor horses made of the whole experience is hard to imagine, but we must endure together. Lucky to be sharing in such a positive, character-building experience - as an Aristotelian in the party would doubtless choose to put it.

There would be no refuge, no port beyond Petuaria we dare enter, for fear their guardians stayed obedient to the authority of Northern Command and its rival Governor-General. Not until we were safely north of Rome's Imperium could we risk landfall again.

Safer in the Kingdom of The Picts than beneath Eboracum's sway.

A fresh line of wooden signal towers newly-built by Bassianus against them stood barely visible - occasional lonely fang on a tilting, linear horizon. Before it fell over them, the crumbling cliffs they fringe once also held our outpost of Praetorio, but today they stay smokeless, their towers' semaphore silent. Reliable sign, perhaps, that we'd kept far enough offshore to float-by undetected. Passing the night at sea but navigating by the moon and stars, masthead beacons left unlit, we recognise next morning from miles offshore a bluish haze of chimney and oven smoke rising high in still air above Arbeia. 'Fort of the Arabs' - supply base and terminus to the Wall.

Last signpost of Rome.

Hoping the busy cooks of Arbeia would never notice the billowing sails of three Roman warships heading north into enemy territory, on a dangerous journey no one has attempted this generation gone. Beyond some vague idea of a hunt for a king, our objective remained a mystery. One our fine admiral, the emperor, declined to share with us:

"When we have arrived. When we are in position to make it happen. Then I will explain."

Beyond Rome's sway, we could risk a changed bearing. One that took us closer-in. Towards a coastline of enormous sands and rolling dunes, sweeping far inland to cultivated realms strangely empty of humanity.

Where that fear of always being watched only grew the stronger.

Watching us was one thing, catching us another. Only warships like ours could tackle a mission like this; fast, superlight and manoeuvrable as they are, with extra-shallow draught. Our enemies have nothing remotely to match them. Sail power having its place of course, essential to quicker progress on the open sea, but it is oar-power which will let us go so much closer inshore. Into more unfamiliar shallows than any sailboat would risk. Oars and a slight keel giving us the confidence and our crews the extra control to beach these galleys undamaged on an incoming tide; whether to take on fresh water from streams running down to the coast or enable a military reconnaissance of locations on the land.

Once nearer to landward, there was so much more to see. I remember the many kittiwakes, or else those stiff-winged fulmars which followed in our foamy wake, floating at ease in the turbulent air left behind by sails. Innumerable shags or cormorants, perched like black priests at augury upon the treacherous tips of rocks. Gathered in silent warning to the hidden danger of their sandy shores.

Thousands of screaming gulls circling two enormous white-topped plugs of pillared rock - one set close on the land, the other just out to sea. Stepped back from the sea and between them like a beached whale rose a third projection - The Dun of Peledur. Capital town and stronghold of the Votadini, client kingdom of Rome and corn-supplier to legions.

Hungry for our bounty, silent witness to our decline, useless to our mission. The one tribe in all Caledonia least likely to cause Romans trouble, but we'd be foolish to imagine them harmless. Common sense warning of one immediate danger – that the Votadini might detain our party in hope of silver; of ingratiating themselves with the current Governor of Lower Britain. Our opponent Bassianus still their biggest customer. So we ignored the siren calls in this chance for shore-leave and kept well clear, staying offshore.

Even if we'd here rebuffed a client, it was apparent from this same point in the voyage how our leader no longer evaded notice but positively began to court it.

Three fine ships a-sailing by, one September day in the morning.

The domed heads of seals bobbing above the waves, black eyed and plaintive like shipwrecked survivors begging for rescue. Lost souls. The spirits of drowned sailors come back to haunt the shoals that claimed them, warning those who follow of a watery fate.

A warning it seems we cannot take, pressing on into danger as we must.

In brilliant sunshine, the river pilot who became an admiral, the admiral who'd become an emperor, gave out his orders for our sudden change in heading. Showing himself still the master of his old craft, reluctant to delegate. On a bearing that would take our little fleet further-in, penetrating towards the narrowest point of that miles-wide firth which Nature carves so deep into the country of the Caledones. A land of hostile alliances, as much against their own as any Roman kind.

Bodotria Aestuarium.

Its wave-flecked crossing overseen by yet another famous native fortress, set afar on a squared-off plinth of dark-black basalt. That distant citadel Caledones call *'Ei-Dun',* their *'Strong Place of the King'*. Where Votadini cease and Venicones grow was always unclear, but in that year our intelligencers told us it should be somewhere close-by hereabouts.

While next year might be different.

How changed it was from those happier, safer days when Rome last occupied and commanded these coasts, a century and more ago. As with the barbarian confederations of the Rhine, so now the Caledones respond - first to Rome's threat and now to her dwindling power. Combining with their own, under a new kind of men like the one we sought today – a breed of charismatic kings.

The word on the wind is of how old divisions and blood-feuds, between farming Venicones and warlike Vacomagi or Monagha, now fade away before the Maeatae. Merging themselves with a secretive hill-people become a new name in the land. One to whose ring even our Votadini friends are said to incline sympathetic heads. And how more distant Caledonian tribes yet are gradually absorbed into that creeping kingdom men call *'Pictavia'*.

How or when any of this crystallised, not even our best-embedded spies could tell us, but we knew its drift for the fluid politicking of a lawless land. On a Caledonian sea where we were intruders and hospitality unlikely, athwart their only road.

If as we guessed it, the unblinking 'Eye of the Venicones' was indeed monitoring our every move, then we wondered for whose benefit. Not for their own, surely, but for some other, greater king - that one Carausius sought? It was miles away but high, and if we could see their Dun, then those on the Dun could surely see us. Yet these watchers of Ei-Dun let us go by with such unlikely degrees of inactivity and indifference as surely spoke volumes. Almost as if they understood our mission and expected it. Even before we did.

As if Carausius wanted them to know.

Eventually leaving this significant landmark fully aft, our steersmen took its cue to turn their oars about. At that point where "...*offshore gulls seem walking, not flying*" how they quaintly put it. Sending the painted eyes fronting our bows to face off and away, finding us a way over and across the waters of this mighty firth. To follow its opposite shore seawards once again, further *"nor'-by-nor'-east"* than most on board have ever done before.

Me included.

To fly the flag and make patrol of a pretty coast whose rich farmland and clustering pine were prelude to our two biremes and single trireme emerging close together under full sail and leaning round the corner. Into a boundless bay. Garlanded to its southern left with sidelong sheets of sharpest rock, angled like black blades to slash oncoming waves into pieces below a line of unscaleable, red or yellow cliffs. Before us and full ahead, that magnificent western wall of level dunes described in old reports. A golden bar of flat and harmless sand onto which we knew three Roman galleys could safely be run for the night.

It might be beyond living memory - seventy years gone-by from the very last Roman armies to march this far north in strength, constantly supplied from the sea as they would have been - but all the route-maps, naval charts and intelligence reports describing in detail every cove and beach, every bay and river-mouth, every hill-fort or marching camp; remain as scrolls in our Army Records Office. On maps decorated with such evocative place names of the uttermost north as *"Horreae Classis"* - 'Granary of the Fleet'. References ready to be consulted and sites available to be revisited by any ambitious army commander with a mind to. Wanting to chance his arm again, if an emperor asked. Which is where, and until the time of Carausius, they have happily remained.

Safely in the archive, unborrowed and unread. Dusty, unvisited, and wisely untouched.

We brought no army, made no invasion force. We burnt no villages. The only soldiers present were our normal complement of marines, four *contubernia* of legionaries, and a small detachment of unusual cavalry. That corps whom Carausius had shipped aboard; more for effect than tactical advantage. A bodyguard, in short.

Ours was a diplomatic mission.

"I have decided it is time to go and see my cousin Fergus...." he announced to his assembled officers from the forecastle. One of the very earliest policy decisions we received from this new Emperor of Britain, our Caesar of the Narrow Seas.

The first recorded incumbent of such office to be ginger.

269

The first recorded incumbent of such office.

'*Cousin Fergus*' was a figure so remote and legendary to anyone living south of the Emperor's Wall, he might well have been invented. This staple of travelling harpists, that semi-apocryphal character: Onengus macFerganus, High King of the Monagha; Swordsman to the Maeatae and now - astonishingly - pre-eminent warlord to the Painted People. An incredible development. One shadowy leader who, by guile and charm, had reportedly succeeded against every odd and a thousand years of hate by forging the feuding tribes of Caledonia and the mysterious peoples of Pictland into a single confederation of common purpose.

One smouldering state of united malice, as may please them all. "*All Men*" indeed, as Germans might put it, and more bad news for Rome. As we decline and fragment into petty divisions, so our enemies merge and grow.

Beyond our target's many other titles and this one, striking achievement, no more was known of him. But our Emperor Carausius knew differently.

And so he should. The man was related.

The Monagha and our leader's tribe – the Menapii or Monapii – were strands of the same line; distant chips off the same ancient block. Found in Gallia, Hibernia and Caledonia, even if totally different in character. There being a perverse strain in the psyche of the Menapii which has had them drawing attention to themselves, getting into trouble, for centuries past. *Vide* that mention in Julius Caesar's book "*De Bello Gallico*" as a people needing sterner treatment from his legions; those multiple defeats administered by Drusus Germanicus later. Yet their blood relatives, the Monagha or Meána, seem a quieter folk. Somehow managing a lower profile among the shifting tribal names and loyalties of Caledonia, they might have remained unknown to history forever, had not Gnaeus Julius Agricola filled their homeland with legions and ringed it with warships in a firestorm of conquest. One which could have stayed permanent if a jealous and distrustful Emperor Domitian hadn't ordered Agricola's sudden recall. Two hundred and two years ago, exactly.

But now we are back.

Where the one thing which hadn't changed was how much it upsets imperial masters when military commanders are seen to do a good job. As our little admiral recently found to his cost. The how and the why of his coming back to Caledonia. As if to compensate for the ancient timidity of Domitian, the modern cruelties of Maximian.

Those obsolete charts from the Record Office showed him how an old marching camp of the Severan campaigns, or maybe even Agricola's, should still be discoverable if not useable. Up there on the dunes which crown tall cliffs to our south, above this enormous bay - a handy beacon-site not far beyond. And if the standard military handbook would dictate we spend the night up there, where earthworks could assure our safety, these relics would do nothing to protect valuable ships left down on the beach. Why it is, and for the sake of viable transport for our return, we stay huddled in their carvel hulls, down there on the ribbed sands. Ships' anchors ready run-out on chain for when tides rush-in at morning.

We laid a long line of big bonfires at a distance between our grounded vessels and the dunes. With a picket of marines as sentry to feed the flames and watch for whatever moves beyond their flare. Knowing there was certainly something when, throughout the night's dreary watches, there would come the occasional shriek, whoop, or call like no nightbird or creature you ever heard.

Ghosts and spirits, or maybe just men.

The *catapultae* mounted on every ship were manned all night and closely targeted on this red band of fire, so that anything daring to step through and into the light would get the neat, square hole of an iron catapult bolt imprinted through their chest bone and out the other side.

Spirit of the Shades or no.

Fortunately for our mission and all concerned nothing ever did, but sometimes, when this strange scurrying and calling in the shadows became particularly irritating, Carausius himself would get up from his cot to stand in the bows of the *'Medusa'* and shout out loud: "Go tell your chief that Caraus of the Monapii is come in peace to visit his blood kinsman, the High King of Maeatae and Monagh, and that there is no man living who should dare prevent their meeting."

271

After he had announced that, we had no more trouble and no more noises before dawn, but it was a frightening voyage we and our galleys were set on, travelling so far beyond the writ of Rome's great power and laws.

With no belief we'd ever get away with it.

"A number of sovereign states uniting into one Commonwealth, and appointing a supreme power to manage the affairs of the union, do necessarily and unavoidably part with and transfer over to such supreme power so much of their own sovereignty, as is necessary to render the ends of the union ineffectual, otherwise their confederation will be an union without bands of union, like a cask without hoops, that may and probably will fall to pieces, as soon as it is put to any exercise which requires strength."

('Dissertation on the Political Union And Constitution
of the Thirteen United States of North America' 1783)

273

In the main passenger lounge on the Rotterdam-to-Hull Ferry, none of the live television monitors were working. The staff had used their initiative to rig-up the central VCR and its player instead so that some of them could show a few old films from the last century. Reruns of popular TV shows. A facility I appreciated but the sight of which only seemed to provoke our younger passengers more. Make them more irritable, left as they were at so complete a loss without the comfort of 'phone or tablet screen to fidget over. The Internet not working well either. Worldwide, or so we heard.

"We need to know what's going on...." a few people kept on saying plaintively to the purser, as if the ordinary crew of a Hull car-ferry could fix an international crisis. All he could do with the persistent ones like this was smile grimly and give out a company form. Mutter something about customer feedback being important to them, before moving on to the next set of moaning minnies demanding their money back.

Why information is so vital to the powerless I did not then understand, but what I knew was going on was that we were all of us lucky to be on one of the few ships heading north. Heading home. One whose Master was old and adaptable enough to remember how to navigate his way from Rotterdam to England and back up the east coast without access to satellites or radio beacons. Relying instead on paper-based charts and sonar, like they used to do in the old days.

The pity of it lay in wondering how many other perfectly-serviceable ships were left confined to port. For want of a captain or owner willing to take similar chances, do likewise. Too many of them registered to the nation of Drake and Nelson - a country grown prouder of her international pre-eminence in Risk Management Consultancy than honouring such names. While according to the operator's brochure I found by the stairs, the normal passenger complement of *"The Pride of Hull"* is about thirteen hundred people, and she's registered in the Bahamas. (So much for my *'Nation of Nelson'* theory....). Whatever the flag of convenience, or insurance implications, it looked to me like a courageous Master had allowed a lot more passengers than that onto his vessel from the hordes thronging Rotterdam's quayside, desperate for help.

There seemed to be people everywhere, sitting in every aisle and gangway with many more left out on deck. Fortunately it wasn't raining, but in the 'Dunkirk' atmosphere prevailing amongst an uncritical crowd only grateful to be rescued, I don't think anyone would have cared too much if it had.

At the best of times this was an overnight fourteen-hour crossing, minimum, but these were not. Why I realised there'd be more than enough chance to talk, interrogate my companion. Having been amongst the first wave aboard, we were lucky to have grabbed a pair of recliners in a corner to see out the crossing. I thought their slight degree of privacy gave an ideal opportunity to broach with Bill that interesting question of all that wandering off on his own I'd observed from him, during the Mille Miglia.

"Doing a Captain Oates...." how I jokily put it.

And when I did, his apologies were as unexpectedly immediate as effusive. Though on whether sincere or true, I intend to reserve judgement.

"Look, I'm sorry, Michael. I really hope it didn't spoil the event for you. Only sorry if you felt it occasionally left you trailing around after me at times, but constituency duties to be done...to be done."

"Constituency, Bill? In Italy?"

"Errr, yes, in the sense of my wider ward. The group I lead at Strasbourg."

"Anti-Europe."

"That's a gross simplification. Unjustly negative. I prefer to say pro-Britain."

"What's left of it. And haven't your little lot left all that separatist stuff a bit late by now? Seeing as we're stuck in a club where once you've joined you're never allowed to leave."

"Maybe we have but people have approached me."

"I saw that. But what people, Bill, who are they?"

"Let's just say they represent a diverse catchment..."

"Oh joy, but please don't give me all that PC stuff. What about the house in the hills? The one with an electronic gate and a Ferrari parked out front?"

"Former Italian senator, now a European commissioner. Someone like me who has climbed inside the machine. If only, as he insists, for the sake of discovering how it works. How best to get his country out of it."

"A kindred spirit?"

"A fellow activist."

"We've talked about this before, haven't we? When the resentment Europe evokes in people risks dangerous as well as honest forms of nationalism. So what do you know about this guy? Is he safe?"

"Yes, that he's a democrat like me. Both of us needing all the help we can get, knowing what we're up against - in our home countries. This is a game that could well get rough, Michael. The Establishment has a long memory, ways of getting you back. Includes some people who don't like dissent, might see me as a target."

"A target, Bill?"

"You heard it here first. Watch out for me, Mikey. Someone needs to."

276

"They tattoo their bodies not only with likenesses of animals but with all kinds of drawing."

(Herodian, Roman historian, writing c.240 A.D.)

- XVII -

In the morning, our vessels rose and floated without trouble and their anchors caught; the screen of marines wading and swimming back towards us from the beach to be hauled back on board, swords gripped in their teeth. It was a beautiful place to be on a sunny day and it seemed that even our shore patrol were loath to leave.

There was an intuitive sense of getting close to those our leader came to find. That we would be wise not to wander too far off or away from their best chance of making themselves known to us.

The anchors were brought up on their cables and then we drifted slowly back out into that limitless bay with only a little help from our oarsmen needed. The occasional stroke given now and then, ash blades chopping through seaweed.

The shiny backs of dolphins and porpoises rose and tumbled besides us, playing with our ships, while gannets and puffins sunned themselves on nearby rocks. Our sailors, more superstitious than any people I ever knew, seemed in relaxed good humour. Taking these creatures' happy demeanour for positive signs against that obvious danger into whose gaping jaws we otherwise thrust ourselves.

Above us, an immense sky of the clearest blue arcing over an azure sea as calm as any pond, the broad strand of the beach we'd quit empty in all directions. Only the northern shore of its enormous curve was yet to greet our keels, so Carausius ordered a leisurely progress be made over there. As if for completeness and to see if anyone - or anything - might be waiting for us somewhere along its length - armed with news of his arrival.

Approaching this next landfall was further off and took us longer than you might expect, slowing while some rowers took their rest. Right across the yawning maw of yet another, second

277

firth, one whose mapped entry we could successfully avoid but incoming currents still deserve a seaman's respect. Could easily drag us in.

That estuary we call *'Teva'*.

About one hundred and fifty years ago, the fertile lands it accessed had for a while - if only briefly and technically - counted in law and operationally as territory within our greater Roman Empire. Under the *Pax Romana* and its blessings. Sadly those days are long gone and now we range deeper into *Barbaricum* than our shrunken British Fleet has dared to do in years.

Enemy territory.

By the time we'd rowed over to the far side of the bay, the shore we're come from had retreated to a distant lilac smudge on the glowing horizon behind. Visible only by squinting against its golden glare. The razor-edged rocks we approached next becoming more visible, potential anchorages fewer.

It was a line of seven stationary horsemen ahead which first alerted us to one likely landing place, a suitably-flat beach sheltered between two flanking headlands.

Sitting and watching.

"Take her in!" said Carausius to the *trierarchus* as soon as he saw them. All three galleys going straight in as he commanded, bows-first and grinding to a halt on sable sands nearby.

Hair and plaids and manes flew in the wind, but the riders never moved one inch until the galleys drove right up the beach towards them, when their horses started dancing.

Unhelmeted. With no shields.

A sign of peace?

"I am Caraus of the Monapii and Emperor of the Romans, come in peace to visit my blood kinsman, the High King of Maeatae and Monagh" he said.

Feet away.

Standing astride the foremast of the beached *'Minerva'*, the chinking shoulder pieces of his scale-mail armour were nicely edged in purple leather, but there would be no barrier could stop an arrow fired at this close a range.

Beyond and behind the horsemen, there was a screen of birch trees and alder scrub that could have hidden anything, or anyone.

Including an archer.

The tension crackled in the air like a taut bowstring until their lead rider spoke up in a halting, broken Latin: "I am Niall The Bringer. Of those peoples you Romani call '*Picti*'. Sent here at His command. To bring you from this coast to the place where He waits. You will follow us now!"

What our leader thought I cannot say, but my own distaste for the man was immediate.

Niall might not have been the brightest linguist in the tribes, but the shining lights of hatred were no less brilliant in his nasty little eyes. Their steady message seemed clear enough to anyone with half a mind to see. Nor did I enjoy reading what symbolic meaning a line of loopy beasts tattooed across his forehead might add to the detail of that one-way journey into oblivion we found ourselves commissioning with him.

This Niall as our chosen guide.

As an infantry-trained officer I could pass the time recognising every classic feature normally alerted-to by the standard tactics manual. Those points we usually take as meaning *"Get Yourselves Out Of There - And Fast!"* As an exercise in good revision, it proved we'd found the set. The only distinction being that we're inbound, not out.....

May Fortuna and Victory protect us!

There was the clanking sound of *catapultae* winding up behind me, our only hope Immortals might. "I am coming with you" I said, climbing up to stand beside the Emperor.

"You and the Nubians" said Carausius.

Getting them and their dozen horses off the *'Radians'* proved a right palaver. Once they and those two more mounts needed for Carausius and myself were lowered down, calmed down, and assembled on the beach our galleys backed out under oars to await developments offshore. Thirty-two legionaries left behind, along with a portable capstan for winching our ships back in and some very clear instructions to dig-in and hold the beach till our return. Against the entire Pictish nation, if need be. Checking their swords and grumpily tightening their kit, as if they really could.

You had to admire their grit. For all they knew, this place might as much mark their end as ours. Somewhere no sensible captain would willingly return to - for anyone's sake.

Despite all this military activity, the line of seven Celts waiting for us on the beach still hadn't moved away. Remarkably confident. At least no surprise attack or arrow came winging-in from any friends of theirs in the bushes before our ships were safely gone.

"It'll be alright!" Carausius had whispered to me from his horse and winked, but I really didn't believe him. This cove or somewhere near it was where we all would surely die.

Fourteen of us and seven of them. We rode off in silence - into another world.

.The path we followed in single file rose steadily up from the coast towards a gentle, wind-kissed ridge. Passing through this dense belt of coppiced birch and waving alder where I and my companions most expected ambush (but found none came) brought us out onto a pastoral landscape of heavily-cultivated fields. Its appearance was quite a surprise. Riding across the stubble of newly-harvested oats or barley, I had thought to see only wilderness and devastation, but instead encountered every comfortable sign of industrious husbandry and productive agriculture. Not what my urban prejudices imagined from a brutish nation whose hatred for the Roman hangs over Britannia like a cloud.

I suppose even Caledones or the Picti must somehow feed themselves.

Hate was one explanation for their lack of conversation, while the language barrier gave a second, but coming in third was pure astonishment. These blue-painted Picti had never seen black men before.

Let alone our Crocodile Soldiers.

The First 'Numerus' of Nubian Light Horse are an exceptional regiment by any standards. Recruited from the nomadic tribes of North Africa, they wear little armour but make up for its lack with the weight of iron they carry as weaponry. Mainly of the throwing type. Come to us via the Tenth Theban Legion whom they faithfully served as scouts and skirmishers, it was only by some fluke of deployment that they were outside Gesoriacum on that miserable, rainy day when Egyptian comrades were ordered south to meet their joyful deaths. Otherwise the Nubians could have expected the same fate, or at least those Christians rumoured to be riding with them would.

280

Men of passionate loyalty, the Nubians were devastated by the loss of so many fellow-countrymen in the legion. Isolated and bewildered, too, in a foreign land - until our new emperor literally gave them a home. Absorbing them into his reconstituted 'Army of Britain & Gaul'. A new home but a cold one. Unimaginably far from baking deserts to which they could never return and always missed, but a safer one for all that.

Or so they thought.

At least until Carausius - their own *'little father'* as they affectionately call him - rewarded an unquestioning commitment by leading a dozen of their best horsemen into what looks like the biggest set-up for an enemy ambush since M.Quintillius Varus took three doomed legions into the bosky heart of Germania.

And it was a brilliant idea. The best Carausius had yet.

In the fog-bound provinces of Britain, even the most jaded student of pageantry will concede the sight of this First Numerus of Theban Nubians in their parade-finery provides memorable novelty. A guaranteed crowd-pleaser, even for the sophisticates of Londinium. So try and imagine what these crouching warriors of coastal Pictavia, these men of forest and bog who'd never seen a Roman ship before and probably no Roman, must make of our black cavalry.

Riding unannounced into their sacred, stinking enclosure, past stones carved with rings. On bigger horses than all Caledonia can muster, adorned from head to toe in the scaly skin and unblinking eyes of a dead Egyptian crocodile. No wonder the men of Pictland we pass seem struck dumb and immobile. Boggling at the sight.

Hard put not to cower down or cry, like their womenfolk or children.

I'd wager no-one present ever saw anything to match it. Just the appearance of our Nubian friends terrifies the enemy. Thanks to them it seems, the momentum of shock they bestow, we ride into the dun unscathed with no-one to stand against us. Dogs howl, warriors blanch, women hide their faces, and small children run away screaming when the Emperor Carausius and his reptilian escorts come a-riding, into the compound of Fergus.

You will notice my word 'compound. Used advisedly, for military intelligence' sake.

Never having travelled outside the empire or into these parts before, I naturally expected a High King to receive us, if receive us he would, inside a fortress. Upon some gale-torn hilltop which generations of his people ringed with those meandering ditches and palisades no tribe ever owned manpower to line with warriors. Those curving contravallations the backward Celt still imagines for the writings of earthly strength and power. A place like Ei-Dun, or The Dun of Peledur.

Well, this was no Dun. Personally, I would have called it a farm, just a glorified farm, but they would have called it a *coria*, a gathering place for the tribe. Its boundaries at least displayed the usual markers all the same. The odd human thigh-bone or piece of upper arm, hung on palings: "*The ghost fence*". So far, so conventional. Delineations of title defending the landholding with magic. Nothing new about that. Likewise the traditional collection of de-fleshed and bleached skulls, impaled by way of decoration over its principal entrance. Discreet reminder to those who enter of what its residents will do to any who cross them. Even their own.

We heard drums to announce our arrival but, for us, the place announced itself. Like the shanties of Rotomagus, the smell of excrement hit us first – human and animal. We passed empty cattle or sheep pens holding some and entered an inner ring of ditches full of more.

Inside them rose a dense cluster of many thatched huts, anchored in a trampled sea of mud. Supported on huge beams, their conical roofs come right down to the ground but don't hide the stone-framed entrance-ways to tunnels running undereath. I'd heard of these subterranean structures and the legends which go with them. Where the Picti live underground, concealed through winter's dark and stoking their resentment of Rome.

If they do, you can hardly blame them.

Even a serious historian like Cornelius Tacitus makes no bones about what Roman rapacity did to these people, two hundred years ago. Read it for yourself in his biography of an illustrious father-in-law. That general who first led the metal legions of Domitian across this rolling landscape, pouring unannounced off ships like ours in an attack of unprecedented scale. Whether you take the words he reports as literal, or merely symbolic, he has the Caledonian leader, Calgacus, addressing their doomed, tribal army before the final battle at Mons Graupius. At the point of our greatest military triumph in these islands, was clever old Tacitus really implying some sort of moral defeat?

If so, how ironic.

A Roman writer placing the ultimate condemnation of our civilisation and its impact into the mouth of a barbarian about to become its latest victim: *"They create a desolation and they call it peace"* what he's supposed to have said.

And maybe he did.

Two centuries on and the tide is turning. We are failing and they coalesce. Now an Emperor of Rome is come to beg, and I knew what form his request was likely to take.

Beyond the huts stood a tall tower, built without mortar from thin, flat stones piled one upon another in the shape of a giant bottle tapering upwards from a broad waist. Like a lookout station or a lighthouse. The nearest thing we had seen to a fortification; a primitive structure which one *contubernium* of eight legionaries could have captured, searched and burned inside the space of half an hour. Killing all the occupants. But not today. Not when one man was seated like a king on a raised mound before it; hunting dogs at his feet and surrounded by his many warriors.

Men who were armed.

To get to the man at their centre we had to ride right through the middle. Looking neither to right nor left, their drumming louder in our ears. Aided by a dozen cavalry, each of them cowled with the yellow-eyed head, grinning jaws and jagged teeth of a Nile crocodile draped round a brass-bound helmet. The beast whose complete and scaly pelt spread out over their shoulders before running down to cover the saddle. The repulsive, reptilian vision which got us in there safe. Through crowds parting with gasps, a people cleft by shock.

That, and kinship.

If his followers were stunned, only Onengus son of Ferganus; High King of All Monagha and Monapia, Hound of the Venicones, Swordsman to the Maeatae, and now deputed War

Lord to the Painted People; only he remained unmoved and sitting down. Completely unimpressed.

Older than I'd expected, above all he just seemed tired. A balding, baggy-eyed and jowly journeyman, about the same age as our emperor.

Almost ordinary.

It was only on looking more closely that I understood how those familiar aspects making him appear ordinary to me were what would make him extraordinary to his native followers.

No beard, no hair. No crown.

Speaking fluent Latin, with a Celtic countryman's burr.

Round his neck on a thong hung a bronze plate of incised script. A metal certificate, recording honourable discharge from twenty-five years' service in an irregular unit of Britons guarding our Danube frontier: another *Numerus*. Roman writing cast in bronze, its meaning more powerful than words. Now its bearer was come back home armed with its experience, empowered by its message. Rome had taught him everything he knew about the discipline of soldiering and soon he would use it against us.

But not today. Traditional rules of hospitality and kinship saw to that. These people may have almost nothing, living in squalor, but their firm principles of etiquette dictate how food, drink and even shelter should always be offered to travellers.

Even to *Romani*.

Carausius dismounted and came forward to the foot of the mound, his bare arms open to show himself unarmed. The High King stood up and did the same, descending its green knoll to greet him as an equal, followed by his dogs. A singular concession at whose sight I saw much nudging and whispering pass along the shaggy lines of warriors. If their chosen words of greeting were ritual formula on either side, I sensed a genuine recognition too; of men who had somehow met before. They hugged like blood brothers then sat down on folding, Roman chairs of lacquered yew. A wooden table of quality to match, obviously part of a set, was quickly brought out then covered with apples, bread, cheese and wine.

I dismounted and stood defensively behind the Emperor's seat, right arm resting on my *seax,* but the Nubians remained on horseback. Fanned out in two neat lines of six upon either side. Curved Persian swords laid on their shoulders ready for action, as if it really mattered. Disciplined professionals to the very end but, just like mine, their ostentatiously-alert positioning was a magnificent irrelevance.

We were all of us surrounded. Surrounded and outnumbered.

Looking up from this brown-ploughed ridge-top, turning back to face the way we had come, I could see our three ships waiting offshore. Bobbing peacefully at anchor, sunlight glinting on gilding. A picture of Roman sea-power and safety. Far beyond catapult range, they could never help us. Miles from the sea, we were outnumbered by a margin of hundreds-to-one and our hosts could have killed us in seconds, whenever they wanted.

Imagining our heads on the gate.

All the more marvellous then, how we Roman soldiers and the enemy warriors could watch and listen quietly while our two leaders talked and broke their fast together, like a private reunion of two old friends. Oblivious to the boisterous horde of watchers around the mound and above them, craning from the tower. A family get-together.

Carausius stroked and pulled at the brindled head and muzzle of the King's biggest dog, a grey and white wolfhound with solemn brown eyes which placed its jaw on his lap. Like a man in a house where he is regular visitor and the hounds have come to know and trust him. As if this old dog recognised him too, one to another.

The High King laughed. There may have been Latin letters stamped in bronze on the plate upon his chest but the thick, gold torcs wound around his neck and arms were pure Celt, stating his kingship and power. A river to his people.

When they drank wine, it must be Roman though. A delicate Rhenus white, drunk from glossy Gaulish goblets. The brick-red samian ware. This Pictavia was a weird and alien world, but not so totally cut off from Rome after all.

Their slaves or servants went along the line, offering pieces of a coarse, dark bread for me and our cavalrymen off a thick wooden board carved in relief with the image of a wolf. Nicely-done, too. Not a Roman wolf, but you could still see it was a proper wolf all the same.

And a golden water which caught in our throats like fire: 'Water of Life' they call it.

"These are fine ships you have brought with you, brother. To think back to when you were just a young skipper out in the delta, and me serving on the Danube. While look at us now" said the king. "With you a Caesar!"

"It was the soldiers' decision. Not mine. The army has spoken. And maybe through them, the people. But if I am to finish this thing, I must deal with Quintus Bassianus, the governor of *Inferior*. And bring his troops round as well."

"The Sixth, and the Wall garrison?"

"Who will be rushing south from their entrenchments to reinforce him fast, even as we speak".

"Empty forts and empty roads. What luck! That great opportunity my people have been waiting a generation for...."

"And the reason why I am here."

"You have something to ask me?"

"Yes, that the tribes do not go south. That you hold them back. That the Maeatae and the Pictish nations do not cross the Emperor's Wall. Not while I deal with Bassianus."

"A Wall where my scouts speak of unbarred gates swinging on their hinges and turrets left unmanned. Of catapults slack and bows unstrung. They say the Red-Crest is gone and the red kite left to roam on your middens. Buzzards where once there were Eagles."

"Even so. It is this that an Emperor has sailed north for; to ask of a High King who is his kinsman in blood. That you do this thing for me, as the very first and probably the last of the Monapii ever to be raised to the Purple. For the sake of our kinship and for our friendship. Mindful of that great honour which Rome's soldiers have done to me, and maybe through me, to you and yours."

"And how far does the writ of that Purple run? One half of Britain and a little part of Gaul. What chance does this Caesar of the Monapii have of lasting any time? When the Rhine and Danubian armies and the best in Italia can be ranged against him tomorrow, what chance does he really have?"

"They are calling me the Caesar of the Narrow Seas. I hold the channel with no opposition because they have no navy, no answer to me. The *Classis Britannica* is all declared for me, along with nine legions."

"Nine *full* legions?"

"Well, three complete, plus several detachments….and I know the Sixth will come round."

"When you have killed Bassianus?"

"Sadly, I cannot imagine it any other way…."

"A provincial governor, a loyal general?"

"Who defies his Emperor…"

"In obedience to another one…."

"A murdering Illyrian barbarian…"

"These distinctions are difficult to make, dear Caraus, and should be drawn with care. Remember, like you I served under Maximianus once, and what will the real Romans make of someone like you, yet another provincial usurper?"

"The answer to Britain's problems. Security and prosperity. Freedom from persecution. An empire for *all* men – even men like us. This time is different – it's what folk are waiting for."

"You stand for all of that? The dangerous life of a separatist, the lonely life? It is a dozen years since what they call the Gallic empire was crushed. That separate Roman state of a northern Europa. Postumus against Gallienus. You and I remember it well. When I was out on the Danube, our officers used to say you Romani in Britannia had got too used to being apart. That it was a good thing when a strong man like Aurelian came along to reunite the whole empire, crushing the Goths into the bargain. Long campaigns I even had a hand in myself, back in those days when I served your rulers. If so, my cousin, is not your latest venture another backward step?"

"No, it will be a forward one! Britain is an island and ships are the answer. With a strong navy I know it can stand alone. Independent from the continent but in-touch and Roman still. Keeping Franks and Saxons off our shores in a way Rome no longer can. No disrespect to my brother emperors, but no-one's tried this before, not like this. I really believe my idea can last, without me threatening theirs."

"You are my brother in blood. My cousin in law. Born of our kin. So I will promise you this. For as long as Caraus of the Monapii is Emperor in Britain, then the Maeatae and the Painted People will never come south. Once you are gone, however distant that time may be, then it will be a different story."

"I have your word?"

"My word. And my peoples' word. You have yourself a treaty. When you are gone, we will come south and then there will be no stopping us. We will sweep the Eagles into the sea. But until then, you have our word."

His warriors watched us go in puzzled silence, lines of blue-painted faces with pointed beards, shaven heads and their curious pony tails - the *ceudgelt* - looking up in wonder as we rode past their serried spears. Visitors they'd never forget.

No longer the enemy. Our new allies.

"Well, I'd call that a success!" said Carausius cheerfully to me, as we slipped out through the screen of woodland and down onto the landing beach.

He was right. And from this distance of years, I can confirm to you now that Onengus macFerganus and his people kept to the promise he made us on that memorable day.

Every last, bloody bit of it.

What number do I call if I want to speak to Europe?"

(Henry Kissinger, US Secretary of State 1968-74)

- 17 -

From where Bill and I were holed-up in a corner of the main passenger saloon, the repeat TV series most monitors showed was a stylish drama about an honest Italian police detective. A public servant struggling to do his duty across a largely-corrupt society. As a fictional morality tale, its timeless parables easily identified with. Why I'd enjoyed watching it so much the first time around. Second only to the old Alfa Romeo its hero charges round Rome in, and a cheering subtext. Middle-aged bachelor of law enforcement wins glorious love interest in shape of foxy, former Bond girl.

On the basis of, if he could, then maybe I might too....

OK, it's pathetic. I know.

LOL.

While Bill, who'd grown bored of the TV, had less need of comforting fantasies. Appeared asleep throughout. Only the noise of a sudden bout of on-screen shooting in the sunlit arcade of a Roman *palazzo* to rouse him. Sitting-up and looking around him crossly while I remained focussed on the wall above me, still absorbed in the story.

On a sofa opposite this bank of dusty screens I was watching lay a crumpled copy of a British tabloid newspaper, several days old. The nearest thing to that *'information'* which everybody on board seemed gagging for. Complacent headlines of titillating scandal and petty celebrity bearing no relationship to serious problems we and millions like us were now grappled with, across half of Europe. Editorial silence over these issues the clearest confirmation possible of a major international crisis coming out of clear blue sky. Suddenly besetting a whole continent in what few days were elapsed since our ship last left Hull, or the Wapping presses turned.

Bill leaned across to grasp the paper. He studied its yellowing pages for a while and then as quickly threw it down: "More lies and posturing! The contract between citizen and state breaking down. The promises they make us. Institutions we trusted...."

"But we're not 'citizens'...." I respond calmly but keeping one eye on the Bond girl, not missing a move. Not willing to be wrong-footed either by so portentous an announcement. Knowing Bill as I did for a man prone to tendentious outbursts, like too many lawyers. Even in normal conversation.

"Don't you remember, Bill? Unlike Italians, we're 'subjects'. Subjects of His Present Gracious Majesty. A simple matter of constitutional law, whatever you feel about it. How things still stand.....even for a republican. Or a Europhile!"

Me being deliberately provocative, but it works.

Every time.

"Constitutional law, Michael? Sovereignty and nationhood? Try telling that that to the kids. A succession of governments selling the UK down the river and our current generation with not even a clue. Not even knowing what they've already lost, let alone what they should still try and keep...."

We landed at Hull in time for lunch but never got any.

Customs took one look at us in the Terminal, and a man in a yellow tabard with face like thunder waved us over into that awful, gloomy concrete side-road where they dismantle people's private cars for pleasure.

Can't really blame them, to be fair.

Xenobia was a bit of a sight, what with her crossed-out racing numbers and peeling Italian sponsorship decals. Car 'two-eight-six' was dirty too, and she had come in direct from Holland like the amateur drug-smugglers tend to. We might as well have had a big sticker saying *"Get Your Coke Here!"* written down the side. And if we had, we wouldn't have been the first motorsport team to use its cars and tool-boxes to conceal an import-export trade. Run as a sideline, if only to pay for the racing.

So fair play to customs.

Information drought or not, it had by osmosis become common knowledge amongst everyone on the ferry that nearly all public and commercial computing facilities in Britain and Europe, for almost any official purpose, were currently knocked-out. Or pretty much struggling. By, what rumour had it, were wave after wave of sustained cyberwarfare attacks currently coming in. And not some solar flare.

"*Denial of Service*" the buzzword going around on our particular boat. One lone hacker's private revenge for some imagined wrong; or the latest way for more than one rogue state to wage their secret wars? The work of Cyber-militias, toiling away in factories of sabotage strung out across the globe?

Either way, "*Europe's got a problem, Houston*" - even without setting the number of worn-out fuel-less power stations going out of service against an exponential increase in new servers and websites starting-up each day. Greedy for power.

Who or what lay behind this phenomenon could only be speculation, but I knew for certain that the few Border officers left available to greet us in Hull would be struggling.

EUROSUR - the European Border Surveillance System - was quite clearly 'down'. Their monitor screens visibly blank as we passed them. So with no watch-lists to compare our names and photos with, I could imagine how completely the state's reliance on electronic border-checking of travellers had been pulled from underneath them by the effects of this crisis. Could see straightaway how much it annoyed them, the officers present that day visibly falling-back instead on those useful hardy standbys - prejudice and supposition.

To be fair to them, Bill and I, plus Xenobia, must have looked a pretty dodgy bunch. Suitable candidates for treatment. So I suspect we were pulled over on no better than instinct. No-one knew who we were and a dead machine can't read the chip in your passport. They were looking out for a chip on our shoulders instead, and running along with a few of their own.

Two police officers standing nearby as if it was nothing to do with them, a man and a woman watching us sternly with arms folded while all this went on. Back-up for the Borders & Immigration people, I suppose, in case Bill and I or anyone like us chose to cut up rough.

As if.

After a while the female officer of the pair walked slowly over anyway, and I thought at first she was going to join in their fun. Go through one of the bags herself. Pull up Xenobia's carpet. Scatter around some tools.

"Is this your car?" she said to me.

No more than five foot tall, max', without her chequered hat. The waist of her fluorescent stab-proof vest so girded round with radio and a personal cell-phone that was probably u/s; plus metal handcuffs and plastic kwik-cuffs, aerosol 'pepper' spray, a *"ruggedised"* e-notebook and similar gubbins. It left this little darling nearly as broad as she was hardly tall.

"No, it's my friend's. The big guy over there, talking to the customs officers. Do you like it?"

My attempt at a friendly smile to thaw her obvious chill was wasting its time.

"We've seen the wording written on your car. And no, sir, we're not daft. Don't like it at all. Very inappropriate, *if* I may say so. Don't think we don't get its meaning: *"Hatred of Foreigners"*. Well, if that's your game, sir, you've come to the wrong place. You and your nasty propaganda. We won't tolerate Hate Crime, not here in Hull. Why I must warn you...*sir*. That's a potentially-offensive public message. And if it turns out that reading it causes *anyone* any harassment, alarm or distress - any witness - then you can be arrested and prosecuted!"

"Inappropriate": the ultimate modern blasphemy in a secular age. Even covers *'rude'*.

I was furious: "No, look, you've got it wrong. You don't understand, that's *'xenophobia'*. Can't you muppets read? This lettering says: *'Xenobia'*. Completely different meaning - it's a person's bloody name. Good God, woman, we've just spent a whole week by choice with a whole load of *'foreigners'*. Do you really think......"

I was hopping mad, almost speechless. Hot, too. Whether it was the sheer injustice or just her amazing ignorance which provoked me the most, I cannot say, but I was undoubtedly on dangerous ground. Foolish to display these reactions when CCTV is watching.

The all-seeing eye.

Cameras everywhere, only no staff. She points up to one, as if to emphasise this point.

"I'd watch your language, if I was you...*sir!* Don't get clever with us, offensive. It's all being recorded. What matters most is not what you say, but how people perceive it. You've had your warning. One more word and it'll be a summons. Anymore, an arrest!"

Tired, hungry and angry, it took us ages, unassisted, to pick up and repack afterwards all the tools and spares they'd left scattered around on the ground. An interlude to make us even later starting home.

"*Big Sister's Watching You-oo!*" Bill sang softly to the dashboard and himself as I finally started the engine. We set off again, past a row of unsmiling yellow jackets bulging with self-righteousness. The black leather gauntlets we were to run folded tightly inside officers' arms. Unmistakable, linear messaging to us of their deep disapproval. Publicly paraded for our undeserving benefit.

"Pillocks!" he adds quietly.

Fortunately they couldn't hear him, while we were too old and life's too short to sit each one of them on our knee and explain the etymology of a long-dead Desert Queen. The story of a remarkable woman who - in memory of a murdered husband, protection of an infant son, the brave defence of her people - stood alone against the tyranny of superpowers. Fought Rome and Persia to a standstill and, if only for a moment, actually won. An exciting morality tale we could have told our puritanical guards all about, if only we'd had the time and they'd had the patience. Gathered inside the damp and draughty halls of a North Sea passenger terminal while our fellow citizens queue behind us in fear of similar treatment.

"Like there's a whole generation of young officers grown-up believing it's thought and speech they were put on this earth to police...." I rejoin. "Won't re-learn discretion....."

"Thought-Crime enforced by Roundheads! Agents of our New Totalitarianism...." grumbles Bill.

"....what politicians taught us, to impose upon each other..." I finish off for him.

Free of the terminal atmosphere of the Terminal, pulling gratefully out from King George Dock, Bill discovers near the prison one of the few filling-stations left locally with fuel in their tanks. Marked out by a stationary queue of other motorists' cars, about a hundred metres long down Hedon Road. Where, finally getting to the pumps ourselves and nearly an hour later, we are lucky to find them not dry. So Bill brim-fills Xenobia as a reward for her patience, not knowing when or if we might get another chance, but using-up the last of our English cash.

293

While Bill waited next in the kiosk queue to pay, I thought to try and call the office one more time from a traditional callbox set across the road from the forbidding gates and high walls of HMP Hull. Using another surviving landline like in olden days, to let them know my progress.

Standing inside its Gilbert Scott-designed lines, this cast-iron Edwardian structure epitome of a tourist's imagined Britain, I was still smarting from our denunciation by another icon of this country, a proper British 'bobbie'. Her public rebuke for that most contemporary of moral conceits, the alleged retention of an unlawful 'phobia'.

But what else could I expect in Hull? Here at the end of the longest railway-siding in England. In a threadbare town robbed of its fishing, tops for unemployment. Where it sometimes seems like nothing else survives beyond her dogged independence of spirit, loveable bloody-mindedness. Where even her Gilbert Scott phone-boxes are painted cream, not red. Love-children of a pre-war City Corporation, the 'phone company that declared UDI from the rest of the UK. A unilateral declaration of phonetic independence achieved through constructing a completely-separate telephone system. And painting all their boxes in the wrong colour, to emphasise the point.

While we were away on our 'jolly' had I forgotten how close my country sometimes felt to falling apart? If I had, then it was poignant to be reminded within only half an hour of return. To find these querkily-familiar symbols of Merrie England so seamlessly combined with the fanatical application of regulation, of thoughtless thought-control. Come fresh from the humourless officialdom which spawns it, and all of it found within the radius of one half-mile. Upon the one occasion.

How I knew I was home.

If this sense of familiarity was as oddly-comforting as it was faintly depressing, I shouldn't have let it. If Hull's unique phone system felt familiar, its municipal eccentricity turned-up trumps for us that day. Showed some real virtue in a world where more than just our social values are changing every week, but also the technology that moulds them. When all mobiles were malfunctioning, but I could be reminded what a mercy it was,

294

here in good old Hull, that not every public kiosk accessing an obsolete wire-based system had yet been ripped-up.

And me with enough credit left on the phonecard in my pocket to use what was probably the last such device left inside an example of Scott's finest that was still actually working. With no resort to satellite. Miraculously unvandalised, and capable of accepting the number I dialled.

My office.

How innocently wonderful it felt to hear a real ringing-tone for the first time in ages. A pleasure as promptly followed by the soothing recorded voice of Young Elaine in our reception. Warmly assuring me in her lovely Geordie tones how genuinely important my incoming call to CPS *englandnorth* really was. Yet despite her promise of priority, but as if to balance any early aural pleasure, she regrets being unable to "*take your call right now, as all operators are busy.*" News not only annoying to me but frankly also perplexing. Because, apart from John, a Sunderland F.C. supporter with permanent depression who occasionally works part-time to cover for Elaine's odd bouts of sick leave (and I do mean 'odd') who on earth were these CPS '*operators*' her message implied we had?

Because I'd never met any.

Frustrating, but probably serving me right. An off-duty civil servant getting a taste of how things maybe now felt for too many members of the public. For police and solicitors, the external agencies trying to get hold of us by 'phone - spending-cuts or no. When there were colleagues I could name who made an entire career out of hiding from phone calls and visitors. Dug-in deep behind an impermeable wall of voice-mail and e-mail, but never actually '*in*'. Never answering for themselves, seldom even seen. The more technology for human contact we devise, the more elusive some become.

A pity then, especially if I couldn't get through to work to tip them off, but we still needed to get back to Newcastle smartish. And if the main priority was petrol, which happily we'd found, in all that messing about at the filling station food for ourselves was the one thing we forgot. While in the rush to leave its forecourt, I also found myself driving again. With hindsight this might have been a mistake, but of course Bill was strictly banned, and him thinking I was the one who'd know the best escape route from a town I never planned-on returning to.

Welcome back, anyway.

We flew over the six-lane river-bridge beside his namesake King Billy's golden equestrian statue, over there in Market Place. And that new one of John Prescott, standing pointing ambiguously to where the brown River Hull pours out into mighty Humber. Passed the Marina on the right, where the red tower of an old Spurn Lightship rises high above a silvered forest of leisure-sailors' alloy masts, tinkering away. The fog-warning bell in its cradle chiming gently with the swell.

"Do you know, Bill, I once had a case here where the interviewing detective managed to ask the suspect - a yob who'd burgle anything - *'If I mention the Spurn Lightship on the Marina, does that ring any bells in your head?"*

He'd laughed politely at the feeble pun and asked me instead: "Are you all right driving....?"

I smiled bravely back: "No problem!"

Traffic-wise that remained true, the roads conveniently empty because the shortage of fuel remained a big issue for everyone. Otherwise, things were rather less bright.

Passing South Cave on the A63 westwards, intending to head across to York via the A64, then A1 northbound, I found I couldn't see properly and had to pull over. Managing to turn off – correctly - at the nearest slip-road but taking the completely wrong turn. Going left, not right – heading east again instead.

"Hey....?" from the passenger seat.

We ended up driving needlessly fast towards some commercial nurseries by a roundabout. The sheets of glass in their shiny greenhouses reflecting the setting sun unpleasantly back as a sickly bronze. Probably why I felt so light-headed, I guess.

'Elloughton' pointed one signpost.

Before we even got that far I'd swerved right across the path of an oncoming builder's van into a convenient lay-by and pulled violently on the handbrake. Xenobia reared to a rattling halt, stalled, and then everything went hot and blurry.

The white van went tearing past us with its horns going and the driver making a 'V' sign.

296

I got out of the car OK but then had to lie down straight away. Full-length on a grass verge beside a large wood. Bill came across and stood over me in frank astonishment.

"I think I've been here before!" I shouted out loud to no-one in particular.

"What on earth are you rabbiting on about, Michael? As faint as this? Or reincarnation....?"

"No, this lay-by!"

Bill didn't waste time arguing.

I've said he was strong. He managed to drag me bodily, back in through the open passenger door and over the sides of its bucket seat. Strapping me in tight with my rally jacket rolled against the headrest to keep my chin up and my tongue right.

Even while he was doing this, and it didn't take long, an angry man in a dirty blue boiler-suit came up to him in the lay-by on a quad-bike. Ignoring me and my presumably pretty-obvious comatose condition, he berated Bill roundly:

"Hey mate, where'd you 'Hoorays' learn to park like this? You boy-racers are blocking the entry into my field and we're bringing crop-sprayers in and out of here all day. So get it shifted before I call the cops!"

Bill just ignored him, jumped into the driving seat and spun Xenobia violently around in the road before setting off north again. Ban or no ban. My head was spinning bad enough already without him doing that, thank you......

Wham.

"Cohors equitata..."

"You're in a bad way, Mikey. Boiling hot and I'd swear you were talking Latin back there. Just hang on will you?"

I think I nodded off in the tightly-enclosing racing seat soon after. When I woke up next, it was in bed at the RVI. The Newcastle Royal Infirmary.

An isolation ward.

"Don't get me wrong, it's a good hospital but any hospital is a rotten place to be when you're feeling ill...." I remember Bill saying at some point.

I'd only been there a few days, weeks, or maybe it was just a few hours - I really couldn't tell - before finding myself sagging and lolling against a locked seatbelt in the back of a speeding

Range Rover. The latest model, I had enough of the anorak about me still to note.

Driven by a woman.

Wham.

It was dark outside, orange street lamps flashing past, but I remember seeing a big green sign for the turn-off beside the speed camera, before blacking out again. "*Kielder Water & Forest - The Roman Wall*" it said.

Wham.

How he got me out of the RVI in that state I'll never know.

"The independent bachelor life has its compensations, Michael, but this minute you're looking at one of its many downsides. Venezia and I can't leave you raving and feverish in your lonely Jesmond flat. Stay over with us for a few days while you see off the worst of it. Venezia's mother's room under the stables' clock-tower will do you fine. Gives us a good alibi too, in case the old bird starts hankering to come back north."

Then I remembered something really important. You see the thing is, it was actually Brantingham where I'd collapsed. I needed to tell.......well, someone.

"You know, Brantingham!" I shouted to the world at large.

"Yes, yes, I hear you...." she called back from somewhere nearby.

Her!

After that, things went a bit fuzzy again for a while.

"The threat of starvation is of far greater concern to a soldier than any enemy"

(Publius Flavius Vegetius Renatus: *'Epitoma Rei Militaris'* - late fourth century A.D.)

- XVIII -

We virtually claw our way back blind, all the way home from Pictland. Closely following the cliffs, rocks and bays of its coast. Carefully floating down through the thick, wet fog that dogs our little convoy almost as far south as the Abus river itself. The smoke of Arbeia or the watch towers above Praetorio escaping us completely on the homeward run. Lost in the mist - invisible. Only the sound of warning bells in the mist to fix their location.

Ideal weather for Saxon raiders?

Sails limp from no breath of wind, this leaves the whole job to our oarsmen. What Trojans they were, but even strongmen need rest. Only extending the journey. Our navigators and steersmen showed their mettle too, saving us with patient craft from hitting any of the many reefs or running aground in the murk. Soundings-men calling out endlessly from the bows of our lead ship every step of the way, their voices ghostly. Care limitless.

It was a cold and frightening voyage we had of it, but the great Carausius stayed buoyant throughout at the thought of a priceless Pictish promise carried in his metaphorical pocket. Cheerful in the fog. No wonder his companions were always comforted by proximity to so gifted a captain. Our lucky leader. One who could never die on water – according to a horoscope as widely known in the Fleet as its truth was universally accepted.

And if his followers' mood matched his own by staying incurably positive, the weather gods fought back with walls of cloud. A sea-fret never abating until we finally crept along the northern shore of Abus, seeking her hidden creek into Petuaria haven. Scraping over spiteful sands.

Till we knew we were safely back in civilisation.

299

Back in that tented city of soldiers protected by palisades suddenly sprawling across a score of urban farmers' enclosures outside the rising defences of Petuaria Civitas Parisorum. An undistinguished, forgotten *civitas* whose trampled vegetable gardens and barley fields now provide our newest Caesar with the most unlikely spot imaginable from which to begin his greatest of great projects. The renewal of Roman vigour across all Britannia and his northern parts of Gaul - achieved firstly through war.

Discovering a few practical facts of government in the process. Including the simplest - wherever an emperor rests becomes the fulcrum to their state. However unseemly the location, their seat of ultimate executive power. Waged here, quite literally, 'in the field'.

Even in the middle of a military campaign there could be no escape from the burdens of office. Now that Carausius was acknowledged ruler in these parts, it was inevitable even the most prosaic matters follow him there. An administrative reality evidenced at Petuaria by bedraggled crowds of lawyers and litigants floating-in like flotsam on every tide. Whether from northern Gaul or southern Britain, Rotomagus or Rutupiae, bringing their impassioned pleas for emancipation and rights. Whole litanies of pleading from the meanest neighbour disputes of Armorica or Aquileia. Those men of means who beg for relief from a tax system he no longer dare mitigate - not now it's all that's left him to feed his growing armies.

Still green around the gills, these petitioners of passage have barely staggered off the boats that brought them than they join a growing crowd of supplicants already camped outside the emperor's tent. Every one of them demanding his judicious settlement of a vital legal issue on the spot. Unfortunately for him, and as these peripatetic lawyers soon discover, the great man's thoughts lie elsewhere. A new ruler with better priorities for his Imperial attention than the boundary of some fenman's field, the inheritance of twins.

The council of war he held to resolve his greater priorities was held in a luxuriously-fitted, general's tent at the heart of our armed camp. I can picture it now, that historic *consilium*. All the key players in his great game present at table, keenly pressing for action.

300

Including Allectus: newly-arrived from Londinium Mint, virtually sweating metal.

What about me, you ask?

Well yes, obviously I was there too. How else could I be describing it to you now?

Sitting at the back and dutifully taking notes - one of my commoner onshore-duties in those days. Feeling privileged just to observe, to listen and learn. Only surprised to find my personal obligations arising from its draft agenda turning out greater than expected.

Memories of a warm and sunny, autumnal day where the front 'butterfly' flaps could be rolled-up on his leather tent. Flooding our meeting with light and giving us long views out over that immense estuary where his many transports ride at anchor. Ready for orders.

Of Marcus Saturninus Lupus; the senior centurion he had promoted to *Praefectus Legionis* then left in charge of expeditionary forces at Petuaria while we were away on our little Caledonian cruise. Ponderously opening their agenda with his painstaking summary of our latest dispositions. Every bit as diligent in their preparation as you would expect from this granite-faced professional, the only crucial thing he lacked that spark our leader always has.

If the Carausius I describe to you in my journal might by contrast with this sober Lupus sound like a man who smiled a lot - as he did, and whom I loved like a father - that does not mean my reader should assume him always a nice person. Or an officer easily pleased. Oh no, he was much more complex a being than that.

When such qualities would only have proved an encumbrance, standing on that dangerous stage where his adoring soldiers had placed him – if not a positive weakness. For if the Emperor Carausius was to succeed in obtaining the total command and discipline necessary to subdue and control that turbulent body of men which is the Army of Britain, then it was unshakeable and unsmiling lieutenants of blood and iron like Lupus who must be his intermediary along the tent-lines.

Not his substitute.

And if choosing then delegating to capable subordinates like M.Saturninus Lupus was another one of those skills making

Carausius so effective a leader, it took till that formative day for me to recognise how much he relied on others to do his dirty work for him.

People like Lupus, people like me.

Even a stranger man like his Allectus, as I came slowest to realise.

Of course more than anyone it was still the common soldiers who took the brunt of it. Whom everyone knew could be relied on to face the greatest dangers on his behalf. Accede to his cruellest and most-severe military punishments. Provided only that the requirement for these pains and sacrifice came from a leader who could guarantee two things in turn for them:

Money and Victory.

While the feverish machinations of Allectus and his coiners could be expected to provide us with the former, it was the careful groundwork of infantry generals like Lupus - when paired with the naval brilliance of Carausius - which would deliver up the latter.

Commanders whose approach to the job would not disappoint on this occasion either.

Covert surveys of the latest situation on the ground in Eboracum, carried out while we were away by agents sent-in on behalf of Lupus, were instructive. Brought us bang up-to-date yet took nothing for granted. Made no casual assumptions about a familiar location at the heart of our military machine in the north for hundreds of years gone-by.

To be fair, it wasn't difficult. We had spies and friends a-plenty inside its perimeter already, but let's recap on their findings. Study the summary given at that day's briefing:

"The legionary fortress at Eboracum is conveniently sited inland on an elevated site some seventeen Roman miles north west from the Abus, a major estuary of the sea. Its tidal tributary, the Ouse, is vital for accessing the city. To its shipping and supply. Vessels can dock at quays and wharves sheltered by a crenellated cliff of bastions in stone, under the fortress defences. The river itself crossed by a principal bridge of timber, springing southwards towards the Colonia of retired military veterans on its opposite bank, where further capacious warehousing stands available....."

"*Carved beside the fortress on a side-channel to its south-east is a tributary of the Ouse. That narrow flow men call 'Fossa' (ditch) closes a triangle of waterways. Protecting the stronghold at its apex while assuring every dockside facility for handling the large quantities of food, military supplies and traded goods needed daily to sustain it. Vital strategic supplies whose onward distribution, inland and northwards, via her wharves and granaries, is crucial to Eboracum's longstanding role as our northern army's hub....*" (you may still read in the archives).

Provided these comestibles can first get up the Ouse.

Their journey normally starts with the larger freighters arriving from abroad to moor in the estuarine port of Petuaria, then unloading and dividing their bulkier cargoes for transfer onto shallow-draughted sailing barges. Until our blockade began, these smaller vessels had usually made the final part of their journey, upstream to the fortress, with the help of horses and oars. Or, in the case of smaller lighters, teams of hauling-men on the riverbank. Leaning on walking poles to steady their momentum.

Heavy work appropriate for slaves and prisoners, but how many more useful jobs can the empire be expected to find for its glut of captured Goths?

Once our emperor's army began its muster at Petuaria, it was these supply barges and their trade we'd stopped from moving. Supplies of grain, oil and wine to the fortress, or anything else, all coming to a complete halt. So that one of the first questions for today's conference at Petuaria must be about how long Eboracum could survive without them.

Our consensus not very long.

Any foreign merchantmen arriving in the Abus - en route to Eboracum but dilatory in divining meaning from an unfamiliar sight, that matrix of a thousand leather tents a-flowering on the flatlands by the town - would suffer for their slowness. Cargo impounded, crews pressed into the naval service of Carausius.

"We have the entire logistical supply-system of Quintus Bassianus and the Sixth Victorious Legion held by the throat. Already they are hungry. If we keep them cut-off for much longer, soon they will be starving" said Saturninus Lupus with an obvious pleasure.

"And when they are?"

"Then I have detailed operational plans drawn-up. Describing your rapid march on the city and forcible recovery of the fortress..." confirmed this faithful wolf of Rome: "No mercy!"

"Good Lupus, I would not expect any less of you..." sighed Carausius. "And hold every confidence in their success. But before we execute them completely, may I suggest a little softening-up for her defenders. Like sending young Triton here inside. Along with a small, amphibious assault group, carrying swords and cash. When he knows his way around the corridors of its principia rather better than most. Has a private debt demanding settlement with Bassianus - or so I hear. Am I right about that, young man?" he called.

From my seat at the back I went red. How he knew, I know not.

All I knew was that my late father had taught me to believe in the importance of contributing to the public good. To *Res Publicae* - if necessary, through warfare. Why serving Carausius seemed the obvious route to honouring the father I'd lost and gaining another. To serving Rome, even if it often left me unclear on where that journey might end. But now I thought I knew.

Probably that point, at this meeting in Petuaria, where the last scales fell from my eyes. When I realised for the first time in my life the measure of my commitment. Saw for myself what my trusted mentor and the 'opportunities' this wonderful new career he offered had finally made of me. Him, and that bloody sword.

A hired assassin on a suicide mission.

Whatever a dead father might make of it, I thought my mother would have wept. But what did she expect an Army career to do for her son and his delicate sensibilities, if not teach him how to kill? Here was no *'Athens School of Moral Philosophy'* but at least I finally understood the latest 'little job' which Carausius had for some time been hinting at. If I did, then he did not seem to want to dwell on it. Preferring to press rapidly on, discuss with my seniors what should happen afterwards.

"Capturing a city is one thing. Holding it afterwards another...." as he told them.

Planning what he and they would do once the garrison had presumably surrendered on our encouragement. When half the demoralised defenders of northern Britannia were roaming the streets of Eboracum in abject want of money, food and orders.

In a lost Province on the cusp of anarchy.

"We will parade their legion and its supporters, those disgraced Wall cohorts who abandoned their posts and duties to come south and join him. Outside the town rampart when they emerge shamefaced to surrender their arms and loyalty. From the *rostra* I will announce myself - my new title and my new name. When, by the way, you should know I will be taking the names of that finest of emperors, the deified Marcus Aurelius, as a prefix for my own. As is only right, I'm sure you'll agree."

There was an immediate murmur of agreement in the tent.

"From that moment, this is how I will be known. By soldiers who will be told by you, my good Saturninus Lupus, and by my ambassadors into the city, that your elevation of me to the Purple is the settled wish of the whole Army of Britain. That here and now is their last and only chance to recover their honour and be restored to our colours. While I do not doubt for a minute what their answer will be, it is that key moment - when we have obtained their oaths and their obedience, stressed the martial fundamentals of duty and virtue - which becomes the proper time. When I should show my appreciation."

"I take it that means money, lord. And where exactly will we be finding more of that?"

"A new emperor should be generous to his soldiers, Lupus, and that is the expectation on which they have raised me. An expectation growing by the day. The *donatio*: my gift to them on accession. So I will justly meet it, as I stand determined. Provide them with a new coinage to thrill and amaze not just the soldiers but also our top people, the *honestiores*. Into whose private coffers it soon will flow, whose opinions it must shape. Important men to be won over by the ideas it carries as much as any metal contained."

"Ideas, my lord?"

"Yes, ideas. Exciting ideas and phrases about the future I remember young Triton first suggesting to us one night in the Wensum channel. His words of the poet on our Golden Age of Saturn. Words I've never read but Triton promises us everyone else has. No-one has tried this approach before, Lupus, but if

305

friend Allectus has done his work well then there will be a distribution upon my accession to be the wonder of empire. East and west alike. Never mind Eboracum, we will be the talk of Roma and Treverorum; of Ephesus and Byzantium. Will we not, my clever *Rationalis*?"

"Yes, my lord, be sure of it. At a crucial moment, starting with the City of the Legion. If our river pilots can get Triton and a detachment secretly by boat under the walls of the fortress by night, his team safely ashore and onto its streets by day, we will see its first distribution. Made by seeming insiders among the garrison of these fresh silver pieces bearing your name and profile. Achieving more in a few moments than siege and starvation could do in weeks. More cheaply, too."

Across the table a glowering Saturninus Lupus suddenly sat up, his interest stoked. Keen to interrogate a rival to discarded ideas of fire and storm: "A bold plan, Allectus, no doubt. One as complex and subtle as its author. But how can you hope to produce stuff like that in a backwater like this, in time for child Triton and his band to carry out their daring mission?"

"While the Emperor was away north, I've had machinery and equipment from the Londinium Mint, along with skilled slaves to work it, shipped here aboard a converted grain-carrier. Found a primitive furnace in Petuaria to adapt. Charcoal and timber a-plenty in the local woods to fuel it."

"You said silver. Where in the name of Fortuna or a robbed and broken country will you be finding enough of that commodity?" said Lupus, disbelief in his voice.

Carausius intervened: "It is safe to say, *Praefectus,* that this is a rainy day the *Rationalis* and myself have long saved-up for. Gathering a scrap of captured barbarian tribute here, the odd piece of unclaimed booty there, we've built a useful reserve in silver and bronze. Plus a little gold. Our modest war-chest."

Allectus nodded: "Which won't last very long. I calculate we need a hundred thousand *antoniniani* just to start with. Twenty for each man. Not only to win over the Eboracum garrison but reward loyal soldiers come up from Gaul or the Saxon Shore."

"That sounds a lot, Can you manage it?" Lupus' tone more respectful, taking his cue.

"We are working the mint night and day. Stamping out coin. If every morsel of recovered or confiscated silver available is melted down, then I think we can. Provided too, as soon as this fortress capitulates, that we seize the military treasury hidden beneath their headquarters and ship it back to the haven. Then I think we shall have the means. Enough to produce it on the scale that's needed. To turn, then keep an army."

"But hardly confined to that?" prompted Carausius.

"No, my lord. Soon it will be out in the towns and markets. Never since the time of Nero will the people have seen coins of this quality. Been able to trade their goods or pay their dues with a revitalised coinage. Weighing and worth precisely what it claims, not some barbarous travesty. Something your brother *Augusti* over the water have never managed. So you are not only setting an example but literally making history. And I for one am certain, lord, it will prove worth all the effort. Your personal message of hope, of a new age. Not only stamped onto these new coins of yours but physically contained within them. A revalued currency able to restore Rome in Britain and speak volumes for your achievement, assure your succession. Resounding to your memory long after we've all gone to dust."

Carausius nodded approvingly and joined in: "As the tribune Triton at the back keeps telling us, it is all about spreading the word. Excepting the Imperial Post and military despatches, the highest standard of information our network of roads carries is whisper and rumour. Gossip and lies, unreliable and inconsistent. But the one source in the world anyone can access is coinage. From the richest villa-owner to the poorest beggar. Provided they can read or know someone who can, then either can grasp its message. Be equal in learning, absorb this information or else have it explained. When they do, I want to be sure it's the same message - whoever reads it. My own personal promise. And our unique opportunity to explain who I am and what I stand for. What my rule means for them - for us. With your help and the gods willing. My oath to Britannia, her promise of better times...."

"My lord, it is a promise we stand ready to help you fulfill...." said Lupus, eyes aflame.

"Truly, I am glad of it. The gods know, people are weary. From the murder of Alexander Severus by one insane soldier, they've lived through torrid times. Last of his line, last of the Severans - his reign the last when citizens knew peace. Fifty years in any one of which our empire could have gone under. One emperor after another. Declared by the soldiers then murdered in quick succession, like no-one could satisfy them. Satisfy us! Fifty years of civil war: our currency declining into a bastardised collection of stamped-out counters the markets value less than barter. Our legions to mutinous rabble. A self-inflicted chaos to play into the hands of barbarians, a series of disasters they've exploited to the hilt. It's got to stop, friends, and we are the men to do it. You and I – this day we draw the line!"

"With money as the answer, Excellency? Not a root of more evil?" This from Hippolitus, that skeletal survivor Carausius entrusts with half our commissariat, on the basis of his adjutant's love of detail, unshakeable Christian probity.

The emperor scowls at this wrong note. Sighs at his piety:

"How else should we buy-in those vital supplies you husband so well? Win back the hearts of men? So yes, Hippolitus, it is! Of that I stand convinced. If we in Britain can put the coinage on a proper footing, its appearance and metal content, restoring its value and our provincial economy along with it, then we can make example to the world. To the continent: Europa and the whole empire. So that one single coin of ours may carry two messages. One, the renewed value of our currency and two, the values of your emperor. What I, Marcus Aurelius Mausaeus Carausius, really stand for. Here in Britannia. What I will do for you, as your Man of Change!"

It would say on the first coins we gave out either "*SL*" or "*SC*", which technically means they were minted at Londinium, Camulodunum or Clausentum, on the lawful authority of the Senate.

Or '*SP*' - meaning almost the same but instead on a procurator's. Indeed, my reader might own a sample example. Well if you do, or collect these things, then let me admit to something else. That neither endorsement is true.

They were all stamped out in a ruinous former iron-works on the muddy banks of the rolling Abus river, during the siege of Eboracum.

And '*SP*' means '....*at Petuaria*'.

Not many people left who know that anymore.

"Matthew, Mark, Luke and John, guard the bed that I lie on."

-18-

That dream again.

Same one I've had for years.

Searching for her. Searching through familiar townscapes, schoolrooms and homes. Going on for ages, my legs ceasing to work.

People saying she was here five minutes ago, must have popped out.

Where I set off again to follow, find tired legs won't go.

My God, how it exhausts me. All that looking and asking, dragging my frame.

Without ever finding.

Suddenly the shape of a shadowy figure outlined in white, standing at the end of the bed. Silhouetted against the brilliant, golden light streaming-in from the tall, pointed window behind them.

As I struggle to come round, I wonder if it is an angel. Am I really dead?

The dream over?

"Mummy, that funny man in grannie's flat! Mummy, mummy! Come quickly and look. I think he's waking up!"

Not an angel, then, but a dear little girl.

God bless her.

One of Bill's.

A Billette.

Sweet.

Billette Doux

Her name was Molly.

And I was still alive.

*"I sincerely believe
the banking institutions having the issuing power of money
are more dangerous to liberty than standing armies."*

(Thomas Jefferson, American President).

- XIX -

The small flotilla of boats he ordered be assembled in the haven at Petuaria for our planned amphibious raid on Eboracum made an unlikely mix. One flax-trader's barge to go lumbering ahead as 'cover' with two flat-bottomed military transports built from nailed planks following-on behind, full of troops in casual order. No shields, no spears.

We gathered inside a large tent pegged out on the dockside as temporary accommodation for the fleet. Carausius was there with the one hundred he'd selected for the mission. Including me, looking at my biggest responsibility ever. Scared and excited, nervous of fate.

I've mentioned before his relaxed attitudes to religion, the observance of augury. 'Nominal' probably best describing the degree of attention Carausius generally gave to divination before dashing off to war. A quick look at the entrails of sacrifice, then away we go.

Today was different – it seemed more important. With the military centre of the whole north at stake, I suppose you couldn't blame him. Since becoming emperor, Carausius had learnt a lot, and something he later told me he'd learnt earliest was to open his speeches with a religious reference: "*It always gets the men on-side. When they so like to have a holy leader, and I so love those hypocritical bastards!*"

From coming to power, there was an existing cult associated with the Mother Goddess of these islands, the personification of our provinces, to which he showed particular attention: "*Genus Britanniae*".

Mother Britain, a holy Britannia.

He officiated at the sacrifice of a lamb to her today with an intensity of feeling not marked in him before. Wine and incense only adding. Rigorous in procedures where the attendant priest

310

came along poor second. The idea of Her was a concept I saw daily becoming more important. And precisely why a female figure to represent 'Britannia' appears on some of his coins for the first time since the halcyon days of Hadrian or the Pious Antoninus.

This 'luck' of the British provinces, their *Tyche*, personifying our island's goddess of good fortune. Of course once she'd appeared on the coinage, she immediately became indispensable. Like leaving her off could lose us her luck, and who would be so foolish?

Equally in how he gave his personal briefing that morning, Carausius seemed as attentive to her divine influence as he was to our mortal input: "I don't want any heroics. Rely on the mother goddesses to see you through, be sure that they will. Our gods and your comrades. Compared with keeping their faith, your mission is simple. And any soldier departing from it not only puts his comrades in danger, that individual will also face the fullest punishments of a military tribunal. If he survives to get back. Better to die than to fail me on this one!"

"We will not my lord!" came the determined murmur back.

"I am putting the tribune Triton in overall charge, with a separate detachment of Batavians under the centurion Aurelius Niger. All of you, chosen men. Honest men of valour whom I believe I can trust. And here is your test."

He lifted a plain sack in the tent onto the wooden table in front of him and when he tipped it out I could see what he meant. A pile of brand-new silver coins shimmying onto the table in a rush.

No wonder honesty was important, men's eyes popping out of their heads at the sight of these riches. I knew that only the utmost discipline would keep their latent greed reliably in check. Part of my job, along with Aurelius Niger - as hard an overseer of trained men as you ever could fear to meet.

"These are among the first silver *antoniniani* ever to bear my name and head. And you are the soldiers who put me there, only your comrades of the Sixth declining. If they are to be brought around to your way of thinking, then I would rather it be by persuasion than pitched battle on the plain. It seems to me we have seen more than enough Roman soldiers killed by their own side - we cannot afford to waste more. So your job is to get

311

up-river and into Eboracum - without a fuss and without attracting suspicion. Your identity that of a late-arriving garrison from high on the Wall, come down on the governor's summons to defend his claim. The governor these coins will unseat: that traitorous general, Quintus Bassianus."

I wondered what history there was between these two men that Carausius always grimaced on his name - the only man I ever saw him hate. Knowing my own experience, I could imagine its roots.

"Tonight there is an exceptional lunar tide. Enough to float you faster, higher and further upstream than normal. Once this and the boats have got you up-river, you will disperse onto the wharves of Eboracum posing as the governor's supporters. Armed only with your personal side-arms and this money, you will infiltrate the town, the *cannabae* and *Colonia*. Perhaps even the fortress. And there, my faithful soldiers, you will spend, spend, spend!"

Eyebrows were raised and we looked at each other in amazement. This was a form of warfare none had known before. Carausius allowing the ripple of laughter that went with it to roll around the tent for a moment before gesturing brusquely for silence:

"Each of you has been issued with one hundred silver coins. While your officers will carry three hundred and hold you firmly to account for what you do with yours. On pain of death. You are chosen, trusted men, but any man who breaks my trust by trying to bury the coin or save it will be identified and executed under military law. Disobedience to a lawful order when your order is to spend. The same going for anyone found drunk. My only limit on your wastefulness is that, whatever else you do, you keep a proper control. Do not waste yourselves for I, like a father, value you all. Remember you are on duty and your lives depend on each comrade staying sober and alert. Compared with the ground rules, the job itself is easy: to spread this coin across Eboracum as fast as you can. Spend it all, on anything you want. Yes, even drink – within reason. On whores, on food, on brooches or buckles, I really don't care. But spend these coins freely and spend them publicly. Money up-front and tips all round. Above all, get it circulating – and you don't need me to tell you there will be naught like women for that...."

"Because I want the soldiers and citizens of Eboracum to be astounded. When we've had no coinage of this quality in Britannia since the days of Nero, and I want any living soul left in town to know that it was Marcus Aurelius Mausaeus Carausius who brought them it. To see my ugly mug stamped on every piece."

"My lord, what if we are challenged? Denounced in the street for bearing your image? You said you wanted no heroics, but we remain armed. What if that gives our only chance – to fight a way out of it?" asked Niger.

"Centurion, you are right, that must be the fall-back position. But whatever else happens, do not imagine yourselves abandoned. While your party makes its way up-river and infiltrates the town, I will be at the head of this army. Marching over the flood-plain from Petuaria to encircle Eboracum. When they smell my money, I know the Sixth will come over to us - quietly without a fight what I hope for. But if they don't, then yes, it will be your remaining job to cause as much disruption as you can from inside, before escaping when we attack from without. And with the thoroughness of planning Saturninus Lupus has put into it, pity any garrison to suffer that assault. They would pay for their resistance and pay for it dearly, but whichever way we take them, I never felt so confident."

"There remains the question of the Prefect of the Legion, their governor, Quintus Bassianus. What is to be done with him, my lord, should he fall into our hands?" A question I only dared ask from my growing awareness that here was a problem he'd implied for a while was coming my way, so it might as well be faced.

"I was coming to that, Triton, but glad to hear you ask me - intending you for my champion. Do this thing for me and I am ever in your debt, I promise it. You more than anyone here knows his way round the fortress. Down the long corridors of its principia. Knows the face of our enemy. That is why it is you I am asking, trusting with this quest. To hunt the rebel down and bring him to justice, wherever you find him."

"Alive or dead?"

The answer I got was clever for leaving all the responsibility on me. Or if necessary, all of the blame:

313

"If he will come quietly, surrendering himself to my Imperial jurisdiction, then so much the better. If you can persuade him, then all to the good. But never forget: he is a rebel against my authority. A criminal we should track down and hold to account. Take as many or as few of these men as you need to effect it. But if you find him defiant and resisting, then you may be obliged to use force. I fear he will leave you little choice. But you are our man, Triton. My skilled swordsman, most-trusted officer. The one I know can always win through, however bad things look. When I hear men are calling you something different now. "*The Slasher*" - is that true?"

This I did not know, and cringed inwardly at their plaudit, Carausius continuing regardless: "You have come a long way from that overgrown child we first met, out there on the eastern fen. Now I choose you to be my special representative, my foremost agent inside Eboracum. And I formally authorise you, Triton, to get inside that fortress with whoever and whatever you need to bring Bassianus out for me – dead or alive!"

I think I got his preference.

High tide that day came on the last hour before sunset. We had already slipped from the haven and worked our way slowly east along the estuary towards the Ousefleet to await it. So the rising waters could lift our little convoy up over the bar and begin to push us inland through the fields. Through the sentries and defensive lines of Carausius's ever-tightening blockade and on towards Eboracum.

Through a no-man's land of abandoned farms and feral cattle left to their own devices by a cruel civil war. Mist rising from riverbank pastures and black cows looming out of its swirl like ghostly creatures from the Underworld as we went floating by.

Those thin cows grazing beside the river looked down at us in astonishment as we came past through the murk. We must have made for an odd sight, even to them, helmeted heads bobbing along at ground level like a row of peas in a pod. No wonder those rowed-transports we rode in that night are called by their crews the '*phaselus*' – a 'bean-pod'.

A fine way to travel to war. Reclining at ease on benches, watching the flat fields of Eboracum's *territorium* steadily sliding-by. Tribal lands taken generations ago for her Colonia's retired veterans to work. The only men working them now are

314

our rowers - the only noise the splash of their oars creaking slightly in muffled mounts, our vessel's wake hitting riverbanks.

And praise be, for once in a ship without nausea, only that hollow feeling in the gut which always comes when facing action.

The tide was strong, the river gods kind, as we slowly snaked upstream. No mudbank or fallen tree opposed us. And surprisingly enough, neither boom nor enemy sentry either. Just a chain they'd left across one of the last loops of the river, that weakly-chinking obstacle we gently lifted out of our way then as carefully replaced. What were the Sixth playing at? Like no-one cared, had energy to patrol.

By the fourth hour of the morning we were slid in darkness under the walls of Eboracum. Tying-up on an empty mooring inside them with no-one coming forward to challenge us. My men swarming like rats in the dark over the sides and away into the town in moments.

I followed them more cautiously with two special companions, Fortis the Batavian, a towering strongman famed among his peers; and chunky Octavius, *optio* of the Second. Three-times winner of Rutupiae's annual bare-knuckle fight. Both of them my personal insurance for any tight spot I find us in, fulfilling Carausius's orders.

An unlikely trio we are to make our way together. Up from the riverside through a sleeping *Colonia* whose last wine-shop has closed, in search of that sheltered spot we finally found. Some overgrown wasteland behind the Temple of Hercules, a suitable place where we could safely wait for dawn among the resting kites.

Predators all.

315

'Difficult it is, suddenly to discard a long-held love'

(Gaius Valerius Catullus, poet & writer, c.84-54 BC)

- 19 -

"Hello" her mother said, when she answered the summons. "So you are with us, after all. Glad to find you back in the land of the living."

"Oh, crikey!" I said.

"Yes, I know" she responded, sitting down neatly and precisely on the very end of the bed "...but it's still lovely to see you conscious and properly awake, at last. We were so worried."

"I had no idea."

"No, well you wouldn't have."

"But you did?"

"Not at first, no. Then I began putting two and two together. He's talked about you a lot over the last few years. Obviously, when we collected you, then I knew for sure. And when you were babbling on about Brantingham, well.... But, no, I've not said anything to Bill.....it's only lovely you both get on."

"I'm really sorry. It's not my doing. An awful coincidence, I promise you. I'd honestly never made the link."

"It's not your fault. A small world. The same profession. You are Bill's friend. He wasn't prepared to leave you there, in that state. Typical of the man, loyal to his friends. True to his family. That's what he's like.....*mostly*."

"I haven't forgotten you know."

"Look. It was a moment in time, a long time ago. My life has moved on, as you can see. As yours will have done. A lot. So how about you?"

"Same old job but wangled a transfer here from Hull. Moved up to Newcastle, flat in Jesmond. Regional runner-up in on-line 'football-manager'...."

"And what's the wheels now?"

"No change there, I'm afraid - still got the red Alfa. Ninety-six thou' on the clock, but the sentimental attachment's too strong."

"No special lady friend?"

"They come and go. Don't last. Maybe it's my fault. Too prone to draw comparisons. You made a hard act to follow."

"Oh, really! Please...."

Her little daughter, Molly, coming back up the stairs and into the room seemed a welcome interruption:

"Is he better, Mummy?"

"Yes, sweetheart, it looks like he is."

"Who is he?"

"I'm Mike."

"Are you an uncle?"

"Err, no. No, I'm not. Just a friend...a friend of your mummy....and your daddy."

317

"I will now treat of ruses that deal with the siege and defence of towns.....Laying aside also all considerations of works and engines of war - the invention of which has long reached its limit, and for the improvement of which I see no further hope in the applied arts - I shall cover the following types of stratagems associated with siege operations....."

('*Stratagemata*' by Sextus Julius Frontinus, c.35–104 AD
Military governor of Britannia, 74-78 A.D.
Inspector of Aqueducts, then Consul in Rome)

- XX -

A few hours spent curled in our woollen soldiers' cloaks behind the Temple of Hercules, hidden among bushes stinking of rubbish, brought the sounds of a town re-awakening to remind us of our mission. Where our comrades had spent them, we could only guess. Similar hides I assumed, unless they'd found women. Some of the charmers in our party could manage that in minutes, from the middle of a desert.

As far as the ships went, and if orders were obeyed, both the narrow 'bean-pods' should have gone home. Retreated empty, rowing away back down the river before their military nature and presence on the wharf became subject of idle comment in the morning.

The bigger flax-boat was different as a common type down there, less likely to be noticed. Allowing its captain and a skeleton crew to stay hidden aboard in case of call. One other option for our onshore parties and their waterborne escape route, if anything went wrong.

The three of us rolled suddenly from our smelly refuge behind the Temple and onto the street as if we'd been there all the time. Brushing ourselves down and trusting to our military dress and carried weapons to merge with a growing crowd in moments. Ostentatiously urinating into broken *amphorae* set at corners for this purpose like we owned the place. Marking our territory like the dogs of war we were.

Town was swarming with tough-looking men like us, doubling the size of the garrison and all here on a governor's summons.

Strangers in uniform whom nobody recognised, no citizen dare challenge. Enjoying the unique thrill that comes from swaggering through a besieged enemy's camp in broad daylight, we savour the moment. Openly gawping at city sights like cousins up from the country. Pointing at statues, reading-out inscriptions.

The Temple of Serapis most people have heard of, its pillars carved by local masons in passable resemblance to Egyptian originals, antiques. I wondered briefly what Theban comrades from the Tenth might have made of that. Christian loathing of the cult enough to neutralise any joy in stylistic recognition, how I imagine their reaction.

Funny how you miss the dead when something comes along to remind of their existence. As if old friends can participate in life from beyond the grave, like father's little commentaries running in my ear. Now there is only Hippolitus left to speak for the Tenth, a living ghost giving body and soul to his clerical military duties, yet stricken with the inconsolable guilt of a survivor. Always praying to his God.

Most of the important city temples were on this precinct; like that of Mars, his image held aloft inside a carved wreath supported by winged Victories. Beside it, the tall circular tower with stone ambulatory round, devoted to the Imperial cult. Dull and dutiful worship of our godlike emperors; followed for form's sake, never belief. I suppose we little people go along with it for the sake of comforting ritual. As a practical means of coming to terms with the awesome power of temporal rulers; done because we have to. Compulsion, not creed.

That one point of obligation to the state over which our Theban friends demurred and, to be fair to him, sole reason for Maximian's slaughter. Claiming no choice when their denial stood equal in his eyes to an outright act of treason. And our law concurs. Men dying over principle, fighting over philosophy. That one, simple, moral and doctrinal question – whether there is any equality between the spirits of gods and men; they ever should equate?

So slight a conceptual disagreement to fall out over, you say?

So high a price in human life for daring.

Definitely not a point in contention here at Eboracum, I thought. You could see from fresh fire-stains on the altar and those shiny marble images of Diocletian and his pal up on their plinths how diligent the resident governor was in ensuring the citizenry observe these important rituals locally. What a pity none of it could save him. Four hundred miles of Carausian control and an impassable sea between the gleaming idols in this temple and those humans they venerate. Imperial mortals unable to rescue their northernmost acolyte.

So where was this High Priest of the Augustine cult; our provincial governor and prefect of the legion; the lordly Quintus Bassianus? Was he hiding out today?

"We'll start with the *domus palatina*...." I told my thickset companions, who knew the reason for my search and swung into line beside me as we forced our way out through the traffic. Beginning a process of elimination before we went for the fortress.

The old Imperial palace built by Severus the African occupies an area in the *Colonia* close to the river-bridge across to the fortress, standing after nearly ninety years of use in some poor state of repair. Today, it looked like the army had requisitioned it as a temporary barracks to house the many extra units pouring down from the Wall, for there is nothing like soldiery to ruin a decent building. Inside, all was confusion. Only the names and symbols of individual units painted-up in black lettering over frescoed flowers or dancing cherubs to distinguish an area set aside for one cohort from another, suggest where to look.

"Where do you gents think you're going?" asked the dark-skinned Spanish cavalryman polishing a row of helmets with bees-wax in an ante-room, when we tried.

"Tribune of the First Batavian Cohort" I said, my two minders moving in around him to underline the point. "*Castra Exploratum*. We get news that bit later, way beyond the Wall. Only arriving last night. Will there be room for us frontier scouts inside the *domus palatina*?"

The Spaniard looked across at our tarnished armour with thinly-veiled disgust, scenting our rubbish-heap rank, then put his polishing cloth down with a sigh:

"Space? Oh, yes, there's plenty of space, sir..." he said. "It's food and rations you gents should worry about. Where your next meal's coming from, not where you will be staying."

"The governor summonsed us, we answered his call. Don't tell me we marched all the way down from the entrenchments and he can't even feed us!"

"Got it in one, tribune. Eboracum is starving. Too few stores to start off with and too many new mouths like yours still arriving. The pirate has stopped any fresh supplies and we're eating our way through the last granary. Then it's the dogs and horses. Unless we force him to battle, the food will run out before the Rhine garrison breaks through his blockade."

"What's Bassianus doing about it?"

"Doing about it, sir? Doing? Have you not heard of the pro-consular games?"

"Games?

"Yes, sir, the games! He starts them today in the city arena. Thinks it will be good for morale. Pacify the soldiers by letting us watch some toothless lions and a few emaciated gladiators circle each other. All of them hungrier than we are. That's his big solution while we wait for help to arrive. An exercise in distraction. Keeping us entertained till the famous Constantius Chlorus comes along. Personally sir, I'd rather eat lion than watch it fed old gladiators."

"You mean I and my men have marched all this way, only to end up in a trap?"

"A trap? Yes, that's probably about the measure of it, sir. No wonder you're an officer. The only fighting you'll see down here happens in the arena, while our Army of Britain lies idle in barracks. It's the biggest military cock-up since Cannae and here we all are, stuck inside it."

I thanked him for his frank advice and handed the cavalryman some silver coins. Because the normal quality was so low, and though he thanked me most politely, it meant he didn't rush to examine what I'd put into his hand. While we made off quickly after that and only just heard the explosion of gratified swearing which erupted when he did.

If Bassianus wasn't in the *domus palatina*, then it must be the fortress.

Going along the street to the start of the bridge we saw banners flying from poles round the top of the arena over the river, advertising the games. Heard the sound of side-drummers drumming. Smelled the odours of frying and boiling. Street-

321

sellers' stalls beside the arena offering a pathetic selection of shrivelled fruits and dodgy meats to tempt the palate of any punter desperate enough to risk them. Dog, horse and rat disguised with spices. As for the people's favourite, their staple, those sea-green oyster-sellers' stalls lying so bare and empty, we recognised signs of our own handiwork. Our work indeed, for the coastal blockade of Carausius had completely closed them down; yet you could sense the disappointment at their absence in those still lingering, hoping for a delivery.

"Why don't we wait around until he appears in the arena, sir, and get him then?"

"I don't know, Octavius, maybe because it might be more difficult in front of a crowd. When the first thing to do is find him. Then we can weigh up our chances, depending on location."

We crossed the timber bridge, marching smartly in step to give a good impression, my two companions close behind. At the twin-arched, stone gateway into a legionary base whose mighty threshold I'd once passed over every day of my brief posting here, a sentry blocked the tunnel of its *porta praetoria*:

"Excuse me, sir, can I ask you for the daily password. Identify yourself and the two men with you. Names, ranks and unit, usual thing - confirm your business in the fortress?"

"Julius Triton, Tribune of the First Batavian Cohort" I said, my two minders moving in around him to underline the point: "*Castra Exploratum*. Hearing news late beyond the Wall, we came with no password. Marched-in alone last night. Come to report for duty to the governor. How he directed and as soon as we could. Will you let us through, soldier?"

"Sorry, sir. More than my life's worth. Instructions to admit no-one. Billet yourselves in the *domus palatina* and await orders with the rest. Someone will come over to you."

There was no point in arguing and our instructions were not to make a scene. Interesting to observe how Bassianus had assembled an army he didn't seem to know what to do with. Didn't trust to approach. I saluted the sentry politely and we went away quietly, back over the fortress ditch but not the bridge. Following instead that line of colossal bastions which guards its riverside prospect.

Here, on flatlands to the south-east of the fortress where its impressive defences end, stands the tall, elliptical oval of

Eboracum's amphitheatre. Already a hollow-cheeked mob of ne'er-do-wells and hungry soldiers milled about on the space in front, looking for food, fornication and fighting. As dangerous a gang as I'd seen in my service, no gathering could illustrate better our great British garrison's world-wide reputation for mutiny.

Or explain more clearly why a martinet commander who once so scared me seemed driven to hide in his fortress from that flood of northern men he's called to his colours.

Obedient to an emperor's briefing, our more-disciplined team of three dutifully split up for a while in search of the women whose acquaintanceship we stood under military orders to buy.

The lank-haired blonde I found and enjoyed in a dark alleyway beneath the arena's arcaded arches seemed listless and thin, giving me comfort but little satisfaction. Though her face shone like the sun once I thanked her with five silver *antoniniani* of Carausius. Empty and heartless transactions like these were all the Army had taught me of women. All it allowed me, in a year where I'd grown older and learned to wish for better.

When my companions reconvened at the ticket booth to josh each other and compare notes on our physical findings, I saw the one I'd just had become the centre of an animated crowd of hawkers and urchins forming outside a tavern over the way. From what we could guess at this distance, any early warmth in congratulation from her friends or owners - for some quality coinage honestly earned – soon teetered on envy and riot.

We its instigators, smiling bleakly at the sight.

"A job well done, sir, if I may respectfully say so. The power of money, eh? That coin of ours will be all round the *cannabae* by midday, just like the emperor ordered. Think my own blowsy redhead's standing over there..." joked Fortis, pointing nearby: "A lady delighted with my prowess and her generous fee...."

"Swore she'd use it for back-rent on that greasy room she has..." he continued. "So her landlord at the wine-shop can repay his vintner; the vintner his Rhineland shippers. One of them bound to carry it over to Augusta Treverorum, out of curiosity and to meet his taxes with. Where, before you know it, the Procurator of Upper Germania will be handing one over without a word for the silent inspection of Constantius Chlorus himself!"

"Aye, Fortis, leaving the great Chlorus rolling about the floor of his palace. Foaming from the mouth at its incredible silver content. Raging at the sight of our man's head and shoulders struck out in bold relief, his *Age of Saturn Renewed!*" added Octavius, wryly.

"Saturn can wait, but we should make ourselves less obvious while he does so" I replied calmly. "Come on lads. Let's get ourselves some seats and mingle inside. The games start in less than an hour. Let's see if the governor shows his face before they do."

"Right-ho, sir, let's go. Get in there and see what's on offer. I could murder a well-cooked rat!" said Fortis, cheerfully.

"Which could as well describe our job with the governor...." my only reply.

The audience of literally thousands waiting inside was military in character but hardly exclusive: plenty of townsfolk too. Half the population roughly, and probably the same proportion from a doubled-up, pent-up garrison. We were lucky, finding a set of numbered wooden seats to match three bone tokens bought on entering. And once the enormous Octavius had ejected with just one glare that pair of pimply youths sprawling over them, we could settle down in good spirits to study its mood.

At first sight it resembled any crowd you might see gathered for the games in any city of the empire. The clothes and bright colours of its many races, tribes and classes; of rich and poor, young and old. More prostitutes and food-vendors, parading up and down between the rows, ready to service every appetite. Calling out the price of diverse wares, each as rotten or inflated.

The bookmakers taking odds on today's card of gladiators' contests, odds they probably settled with their trainers several days before: "*Any good, any good, you ashk?*" had said the man with no teeth on the ticket booth. "*By Ashtarte, they jolly well should be – they've been practishing with eesh other all week!*"

Then once you get used to the wall of noise and shouting, of drums and music, you start to home-in on the faces. Noticing how many seem gaunt and drawn. The individual, whether soldier or civvie, who gnaws at their hands or chews at their tunic. Skin disfigured with sores. The women with black shadows under their eyes, babies squalling for the milk that's never forthcoming.

All of them hungry. Hungry for bread, meat and flesh; hungry for blood.

Even before what happened to my father, I never could stand the games. I'd seen and disliked what it did to my peers. To decent young men who'd never seen a battlefield in their life but turn up with friends in holiday mood, then creep out alone and twitching halfway through. Hot, red-eyed and agitated from all that blood and screaming. Secretly craving more and yet grown so sated with the sight and sound of killing that all they can think of is running as far away as possible. Off to bury their head in a blanket or some convenient harlot's chest. Until the next set of games are called on when, privately hating themselves, creeping back they come. Liking it better, staying on longer.

My responses were different, those of a soldier sent on a mission. Here to obey and execute orders - not gratify a filthy, stinking mob's delight in watching innocent others suffer and die for their public entertainment.

Corrupting, I thought it.

Decay.

The festering heart of Rome and her ageing empire, that vicarious taste for public pain which saps its vigour and taints our populace. Seduces its moral will. If these were my private thoughts, too many would disagree – including probably every soldier I ever commanded. Men enlisted in a time of peace for whom the pleasure of the arena provides a cathartic mirror to their fleeting sights of combat in the service. Killing the odd Caledonian or Saxon, out on a distant frontier, then coming back to boast - as if they were Alexander.

And the sort of commanders who will always insist that soldiers with hardened hearts should be the only type of Roman. That cruelty is duty. A proposition and point of view I knew for a fact to be embraced by the proud official we suddenly saw parading to the sound of trumpets into his governor's box above us. Large escort of legionaries following.

Quintus Bassianus himself had arrived.

Not so reclusive after all?

I studied the crowd for reaction, but could divine little. Opposite, I spotted Aurelius Niger and a cluster of Batavians casually grouped in his general vicinity. Niger saw me too and tipped me a wink to more of his boys sitting right below the 'Imperial' box. Well sited and well done. The plan was moving on.

I did a little count of what we had and told Octavius.

"Say seventy from our chosen hundred are in here with us. What do you reckon?"

"That Bassianus holds the advantage of number. Seems like half an armoured cohort has brought him to the games. Maybe more. Not forgetting his own soldiers among the audience. What should we do, sir?"

"Nothing at the moment, lads. We can't climb up there – his guard would cut us to pieces. Let's watch and think. What more could silver do?"

The trumpets blared again as Bassianus stood up to give the signal for his games to begin. Dropping a kerchief. If the cheers from the crowd in response seemed ragged and half-hearted, who could blame them? Bread might have been a better gift than this circus.

After a Priestess of Nemesis had blessed the arena with incense and bells, the first attraction on the bill seemed pretty routine, the execution in novel ways of the latest crop of condemned criminals. Something the crowd regarded with composure; talking loudly over the herald's description of their crime preceding each disposal, let alone the actual event. The routine elimination of felons. Only the case of two women strangled for stealing food caused the audience particular notice and dimmed the hubbub for a moment, briefly. Perhaps they identified with the crime.

"May the Gods Bless them, poor loves, wherever they're going" said a few of their own sex from the crowd. From up here, it looked likely to be Hades.

A man who'd assaulted a tax gatherer was tied to a wooden pole then a tired-looking bear let in. I don't know where they'd got the bear from but it must have been the only living thing in all Eboracum that day which wasn't feeling hungry. It sniffed around the margins of the arena instead, looking for an exit and showing little interest in this man the organisers set for him, who sagged on his pole as if passed-out from fear. Or else its vile breath.

The clincher was the bear's reaction when it heard the noise of some street musician drifting-in, presumably playing their pipes in the arcade under the amphitheatre for the charity of passers-by. The bear pricked up its ears then stopped to listen, before standing up on its hind legs to dance, causing the first signs of humour I'd seen in our audience. They rocked with laughter while the beast, further encouraged by this favourable reaction, now pirouetted dreamily into the very centre of the ring.

Bassianus's face was a picture, fury written all over it. I could almost read his lips: "What idiot chose this animal?" Then he gestured for action.

The bear was driven back out through the archway it had entered by, gingerly pursued by two daintily-winged attendants dressed as Mercury. The felon being cut down from his pole and falling into the sand like a mariner onto a beach. When he looked up from the ground revived there was a fleeting hint of joy, as if he thought himself rescued from a nightmare worse than any shipwreck, but Bassianus's quick gesture across the throat to the masked attendants made his long-term future clear.

After two blows with a hammer, 'Mercury' takes him out on a hook.

It wasn't enough.

The crowd stayed restive and something good was going to be needed, if they were not to start throwing things.

At the other end of the ring a herald came in to announce a proper contest: *Secutor* against *Retiarius*. The classic bout: sword-and-shield-man against net-and-trident-man. For a moment its prospect settled an edgy mob, but everyone knew that keeping their contentment would be contingent on the quality of scrap which follows.

The bookmakers closed their odds, the doxies their legs. Flautists stopping fluting, drummers drumming, hawkers their hawking. Leaving we three, plus Aurelius Niger and the Batavians over, not betting on anything and all of us holding our breath. Waiting for an opportunity.

327

From the other end of the stands, we watched the *Secutor* being ceremonially armed in advance of the fight. Handed his visored helmet and then the rectangular shield which gives this type their ancient title. Breastplate and leg-guards.

Who he was that day or the individual's 'fighting' name I cannot now say, and nor could we have guessed whether he would prove any good. Too far away to judge. All I can say is, as a soldier and swordsman myself, that the *Secutor* is traditionally more heavily-armed and armoured than his usual opponent. So he might be thought by some to have an advantage, as a type more resembling and equipped like modern soldiers.

His lightly-dressed opponent, *Retiarius*, was led out into the sandy centre of the arena by the umpire; usually a retired gladiator himself, the *Rudarius*. Where they assemble in the middle there is always a stone block with an iron ring to which any reluctant fighter wanting to run away can be chained, though neither of these two looked likely candidates for its humiliating restraint. To be fair to them both, a pair of experienced professionals who could be relied on to give the punters of Eboracum a proper fight for their money.

The best bout of the day and their sponsor Bassianus's best chance of winning audience satisfaction from his resident population or their swollen garrison. A lot at stake, in short.

What about the other fighter?

Well, the advantages of *Retiarius* lie in the long reach of his trident and the unusual potential in his weighted net, should he ever get opportunity to deploy it against a heavyweight opponent unable to move so quickly. His weakness apparent in an almost total lack of armour – hence his agility.

And don't forget he also carries a sword.

The reason why this deliberate mismatch of weaponry and equipment between the two types makes the unbalanced contest resulting so absorbing for *afficionados* of the arena.

How would it pan-out today?

The *Rudarius* brought them calmly together into the centre over the ring-stone like a teacher his pupils. To receive some judicious words of quiet advice we couldn't hear, before tapping its iron with his wooden wand as signal to begin. When the stone rang.

It started gently enough, these two gladiators circling each other carefully for a while in the usual way. Getting into it and scuffing up the sand with squirming steps while they did so, before the *Retiarius* boldly and unusually attempted an immediate throw with his net.

The crowd gasped at such a reckless opening and while the *Secutor* might be weighed down with armour and equipment, at this stage in the combat he will always be fresh and lively. Even the most ponderous of their type can usually jump and dodge, at least to start with. As this one did this time.

Bad move for someone.

The throw fell short, leaving the unhappy *Retiarius* regretting his early impetuosity.

Naturally he tried to recover the net but *Secutor* wouldn't let him, hobnailed boots firmly pinning its mesh hard into the arena floor.

Faced with its loss, *Retiarius* retreated, trying to draw the sword-and-shield-man after him on his faint hope of maybe recovering this essential piece of kit, doubling-back for it later. If that was the plan then *Secutor* had realised it, for he took the unusual step of picking up the net and running his sword blade clean through its fibres, lead weights breaking loose and falling to the floor.

The audience hooted at this novel stratagem, while *Retiarius* reconsidered his worsening position from slightly-further away.

The net now useless and in shreds, *Secutor* came looking for its owner. Lumbering towards him like a legion of one. Heavy infantry on an irresistible charge, his face invisible and inscrutable behind the perforated bronze visor.

Inhuman.

In an oval arena, *Retiarius* had nowhere to go. Running away was all right up to a point but the patience of the mob would tolerate it only briefly. Right in front of our part of the stand was where he finally decided to face up to his faceless opponent.

In a momentary pause from the yelling of the crowd, so close I could see beads of sweat running down the net-man's back, I heard the panting of *Secutor* inside his helmet as he approached. Maybe he was not so irresistible a killing-machine after all, probably as half-starved as everyone else round here, inside all that armour. An ageing gladiator in his last fight, as much to be pitied as the unprotected man in a white tunic he'd brought to bay in front of us.

Poor old bloke, I thought.

On that moment, I felt sorry for him, even though he couldn't lose. The net-man held his trident out ahead of him like a magic charm, as if that was all he need do to fend *Secutor* away. Like the boatman a river bank, but *Secutor* had recovered his breath from the chase and wasn't having any of it. He barged its line of three barbed prongs contemptuously away with the rim of his shield like the weapon was an annoying fly, and moved in for the kill.

People often forget the net-man's sword. His trident too long for close-quarters fighting, *Retiarius* recognised the time was come for his last line of defence and drew it. Blades clashed and sparks flew. The mob was on its feet, red-faced and screaming for their particular favourite but, whatever the outcome, some wouldn't like it. When, as the Gracchi brothers used to say, you can please some of the people some of the time....

Secutor drove forwards regardless.

Retiarius tried bravely to parry his flurry of sword blows with a flat blade but the astonishing forces coming-in on him clanged so hard and shivered so violently down his arm that he couldn't but drop it. Vainly he dived to the floor to recover the fallen weapon but *Secutor* beat him to it, stamping his boot onto his opponent's blade and pinning *Retiarius* down beside it as firmly. Held by the tip of his own short sword, a *gladius*.

The umpire came hurrying over to intervene whilst *Retiarius* took his arrival for the best chance of crawling away. *Secutor* now had two swords in his possession; one in his sword hand, the other gripped beside the shield-boss.

The panting *Rudarius*, finally asserting his official authority, used his wand to separate the fighters. The crowd was stamping and roaring its approval of *Secutor*'s style and achievement, so he was obliged by convention to turn around and gratefully receive their adulation. Folding back the hinged visor of his helmet, he held the captured weapon and his own aloft for their public inspection.

"*Secutor-two-sword,   secutor-two-sword!*" chanted the spectators, thrilled at the whirlwind speed of his crushing victory.

I saw no joy in his tired face. While he turned towards each corner of the stands in turn, neither *Secutor* himself nor the *Rudarius* could have noticed *Retiarius* creeping lizard-like along the sand towards him, trident still in hand. They certainly did once he'd slashed him - soundlessly dragging its triple points across the brown, unprotected backs of *Secutor*'s knotted calves.

Secutor grunted and fell like a tree, the gasps and sympathy of the crowd falling with him. "What a dirty trick!" said Octavius, disgusted. "What in the Name of Nemesis is the umpire going to do about that?"

The man we'd thought our victor now lay in the sand with blood on his legs, crippled for life. Unable to rise but still hanging grimly onto both swords while looking bravely into the eyes of an upright *Retiarius* whose sharp-pronged trident was pointed straight at his throat.

"Mercy!" shouted a sentimental mob on the edge of tears. One which had already viewed half a dozen deaths before with utter equanimity, but now felt deeply-moved.

Rudarius and the rest of us looked across to the 'Imperial' box for a decisive ruling on an unusual case. Justice delayed is justice denied and Quintus Bassianus was never a man troubled by self-doubt. He didn't hesitate or flinch from the question for one moment: drawing himself up in his gilded seat straightaway to make the traditional gesture for a kill.

"A kill?" said Fortis, "I do not believe it! What on earth does the governor think he's doing? To kill the real winner? He cannot be serious!"

All around the stands, people were stunned by his decision.

"You cannot mean it!" they shouted.

Was the governor daft? Did he not understand the Rule of Blind-Side?

In the sudden silence that followed the heralds' official repetition of this remarkable ruling, I found myself standing to my feet and yelling out loud with all the force in my lungs I could muster: "One hundred silver *antoniniani* for the life of the *Secutor!*"

331

People turned around to look at me, astonished: "In the Name of Jupiter, man, this is the arena, not a slave auction!" said a notary next to me.

No matter, I'd caught the eye of Aurelius Niger opposite while I did so, No sooner had I finished than he'd grasped the plan. Up and doing the same thing. Standing there and shouting with all the priceless resonance of a man whose whole professional life is spent out on the parade ground: "One hundred silver *antoniniani* for the life of the *Secutor*!"

If Bassianus hadn't heard me, then he'd certainly be hearing Niger.

I saw the Governor and Prefect of the Legion lean across to his officers and advisers, as if he wanted to check with them what everyone else had heard. Like he didn't know what to do. Didn't really believe that anyone in the crowd would dare to question his judgement.

Bid so much for a hamstrung piece of gristle.

Octavius beside me joining in: "And my silver *antoniniani* to save him, too! Add my one hundred to the total bid: make it three hundred silver *antoniniani* for the life of the *Secutor*!"

There was consternation in the 'Imperial' box.

I could guess one obvious question immediately exercising them. Since when were *antoniniani* stamped out in proper metal, let alone silver? The correct answer: *'two centuries'*. And yes, if Imperial administrations had cynically run our currency steadily down for generations, to the point that even government no longer accepts the product of its own mints to satisfy taxation, then what on earth did these bidders intend? What sort of madmen stand up inside the arena of a besieged city to offer insane amounts of special issue for the one-off purchase of a permanently-crippled gladiator?

"Sir, I think it's time we showed them the colour of our money...." stated Fortis.

He was right and its brightness was blinding.

I reached into my bronze arm-purse for the two hundred and eighty-six examples left me, after whores and miscellaneous expenses. The governor in his box was too far away but an artist's still-life of a wounded gladiator stood-over by his vanquisher remained well within my range. As if white marble, frozen below. So I lobbed all but one of my remaining ration towards this touching tableau in a shining shower - some falling straight onto them, the others short and into the audience. Aurelius Niger and his lads doing the same from their side, successfully directing a hail of coin into the 'Imperial' box itself. Confused, the governor's guards put their shields up against it, as if these were silver arrows.

When the fighting in the crowd had stopped and people examined what they'd won from each other, or the sky had gifted, there was complete pandemonium.

"Is this truly the coin of Carausius? The money of a pirate?" asked the middle-aged farming type seated beside me, in a quiet tone of wonder. "They told us he had nothing."

"Yes, it is" I said "And there's plenty more where that came from...."

If he was a farmer, then he must have been a gentleman farmer. Maybe a villa-owner like Justinianus. One who'd been to better schools than I had. Turning the shining coin he'd caught from me over, he knew its reference straight away: "*Expectate Veni!*"

"*Oh Come, Awaited One!*" I said.

"Yes, yes, I do realise!" he said, testily. "I have read Vergil, you know, I'm not that stupid. And this abbreviation, this '*RSR*' on the other side?"

"*Redeunt Saturnia Regna:* The Golden Age - of Saturn of course - is now returned us."

"Mmm, that's what I thought it would mean, I didn't need you. It follows naturally on from the texts...." he said more kindly. "And with beautiful coinage like this, maybe it really has."

It is no exaggeration to describe the psychological effect on their hearts and minds of the high-quality silver coins we showered onto the starving people of Eboracum that day as absolutely devastating. Nothing we could have done, neither military victory nor contrived family tree, could have more vividly proved to them the absolute legitimacy of Carausius. His entitlement to rule the three provinces of Britannia and Lower Gaul was clinched in that moment.

Including with the soldiers.

I looked up at the 'Imperial' box. It was empty, though I saw the back of one legionary filing slowly out the door.

"Quick!" I called to my companions. "Our man's getting away!"

We turned and ran for the stairs, throwing more money and barging people out of the way. Over the other side, I was glad to see Aurelius Niger and his lads doing the same, plus another knot of our men from the ships not spotted before. If we were to dare intercept the governor and his guard before they got back into the fortress, then I was going to need every man-jack of them.

"Do I know you?" said Quintus Bassianus haughtily when I stepped out to bar his path along the river road. A provincial governor at the head of his men, confronted by one junior tribune and the scrapings of the Fleet.

"I once brought you sealed despatches from the Pennine forts...."

It meant nothing to him and he looked back at me blankly.

"Get out of my way, boy, before I have you arrested!"

The street was lined with people, shadowed by the mighty towers above us. For a moment there was utter silence. I broke it with the last coin I'd kept back, a silver *antoninianus* with the chunky profile of his enemy stamped off-centre onto it by the Petuaria Mint, which I flicked towards him to show my contempt. It fell clinking at his feet and he looked involuntarily down to its gleaming in the mud, the face of his nemesis, before jerking back upright at my reply:

"Not this time, sir. Now it's the other way around. The man on that coin is Emperor of All Britain. He sent me here to arrest *you*. Any one of your soldiers who comes round to his cause is promised a hundred like it straightaway!"

Bassianus scowled and gestured to his officers: "Clear these water-rats from our streets, men! Take this upstart to the cells. We can draw more detail of his master's insane strategies out of him later. Cure his insolence with hot irons."

Nobody moved.

Bassianus was stunned. He could not believe his order had not met with that unquestioning obedience he'd always demanded and won throughout a long military career. Perplexed, he turned to look at his escort. They were still with him all right; standing smartly to attention in parade armour, the scarlet horse-hair crests on their helmets waving gently in the breeze off the river, but no more movement than that from any of them.

Cursing their idleness, he drew on his sword with a rhetorical: "Must I do it myself?"

Sensing a pressure on my chest, I pulled back my soldier's cloak and looked down to the *seax* strapped across it. Her hilt glowed redder in the sunlight, like she smelled danger and would draw my hand to hers for comfort. Which I did.

Spatha against *seax*.

As we faced each other I realised how very much like that other brute, Maximianus, this Quintus Bassianus seemed. How big he was. Another bullying martinet whose sheer physical size had been crucial to their early progression. And then to staying in office. He towered over me, bulking-up over-trained muscle like some wrestler at a country fair.

"Is that really necessary from an officer – what a shocking way for gentlemen to behave!" - I could almost hear father's disapproval, imagined in my ear.

The crowd parted and made a space, relishing their luck. Who needs the amphitheatre when a bout of this calibre is opened up for free beside the public highway? An Imperial governor in person, down in a street-corner tag-fight with some jumped-up subaltern from the frontier. There were catcalls and jeers but for whose benefit, I couldn't really say.

I knew my men were invisible but behind me, though unsure of their reaction. Would they passively stand back like the mob and his legionaries already had, committing the fate of their young commander to the divine whims of Fortuna?

However those went.

On that pivotal moment I felt most scared and alone. That didn't mean I wasn't.

Bassianus advanced, his army long-sword in hand, its hilt carved in ivory like the head of a bird. An imperial eagle. I held my shorter *seax* up but feared for the exceptional reach of this unusually-tall man, almost six feet. His greater strength and cruelty.

We stood there fleetingly, face-to-face and blade-to-blade, and I tensed for the first blow given. Then a small trickle of blood came out the left side of Bassianus's mouth and trickled down his chin, while his body rotated slowly like an Archimedean screw and he collapsed neatly under a rain of blows coming-in

335

from his own side. His eyes turning white into his head as they rolled upwards and he as suddenly fell.

The governor's escort detachment from his Sixth Victorious Legion, The Faithful, had swiftly reviewed their position, and decided to go with the money.

From standing facing me, their erstwhile commander instantly went down in a flurry of dagger-blows to the back, his soldiers not even bothering with swords. Like it was an outlet for all the years of hectoring and bullying, of privation and punishment, endured at his behest. So great in their ferocious vengeance, they nearly took his head off.

In no time at all, what had once been the Imperial governor of *Britannia Inferior; Praefectus Legionis* to *Legio VI Victrix Pia Fidelis* and a *Sevir Augustalis* in the Imperial cult; resembled nothing more than a tawdry heap of soiled rags, lying at the side of the road.

They gave his corpse Carausius's coin to pay the Infernal ferryman with, then unceremoniously cut through the rest of the neck cord and dumped his head with whatever else was left of him on a rubbish tip, under the fortress' west-walls. Left for dogs and crows to do the mourning over.

"I think we've just captured a city" said Aurelius Niger. "Will we get *Corona Muralis*?"

Medals were the last thing on my mind and I was sick of killing. All I wanted from anyone was the chance to get home.

336

"However, the....case was referred to the European Court of Justice by the House of Lords, and after the usual two-year delay, the oracle at Luxembourg, in the form of a Grand Chamber of thirteen judges, gave an unusually clear and decisive answer. The Grand Chamber held that the Court of Appeal were entirely wrong."

(The Honourable Mr Justice Bean
in <u>NHS Leeds–v-Farner</u> [2011] UKEAT)

- 20 -

Once they were satisfied I was well enough to leave and not falling over any more, Bill and Venezia responded to my insistence I went home to Newcastle with an equal insistence I let them drive me back together. Travel in their Range Rover on the Sunday night, rather than get the last eastbound-train from Hexham, slowly alone.

Venezia was a fast driver, something else I hadn't known before. In what seemed like no time at all we were pulling up outside my first-floor flat in a leafy side street off Osbourne Road. Lucky among the student or academics' hatchbacks to find any space big enough for parking so large a status-symbol as their boxy 4x4.

On one of those sunny May evenings when life holds fresh promise and pollen dances in the air like visible grains of goodwill, making everyone feel happier. Except of course for that overweight man in the grey and blue *gauleiter*'s gear of a *'Parking Control Warden'* I'd noticed sliding under the nearby cover of a weeping-willow to watch us unload. Keen to strike the moment our twenty minutes expired. So keen in fact, after only fifteen minutes at the kerbside, that he's already taking multiple pictures with some hand-held device. Oddly premature, but then it's expensive cars like Bill's which most attract the peak-capped servants of a cash-starved local government regime at war with its citizens.

Legalised extortion and war without end, waged by an army of jobsworths. Including that rotund punk whose day we had no intention of making.

337

While Bill leaned in through the open rear window of the Range Rover, Venezia gave me a quick hug and peck on the cheek, handing over a supermarket carrier-bag: "I've put some milk, a frozen pizza, and some oven-ready chips in there with a few other bits. To tide you over before you can get to the shops for yourself. Take care now. Look after yourself."

Bill passed me my leather rally-bag containing all the clothes and kit I'd used to live out of *Xenobia*'s boot during the event, clapped me heartily on the back, and then they were gone. I waved them off to the end of the road then let myself in while the traffic warden waddled off down the road, radiating disappointment. Looking instead for a hearse outside a church he could ticket, or an ambulance at a road accident. In a city littered with abandoned electric cars, surely he could find enough elsewhere to be going on with?

When I got in through the front door, the floor mat was covered with several layers of official post. No-one else writes these days, so mostly they were of the threatening brown envelope variety. From various institutions, one of them postmarked *'Communita di Siena'*. Another from my student-loan company of a dozen years ago, still hounding me with final demands. And an £85 instant fine from the vehicle-licensing computer in Swansea.

Chilling taste of a future where all prosecutions are run by robot, putting honest lawyers like me completely out of work. Heartless machines lacking my 'discretion' option, automatically convicting of the 'crime' of not notifying them by the first of this month that the road tax on my wrecked Toyota was not to be renewed. The agency's indifference to my trinity of reasons:

One, that it's in pieces; two, permanently off the English roads; and three, currently in police custody at a secure compound inside Milan airport.

Typifying that irritating, petty, bureaucratic tyranny now encountered everywhere which still so winds me up. Why, when every curtain was closed, it was important I took urgent action to lift my flagging mood and lighten my life despite it. Dragging them back to let the last rays of daylight flood into my empty sitting room, restore its cheer to a gloomy interior. Put on a bit of Bob Marley, too: his *'Natural Mystic'* to warm the air and brighten me up along with it.

338

Time to unpack.

To my surprise, when I unzipped my rally-bag all the clothes inside were freshly laundered. Ironed and folded. This was embarrassing: I was a New Man in an age of crease-free shirts. No woman had done this for me since my mother died.

Either a harmless act of selfless kindness, or a symbolic gesture towards something else?

Nod to the memory.

Something too complicated to contemplate this minute.

I sat down in an easy chair with my head in my hands. This was getting ridiculous - I could almost have cried.

Getting back into work tomorrow should cure me of that.

Or really give me something to cry about.

"The retreating pirate seized first the Fleet which protected the coasts of Gaul, built many more besides in Roman style, seduced the loyalties of a Legion, cut off whole divisions of Provincial troops, recruited Gallic merchant traders to his service, won over hordes of barbarian forces with spoils from the provinces themselves and, through training given by those who supported him in his disgraceful acts, prepared them all for naval duties."

(From Eumenius the court poet's panegyric
on the life of Constantius Chlorus: 1st March 297 A.D.)

- XXI -

When he was still commander at Rutupiae, they say Carausius had insisted on living an ordinary domestic life with his large family of women, whatever daily dangers he was facing out at sea. Billeted in an extensive but sparsely-decorated town-house set just outside the fort walls. An unassuming but charming old *domus* from whose back-door onto a side street his wife and elder daughters would famously sell to passers-by their onions and purple cabbage, grown on adjoining allotments.

Once he'd finished recovering Eboracum and ensured control of Londinium, and now that he was a proper emperor, such homely arrangements clearly wouldn't do. But neither, announced Carausius, should we expect to find him occupying Londinium's dedicated palace for the governor like everyone imagined. His whole family would be moving across instead to Calleva Atrebatum. My home town. A place where, apart from the walled security of its inland location, he could point out practical advantages for his supervising certain urgent works he'd commissioned with the shipyards of Clausentum.

Doubling the size of our *Classis* by next spring.

With no sign of my intermediate officers offering me leave, or any looking likely, one benefit of my Commander-in-Chief's latest change of address lay in its hope for some official errand giving me chance to get home anyway. My first since joining-up.

And I will always remember when it did.

340

Officially provided with a series of worn-out horses from Imperial Post stables along the way in order to obey my imperial master's call into his presence, these nags left me making slow and lonely progress along an ancient road which snakes west over the downs like a serpent's back. At which point I'll readily admit to not being the world's greatest horseman - treating them more as means to an end, as transport not friends. An ambivalent attitude to horseflesh doubtless traceable back to father's tired joke about *"dangerous at both ends and uncomfortable in the middle".* Creatures whose necessary use for sport or travel was never transformed in my case into anything resembling enthusiasm.

The latest beast I'm issued with probably didn't help, its limping gait further slowed by the squalls of a prevailing westerly. Plus my eventual decision on hitting the woods to fall-in for safety with a gaggle of other road-users. If these travellers I joined showed little urgency, it was interesting to note how many travelled to petition the same important person whose summons I answered. Illustrating if nothing else how his recent elevation filled a decision-making vacuum which a succession of corrupt provincial governors never properly met.

Being readily accepted by the people as emperor, it fell increasingly to Carausius, and in natural extension to his military authority, to exercise a growing range of powers. Whatever citizens wanted, in fact, like sitting in court to take cases. Manumitting (granting the freedom of slaves) by hearing their story, then bestowing a bronze certificate - or deciding on boundary disputes, blood-money, contracts, and so many civil matters. Exercising in short, and to all intents and purposes, what I think our local Atrebatean tribesmen had translated in their own minds into the inherent powers of their former kings.

Traditional rights traceable from centuries ago.

If my fellow-travellers were from further afield, some even from Gaul, they were mostly in pursuit of the same jurisdiction. Merchants, lawyers and supplicants. Like at Petuaria, a guild of wayfaring litigants looking for a court.

Provincials mainly and hence - unlike me - people with no local knowledge or understanding of the Great Forest through which this important trunk road cuts its linear swathe. All of us feeling safer in company and a country where bears, boar or robbers represent an equal danger. Even for someone who once hunted here, the threats against which we all band together. Thinking to that extent our new brotherhood of the road has nearly done its job, if not for an ambush we so carelessly fell into where the forest began to thin and our vigilance relaxed.

The embanked road had levelled out and, high on its *agger*, we were jogging along perfectly happily together. Engaged in harmless chat. Pleased to see the encroaching trees starting to draw back, more open landscapes up ahead, when two groups of armed men who must have been hiding - crouching down in deep drainage-ditches either side of the road - suddenly burst onto the carriageway.

There were two of them to every one of us: armed to the teeth with axes and swords. Resistance seemed pointless and they took each horse by the halter.

Barbarians.

Their leader, or else the one who shouted most and loudest at his comrades, was a tall man whose thin moustache drooped down past his chin. He turned and sheathed in a broad belt the sword he had just waved in our faces, as if to show his contempt for the threat we didn't offer.

"What do you think you are doing, holding up honest passengers on the Emperor's highway?" I said, dismounting, and suddenly the only one of my companions with a tongue.

Presumably assuming he could subdue me with one watery glare and a blast of bad Latin, he looked me in the eye and snarled:

"I am Hnaudfridus the Frank and these are my men. Free-born men, now your *Numerus Hnaudfridi*. Roman soldiers in the service of an emperor's coiner, your great *Rationalis*. These are my men and this is our roadblock, his official checkpoint. If you don't believe me, get yourself back to Londinium. Ask our master, Allectus, he will tell you. Whose rules are simple - if you want safe passage, then you must pay our toll. We only accept silver and we give no change: jewellery or coin, anything will do. If you have no silver - then you cannot pass, must return to the woods. Understand me? If you have no silver but try to push past against our orders, then we will kill you. And who are *you* to be questioning men like *us*...?"

I drew back my hooded cloak and dropped its hood so they might see my face and uniform tunic, the blue lighthouse badge of the *Classis* stamped on its creamy cloth. Whether that impressed them, I cannot say.

More interesting to Hnaudfridus and his men seemed the red garnets suddenly glittering on the pommel of my *seax* as the light got in. Those stones to which their greedy eyes straightaway glittered back with retinal cupidity. Mistaking their chance of imminent loot. They were ignorant fools not to know as I her keeper grew to, that she only shines like that on the sometime: when there are bare necks ready for taking. On the subtle scent of unguarded throats, left open for slashing open.

When she smells blood.

Like that windy day on the road to Calleva Atrebatum, when some Frankish mercenaries of Allectus tried to rob my new-found acquaintance of their little silver.

She'd put herself into my hand and was dancing across the first row of the Hnaudfridi before a thought to go with it had even entered my head.

Immortal Gods – how it pumps from a neck wound! And what a bloody shambles.

The rest of the Franks fled.

When they had, I sat wretchedly down by the side of a stone road, drained and appalled by whatever comes over me. Grateful companions slapping my back.

Me put hopelessly in mind of a thing once read long ago in a History of Herodotus. His tale of how the Greeks of Socrates' Athens would prosecute as if a live defendant before their courts the very sword by which some man of their city had come to be killed.

As if it could bear a guilty mind of its own, be culpable as such.

Here in far-away Britain, hunched on the damp edge of Spinaii Forest, I was forced to acknowledge the sense in those ancient jurists' reasoning.

That someone self-possessed like me could wake up, to find himself bewitched.

Obedient instrument to this, his overpowering weapon.

343

- 21 -

When I walked into town from Jesmond, there were multiple newspaper hoardings propped against the building line. All the way down from Eldon Square to Grey Street and each one of them announcing: *"TYNESIDE MEP ROCKS EU WITH 'GOLDEN AGE' PROMISE"*.

Instinct immediately told me its slogan must involve my old friend Bill. Back in the fray straight from our return, even in the week or so I'd lain comatose and out of things. What it couldn't do was tell me what story lay behind this extravagant claim.

I bought the new-look *'Newcastle Journal'* which should from the old man whose open kiosk has huddled beneath the towering base of Monument, by the Metro entrance, for more years than I can remember. This time, there was a queue. The online edition was currently out of service and, with the amount of disruption the worldwide web kept on suffering, it was interesting to see how promptly even the younger generation would revert to traditional newsprint for getting information instead.

Or how happy it makes our Geordie press-barons to find a local lad like Bill Cariss right at the heart of national and international politics. For the first time in a generation. Someone who understood their media priorities, whose self-penned press releases assure the latest crop of 'management-buy-out' editors a regular source of reliable north-eastern copy. When half the digital sources of stories fit to follow from a desk-top have somehow dried-up, and old fashioned legwork is back to take its place, self-publicists like Bill could offer local gold.

"There you go, sir" said the newspaper seller, rolling my copy tightly.

This time and for the first time, he truly was right. I really *was* going. No argument, no pausing to take my change from him. His newspaper one of the few things left in this world you can't pay for using a 'phone or a pad - from an old geezer only accepting cash. Even if I had no time this minute to stop and read the story behind his banner's interesting headline, about my old mate Bill. Not if I was to arrive bang on schedule at work as planned. Monday morning, eight-thirty on the dot, and only two weeks late.

"Hey, what's a couple of weeks between friends?"

When I made it across to our deliberately-anonymous CPS office's front door, either I'd forgotten the security code on the lock or else they'd changed it while I was away. First time in years. And their facial-recognition thingy would be no use either. That device stopped working barely two weeks from installation - probably thanks to the piece of used chewing-gum some Geordie clubber forced into its aperture while doing something similar with a girlfriend in our doorway. I sighed heavily – another clever piece of kit broken. Nothing electronic seeming to work properly anymore, certainly not these days. Leaving me with no alternative.

Instead of slipping quietly in, I was going to have to press the buzzer with a thumb and put my looming face to a grill. Beg through its intercom to be let in. How embarrassing is that? Not what I'd wanted at all for my return, making any sort of fuss.

The white box of a CCTV camera looking down on me from a forty-five degree angle, its lens the picture of glassy indifference. What a way to arrive!

"Well, hello, stranger!" replied Young Elaine from reception, through an intercom clear enough to catch her crackly sigh on hearing my request for some physical action from her. Prelude to a lengthy pause before she reluctantly abandons her post, slipping daintily down a short stairwell to open the security door only but slightly.

"Be quick!" she hissed, nervous of the outside world. "Whatever happened to you?"

"It's a long story…"

"Yeah, whatever!" she said, looking down to check she'd not chipped a sculpted fingernail through heavy manual labour, before the reception phone rang out again to interrupt her warm concern and hasten our rush upstairs.

"The prodigal returns..." called out admin's James from their side room, as I marched down the main corridor towards our team office: "Kill the fatted calf!"

"Oh, hallo, *daaarling*!" squealed Victoria, a barrister in the adjoining 'set' as I crossed the overcrowded, under-decorated, open-plan room which pens our various lawyer teams together between ever-growing towers of paper. "*Wherever* have you been.....I've been *so* worried about you, my darling. Simply *pining* away!"

I knew full well that Victoria would iron my clothes and a whole lot more, anytime I wanted, but could never face the likely sacrifices involved. Being vetted by her terrifying mother only the first of them.

"Vicky, babe, Light of my Life, why else do you think I fought my way back here across half of Occupied Europe - if not for the joy of seeing you again!"

"Hey man! We'd given up on you...thought you'd gone and emigrated...." said Sanjay, one of the senior lawyers in my team: "Thought we were going to have to cancel your invite to my wedding reception, this Saturday coming...."

"No, no, Sanjay. Please don't think that. Remember, I always said I wouldn't let you down, didn't I? Mille Miglia or no Mille Miglia. Besides, it's an honour - I've never been to a Hindu wedding before. Still at the same venue - Saint James's Park, isn't it?"

"Sure, man, United's main hospitality suite. And no, not *on* the pitch, remember. All the same, a shame there'll be no home match on - we could have watched it during."

"They'd be sure to lose...." said James, following me into the room.

I had worked in that particular prosecutors' office covering what we once would call the '*Northumbria*' police area, for a good few years by now. Ever since my transfer up from Hull and long enough to grow pretty-much used to most of the people there. Like most offices, an odd and varied bunch, but not so bad a selection of professional humanity when all was said and done.

Almost family - good, decent people; capable lawyers and committed public servants. Including my learned and eccentric old boss in Newcastle, a senior solicitor of integrity who knew her law and had somehow managed to survive on the basis of a pragmatic approach towards applying an ever-more rigid policy book of centralised correctness.

"Never mind what the law says, never forget we are civil servants, too...." she'd laugh.

Until last year when, like almost everyone else I ever admired professionally or took for example in my early career, she was suddenly got rid of. As if it was all my fault - as if earning my respect only guaranteed a mentor bad luck. Hardly auguring well for my own future, either, if this was the fate of my every professional exemplar, of every professional. But so long as I stayed young, in outlook at least, I could believe it wouldn't be.

For them or me.

Leaving us to wonder what fresh example her successor might set? For a while, and after my wise old mentor was prematurely retired in this way, no-one could say. As a vacancy, left unfilled; coincident with various other CPS geographical areas further regionalising, to save us more money. To match that modern, unified policing machine which Home Office mandarins now demand be forged from the former Northumbrian and Durham forces, plus several others adjoining.

Until someone found some cash at the back of a drawer in Whitehall.

That point when we were told of a brand new Chief Crown Prosecutor to be appointed for the whole northern region; of our re-branding as *'CPS englandnorth'* – as an east and west combined. Our new leader to be based at a *"state-of-the-art hub office"* converted at massive public expense from a derelict hotel sited beside the A1, near to Scotch Corner.

The middle of nowhere, in short, and handy for no-one but herself. In her own words: *"A higher vantage"* - how even she admitted it. More importantly, somewhere safe where performance indicators and Byzantine pronouncements of latest policy could remain her uncontested speciality. Fiddling while Rome burned.

And while we waited to find out more about how this new incumbent would tackle these peripheral things, someone from her old office in Manchester I met on a training course offered some idea: "You won't like her style.... " said Ajaz.

"If she doesn't bother the troops, she can do whatever she likes..." my calm response. "Watch with beady eyes from a distant tower while we footsloggers down on the front line get on with the real job. That little business of practising proper criminal law. Potting villains..."

Since her new job description gave her the whole of an immense new northern 'Region' to supervise, both side the Pennines, then the good news was that by definition we would never see her much. Constantly flitting about like a mad thing as she must. No wonder she could never remember anyone's name. "*Catch you later...*" the eternal catchphrase of her corridor collisions. We her minions, smiling blandly back, as firmly hoping she wouldn't.

"*Not if I can help it....*" what we really thought.

Staff, eh? Where on earth do we find them and, to be fair to her, who would be their manager? Herding the proverbial cats.

"*I have a passion for efficiency....*" was her memorable announcement on first arrival. Doubtless what she told the interview panel. A motive we readily understood, and yet a sensation we couldn't imagine her discovering in any other way.

If bosses come and go, all working life goes on. Everyday life for us prosecutors in those local courts not yet closed through savings-cuts continuing much the same as always. The same old defence solicitors popping up to defend the same old defendants: generation unto generation. The same old tired excuses for the same old names, falling on the same deaf ears.

Some of the men – and it was still mostly men – our magistrates and district judges were jailing could trace a direct lineage of crime and family all the way back to the Border Reivers. As could a surprising number of their solicitors. Notorious names whose lawless Armstrongs, Nichols, Grahams and Elliotts had terrorised the Borders for centuries.

Pity so few of the region's courthouses survive intact to show the same resilience. When neither our old English county police forces, nor those homely, local courthouses once administering local justice to their peers, can match a homogenised European model being silently smuggled-in, '*Grotius Project*' et al.

When austerity and a dwindling tax-base provide the ideal cover story and excuse for a government doing away with both.

But, whatever the dilapidated state of our regional infrastructure or those staff still working it (and from a personal/professional point of view) we saw the worst of times on those rare occasions when this important supervisory bird flapped over to inspect us, from her new perch near Scotch Corner. Rarely making for happy meetings, if only because of a palpable lack of corporate feeling. And an unfortunate manner, where she was as tactless as we were surely resentful.

Socially, these were excruciating encounters for everyone.

Including her, to be fair.

Morale in the office was dipping low, money tighter and inadequate staff numbers reducing further. Growing managerial distance and alienation one result of endless spending cuts; although the demoralising upheavals these caused were something she took particular pains to assure us - during those strange *'consultative'* meetings with staff, where no direct question ever met with a direct answer - were her *'number-one priority'*. Yet if we doubted her sincerity on that, I don't suppose the name we applied behind her back did much for our side of an increasingly-unsatisfactory bargain either:

'The Mummy'.

At first, I was even sorry for her.

How old she was is hard to say and ungallant to guess. Even I could tell her clothes were expensive, seeming more appropriate to attending the theatre than our knock-about law office. With unkinder, female members of that office (I really mean Victoria) swearing 'on oath', one hand placed on the Policy Manual, that they'd "...*seen her on Northumberland Street, wearing Dalmatian fur - pale as her deathly pallor.*"

True or false, a mental picture to clinch her popular cartoon image. Provide the alternative nickname. That *alter ego* for which she was our dead-ringer, and to which a glazed mass of dyed and tawny hair fringing alabaster features only added authenticity. Those bags beneath blackcurrant eyes, tormented expressions below.

No yummy-mummy she, our latest boss seemed as dry and desiccated as the cadaverous resident of some Sicilian catacomb. An obsession with numbers - not quality - the

349

preferred benchmark, her chosen path to spiritual karma. When CPS HQ at Ludgate Hill had clearly chosen her, not for any lawyer's skill, but the demonstrated morality of a natural assassin. As their Thomas Cromwell to our Anne Boleyn.

And an uncanny ability to promote the state's retreat from responsibility as if the ultimate triumph of our public's will - civil and servile to the core.

About the only positive impact I do remember her having on how we Geordie staffers organised ourselves came in her introduction of the much-vaunted *'twenty-second rule'*. This performance-management gem not only winning us *'efficiency savings'* and brownie-points from the inspectorate (over how we field incoming 'phone calls) but also providing the principal cause of my difficulty getting in from the street that day.

When it took a courtroom advocate of my calibre to persuade Young Elaine *via* the intercom to relinquish her place at the workstation in the first place. Even for a minute. Just to come down the stairs and open the door for me.

To descend from that seat where she crouches in permanent hypertension over an illuminated switchboard - watching for calls like a kestrel for voles. And no wonder she never has time for lunch, nor chit-chat with me, must go scuttling back. Almost as if frightened: frightened of criticism, fearful for her job. Which she rightly was.

While what our opponent solicitors or a long-suffering public made of it all was a *'customer-service issue'* the Mummy had long ago resolved to ignore - whatever latest Mission Statements claim. As she announced to us herself: *"When money is tight and resources are tighter, I'm afraid everyone's job's on the line. But through a constant search for innovative improvement, we will drive our public service forward...."*

Where maybe even bosses felt a little frightened, too?

No less than Elaine.

Yet if we knew our newest Chief had already sold her soul to London, there were other prices to pay. In her case, the strain of maintaining the pretence to purpose, printed all over her face like a down-payment on reward. Those finely-tailored suits and glossy German saloon, her executive trophies to an endless peregrination. Badges to her restless wandering from meeting to pointless meeting, badgering middle-managers.

Meetings, that reliable substitute for work.

Including the one she'd called me in for.

Waiting, I looked wearily out the window of our second-floor conference room to a rain-swept Quayside. Down to where a tight knot of protesters bearing placards battle wind and traffic noise to make their voices heard.

Men and women, workers from Alec's shipyard, trying to draw wider attention to their imminent plight as the last working slipway on the Tyne. *"Let Us Build You Your Ships!"* they shout, as if shoppers and office workers hurrying past them in the drizzle just happen to be buyers. In the market for oil tankers, hunting for frigates. These demonstrators were wasting their time, I already knew that.

Bill's message left on my phone the night before had tipped me off: *"Mike? It's Bill. You're not in? Just calling to tell you that test case is listed for Tuesday....Yeah, you know, Article One-Oh-Seven. Thought you'd be interested...yes, set down for hearing at the Supreme Court, England & Wales....ten-thirty sharp....You know – the old Middlesex Guildhall, as was. Don't suppose you'll be able to get down there? ....No? Oh well, we both know what'll happen anyway, don't we?....Yeah, like we said in the article. If they confirm what you and I thought inevitable, based on European rulings, as I think their lordships must....then Alec's people are out of a job. The shipyard must close. Oh, well, at least Diane will be pleased with us...."*

Bill was right.

And if some private reasons were not entirely noble, for why he and I, on the encouragement of a certain academic up at the university, agreed with her to pen that joint article about the technicalities of Alec's case for her shiny legal magazine, let's overlook them now. Though we did cite *'social justice'* and try to target its strapline to catch the eye of a few national broadsheets. Where, ever the slow-learner, it only dawned on me later how airing this controversy with them could help with Bill's political ambitions. But also knowing full well, whatever the true motivation, that our dry legal critique could never save Alec's yard.

Hard times indeed.

But I wasn't put up there to watch demonstrators, even if they did start chucking cobblestones. The reason I was sitting in our

351

old boss's former office was for interrogation by her successor. When *'The Mummy'* was back in town and one of many minor boxes she must tick on her relentless trajectory towards head-office glory was my annual appraisal.

My PDR: that *'ferret's fandango'* (*pace* Victoria) they call a *'Performance Development Review'.*

Of course *The Mummy's* own performance lay beyond question, what got her posted onto us. This shooting star of CPS - ahead of each development, mentioned in every review. When our new boss operated in a higher league altogether, and we understood why. Everyone acknowledging that leading role she'd played in prosecuting the notorious *'Channel Zed'* case, in making hers a household name.

The shocking outrage resulting from a popular TV programme. One which at the time seemed like everyone's default peak-time viewing. Subject of a million web-posts; argued over in parliament. That nightly-fix folk got from a confidently-daring, always ground-breaking programme the whole planet came to know as *"Arena2"*.

Call it what you like - adventurous anthropology or naked voyeurism – it proved a world-wide sensation. Massive money-spinner. When it seemed like there was nowhere on the globe you could hide from latest news about it. With hindsight, all their other options gradually used-up, what they finally brought us seemed inevitable. That memorable Sunday night in November when the ultimate media-crime happened right in front of us. Committed in their own homes before a gasping public.

The tipping-point.

When reality TV finally and inevitably crossed the last taboo: *"live sex being so very last year"*. Finally crossed the Rubicon. Treated its jaded viewers to the very first, live and on-screen killing ever shown on British TV, outside a news broadcast. Filmed as it happened in a converted Lancashire cotton-mill with all the sophisticated gloss and digital wizardry twenty-first century entertainment can bestow. Made broadcasting history.

Their only mercy or restraint shown in keeping it right side of the 'watershed' - after nine p.m. The only saving grace. So at least a minority of children, or those under eight years old without a TV in their bedroom, were probably spared seeing it.

That fatal moment when two equally-pitiful individuals - a matched pair of inner-city refugees believing five minutes of fame from one week's appearance in this human zoo promised them celebrity for life - were steadily, gradually and quite deliberately wound into so much nervous and emotional anxiety by their TV 'handlers' that they were literally at each other's throats by the last and final programme.

Convenient to the ratings 'war'.

Grappling for our vicarious amusement. Using two ornamental oriental weapons, *'accidentally'* left handy on the walls of that laboratory-like and overheated set in which they've both been penned-up together, right throughout this week.

Fighting to the death.

Bang on time and dead on schedule. No thought for the consequences.

"TV Gladiators!" screamed the redtops.

"*Murder....?*" thought the cops.

The surviving inmate, the programme's sexy female introducer, one director and the whole production team. All arrested in dawn raids then indicted together at the Old Bailey in the most media-perfect prosecution ever seen, Fronted by a cover-girl QC with bee-sting lips and run by a team from CPS HQ's Special Casework division under the expert guidance of ....guess-who?

After a six-week trial, the jury were out for fifteen minutes and back in time for tea - the early evening news. She'd truly nailed the lot of them, and nowadays the modern prosecutor comes outside to gloat, where once 'twas thought improper.

"Justice has been done and our thoughts are with the family" as she told us from the steps.

A thorough-going triumph, or at least it was for her.

In a case so celebrated, multiple audiences across the globe were soon demanding yet more hours of TV coverage. Chance to digest social meaning. Their first opportunity coming in the form of a lumbering documentary quickly thrown together with police help by the offenders' biggest commercial rival - "*Arena2: The Inside Story.*" As opportunistic and emotive a piece of reportage you'll ever see; probably attracting about the same catchment as sat unflinchingly through the original without one twinge of private conscience in the first place.

Every gory detail run by us in detail for sake of anyone missing it first time. Especially the final blow. The full inside-story all over again, with no-holds-barred and repeat clips of the killing included for morbid good measure. Garnished with its producer's disapproving tone throughout but guaranteed to clinch another million viewers through this prurient re-run, the respected anchorman fronting was still considerate enough to warn us this *"might contain some scenes of flash photography."*
In addition to a death.

"How lucky we are, living in an open society. Still able to rely on our journalists to bring us serious investigative broadcasting to this high standard. On disturbing issues like these..." intone next day's editorials.

Like the media moguls behind all this had done us a favour: *'In the public interest....'* as their narrator kept on reminding us. A familiar term we CPS lawyers knew well: that phrase we live or die by, so to speak, in our own line of work. Now applied as camouflage by a society rediscovering the art and entertainment to be had from watching public killings obtained through combat – presented live and for pleasure.

Not to mention the money.

Yet it's an ill wind that blows nobody any good, and while the victim's family were still placing flowers wrapped in cellophane before the padlocked gates of Channel Zed Enterprises Ltd (In Receivership), *'The Mummy'* was looking so much more gorgeous on film than she ever did in life. Archly-silhouetted and tastefully back-lit against venetian blinds in studio-sets chosen by the documentary-makers more for their resemblance to an out-of-hours abattoir than CPS's Ludgate Hill. Pouting her way through the seven year-old's guide to whatever legal complexities had beset her team, *en route* to final victory.

The perfect legal eagle and ideal foil for its po-faced narrative, or else those police officers in the team who'd done more of the legwork but wisely laid-claim to none of its transient glory. Probably our country's first celebrity-prosecutor: interviewed on radio, BBC *"Womans' Hour"*, about her choice in shoes. Short-listed as a runner-up in *"Lawyer of The Year"* - search her name on the internet and there are 5,473 mentions. (When it works).

No wonder why, within a calendar month of these programmes going out, her rising star rode so high in popularity ratings up at

Ludgate Hill that our latest Director of Public Prosecutions - a fellow, female barrister - was promoting her sister-in-law to head this brand new mega-region of ours. Sent up in triumph to front '*CPS englandnorth*'.

High enough, too, for everyone conveniently now to forget whatever earlier public harm she'd once done herself. Those unwise announcements made from lower down the food chain. Backing a mooted name-change in the service's corporate title, for instance: its suggested slide from '*Crown*' into '*Public*'. An ambiguous concept if ever there was one, still sufficient in post-Olympic years to be thought too Marxist to swallow. Even if, now a fresh decline threatens, still an idea whose time may come. Make sinister resurgence.

Either way "*Manchester's Loss is Geordieland's Gain*" how our in-house CPS 'magazine' breezily trailed its fawning online hagiography. The news it cascaded merrily down to us, shortly before being axed itself in yet another efficiency-drive.

Though if that imminent posting its e-pages foretold soon became a decision we were stuck with, there was always comfort to be had in how easily and inevitably "*Time Changes Most Things*". Maybe it can and sometimes it does, but nowadays a streamlined and invigorated Court of Appeal can generally be relied on to do the job rather quicker.

Whose Lordships had, by the time a calendar year was over, systematically overturned virtually every one of her hard-won and much-trumpeted convictions in the original '*Zed Case*'. Except of course for the swivel-eyed swordsman himself, that loner now lodged for ever in a Broadmoor painting-class. Arguably as much a victim as the poor guy he killed.

Yet by the time their Lords of Appeal in Ordinary turned to procedural issues - and used a Practice Direction to voice their definitive disapproval of her CPS team's inexplicable failure to disclose to the defence certain vital '*Unused Material*' only found later, inside a police evidence bundle - it seemed Ludgate Hill had forgotten not only about him, but also her.

About '*The Mummy*' herself and why they ever thought it wise to post her up here with us, we barbarians of the frozen north. Now just another piece of top-brass, those waxy managerial mannequins propped for a lifetime, she appeared immovable. The sack not in prospect, whatever Their Lordships may say.

"*Not how the service does business...*" as we heard.

Even if - and considering the amount of crockery reportedly being thrown in regional meetings held beside the A1 at Scotch Corner - even London was beginning to realise it was time to move her on again.

Off to a fresh set of mistakes. ('*Challenges.....*' I mean).

Somewhere else.

Though one thing was for sure.

If they were going to, then it wouldn't be in time to save me.

"Although they could have held even Britain, the Romans scorned to do so, because they saw that there was nothing at all to fear from the Britons (since they are not strong enough to cross over and attack us) and that no corresponding advantage would be gained from taking and holding the country. For it seems that at present more revenue is derived from (our) customs duties on their commerce than the tribute could bring in, if we deduct the expense involved in the maintenance of an army for the purpose of garrisoning the island and collecting the tribute, and the unprofitableness of an occupation would be still greater in the case of the other islands around Britain."

(The Geography of Strabo: Vol. II Ch. V Paragraph 8:
pre-conquest, late 1st Century B.C.)

- XXII -

Funnily enough - and long after the last scribe's minute from formal meeting or dry court proceeding is forgotten and consigned to the conqueror's bonfire - of all the admirable features to that golden age when Carausius saw to our public administration during his time at Calleva, the memories staying with me the longest are rooted in ordinary, human detail.

Of indigenous tribesmen down from the western hills, whose way of life hasn't changed in centuries, squatting in the basilica square while waiting for their chiefs or elders to obtain audience with him. The spectacular parades of legionary and auxiliary soldiers saluting him at the *rostra* during the veterans' annual march-past; local women sitting weaving at the base of that marble statue of Postumus he resolutely refused to pull down.

Their chantings of greeting and praise.

At every level of society, I think most people had come to believe in him. So far as you can place a trust in any human leader, that is. The man who, for a while at least, seemed to be delivering what he always promised he would. A strong and independent state to hark after the glory days of Rome.

Under the first British emperor in history.

The irony of it all. This despised and forgotten island on the very edge of nowhere, suddenly the best hope for traditional Roman values. Standing alone and self-sufficient among inhabited lands. Representing values visibly buckling elsewhere beneath the tide of enemies and invasion which assails a world empire.

Paying our own way, into the bargain.

A minor economic miracle powered mainly by optimism and a little vein of silver, even less of gold. One where I still flatter myself people's renewed faith in money was bolstered as much by the stamped captions I helped him devise for it – all those promises about *"Peace of the Augustus"* or *"Protection"* we embedded in their skulls – as by the sterling efforts of Allectus. A clever man who reversed two centuries of decline in a month by restoring a proper coinage. Circulated the discs that could broadcast his master's message to anyone who'd read it: coins minted from a matchless quality of silver the *Rationalis* conjures up as if out of nowhere. Almost by magic, with only the occasional help of his hired Frankish friends?

"*The mines of the Silures work overtime...*" our magician would assure us when pressed. *"Efficiency is all."* Any other sources he had for it, I know he never mentioned.

Indispensable – that was how he seemed then: the marvellous Allectus. Our emperor's right-hand man: poring over his books of account, keeping everything going. That cunning moneyer whose Treasury every public officer is sent to, cap in hand, if they want anything doing that costs. Paymaster for the whole circus that our 'British' empire has suddenly become. *"Mere Spring to His Aqueduct"* how he styles himself, with a false modesty that's overweening already. No wonder our brave emperor won't hear a word said against him.

Maybe he daren't.

Whatever secret companies Allectus might in private choose to keep.

Those harsh realities I finally faced-up to, that night I came home to Calleva. Returning to the town in the woods where I had been brought up: suddenly an imperial capital. What a terrible condition to find myself in for such a happy home-coming.

Covered in blood.

It was an unenviable choice. Did I go home and present my widowed mother with a terrifying spectre at the door, clothes black with gore; or turn up at my commanding officer's palace with an explanation for my bloody appearance which I knew he'd never want to hear?

Fortunately, one of the travelling merchants I'd saved from the Franks had an elder brother with a big house outside the city walls - Sorviodunum road south. A well-off local resident with private baths. A man whose social circle would hardly extend to the poverty-stricken widow of a nobody-clerk, but whose brother's hospitality could get her wayward son cleaned-up and clothes changed before she ever saw him. An invitation doubly-welcome for sparing my mother and her nosy friends from hearing of my difficulty on the way; and a busy emperor needless word of more worrying aspects into the bargain.

Unfortunately, when we got there elder brother was out and the gate guardian his trout-faced wife. Someone equally displeased at greeting either of us, her disgust more open at the sight of my darkly-spattered clothing. A sensitive person perhaps considering this show of blood a thing best reserved to the arena, the prerogative of butchers.

Whether sister-in-law - and then a sister - thought these marks of blood ill-omened, they clearly gave even less consideration to my other status. A returning local hero, safely back from the war. And if being received coldly in a private house was once an encounter to embarrass my younger, more self-conscious self: no longer. Not when as public officer I could have demanded by right and force of arms what new friend Publius offers me by grace. Yet if too few soldiers are nowadays left to feel as welcome as they deserve in the households of citizens grown fearful of the billeting officer, I was still the one wondering how often or how far these stuck-up townies planned on journeying beyond their walls?

Or what they would make of a gang of robber Franks, encountered alone on the road?.

At least she met the basic rules of hospitality.

Grudgingly directing her slaves to provide me with the tepid bath, hottish meal, and clean bed I'd already overheard from the atrium how loudly her husband's troublesome brother demands I receive. Probably thanks to him, too, that my bloody uniform is whisked away to the fullers before it reaches the bath-house floor. In its place a Gothic-looking slave girl carrying a scratchy tunic of grey wool to win no prizes for style but cover most essentials. The girl herself, little more exciting.

After everything I'd been through from joining the Fleet, their urban-suburban reactions didn't matter. Only amused me the more, lost uniform with it. When all I needed to retain a professional identity was my military belt, a unique sword, and those other trappings of a soldier which are only made in metal. At first light tomorrow, I'd be presenting myself smartly and armed with all three before an Emperor's court. Where if Carausius approved a short release from duty afterward, perhaps before sunset I could be visiting my mother.

All credit to him, friend Publius was the model of hospitality. Repeatedly apologising for the shortcomings of his in-laws, and if they criticised him afterwards for dragging this stray in from the streets, not a prospect to trouble him much.

360

So we sit apart from his snooty female relatives in their honeysuckle-filled garden. Drinking as much *in absentia* of his brother's quality wine as we possibly can before a westering sun disappears behind enclosing walls. Not without company either, for two of his smallest nephews come sneaking along to inspect us. Wide-eyed at our laughter and shouting. Delighted to discover their young uncle and his friend's boisterous willingness to play ball and then chase them round the apple trees, at least till bedtime calls.

After a few hours of this harmless fun, I feel more relaxed than in ages. Forget about the Franks. Shuddered by constant warfare, it took the brick-walled shelter of a Calleva flower-garden not even my own to begin therapeutic processes long overdue. Restore a sense of youthful optimism. My hopes for a better day bolstered by his brother's wine, their children's happy smiles, those last lancing rays of late-evening sunshine.

Enough to feel encouraged about tomorrow's likely course by an interlude of calm out of kilter with the times. Intermission only, no more than brief respite, its auspices taken for good.

Though if I'd known what next I'd be led into, how much of my future this day to come would shape, perhaps I should have been more cautious.

Consider not turning-up.

"You have adopted the right course, my dearest Secundis, in investigating the charges against those Christians who were brought before you. It is not possible to lay down any general rule for all such cases. Do not go out of your way to look for them. If indeed they should be brought before you, and the crime is proved, they must be punished; with the restriction, however, that where the party denies he is a Christian, and shall make it evident that he is not, by invoking our gods, let him (notwithstanding any former suspicion) be pardoned upon his repentance. Anonymous informations ought not to he received in any sort of prosecution. It is introducing a very dangerous precedent, and is quite foreign to the spirit of our age."

(Letter XCVIII, Emperor Trajan to Pliny the Younger.112 AD)

Clicking her biro top endlessly in-and-out in unconscious illustration of the perpetual agitation of the soul which stalked her, my shrivelled interrogatrice beamed coldly at the light-fitting above my head before opening for the prosecution:

"I hear from the Branch Manager you were reported absent without leave...."

What a very nice introduction to my PDR, I thought to myself. Nice to see you're back, too.

And why does she have to talk like that? Letting the end of each sentence fade away into a higher, softer pitch - querulous and inaudible. So that what starts out as positive assertion falls away into a faint diffidence the uninitiated might take for question, even doubt. When I knew it was neither but answered like it was:

"I was trapped in Italy when the satellites went down. Galileo and the rest. Sorry, boss. It took me another week to get home."

"I see. How very unfortunate. Well, if you do ever find yourself in that situation again, can I suggest making sure you let our local office know. It only takes a 'phone call, after all. God knows, with staff numbers only set to get tighter, you'll realise how much pressure simply not turning-up puts busy colleagues under. I'm sure you understand my point, Michael. It's about corporacy. Having a corporate attitude, loyalty to the team."

"Then I got a bug or something. Put me in the RVI for a while."

"Well, let's leave it at that. With saying that you need to be more careful of the sort of sick-record you accumulate. Fortunately, once we can get you into the courtroom, I hear nothing but good reports from the judges about your work. And the lay justices, too. I know you are one of our most experienced advocates, and it is your advocacy skills which are the public face of the service. Especially in the Crown Court. So thank you for making it so easy to be so positive about that side of things, Michael."

This was clearly the good news. I wondered what form the bad might take.

"Now....to the question of casework....."

"Yes, a major part of the job. Which I enjoy, of course. Although it's always a struggle balancing that with the prep' needed for going to court. And my team does get through a lot of files. Productively, I mean. Reviewing the evidence. Preparing them for court use, trials or committals. Advising on disclosure. On what is to be done with unused material. Fitting in all the telephone or written advice....."

"To the police..."

"Of course."

"Yes, that's particularly what I wanted to talk about..." she squirmed on narrow buttocks.

"Right....boss. Which means me applying the Code for Crown Prosecutors - carefully of course. As well as interpreting the law itself, naturally."

"Obviously. Splendid, splendid. Now that's the area where some of your decisions....."

"Is there a problem?"

"....have drawn a bit of controversy."

"It's a controversial area. People don't like it when your advice means they get to stand before the beak, facing a charge in court. And police can get upset, too."

"Yes, God knows, I'm perfectly aware of that effect, thank you. People. The police, complainants and defendants. Our 'customers' were the same in Manchester you know. But it's where you've recommended no prosecution that there have been concerns....."

"The CPS Policy Manual doesn't say we must criminalise every single person whose behaviour ends up subject of a police file, does it? There wouldn't be any teenagers left at liberty if we did....."

"No, no. I'm not suggesting otherwise. But there was one case..."

"The old man on the soapbox?"

"You are so there.....ahead of me as always!" she gushed. Nearly falsetto.

"It was never against the law of this land for Christians to preach in public. Even the pagans tolerated that – we know this from the Bible. And when we are...sorry, we used to be..... a Christian country, weren't we?"

"Oh...*gosh*, and now you really do mean the *proper* Bible, don't you, Michael? O-M-G ...Oh yes, gotcha! *The* holy book. So sorry - thought it was your little joke for a moment there, reference our Policy Manual. No, Michael, and let's be serious now, I'm really *so* with you. All the same, we're not Christian ourselves are we.....by any chance?" she said, looking sidelong at me for a moment as her voice faded again.

"No, no, not personally...."

"Oh, thank God for that! I do mean - and *so* don't want to cause offence - but you will know they can sometimes be *such* bigoted people. In a vibrant society where we're all entitled to a diversity of faiths. Of course we are. To our personal belief system but really, sometimes....."

"No, and I'm not *jedi*, either.....though that doesn't mean we should pick on them....."

"Prosecute according to the law, you mean?"

"....persecute for strongly-held belief."

"For remarks offensive to anyone from a minority or multicultural background...."

"Yes, yes....*if* they truly are. But why are you raising this particular one with me?"

"Someone has complained about you."

"About me! Who?"

"Oh, I can't tell you that!"

"Anonymous?

"Effectively, yes."

"Welcome to the world of Josef Stalin."

"Oh, *God!* Do you mind, Michael, that's like, really *so* not on. So unfair. Now look here, let's get real - a public complaint's come in. Surely you can't expect CPS to ignore that...."

"If it's anonymous, unsubstantiated and malicious, why not?"

"I'm not going to tell you who. What matters is why."

"Well, let's try an educated guess. Since the only witness statements on file were those of three police officers, directed there in response to yet another, equally-anonymous and doubtless just as public-spirited, denunciation of a fellow citizen. On the strength of one 'phone call from someone who wouldn't identify themself. Does that make the cops into complainants in their own right? Sensitive souls, entitled to be upset?"

"You know perfectly well how they've changed the law. The last Criminal Justice Act...but one. That police officers can now be personally offended. Feel harassed and alarmed."

"Hell, this guy was evangelising in the street, that's all. Didn't John Wesley or the early saints do similar? And that first officer seemed determined to provoke him anyway. Make him say something - something outrageous. Drive him into the position of making a statement in a public place about matters of religious conscience. Then to nab him, teach him a lesson. Him and his kind. Wham, bam, thank you ma'am! Since when did it become the role of the police to go round quizzing people in public on their private beliefs? Provoking dissent? Those issues this particular constable deliberately went over to quiz him about. Wanting to wind him up and watch him go. Looking for something from him – for answers - she could then characterise as breaching the Public Order Acts."

"Causing *harassment, alarm and distress*. Which he surely did...."

"Offensive is as offensive does. In the eye or mind of the beholder...."

"To the officer it was. Personally. Who could doubtless refute your interpretation."

"Who was virtually egging him on......"

"Let's move on, shall we? To when he was arrested and you got the advice call?"

"Yes, and how could this first officer, and then the whole PSU that came along next - all those other cops turning up mob-handed in an armoured van as 'support' for her afterwards - call it a proportionate response? To one old man on a box? In a quiet Northumberland market town. Just for proselytising his faith. Like others do their different values...."

"*Northumberland*? How quaint! You're like, so out of date there, aren't you Michael? I really don't think even the postal service bothers calling it that any more. Please do catch up, try and sound a bit more corporate. More modern, at least while you're present here at work. We're part of a global society now, and it's our *Region* that matters most with government. While you still sound *ever-so-slightly Christian-ish* to me...*I-M-H-O*"

"*In your humble opinion!* Well, let me assure you, boss, I'm certainly not. These terms I use....he used....were once common property. Everyone's....."

"Everyone's?"

366

"Yes. When Biblical references were commonplace, not an embarrassment. Like Shakespeare. For signalling between warships, factory-floor remarks. Still are, I suspect. Common cultural allusions tying a civilised society together that's no longer aware it's using them. Terrified when it dawns. Like it's grown ashamed of the source, a post-Christian culture abasing itself before any-old alternative. Pagans and *jedi*. Equality cuts both ways, you know."

"OK, I hear you, but there is nothing like a passionate denial to make me suspect otherwise. Almost the opposite....have you got something to hide?"

"Look, boss, I thought this was my annual career-appraisal, not a lie-detector test for thought-crime. How many times do I have to tell you? You've had two denials. Watch my lips a third time. No, I'm just a practising solicitor; not a practising Christian. One who's employed to fulfil the duties of a prosecutor. Properly, if I can. What they used to call the *"Disinterested Minister of Justice"*. So I gave my disinterested advice to the police."

"And are you?"

"What?"

"Disinterested."

"I think so, more than that officer. Reason why I told them how it reeked of entrapment. When anyone who's done a trial could see the defence would cut their first officer to pieces in the witness box. And serve her right, too. So I gave them my advice - that their case was sure to fail. A shame they didn't like it, though I didn't expect the Spanish Inquisition...."

My attempt at humour wasted:

"Entrapment! A trap? Oh, really, come on, Michael! Surely that's an overreaction: OTT. Melodramatic. When this man was *so* like, asking for it, wasn't he? Being offensive about people whose interests the CPS promise in public consultation after public consultation we're doing so much more nowadays to protect...."

"Presumably why you and the cops believe I had no choice but recommend his prosecution? Make an example of him, however weak the evidence. Just for being 'rude'? The persecution of one minority to satisfy some others? Isn't that the choice Pontius Pilate gave the mob? *"Which one do you want: Barabbas or Christ? Makes no odds to me or the state."* Not because of what the law demands, but to satisfy *'popular opinion"*. With the added advantage of avoiding any bad PR for our organisation, of looking good in the press. Is mob justice what we're put here to deliver now? Support government's aim of policing more closely how ordinary people think?"

"Now it's you being ridiculous! Community engagement is our core duty. And that whiff of religiosity still bothers me, Michael, even counting three denials. Too much at ease with the biblical references to my mind, too ready to come out with them in the workplace. Frankly it gives a bad impression - not the *'Indicative Behaviours'* we want to see in our staff. Always remember, you are put here for all faith groups, Michael. So think carefully, reflect on yourself. Like, do you hold inappropriate prejudices? Are they coming to affect your professional judgement? They're the important questions I want to see answered: do you need more training?"

"Those are ridiculous statements. I *am* trained. This *was* my professional judgement."

"That there was no crime. OK, it's your call. But why did the man arrested have to say what he did? What is it with these people, why can't they just get along with the modern world? All they need do is update their world view a bit. Keep quiet if they can't. Put up or shut up - is that too much to ask? Acknowledge our contemporary rules and social conventions. So why do they always have to cause trouble? Always. Obey the law - including our own equality laws, obviously - and these Christians will find themselves enjoying no less protection than any other minority or faith group. Keep themselves out of jail into the bargain. We do live in a democracy after all, don't we?"

"Hey, are you my line-manager reviewing performance, or become my moral guardian?"

"Look, Michael, I think we're getting away from the point here. Fact is, the officer in the case wasn't happy with your decision: *'What the CPS decided'*. Bad for the image of the Service, bad for this region – he's probably blogging away about it on the web right now, provided it works. So when his superviser, the local Inspector, e-mails me about it, I flagged this meeting up as the appropriate opportunity for gently sharing with you some critical customer feedback. That's all I promised them, all I'm doing now. I do hope you haven't got a problem with that. I'm sure you'll agree it's only reasonable we at least discuss it......"

She quickly changed the subject after that. Straight onto PIs - Performance Indicators - and AOs - Annual Objectives. Customers and Stakeholders. I knew the score - if people like me in the branch offices don't deliver on the figures, she won't be getting PRP: 'Performance-Related Pay'. Her bonus in short, extra cash.

One thing was for sure, I wouldn't be getting any.

The new Chief Crown Prosecutor closed the buff cover of volume one to my burgeoning personal file then set her glossy, black-painted nails into two prehensile, skinny claws. Delicately drumming their chiselled tips across it to symbolise our meeting's closure.

"Well, thank you so much for your time, Michael. I really do think it's been the most enormously helpful discussion we've had today. 'Full and frank', as they say at the FO. And I'm sure you know how much the service values all your hard work. Your professional commitment. Since I came north, I've had several people tell me what a good job they think you do. So I'll be writing-up a short note to summarise the 'Key Objectives and Targets' we agreed on for the coming year, the 'K-O-T's, then passing them across to you for formal signature. Recording what we decided on today. Other than that, it's just a case of us all carrying on as before...of Keeping-Up-The-Good-Work!" she trilled in girlish fashion.

I took the hint and quietly stood up to go.

Or 'FO', as they presumably say at the FO.

She looked up at me in what she probably believed her most seductive way, and put a scrawny hand to her tousled head as if she'd just remembered something minor.

"Oh, and by the way. There's someone waiting here to see you. An official. Asking if he could have a word. So I told Elaine to put him in the interview room. I think we should help him...if we can."

"We?"

"You, Michael."

369

"Their enrolment having been completed…those of the tribunes on whom this duty falls collect the newly-enrolled soldiers, and picking out of the whole body a single man whom they think the most suitable, make him take the oath that he will obey his officers and execute their orders as far as is in his power. Then the others come forward and each in his turn takes his oath simply that he will do the same as the first man."

(Polybius: 6:12, mid-second century BC)

- XXIII -

Presenting myself by first light as commanded before the studded gates of a one-time inn for official travellers now the 'Palace of Carausius' - set on an *insula* of its own in Calleva's southernmost grid - it was left to the elderly centurion of his guard to explain why early arrivals like me should expect a long wait: "The emperor spent last night in the shipsheds of Clausentum. Hobnobbing with the guild of shipwrights, inspecting new galleys being built for him there. Why he's not expected back here till late afternoon at the earliest and you should make yourself scarce….."

The old n.c.o. laboriously inscribed my name and rank with crabbed handwriting into the duty-book nonetheless, while I confirmed an intention to return later: "In the middle of the day once I've been home to see my family. When you may be sure to expect me, centurion, returned on my lord's order."

Now there was no hurry and he was at ease, I found myself lingering a while longer, chatting with this amiable officer. A veteran of the Second with amusing tales a-plenty from his lengthy career, free to any palace-gate dawdler willing to stay and indulge him.

It was while sharing anecdotes in this way that a sudden commotion occurred indoors. When a complete party swept out and passed-by us, sufficient to have the whole honour guard out of their room by the gate at the double and standing at once to attention.

Surrounded by a screen of household slaves armed with staves, three gentlewomen of birth came laughing and singing

370

out of the house and into the public byways with such airy grace of movement and lightness of being I felt immediately transfixed. Judging by the baskets and trowels they all dandled, their common destination was a garden, but it was the most slight of the three who plants my instant focus.

"Who in the name of heaven are they?" I begged the leathery centurion watching them float away down the cobbles with almost as much pleasure as I did.

"The girls? Those lovely girls? What, don't you recognise them, young fellow? The daughters of Carausius, my boy, the famous daughters of Carausius. His 'Three Graces', how he calls them. Our little emperor's sainted darlings, all of them his issue. Leaving their great father without one single son of his own to inherit the family name...."

The one whose glance caught my eye so sharp she might have put a jet hairpin through it was probably the youngest. Caught it and played it like an angler with a fish. For a twinkling moment that's so brief I'm hardly out the river before she's returned me to its flow. A no-one, a nothing, put back in the street. Like she never saw nor hooked me, yet still for long enough.

There was such a way she had, I knew her at once for someone I'd die for. Could never live without. As acute and pleasing a vivacity men could surely bottle it, shining like a light. I never saw a girl before so striking me with intelligence and beauty, nor ever so quickly. Me the shabby wayfarer, standing in the shallow shadows of this street she passes through.

"Who is she, that one with the dark hair, the black eyes?"

"So she's the one as takes your fancy, is she, sir? Not her strapping red-head elders?"

"No, her! The auburn lass...."

"That's Diana, that one. The people of Calleva love her specially. His wayward youngest. They say our emperor was so much for the hunting of Angles, Saxons and Franks or else of the boar, that he named her for his patron. For the Goddess of Hunting herself. A pious dedication and a nice touch if true, but no suitable quarry for soldiering nobodies like you and I to chase after, if you'll pardon my saying so, sir....."

I'd see about that, was my private reaction.

And if Vitalis was right - that I must have seen her before, if I'd served at Rutupiae where once she had lived - then it would only be as a child, not drawing my eye. Now she's grown up and as suddenly I saw. If her name was Diana then it was to another goddess, to Aphrodite, that my prayerful thanks were owed.

For a miracle.

For touching the heartless soldier I'd feared fast becoming with the heart-stopping sight I'm suddenly shown. Enough to inspire and change my life. Instantaneously, forever.

Promising myself I'd soon be back to find her - armed with an old debt from her father and a novel thought breaking of what priceless currency could be imposed for repayment - you can imagine how reluctant I felt to quit this Palace of Carausius.

For a meaner dwelling I should visit first.

The home of my parents lies in a minor lane between the temple enclosure and the street of the metal workers. If there are plenty parts of Calleva to stink as bad as any Pictish compound - those drainage ditches full of dead dogs and excrement, fumes off the foundry - there are sweeter tangs too. The scent of fires fuelled with applewood, of wall-bound lavender or my own mother's baking. Yet if I can find my home and its odorous location with a blindfold on, it would be wiser to approach it all with caution.

With nearly a year gone by since anyone there saw me, who knows what changes Fate might have brought in the interim? Accident, disease or bereavement. Neither did I want to cause a shock – least of all for my mother, who'd have had no warning. So it was very carefully I pushed on the yard gate and put my head round its creaking laths. And there she was, one year older. A woman in a thick woollen dress with her back to me, slowly grinding corn on a hand-turned millstone under the shelter of a modest portico. My own dear mother, busy and productive as ever.

"You have changed a great deal from the brave boy who went laughing down the road to Glevum depot..." said my mother gravely. After I had hugged her tight then stepped reluctantly back for the overall inspection she demanded.

"Yes, mother. It's been a whole year, so expect I have...." was all I could manage, and wisely didn't add *"...for I have lain with many whores and killed seven men."*

Reading in my eyes the information withheld, it was all the more typical of her loving generosity she could look this dusty military wanderer up-and-down in his borrowed clothes and burst out: "Your father would have been proud!"

"I hope so, mother, though I doubt the Fleet was ever in his mind."

"It does not matter – the navy is as much a proper soldier's calling as any cohort. He always thought the less of himself for never having served."

"With his eyes and his foot, you know he never could."

"No, my son, we all knew that. But now you are, he will be watching. His last surviving son. Remember him as I do - brave in a different setting, but in his official duties always principled and firm. Then and in how he met his end, a loyal servant of the state. Fighting all his life to provide for his family as best he could. Despite those frailties gods impose, their betrayals of ambition. And when magistrates of the council sent officers to arrest your father and hundreds like him - on the Edict of Diocletian and the say-so of informers we once had counted friends - he stood in line with the best of them. Looking death in the eye and smiling with the unshakeable firmness of a man who might have been a soldier all his life."

"I know it, mother, stay truly sorry. Father deserved better, but we will never forget and I cannot pass an arena without remembering what he suffered. But our world is changing and I am lucky to serve a greater man, promising us protection from the injustices father endured. A respite too, whether from the persecutions of Diocletian and his thugs or raiders from the sea. Protection for Britain, protection for honest folk like us. It means the return of happier times, mother, his promise to us of a new age that's coming!"

"Protection? *Tutela*? I don't know about a new age, my son, though I've seen what it says on his coinage. You'll find precious little of that around this house but I can see the army has hardened you. Changed you as it's bound. At least we brought you up well before it could. Your father insisting on a proper education once Flavius died, even for your sisters. All of you the apples of his eye, never you forget. Where he found the money from, once family lands were confiscate, I'll never know. But he did and we clung on. He was like that, you see. Determined you would read Horace and Vergilius at eight. What's more, understand it. And you being such a clever boy, I expect you probably did….."

"I have used that learning, mother. Used it well, even in the service. He would be amazed. It was money well spent."

"I am glad, glad for your father's sake…" she said vaguely "but will you avenge him?"

Like respect for my ancestors was no longer enough and everyone, even my mother, wanted me out there.

Killing still.

"The European Commission is building a security system to issue early warnings on threats of extremism, xenophobia and other forms of radicalism."

(EC spokesperson, July 2011)

- 23-

"Elaine, the boss says there's a man here to see me? Is that right, and where's he from?"

"Err, yes, there is. He's in the interview room outside. From? Where's he from? Oh, no, I don't think I asked him that, Mike. But she said he's definitely an official visitor, so I'm sure of that. That he's OK. Is it Belgium? Yes, yes. It might have been Belgium....."

Young Elaine might not have been the sharpest blade in our CPS knife-drawer, but she had a good instinct about people. No wonder we'd made her Office Fire Warden. Her little guess seemed right but I made sure to check him out for myself, using one of the internal CCTV monitors set on Elaine's desk to cover the glass-walled room she'd put him in. Seeing his head down and studying the CPS mission statement on '*Common Purpose & Values*' we leave in there as special treat for visitors, like he was about to do an exam on it.

Looks like he really is Belgian. Good old Elaine. You should never underrate anyone.

Still wondering how she knew.

Maybe because he seemed so pale and grey. Like rain in Arras. Even down to the raincoat.

As he rose slowly to his feet to greet me when I entered the interview room, I could immediately work out his genesis. Conceive his nativity. After the latest monetary crisis forced fiscal union from aspiration into an inescapable certainty. Once the former European iron-and-steel confederation-cum-community turned super-state had decided on a new, standing army of its own to maintain its status; the establishment of a separate EU diplomatic mission became essential corollary to growing its role on a world stage. And once they'd got one of those, then you could almost excuse its satisfied creators for

375

considering a dedicated internal security service their very next, 'must-have' accessory.

Equally indispensable.

Why the shadowy man tracking me down to my employer's office in Newcastle that memorable afternoon - with her active co-operation and permission, I was interested to note – had all the signs of this fledgling service's first appointment. Their pathfinder. Someone wanting to assert an efficiency and capability in his new role to managers and minders up in Brussels, or wherever it was he's sent from.

To prove himself, and them.

I still wondered what particular enquiry could have brought him here. To me in particular. Being slow on the uptake, I found it hard to imagine. With little personal knowledge of Europe beyond my summer holidays and no involvement from work, I could only think back to what I might publicly have done or said upon the subject in my private life.

Not that there has been too much of that to report on lately.

Why the few possibilities available reduced a shortening list of three down to a poorer choice of two. Including that obscure legal article on EU State Aid which I'd been egged-on by a certain Newcastle academic to pen for her even-more obscure legal journal.

In company with Bill.

And our even more boring follow-up for their next edition. About the use of EU rules and institutions by international corporate bodies: either to avoid taxation or else obtain double allowances in two or more jurisdictions for the same transaction. Bill majoring on the dull bits, the UK tax part of the racket, and me on the interesting potential criminal implications, if any.

Me and my big mouth.

But surely no-one reads this stuff? Apart from the sort of man I had in front of me. Or the big corporations in question. And if they do and don't like it, or the kind of people who produce it, then I suppose they wouldn't like my authorial friend either: that minor tax-lawyer and MEP who helped me write the two offending articles. About an entity incapable of accounting for what it does with its money – sorry, *our* money!

Like Bill often said, if it *was* a UK limited company, then Companies House would have closed it down years ago and probably jailed half the directors, for failing to file. Then I remembered what they allegedly did in real life to that woman accountant who exposed the apparent state of EU book-keeping, years ago, and my state of unease grew stronger. Thinking I'd try harder to be careful, sound helpful.

When the visitor shook my hand, it was like gripping a wet haddock. One that couldn't wait to slide back into the sea. The North Sea: *Oceanus Germanicus.*

"My name is Tommas van Rijn. I am come off the ferry for this day to see you here at your place of work. For purpose of investigating cross-border crime."

I was a public officer, criminal lawyer and law enforcer myself, so why should I feel so shocked on hearing these ordinary words? Because there was a different ring about them, one that breached my professional detachment. When it felt threatening and I knew at once that the crime he had in mind somehow concerned me. That his visit was personal.

"Sounds serious…"

"It might be. This is what we need to find out."

"Find out?"

"If you will help me. My Commission requires Member States such as yours to assist with evidence-sharing. As an investigator seeking evidence in another EU country, I must rely on a fifty-year-old mosaic of rules."

"Mosaic, you say….?"

"Yes, do you have problem with that word? It means how we use varying legal forms and procedures to obtain different evidence. Authorities across borders can ignore our requests or specify how they are made, set their own deadlines, but your boss says you will help.".

"Oh! And where exactly have you come from to make this important request?"

"I work out the offices of EUROPOL in the Hague's Statienkwartier. On attachment only. Do you know EUROJUST?"

Beside the acronyms, this list was Holland and he was Dutch. Not Belgian after all. So much for relying on Young Elaine for office risk-assessments. What a good thing there wasn't a fire starting. Not yet, anyway.

The stranger reached across and handing me his card gave me time to think. I looked at a nice picture of the EU flag in full colour and noticed there was more than just his name on it. This Van Rijn was a police commander.

Or had been.

What he did now was more obscure. Secret squirrels?

"Do I know EUROJUST? Of course I've heard of them. Of it...I mean. Why, in Newcastle office, we speak of little else..." I gabbled, trying not to sound like a provincial hick in a northern backwater. While Tommas looked wanly across at me, just as if I was.

Which was probably fair enough.

"I'm sure you do. Also, you will know how we coordinate criminal investigations between European countries. And how, since twenty-fourteen, with Lisbon out of the way, our role has been massively expanded."

This passive sense was interesting. As if their relentless expansion was a natural, spontaneous and organic development. Like mould. So maybe Bill was right. If they were all like him, I guessed they'd put a lot of effort into making very sure it was. These people in macs were door-to-door evangelists, come over here to proselytise. Tell us what to do.

What to believe.

"Of course. An FBI for the EU?" how I actually responded.

He carefully arranged his lips into two parallel lines across his face, in a manner someone kind like his mother might once have suggested was the best way of making friends. If she had, it was mistaken. He would have been a disaster at speed-dating.

"No, I do know people sometimes say that, but we prefer to see ourselves as facilitators. Helping proper coordination between national prosecuting authorities like your own. Also, we support criminal investigations into organised crime cases...."

"Which has got to be good. How else can our national police forces deal successfully with cross-border criminal organisations? Round up mafia barons or international terrorists? Bad people, not bothered by borders."

Their best argument and my personal effort to be polite to a visitor. Genuinely. On my best behaviour over a subject whose more obvious positives only help conceal some mirror-image negatives. Equally scary. Those sinister issues I knew better than to mention right now to Tommas The Smiler. The darker side of his same coin - the notorious European Arrest Warrant. Why I thought of it then, I really don't know.

Maybe you could call it intuition.

The dreaded EAW: '*Ee-aw*'. The law might be an ass but I fear this for its ultimate donkey. And no laughing matter. Like Bill says, it could be any of us. Ordinary British holidaymaker or sophisticated businessman or woman - convicted in their absence by some ramshackle Balkan court. People like us. Teenage hacker or middle-aged motorist. Those defenceless people government allows to be plucked from home and family for their meek surrender abroad into the living nightmare of policing and judicial systems hardly deserving of the name. For years on end. Sacrificed for the sake of good relations with lumbering institutions accountable to no power in these islands.

Like Bill told the Orpington gardener.

I.M.H.O. of course. My personal opinion, no more. And his. But as a professional English lawyer, I'll make no bones about it. Admit it upsets me privately quite as much as we know it did old Bill. And all credit to him for alerting to a legal phenomenon that's disturbing like no other. But no, I wasn't daft - knew better than raise it now. Trying to tell myself inside my head. How my friend would, if he were here beside me now: "*Not now, Mike. Not something to argue about with him today, eh? Besides, it won't be relevant, will it?*"

Tommas at least agreed with my outward show: "Your point is a good one. Apart from domestics, there's eighty per cent of London murders have some international element, need enquiries abroad. Why you need us. Also, we coordinate co-operation with the European Judicial Network. The EJN in case you forget, gives a valuable network of judicial contact points. Set up between member states, between public prosecutors."

"Such as my own service?"

"That is correct."

"None of which explains why you came over here today, or to see me in particular."

"We are concerned about a friend of yours. Someone INDECT points up. The lawyer, William Cariss. He is of some interest to us and we were wondering if you could help."

"Me?"

"Yes, you, Mister Tryton! We know you know him well."

He pushed a single sheet of white A4 paper across the desk towards me. A set of six digital photos taken in the street outside my flat had been badly printed onto it. The colours were dull and leaching into the fibrous paper but Bill's big black Range Rover and me getting out of it were clear enough. Bill shaking my hand. Me getting a white carrier-bag out through the rear hatch. All in telephoto - including a rather tasty image of Venezia stretching across to give me a juicy peck on the cheek. Particularly pleasing, but not one it seemed the right time to beg him for some reprints of: "*Two 9x6 in glossy, say?*"

"Since when did Europol run parking-enforcement in Newcastle?" I ask him instead.

Tommas wasn't much amused by that quip either: "We have our sources. Know you deal with him a lot through your work. Instruct him on behalf of your service. Encounter him as an advocate. Also that you have built up a friendly relationship and that he trusts you."

"Which you presumably would like me to betray?"

"You are an official of the state. A civil servant. An officer of your English courts, with higher duties than just to your friends."

"What do you mean? To God?"

For the first time in our meeting, Tommas actually smiled like the rest of us do.

"No, not quite that high. To the law. To justice."

"I don't need you to lecture me on that. What is your interest?"

"Enough to open an AWF on him."

"An AWF?"

"An *Analysis Work File* – opened by Europol on a specific area of crime where at least two EU Member States are involved."

"At least two?"

"Yes, the United Kingdom, while it remains so. And the Republic of Italy, also."

"Oh, Italy. Right, I see..... so what have you got against him there? Sorry, don't look so cross, let me put that another way! What area of crime do you have in mind?"

"We're not entirely sure. Money-laundering maybe, but the trade in stolen antiquities more likely. What we started with, the algorithms suggest."

"You're not entirely sure, but you're investigating him anyway! That seems a bit off?"

"His wife is a qualified archaeologist who runs an international consultancy. In the course of her business she sometimes has reason to move artefacts around the globe. An ideal cover, if some of them were stolen. And she has drawn attention to herself by poking about at historical sites up near the Alps. Where her husband also travels. Including, most importantly and on an annual basis, when he goes to Italy with you. Coming back by car, what we gather."

"The Mille Miglia?"

"I hear it is a fantastic experience. This year there was a car from the Dutch Royal family."

"This year was not so great. Our journey back was a nightmare."

"You were searched at Hull?"

"To the point of extinction. But not at Rotterdam. Sounds like your people there missed an opportunity. No-one found anything, probably because there was nothing to find."

"Even so, I would like you to keep an eye out. Tell us of anything odd."

"It would be my public duty. But where does his role in the European Parliament come into all this? Funny you never mention that. Is this other stuff your cover?"

"That fact is unfortunate, I know, but unrelated to our inquiries - I can assure you. Beyond providing him with a convenient excuse for regularly crossing borders......"

"An *excuse!* Are you sure? Has Bill upset someone? Is this their smear campaign?"

"No way! Your suggestions are unworthy, Mister Tryton. This enquiry is for real. There are priceless artefacts going missing in Italy from Roman or Etruscan tombs - statues and grave goods - and my office has been directed to help national forces investigating where they end up."

"You seriously suggest we had a stolen statue in the back of Bill's Aurelia?"

"Not a statue but maybe information. Money or information. Some of it returning the other way. You see we know about you also. Your own personal interest in mosaics - a stolen one in particular. From a place called Brantingham, although a very long time ago. An interest common to his wife and placing you both near enough to a trade in stolen antiquities. Maybe attracting the organised criminals my agency plays a key part in fighting. Our information sharing system, SIENA, is vital in that battle and I can promise you, Mister Tryton, that any information you provide me with *will* be shared. Go directly towards it."

"Siena? That's a nice town."

"*Shared Information Europe - National Agencies*. We combine crime and personal information extracted from different EU countries' police forces to build up a rich picture of criminality among their citizens. Use it to formulate organised crime threat assessments – what we call 'OCTA' – we then feed into the new ECIM: *European Criminal Intelligence Model*. The business model for what we do. Under our main Mission Statement, naturally."

"Naturally, and coming armed with such great acronyms. But beyond the bureaucracy, do doors get put in? Does anyone actually get knocked on the head and arrested?"

"Sometimes. But only if the public help us with information. Or people like you."

"How public am I?"

"More than you think. Our machine got lots about you off the web. Though we make this approach in your private capacity, aware of your public office. Through an employer who has been very helpful. Like you said yourself, it's a question of duty."

"What if I don't play ball?"

"We don't think there's any question of that..."

"But if I didn't?"

"You put me on the spot but from information-sharing, let's say we have a few files....."

"Files?"

"Where to begin? The *Polizia Stradale* have quite a thick one over a terrible bit of driving apparently happening on autostrada eight. Just outside Milano, only last May. So bad they've kept the wreckage in store at Malpensa: a red Toyota and its trailer. What a mess!"

"A mess?"

"The one you're in. You should see their photograph album, Mister Tryton. Its pictures include several showing officers measuring some incredible skid-marks. Showing their full length – all the way across three carriageways. Then right into the crash barrier, without even stopping. *Bang!* Say they've calculated the co-efficient of friction from them to show you were driving - minimum - one hundred-twenty kilometres per hour. At the point where you first brake really hard. And how irresponsible a speed is that, they are asking their prosecutors, for a loaded trailer on a busy autostrada?"

"I was not speeding!"

"Not what the maths says. Potentially you are looking at a lot of trouble, my friend, and over there, they like to take time to decide. Different rules, no rush. Not that six-month limitation period you fair-minded Brits stick with over here. Basically, the Italian investigator is calling you a reckless idiot. Putting lives at risk. Full admissions present on the file and now he's found someone who says they were injured. Quite badly it seems, to the neck. Aggravated whiplash. Says the evidence looks sufficient and they are thinking of issuing a Europe-wide warrant for the dangerous driving....anytime within the next two years...."

"That's a complete lie! No-one was hurt when I went off. There wasn't even another vehicle within a hundred metres of me."

"Not what the *polizia stradale* are telling us. Not now a victim has come forward....."

"Victim, my foot! But you said files?"

"I did."

"What else have you cobbled up?"

"Not me. I think it is all your own work, Mr Tryton. Your own doing. All catching up with you now like sins for judgement. Because there is a question, also, about a recent article in an online magazine. You and Mr Cariss together."

"An article? Since when did writing an article deserve opening a file?"

"The Commissioners don't like it. Don't like what it is suggesting. See violent attacks on EU institutions as implicit in the text. Equalling *'seditious libel'*, say some. There are some hawks in Brussels, you see, who can be very quick to take offence. Especially when the thing that upsets them comes from a serving public officer. A civil servant. Someone who should know better. Presumably hoping to retire one day on a proper pension...."

"Seditious libel? A criminal offence akin to treason! Towards the EU? This is pathetic! You are just threatening me. Over a boring lawyers' article about the technical application of contracts and procurement law? Come on, you've gotta' be joking!"

Tommas was never one of nature's jokers and I knew he wasn't. He didn't crack a smile, just looked steadily back at me. Intimidating it was.

"OK..." I said with a sigh "You've found me. I'll do what I can."

What I never admitted to Tommas van Rijn was how much I knew already.

After all, I'd been carefully investigating Bill Cariss and his foxy wife myself, for several years by now.

They were sitting at a metal table in the window of the wine bar with a good view of the Old High Street and people going by.

"You've been very helpful" he said.

"A pleasure" she replied. "Least I could do. Thank you for the drink. So what have you discovered as a result?"

"That the villa was completely destroyed by the quarry and there's no trace left of it today. That nobody ever wrote up a proper report of the site, even if all the finds – well, nearly all the finds – are in the museum over the road. And, of course, that one of the mosaics was stolen, shortly after the war."

"Yes", she said, "the locals still think the Americans took it."

"What do you think?"

"I don't know. How do you move something so big and so heavy? What made you so interested in the site, anyway?"

He smiled: "The villa. It's an interesting story. And there's a link. My grandfather was a policeman in Hull, just after the war."

"Oh, really", she said, "and what was he like?"

"I don't know. I never knew him. I think he was an Inspector."

"Well, you've obviously had a good day. Do you think you found what you were looking for?"

He rolled the last of the red wine around in his glass, refracting its colour across the aluminium table top, then looked directly across at her and smiled:

"Yes", he said, "I really think I have."

They were walking across the car park by the Marina, the wind from the sea on their faces.

"It's the red one" he said.

"Nice car."

"It's an Alfa Romeo. I'm trading it up next year for the new model. More power."

"Mmm, leather seats" she said, sliding in and stretching out her legs.

They were travelling fast on the dual carriageway out of town, the ruinous fish docks and beyond them the estuary flashing by on the left. He was trying to impress her with the car's acceleration.

"Where are we going?" she asked.

"I know a nice little hotel in the centre of York. It's Georgian."

"Now why should I like the sound of that so much?"

She smiled happily and reclined her seat slightly, strands and filaments of auburn hair spilling out over the back of the headrest to catch the sun.

(**'MOSAIC'** - Clive Ashman)

We all need to know where we come from, but the most definite fact I have about my grandfather is his date of birth on a birth certificate. A post-First War baby who was presumably lucky to avoid the Spanish Flu' which killed millions across western Europe.

Like that remark itself, much of the rest is supposition.

Born as his name suggests on Saint Michael's Day, September 1919, at Rouen in northern France to a serving British Army officer and his glamorous French wife; to the father who eventually left them both in the lurch while Grandpa' was still at school. Ran off with an actress so they say, fifteen years later. And probably the reason why Sandwich Grammar School in Kent was the last place we traced Grandpa' to; there and a house in Richborough, before he joined the forces himself. Following his Dad's example in an earlier conflict. Disappearing into World War Two.

How do I know even that much? Well, there was a period in my own life where I put quite a bit of time and effort into trying to find out about him. About a man who seemed to be at the heart of our family's little mystery. Searching on the internet and all those genealogical websites that are out there, hoping to discover some more specific information.

Not to any great effect.

Grandpa' had always been a bit of a family legend you see but when you got down to it, the closer you looked, the more he faded away, The less about him seemed certain or survived. Only his name, written out in faded cursive ink on that tattered birth certificate. All we had left to show that the original 'Michael Tryton' ever lived. He really existed.

Those names my parents rather unimaginatively passed on to me, as if they wanted to carry on the line. Because like him and rather uncannily, I was also a Michaelmas baby. Almost as if the name and the date was something inescapable. Forced onto them by fate. Onto all of us, as if it was meant. What always gave me that strong sense of a connection with him even though we never met. But whether it was a name worth maintaining, worth commemorating, well that was a different question.

387

No-one could answer.

The one big thing we did know about Grandpa' was that he'd been a fighter-pilot during the Second World War. Yes, I'd always liked the sound of that. Defending his country. Flying Spitfires with a New Zealand squadron based in Yorkshire. Along with our other fine friends, from across the Atlantic, those magnificent Canadians.

Up in East Yorkshire to be precise, at RAF Leconfield.

So in theory then, a hero. As we'd always assumed. And not a rotter, though the reality no-one really knew. Even if Mum found some of his medals hidden in a drawer.

DFC: *'Distinguished Flying Cross'*.

And a little gold badge: *'RAF'*.

So was he?

Mum wasn't impressed with these artefacts, saying he'd been a terrible womaniser. Something she was always a bit stern about. How she knew that part, I really don't know, but the strain certainly ran in the family. Considering she'd taken a bit of a risk herself by marrying into our lot - and remember she was Dad's third wife, even if the one that finally lasted - it still seemed a bit rich. Maybe that was precisely why she always disapproved.

Her own sense of insecurity.

Anyway and as far as dear old Grandpa' is concerned, after the war the trail goes a wee-bit cold. The Second War, that is, and at least in the official records. With no family photos either. No diaries, no nothing. Almost like a ghost, a will-o'-the-wisp he was. A wanderer. The harder you look, the less you find. Until he pops up again a few years later, serving as a post-war policeman in Hull. That run-down port city on the Yorkshire coast where I'd ended up working as a criminal lawyer for several years. Coincidence?

Almost like I was following in his footsteps without even realising it.

Or why.

And where I learnt to fly myself, in the city of Amy Johnson.

So it's complicated, you see.

My own father was born in 1949, but by then Grandpa' was already dead. Leaving a bit of a mystery about that departure of his trailing behind as well, plus a definite whiff of woman-chasing. And Dad an orphan.

Oh yes, and a forgotten unsolved crime.

Notorious, in fact.

We found the police records about him in a local archive. One unfortunately burnt down since by Hull vandals. During another of those minor urban riots the pundits tend to blame on economic meltdown. Like almost everything else involved in this case, the records unexpectedly disappear, but the fragments we were lucky to inspect before they did showed him being promoted to inspector. Ending up as a senior detective. So his bosses must have thought well of him, whatever my old Mum said. Or thought about him herself.

But no, we don't think he ever found out - or not so far as we know - what really happened to that Roman mosaic. You know, the one stolen overnight in 1948 from Brantingham. From a quarry near Brough-on-Humber. In all the papers at the time.

The guy who's helping me research this book you're reading now wrote an earlier one about that little mystery, calling it '*MOSAIC*'. With our family's help, obviously. Yet another lawyer: what the trade calls a 'ghost-writer'.

Not that I thought we really needed *him*.

Fiction of course, but he based it on the true-life crime in 1948 and what little else definite Mum could say at the time about good old Grandpa'. Or else dared to. Including the womanising, I guess. Before Dad came along and Grandpa' exits stage right in circumstances unknown. The rest of it? Well, don't blame me. Blame that 'ghost-writer', who made up large chunks. Claiming little choice. "*Necessary...*" he said "*...to fill in some pretty big unknowns.*" Ones we'd apparently left him stuck with at the time. Changing the names and the story to protect the guilty, not the innocent, what myself and a few others thought about that.

Not how I'd have done it myself. No, of course not. Not now, anyway. All that stuff about a stolen Roman mosaic incorporated into the floor of some English country house which then burns down. I don't know where he got that bit from. Really can't say. Personally I wasn't convinced, didn't agree, but as he would often remind us, no harm in a bit of "*artistic licence*" to fill in the blanks. What he'd always say if you tried to press him about anything.

Whatever.

What I do know is how some older, local people around Brough at the time had plenty of other ideas. And passed them on to me. Their suggestion, for instance, that the stolen mosaic was taken out, rolled-up in resin, inside the bomb-bay of a home-going American bomber. Flying back from Lincolnshire, late 1940s. Or else the claim it was simply broken into pieces then thrown away overnight - but why would anyone bother doing that? And then there was one man, briefly a copper, who even suggested that it might have been taken all the way to northern Italy, home of the Romans. That area called Venetia just under the Alps, where I heard she later went to check.

For everyone you met, there'd be another theory. For every rational thinker, another crank or conspiracy-theorist. No-one knowing anything, as I saw it, or not for definite anyway.

But what I can confirm for sure is that my Dad was already forty-one years of age when I was born; Mum only twenty-eight. I told you he was a bit of a lad. Still, if it wasn't for them both suddenly mentioning it the once, many years later in an Italian pizza restaurant while I was still working in Hull, I might never have got onto the trail of good old Grandpa' and his strange unsolved case of the stolen Roman mosaic.

Or ever found Venezia again.

I've told you this was complicated.

I'd first met Venezia when we were both sixteen. Maybe I was only fifteen, and she already wasn't. Why she found me so boring, so soon. Didn't know what I was doing, why I was 'dumped'. All very nicely, but dumped all the same. Traumatic for any teenager and I was the one who never got over it, not her. Hard-wired into my brain.

While she never remembered.

Until that fateful day when I was standing in the entrance to the Hull & East Riding Museum, asking their helpful staff in my inexpert way about the famous Brantingham mosaics. And she just happened to be passing.

"*You need to speak to this lady*" they said. "*She's the one to ask. The real expert!*"

Mega was.

She certainly knew her stuff. Hot, hot, hot! Whether she recognised me at first, I cannot say, but I clocked her at once. Couldn't believe it after all these years.

Wham!

Certainly knowledgeable and with good recall for archaeological fact, if not old-flames.

As she should, having apparently qualified as an independent consultant in *"finds-identification and their sustainable preservation...blah-blah"*. Reason why she was in there on that fateful day, acting as a bought-in adviser to the museum. Saving them the cost of permanent staff and providing the sort of expertise which provided her with such a nice little earner. Or covering for retained staff they had who for whatever reason could not sort it.

Her nice little line of business, a proper consultancy. Charging shed-loads of cash.

So when I told her what I was there for and the almost mythical story of Grandpa's determined efforts, made shortly before his mysterious death, to find out what happened to the missing Brantingham mosaic, I thought she was going to pass out with intellectual pleasure. Or something of the sort.

Penny beginning to drop?

And yes, me. Standing there giving her the subtle once-over, sneaking a look at her slender ringless hands. Seemingly still single.

After that, it all happened pretty quickly. Huddled close together in the archives. Almost hearing her heart. Hunting out the museum's few records left from the Brantingham digs.

Bugger-all, in fact.

A small chunk of painted wallplaster. One battered coin of the beatified Helena, Constantius Chlorus's saintly wife. (And me still running without one....). Plus whatever's still displayed on their walls. From an excavation no archaeologist ever bothered to write-up, of a Roman villa feeling cursed by its proximity to a town forever damned.

If only by Philip Larkin's: *'Cold, and smelling of fish'*.

Not long before a Royal Navy which once sank *'The Bismarck'* could, on politicians' orders, let a few Icelanders steal everything of value. Our last glittering cod. From a city whose defining tragedy is *'The Gaul'* - that Hull trawler sailing off in search of them. Into an arctic tsunami with its hatches left open. Robbing families of futures, all hands lost.

Fish and its future, it sometimes feels like Hull has been robbed of everything. Not to mention its Roman mosaic. Despite me and an old girlfriend poring through past museum records, thinking we'd solved it.

Breathing in her scent, thinking I'd cracked it.

I do not know to this day whether the car clinched it. Maybe not. With some girls it does, while others stay indifferent. *'Alfa-Romeo-Milano'* bonnet badge with the armorial serpent of the Visconti family swallowing a live man. Cross of Saint George adjacent. Bodywork in authentic *rosso corsa* – racing red.

I remember walking across town towards it with her hand light in mine.

Wind off the river.

Swallow me, I thought: I am that man. Devour me completely!

The Alfa waiting quietly for us in the car park by the marina. At rest, awaiting my call.

"Nice car" she'd said, its engine rasping.

We went straight to York. Don't know why, just that it seemed right. Almost inevitable, like fulfilling a prophesy. Her eyes were grey and full, I hugged her tight. We walked on the walls, traversed its ancient streets. Felt the drumbeat of centuries. City of the Legion.

Our sense of wasted chances.

The hotel was Georgian, its interior a symphony in flock and nylon. Laminated fire notices pinned to the door. Its choice maybe where I went wrong, hadn't done my homework. Despite the disappointing décor, we still made love.

I don't know about her, but I'd been waiting for Venezia by and large ever since I was fifteen, and the wait had been worth it.

Cataclysmic.

On the Sunday morning, I woke to sunshine across York. Bells from the Minster and a great sense of joy, but the space beside me was empty and cold. One auburn hair left on her pillow, like a fine black wire. My keys for the Alfa were gone and in their place was a handwritten note: *"Sorry, Mikey. Gone back to Hull. Need time to think. V V xx"*

'V V XX'?

'XX VV: Legio XX Valeria Victrix' I thought wryly to myself and got the afternoon bus back alone. A half-smile playing across my face. By the time it stopped halfway at Wilberfoss, I couldn't cry any more. The other passengers looking across at me pityingly.

Who could blame them, when they were not to know and here was their stop.

This time was twice!

The kind man on reception at the museum in Hull's Old Town passed me a brown envelope containing a set of car keys, with the words: "*She left these for you*". I thanked him inaudibly and went out to the river, considering its embrace.

The fate of a Gaul.

Needless to say, I didn't have the guts.

"Don't worry, I'll find you...." I told brown waters instead.

"One day, I'll find you. Not lose you again....."

"This question of legal plunder must be settled once and for all, and there are only three ways to settle it: The few plunder the many; everybody plunders everybody; nobody plunders anybody. We must make our choice among limited plunder; universal plunder; and no plunder. The law can only follow one of these three."

(Claude Frédéric Bastiat, economist and theorist
in '*The Law*' - 1850)

- XXIV –

I was in a strange and sombre humour on leaving home, and not just from my frantic desire to get back to the palace, discover that Diana again. A mood-change oddly reflected in threatening skies assembling above me. And when I see my new ally, the centurion of the guard at its gate, an unhappy temper he detects in my face. As an ancient soldier who'd seen it all and, perhaps because he had, grown unusual kind from the more common holders of this ferocious rank. So he lays his twisted vine-stick down on the desk with those knotted purple hands which match it and looks solicitously into my eyes:
"Are you all right, sir? No bad news, I hope? Everything, everyone, alright at home?"
"No, I'm fine, thank you very much for asking, centurion. I mean, yes, they're all fine. Everything's fine, honestly."
"Visit not go well, sir? Family being difficult? You look bothered….listen, sir, don't worry. It's often the way. Like we think they're different when really it's us. The service changes you like that - and to be expected, isn't it? The life of a soldier, what civvies never know. Things we see, the things we do. Especially such a young fellow as you are, with respect. First full year with the colours, actions you've come through. It's natural, sir, don't worry. Done well for the emperor what I'm hearing. Well, really well. Made quite a name for yourself: the reason I knows you once you presents at our gate. That strange sword you carry. So then, how best to cope? Well if being a hero has its price, it's nothing you won't get over through a few drinks with the lads. Young officers like yourself,

394

some nights on the town. Take my advice, sir, get out there and enjoy yourself. You'll be right as rain, believe me."

I hoped he was right and thanked him for his kindness. He went back into the guardroom and slowly wrote my name down in the visitors book again before patting me on the shoulder. Signal for one of his soldiers to lead me off inside the palace to a waiting room beside the central courtyard. At least he was right about the rain - it started as we entered. Quite a storm, hailstones for good measure. Very unseasonal. You could hear them rattling down onto every clay-tiled roof we passed under, and it was good to have their shelter.

"How old do you think he is, sir?" asked my escort above the din. A beanpole of a legionary younger than me, trailing his shield and javelin along like unwelcome luggage.

"How old is who?" I replied, irritably, and then pedantically added: "Whom?"

"The centurion Vitalis, sir. Marcus Aurelianus Vitalis. How old do you think he is?"

"I don't know" I said, shortly.

"Go on, sir, guess! You'd be surprised. Go on, have a guess!"

"Oh, I don't know. Fifty-five. Sixty?"

Few people of any description live as long as this nowadays, from any social class. Even with the regular routines and benefits of army life, its certain food and guaranteed accommodation, not even soldiers. Soldiers who've never seen battle.

"You'll have to do better than sixty, sir. People always think that. Have another go!"

The lad was getting on my nerves but I could not but humour him:

"Alright - sixty-five. My final bid."

"Wrong, sir!"

"Wrong?"

"Yes, sir, wrong! He's seventy this year. Honestly. The centurion Vitalis is seventy this coming Kalends. Can you believe it?"

It was surprising so I could see why his kindly commander might become a local curiosity. Point of a quiz. I knew there had once been a serving Centurion of the First Spear down at

Glevum depot, dying in harness beyond that age, but it was still pretty exceptional.

"He seems a good man. You are lucky to have a boss like that."

"Lucky, sir, lucky? You can say that again. Compared to most of the crackpots they give the vine-stick out to, you're dead right there. The sort of men who'd beat their soldiers half to death on the march before they ever met the enemy. No, I've been at the mercy of bastards like that before and I can tell you, sir, it's murder."

"Well look after him, soldier. Keep him out of trouble. In a nice quiet posting like Calleva, there shouldn't be too much risk of that."

"You can bet on me, sir!"

The visitor's waiting room where he left me was an open cell whose plaster walls were painted crudely to look like different sorts of marble. I must have passed a whole hour in there alone. Kicking my heels without anyone coming to find me. Taking in the decorations. You could tell that only last year this building was still officially an inn, although someone was trying hard to tart the place up quickly to a standard befitting its new status. Fountains and statues. Mosaics and wall paintings.

To think that vision of this morning could be somewhere inside the same premises. Breathing only feet away. Maybe bathing or undressed. Would I be turned from human into stag like the hunter Actaeon, for catching sight of a real goddess, bathing naked in the woods? And wouldn't chance be a fine thing? Back in the real world, what were my chances of seeing, let alone meeting, a gorgeous girl of her standing? How would I cope if I didn't? Never mind drink, she alone could make me better. Just thinking about her.

The adorable Diana.

But instead of any bathing beauty, all I saw was the occasional slave or servant, fully dressed, hurrying down the adjoining corridor. No-one who's interested in me. Maybe the emperor was still at Clausentum: counting his ships, his visitors forgotten.

By now I was really bored.

What did the emperor want to see me about, anyway? Why had he summoned me to travel all the way from Rutupiae?

Perhaps, now he was an emperor, making such impulsive requirements became part of the fun. Who knows what effect the enjoyment of its powers would have, long term. Even on a decent man like Carausius.

I stood up and paced around the room again, as I'd already done a dozen times. Then I stopped and put my head out into the corridor. Nobody about, only voices in the distance. The corridor was colonnaded down one side; a pillared, covered walkway giving onto an open garden in the centre of the building, the fountain and water tank to its centre filling-up with rain. The downpour deafening.

Countless rooms like the one I languished in; large and small, private and public; were accessible off the main corridor going all the way round it. Some with no doors at all and open to the elements; some with doors which were locked; and some with doors which would quietly open if you carefully turned their large bronze handle or a key left in it.

In my defence I would say I did what I did out of boredom. The reason why I set off down the colonnade finding which ones would.

Some were offices; some were bedrooms; others different types of audience chamber, furnished for display. It was in one of the latter type, a windowless ante-room just off the atrium, entered through a side room or secret passage, that I finally found her:

I have to say, it came as quite a shock.

Her standing there like that: completely naked. Only the lamps to show.

So beautiful, too. Beautiful beyond what an ordinary fellow like me has realistic right to imagine. And, ye gods, how often had I imagined someone like her from my sleepless barrack-bunk or those tedious channel-crossings on 'Minerva'.

Someone with the body of a twenty year-old female athlete but that intriguing hint of deeper wisdom in her face. More to be expected in a goddess. Honestly, I can tell you, she caught me completely by surprise. Standing there without a stitch on - as her kind often do to capture souls like mine. This silent siren. Yet never had I expected it for myself, never in a thousand years. Out of the blue, taken by surprise. Stunned to find her waiting inside this gloomy room, bold as brass. Unashamed before me, displayed to me like this.

Ready; ready and still.

I was shocked, shocked by the questions she raised but gratified by the sight.

My eyes pleasuring themselves for a moment - running slowly, slowly down from her jewel-bright eyes. Traversing the smooth skin of her cheek bones to slide off coiling ringlets onto flawless shoulders. Savouring their laggardly journey towards the floor.

If my eyes ran down, her breasts looked slightly upward, mirroring the upturn in her face and just as alert. Her stomach with that smooth firmness of the young and childless, her legs descending long and lithe into all she wore. Prosaic that. Just a typical pair of outdoor sandals, all the more touching for their ordinariness. Nothing else.

What a wonder she was and for how long had I waited in vain for such a vision of perfection. So perfect, so human, with her perfection suitably marred by that one homespun detail to clinch it. As if it could only enhance her peerless beauty with this single mark of earthly fallibility. Of helpless imperfection, her own unique identity.

How I knew her at once.

From all these features I've described - and that badly-welded plate on her left buttock. Cloak over her shoulder, still frozen mid-breeze. Only the golden bow-and-arrow missing from her dainty hands, but we can all guess where they went.

Into the Mint.

Their Green Goddess, his holy huntress:

"Diana of the Downlands".

What was she doing in this ill-lit room and how had she got here? Where had she been all this time? And what was the link with her namesake?

I walked around her several more times, studying her frozen details by the light of a few pendant lamps. She really was an utter beauty.

Craftsman-cast.

There could be no doubt, this was the stolen statue. The one I'd been sent out into the marshes last year to find by a now displaced and very much disgraced governor of *Britannia Superior*, the late-lamented *'Squintgob'*. And the very statue which Carausius swore at the time that he and Allectus never had sight nor sound of. The one for which we'd searched his squadron, and an entire fort.

What a complete fool the sight of her concealed in here left me feeling. Stolen plunder.

I don't know how long I'd been left alone in the anteroom, brooding on these unwelcome thoughts or their worrying implications, when its door creaked open. Accompanied by a cloud of indoor clerks, a short but burly man in an oilskin cloak wet from the road, burst in:

The emperor.

I fell to one knee.

"My lord!"

"Triton, young Triton! Is that really you?"

"My lord, it is. Did you not order me here from Rutupiae?"

"I did indeed. But not into this room."

"No, in faith, I can't claim that."

The clerks took his cloak and he ordered them out. The usual smile was there, the old Carausius still. Bluff and cheery but getting older. And now more things had changed than just the day. I was the man who'd captured Eboracum for him, along with one hundred others, and he was a man who owed me.

Until a Diana came to stand between us.

"The statue, my Lord..."

"Yes, Triton, I know what you are thinking...."

"How did you get it?"

"It was a quality house. Out near Cantiacorum. Raiders further inland than ever before. The owners got word and escaped in a carriage, nick of time, but their slaves and bonded labourers stayed to defend it. Brave, but probably with nowhere else to go anyway. No transport, poor devils. No choice, defending their own families on the estate as much as anything else, armed with little better than billhooks and scythes. Didn't stand a chance. You know, Triton, it's some of the things Saxons do to those few who stand against them which make me hate them so much. Which drive me on. Why we've got to stop them coming, no question about it."

"Well, they didn't do anything to the statue, did they?"

"No, but they did get it outside though, and onto a wagon from the farm. Presume they were trying to get it back to their ship, to hack to pieces for scrap. Then our lads turn up."

"And recover it?"

"Yes, of course, once they've hunted down and killed everyone from the gang who'd attacked the house, that is."

"Too late to save the staff?"

"'Fraid so."

"And when Londinium sent me out to Garrianonum via Venta to find her, where did you manage to hide it?"

"Out on the Great Fen. Propped up like a wildfowler she was, out there in the marsh." He chuckled at the recollection. "Bow and arrow in hand, looking like a good-un. So it was strictly true when me and Allectus said there was nothing like her to be found on the squadron, or inside the fort."

"But not the whole truth?"

"No, I suppose not. Look, I'm really sorry, Triton. And this from your emperor! You have turned out one of my best officers, and if the governor hadn't sent you out to us that day we'd never have got you on the strength. Grown quite fond of you, like the son I never had. And you've played a key part ever since, in incredible events bringing us here. Especially at Eboracum. Where you know I'm the most grateful of everyone for what you achieved, what you managed. Not to mention your invaluable advice on how we should style the coinage. So it's a case of grateful and, yes, sorry too. Sorry to have led you a bit of a dance."

"Why did you keep her, my lord? You were always telling me how much you resented any allegation you were keeping back recovered booty. How unjust they were. The claims of Constantius Chlorus and Maximianus. Why did you do it? The very thing you denied?"

"Sometimes Triton, as you will find yourself one day when you have a command, it is a lonely place. Somewhere the Gods force you into difficult decisions. Decisions which with hindsight you might come to wish you'd handled differently. Or simply have no choice about. Decisions and deceptions. It's an unusual situation for an emperor to be apologising to a junior army officer, but I value your loyalty and think you have a lot of potential. Which is why I have always been willing to talk openly to you about important matters of state. Even one like this...."

"My lord, I know and value the great honour you do me. Proud to be in your service. Which is why it grieves me all the more to feel deceived. Why did you keep her and are there any other examples? Similar deceptions to feed the grievance of others, not mine?"

"The one-eyed priestess in the woodland Temple of Apollo and Diana, outside the walls of Londinium, is the same seer who reads my horoscope, tells me I'll never die at sea. Says I am born to hunt: men, not beasts, as a true son of Diana. Why I am tattooed with her special sign on my forearm. See here, below the army's mark. Same reason why I carry her symbol on a flag at my masthead. The crescent moon. And dedicated one of my beloved daughters to her special cause, to my own patron goddess. So that when a patrol ship of our 'M' squadron arrives unannounced in the Wensum channel one moonlit night with a life-size figure of Diana standing strapped to its foredeck, I was overcome at the sight. Overcome without any warning. Like it was a sign to me, a personal message from the Gods. Incredible, hitting me like a body-blow. Walking up and down the quay in the moonlight, back and forth. Just looking at her, bathing in her own glow. An absolute marvel, a miracle beyond question. Not knowing what to do, where to go, who to ask; what it all meant."

"So what did you do, my lord? Where did you go?"

"Well, I took advice from the augurers and priests, discussed it with Allectus. Wrestled with my conscience. Yes, young Triton, even a rough Menapian has a conscience! And what were the alternatives? Nowhere to return her to, the house all burnt, its owners fled. If I surrender her to the Public Treasury, then I might as well commit her to the furnace myself. Melt her down for coin, an act of total sacrilege. The Gods know, I am no art lover, but she is so perfect. Crafted so finely the Gods might well have made her, not men. So who are we mortals to destroy her? In a world full of destroyers, I realised she is sacred. Sacred to my own Goddess, and that I must protect her."

"By keeping her?"

"Yes, indeed. A sacred duty!"

"I see. One in which the Gods left you with little choice?"

"Exactly! I knew a clever lad like you would understand."

"And Allectus, what did he say?"

"Only that he disagreed, naturally. When all he could think about was the flaming metal....."

"Melt her down for your 'Rainy-day Fund'?"

"If he could. But I told him straight: the lady's not for burning!"

"If you had, lord, no-one would have known. No proof left for your enemies to use. And has there been other stuff like her? Metals and booty you've kept back?"

"What do you think?"

"Yes?"

"Yes! There was never a general in our history not obliged to let his soldiers hang onto at least some of their loot. And what a good thing I did. We couldn't have managed half of what we've done with the currency otherwise. Allectus too: we couldn't have achieved it without him."

"Do you trust him, lord?"

"Eh? What do you mean, Triton?"

"What I say, my lord. Do you trust him?"

"Look, he's the right man for the job. An accountant. A specialist, like you with yours. Don't I trust you? Like you, Allectus is doing his job well. While he does, I'm happy."

"With the Frankish irregulars he's recruiting? Whose name actually means 'destroyer'?"

"Triton, you know we're desperately short of men. Even shorter when madmen like Maximianus butcher our best like chickens in a coop. These big forts I'm building down the coast are raised as much against him and Chlorus as any coastal raider. And I need troops to fill them with. Otherwise, what's the point? When Rome has used its former enemies as expendable front-line troops since time immemorial: why I was happy to let Allectus recruit mercenaries from along the Rhine delta. After all, I grew up with these people, I know them. Whoever they are, whether Menapii or Franki, I know their loyalty will last - so long as we have the coin to pay them with, that is....."

"My lord, you called me here. I rode from Rutupiae without stopping, on your order. For whatever is it that you want from me next....."

"There are three things, Triton. First, the design for a new issue: Allectus has sent me some sample dies from the

Londinium Mint showing the spirit of this province. Holding a shield and spear, but I want words to go with her image. The right sort, mind: *'Holy Britannia'* with the sort of stonking captions you gave us before. Fine words from Vergil. The palace steward has made a library here, though it's a room I never enter. I daresay you can find the references you will need somewhere on its dusty shelves. Whatever you come up with, my boy, just make sure they're as good as the last lot. Have the same type of impact."

"I will set to immediately my lord; offer you a short-list of suggestions before evening. And the second?"

"I owe you a great debt in the capture of Eboracum and submission of the Sixth. You know how important this was to our cause and I have done nothing yet to reward you. That does not mean I have forgotten."

"Reward, my lord, for only doing my duty?"

"That was my promise and I am a man who keeps them. An emperor. If there is anything the Caesar of the Narrow Seas can bestow on a brave and dutiful officer, then he should claim it…" he said, opening his arms expansively.

"Anything, my lord?" I pressed gently.

"Anything falling within my power and possessions. If it does, you only need name it."

I took a deep breath and looked him in the eye. He beamed back, not knowing what was coming.

"Her name, my lord, is Diana and I do not mean the statue."

I saw his face redden with trouble and confusion while a thought he'd never contemplated trickled through his brain:

"My daughter, my dearest, youngest girl?"

"Given as my wife, if you will. I have seen her now, my lord, and never will be happy until I do again. And again….."

"Oh….I'd never thought of that!" and he put his arms back behind his neck, splaying huge fingers over a chestnut dome wrinkling with concern. Cracking his knuckles at the ceiling then chewing briefly on a stumpy nail, before looking me sternly in the eye once more. Disconcerted by a new severity, I look down and begin to apologise:

"I am sorry, my lord, if I presume too much on the great generosity of your offer…"

403

To be reassured when he suddenly smiled again and put his big hands onto my shoulders: "By all that's holy, I'd never thought of that for an idea. Just took me by surprise, my boy. Needed a moment's thought, and now it's done. Listen to me, Triton, I swear you shall have her! Nothing could please me more!"

"And Diana?"

"Oh, she'll come round to it, I'm certain. You and her, eh? I know you'll make her very happy, a fine lad like you. And her mother, too. What else could be better? Why in the name of Aphrodite did I never think of that myself?"

I think I was as overwhelmed by the idea and my daring as much as he was, but still managed to stutter: "You mentioned a third. What of the third reason for your summons?"

Shoulders shaking, Carausius roared with laughter and banged on the wall in his glee:

"Why, you horny devil, you've beaten me to it! Beaten me to it. Arriving at nearly the same destination, only over different roads. Damn your impertinence!"

"I hope you don't....."

"No, no, my boy, don't mind it at all. Not one little bit. Come up with the solution to my dilemma. By a different route, that's all."

"Solution, my lord?"

"Yes, the solution. To having daughters, don't you see!"

"What? I can't marry them all...."

"No, you damn well won't, you randy satyr! But I am a father of girls and left without an heir. That is bad enough for any property-holder but now I wear the Purple it grows a problem of a different colour: how to preserve the succession. So I had been brooding for a while on how to get a son, with all my legal advisers recommending adoption. Which is how I arrive at you. Third reason for my summons."

"Adoption, my lord?"

"Yes, someone young enough to last. True enough to trust. Clever enough to survive. That's you to a 't', Triton, if it's anyone. Now you're grown into a proper man of the fleet and a doughty fighter, too. Out of all my many good officers, still the obvious candidate. Why I would like to proclaim you as my son and heir. My imperial successor."

I've said this was the day to change my life forever.

Doubly-so.

The weight and enormity of what he was offering came down on my shoulders like a collar of solid gold. The danger as well. But if I wanted his Diana, then I could not refuse his second gift either. One went with the other. If I was to have the person I most desired in the world, then I must take on a role and position I desired the least. One where very few succeed and even fewer survive.

"Are you all right, my boy? Have you nothing to say? You've gone very quiet."

"I'm sorry, my lord, it's a fearful lot to take in. And the greatest honour imaginable."

"Fearful? The Conqueror of Eboracum?"

"Of the succession, of what it may ask of me, I suppose. Because I'd never even thought..."

"Look, Triton, neither did I....I never set out looking to make a British empire. Or defy a greater one - only to survive the day. As any seafarer hopes. When this is just the next step in a bigger game where you and I already stand committed. Ever since Gesoriacum, and no worse a step than all the others. Our names are on Maximian's little list, our stories will be history. Marry my daughter and you're family anyway. So what is it to be? You can't refuse me!"

I thought of that lovely girl going down the street outside and knew I'd do anything. Wade through blood to get to her, or else to keep her safe. History? Just one damn thing following on from another, as my dear old dad used to say. What did it matter?

Alea iacta est.

My own personal Rubicon, and of course Carausius was absolutely right.

I couldn't refuse.

*"It was a safe bulwark, having the Picts Wall on the north side,
and the River Tyne on the south......"*

(William Gray, Newcastle historian: *'Chorographia'* 1649)

- 25 -

If latest news reports were right, that developing crisis in
Europe which - only the previous month - Bill, myself and
Xenobia felt lucky to escape, still stood at its height. On that
bright day when I arranged to meet up with Bill on the
pavement outside Newcastle Crown Court to mark his unusual
farewell.

The night of Bill's last trip to London.

His unrepeatable chance to make triumphal appearance
before the Palace of Westminster. Arrival there by means
unique, a transport no other modern politician would probably
dare contemplate. Let alone arrange or access. Sent there on a
popular brief whose message he knew its self-serving denizens
stood certain to oppose. Symptom of Bill's rocketing career
across a fragmenting country. Our desperate want of leaders.

Of giants, not pygmies.

To make this appointment, I'd jogged down Grey Street after
work. Cut across towards the mediaeval cathedral of St
Nicholas beside the castle keep, then turned right and ducked
downwards through broken city-walls onto King Street. Past the
Georgian steepled church of All Saints at Pandon, reputedly
built on the site of a Roman pantheon, its stained-glass now
barred with grilles against the same heathen once gracing this
hill. From whose churchyard I can finally descend via a flight of
stone steps, running steeply down between Victorian offices
and shops, to enter by its flags that unique urban panorama
which is Newcastle's famous Quayside.

Nineteenth century high-rise, our Geordie Manhattan.

To the right stand four separate Tyne bridges. All of them
crammed into the tight visual framing made for them by this one
narrow gorge. A spectacular sight never failing to move me. The
cantilevered, overarching upper span of Tyne Bridge itself
leading southwards across the water to Gateshead Parish

406

Church. Its green-painted access ramp wading across whole streets on cast-iron pillars higher than the tallest Victorian warehouse, like the legs of a Martian invader. One single span sprung from cylindrical stilts, made-to-measure like trousers by some long-gone boiler-maker of Olympian skill. Pimpled with rivets.

Below me in the bottom of the ravine - where the Romans built theirs for *Pons Aelius* - rests Newcastle's oldest bridge. George Stevenson's revolutionary *'Swing Bridge'*, its control room astride like the pagoda on a Chinese emperor's galley. Above them another creation of the great railway engineer: his *'High-Level Bridge'*, its open-sided stone-colonnaded corridor for road traffic supporting the mainline railway above. Beyond them but visible in the distance through High-Level's squared pillars, are blue angled spars of the modern *'Metro Bridge'* at Redheugh. Toy-like yellow carriages from its semi-underground light railway bustling commuters homeward on strictly-rationed fuel.

Typical blustery example of Newcastle's lacklustre approach to June, the city grateful for a wind off the North Sea to keep clouds moving along. Good enough to keep things dry if not positively sunny, and for me to rest awhile on a metal bench facing south across the Tyne to Gateshead. Time to kill before our appointment, a chance to catch him passing.

Behind me the apricot stone of the Crown Court was massing silently. A palace of terrible deeds, my frequent place of work. Glowering down from below lead-capped eyebrows as if the structure itself sat in judgement on the manifold crimes of a sinful city.

Where Bill was based, his own chambers, stood nearby as a new set built on a former bomb-site. Not far from rather longer-established rivals in the Old Custom House of 1766. Both of them places I visit many times on business, but Bill's *'Carvettii Chambers'* on Trinity Chare definitely the coolest. An ultra-modern structure of tinted glass and transparent lift-pods now featuring in every design magazine. Their award-winning architect's daring open framework self-referentially deployed to reflect a Quayside location through needless traceries. All that silhouetted steelwork he calculated to ape in miniature the supporting towers and latticed girders of an iconic Tyne Bridge, vaulting heavily above.

Trying but failing, when set against the sublime.

For a moment I consider popping-in there and button-holing him. Asking one of his many charming and hyper-efficient female clerks if Bill has come back? Then realising he'd probably prefer not to draw more attention in chambers to his meeting with an *apparatchik* of the state like me. Not on the eve of Bill's most important and high-profile venture ever.

An adventure where a friend like me should at least show support, be his distant spectator. Wave him off on a private assignation nothing to do with my daytime public duties, while at the same time staying careful to avoid any more obvious sign of aid or assistance which the more-tetchy in CPS management could seize on. Spiting a Tommas-the-Smiler whom riverside air has already blanked from my mind.

Whatever chaos and confusion exists beyond, in the rest of the world, I enjoy being here. That sense of occasion never far from this place. Cheered while I wait by the minutiae of life and legal business continuing as if nothing could change. Snapshots from litigation of a different colour disclosed on the next bench to mine: two office-girls discussing one's divorce: *"It's not you talking, Carol, it's them solicitors. Spinning it out, making it worse at your expense. Tit-for-tat between them."*

Almost as if scripted, the epitome in a pinstripe suit stalks-by us on cue. Spitting image of the type described. Barking harshly into a 'phone as if the world cannot hear him, his commonplace delusion: *"We need to stop their nit-picking, Martin.... take it or leave it! I tell you, if it's not put to bed by tonight, presume a full trial on Monday. I'm in the office all day tomorrow, but it's down to you to see our trial bundles are right. All witnesses warned!"*

Instinctively I recognise the feeling. Pity Martin - whoever he was - not to mention Carol: *"Can you hear me, Martin? You're breaking up.....!"*

I should imagine he was, working for a tyrant like that.

Sitting on a bench, watching and listening while the workaday world passes-by beneath so enduring a townscape, gave me time to think. To focus on the safer micro' in a macro' world gone mad.

On this river and its bridges, the Norman *'New'*castle was raised-up on its mound, right over Rome's *'old'*. Beside their cathedral, now cleft by the railway. Changed by each generation but somehow unchanging, these rugged northern relics thinking themselves too far away to worry over a continent on the brink. Too old to care.

Normally by this time, late afternoon, I should be witness to a maze of queuing cars. Rush-hour traffic struggling through a brutal one-way system bequeathed Tyneside in the latter half of the twentieth century, distant 1960s. By a forgotten era whose T. Dan Smith of happy memory and ruddy complexion was its unstoppable local government visionary. A man called John Poulson his corrupter; best-architect-mate. Doing deals together: *'Our Friends In The North'*.

Slashing new canyons for cars through the sight-lines and fabric of Georgian streets or mediaeval city wall. Tiny Jacobean buildings marooned beneath reinforced-concrete. Underpass and office block. Turfing bewildered occupants out from terrace and tenure, rehousing them in high-rise.

Smashing through history with an utter contempt, turning an older Newcastle into Smith's fevered modern image. His ego's mad conception for our *"Brazilia of The North"*. Ridiculing those who stood in his or progress' way, when really it was graft.

Crooked as 'owt.

Taking Michael Caine's *"Get Carter"* as a cipher for their crimes. Capturing this city's fast-disappearing monochrome as a backdrop to glorious technicolour, during her time of change. The Cortinas and Minis, Bedford vans and E-type Jags, once filling these lanes.

Now there are no cars, no rush-hour to speak of. Only a lonely ambulance, the occasional hybrid or smug electric car. Not when the latest fuel crisis, so long as it lasts, leaves less and less petrol for we ordinary commuters. When whatever arrives - Straits of Hormuz permitting - is sold at ever-increasing rates to a privileged few. Or doctors and councillors, nurses and politicians. The priority given to *"maintaining public transport and the emergency services until normal deliveries resume"*.

Which everyone assumes is soon.

Hardly the first transport revolution this key ravine has seen. Not when the river itself enjoyed its turn at greatness, was once our real roadway. Ran on sail and coal. But now look at it: a place of silence. The preserve of old men fishing and bench-sitters like me. A few bored professionals, accountants and

409

lawyers '*working late*'. Looking vacantly out from their bronze-mirrored prisons, new ramparts of commerce, and wondering how anyone will manage, getting home tonight.

Today the river we watch is as empty as these busy roads have grown. Stone dead itself, a life-blood of trade and heavy shipbuilding gone inside a generation. When even the night ferries to Norway no longer even run, ending over a thousand-years' traffic. When it was always Scandinavia this city looked to, and never blooming Brussels.

Precious few pleasure vessels left to work the river either. Superstructures of those few which do garlanded with orange lifebelts and capsular survival-dinghies. Medals of a health and safety culture now become ingrained, however badly folk behave. Bobbing restfully with the tide, awaiting night-times now suspended pending the Emergency. Tied-up and useless. Longing to renew their booze-cruises downstream to Ouseburn and North Shields. That rough trade in shrieking girls and throbbing discos. Italian beer bottles lobbed by louts into a rivermouth once entered in state by Roman emperors. Riding galleys rowed by slaves.

Where *is* Bill?

Quarter-past six and I should have seen him by now. Intercepted him walking over from chambers past my monitoring bench. So I look out across the river to the location opposite where I know he's due in. The RDV, our rendezvous. Where floats our last naval hurrah - Tyneside's lingering reminder of a vanished age when Britannia Ruled The Waves.

"*H.M.S. Calliope*".

Hardly an obvious salty name - one of nine artistic 'Muses' to the ancient world – though some sealord at the Admiralty must once have thought it so. Back in the nineteenth century when they first stuck it on a ship. In an era when I could imagine everyone who worked there readily knowing Vergil. Reading bits of him out to each other, over long lunches.

A name nowadays emblazoned across the redbrick wall of an R.N.V.R. training-centre visible across Gateshead-side. That "*stone frigate*" in front of which their eponymous minesweeper moors. Where forty-five reserve volunteers attend on her weekly, learn how to be one crew. Guarded today by a matched pair of smaller patrol-boats I knew to have been built in Alec's

410

doomed yard. Floating neatly in line behind her as both escort and company; one linked to the University whose crest and name it sports, equally unarmed.

"*Minesweeper*" - so long a word for so short a ship. Latest jargon even longer: '*MCMV: Mine Counter-Measures Vessel*'. But their's a dangerous job, whatever you call it. However you style them. Tiny in naval terms, but these days probably the largest vessel of any sort, civil or military, to sail so far west into Father Tyne's reaches. Symbolic too, in this place where cranes as high as the city once unloaded the largest ships of empire. Whose men built the ships; sons hewed and loaded the coal we relied on to fuel them.

If she could not be built on Tyne, which stayed a crying shame, then you could at least say this latest '*Calliope*' was made somewhere in Britain, not abroad. Her carbon-fibre hull and state-of-the-art electronics this year's output of a 'high-tech' Solent yard likely soon to face closure. '*Prospers*' of Bitterne, receiving our country's usual reward for excellence.

Apart from a 'town-twinned' RN frigate, permanently out on station in the Gulf and rarely seen up here, the sight of something like '*Calliope*' berthed in an urban setting like this is unusual. A natural cause for wonder. So did their recent decision to post this new minesweeper up to Newcastle represent government's final nod to the glorious heritage of Tyne and its people, their ultimate link with a proud maritime history? Granting them this last opportunity to train a few token volunteers in a naval craft which thousands of their seafaring forebears were once synonymous with?

When "*Join The Reserve Forces in the North East*" on a plastic banner the length of its longshed has become their feeble plea. And "*Not If it Sends Me off to Some Pointless Eastern War...*" the likely riposte from too many desk-bound cowards like me.

From where I'm sitting reading that today, to the extreme left of H.M.S. Calliope but on the same, opposite bank, you can also see '*The Baltic Centre*'. Still one of the biggest, tallest buildings standing south of the river, and only available in white, like all good delivery vans. Once a busy flour-mill visible for miles, they say it gave a welcoming marker for Luftwaffe bomb-aimers crouched in the glazed fronts of their Heinkel 111s.

Come over in gangs on daytrips from Occupied Norway to devastate the Tyne. Nowadays it's an art gallery, those bomb-sites the Heinkels brought us built-over, the Baltic trade over.

Adjacent to 'The Baltic' but directly above 'Calliope' squats Gateshead's other major arts development:'The Sage'. Shimmering on the bank but best viewed from Newcastle side, a gigantic glass armadillo about to slide into the river. Its silver body's reflection of the city and sky my favourite photographic image obtainable locally.

With no sign of Bill, it's time to walk over there and find him. Standing up from my bench, I look to scan the heavens, re-assess the weather. Thousands of feet overhead, the spreading vapour trail of a single executive jet streams out behind it. One lonely stripe in the sky.

At least someone's still flying, whatever the BBC keeps on saying. Not all planes grounded then, as the Jeremiahs would have it. Light perceptibly starting to fade even as I watch this solitary jet heading steadily west up-river, as if tracking its source. Starting a gradual descent towards the airport at Ponteland, an upright tailfin reflecting fingers of sun.

Wondering idly who might be on board.

What they are and where they are going.

Over to my right, a trendy pavement bar tries vainly to lure outdoor custom in, with music piped through giant speakers. Serenading scattered diners protected from the breeze by flapping parasols, but inadequate to suppress the croaking calls of a wandering drunk and his out-of-tune guitar.

Busking incoherently to empty riverside walkways and an unappreciative silence, his violent hand gestures towards any passing car make it fortunate there are so few.

Nearby are serried lines of olive trees in ceramic pots, climatic anachronism and an Etruscan form to serve our modern health & safety. Make a mediterranean boundary to al fresco dining, prevent any patron or waiter from stepping backwards into a roadway. The path of an odd taxi, what few buses are running.

Beyond their terracotta, but cast in counterpoint, rear vast perforated sculptures. Tall bronzes of unknown meaning. The vaguest hints permitted to a rumbustious maritime heritage, our glories of Tyne. To a past our media and the eurocrats would rule too incorrect to celebrate, improper we should know.

Monuments to decline's permanence echoing more explicit prophesies yet. The financial forecasting to be had from a forest of *'To Let'* boards across riverside apartments. Hung on once-fashionable accommodations for a vibrant demographic now cast out from this place. Casualties of a service-sector these empty pavilions can no longer support; fled from a nation that sold its island-soul to the God of Financial Services. Sacrificed its manufacturing base and a control of the seas for this proverbial *'mess of pottage'*.

Wearied by my own negativity and still with no sign of Bill, I finally lose patience and set off to walk. Stretch my stiffened legs. Time to get on over the river and find him for myself, courtesy of the Millennium Bridge - Gateshead's *"Blinking Eye"*. Pedestrians only, its span quivers like a living thing from the moment I cross. Arching over the river like the jawbone of a dead whale, convincingly-strung with high-tensile threads to form its steel saliva.

Following its arc, then turning westward along this southern bank, has me directly approaching the mass of the minesweeper, close by its bows. Now she's more imposing, purposeful and lean, this slatey hue her uniform. Slight plumes of white exhaust-smoke already venting out the sides, wafting away from the funnel as they run her diesels up. Crisp commands through loudspeakers to toiling figures on the deck.

The thirty-millimetre cannon in her gun turret makes a stark point, aimed east like a signpost. One general purpose machine-gun flanking each side, both covers removed.

If Calliope is this ready for sea, where is her best-known crew-member?

Venezia must have brought him down in the Range Rover because I can identify its square, black bulk parked inside the security fence of the compound around *"Calliope"*. Distinctive beside the helipad and olive-green army trucks, I convince myself I can see her mane through a tinted windscreen despite the distance. Auburn in my mind.

'MINISTRY OF DEFENCE AREA – KEEP CLEAR' say the signs but I ignore them.

Walking past and through the spiked outer fence onto a tarmac-covered jetty, I see two access gangways walled in white pvc. Going upwards to the deck. At the foot of one I discover him in conversation with a uniformed naval officer, Bill still in civvies. He greets me with the usual enthusiastic handshake then introduces me to the other. Surprised to find it's Alec Cadwell - that hobby ship-builder, big-time hotelier and small-time motorsporting pothunter I so much dislike. His fellow reservist. Leaving us limited to exchanging a few polite comments about likely sailing weather, before Alec gratefully ascends the gangway, leaves me alone with Bill.

"Calliope has been recalled" he tells me. "Ordered back to London. Patrol on the Thames."

"You mean there's no rioting in Geordieland?"

"Seemingly not. But plenty in Putney!"

"It tells you a lot…." I add "…about Newcastle compared with London."

"Maybe it does…" he responds "…but that's where we're ordered. Where the problems are."

"What will you do?"

"I hold an RNVR commission…" says Bill "and this is my ship. If she's ordered south, then I must go with her. That much my duty."

Whither Thou Go'est, I Go'est….." says I.

"I beg your pardon?" goes Bill.

"Song of Ruth, Old Testament" I reply. "Not to be mentioned at work."

"But you're definitely not coming…..?" he asks as if my last comment left him uncertain.

"Sorry, mate. I know you're pleased this trip coincides with your party-invite to Whitehall, but you'll have to juggle that with whatever the service expects, alone. There's no chance of me attending, sneaking on board. More than my job's worth, or probably your commission!"

"That's a real shame, Michael, although you're probably right. Could have done with some of your political instincts, the usual wise advice. About what I should tell the press, say to the minister."

"You know I can't get involved…." I reply firmly. "Got enough stick last time, just for being in hospital. You know how much *'The Mummy'* hates me, dislikes my opinions. Why I daren't risk it…" Bill looks pained but I continue, stressing the point: "Know I

414

would definitely lose my job if I went missing again. But go on, tell me all the same. What's the angle?"

"Remember that trip we made to the Home Office together?" he says.

"Yeah."

"Invited down to see the minister?"

"Of course, how could I ever forget?"

"Well, it seems we made an impression."

"Well, on someone we did..." I insist. Adding cryptically "....a man in a hat."

Bill looks quizzically at me but probably has no idea.

"Whatever, and even if belatedly. Got them to take on board at least some of our views. Consider rethinking our fundamental relationship with Europe. Before it's too late."

"With all that's going on at the moment, Bill, I should think they're pretty desperate for any sort of political support. At any sort of price, and not left with much choice."

"Maybe so. Why they've invited me down to Cabinet, suggesting I might have a role."

"Unelected, of course. And presumably not in uniform?"

"No, of course not, Michael, I mustn't do that. Dishonour the service. Part of what makes it so complex, keeping the two roles separate. But you know how they would get round it...."

"Yes, with a place in the Lords. Baron Cariss of Redesdale?"

"You jest, Michael!"

"But you wouldn't be averse to that, would you, Bill? No, I think it rather suits you."

"Why not? Not if it helps my country in its hour of need. Not if it gives us a foothold from which to counteract some of the insanity coming out of Brussels!"

"With baubles men are won."

"Eh, that's not 'Ruth', is it?"

"No, Bill, Napoleon Bonaparte. An early EU enthusiast."

"Well, no-one's '*winning*' me! And my ship's ordered south, so I'm headed there anyway."

"With all roads in that direction apparently in the same state as the A1, that's got to be best. Blocked with abandoned cars. People who've run out of petrol, lorries out of diesel, 'leccy cars with flat batteries. Why the sea's your best option, Bill, and probably the only."

"Yes, I know, Michael. For a crisis like no other. You know the list. No fuel and a hostile power hacking into half the servers running CNIs: "*Critical National Infrastructure*". Water, sewerage, and gas pumping-stations. Personal computers and 'phones. Cyberwarfare fomenting chaos like there's someone with a plan. Throwing everything they've got into making it happen, through a new form of warfare. I'll tell you, Mike, and never mind the government, it's ordinary business people that are being driven completely spare. Economic sabotage what they all call it, even if everyone's still arguing over who's really to blame."

"*Cometh the hour, cometh the man*" I said. "Be surprised if they don't end up putting you in charge of the whole Navy after this. What's left of it, anyway. Your big chance, Bill, help them get over the embarrassment of Argentina recapturing the Falklands. And who'd begrudge you the opportunity? Can't imagine anyone better placed to save us."

"That's very kind of you, Michael, just hope that you're right. Look, gotta' go now, so wish me luck. We won't manage contact again for a while, apart from maybe by landline. Either way, I'll try and let you know how things go. What progress is made with the government, or not...."

"It's great you've got the chance, Bill, and what sounds like the only reliable means available for getting there. Good that you've got it at your disposal. Honestly, I really hope it works out, that this time you finally get them to listen. Accept it's time to stop selling the country down the river. Get a bit more protection for ordinary people. And, yes, that things do calm down a bit in the rest of London, obviously....."

"Well that's the primary reason for our going. Keep order from that river you mentioned...."

"Yes, but getting your appointment in Whitehall is a real bonus. No doubt about it. Shows at least they're willing to listen. So if there's anything I can do, anything you want finding out from here. Research on any legal points you want to make but wonder how best to, or else can't get the source for. Don't hesitate to ask, I'll look it up for you. Probably in works time. Even if our normal servers get knocked out again, you should be able to get hold of me on a landline in the office. Just call me at work."

"There is one thing. I'll be worrying about the family, you know. Ness and the kids…. "

"Right. So what do you want me to do?"

"Keep a bit of an eye on them for me, Michael, could you? Check they're all right up there. Now and then would do. She's back and forth to town a lot anyway, but I'd be glad to know there's someone else with a watching brief. Someone I can trust."

"Yes, of course, if that's helpful. Whatever you want…."

"You're a good fellow, Michael Tryton. Absolute salt of the earth. Always said that. Knew I could rely on you!" he says as he starts climbing the gangplank.

I knew it was a genuine statement and he didn't mean it to sound patronising. Though when Bill speaks like this, in that public school-style still surviving at our English Bar, there will always be people whose hackles start rising. Will treat it as enough. Soured souls still carrying that chip on their own shoulder. Individuals for whom even a whiff of *'Received Pronunciation'* is sufficient provocation. Red rag to a bull. Maybe some do, but face-value was how I chose to take it.

Along with that growing sense, something like guilt.

"You're the one who should be taking care, Bill, my lad…." as the best response I can manage: "So mind how you go…..and remember what I say. Never trust anyone!"

He turns at the top of the deck with a broad smile and gives an exaggerated naval salute before disappearing out of sight beyond a stanchion.

Answering duty's call.

It is night but the ship and its mooring are floodlit, the Quayside's bars orange with neon. Gangways are dragged away, the last line thrown; *'Calliope'* giving a long thundering blast on her hooter that echoes hauntingly right up the Tyne. Loud enough to have stopped them in their tracks on the Town Moor or inside St. James's Park, whatever the latest owners call it now. My neck prickles and I'm surprised to feel a lump in my throat, a catch in my breath.

Watching the the dark shape of the warship go with an unexpected sense of sadness. Melancholy feelings. Wondering if she is the last Royal Navy ship ever to be based here. Slipping her moorings to float slowly and sideways out into the

417

current, then drifting downstream past the business district and those empty flats looking so smart and trendy from a distance, shabby close-up.

Heading out towards Ouseburn and then the open sea. Smoke from a black-topped funnel trailing back down the ravine to Redheugh, a large white ensign fluttering at her stern.

While she manoeuvred into the centre of the river then moved off in this way, I had begun to climb slowly towards The Sage, walking upwards and alone on a darkened footpath. Looking back behind me all the time to keep track on 'Calliope's illuminated progress. People coming out of buildings along the Quayside to line its edges, forming quite a crowd. Waving flags and hankies as the vessel glides by, whatever they've got to hand. The sailors lined-up smartly along her stern under an unfurled ensign, waving white hats back.

I wonder if these people on the opposite bank hold the same thoughts. Share in that same sense of impending loss. The deep-rooted concern that things should become so bad in London we need warships on the Thames. "If only as a precaution..." as a succession of BBC announcers hourly insist. Extra reassurance to the capital, if reassurance were needed, of the centre's utter determination to preserve our public safety.

Maintain the firmest control.

Climbing up and reaching the empty carpark for the Sage, I encounter better prospects. Built over the ramped brick arcades of a Victorian wagonway, it overlooks the whole scene. I stand absolutely still there for a while, watching developments from its edge.

Probably making me pretty prominent to whoever's down below. Silhouetted there under the lights until 'Calliope' has finally turned the corner, disappeared from sight. When she's gone the crowds on the Quayside quickly disperse, returning to the brightly-lit bars, restaurants and offices they'd emerged from. Markedly subdued, even at this distance.

Like they could recognise that sense of something important gone forever, not just me.

As I finally turn to go myself, feeling this odd reluctance in my soul, a familiar black Range Rover with tinted glass comes speeding up from the road and turns sharply onto the ramp.

418

Stops right in front of me with a thump, headlights blazing brilliant white. So I am caught in their glare like a rabbit on the road, frozen and transfixed.

The nearside electric window hums downwards and now I can see inside. A woman driver is lit-up, leaning across towards me from the wheel.

"Want a lift anywhere?"

"Bill said I should keep an eye on you...."

"Well, here's your chance!" she says, patting the squab of the passenger seat invitingly.

"Necessity is the plea for every infringement of human freedom. It is the argument of tyrants, the creed of slaves."

(William Pitt, British Prime Minister, 1783)

– XXV –

It was three years following Carausius's elevation to the Purple, and only after he had declared himself Consul and our Chief Magistrate for the second time, that we started to get word from dealers and merchants of a full scale invasion fleet being assembled away up the Rhenus. Of wide-bodied transports and sea-going, ballista-carrying war galleys built along its banks.

Knowing full well what they were meant for.

It made disappointing news for everyone in the province but left no-one surprised, even if some lost their nerve. Like two ships from our Dubris patrol suddenly defecting to the other side, fearful of what was to come. Some say Maximianus publicly showered their crews with golden gifts; while others claim that, if he did, then he had them privately murdered in Treverorum no sooner, very shortly afterwards. Nothing to be surprised about from the type of ruler our western empire enjoyed over there.

While our leader over here, Carausius, had tried hard to win some acceptance of his *status quo* in Britannia, a formal recognition even, but Diocletian and his co-emperor were harder nuts than that to crack. These men Carausius vainly called his *"brothers"* were having none of those conciliatory messages to the world which their irritating usurper regularly issues on his gleaming coinage. All those *antoniniani, denarii* and *aurei* we embossed in relief with *Pax Augusti* - 'Peace of the Emperors' - in the hope our upstart pirate might gain some equal part with them, were simply ignored.

We even produced one special coin later on that showed all three of them standing side-by-side in profile. An event never occurring in real life. Head and shoulder portraits of *"Carausius et Fratres Sui"* as it said round the rim: *'Carausius and his Brothers'*. He was wasting his time of course, both at home and abroad. Nobody believed him, but no-one can say he didn't try.

420

For some peace and harmony with the rest of Rome's empire, a solution involving them all.

But what else did he expect? As the impertinent rival who successful defied their universal authority, made them both look small. Effectively defeating them at sea, if only through that classic expedient of never meeting them in battle. Another *Cunctator* to go down in Roman history, like that great *'Delayer'* who once opposed Hannibal; a Fabian reborn.

Couple this with Carausius's remarkable economic achievements at home in stabilising inflation and revitalising the currency. As compared with his continental equivalents' only making Diocletian and Maximian appear ineffectual, never mind brutal. Their hated comparator: a rival needing to be eliminated not emulated. For the sake of achievements they could never forgive, let alone match or be reconciled over; his excellence their affront.

However quiet our relations with Europa currently seem; however settled the cross-channel traffic our naval patrols so politely control, however mild our customs tariffs; that sense of building danger grew. They say that when his coinage inevitably percolated into the markets of the Rhineland, a new decree was issued from Treverorum. That a trade blockade would be mounted and any trader found in possession would have their hands publicly-pinioned, our coins melted down and poured onto them. As if even the sight of our admiral's engraved image could reduce an Augustus to insane extremes of fury. Retribution beyond reason.

Now they plan a final reckoning: the attack we'd always feared.

And me with a wife and family to worry about. Not only his son-in-law, but now his adopted heir. All of us in it up to our necks. Even my little one.

Diana had taken to me and the idea of marriage with far more grace and enthusiasm than the stalwart of the fleet I'd become had any right to expect, especially from an independent-minded girl of wit and beauty like her. Yet the betrothal ring I gave was carved in jet to special order by a workshop high on the north-east coast out of that magical, glossy ebony they mine from fallen cliffs.

If I knew I had precious little else to offer an Imperial lady or her powerful family, it made for good choice all the same. Its pooled blackness reflecting a mane like raven's wing, that glossy tint of red. Why I thought the kissing couple I ordered be wrought in relief on its face would give a pleasing foil to her secret, softer side. Still like to remember her sitting in her father's house at Calleva, turning it over in her hands. Silent but delighted, grey eyes full.

We signed the marriage contract together three months later. Before her fond father in the law courts of Londinium, with all the pomp and majesty available to his rebel, British empire. Soldiers and choirs: *"Hymen, o Hymenae, Hymen"*.

A great occasion, though I remember being annoyed at how quickly the evening ended for the father of the bride. Soon ensconced in conference with an uninvited guest arriving at our feast. Its spectre the shadowy figure slipping in through a side door; his equity partner in our Brittannic enterprise come to add his own crooked blessing. Gift of a Frankish cup.

The *Rationalis* Allectus come across in a litter from his nearby palace; both of them huddled close together at the back, conferring in low tones about affairs of state even at our nuptials. A physical closeness somehow emphasising their increasing alienation from each other. Allectus alone in his great palace in London, hoarding his metal and consoling isolation with the bizarre bacchanalian revels that make him talk of the town. While his emperor rode the chalk cliffs or spent his days with shipwrights, counting nails and cordage.

Yet if Carausius was his leader and our chief of men, then no one could forget that Allectus was still the paymaster; ultimate impresario. The man financing this whole show - though it did not prevent Diana showing her displeasure, on seeing him at our wedding. Whatever you thought about him, she like me knew that without the ingenuity of Allectus, his ability to conjure up resources and supplies from nowhere, then our successful defence of Britannia together could soon become impossible.

And I'm forced to admit theirs was a project Carausius had tied me into very nicely. One way or another, and not just through marriage - as I saw him manage with nearly anyone he ever needed or required to serve him. It was no longer a case of my private promptings of personal loyalty, that military creed of duty in a professional officer, which turned a willing volunteer into one of his most devoted servants. Now I had been transformed into something else: a significant member of his regime.

Family, in fact.

Contracted-in. Built at my own request into his edifice of blood. A partner in his great project of rebuilding Rome and Roman values from the outermost edge of empire, her remotest province of Britannia. That island of fog and mist nowadays proclaiming itself as a moral lighthouse to all the rest.

Fine work while it lasted, but for how long would that be?

If a sense of insecurity may have become our way of life, and my wife a princess, everyday life went on regardless. Diana and I hardly needing to look at each other before there were children on the way; we never had any problem on that score.

By the year of her father's second Consulship, Diana had borne me a daughter, Lucia, and showed another child on the way. I loved Lucia well enough, growing a spirited girl like her mother, but still hoped for a son. For a boy who could come to run and hunt as I once did, a bright cherub to share in his father's new-found enthusiasms for the sea and for ships. Learn to handle a modern sword, appreciate an older one.

Inherit a magic blade?

Living how we did, imagining these outcomes seemed harmless enough pastime. Innocent domestic ambitions projected onto the place she'd grown-up. Her father's old house beneath Rutupiae walls, now our first together. Where she "*kept the home and spun the wool*" as the law has always had it. Its old-fashioned plaster decoration and classical mosaics redolent with similar reassurances of familial or social continuity. Hard-won, but what better location for a new-made family like ours to grow and find its feet?

Except we were only living there for one important reason. Because I am the emperor's adopted heir, his son-in-law and one-time junior tribune. Granted a senior command suitable to match my new status, put in charge of a squadron. Family, that's how the top jobs were starting to be given out, and people were beginning to notice.

It's not as if I'd even demanded, or begged it for myself. Me, '*Triton*', ever the seasick passenger, now put in charge of ships!

423

The Rutupiae section of his undefeated British fleet to be precise - my own precious 'C' squadron.

Ten brand-new biremes of Anderidan oak, fresh off the slipways of Clausentum and no finer sight on all the coast. We named them 'Casseopia', 'Carausius Victor' and 'Colossus' (a vessel heavy with catapults) or 'Caius Volusenus' after the surveyor-tribune of Julius Caesar's first reconnaissance in strength. Not to mention the 'Cassandra', 'Corona', 'Caesaromagus' and inevitable 'Clausentum'. Plus the agile 'Coria', crewed solely by northerners. And last but not least, that special one I chose for their praetorian flagship. From whose decks I would lead them.

My very own 'Calliope', mother of all muses.

Their task between them to guard our closest stretch of coastline to Gallia from their base over here. From beneath a decaying monument some forgotten emperor once raised to commemorate his role in our island's story. The tetrapylon, its stump eroded by war and weather into nothing more prosaic than a simple watchtower. Guarding those sacred grounds where Rome first arrived, the first of her Caesars made his original landfall full three centuries ago. And where we modern Britons are called upon once more - reluctantly withal - to stand in arms upon its chalky beaches.

Romans standing against Rome; a Rome run from elsewhere.

History repeating itself? Holding under Roman flags that same front-line of sea and shingle my tribal ancestors once walled against foreign ways. Against those ways of Rome we now would willingly die for. Promising to restore her glories in Britanniae but determined to prevent her return: contradiction building upon contradiction. Opposing sides in a Roman civil war; what man-made madness more bitter, more ironic than that?

Yet before he could finally turn on us and our "Imperium Brittannarium", the Augustus Maximianus and his faithful subordinate, Constantius 'The Pale', must first defeat certain rebellious tribes along the Rhenus. Peoples nearer the sea who stayed loyal to Carausius as a son of their shores. Friends identified by Treverorum as their most recalcitrant foe; in most immediate need of condign punishment and a savage suppression.

424

"The longer these folk hold out, the more of a breathing space they win for us in Britain!" Saturninus Lupus insisted to one of our regular councils-of-war: "Time in which to prepare, now the coming threat is realised......"

If he was right, the ferocious storm of iron and blood raining down on friends across the water from Maximian's Rhineland legions would not leave us very long. When these allies on the edge of empire were soon taught to bow the knee once more.

Those few they left alive to do so.

"How ready are we?" asked Carausius.

"It is all in hand, believe me, lord...." Saturninus Lupus told our worried conclave. "*Gesoriaco quod nunc Bononia*, our headquarters over there and the satellite forts of northern Gaul; such places as Grannona and Marcae, loyal cities like Rotomagus; are being strengthened all the time. Armed with every precaution and device against the type of avenging Imperial force we know is like to come against us."

"Whether by land or by sea....." growled Carausius.

Over here on the southern coasts of Britannia, now it was returned to a single administrative entity under our control, the bright new blockhouses of brilliantine flint he had called his 'Saxon Shore' were filling-up with grain. Ready to feed the fresh troops we were amassing there, whole towns of tented leather.

Gathering against Romans, not raiders.

Long before he did come, we'd already heard how often Maximianus had been in the habit of boasting to his courtiers at Treverorum how easily his armies could cross our narrow sea. "As *if it were a canal...*" he'd say. Imagining it his prelude to reducing these rebel provinces to obedience within the space of merely weeks.

A boast silently echoed by the geographic closeness of my new command at Rutupiae to several likely spots for landing. A proximity innocently emphasised by fading maps on the wall of its centuries-old headquarters. Painted in a distant age when 'Rhenus' rhymed with 'friend', but assuring the inevitability of my beloved '*C*' squadron being the first called to battle, when that time of asking came.

It did not take long.

In the month of summer we dedicate to Divine Augustus, I remember us entering an extended period of settled weather. A fisherman's dream of millpond seas, cloudless horizons and reflecting sunsets in the west. The land baking under a steady sun and the harvest coming-in early. So much easier to gather without the wind and rain normally battering our province during its apologies for summer. A golden time capable of proving as much a curse upon our safety as it was a blessing for farmers. Blue skies and calm seas.

Ideal for invasion.

How long would it last? Only the gods could say, but which should we ask?

There is a Syrian variation on our ultimate King of Roman Gods, one Jupiter Dolichenus, retaining a surprising number of adherents in today's army. And in this context worth recalling for another important role - as powerful weather-god. Riding-in on horseback, bolts of lightning in hand. The very reason why Carausius consulted the more cerebral of his officers known to favour this cult for their best recommendations and advice.

About where their commander could find reliable divination regarding a singular, vital question: *"When does good weather break?"*

Having got one unspecified answer about it from this Thunder-God, via their chosen man, the next thing we know he is galloping off to Londinium. Gone in person to his oracle. For another consultation with his favourite sage. To the Temple of Diana and Apollo in their wood beyond the walls to see that one-eyed seer who does his horoscopes, now trying for another.

That keen for reassurance?

Anyway, it must have been worth the journey, not to mention the price of an altar, if the forecast he got from her satisfied him better. For I heard along the grapevine how soon he and his companions on this errand were back home in Calleva. *"By the end of the week, brimming over with enthusiasm and confidence..."* what I was told.

"Now for the enemy!" he'd said.

By the time they finally came against us, there was not a shred of surprise left in it. Our spies along the Rhenus, friendly traders of the seas, military lookouts on the cliffs, Carausius and his seer; they all saw to that. Told us what was coming.

One thousand ships.

Carrying the Army of the Rhenus.

When the word came, it was early evening and I was eating at home with the family. We had just heard the first rain in weeks, pattering on the roof, then soon after a loud banging from the front doors. Bruccius, the house steward, came bustling into the dining room, our *triclinium*, with worry printed on his face.

"My lord, please forgive me interrupting you at this hour but there are men at the door...!"

"That's all right, Bruccius, who is it?"

"My lord, it is Fabricius the Thracian, captain of '*Colossus*', and Tertius off your '*Calliope*' come along with him. It seems important."

"Show them in, Bruccius, show them in. Don't keep them waiting at the door, let them get any more wet!"

When Fabricius and his companion came in, water dripping off their clothes onto the mosaic floor, I could tell by the former's face what's the news. Without even asking. In a way, it was almost a relief.

"They are coming?"

"My lord, the tide turns and the weather with it. And, yes, they come! The Emperor of the Narrow Seas commands his several squadrons to put to sea. Upon no other timing or co-ordination than everyone at once! He commends his own safety, yours, and that of all Britannia to the valour of our crews and his trust in the Goddess. He wishes us to know that the Jupiter of the Syrians has smiled on our voyage; Apollo and The Huntress too. That the *Classis Britannica* should convene in the centre of the channel and the heart of the enemy's force. Between here and Gesoriacum, where we and the Weather-God will despatch the tyrant together."

"Beyond that, no other order?" I ask.

"Only to keep a watch everywhere for sign of his squadron, lord, his flag the crescent moon. And until then, till his arrival, we are always to attack. Only attack!"

"Well then, let us call every man to his post and proceed to sea immediately."

"I am grateful to you for receiving us promptly, commodore. Acting so quick. I think this the beginning of that great thing we waited so long for - the reckoning. Your squadron, lord, its vessels and crews, stands ready. Awaits your kind disposal..."

said Fabricius, who could add to this complement an extra armoured ship. That *navis tecta* he'd come across from Portus Dubris in, now moored on our harbour.

"And did the emperor tell you our password for the day?"

"It is Diana's, my lord: *'Diana'*. For however many days the fight may last!"

Now there was an idea a man might fight for - far more than any fancy promise of a *'Golden Age Renewed'*. As if she wasn't what I would be fighting for anyway, password or no password. As if she hadn't heard it all, standing beside me in the *triclinium*, leaning back with hands on hips to ease the weight of the unborn child she carried.

"Now is the time of asking." She said. "You who are a soldier, praying for Victory and Glory, as I will be praying to Neptune and Salus for your safety. All of us praying together - myself and Lucia.....and your son-to-be."

(Women, eh? How did she know it would be a son?)

"As I will be praying for you, dearest wife. Be brave for me my darling, and trust in the Gods. Do we not sail with your father, the luckiest admiral ever - Carausius the *'Felix'*? I love you, Diana, and beg you to have faith in me. To trust in my return. Don't ever doubt me, Diana, I promise to be back. For you and ours, whatever else happens!"

My oblations before our household gods, the *lares*, were brief but sincere. With an extra prayer to Jupiter for her peace of mind and our victory. Then I kissed my wife and hugged her tight. She kept her dignity, even if her eyes reddened. Filled-up. Keeping her back straight and her chin out like a proper Roman lady, she drew Lucia in between us and we three held each other for a fraction, before I must go out like a soldier.

Precious Gods! How it pained me to go, but go I did, without one backward glance.

That thing I regret most.

"The EEC treaty is the supreme law of this country, taking precedence over Acts of Parliament. Our entry into the EEC meant (subject to our undoubted but probably theoretical right to withdraw from the community altogether) Parliament surrendered its sovereign right to legislate contrary to the provisions of the Treaty on matters of social and economic policy."

<u>R-v-Secretary of State for Transport ex.p. Factortame</u> (1991)

(Decision of House of Lords judicial committee,
on ruling that the UK's Merchant Shipping Act 1988,
as passed by Parliament, was contrary to EU law).

The French theory about it (from a nation generally accepted as expert in these matters) is that it is the hasty and excited chase upstairs – glorious prelude to bed and whatever happens in there – which really is the best. Anticipation as high point.

While the rest of the world took seven steps nearer to madness, what felt to me like our calmly climbing the stairs together had begun with a forty-mile journey in her Range Rover. Heading out of Newcastle on the A69 up to Hexham, then turning off for Chollerford, Otterburn and Kielder. A glorious journey with Venezia at the wheel, storming past dawdlers, scything through the lanes, her exquisite features always in profile. Lit round the edges, sculpted by God.

My beautiful statue, me worshipping at her shrine.

Looking fixedly ahead to the centre line, as if its relentless white dart could provide some neutral focus for all those passionate thoughts I'd been waiting so long to share with her. Still struggle to express, although dying for the chance. Help me formulate some painful concepts, make sense of five years spent hoping. All those quiet hours imagining another opportunity, brooding on her loss.

Ever since our first and last attempt to renew a shaky teenage romance, I'd thought of nothing else. How we - I - might reconstitute an ancient infatuation together. Bruised by the thought of my clumsy early attempt to reconstruct something we'd never properly got to. Even in the first place. That thing our generation calls 'A Relationship' - like these are machines or engines you can publish an Owner's Manual on. With that well-thumbed chapter you go to at the back, headed 'FAQs and Fault-Finding'. That section I'd turn to first, in the hope it could explain what went so well and truly pear-shaped inside a bad hotel in York, the last time I'd tried. Struggling to divine reasons in her mind a ponderous male psyche still fails to fathom, she probably thinks obvious.

Torn between honour and hope. Wondering what buttons I should press, while all the time I keep on scrupulously avoiding them. Passing the journey in meandering conversation; clinging to honour, entertaining hope.

"Let's hope Bill gets the answers he wants this time… " I said to the dashboard.

"Yes, let's!" she replied, cutting across a bend. "It really looks like our best chance, Mike, both his and the cause. If government won't listen, if he can't turn the tide this time, then he says the country's done for. Decline come to Fall. Ruined, finished, sold down the river!"

"I'm only sorry not to be going with him. Giving moral support."

"Yes, it's a shame, but I'm sure he understands. Values what you've done already. William couldn't do without your contributions, you know. Your support and advice."

"One of Trotsky's useful idiots."

"Oh no, not at all. His '*Just and Faithful Knight*'…"

"Steady on, pet! A bit fanciful that, much too Arthurian. But what about you? Your role?"

"Following the faith, believing in the cause. Keeping the family afloat….holding on here."

"Ah, yes, as his Guinevere. But still managing an interesting career as well, so I hear?"

"Oh, really, Mike, and I'm not even blonde! But, yes, at least one of us has a vocation. All his seems to mean to him now is just a job. How it looks to me. No disrespect to you guys, but it seems only an idiot would want to join the legal profession in England nowadays. Tyranny by regulation, with us gold-plating Europe's, as if theirs weren't bad enough already. Looking for complexity, extra things to do. You'll know what I mean, but it's supply and demand isn't it? Our universities produce so many lawyers, the specialist technicians servicing William's Range-Rover get more money and respect than you guys seem to get now. And have you seen how many new law graduates come out of Newcastle every year? All of them needing somebody to sue, if only to put food on their own table."

I grinned at her sarcasm, knowing it was true. Enjoying her vivacity.

"Getting like America, you mean, where they joke about '*More lawyers than rats'* ?"

"Yes…." she agreed with a delicate smile best seen from the side: "Too little trust left in downgraded professionals. What my parents said was done to teaching in their day, before it became our turn. Archaeologists and lawyers. No, whatever I do is done for the children."

"And the horses?"

She laughed.

"All right yes, Michael, maybe a little bit for the horses. At least they don't answer back. But never so many of them as he claims to exist under the bonnet of William's *Lancheea* – that bloody Aurelia you and he so dote on. Even counting the vet's bills, I'm sure they cost us less to fix!"

I couldn't credit that last point but thought it better not to argue. Part of my new charm offensive.

Coming off the Otterburn road, we began climbing that interminable hill which leads for several lonely miles into the Cheviots and up towards Stipend Howe.

It was bouncing along this lane that the swinging headlights of the Range Rover would occasionally capture sight of some of those horses she meant. Standing stoically alone in the darkness, their long manes hanging down over the neck like a melancholy maiden's. Nags more resembling ponies than any normal horse I knew. Lit against the dreary tan of bracken and heather, we must have seen a dozen or more examples of this rare local breed.

Bill had told me how they'd been saved from Darwinian oblivion at massive expense, now resell at a premium to equine collectors. Reckoning their contribution along with however many her livery business takes in as another lucrative little sideline of the Cariss family, it looked like there was enough horseflesh assembled out here to mount half the Household Cavalry.

The harsh message contained in all these signs and trappings of wealth. One maybe only dawning on me then - if it had not already while I stayed here before, convalescing in the clock-tower. Floating in a fever. Something it pained me to recognise.

How she'd never have got all this, living with me. Married to a minor public servant.

None of it. Not this house nor these horses. The antique furniture and Victorian paintings. The stables, vast tracts of land, and collector's cars. The isolation and privacy.

Money, the ultimate aphrodisiac.

Bill might have big feet but he remained a real catch, while a loser like me never would be. Not for the rare beauty she was, anyway. A breaking realisation set to hurt me all the more. Though it was while coming to terms with its reality, standing out there on the front doorstep and about to go in, looking back across their floodlit paddock at yet more of this unique breed of horse, that I had a brilliant idea. One we'll come onto later.

I turned towards the open door with its thought still stuck in my head and saw Venezia standing there. Looking at me sideways in an odd sort of way, strands of auburn hair streaming over her lips, hands on her hips like she'd had another of her own.

"Well, are you coming in?" she'd said.

I don't remember how we ended up upstairs, but I blame the French.

Location: a main bedroom in the Victorian wing.

"I knew I'd find you again..." I told her at one point in the tumbling, remembering a vow made on the banks of the River Hull a long time ago. In remembrance of '*The Gaul*'.

Venezia moving across and suddenly straddling me. Lovely big bed.

Her saying: "I don't know why I'm doing this, like I'm going mad. Knowing it's wrong. Oh, God, please help me, Michael. I'm terrified, can't help myself. Take care of me, hold me!"

Taking off her t-shirt with no help from me, before I even got chance to try. Wishing to all the same, against both our better judgements.

Things were looking up.

I brushed my hand over her upright nipples and she sighed heavily before pulling me closer in: "Such an incredible coincidence! You and me finding each other after all these years. Like it is meant. And, yes, despite what happened in York. Honestly, I am so sorry about that. About what I did to you there.....really sorry. It was all my fault. I was such a fool..." she breathed. "My darling....forgive me!"

I do not respond to that but simply kiss her on the mouth.

And the rest.

"The pirate must now lose heart, when he sees that your armies have almost entered those straits which alone have postponed his death until the present, that his men have abandoned their ships and have followed the retreating sea. Is there now any more distant island he can hope for, any other Ocean? How can he escape punishment for treason, without being swallowed by an earthquake or swept by a hurricane onto lonely reefs? Splendid fleets were built and equipped, which would head for Ocean simultaneously by every river; men not only competed in their labours to complete them, rivers suddenly rose to receive them."

(Claudius Mamertinus, a court poet's panegyric in honour
of the Emperor Maximianus Herculius, 21st April 289 AD)

- XXVI -

It is a special naval commander who can successfully lead five separate squadrons while scattered out at sea. Rarest of mariners and hardest to find: being born, never made. While that quality became his by nature, there was in those days no citizen in these islands who would not have stood to hail Marcus Aurelius Mausaeus Carausius as the Caesar, their ultimate scion of this uncommon breed.

And by the time it came about that I found myself witnessing his proof, it was from the privileged vantage of a squadron commander. Selected by him for our ultimate test. Sailing together into the heart of what he always told us would be the greatest sea-battle since Actium.

Yes, I know - I've told you already - but my pride never wanes.

When I couldn't believe it myself. Promoted to a sea-going command, now his *navarchus*. Me, that country boy who became a commodore, despite a disability at sea. The commander of a combat squadron who must always go below on leaving port, only emerging later. But if this initial routine sounds like my handicap then I will insist otherwise, no man living tell you different. No, to the point it hardly did matter - not now I'd worked out a practical method, my own ways to cope. Tamed the discomfort and sickness in my mind so well it became unimportant. Just another background circumstance to be worked around and against. Mere vicissitude of war.

The important thing was that I always did manage. Recovered my sea-legs within the first hour or so afloat, long before battle was joined. Like some mental and physical barrier I must first negotiate - an ordeal Mithraic in its tests. Finally reaching that point in my career where I could welcome its sensations like a familiar foe faced-up to, more the blessing of experience than any gift of gods. That point in life where, like death or fear, I can greet this sickness of the sea like an old friend come in from the shadows. Look in the eye and smile.

Where an unforgettable August evening, three hours out from Rutupiae, found me on '*Calliope*' and shaking the bony hand of all three nightmare familiars together. Wondering which one of them would choose to take me first – whether sickness, fear or death.

435

That day when ten priceless vessels of my brave 'C' squadron found themselves pitched full-tilt and alone into a teeming epi-centre of the entire Rhenus Fleet. The red sails of their expeditionary force covering the whole of an evening sea like butterflies on a flowerbed; countless in number. Only when we finally see them do I realise the extent of our madness. Ten against a reputed thousand, and we with time to count.

The closer-in we get, the more obvious it becomes how grievously a raking fire from *catapultae* or *ballistae* ranged along the sides of Maximian's lumbering transports will devastate our open decks. The moment we venture in range. So I consult with Tertius, the experienced *trierarch* of *'Calliope'*. Agree that if our squadron forms a narrow column and attacks our opponents at a right-angle to their current line of sail; if we can but keep nerve enough to pass close behind the stern of each enemy vessel; then the *ballistae* on our deck-towers will be able to unleash such a barrage onto ships packed with soldiers. Inflict degrees of damage out of all regard to how few we rebels really are.

And whether we survive this reckless ride afterwards. Live it out or not.

So my ship's trumpeter, our talented *bucinator*, puts up the standard huntsman's signal for *'Follow Me!'* so clear and bright it rings in the air like a struck glass, our little convoy forming up in line very nicely and no time at all upon its cheery command. Obedient to a man, we drive on regardless together, into a mighty host.

Jupiter, I was proud of them!

Against so many, my plan - such as it was - was consistent with our orders. To cause the most disruption and confusion possible to the whole which might result from our attacking so ferociously just some. Taken together, it would be the accuracy and rate of fire of our catapult crews; the relative manoeuvrability of our Clausentum biremes against their longer, Rhenus transports and the perfected seamanship of well-trained officers and men; which were all we had to tip the balance.

As we bore down upon the enemy at maximum speed, one hundred and fifty of my embanked rowers straining to their oars on *'Calliope'* under the bearded baritones of Didius our rowing-officer, calling time, I had no idea whether any of it would work.

"*Alea iacta est!*"

The *trierarch* looks calmly across at me from our position high on the steering deck, as the *Calliope* rears on her pretty haunches at their push, then he spits into the sea.

"Now to discover how hard our Anderidan oak is - ground on the greenwood of Germania!"

"Whoa, Tertius! Today your ram and grapnel must be our last resort, never the first. Not a battle of contact but a contest of firepower. Get alongside any and they would flood us with soldiers. If we can but hurt the transport and evade their escorts, every one that we sink dilutes the force Maximian lands. These ships are set for carriage, Tertius, not for fighting back - and we will knock them down like skittles!"

Our column makes for a narrow-enough target when their iron bolts start coming, but some must hit and when they do it is savage, tearing through sinew, armour and timber like an augurer's knife through entrail. Why it is an officer drawn upright to direct a dozen archers waiting on Calliope's deck, his men kneeling down to dip their arrowheads in troughs of heated bitumen, who receives their first. Taking it so hard in his back that he is thrown along its entire length, coming to rest pinned and stone-dead against a cabin wall. Right beneath where Tertius and I are standing.

A sensible man in his forties with sad eyes: Hyginus, the deck-officer, who has a young wife and three children down in the town, but now she is a widow and they are left fatherless. The *medicus* closing his eyes and covering his impaled corpse with a tarpaulin, then going looking for others to help.

Soon there are plenty.

Even if most incoming bolts hit nothing more vital than superstructure, the sharp splinters which fly-up when triangular snouts are buried in timber can wound those nearby as badly as an arrow. Painful cries coming, as soon as they do.

"I'm going into the tower...." I yell to Tertius "but don't change our course!"

He nods gravely and turns to face the starboard-quarter's steersman just as a ballista bolt goes through the latter's neck. Tertius grabbing his body then taking over the oar.

I rattle down the open steps onto the main deck anyway and run across its length, heading for a ladder into the catapult loft. Up behind the flimsy wooden battlements of its tower where its crew, the *ballistarii*, are straining to load and prime their powerful weapon. Ready for when our opponent's stern appears in plain view, ready to rake sailors and steering gear. Crouched behind the painted masonry of a wooden palisade that's all they have to protect them, they grunt dutiful greetings when an officer arrives.

"How many shots can you give them, when we go by?"

"Two, maybe three. Where do you want them, sir?"

"One for the captain, two for their steersmen, then we'll go about. Come back for more!"

I see the *ballista* men look at each other like I'd asked them to split an apple on the head of a baby, but know they'll give it their all, so I clap each man on the shoulder and rush back down to the deck.

The archers are holding their composite, Parthian-style small-bows in horn and sinew taut, loaded and ready. Each one with an arrow cocked to the string. Waiting for that time when we are closest-in to the nearest transport and they can light them, their questions the same:

"Where do you want them, sir?"

"Into the middle of their deck. Wherever their soldiers cram the closest. And anywhere that starts a fire!"

By now, *Calliope* is at too close an angle to their line of battle for the deflection on our enemies' artillery, so we get a fleeting respite. Now it is *Colossus'* turn behind us to draw their incoming fire. At the same moment our archers finally stretch their bows and let fly with burning arrows, onto the ship whose sternpost looms above – while our own catapult bolts are whizzing over their heads and into the enemy's poop deck, mowing down crew.

Then we are out and past her, the *Colossus* still taking her turn at it, more fire-arrows pouring down. The invasion convoy is several vessels deep and the next one in is dead ahead, closer than expected. So close we cannot swerve round her or return. Tertius looking quizzically at me after what I'd said about contact, and me grinning back:

"Yes, this one we'll ram!"

It is like those onboard have read our mind, heard drumbeat's command. Even before the bronze ram fitted to *Calliope*'s forefoot has appeared out the water on our oarsmen's increased acceleration, she is straightway starting to heel in anticipation. One hundred terrified legionaries rushing to her furthermost side, trying to flee the impact.

Too late.

The *Calliope* hits their transport at full speed and its shock completes a roll already starting. The Maximian troopship turning-turtle in a flash, breaking its back as it does so. Suddenly we are at rest in a patch of boiling water, rowers lifting their oars for safety as our hull and keel-strakes grind over a barnacle-encrusted dome that's all that's left above water.

Where we see several soldiers in the sea, swimming for a few seconds before the weight of armour drags them down. Roman soldiers looking their countrymen despairingly in the eye for the one moment of life that's left before Oceanus swallows them up for ever.

Now is no time for sentiment. We cannot stop.

I get a momentary glance aft at the first transport we passed, now a pillar of flame on the ocean, then hear the voices of Tertius and the rowing officer together. Demanding fresh strikes from our oarsmen, as if they have not given enough. Knowing we've hardly begun.

Another ship ahead.

This one tries to turn away from us and all we can see is stern, carved and gilded *aphlaston*, but in his panic he crosses the path of a neighbour. Their two allied ships tangling, then both starting to sink. Sailors jumping into the water, soldiers frozen in fear.

A hail of arrows is coming-in from that quarter too, then the occasional bolt, and I see the frightening sight of an armoured warship, a *cataphract* as we call them. One of their biggest escorts, turning mid-stream under full press of sail in order to set her artillery and archers loose upon us. Tertius has seen her too and orders a rapid turn-about, two banks of oars straining on the one side, left feathered on the other.

Calliope shudders from stem to stern and turns on her axis like she's centred in a whirlpool, then lurches forward on a new bearing. Showing her tail to this heavyweight, we are

439

minimising our target, shrinking from its fire. Head-on to the wind, too, and momentarily left struggling, but oars can take you where a limp sail cannot and suddenly *Calliope* is tearing back down the centre of the whole invasion fleet, leaving the *cataphract* behind.

The oncomers dare not fire at us for fear of hitting friends adjacent, but we are letting-fly at them with everything we have; bitumen, metal and fire. Creating such chaos among these matrix formations of the Rhenus that oncoming troop-ships, transporters and escorts go scattering wildly. Swerving off to left, right and centre, any which way but loose.

Looking aft again there is smoke and flame drifting across the convoy's path and fresh wreckage on the sea, but I am amazed to see, powering triumphally out and through it, what appears to be the complete '*C*' squadron. Following my earlier "*Follow Me!*" to the very letter, may the Gods praise and protect them. All of us heading east through the breaking centre of a westward-sailing fleet, ramming and firing and burning as we go.

Looking east, I see another thing.

If we had left a world of sunshine, evening draws on. The backdrop frieze to a tyrant's petty show of earthly force, these glowering walls of grey. Limitless towers of cloud building higher into the stratosphere, divine citadels of the Weather-God raising his ramparts in tribute to an irrational anger like to exceed any emperor's. Works of a god whose winds will only blow stronger, grow heavier with water, as a new force rises up on the sea. Raindrops spattering across my face, the scent of them sweet.

Harbingers of victory?

Not now, not yet.

If we have broken the enemy's formation, then the price of doing so is to place ourselves at its very heart. However many we sink or ram, the simpler mathematics of our situation are starting to dawn quite as fast as the sun may be setting. Upon them, as much as on us.

We are surrounded.

The transports are still drifting slowly by, crammed with soldiers and horses fearing the sea more than us, more curious than hateful, but their armed escorts are gathering. Circling, slavering, like dogs round a badger.

They fear our jaws but gain courage from numbers, and all the time the incoming fire and oncoming wind is increasing. Reducing our momentum, weakening our crews. Killing our men. If that feels painful and takes more from our strength every minute, then what they really want to do is grapple. Take hold of us tight.

A Dance of Death. Stop moving and we're done for.

The first is to go down is *'Coria'*.

Its crew from the northern coal-trade under Intrepidus are still relative newcomers to warfare. Good men, perhaps not hard enough in their hearts, not ruthless enough in reaction. So that when the first *korax*, a grapnel, comes in over the side from a *cataphract*, it seems like her axe-men aren't quick enough to cut its rope. Then suddenly there's another one biting their rail, then another and another. Too many for axes. The *cataphract* has her now, like a spider its mate, and hauls the *'Coria'* in for a kiss that will kill her. Now in its close embrace, the spiked ramps come down and there are fully-armoured legionaries pouring onto her deck, killing everyone they can find and torching the vessel.

I cannot bear to watch her sink, and look instead to Tertius to ask him: "How can we get out of this nightmare?"

Tertius is from Sicilia, which I hear is a hot country, and so a man who never hurries. He looks calmly round instead at these *cataphractae* closing in from all sides. Like he is the landlord of a soldiers' inn wanting to shut, and points to the south-east where a pin-prick of yellow shines faintly on its darkling horizon.

"Gesoriacum Light" he says, laconically. "Can you see it? Our people. Their own squadron fighting a way over here, you can lay bets on that. So let's force our way out and through to meet them while we're still left a gap. Then return together in strength to renew the party."

I smile back, my confidence restored, when a stone catapult ball from one of the Maximian escort ships smashes in through the deck-shelter, tearing through steering gear and shrouds like they are papyrus. Tertius takes it full in the chest and falls to the deck, myself and a marine next to us bending to try and lift him up.

It's pointless, no good, and we know there's nothing useful to be done - but trying to get his crushed and bloody frame into

441

more comfortable position, he whispers hoarsely into my ear: "Sorry to be leaving you during business hours, my lord Triton. Rest certain you'll be fine. Only do as our little emperor says: attack, only attack! And let the lads look after you....they will see to whatever needs doing....just trust in them to know it."

The last thing Tertius ever says to me, but still he lingers, breathing on. Blood bubbling round his chest. He never spoke again but at least I made sure he didn't die alone. Staying crouched right by him, there on the wrecked poop. Only standing up to call out the sort of commands I fondly hoped he'd approve. Consulting and involving him to the end.

Though in all the din I cannot tell you when he finally slipped away. Over the Stygian River with a coin of Carausius in his mouth, fine payment for the ferryman. Another honest soldier of Rome needlessly lost; slaughtered by the tyrant. Another murdered comrade whom I'll always miss; another friend to avenge in that line of shadowy men headed by my father.

And, yes, by Jupiter, his lads do look after me. Know what needs to be done. Where I might be at a loss to devise on the spot some of the more technical, sailing solutions necessary if we are to smash a way out of a ring of Imperial warships determined to stop us leaving, but the second officer and the steersmen and the rowing-master are making-up for it between them, working as one.

The wind is blowing harder now, coming in as increasingly-gusty squalls. Rain like smoke and smoke like rain. We drive hard for the south-east despite it, compressing our battered formation into a tight phalanx of nine rebel ships. The most damaged to the middle, one already on tow. Heading through cloud for the last, narrow space that's left in sight between two careless *cataphractae* standing over that way. Not knowing how heavy a price we are about to pay for asking them to move; how much longer our exhausted, boxed-in rowers can be asked to keep us going forward, at any sort of speed.

'Calliope' is still leading and it is from her foredeck where I am amazed to see the *cataphractae* parting, getting quickly out of our path. Poor seamanship or just too frightened of barring the door? Whatever it is, the gratitude they receive is minimal, their opening momentary. While we go through it, our remaining archers and *ballistae* crews are pouring down such a torrent of burning missiles onto these two gatekeepers that they must wish they'd gone away sooner. Suddenly under this hail, the nearest one spontaneously ignites and then seems to lose control. Oarless and rudderless, it is rushing back helplessly onto us, borne headlong by the westerly current. Entirely on fire.

It is brave *'Colossus'* of the battles, first to come and last to go, which is once again our rearguard and stands full-square. Taking the brunt of it. Tangling with the runaway, blocking its route into our formation, the fire leaps from vessel to vessel faster than any soldier could. Illuminating night.

Held as prisoner where earthly elements collide, I hear the screams of men. Whichever side they come from, it seems they sound the same. Caught in the ultimate nightmare of fire flowering on water, the shrill despair of men who have been left to choose between a burning or a drowning. Many getting both.

Hell and high water.

Then we have broken free of their horrors but now are only eight. Heading together into the dark for the *pharos* at Gesoriacum. Its guiding light eclipsed in the blackness by the bitumen brilliance of vessels burning behind us, some of them ours. The *'Colossus'* turned into a death ship we never shall see again, its bonfire a pillar. Making us the gladder, despite these losses, to encounter the friendly lamps at mast-top of an allied squadron coming over in the other direction towards us. Feeling their way through breaking waves.

Because of and not despite these desperate circumstances, it is a joyful reunion we make in the darkness with our companions of the *Classis*. Dropping anchor and mooring alongside them in a rising swell, the interlinked line of ships helping stabilise and calm an angrier sea. Conscious of its bigger heave, out on the inky-black seaway, I should say my determination at this point was for our prompt return to battle. To take a brief pause only towards regrouping, re-victualling, and some little rest.

For too many of our gallant company, a respite eternal. Tertius and Hyginus are buried out at sea by the flickering light of oil lamps, along with all our other dead. Joining good friends like Fabricius from the still-missing *'Colossus,'* somewhere deep in ocean. Consigned to the mercies of Great Neptune Himself according to the ritual of mariners. As tough and as kind a brotherhood of fighters you could ever hope to meet. That one to which I'm proud to be irretrievably joined, this land-bound lad from Calleva.

While more vital than fresh food and water, this Gallic patrol brings us clearer news of a continuing battle. Plus an interesting new order, direct from our emperor.

"A fast cutter of his '*M*' squadron got through to us from Vectis Isle, late this afternoon" says my opposite-number, the commodore of Gesoriacum in conference on his deck. "Between us, we have successfully scattered elements of the Imperial invasion-fleet, but Carausius wants his squadrons to pull back from further attack. For the moment at least, to find temporary safe-haven. When his advisers have convinced him how the gods stand ready to intervene on our behalf, poised to answer his prayers with a storm. Why you and I should get back to Bononia. Somewhere to sit it out in safety together. So that when Jupiter and Neptune have done their work, then the *Classis Britannica* can return. Finish off the job!"

Our brightest military strategy is built on prophecy, but who am I to disobey?.

Tertius had been right.

Whatever turbulence the gods bestow could be no substitute for the hard slog of battle. Whatever dangers we survive or the promised storm inflicts, when tomorrow dawns we secessionists must rejoin what brave Tertius had laughingly called his '*party*'. Like it or not, and however wild these seas remain.

Heading back into a running fight against a mighty fleet whose true ferocity and incredulity of scale I knew we'd so far only tasted.

Under the cover of whatever temporary disruption an obscure weather-god, some Syrian fashionable with officers, might manage to drum-up for us in the meantime.

Operating like us, so dangerously far from home.

*"The further back you can look,
the further forward you can see"*

(Winston Spencer Churchill)

- 27 -

"It's wrong what we're doing" she sighs "…. but serve Bill bloody well right. After his squalid little affair with that trollop Diane, up at the law department. It nearly broke us!"

Whatever she was confessing to me about his, I was certain in my own mind that I would never tell her what deceptions of my own had brought me here. How I'd really got into this house. Into this bed. How long it had taken me. How hard I'd worked to make it happen. What fiddles I'd worked. How closely I'd been following her upward progress, ever since York. How easy it had been. A doddle in fact.

Dulce et decorum? Not any more. Decorum went out the window years ago.

People put far too much information out about themselves, don't they? Companies and government demanding even more. Out there on the web, like they've forgotten decent discretion. Any sense of what's seemly, any thoughts of decorum.

So what do they expect?

New social rules apply and they are simple: like anyone born after the millennium simply doesn't care. Can't envisage the downside, doesn't know different. The original *'Facebook'* and whatever else came after it. Names of the latest websites come and go, preferred social media, but their basic principles don't change. Forget about the family, eat dinner alone. Watch the screen till midnight, responding at once. Spill it out to millions. None of whom you know, but some of whom are psychos. Tell it like it is. Public confessional, online-petitioning, and beggar my neighbour. *'Like'* or *'Unlike'*, as the fancy takes you.

Voting that repulsive snake-charmer *'In'* or *'Out'* of the house. Your personal chance to make decisions about trivia, forgotten once made. Be part of something greater, feel like you count, on issues that don't. Marvelling at the transient wonder of a digital democracy while older rights and duties die quietly alone.

445

Unlamented, unnoticed, by the peoples of the screen. Hunched over monitors while their downstairs door goes in.

Liberty leaving by her windows.

Busy logging every tedious detail. Advertising self to a nation of lost souls. The diary of a nobody, contained in status-checks no-one reads. Birthdays, partners and family; work and qualification. Appointments and engagements. Highs and lows; moods and rows. Where to find me next, a stalker's delight.

They don't get it, do they?

Caught up in the craze.

As if spiritual belief's gone digital itself. Believing it the only way to live. The only worthwhile existence in whatever crosses an ephemeral stage. Their only test of worth. When Death takes no crueller form than *'No Updates'*, the only *'Status Option'* programmers deny. The flickering screen promulgating to millions their individual delusions of Immortality. Denying death any status whatever becomes of Steve Jobs. In an elsewhere place where real life and real people have become the true *'no-no'*s. Too tricky to face.

"With no time to live, let's get on and do it online."

OK, you think I sound harsh? Not me – an enthusiast! Because it's an ill wind blows nobody any good and this progress in how we live proved such a boon to my own.

My private investigations.

When without it I'd never have rediscovered Venezia.

When, after York, my first enquiries were no more than haphazard. Made with no guilty intent - I'd swear it. Casual, maybe - idle, yes. Starting with an online search, only the one. No intention to repeat. Like I was kidding myself, saying it didn't matter. No harm just looking, is there? Wanting to know she was OK, wherever she'd gone. Not meaning any harm. Just to find a picture of her face. See if she'd changed.

When I did, it left me seeking more.

The face that launched a thousand searches.

Her archaeological consultancy had its own website, packed out with facts, and I memorised every one. Its riches all the easier and quicker to find after our unexpected re-encounter in Hull. That unforgettable Saturday night in York which had ended so badly and abruptly one sunny Sunday morning. An event which hurt me so badly, left me reeling by Wilberfoss, but told

446

me so much more than I already knew. Drove me on to track her down again. To find I couldn't stop.

Compulsive, *moi*? A stalker? Oh no, no, not me. That's ridiculous, outrageous, unfair.

So mind what you say.

No, just an old friend, keeping track for a while. Checking she was all right.

All I had in mind.

And if most of the online history and archaeology sites I went to next had not offered a helpful facility, probably where it would have ended as well. I'm sure about that. If not for those temptations they placed in my way. But once I'd ticked that box, they simply wouldn't stop. Wouldn't leave me alone. Any future mention of her name and they automatically sent me an e-mail, a hyper-link to their article. Soon I was showered in them. Conference speeches and learned dissertations, opening ceremonies and new members of staff. Wine bars and leaving do's; tags, blogs and twitterings.

Like she was pursuing me.

And always with photographs - attachments increasing mine.

Where she looked radiant at Cardiff, dusky at Naples, chilly in Carlisle. Tired at Trier. So what was a man expected to do? Knowing that one right 'click' on *'Save As'* and I had her for ever. Soon had a file-full.

Looking at them for hours, studying her life.

I love her, you see. Always will. Like Lancelot and Guinevere, equally tragic. Freighted with treachery, born out of goodness. The loyal friend who betrays his king?

Sorry, no! Don't *you* let *me* fall into that sentimental Arthurian-analogy thing. We all know it's rubbish, whatever people say. You know it and I know it. While this thing is real life, twenty-first century. Digitally-based and nothing like chivalry. Passion for Venezia hardwired into my brain, with nothing left that moral sense or the internet can ever do to undo it.

Not now.

Not when I make no excuses for the natural results of formative experience. OK, if you prefer it, for an old fashioned, high-intensity teenage fixation preserved to the cusp of middle age. Sad maybe, but isn't that how love goes? Add the white heat of technology, laser-cutting her picture irrevocably into my brain, and there's permanent cell damage here. Leaving me wrecked.

Why I couldn't stop looking, leave her image alone.

Mental and digital, not some portrait in oils.

Christina Rosetti.

To that point where - just a few months after York - I learnt via my tireless robot friend, the search-engine, that Venezia was engaged to be married to a successful Newcastle tax-lawyer. It came as quite a blow I'll tell you. Couldn't eat, sleep or rest. Wandering round generally in a bit of a daze. People at work and in court asking me: *"Are you alright? You look terrible. Has something happened?"*

Even some defence solicitors showing me concern. Now there's a turn-up for the books. Of course, I fobbed everyone off with my cock-and-bull story about a death in the family and people soon forgot, even the kindest. But I didn't. Though that was genuinely how bad it felt at the time. Like news of a death.

That it should have been me.

As I'd have shouted out in church, given half the chance. Except I'd left it too late of course, the story of my life. Always too slow to respond. To news that this time did spur me into action. Into further e-research, more digital dredging. Going through the online silt down at the bottom of an endless river. Getting into her private webpage through the clever harvesting of certain shared *'friends'*. People I'd never met, it goes without saying, but now they became mine quite as surely as she'd once assumed they were hers.

Learning from them that it's true, she's definitely spliced.

Checking out next the guy that she's married, his entries in the Bar List. Hating his guts, but gritting my teeth and going on to cultivate his professional company anyway. The new husband himself, more likeable than expected.

Good old Bill.

Their whirlwind romance and my Trojan Horse. Bill needing me as a contact inside CPS, a regular source of work, while we of the Crown just needed an advocate who could win.

Don't get me wrong – we became genuine friends, it wasn't all parasitic.

Symbiotic?

448

We got on well together and both had something to offer the other. Sharing a common interest in motorsport, too. So that as long as he needed a driver, then I'd need a navigator. One who knew his way round a map, could help us win together. And why it was fun while it lasted.

Pending my other, long-term goal of winning access to his wife. Yet if Bill hadn't taken my girl, none of this need have happened. Or would have. The good and the bad.

Finding out their precise home address in remote Northumberland transformed into my next and overriding priority. Without having to wait for whenever Bill felt he knew and trusted me enough as a colleague to mention even its general location. Well, hard cheese, Bill. By the time you finally did, I already knew. To the nearest metre.

God Bless the DVLA, whatever they call it now.

You can track anyone through this system, citing their car's number plate. Now they've closed all the others, those helpful people at Swansea's vehicle registration office will tell you all you need to know about anyone. Locate your chosen target.

Provided you pitch it right.

Telling them it's information necessary for serving the registered keeper with notice of some vexatious legal action you've currently got in mind. How the crooks and car-park owners do it every day. Claim illegal parking outside some ropey nightclub say, or anything like that. Of course it's a national disgrace but the fact remains, that's all you need to do for it. When it's a public resource, but not quite the sort most decent motorists envisage. Now privacy is dead.

Oh, hadn't you heard?

Believe me, nowadays, Swansea won't want any more than that, because they helped to make it so. Not even caring whether your reason for requesting disclosure is true. Whether the registered keeper's car did make the fatal mistake of parking on your scrap of unusable wasteland for under ten minutes. Whether you really will sue them for it in the courts on some trumped-up trespass or breach-of-contract suit.

No, don't worry. Register with the right parking bodies and vaguer grounds than that will get chapter and verse about the driver from Swansea's giant brain. Or, in my case, location details behind the serial of that old Volvo estate I saw Bill often using for out-of-town courts. Claiming parking enforcement what did the trick for me, seemed good enough for Swansea.

And once I'd got the precious private address that went with Bill's registration plate, they might as well have given me the key to his front door. With the world-wide-web to thank for my immediate chance to try it out in the lock, make a tour of private premises. Cue that special mention in my credits now to what we'll call 'The Company'.

An international corporation which, several years ago, decided it was high time they filled a longstanding minor blank on their limitless global screens, by despatching one of their camera-cars. A German hatchback running around England on Spanish registration plates. Sent to arrive unannounced and without invitation in the darkest heart of Northumberland, where the tarmac runs out. Here in Bill and Venezia's secluded valley, so that one day the hunter I'm become could do virtually the same. Free, *gratis* and for nothing. Paying nowt for owt.

Whether that last is correct, here's another company paying little tax in Britain. Happy to use for their commercial purposes that same disintegrating road system which the rest of us must subsidise with taxes. To help company men get anywhere they fancy no harder than ourselves, Spanish plates or no.

"Quicker than a raid by Border Reivers, but vastly more ruthless. Piloted by some melancholy driver they probably borrowed from Langholm jobcentre for this one sneaky mission...." how I remember Bill regaling me about it later. During one of our regular sessions in a Quayside pub. Making weak jokes about an experience he clearly still resented.

About the black car's sinister appearance, and how it sneaked up. Raised its twelve-foot camera-pole like a U-Boat its periscope, then stole a full three-hundred-and-sixty degrees' worth of digital detail for continental masters, just how they like.

"Quick as a flash. Photographs our whole house in less time than I expect it took his bosses afterwards to sack the bloody driver. On the obvious technical ground he's now functionally-redundant, their mission's a success..." how Bill put it to me then: "Once he's captured every detail of a house that always stayed hidden, full five hundred years. Before its poor old proprietor could even realise what's happening. Had time to spot this flipping Opel from my study window and run out across the paddock, waving my arms about like a fool. Not that it did me any good, mind, I'll admit that to you now......"

Unaware of how my private interests ran, I remember Bill's blow-by-blow account of the unprofitable conversation he'd enjoyed with its driver. Discourse never got over. What pieces of his mind he'd shared with this guy, what little interest or concern his outrage won him back:

"This blooming camera-car of theirs was a base-model 'Opel Astra'. Horrible-looking thing, it was. Ugly, covered in dents and I can see why. A travelling outcast, a scapegoat. People only wanting to kick it, wherever it goes. I know I did. When these people leave you feeling so flaming helpless, Michael, so powerless. As any media baron can. Because there's really nothing else practical you can do about them, to stop what they do. Like nobody cares, least of all government. Even after Leveson. About what's a foreign invasion, an invasion of privacy. An invasion of our country to which we've already surrendered. Nothing you can say, nothing you can do to stop them. Apart from maybe blowing the bloody thing up. As if they'd be bothered anyway.....and you'd just be jailed."

"Nothing that's legal, no. But didn't you try? Ask their driver to stop taking pictures?"

"What do you think? Of course I did! Wasting my breath. Too late and he wouldn't anyway. The pictures were already taken. Just sitting in his god-awful car looking sadly up at me like a bloodhound. Handing me an already-ringing phone without another word."

"A mobile?"

"Must happen all the time. People banging on his bonnet. Demanding to know by what right the black cars come round, start photographing everything. Private property. People's homes. Horses in the paddock. Our cars in the drive."

"Who was he ringing?"

"Geneva, blooming Switzerland. I ask you! A man answered it, and he was Scots too, believe it or not. Head office patiently listening to my rant like they'd heard it all before. Claiming my comments were valued and would be *taken into account*. Knowing they wouldn't be...."

"Well, were they?"

"What do you think? Have a look on the web. It's up there all right. The whole of our house."

"Yes, it's an outrage, I can see that. But can't you complain? Or else go to law?"

"No chance!" Bill had said, with uncharacteristic bitterness in his voice. "It's Switzerland – completely out of the jurisdiction. Parent company American. Answerable to no-one, not even governments. Something my new job is teaching me applies to the whole EU. But you're a car-lover, Michael. Someone who I know will get the underlying symbolism. Recognise the subliminals. When it was a black Opel they used, of all things....."

"An Opel?"

"Yes, I ask you, how could they be so crass, Michael? So insensitive? Black, with a silver lightning symbol stuck on the radiator grille. Right in your face like an SS badge."

"What are you saying? That it's a Nazi car – like Fritz Huschke von Hanstein's?"

"No, that would be silly. I don't expect anyone at the corporation even realised, gave it a second thought. At least I hope they didn't. But what I do know is, there are plenty other people who will."

"Will what?"

"Realise what a bloody-awful logo it was to choose for such an intrusive job as this. When it signifies like crazy. Even over a sensitive historical point which someone in Geneva - in a neutral country which opted out of all that bad stuff at the time, some twelve year-old in marketing - might not necessarily be expected to know or remember."

"Remember what?"

"That in World War Two the 'Opel Blitz' was Hitler's army's - his Wermacht's - favourite truck. The SS used them too. That 'Blitz' is 'lightning', just like in their logo, and that 'blitzkrieg' means 'lightning-war'. Or that there must have been tens of thousands of Nazi victims loaded onto canvas-covered lorries carrying this lightning logo on a field-grey bonnet. In 'Feldgrau' - a grey so dark it's nearly black. Honestly, I ask you, Michael, how could they do it? Not just destroy mine - an Englishman's retreat, his own home, the last vestiges of his privacy - but choose that particular badge with all its offensive overtones to do it under? In the colour of a bloody SS uniform..."

"God! I can see what you mean..." I remember venturing carefully. Feeling we were on difficult and sensitive ground for various reasons. Including some I hoped Bill might not fully appreciate: "Now you point it out. That it's a weeny-bit unfortunate, a bad bit of branding......"

"Too right it is, but we're not only talking branding. Why did the thing have to be registered in Spain for God's sake? Running around for free on Spanish plates. No road tax in the screen, while we have to pay hundreds. Talk about adding insult to injury......"

"Getting their own back for the Armada, I suppose. You as a naval man should appreciate the irony in that, Bill. Just another consequence from globalisation. Showing us how their fleet finally won, even if it took them five centuries to get around to it. But, like you say, *'insult to injury'*....."

He'd just huffed at that.

"But what did you do about it, Bill? I mean, what exactly did you say to this Scots guy in Geneva to cause them such offence? Make them home-in on you, like they did later?" I'd asked him as the pub filled-out. Still interested despite myself.

What reply he'd made to that last question, I can't honestly remember, having rather lost the thread. Feeling Venezia his wife arching astride me, right now didn't seem like the best moment for mentioning this interesting build-up for my visit to her either.

She was worked up quite enough already.

"Your troops in contrast, though in valour unsurpassed, were nonetheless unused to naval action....On top of this, the crime so long unpunished had fanned the insolence of those reckless men to boast that roughness of the seas, which by constraint of fate delayed your victory, was a cover for your fear of them. The war had been abandoned in despair, or so they believed, not postponed as a policy decision....."

(Claudius Mamertinus, a court panegyric
in honour of the Emperor Maximinanus Herculius:
Pan.Lat.viii(v) 12.1-2. 289 A.D.)

- XXVII -

We were told, and probably believed, that the promised storm which did indeed blow-up overnight and on cue was the veritable Work of Giants. A terrible thing they could build out of nothing more substantial than sheer divine fury inside these massing walls of cloud. Its booming reports constructed from those echoing towers of thunder we glimpse being raised the previous night. Endless volleys of electric shards whose sheets of blue lightning He hammers out for His use on the anvils of the Weather-God. All to be unleashed upon the Imperial fleets of Maximianus Herculius while they scurry through the Channel.

Watching how our ships tossed and writhed while riding at anchor inside the shelter of Bononia, shielded from its westerly-worst by the ramparts of Gesoriacum above, I could only pity any poor sailor with nowhere left to go. Left outside on an angry sea.

Let alone the Army of the Rhenus.

Sitting out there facing what our older mariners in Bononia claimed for the most severe August gales seen in forty years. Rising tides and a wind of implacable velocity which rage against all the southern coasts of Britannia like they never will end. Howling through our rigging in harbour, how must it feel out at sea? Its offshore waves topped-off with white, climbing higher and higher till they could be seen standing to the mast-head of any Rhine-built transporter surviving.

And there's the nub, already noticed from our skirmishing. How the ships of Maximianus were made for him by river-men, his shipwrights of the Rhenus. Land-locked artisans who'd never contemplated full violence of seas, could never imagine the anger of those gods. Ships whose serried rowers ride open to the weather by design. Upon wide decks and narrow hulls so notable for lacking that extra protection and strengthening which Clausentum builds-in without asking. Without us even ordering.

Our enemies' nemesis, crafted by themselves. To be abroad in such narrow, lightly-built, and over-loaded ships, cowering beneath towering seas. What fate could be better, more cruel? Maybe the gods had ordained it for our benefit after all, vengeance their calling.

If these men of the Imperial fleet obey Maximian's orders by persevering to their designated target - steadfastly aiming for Britannia in unsuitable vessels through such appalling weather - this old-fashioned military devotion and courageous obedience seals their destruction. When persistence is not always a virtue, no-one can row on such seas.

Seamanship and sails cannot save them either, not in extremes like these. Its orders inaudible in a typhoon's scream, their sailing gear unmanageable on wave-breached decks. Their valiant attempts to keep going from those wet-through crews who somehow do - tacking one way and then another - offer little more than hopeless mitigation to the powerful blasts driving them headlong. West-by-north-west. Prolongs the inevitable, every change of direction only importing another confusion. Driving them further off-course, more dangerously inshore. While the best compromise left a harassed captain is raising enough sail to keep him off an invisible coastline, yet not so much as gets it torn-away completely. None of which will finally save him from running onto the endless miles of jagged lee-shore, of treacherous bays and rocky shoals with which Britannia waits to ensnare his vessel.

Out there in the dark, for ship after ship.

Those riding the surge last out the longest. Aligning stern and steering-oars with the tide but only sealing their doom the more surely, warship and transport alike, as they come charging in out of control - at such impossible speeds. Hitting a hostile shore head-on. Where if they are lucky it is shingle, but for most unlucky ones it's cliffs or rocks. Often both. Breaking their ships to pieces in the night-time surf.

The flower of Rome's German garrison is drowning and dying out there, all the way down Britain's darkening coast. Even while his poets proclaim to an emperor languishing on a gilded throne in Treverorum their absolute certainty of Victory, the greater glories to be His.

We in Bononia wake before dawn to a smoky sky of yellowing green and a series of successive squalls from the south-west, each one seeming worse than before. The wind turns to the west and visibility plummets as I go down to the harbour with my crew to inspect the squadron, cloaked men looking up at me with fear in their eyes.

The rigging hums and sailcloth rips, flags cracking, as I stand on '*Calliope*' looking out along the Liana River. Past the dunes to an empty sea. Thinking what's to do but only seeing Thebans. Rain which never let up all night pelting down, a sinister mood to the day.

Where the *navarch* of Gesoriacum squadron comes smartly up our gangplank and joins us, looking glumly with me across an ominous sea decorated with white horses. We know our duty is to get out there and pursue but dread its challenge to the very pit of our stomachs. What is different today is that I am the commander, my opposite-number deferring to the Emperor's adopted heir. Obliged to set an example, the man whose sole responsibility it is to make vital operational decisions on which his own safety and that of so many others depend. When I desperately do not want to reach the wrong one but know I have no choice, hold only one order.

"Attack, only attack!"

"Will you consult the augurers?" the *navarch* beside me asks hesitantly and for a moment I flinch, thinking him the spirit of Tertius come back to guide me. If his tempting suggestion is based on private fears, or else an understandable hope our delay for ritual might give the weather a chance to improve, I am shamefully slow to reject his caution. A superstitious sailor too chary of sacrilege. Muttering something suitable instead about the ineffable wisdom of Jupiter, Best and Greatest, while I try and decide between these mirror-image dangers. Between being remembered as the idiot who lost his squadron in an epic storm, or else that coward who let an enemy escape. Which is why, if only briefly, I entertain the *navarch*'s idea of surrendering my decision-making duties to the arbitration of divination. Until a shout is heard which resolves my dilemma immediately:

"A ship, my lord, a ship!"

Out of the sickening gloom there comes a shape, a greyish mass. And then a hint of glitter to define where its railings are decorated with gold paint, a head adorned with writhing snakes grinning from her foredeck. As does its captain, another face I know as well. The '*Medusa*' herself, with his hunter's golden pennant of the moon goddess, Diana, ripping and flashing from their mainmast.

Carausius!

Alone with his crew - no escort.

He tells us he has come from Clausentum, right through the enemy, and is laughing and roaring with great good humour at the joy of it, the utter fun. At seeing a mighty fleet which the Master of the World has sent for his own destruction, disintegrating upon the sharpness of that land mass it sailed here to take. Upon the courage of his sailors, the anger of his Weather-God. So wild-eyed in his pleasure, so ebullient, you might have wondered if he had not taken strong drink. If you were a person who did not know him better, as I then thought I did.

Standing there before all the cheering soldiers of his *Classis Britannica* whose mood he's transformed, dressed like them in an ordinary seaman's cloak of green oilcloth. Revelling in their brave company and unquestioning loyalty. In all this awful weather and the astonishing certainty of a priceless prophesy given him by a seer. That personal priestess so little short of a witch, from a Temple of Apollo and Diana beyond Londinium Walls. The irrepressible confidence of a man who has made some private pact with God and knows he will win.

In an extravagant gesture I'll never forget and which so sways the crowd, he grabs a long piece of seaweed from the dockside wall and drapes it round his shoulders.

Telling us he is a creature of the seas, a child of Oceanus. One who is riding and loving its greenness and violence, those natural features which are to him no more than the caresses of his Mother. Their admiral of Britain who is come to rally his faithful troops and lead us out to embrace Her Seas once more. In a British fleet which will outride any storm, crest any wave.

Returned victorious to harry and hunt the evil forces of Maximianus, the Beast of Treverorum, until not one of them survives alive to threaten our '*Golden Age Reborn*'.

There was no question. Did I not say we would have followed him into the Mouth of Hades?

That day we surely did.

'A balancing act is needed in extradition cases, between the Article 8 (European Convention on Human Rights) rights of the individual to a family life, and the interests of the extraditing state in culprits avoiding a safe haven and accounting for actions..... The public interest in extradition weighs very heavily'

Lord Justice Phillips in the
Supreme Court case of <u>Norris-v-United States</u> [2008]

When the plane fell, the pretty young flight attendant in the aisle stumbled but slightly. Let a frown cross her perfectly-powdered features for a fraction only before she grabbed hold of a headrest, recovered her balance and composure with it. Continuing calmly forward and uphill to check on each of her charges' seatbelts as if nothing had happened. Where, towards the back of them and among those be-suited types from whom he seems so indistinguishable, sits Lieutenant Angelo Di Romagna of the Carabinieri's specialised Art & Antiquities Squad. A man disliking air travel so much that he could not help grimacing openly and loudly on experiencing its alarming sensation.

Angelo was a man who liked to feel in control of any situation, so that when the Hawker HS125-800 of his unscheduled charter-flight, carrying the seven other businessmen originally commissioning it, suddenly dropped several hundred feet straight down without warning, falling earthwards through an invisible pocket of emptiness, he'd never felt less in control in his life. The passing air hostess turning around at the involuntary groan Angelo emitted when it did, their eyes meeting.

"*Turbulence*" she'd said, twinkling back. "*Is normal, no problem, and now we will land!*"

Of course she was perfectly correct, it had come right on the moment and Angelo felt embarrassed. A combination of the pilot's skill and some better air caught the plane like a sail and their more measured descent could now begin, onto Newcastle, England.

In fact and truth be told, the air hostess was actually lying. There was a problem, and a big one. Also arising during their approach, less easily resolved than turbulence.

What she and the flight deck knew but made sure their passengers did not was that all air-traffic control and radar were '*down*'. That they were coming into Newcastle on nothing better than their instruments, the radio, and the co-pilot's success in keeping a 360 degree look-out for other incoming aircraft, whether military or civil. Relying on antiquated method and that indispensable instrument his sardonic Sardinian first officer christens "*The Mark One Eyeball*", they were coming in on a bearing just as if their destination was some grass airstrip at a local flying club. Not an international airport.

Somewhere out there, a malign intelligence was waging an intermittent and undeclared war on the computers and connections of European airspace, A secret war of cyberspace. Until its efforts were resolved or thwarted, the culprits found, most aircraft stayed grounded. While those still in the air like this one must struggle to get down. Unassisted and as best they can.

A conspiracy of silence leaving the passengers on board this executive jet with nothing more important to worry about than their collective sense of disappointment. Their dismay on realising that this special charter so costly to arrange was delivering them – by choice and at their own expense – straight from a land of blue skies and brilliant sunshine into the crepuscular world of cloud and drizzle that is northern England.

After cruising over at speeds exceeding four hundred miles per hour, the plane was now going down very steadily and smoothly indeed, thank you. Flaps and hydraulics whirring away in the wings. Instead of putting him at ease, these regular clunks and sounds of mechanical repositioning only reminded Angelo of the worst bit yet to come – the landing itself. That involuntary clench he gave to his frame at the very thought of it as he hunkered down into his individual leather seat beside the window. Unconscious personal preparation for hitting the tarmac, its slight increase in spinal tension rewarding him with telegraphs of pain.

Angelo had never enjoyed flying and was hardly here through choice. Even though he knew everything was under control, he always hated landings most. Feared them in fact, especially in smaller aircraft like this HS125. Reminding him too much of a car crash, and hadn't he seen too many of those? Including the one that invalided him out of the motorcycle section.

Angelo knew he had no choice. He was a man on a mission - a European mission.

A knowledge of its potential international significance doing little to improve his enthusiasm for the difficult job he's set. Executing a European arrest warrant was prickly enough business in any country, even without the requesting nation's own cops turning up to witness the spectacle. Time was when that was a complete 'no-no'. When the only way a British cop could land in France or an Italian one in Britain, without being arrested and put on the next flight home, was with a "*Commission Rogatoire*" snug in their briefcase. Nicely typed-out in enough languages to say '*pretty-please*' twenty-seven times below a brace of official stamps and signatures.

Mediaeval heraldry? Virtually, yes. A ceremonial piece of diplomatic mumbo-jumbo still serving sensible purpose. An ambassadorial letter of introduction requesting free passage. Diplomat speaking unto diplomat, nation deferring to nation - and the only fit job for a cop being to carry their message in a forked stick. Now only Angelo's bosses could remember when ComRogs were de rigueur for the visiting side. Potent symbolism to remind us of the score. That if you want our co-operation, then first you must recognise our sovereignty. And show the beginnings of a case. Nowadays, neither seemed to matter much. Not least for lackadaisical Brits, unembarrassed by that '*sovereignty*' thing.

Typically the French take a rather different line, as he'd experienced for himself only the other day. When they closed the border at Ventimiglia while Angelo was chasing three North Africans with some Roman stuff stolen from Syria - Palmyra - during a civil war. So much for the EU dream, its idea of free movement through open borders – the Schengen Agreement. With orders to keep illegal immigrants and refugees out of France, he thought those bone-headed gendarmes had managed to prevent him doing France a favour. Actually extracting some.

What seemed to matter more, operationally speaking, with these international warrants was orchestrating what local people actually saw. What the home press somehow picks up on, not that secret score we play behind the scenes.

"What the mind doesn't see, the heart doesn't grieve over. Believe me, Angelo, you'll have no trouble with these *Inglese*..." General Massimo Biscaretti had told him over a cigar in the *Questura* the day before he left.

"But what have we actually got on him?" Angelo had asked his boss, *il capo di capi*. "What will there be, apart from whatever's incriminating we can find in the the house?"

"Money-laundering? With his wife an archaeologist, seen poking around in the Venetia hills again, asking after some mosaic stolen in 1948, we're bound to find signs. Believe it my son, and INDECT does already. Plus whatever you discover from seizing their home computers. Expecting more from international phone-calls made during the race - when he was over here with that other stupid lawyer. Made from mobiles with non-Italian SIM cards we know they used around Brescia. Dozens of phone calls already intercepted, our girls down the *Questura* busily transcribing them this very moment. Bound to be a goldmine, find good stuff in there. Before we even start knocking doors-in at his home, trawling their laptops."

"But will they be enough?"

"Of course, my boy, of course they will. More than enough. This warrant from the Office of the Prosecutor attached to the court in Rome counts to all intents and purposes like a homegrown British warrant. Believe me, no problem! All that his domestic court and prosecutors are allowed to do is satisfy themselves the right person is detained - the one we name on our warrant. That its wording is technically in order. Easy or what?"

"Surely they'll want rather more than that, sir?"

"OK, maybe a little. As the *'executing judicial authority'*, they can check its indictment is for a recognised offence. As ours definitely is - so *'check'*. Yeah, yeah, *'trading stolen art'* - *'check'*. And that the man we're after is not already tried for it. Which of course he isn't, Angelo, because we know he's clean. As he'll be keen to tell you straight away, playing into our hands, so *'check'* again. But make sure you note that fact, as soon as he says so - even before, if you can. You see Angelo, unlike the extradition cases you're used to, the beauty of these European warrants is – there's no requirement for anything. Not even *prima facie* evidence. None at all, believe me. Of course, we can go and look for some later, once you've arrested him. So I ask you, Angelo, how easy is that? On even less grounds than I expect their own laws would require for lifting their own people off their own streets. I tell you this job's a cinch - a doddle, my boy. We'll worry about evidence later."

"But what if the *Inglese* do try and stop me taking him away? Claim it's oppressive?" his *'boy'* asked him uneasily. Still not fully convinced despite the general's bonhomie.

"No chance of that. Believe me, Angelo, no problem. They're such a soft touch on this sort of job - truly it is incredible. I know this from that stolen Leonardo case. Desperate to co-operate – falling over themselves at the sight of any foreign warrant. On our side already, now their government is hacking this guy's internet at our specific request. Once they signed up to Amsterdam, probably thinking they've little choice. And boy, you should see them with the Americans. Like Yanks can lift anyone they want out of that little island: cripples, psychos, women, teenagers. You name it. The more vulnerable the better. Not even needing evidence. So don't worry, Angelo, just be careful. That's all I ask, my son. Expecting you safely back home in Italia with our man handcuffed to your wrist. So I can phone-up the Justice Ministry on behalf of the squad, announce *'Milord!'*"

Not how Angelo remembered the first time he'd gone over on a job like this, not how it used to be. When you had to stand discretely at the back in plainclothes while the local lads did the business. Now the EU is bolder, wanting people to know it has a Europe-wide reach and legal powers all its own. So how could old Biscaretti expect him to stay discreet at the same time? A question soon resolved when it turned out he didn't:

"Don't you worry about hiding from the press, Lieutenant. No problem. Show your face, my son. Smile and give the squad a profile. Stand up and be noticed. It's all about globalisation now - the days of the nation-state over..." said his General, beaming at him: "After all, my boy, it's not as if we Italians had our own to enjoy that long, eh? It's a federalised world we work in today, Angelo, mark my words. What once were countries are now just cantons, regions of Europe. Toe-rags don't pay attention to national borders so why should we cops? Or the EU?"

Corpus Iuris.

So Angelo Di Romagna, the keen motorbiker who'd always been scared of flying, had kissed his sleeping wife and three beautiful children goodbye at half-past two that dark morning in the third-floor apartment they shared together on Via Orti di Trastevere. Taken a long ride on some graffiti-covered all-night trains, then the one, red ATAC bus running for a last hop over to

'*Aeroporto Leonardo Da Vinci*' and its first flight of the day. On an executive-jet whose passenger-list of seven local businessman accepted Angelo's superficial cover story about visiting a tyre factory without a word of challenge.

Flying to England.

So he could do as directed and stand in a prominent position at the very front. Smiling for the press while the TV crews he knew were invited film British police using a metal tube to batter down the side-door of a Northumbrian 'bastle-house'. Arresting some big-wig lawyer-politician inside on their Italian counterpart's suspicion of handling stolen artefacts, arranging for more. Plus some 'off-book' payments they imagine associated.

The press?

Nothing to worry about there. If all went really well, Angelo thought it possible he and his prisoner could be back in Rome before tomorrow evening's TV bulletins went public. Not his problem, whether or not some sort of a row might blow up later.

Why he thought he could probably chance being filmed supervising personally the search of this old house whose stone exterior and small, mullioned windows the wonders of the Internet had enabled him to circumnavigate and study so many times before already. Toured from the comfort of his reclining detective's chair of chrome and black leather. From inside their centuries-old HQ at the Palazzo Sant'Ignazio in Rome.

Angelo had been born and brought up in Palermo. In a succession of rented modern flats and post-war apartment blocks built by the Mafia around Sicily's densely-packed capital. So that communal urban living was all he had known, all of his life. He didn't blame his parents for it, not when that is how most people live. In a way, he would once have felt lonely and ill at ease not to be living with people all around him like they had then. It was only now that he had a family of his own that he first started to feel bothered. To wish for peace and quiet. For some respite from trains and cars and motor bikes. From shouting and banging and endlessly being the unwilling party to so many other peoples' noisy conversations, their arguments and lovemaking afterward.

Why he'd started wishing for better for his own children. Especially for the girls – they shouldn't have to put up with

465

hearing that kind of stuff anymore. And a proper garden for Luca to play football in, wearing the replica orange 'AS Roma' shirt that was undoubtedly counterfeit, but his father happily bought him anyway from a smiling African street-seller. That vivid shirt Luca was always so proud of. To the point they sometimes had to tuck him up in bed asleep in it, whatever Sophia thought about its cheap nylon next his porcelain-perfect skin.

Their "little lamb" like she always says: "Agnello."

While Angelo sat there in his crowded office on the second floor of the venerable Palazzo Sant' Ignazio looking down at pictures appearing on his computer screen. Pictures of a beautiful English house probably older than this Palazzo. The place their enquiries led him to - one where he was mature and self-aware enough to acknowledge the possibility of resentment. Feelings Angelo could accept as probably inevitable. Material greed, unworthy thoughts deserving mention at his next confessional. It wouldn't be the first fine house his police career had taken him into, explored with a sense of wonder at how the other half lives. Recognising how just a few pictures of another's dwelling might provoke unwelcome comparison with his own modest home. Less unhealthy than comparing his wife with the images he'd caught that useless sergeant of his, Di Ruffio, secretly looking at. Spending half his day surfing the web for, from an adjoining desk - instead of getting on with paperwork.

The moral dangers in comparison. Envy, even. He'd have to be careful about that.

With the core-nominal whose house it was. His target, the successful lawyer they were investigating: a clever politician. This Englishman who'd found himself a secure and isolated home, far from the madding crowd. A refuge where he at least could rest assured his wife and children need never put up with what Angelo's did every day.

Listening to their neighbours running about or stamping above their heads while they argue, noisily washing-up pans. "At two in the morning for God's Sake!" Revving a Vespa scooter in their communal stairway at half-past five, just to go to work. Before dragging it out into the courtyard with so much metallic banging and crashing, clatter and smoke, that the smell of its exhaust fumes penetrates upstairs. Sidles in like a cat through windows left ajar against their baking Roman heat.

No, this Englishman's home was almost like a small castle – a *castello*. Reminding him of those fortified farms or hilltop watchtowers turned into time-shares and *agriturismo* all around Tuscany. Except this example was set in a topography vastly more rugged and lonely. Bleak and desolate. How remote and far away from other people and their noisy affairs the peaceful valley it stood in seemed. How green its woods, how purple the moorland. Enviable aspects he prized at once in those satellite-based photographs Angelo downloaded from the worldwide web, on one of those increasingly rare occasions when the wretched thing still worked properly.

When Angelo clicked on the icon and zoomed-in from outer space to grab more detail, he found he could study every twist and turn of the meandering single-track public road which led up to it. Following the graphic of an arrowed line through the yellow gorse to the head of the lonely Northumbrian valley the house commands. Then he could change tack and click on a whim onto a ground-level tour of its private gardens and tennis court, stable yard and paddocks. Viewed from the roadside of course, but from four metres up you could still see more than enough. Every detail and the layout of a location which only a moment ago he'd been scrutinising from so high in the air.

When the graphics caption would open-up on his demand, a 'click' produce its name below the arrow: "*Stipend Howe, Horsley, Northumberland, EU; England's NE Region*". A place name he attempted pronouncing but failed. Left him chuckling at the ease with which he'd found his target even if he couldn't say it properly. Though he would soon learn; a name coming to mean so much through the wonders of modern technology.

Angelo was a man brought up to expect very little in the way of social privacy or personal space to enjoy. Why he found it all the more ironic to be realising, only at that point in his adult life where he's finally learnt to value these qualities for himself, how quickly and recently their complete destruction had occurred. For everyone, worldwide.

While he wasn't looking.

This Englishman they tracked must be a man of means. Sufficient to buy a period house of charm and character in so remote a location he must have surely believed his personal privacy assured forever. And judging by the blockhouse tower forming one end, the tiny slit-windows high in golden walls, close to an absolute security. So near the Scottish Border that even a distant outsider, a foreigner like Angelo, could imagine how ideal this lovely old place must once have seemed to its builders. How secure and impregnable for men living through a violent, lawless age where privacy and defence were more than luxuries. Essential, a matter of life and death..

How oddly physical it became then, that historic realisation when it personally dawned on him. As if the mere by-product of his current investigation. When he finally recognised, with an intensity Angelo thought he could taste on his tongue like the fumes from their neighbour's Vespa, how thoroughly and completely the unblinking eyes of satellite surveillance, of modern digital photography and a worldwide web, had together combined to kill it. Once and for all, like he'd witnessed a death.

Not just for this eccentric Englishman in his remote northern *castello*, but for everyone everywhere. Even in their teeming flats of Rome.

The Death of Privacy.

Though if that discouraging finality was true, then today it must remain by-the-by. When there was still a professional policing job needing doing - what he did best. What he enjoyed. And Angelo's preparations had been thorough, as always. Feeling he already knew his way round the target premises as well as someone who's actually lived there. Now he was looking forward to action, to playing his part. Going in, getting the chance to show those *Inglese* cops - who would not know a terrabyte from a terracotta - what to do. What to look out for. Whether on the suspect's computer or hidden in his desk drawers.

And from the wealth of pictures downloadable from the Internet, he'd even worked out where that desk probably would be. Astonishing the detail you can see from two thousand miles away.

His quarry's home, hidden in the middle of nowhere in far-away England. So completely and instantly available for inspection, for anyone's casual surveillance from anywhere, it was almost indecent. Voyeuristic, like Di Ruffio's cavorting women. And here he was, sitting in a sultry Rome on his lunch-hour, virtually walking round the whole outside. Checking out the fancy SUVs parked in the drive beside a shiny classic car. Distinctive - no, unique vehicles. Their number plates pixillated out as a minor sop to data protection laws, as if they thought it would stop you recognising any of them again.

As if it made any difference.

Then putting it onto zoom so he could look through all the windows. Including that big modern one where you can so easily see the corner of their target's computer monitor peeking out the side. Yes, excellent. They'd go for that room first. In through the window of a fascinating house he was learning to call *'Stipend Howe'*, already felt so familiar with. And since it appeared double-glazed, then sledge-hammers would be best.

Angelo knew how, once this job was over, the press office of what General Biscaretti calls *'Our Partners'* up at Interpol in Brussels or Europol in The Hague, would probably put a nicely-upbeat circular out about it. Something generic along the lines of: *"Operating jointly in conjunction with Italian officers of the Carabinieri's elite art squad through EUROPOL, English police from their northeast regional force carried out a series of raids today on private premises located near the Scottish border. Seeking evidence of an illegal international trade in Roman antiquities. One man arrested is being extradited to Italy under accelerated procedures to assist authorities in Rome with further enquiries into missing property."*

Wasn't it always *"officers of the carabinieri..."* (plural) in those dry, official releases? The press office preferred it that way, said it was important. Made it sound like a bigger deal, when in reality they know how few there are of them in the squad to go round. Even when it was only good old Angelo on his lonesome-ownsome, dying to get the job done then back to his lovely wife and adorable kids, *il ragazzi*. Before bedtime ideally. Not that he'd much chance of managing that tonight, however quick the turnaround.

Later on he could imagine General Biscaretti, the Interior Ministry and the Department of Cultural Heritage & Activities, getting round to reading Interpol's release. At which point they would call him in to profess satisfaction over his close involvement in their mission, its successful outcomes. Perhaps he'd finally get a long-overdue promotion out of it. A promotion and a pay rise. So he, Sophia, and the *ragazzi* could move out of that cramped apartment on the third floor in Trastevere and maybe get to rent a house with enough bedrooms for all of them. Nearer to her parents. Somewhere much further out of town and nearer the hills, with a proper garden where the kids could play outside and have a dog, like little Anna kept on begging for.

"This job will do you good, Angelo, and me good. Good for the profile of the squad, and good for the Minister. Important you get it right. Get home with no problems...." said the General, lighting one cigar and passing him another.

Angleo had joined the Carabinieri to get away from Sicily and an insular world offering few worthwhile opportunities for the bright and university-educated. To Southerners like him for whom the Italian public service allows their only realistic route to success on merit in a society too often riddled with patronage and graft. And the best thing he ever did - so that what seemed at the time like his disastrous departure from the motorcycle unit was turned into a real stroke of luck. When it led to him getting onto the elite Art squad. If Angelo was ambitious and wanted to get on any further, then keeping here in the squad and on the right side of his important boss, the General Massimo Biscaretti, was essential. Why he is demonstrating such close attention to his lecturer:

"Don't let the *Inglese* cops screw it up for us, Angelo, introduce stupid irrelevancies. Just remember, since 2004 all they're allowed to do is check you've detained the right person. That the warrant's in order for a recognised offence and your man's not been tried for it elsewhere. Concentrate on these three key points, Angelo, and they can't block you removing him from their country.....like because you can't produce any evidence, say. No, you can't lose and I hope you realise just how lucky you are at having this big chance. All your own show, with the whole squad relying on you for a good result."

That sensitive question of the profile of the squad.

It had even been suggested to him by Biscaretti at one point in their discussions that he should consider going over in full uniform. The peaked cap with flaming grenade, red stripe down the trousers. Assert the interest of his force and his nation rather more publicly – not to mention a global interest in stopping the illicit antiquities trade. No, of course, that goes without saying. There was no police unit in the world done more than his country's to counter the international trade in stolen and looted artefacts from archaeological sites. Millions of euros' worth. He and they were rightly proud of that.

But go to England in his uniform? No way. That was taking it too far, he realised. Pushing their luck. Even the English might find that sight too much to swallow. Besides, Angelo was a detective. Apart from weddings and funerals of colleagues, he hadn't worn his dress uniform, hanging under its nylon cover inside a mahogany wardrobe in the corner of his children's bedroom, for nearly ten years. And didn't plan on doing so now.

No, he would appear in their cold and foggy city in his usual lightweight grey suit and silk Armani tie, smile brightly and introduce himself in that flawless English which was key to his charm. Turn up with the local cops in their lead van when it storms up the drive then do the search, grab the prisoner, and get the hell out of there. With their biggest worry still some fancy English lawyer getting an urgent application into court to try and stop them leaving the country with the target. Getting blocked on other grounds.

"No chance of that..." promised General Biscaretti. "It's these white-collar criminals who are easiest to remove. Especially the *Inglese* middle-class, who seem conditioned from birth to co-operate with police. Whatever their underclass get up to. If only more Italians could behave like that over here...."

If the General was correct and they could get back to the airport quickly after a quick court hearing; and if Angelo could be home the following night at least in time to kiss his sleeping children; then that was all that mattered. Whatever else General Biscaretti or the Minister himself; or INTERPOL, EUROPOL, EUROJUST or any other acronym you cared to name, whether in Rome or The Hague, might expect from Angelo's little errand.

And since everyone was promising him the *Inglese* would be falling over themselves to help, as they apparently always do once you mention the magic words *"international cooperation"*, then these ambitiously-short time-scales in mind for his little 'Away-Day' might not be so completely out of the question after all?

471

Looking down, the world was still in darkness, but out of the window he could see orange street lamps illuminating long lines of identical, red-brick houses below. They were close, Angelo tightening his seat belt yet again as the plane dipped for its final approach.

Just to be sure.

Besides, there was no hurry. It was not as if they would have to discover or decide on every piece of evidence today. No, there'd be time enough for that later. Months and months of the case crawling gradually through the Italian judicial system would give everyone involved plenty of chance to get the paperwork organised. Get round to reading and sorting it from whatever material they took away today. At their leisure.

Even the prisoner and their legal team.

Most of the foreign defence lawyers he came across in this line of enquiry seemed delighted at the chance of getting a year's guaranteed business out of it. The anticipation of several comfortable visits to the best hotels in Rome. And that was just for the preliminary hearings – these cases could go on for ever.

"What our case needs is more time to prepare" they would say, standing up po-faced and serious to apply for one of those lengthy adjournments judges always seem ready to grant. Given the defendant's overriding human right to a fair hearing and everything else the Republic's courts are obliged by the European Convention on Human Rights and its caselaw to take into consideration, our Italian judges feel left with little choice.

While whatever the unfortunate client might feel about the matter, or the prospect of another year banged-up in an Italian jail while they wait, unconvicted or no, the professional outcomes for their busy lawyers are never less than appealing. All those self-important trips to Italy to look forward to. The chargeable hours spent in Rome's finest hotels, poring over points of law with congenial colleagues in the restaurant. Working their way through the wine-lists. No wonder these foreign lawyers were always so keen to get the brief; so obliging to the police, ingratiating to the courts.

Angelo knew their boss was right. As long as they could get the Englishman home to Rome, sorting his case out afterwards would be a long drawn-out job. One the authorities could

472

complete at their own pace. There really was nothing to worry about.

"No problem…" said General Biscaretti yet again from across the empty surface of his enormous rosewood desk, as if to reinforce these unspoken thoughts once and for all. "If you keep in mind what I say - if you don't forget we're a *European* gendarmerie now - then it is these rules which make it do-able. So off you go, Angelo my son, carrying my prayers to The Virgin for your good fortune. For good hunting!"

At which Angelo had saluted smartly then left, another cigar tucked paternally into his top pocket. The General's parting gift he'd told him, not to be smoked until he came back with something to celebrate.

As they came in to land at Newcastle in the darkness and the wheels hit, tyres chirruping, Angelo crossed himself and offered up a short prayer to Her for safe deliverance. Then he went back to his happy daydream about renting a secluded house in the shadow of the Lazio hills. A place of their own at last, where Anna and baby Laura could chase a puppy round its garden in complete peace and safety.

And little Luca kick a ball about in his bright orange 'AS Roma' shirt with the suckling wolf on - to the upset of any Lazio-supporting neighbours.

"The provinces are won by the blood of the provinces"

(Julius Civilis in Cornelius Tacitus's
'Year of the Four Emperors')

- XXVIII -

On the morning after the Great Storm, and if you count his *'Medusa'*, we manage eighteen fighting ships operational out of Bononia, working close together. Compared with the scattered Imperial fleet which Carausius led us into the heart of that day, ours was the formation more adequate to prevail, most cohesive on the sea.

As the weather eases if not the rain, our battle confidence grows along with the scope for what we can do. To an extent, the same could still be said of some of our opponents. A few.

They were not a push-over.

Every single enemy ship, every group of ships we found, was fiercely attacked - but you should not imagine we had it all our own way. Enjoyed overwhelming numbers at every skirmish, suffered no further casualties.

The *'Caesaromagus'* we lose to the weather, along with a dismasted bireme of Bononia, but at least we rescue their crews, while enemy arrows and ballista bolts are still finding targets on our decks. All of us taking water and everyone struggling for headway. Despite these further setbacks, we know the grand Imperial fleet is broken. That those of its remnants who have not been driven onto British shores are being blown helplessly away to the west.

Away from inhabited worlds.

For all these signs of Victory, Carausius stays concerned that Maximian infantry might have survived to be landed on the gentler, shelving beaches running west of Portus Dubris. Enough to constitute a serious threat. So we tack northward for several hours against difficult blasts, heading over to that quarter as much for respite as anymore patrolling.

What we find there proves him right, if only after a fashion.

The Maximians have been landed all right. Their broken ships and barrels and sodden stores line the tidal-reach like giant

474

strips of blackened seaweed. Bodies of soldiers and animals bobbing bloated amongst them like swollen pods of kelp.

At my emperor's signalled request, I put myself and a dozen marines off *'Calliope'* onto one of these lengthy strands of shingle, to see what we can see. Small groups of other men have been observed from offshore, picking their way slowly along the beaches and through all this debris, and Carausius wants to know who they are. What they are up to.

We assume they are locals, out early on the sands and looking for loot, salvage to plunder, but need to know for certain. Satisfy ourselves of no survivors. No more enemies at our gates.

When the rowing-boat's bow graunches onto the pebbles and I step out into water with my marines following, I can imagine myself for a moment as the first Roman soldier who'd ever landed here. One of the legendary legionaries of Julius Caesar, invading Britain against the yells of my ancestors. Onto this very beach more than three hundred years ago.

A harmless imagining soon cruelly broken on a tide awash with legions.

By hellish scenes.

Recognising the importance of military intelligence, we need to know the identities and type of units which have been sent against us, estimate the damage to their strength. I carry a small, wax-on-wood notebook in which to record what we find with a stylus, account for the numbers, and it barely takes me more than a few steps along the foreshore before needing to begin.

.A man, a soldier, lies face down in the water nearby, half-floating half-resting, in the bleached woollen uniform of a Rhineland legion. He has no equipment, no armour, and even his boots are missing. One of my marines turns him over with his foot so we can check for a legion's badge, though I avoid looking at his face.

Stamped onto his shoulder with a waterlogged red dye now running away like blood is the distinctive ship-shaped badge of Legio I Italica. Like a bireme's prow, mark of the First Italian Legion, recruited originally from sailors on the Danube, few of them Italians.

Men like us, dying a long way from home.

Within the space of less than a hundred paces we find another hundred floaters like him, rising and falling in the swell, plus several more from the Upper Rhine and their Legio XXI Primagenia. A nautical legion with similar recruitment policies in place. What background skills their centurions went out through the taverns looking for.

Skills which haven't done them any good.

All of them drowned, yet not a wound between them. Infantry who'd never got a chance to fight. Dying pointlessly out at sea for the glory of Maximianus Augustus, our little emperor's 'brother'. His victims, as much as any storm's.

Further up the beach and in the distance, we see another one of those small groups of men we'd noticed from offshore, bending down and searching much like we are.

"Let's go and take a look!" I say to mine and we head off briskly towards them, our armour and metal fittings chinking in time with the crunch of white stone under hobnail.

As we get nearer, I can see they are dressed generally the same, carrying round shields and primitive weapons. Soldiers of a sort, but not a type I recognise. Irregulars.

Mercenaries, in fact.

Franci.

The men of Allectus.

I sense the tug across my chest from the *seax* always carried there, can guess how her garnets glow beneath my cloak, but advance unarmed with my marines fanning out behind me. Raising my empty hand slowly, as if in gesture of friendship.

"Ave!" I drawl, aiming for condescension, the careless arrogance of victors.

Today, I'm no anonymous civilian, no harmless traveller safely to be robbed in the privacy of woods. Today I am a Roman officer in a scarlet cloak, its colour imperial, under a crested helmet. Advancing on them with the potent authority of Rome, my soldiers come with me.

Amazing what difference it makes.

The Franks recognise my power and the threat in my soldiers, their imminent danger from hard-bitten professionals. Become subservient, bowing to my rank, fawning and deferential. Making eyes at their leader to get them out of this mess. The man I address:

476

"What are you men doing?"

"Excellency, obeying orders. Only obeying orders, on a great day where the gods have brought us victory!" starts their bearded leader, soon growing fearful at my look and lowering his gaze. A man vaguely familiar, though one filthy Frank looks much like another. I glare at him:

"What orders? From whom?"

"Perhaps the same orders as yours if I may dare suggest, Excellency? Because His Perfection, the Rationalis, has ordered it of us. Has sent us all the way down from Londinium to protect your peoples living inland. Prevent the worst of your enemies from getting ashore. Motive for the firm instructions he gave us, I promise you, my lord!"

"Which were?"

"To kill any breathing thing that attempts to land, whether man, dog or horse, and rescue all metal. Protecting and gathering it carefully for the Rationalis and his exchequer to use. A simple order which I hope, Excellency, one day soon you will confirm to him how closely we followed."

"And you are?"

"I am Hnaudfridus the Frank and these are my men. Free-born men, Excellency, now your 'Numerus Hnaudfridi'. Grateful servants of an emperor's coiner, your noble master the Rationalis. He who has commissioned us, humble soldiers in his service."

Suddenly there is a commotion down by the water where some of his men are still ratching through the debris and flotsam, tossing stuff to one side. Frankish barbarians dragging the bloated bodies of Roman soldiers up from the beach by the leg so their cronies can strip them of clothing, valuables, or weapons. Before dropping the naked corpses back down anywhere like so much abandoned rubbish.

Is this what we fought for?

A man is calling weakly, querulously: "Leave me alone, leave me alone!"

We turn and see a tall man they have pulled upright who is pinioned by the arms. Six Franks are holding him, one with a knife across his throat and clearly about to use it.

"Stop!" I shout, and move quickly across to this group, followed by Hnaudfridus and my men, wanting to identify their prisoner.

His uniform and leather under-cuirass are stained black with seawater and blood, but I can still see where woven, golden threads are embroidered onto his pteruges, the leather flaps which edge where armour rubs. This is an officer, and a senior one at that.

I step forward into his vision, a gang of Franks still holding him but increasingly nervous and ill-at-ease while they exchange comparative glances between Hnaudfridus and myself. Guessing what's best to do.

Kill him or not.

The officer's eyes appear unfocussed but I stand closer. Trying to engage, wanting to help. He seems to take in my familiar helmet, its difference from his captors' and there are slight signs of recognition, but he is sagging in their hands and I wonder if he is dying.

"Who-are-you?" I ask him slowly. My mouth placed inches from his shivering face.

"I am the Army of the Rhenus!" is all the response I get.

Then Allectus's Franks relax their grip and the man collapses head-forward onto the white shingle, its rocks cutting his face. By the time my marines pick him up again he is stone dead already.

This is how it really was, even on the day of our greatest victory.

Rome destroying itself and all of us complicit, with only barbarians winning.

478

"Come the three corners of the world in arms, and we shall shock them"

(William Shakespeare, 'King John')

- 29 -

There they all are. Assembled bang on time and well before dawn that cold morning. Ready for an early start. Gathering inside the brick-walled yard of some northern police station that's already crammed with blue and yellow patrol cars or the more junior officers' personal transport, cheap commuting-cars. Barely visible in the dark, camouflaged against it, at this time of day the milling crowd in black overalls provides our only sign of life.

Compared with the drug-dealer's confiscated BMW - sinister in gunmetal grey, its windows smoked and a bloom of white cocaine-mould across its dashboard - or the '*Crime Prevention*' caravan jacked on its axle over by the gate, where a wheel went missing-presumed-stolen, there's only the sensible saloon of their duty chief inspector to provide any contrast. The baby seats across its back, his young constables' motorbikes or sports cars, to evoke more innocent existences. Lives lived far from here, well away from crime.

Even cops have human rights, you know. To the enjoyment of a private and a family life.

Except for 'POLICE' markings and blue lights, the two plain vans these overalled officers are busy clambering in and out of could appear the typical crew-bus. Just the large lettering, perspex side windows, and a heavily-framed, black-mesh grille slid back on rails above the windscreen, to distinguish them from the more anonymous commercial. These vehicles are armoured for good reason and about to be used in support of the type of raid where such protection is usually required, at least in the tougher estates off Newcastle's West Road.

Except that the briefing they are filing indoors from the yard and into the constables' parade room to receive from Chief Inspector Steve Ryton will stress a rather different character of 'job'. One that's almost genteel:

479

"Good morning, ladies and gentlemen. Welcome to '*Operation Milano*'. Or should I say, to our very own antiques road-show. Got an interesting one for you today by any standards - and glad to see you appropriately dressed for it. Following the revised Force Order on health and safety, it's black fatigues and combat boots for everyone. Chequerboard baseball caps will do, no need for stab-vests. Yes, we've done a thorough risk-assessment and there's no need, so good to see you've got the message. Standard operating procedures will apply - including Code D of PACE. And by the way, there's enough food for everyone carried in the vans, so make sure you help yourself to Max-Packs. From what I see, most of you worked out how to get them mega coffee-cups filled-up inside the station. By, anyone would think there were some regular detectives turning out with us today....!"

The atmosphere is low key and relaxed, his younger officers taking a cue from their middle-aged superior and slouching against the wall.

"Right then, on to '*Operation Milano*'. Today you're executing a European Arrest Warrant at a big house in north Northumberland. And no, we're not talking inner-city, so some of you Geordie lads who've not done the CROPS course will find things a bit smelly and muddy in our real countryside. Compared to what you're used to, an education. Top end of the old county, slogging north up the A68. And remembering how close it is to the Scottish border-line, let's be careful keeping ourselves and the target right-side. No diplomatic incidents please, we don't want to offend anyone. Upset the Jocks post-independence now these things matter so much. No shopfronts smashed in reprisal..." he paused briefly.

"OK, enough of that dreary background stuff and onto introductions. This nice gentleman standing here beside me is Lieutenant Angelo Di Romagna. Welcome to England, Angelo, and to our northeast policing region - I do hope I pronounced your names correctly....."

A lithe man in fashionable light-grey suit had stood to one side and apart, shivering slightly while the Chief Inspector spoke. He smiled brightly with perfect teeth but spoke quietly:

"I flew in just an hour ago but am really glad to be here. A privilege to be working so closely with you. I feel like some of us know each other as friends after our video conferences but it is good for me to meet you in person. Everyone has been so helpful."

"We're all cops together on this job, mate. Angelo has come all the way over here from Italy to see what we can do for him today. From the Carabinieri, their specialist Art squad, believe it or not. Named the operation in your honour, if you don't mind, Angelo. Otherwise the next name off our op's list would have been '*Macmillan*'....Harold, I suppose! So what with that and the Euro' warrant, it's going to be a bit of a first for us out here. Big day for the BCU. Right, now I know half you lot wouldn't know art if you fell over it – and I do especially mean you Jason, hiding there at the back - but let's show Angelo how well we can do things over here. I want to see a nice, tight, professional job. Done tidy, with no accidents, no runaways. No unnecessary damage either, thank you very much...."

"Who exactly are we after, sir?" asked the unsmiling sergeant with shaven head at the back of the parade room who'd just been pointed out. Standing beside that prop-forward in a charcoal-grey suit who never spoke, only grinned. That big fellow in a neck-brace whom no-one else knows, but C/I Ryton doesn't bother to introduce either. Jacket bulging like it's going to split, whenever he folds his arms.

"We've been tasked, Jason, with detaining a named individual. The guy in those pictures on the wipe-board - of which more in a moment - then doing a PACE search of the premises. Looking for evidence and missing property: antiquities. That's 'old stuff' to you."

The unsmiling sergeant smiled even less at this. Sometimes, Stevie's banter bombed....

"Angelo will direct us as to what. He has brought along some pictures of certain things we might expect to find. What his people are missing. In a good-class dwelling house whose occupiers are not expected to cut up rough on our arrival. Posh people, naturally polite. Taken by surprise, they're bound to co-operate, believe me. Our target a lawyer with no pre-cons and no warning tags. And more importantly, a politician. An MEP. That's European parliament, to those not in the know, but by-the-by. To date, he's respectable. Clean. But depending on whether she's there and what we find, bear in mind we might

481

decide to lift his lady-wife as well. That rather nice brunette on the back wall....."

A female officer shouted something from the floor and he looked sheepish.

"OK, sorry Chantalle. I'm sorry.....*auburn!* And yes, *'woman'*, not *lady!* Anyway, Angelo's lot think she's the front for any dealing, the archaeological expert. Even if she is, he's still the traveller. There's no weapons-related intelligence although the husband is one of our registered firearms certificate-holders. Only for two sporting shotguns, nothing bigger than that, so we're not bringing any either. Keeping things low key: *'Reasonable, proportionate force, blah blah...'* Usual Human Rights Act considerations apply, it goes without saying. So there's no worry on that score, says the local bobbie, Mick Armstrong, who knows him well."

There were satellite photographs of the house and grounds blown-up in full colour then pinned to the wipe-board with blue magnets. Angelo recognised these images as familiar from many hours spent trawling the internet in the Palazzo Sant'Ignazio, along with ground level equivalents downloaded from the same source. The English senior officer running the briefing pointed them out individually to his officers and everyone turned to look, although Angelo got the impression most were professional enough to have studied them already.

"Where did we get these aerial pictures from, sir? Dead neat, such a lot of detail. Helpful to the mission, ever so clear. Was it the Force drone, sir, flown over the target from HQ?" asked a pixie-like officer in love with technology, his pointed features and spiked-up hair a cipher for youthful keenness. One earring for something else.

"The Ponteland Drone? Now don't let me hear you refer to our new ACC (Ops) like that in future..." answered his Chief Inspector archly to a smattering of dutiful laughter. "No, Danny, she won't be thanking you for that. No chance, but no - joking apart – they're only downloaded. Easy-peasy stuff. Public access, straight off-of the good old Interweb. Free and for nothing. And with Home Office and the old Police Commissioner nagging us for another twenty per-cent in efficiency savings this financial year, I don't think HQ would thank us for putting their expensive UAV into the air for a wee job like this one. Would they? Not when we can get our hands on quality images like these as cheaply as nowt."

Danny thought he held a rather better understanding of the laws of copyright than his boss, and suspected it not quite that simple, but the Chief Inspector ran this show and Danny knew not to correct him in front of others - let alone visitors. That would hurt his PDR.

The Chief Inspector would have agreed. Despite his relatively-elevated position in the rigid hierarchy of policing, Steve Ryton was a fair-minded man who liked to think he'd kept the common touch on his way up. That unique sense of humour so often commented on inside his own family, especially around Christmas - coupled with what he thought a natural democrat's willingness to 'get down with the kids'.

Features central to the pacey team-building style he's adopted with the junior ranks. Just that bit edgy. The breezy informal tone he would set from the outset - first names for everyone and plenty of banter to go with it. "Discipline? Days of the dinosaurs, man, irrelevant to modern policing. Nowadays it's more like football, winning hearts and minds."

If his bosses up at Ponteland's north-eastern HQ sometimes wondered if their 'Action Man of Ops' sometimes allowed too much familiarity with his staff, their buoyant Chief Inspector suffered no such private doubts himself: "You can't go wrong with that formula...." he would frequently insist to his loyal wife at teatime. Oblivious to some slight but unspoken concerns she'd sometimes share later over a glass of wine with a few police wives she trusted. About Steven and all those younger female officers in his team – what with their swimmers' physiques and no stretch-marks to mention.

"That's what makes me such a good operational commander, my love. Best on the BCU. Why my search teams always get the amazing results we do...." Steven would boast to her, over the kitchen table along with the kids. Others in today's captive audience might be taking a different view. Wondering privately why they should respect him, let alone listen, if he showed none for others higher. Those few who did kept their own counsels. Their duty Chief Inspector held the floor and they did not, so on he went, like the very worst that Ponteland or Force HQ could ever muster.

483

"Two-eight is the Airwave channel we've got for use today, so make sure your sets are switched onto that frequency. Six the default code. Don't expect your mobiles to have much in the way of reception out there by the way, but I think Airwave should stay OK. It's got a booster aerial above Rothbury, whatever trouble's hitting civilian networks currently. The important thing is, you should know your way around the location before we arrive. There's pictures of the target premises on the white-wall I've already mentioned. Make sure you check them out before we go, if you ain't already. And everyone has a floor plan in their briefing pack. Based on the photos. When we hit, entry by 'Enforcer' will be made through the side door at 'A' – that's your task, Martin, so you'll carry it. So far as the firearms go, and to be on the safe side once the door's gone down, Jamie's search team will go in first and secure their locked cabinet and its contents straight away. Including ammunition, of course. The gun cabinet's located at point 'B' on the operational plan you have, by the way. In the kitchen corridor. And there'll be a circulating AFV available within call, should we change our mind or the threat-level changes. So don't worry on that score."

"Sir, can I just remind anyone who's forgotten that I'll be functioning as Exhibits Officer today?" interrupted a small man with a pasty complexion and short, black hair dyed a sodium blonde, whose roots were showing.

"Yes, don't forget Dominic, everyone. He's the boy! We've got three dedicated evidence-gathering teams in total, feeding material onto him. Chantalle is leading the documents team, who'll be grabbing anything resembling a computer for downloading later, and looking out for paper evidence of an illegal international trade in archaeological relics. Think time-team, Jason, while your own crew will be going straight into the garage to secure the target's vehicles. Stop them being driven away. A newish Range Rover with a personalised number and some rather tasty classic cars - if the DVLA have told us right. Seizing those under the Proceeds of Crime Act if anyone asks. And any more questions from you lot?"

"What about the gee-gees, boss?"

"I'm glad you mentioned them, Martyn. You've noticed there seem quite a few in most web pictures of the paddock. Quality bloodstock. Not to mention a few dogs. Don't worry. Their welfare's all covered - we've got an RSPCA team on standby, to come in and take good care of the lot once we've left."

"And any kids?" asked the woman with an inspector's silver 'pips' on her black shoulder epaulettes, coldly. The one he'd called Chantalle.

"Oh, yes, kids..... Well, none are expected. Probably away at boarding school with people like this. Perhaps you could look after that issue once we get in there, just in case. There's always social services, isn't there, assuming they can be bothered to answer the phone?"

Judging by the face he saw her pull, Angelo thought she felt that an unwelcome comment, addition to her list of responsibilities, but Chantalle said no more and seemed to accept it.

As *'the troops'* filed outside after the briefing and followed the gorilla in a neck-brace back into the station yard, Angelo and the chief inspector encountered a slim, blonde journalist from the local TV station whom the Force press office - correction: *'Media & Marketing'* - had invited along to capture the action for tonight's regional news. Waiting nervously for them in the yard beside a pile of equipment. Smoking a cigarette on police premises in an obvious breach of force rules no-one bothered to challenge.

People who'd seen her on the regional newsround were sympathetic to her vice. Reporter, interviewer, sound-recordist and cameraman combined, they knew she had to manage and carry all this gear alone. An arrangement saving her employer considerable sums of money but doing nothing for her back, gym or no gym.

When she'd finished her cigarette and thrown it down beside the BMW, then seen her equipment finally loaded aboard, she came around to the front of the lead van where Chief Inspector Ryton and Lieutenant Di Romagna took their places on the first bench seat.

"Where would you like me to sit?"

Chief Inspector Stevie Ryton, in whom middle-age had failed to break the habit of a lifetime, gave her sinewy frame what he thought a surreptitious once-over, up and down, then gestured to the remaining space beside them.

485

"Up here with us" he smiled warmly, pointing to a slight gap between him and the driver.

"What?" she said. "Leading the mission?"

"Why not, pet?" he replied. "Riding shotgun!"

*"The fact is, as an island nation we will indefinitely be
dependent on the security of the seas,
and that never is going to change"*

(Vice-Admiral Charles Montgomery,
Second Sea-Lord and Commander-in-Chief, Home Command:
onboard HMS Victory, Trafalgar Day, 21st October 2011)

- XXIX -

By the time I finally brought *'Calliope'* and what was left of 'C'
squadron wearily up the Wantsum River and into Rutupiae to
dock, we'd seen enough blood spilt to last every butcher's slab
in the empire a twelve-month, but at least we knew we'd done
it. Britannia was safe.

'Rutupiae Light' atop the tetrapylon was flaring and fizzing in
celebration. Erupting blue and green sparks from some special
shavings one of the Greek traders down in the town had offered
to their legionary guardians in gratitude. Magic metal they
donated to brighten its flare, give thanks to the gods for our
emperor's safe deliverance.

Meant in good spirits to enliven the fire, mark out from afar our
triumphant arrival, at first it only alarmed me. When you've
spent days out at sea in fear of the enemy and in such a high
state of readiness, constantly vigilant for danger, sometimes it's
hard to come down.

There was a large crowd down at the dockside to greet us with
much cheering and waving, warehouses and wharves
garlanded in welcome. So many people calling out, in fact, so
much by way of backslapping, whistling, or flowers raining
down, that our seamen vaulting onto the bank could hardly get
hawser over mooring-stone, gangway onto deck.

Getting off the vessel through this press was even harder but,
once I'd supervised the secure docking of my squadron and
formally released its men, getting home was all I wanted. For
myself as much as anyone. Not this pale parochial shadow of a
proper Roman triumph, Roman citizens in rejoicing over the
killing of other Romans.

Eventually however, their hubbub did die down and I felt able to escape. The shouting throng left me in peace, breaking into smaller groups and heading off for different taverns. Allowing me to walk the short steep path uphill, alone and unhindered. Away from where our burnt and battered ships were moored below to my own little house, set back from a noisy riverside.

Where quiet was how I found it.

All the shutters were closed but the main door swung easily enough when I pushed it open. Too easily perhaps, meeting my porter waiting for me inside the *atrium*.

"Brucchius!"

"My Lord, you are come home safe from the sea! How good it is to see you back…" he says at once, a sadness in his eyes not matching the warmth of his words. By now I am already kneeling before the *lararium*, shrine of our household gods, giving proper thanks for return, but I pick up on his mood immediately. Look around the *atrium*.

"What is it, Brucchius? What has happened?"

An old woman in a filthy apron steps forward from the shadows. I recognise her from the town and know her by her calling. It is Margarita the freedwoman, a midwife of sorts. See her holding a linen bandage or parcel which she unceremoniously places into my arms. One heaver than it looks and why I glance back at her, uncertain what it means. Margarita is impatient and instructs me abruptly:

"Take it, my Lord, for this is your son!"

A swaddled, sleeping child.

Swaddled so tightly I can hardly see the infant's face, but what little of it shows resembles a red-faced old man. Blissfully fast asleep, white down on his cheeks, while I his father – a victor home from the sea – struggles clumsily to win any proper hold on the unfamiliar package containing him. Unwieldly, his treacherous linen in serious danger of unwrapping, of snagging on my armour.

I, the soldier who has never held a son before, but now stands holding mine. In my inept fumbling, leaving him nuzzling on the jewelled hilt of a *seax* worn high. Gazing on garnets, their glint in his eye. Turning and kneeling, I place him on the ground in front of the *lararium* in time-honoured fashion: his formal introduction to our household spirits. Before I can take him up again he gives a strong little cry, firm proof of a child worth rearing. My son!

The elation on this realisation was briefly so sweet. My joy so nearly complete. Then I remember the eyes of Brucchius and the chill in the midwife. Notice the blood on her apron. What a lot there is. Look up at them both.

Understand it is hopeless.

Our daughter Lucia is nowhere to be seen but these two take me to where Diana is lying. On a bronze-framed bedstead in a private room of the very house she was born and brought up in. Her father's house that's now become ours.

The freedwoman's wooden birthing-stool lies discarded in the corner. Bloodied, its job as complete as the stained deck-planking of any Clausentum galley you might care to name, returned today to port. Docked.

Finished.

It is done. She and the Mother Goddesses have given me a son but their price is too high. Bearing the name of that huntress who also protects women in childbirth availing her naught, not even one *iota*. Dressed by her servants in an elegant red shift coming to her ankles, belted in gold with knotted straps whose solid ends hang down off the bronze frame of the couch, my beloved Diana is cold and still.

Over her heavy eyelids have been placed two glittering coins and I knew at once what issue they would be. Two silver *antoniniani* of her own father, embossed with the words *'FELCITANI AUGUSTII'*.

'The Luck of the Emperors' laid onto one of his daughters with kindness not mockery. By good, ordinary folk who'd fought for her all the way while her absent husband fought another battle, thinking only of himself.

Coins stamped with an image of a victorious galley crewed by soldiers like him - epitome of her great father's unbeaten British fleet. Once minted at Petuaria to suborn a legion but now called-in to meet another, private debt. As her fee for Charon, the infernal ferryman on a lonely voyage over the River Styx it seems I am unfit to share. At least for the moment, and not for want of trying.

489

On the point of our greatest victory. At a time when there should only be joy yet all I have come to taste is gall, the loss of my darling grey-eyed beauty feels impossible to bear.

The spark that's gone. The sheen that fades from auburn hair. Showing her our little boy and babbling utter nonsense, I kneel there in my filthy salt-rusted armour beside this bed, holding a lifeless hand gone cold as the sea.

Weeping for her and our children, not me. For an innocent soul that's fled and two others left motherless.

How it came to be, at the age of twenty-one, I found myself a widower.

"Quis est iste qui venit?"

Who goes there?

(Restoration of a Latin motto carved into stone door-lintel of sixteenth-century tower, Stipend Howe, parish of Horsley, Northumberland, former United Kingdom).

- 30 -

Sadly hacked-about perhaps, but resilient survivors they remain. That mediaeval tower and attached stone bastle-house which, despite the odd Victorian accretion,still stand to this day under the mapmaker's name of *'Stipend Howe'*. Clinging grimly to each other like a pair of orphan-twins. Lost in a Border wilderness, waiting for a rescue which never comes. Upright on its fading expectation.

Lost at the head of a forgotten valley far beyond the remotest hamlet of Redesdale. Just below that distant horizon where they were perhaps first noticed by Leland himself. Their visitor during the long hot summer of 1539 who mentioned *"a pretty castell or pele built high above a minor springwater of the Coquet that is held by sixty men and horse under Sir Christopher Nicol as the uttermost house in England."* *('The Itinerary of John Leland in or about the Years 1535-1543').*

Next in the Bowes Report of 1550 to the English Crown, concerning arrangements for the defence of Wark in Northumberland against the Scots; its passing reference to a *"strong tower with a stable beneath and lodgings above, able to contain many armed men and horses, in circate about it a large barmakin for safeguarding cattle."*

While in 1583 State papers were recording this isolated pele-tower as held on behalf of the Crown by a Warden who was *"strongly enjoined"* to be *"a true, able, sensible and sufficient man who will keep the pele and see that all borderers and tenants appertaining be as well horsed and armed as they are in the defence of that country bound to be; and that some watch nightly at the fords for the keeping out of the Scottish thieves that commonly ride in the night through the said barony; to break not only poor mens' houses but also their hearts, bereaving them of all they have and worse, their lives also."*

Quaint entreaties and obscure facts only mentioned now, not as an enthusiast swotting-up to gratify his hostess, but because no visitor, not even the most ignorant, could stay one night in this remarkable house without coming away with an inkling of its past. Some feeling for its history. Least of all when proud modern owners helpfully mount copied extracts like those above in clip-frames, along its corridors and walls.

Example the one found on entering an en-suite bathroom in the pele tower, electric toothbrush in hand. Where I become absorbed in the literary account of that sensitive, eighteenth-century visitor, James Buchanan.

His seminal work *'Gentlemen's Houses and Demesnes of North Britain' (London, 1751)* betrays a man more used to the coffee-houses of Edinburgh, someone more concerned with ingratiating himself with influential proprietors than any proper architectural critique. And, as Buchanan's extravagant account of approaching this location reveals, a reluctant and fearful visitor, glad to get away:

"To a fortified stone dwelling in the Parish of Horsley and the loyal County of Northumberland: namely Stipend Howe. Long-held by the lawless and thieving Nicol name of Liddlesdale and lasting ill-fame, but now more graciously disposed to the profitable rents of the absent Dowager Countess of Corbridge: a lady of pious repute and the foremost consequence. Invisible from their Dere Street to the Old Roman below and set high above the summer-steadings of Redesdale, this former pele commandeth the loftiest of settings to head a closed Valley among Cheviot Hills. A place whose Pass affords the driver of Scotch cattle their secret route to market, it stands best viewed by devotees of the Picturesque from the South-west; a perspective coincident with the only approach available for horse. Gained by a stony access riven in dry weather by rocky Ghylls; near washed-away in wet; those Gentlefolk persevering against these discouragements of an Unprofitable Wilderness [the Danger of Ambush from Moss-troopers and Reivers; Rogues, robbers & Scotch raiders infesting these parts until lately] discover a Veritable Valley Of The Shadow of Death."

"Find themselves drawn up before a rough-cast Façade of no decoration and little penetration by lights. Fierce beyond Husbandry; though its lesser to a Brother over westerly mosses, to Bloody 'Hermitage' itself; this blockhouse shows us Frontage carved only for Defence. Made by Countrymen without care for Domestic Comfort or what Lonely Tenant it may incarcerate, but drawn in simple Blockwork and Machiolations sufficient of themselves to describe in stone those sanguinary Border Wars plaguing these parts for Centuries. Smoothed by Wind and butchered by Man; a Structure built, ruined, and then rebuilt so often there is neither Yeoman in the Locality nor Register surviving which can ascribe History, Author nor Year to its multiple Amendments. Fortress to a land where Rude Agriculturals see out their days in secret places marred with Terrible Memory; this primitive Domus whose Arcaded Groynes echo through silent mouths to a Visitor the Manifold Cruelty of Days-Gone-By."

Collectors fortunate to own one of the few first-editions surviving are compensated for Buchanan's prose and his frustrating imprecision over detail, whether of the site or its history, by the magnificent engravings of Joseph St.John Baxter accompanying.

Nowadays, a framed reprint of one of these fine illustrations can be found hanging over the freestanding tub with claw-feet that commands the pele tower's pink-papered, floral-curtained bathroom. By the look of it, Baxter - an architectural draughtsman and engraver of repute, known to have trained in Rome under Giovanni Piranesi - was an artist we can rely on for accuracy. His contemporary view towards the south prospect of Stipend Howe as our evidence that he at least must have visited here in person; whether or not a timorous Buchanan ever did. An engraving that's as useful to modern historians and architectural students for confirming how little the original parts of this historic Northumbrian building have changed over succeeding centuries.

Including those *"Arcaded Groynes"*.

An integrity of line surprisingly-little spoilt when, later on, the Victorians decide to make their own addendum at the back. In the shape of that stubby, half-timbered residential wing still so completely out of place, provided you go round the back to discover it. Followed a century later by the solar panels, security lights, satellite dish, tennis court, and triple-garage in reclaimed stone with powered roller-shutter doors which Bill and Venezia have discreetly added to their beloved Borders refuge, nestling into the hillside. Twenty-first century technology beyond anything a sophisticate like Buchanan ever dreamed of, let alone the hardy Border Wardens, yet hardly diluting that powerful sense of a dramatic past surviving at Stipend Howe.

Haunting its rooms, lingering in the walls.

All the more disappointing then, and for whatever reason - whether because of these modern additions, its inaccessibility by road, some metropolitan confusion over its location in relation to the Scottish border, or else the lack of a coherent architectural scheme - that such an interesting and characterful dwelling remains continuing omission from the relevant volume of Nikolaus Pevsner. His authoritative 'Guide to the Buildings of England' that covers north Northumberland.

Perhaps it was just an oversight by some revising editor. Maybe they didn't realise it was there. Or maybe, like Buchanan, they simply didn't like it. Consider it a mess, now that modern aesthetics and priorities in architectural heritage have changed so much.

What's for certain, before the memorable dawn in question, is that I was comfortably granting my own approval from the inside. Ensconced warmly in bed but imagining what glorious panoramic views will grow visible down its ravine of a dale. And judging by the bright rays suddenly penetrating heavy curtains drawn across a stained-glass window, put there to illuminate with Victorian splendour this principal bedroom to Pevsner's offending wing, a dawn not long in coming.

One I must await: restless and awake.

In bed with a beautiful woman, the proprietor and hostess.

My best friend's wife.

While from downstairs, there comes a loud thud.

"What the hell was that?" I ask myself. Quietly, but nevertheless aloud.

"Be Ed, the groundsman. Come in for Bill's gun. Gone out rabbiting, I expect...." the sleeping goddess beside me murmurs before rolling over.

Thank goodness it wasn't Bill himself.

Then I check the time on my 'phone and realise with surprise that I was wrong. Half three. Definitely too early for dawn. And that this glare through the curtains was caused by a line of hidden security lights mounted above the front gateway, suddenly coming on.

Not some premature sign of sun.

So that when these lights went off again, as quickly as they'd lit, dark and night returning, I must have gradually nodded off.

Neither as troubled nor as wakeful as I'd thought myself, after all? Hmm.....

"The intimacy of kings is dangerous; I court it no more; the most distinguished of mankind have well compared it to a flame, which illuminates things at a short distance but consumes them if they come within its range."

(Letter from Sidonius Appollinaris
to his brother-in law, Ecddicius, 474 A.D.)

- XXX -

Our defeat of the Imperial fleet gave us another three years' respite, if not a formal peace.

Leaving the victor, my adoptive father Marcus Aurelius Mausaeus Carausius Augustus, to enjoy them as our undisputed *Imperator*. Ruling over what felt like a separate country. A land at peace.

Freed from the bloody tyranny of Maximianus and his puppeteer, the cruel Diocletian. Free of their terrible persecutions and grinding central power. Separately governing the separate provinces of Britannia, aligned with Gallia Belgica and Lugudensis, as an independent state. The master of self-reliant Roman territories whose wealthy landowners, the *honestiores*, had once looked down their noses at him, but now must change their tune.

Finally realising which side their bread was come to be buttered, it was these influential magnates; these self-important villa-owners, retired soldiers, and magistrates from the south-west; supreme tribal chiefs or mine owners from the north, and prosperous east-coast cereal-farmers alike; who convened in an unlikely caucus held at Londinium. Gathering together towards the one patriotic end. Rejoicing to announce how their great and valued personal friend, *'The Most Fortunate Carausius',* should enjoy as enthusiastic a political support; and as deserved a degree of public recognition among the civil population, their grateful tenants, clients and *humiliores*; as could mirror his devoted adoration by our Victorious British Legions:

"Ave, ave, ave!"

Publicly recognising and confirming for the first time, as these long-winded civilians finally must, how conclusively *'The*

Menapian Candidate' (as they once so condescendingly called him) had become their best and only hope.

Theirs and Britannia's both.

Not only protecting them from Frankish or Saxon raiders in from the sea, but those rapacious fiscal demands and ingenious physical cruelties we hear are being visited upon his unfortunate subjects in the continent of Europe by the Western Empire's official ruler. Maximianus himself, the Butcher of Treverorum, increasingly taking it out on his own. That unspeakable Illyrian from whose tyranny and hooded eyes the brave Carausius shields us. So that if human gratitude might normally be ranked among more evanescent of physical phenomena, along with ghosts and mist, its manifestation by the people of our sheltered British isles might now manage slightly-longer legs.

These foreign dangers partly why; their other reason, money.

While inflation continued to rage unchecked across the whole continent, along with Maximian's fury at defeat, here in Britain we enjoyed an unusual period of economic calm. A growing prosperity, too, for at least as long as Allectus and his mines could keep on churning-out a range of more than decent coins with a proper silver content.

Yet if the Western Augustus could not invade, at least he could blockade.

And if our own rebel possessions, our cities and strongholds across in northern Gaul, could still give our shippers something resembling an import-export trade, they could never penetrate a greater empire further. No, friend Maximianus had been sure to see to that, condemning any private citizen or merchant found in possession of Carausian coin to a grisly death in the arena. Melted metal down the throat. No wonder there was so little taste beyond the besieged walls of Rotomagus or Gesoriacum for accepting our currency in payment, under or over the counter. However high its precious metal quotient, conciliatory in concept my captions.

Barter or bullion were a different kettle of fish-paste; how we still got so much of what we needed from Germania and Narbonnensis. Including the occasional amphora of their famous sunshine wine. (Always better than that acid British stuff, from the valleys round Corinium).

I've called it a blockade, but it was in reality more of a customs' trade-embargo. Restricted to the land now Carausius controls all the sea-roads.

Seas our galleys never stop patrolling, as much against Roman as Saxon, while the construction and expansion work continues on land; strengthening his massive fortresses along our 'Saxon Shore'. Activity as necessary against an enduring threat as it was good for keeping this scion of the ruling house, senior member of his defence staff, never less than fully occupied.

Stop me dwelling on the past, as I was otherwise prone.

Even with a household of domestics for *familia*, my two tiny children deserved a better standard of care and attention than a combination of these good folk and a busy naval-officer father could hope to offer between them. Fortunate indeed his dear old mother agreed to move across from sheltered Calleva to windy Rutupiae to supervise their regime. A big upheaval for her and even bigger for my servants, once she arrived, but soon they had unloaded her cart and she was in the thick of it. Happy bossing them all about and finding along the way a new wet-nurse for baby Victor. A tutor for Lucia, who was turning into a spirited little madam to remind me of her mother.

As if I needed reminder.

We had buried Diana in an embossed lead coffin lined with imported white gypsum, a miraculous material which the priests and undertakers swore to me would keep her complete for centuries. Including they insisted, her iridescent, ruby-black hair. Awaiting that bodily resurrection of which Hippolitus of the Tenth and his few surviving friends remain so utterly convinced.

Gypsum and auburn.

Her coffin was placed in an impregnable brick vault I ordered be constructed specially to receive it. On a prominent plot in the public cemetery bordering the Londinium road, sited about half a Roman mile beyond the twin towers of Rutupiae's Northgate. Outside the walls in compliance with law, but somewhere I could readily visit. That I could afford all this, one of the few blessings of any value from my rapidly growing wealth.

And there Diana lay. Day after day, night after night. Beside the wheat fields by the busy, poppy-lined road and its unthinking travellers, in an unmarked tomb. Hearing the marching men, the cursing carters and their mule-trains heading north, the horse-litters and pedlars. The melancholy winds, howling in off the German Sea.

Cold and alone, with me down here in her old house beside the Wantsum Channel. Brooding about how she had no other memorial upon this earth than our two little darlings playing quietly in the garden. No finer either, but never to see their beautiful mother again.

It preyed deeply on my mind, you know.

As it did with Carausius, who one day sent me a gift. A new slave.

Barates the Palmyrenian was an old man, a stone mason skilled in lettering who'd probably learnt his craft in a desert kingdom on the other side of the world. In an arid land of red sandstone and sand whose cities thrive despite it. His weather-worn face lined by age and hard labour. One of our last surviving captives from a forgotten campaign of years ago; when the late, great Aurelian and a younger Constantius together suppressed the rebellion of Xenobia. A reluctant prisoner still finding our island cold.

It was easy to guess how his Imperial sender's intentions had run. How his arrival should get this elderly fellow set on carving that formal tribute and memorial Carausius knew his daughter's vault on Londinium Road was still so grievously lacking. Maybe he did, but for some unknown reason another idea altogether had dawned as unexpectedly in my head.

Instead of this slave producing it for me, to order in the normal way, it was my conceit that Barates could teach me how to make these letters in stone myself. An eccentric arrangement I know, but one enabling the grieving husband to chip out his own slow lament in person. Turn the strike of metal on quartz into rhythmic accompaniment to his pitiful wails and tears. So that wherever she was, Diana might know. Might hear its sad percussion and recognise in its relentless beat that message of love I am sending to her. Wherever she is.

Why for her sake I have enured myself to the work of slaves. As if through hard labour, through setting myself to chiselling out her name with irons into the hardest materials on earth, I can somehow assuage the guilt that plagues me. Make good some of my fault.

And through it all, that she may live forever.

He was a slave and I his owner. A general, an emperor's heir, with the power of life or death over many more men than he. Full fleets and cohorts.

Yet we chatted cheerfully enough together down there in my garden. Squatting like equals on a slabbed square of Silurian bluestone I'd had laid down to give Diana and myself an outdoor dining-area. For those three days a year when doing so is bearable, out here in the salt marsh.

When there is no decent stone to be found anywhere near Rutupiae, so all must be shipped-in. Apart that is from the rough flint and shingles which almost every other building in the town is constructed from, that thing we worked was special. Barates identifying and sourcing for me a superb slab of red sandstone via some contacts of his in some quarry of the north country. Set on end here in the garden on arrival, as it now stands in readiness for working, together we would turn it into her lasting memorial.

Adjoining it were a group of offcuts from the same quarry which Barates told me were intended for practising-on. If I knew he chose this material for its resemblance to the stone of his homeland, I indulged his choice and met the shipper's fee without argument, for its delicate texture and colouring felt almost as pleasing to me.

Its redness an echo of that sheen to my darling.

And yes, if I call it 'red', truth be told this grit was nearer pink. While wherever the chisel strikes it almost turns white, weathering away slowly to salmon. Granular and crystalline, its glittering quartz-crazed softness should prove easier for the tyro that I was to work on. Though my main worry remained how long these carved surfaces or the grieving words I'd shaped might last, it was my hollow-eyed adjutant, Hippolitus and his followers, who insisted how much this fear was needless. Who begged me not to fret. When that resurrection and imminent second-coming of their *Christos* which was all they ever talked of would soon be transfiguring our world.

Prefigure its erosion.

Barates brought chisels and hammers of his own and requisitioned a spare set for me from a military mason in the town. But first he spent a long time sitting in the garden just

500

teaching me about stone and how it goes under blows, showing how different types may flake and shatter, before we ever picked up one. Explaining to me the philosophy of carving and how a plain man may bring life and the human form out of a living rock in the way that only gods ought. Why a proper fear of God or the love of lettering should be as integral part of this work as keeping a steady hand or a good knowledge of muscle.

If he offered me these priceless insights into a divine craft, what I offered in return was mutual respect and the persistence of a determined student. Plus the merest whiff of talent. To the point we were almost like friends.

How I came to win his confidence.

This captive Barates, as I discovered while we chipped away, was not only a good teacher in the art of stone-carving but also a great conversationalist. Nor this his given name. Encouraged by our friendship, the emperor's rebellion, and what distance an independent Britannia could now place between him and those stern men once his conquerors, Barates flattered me with frankness when I enquired about his past. The time of enslavement.

"I was captured on the banks of the Euphrates by your emperor, the mighty Aurelian. Your greatest-ever general, *Dominus*, and the only one who could have saved Rome."

"A man we murdered for ourselves...." I acknowledge.

"Rome's constant response to virtue. What is it with you Romans? Why must you destroy your best chances? Those men of valour or principle who could most restore your empire."

I knew he had a point; why I worried about Carausius.

"How old are you, Barates, how long have you been in Britannia?"

"I am an old man, lord, who has seen forty summers. Twenty-three of them spent in your island, freezing to death, but my real name is different and once I was a prince in warmer climes."

"A prince? Surely not. Of where.....are you from Thebes?"

"No, my lord, a prince of Palmyra. My father was a king, my mother a warrior-queen."

"A king? Are you serious?"

"Why should I lie? I've got away with it this long."

"The king of Palmyra?"

"Of course, my lord. King Septimius Odenathus, consul and lord of Palmyra; faithful protector of Rome's eastern flank from the hostile Sassanids and their evil empire."

"The Persians."

"Yes, our mutual, ancient foe."

"And if he was your father, then....."

"Xenobia was my mother....."

I whistled through my teeth in astonishment. Words were superfluous and here I was lost.

".....Julia Aurelia Septimia Zenobia, to give her Roman name and its spelling in your tongue" Barates continued. "From a line directly traceable back to Dido, Queen of Carthage and Cleopatra of Aegyptus. Related to the High Priests of Emesa and also Julia Domna, wife of your famous emperor Septimius Severus, the African."

"A fine lineage, but it didn't do her any good...."

"It was father's murder which turned her. By my uncle when I was one year-old. She took over the army and restored order, ruling in my name."

"Which is?"

"Lucius Julius Aurelius Septimius Vaballathus Athenodorus."

"Quite a list... and for short?"

"Just call me Vaballathus - it means 'Gift of the Goddess'."

"The same 'lady' who invaded Egypt, beheaded our governor. Threw us down a gauntlet?"

"Rome was weak, her armies bogged-down in endless eastern wars, yet my late father could beat the Persian Sassanids, capture Ctesiphon. Prove victorious across the same deserts where your own legions and their betrayed emperor Valerian could only meet with failure. Become the Sassanid's prisoner. When the whole of the East could have fallen to Persia, if we in Palmyra had not filled the void Valerian's capture left everyone else facing."

"Thank the gods for Aurelian, giving us a strongman. A man able to reunite an empire...."

"Including by reconquering their separatist Gallic Empire. One seeming little different to what your father-in-law would nowadays recreate. No lessons to be had from history, lord?"

"What Carausius is doing is a completely different concept, believe me, Barates. But your mother was playing with fire..."

"Not how things looked to her at the time. Perhaps not until that point where our army had captured all the camel routes. Finally getting us Palmyrenes an empire of our own. Controlling half the cities of the east while Aurelian was away sorting-out Gaul."

"An affront to Rome!"

"An empire that could have been mine. As its juvenile Augustus. But look at me now....."

"I don't understand how you survived?"

"When I was seven years-old, my mother's army was destroyed by Aurelian at the battle of Antioch. We fled in a camel-train across the desert, carrying as much treasure as could buy us into safety, but were intercepted by your Roman cavalry on the banks of the Euphrates."

"I don't know why you weren't both executed straightaway. There and then...."

"Aurelian wanted my mother to star in his triumphal procession back in Rome. Whilst the Roman gentry doted on her beauty. Sparkling black eyes and such a cultured intelligence she had, though I have seen her happy enough to march with the infantry when we were out on campaign. No-one could bring themselves to see her dead..."

"I knew a woman like that, once...."

".... Whatever she'd done to your *praefectus* in Egypt."

"Tenagino Probus, the unfortunate fellow she beheaded."

"You Romans never understood Xenobia, nor *'Tadmor'* as we call ourselves. Thought she was just a figurehead to yet another compliant satellite-state. Not even needing conquest. Complacent about it. Patronising our exoticism, not recognising our game."

"Game?"

"Yes, it's all a game, isn't it? Diplomacy and war. But maybe our's was the one your British emperor might do best to learn from. How Tadmor pretended to be Roman, an ally, but never really was. How we secretly kept hold of our own freedoms and sovereignty. Right underneath your noses, right to the end. Until we rebelled. Pretending to be like you. Dressing in your style and aping your buildings. Togas and columns. Affecting your ways. Outwardly conforming to your endless stupid rules and regulations, when we were nothing like. The *'indomitable town'* as the name of Tadmor really means in our tongue, repelling all invaders."

"Simply by soaking them up?"

"Exactly, my lord."

"It doesn't explain your own survival."

"No, because even if Roman high society was seduced by my mother, they would have had no compunction strangling her only heir. So a secret swop was made early on in my captivity. Between myself and another prisoner. A merchant's son who resembled me."

"Barates?"

"Yes."

"And what happened to him?"

"I think you can guess, *Dominus*, though they waited till after the Triumph. The usual place: Mamertine jail under the Capitoline."

"Strangled?"

"Of course. When it's traditional, is it not?"

"Poor boy."

"One of many. Rome's vengeance has always been terrible."

"But not on your mother?"

"Not so I'm told. Seeing out her days in a fine villa of Tibur, up in Lazio hills."

"But you never saw her again?"

"No, certainly not in the open stoneyards of the Dumnoni where I've seen out my time. Collected this cough. People like me don't receive visitors of that quality…"

"I am sorry. But you will carve me out my angel?"

"Yes, willingly. And teach you the special strokes needed for those fine words you've chosen to go with her. But all of it on one condition."

"A slave who lays down conditions? What an impertinence, can I believe my ears?"

"One only, my lord. That you give me my freedom….."

"And a mighty condition at that. Of course I will, my friend. Willingly and deservedly. With a deed of manumission on finest vellum to prove it, when your commissioned work is done."

"….and a free pass over the Fretum Gallicum, a few denarii to bring me to Tadmor?"

"Yes, yes, all of it; and more than a few! A deal, Vaballathus, a deal – although from what I've heard in Gaul you will be sad at what you find of home. Now that the tyrant Diocletianus has covered your city with legions. Converted colonnades into ramparts, temples to barracks, made a blockhouse of her beauty. A fortress against Persia."

"I am grateful, my lord, but she remains where I belong. With a towered tomb to hold me once a dry, desert air can soothe aching lungs no longer. Though first we must be carving out your lady, you and I together."

Her sculpture was his work. He made a head and shoulders in high relief, proud against an architectural niche as if she was sitting in a scalloped alcove on a wicker chair, its high back visible behind her. One of Diana's attendants showed him her finest dress, modelled how it once fell on her shoulders, and this magical easterner could engrave it to the life. Onto the living stone. Her hair that was her glory, laid up in latest style.

In one hand she held a dove, in the other a trowel – my little joke about a spirited person happier in her garden than holding court to guests in our *triclinium*. Our two small children, Victor and Lucia, represented as miniature figures below her.

Pathos of the bereaved.

All this took time, but the hardest part was the face. For me as much as her sculptor. We had a death mask to work from but it was oddly lifeless. No more like Diana than anyone else in that unhappy position. So Vaballathus beavered away on my weeping instructions. Refining a cheek bone here, strengthening an eyebrow there, until I was content.

Which I never could be.

After three weeks, he said the stone itself could take no more, its guardian spirit surrender nothing nearer life. Now was the time for words.

Their first bit was simple: '*DIS MANIBUS* – To The Gods Of The Shades'. Abbreviated to a laconic '*D M*' in the usual way. What came after was harder, but eventually I settled on:

"…..*and to the memory of Diana Aurelia Carausius, daughter of the Imperial Caesar Marcus Aurelius Mausaeus Carausius, a matchless wife living twenty one years and seven months. May the earth lie light upon you. I, her inconsolable husband, had this made.*"

Now came my penance. Chipping all these letters out.

The more I did, the better I got, so that I could go back and improve with more confidence on what I'd already done. Taking a perverse pride in my new-found skills. In what I knew polite society would dismiss as a manual labour, fit only for slaves.

Making the whole job longer. Adding a flourish here, a curving tail there. How my off-duty hours spent in the garden grew into days and still she wasn't complete. One night I'd been crouching down by the stele, trying to catch the fading light enough to add an extra discrete bevel to the sides of a capital 'A', when I heard footsteps on the gravel and felt a hand on my shoulder, so that I started:

"Come, my lord…" said Vaballathus, quietly. "I really think it finished."

"You want to leave for Tadmor?"

"Diana wants her memorial."

And then he coughed. Badly and painfully.

I knew he was right. Without the abode for her spirit which his remarkable likeness would give, her soul would be restless. Likely to stalk abroad. It was high time we provided it, he said. For our sake as much as hers.

I liked the finished stone well enough as it was, but Vaballathus' firm advice was to respect tradition. Have the figurative part and lettering painted-up with bright colours to bring her dimensional image fully to life. He spent another week on this aspect alone, carefully mixing the correct colours from earths and plants then applying them with brushes specially made. A job he did equally well. Only once it was dry and the stele been transported beyond the town to its final resting place by the road, did he actually ask me to fulfil my original promise.

To let him go.

I accompanied him down to the quayside at first light. Looking like any ordinary traveller. Vaballathus the son of Xenobia, once a prince and now a freedman, would take a coaster heading for Armorica. Carrying the official furlough I'd provided, and warned him to destroy as soon as he left our territories, in exchange for a bagful of chisels I would always treasure. Wearing enough gold in one form or another to get him back to Syria, one way or another.

In theory.

In practice, I doubted he'd survive the journey.

When the ship had gone and I'd waved him off, I walked alone around the outside of the ring of double ditches which circle Rutupiae's flint walls and bastions, then onto the Londinium Road.

Going to sit and admire his vivid portrait of Diana.

Tell her the latest news.

*"No foreign power, prince, potentate or state hath
or should have any jurisdiction, authority or pre-eminence
within this realm"*

(Act for the Declaration of the Bill of Rights 1689)

- 31 -

This picture of a wax-jacketed farmer holding a phone to his ear while astride his muddy Japanese quad-bike, ears of two panting collies bobbing-up from a box-trailer behind, could have been culled from some lifestyle magazine. Publishing's idealised embodiment of a remote northern rustic. How they're imagined from Surrey. Nobly struggling on against every modern odd. Tradition and technology combined, this watcher's vigilance directed not to his stock on the hill but signs of movement on the main road below.

Watching quietly as the headlights of two white minibuses come belting up from Otterburn in the earliest lights of dawn. Seeing them move more slowly right. Turning off from Dere Street onto a single-track route. From an ancient Roman road and mediaeval invasion route still the main road into Scotland, the A68, their chosen turn-off diverting to follow a stream he knew well. Bordered with gorse bushes all the way up to his home.

"Police! There's a rare sight for folk out here. What do you think they are up to, at this time of a morning, eh, boys?" he wonders out loud to his sheepdogs.

He in particular had a vested interest in the likely answer. With wool prices the way they were, barely a pound for a whole sheep's, little wonder he'd had to diversify into a lucrative little sideline. Earning double what he ever did from sheep-farming, but one to make him naturally uneasy at seeing cops entering his valley. Now that he was permanently moved up here from Gwynedd, come to an ideal location for dismantling stolen Land Rovers inside the privacy of his grant-aided barn. Selling parts over the internet to buyers who care little for provenance. Why the very last thing he wants to see up here is *'The Filth'* crawling all over his patch.

He sincerely hoped they weren't coming for him.

As the little convoy began its gradual climb higher and above him, he knew they would find the road surface getting worse and worse. Hoping they might even become stuck. With money tight, little-used routes like these had virtually been abandoned by the highway authorities. First it was their unspoken policy of only filling the biggest pot-holes, just a nominal dump of tar and gravel, then it was nothing at all.

This dead-end road soon passed his farm, on the tedious twisting way up to Stipend Howe and its distant head of the valley, but was typical. Pockmarked with the scrappy half-hearted efforts once made by unsupervised council road-gangs. Overweight men in flourescent jackets who spent most of their time hiding inside a warm van parked in a field entrance. Reading a sports paper with their feet on the dashboard. Those crumbly patches of sticky 'goo' they finally dropped from a shovel onto his road in the last ten minutes of their working day rarely lasting a month, let alone a whole winter.

That was in the good old days. Now he'd seen four complete winters pass, a succession of icy onslaughts whose cumulative damage stays unaddressed. Municipal shoulders shrugged. Excused as *'Public Spending Cuts'*. Saying that if you choose to live out here, backing onto hundreds of square miles of empty unproductive nothing, then it's a question of choice. That if you insist on running the environmentally unfriendly vehicles which are all that's capable of getting over cratered roads - like those old-style Land-Rover Defenders he hides, strips and 'recycles' for some scary Scouser 'friends' - then expect to pay the price.

Because when they are not being stolen, the tired old warhorses on which rural types round here tend to rely, are all they can afford, also happen to be those big-engined, petrol four-wheel-drives which governments proscribe. Pick on most for not being sufficiently *'green'*. So inappropriate for Chelsea or Fulham, the school run, they think. Hammered for Road Tax as a result, but dare complain and what they suggest instead is the type of dainty electric car now clogging up our towns. Tax-free but completely unaffordable, certainly to ordinary men like him. Or anyone he knew. Though he already had an acquaintance in Liverpool who specialised in stealing them, for anyone daft enough to buy.

"Clown-buggies with no ground-clearance and even less traction. Hopeless hybrids run off nuclear...." he mutters to the dogs, pink tongues panting their fond approval back. *"Twenty thousand quid's-worth of Chinese battery, a rolling shell for free. I'll tell you both, boys, a ninety-mile range will be max'. Run off precious metals out a Congo slave-mine. Terminally-flat inside five years. Flimsy capsules fit for ponces to troll round Westminster in, and 'bout as much use as a ferret on a treadmill for ordinary folks like us. Out here in the wilds."*

It was solitude and a spell in prison which had made the farmer accustomed to talking and debating the big issues of the day like this, with himself or the collies. Much as he did now. Or sometimes with the radio. Shouting down its presenters as *"....arrogant, self-important twats!"* Not as if he had anyone else to spar with, no female company; and if there were moral distinctions to be made between his own dishonest activities and the depredations of a desperate Revenue, the recurring scandals of politics or banking, then he couldn't see them.

"Nicking cars and fiddling expenses - what's the bloody difference?" he'd say to any dog who'd listen, but the unwelcome sight of police approaching his upland hideaway suddenly made him a bit less confident about those bombastic positions. Triggered some of his deeper and more bitterly-held resentments, at an hour of the day they're least expected.

No-one heard his private debates, they never did, but loneliness was grown his friend. Ensured his arguments prevailed. The only way he could, with no woman to put him right. Yet in the outside world he knew the reality: that the votes and opinions of northerners, of country folk like him, were valueless anyway, compared with a teeming south-east's. Unheard like he was now. Why he could somehow lie and justify to himself what desperate measures he found himself following for a living. Why he guessed that these police vans would go straight past him without looking. As if to prove a point. Like they knew where they were going and that he was going nowhere. Didn't matter, not even deserving of a wave.

Country people like him always waved, whatever they got up to at home.

"Are we on the right route, sir?" said the driver of the lead-van. Ignoring the muddy peasant sitting on a stationary quad-bike, mouth working away, who appeared momentarily beside the road in the corner of Damian's eye. That phantom face looking mournfully up at him out of the gloom for one fleeting moment. Fearing a search-warrant on his barn - did they but know.

("*No need to bother him for directions*" their driver was thinking. "*No, not with the boss doing navigation duty....*")

"Yes, of course we are, Damian..." Steve Ryton had said, in answer to his question, rustling their map just to show.

Steve was always like that. Confident even when he wasn't, but recognising the importance of always conveying a positive image. If nothing else, at least they'd taught him that on the last course he'd been invited down to Swindon for. '*Future Leaders*' it had said on the programme, his chest still swelling with pride when he occasionally re-reads it: "...*Working Together To A Common Purpose*".

Yes, he liked the idea of that a lot. Those words had a ring about them, always sounded good: "*That's you to a 'T', Stevie. A born leader if ever there was one. Good at winning people round, persuading others to work together.*"

For his own benefit of course, in a personal career trajectory that's only going upwards. So where would all this '*Accelerated Development*' and their '*sat-nav*' lead his team today, before dawn even showed? With the satellites playing-up again; frankly, only God knew!

It was a long time since he'd last had need of a paper map, but Stevie was having to relearn the old-fashioned navigator's craft all over again. Use one he'd found in a desk-drawer at the police station, brought along as insurance. Not making for happy reading either, was this tatty OS map of his. Must have been twenty years-old, revealing the sort of unsettling place-names passed to the side no satellite would trouble to mention. Sinister titles the neat suburban Stevie preferred not to see, would rather not know.

Those authentic but discouraging Border landmarks cropping up all around them like curses at a horse-fair: '*Pity Me*', '*Lousey Law*', '*Foulplay Knowe*', '*Flesh Shank*' and '*Witches Edge*'.

It might well have been the right route but the road was as awful as the place-names. Their van bouncing all over the place, headlight beams waving over empty fields. Wheels crashing in and out of potholes. Impacts jarring up through the chassis to set everyone's teeth on edge. Steve grinning back at Damian, their driver, who is making a face:

"Hang on in there, my son!"

Then they came around a corner and there was a passing-place with a black Audi parked right across the road, instead of in it. A black car left on a wet, black road in the dark and streaming rain. *"What the f....?"* Almost invisible and a miracle they didn't hit it. Damian slamming on the brakes and their police van coming to a sideways halt. Swerving into the passing-place followed by the one behind it. Half-asleep crews asking the same question: *"What sort of idiot parks a car like that at dawn, in a god-forsaken location like this one?"*

The answer and their culprit came in the indistinct shape of a man standing beside the Audi, holding up his hand. His spread palm white and almost ghostly in the gloom. Caught in the headlamps but his face invisible, strangely shadowed. Some local in trouble?

"Excuse me, pet" said Steve to the reporter, squeezing her leg gratuitously as if to request space before clambering out onto the road.

Her fleshy shank. Fit.

Nice.

Once he got out and closer to the back of the offending Audi, he could see that it wasn't even British-registered. Small bulbs illuminating two tiny letters on the blue bit at the right under EU stars: *'NL'*. Dutch, eh? He'd always found them nice people but what was a Dutch car doing out here in the wilds at this hour? Why was its driver flagging them down?

"Hang on, Stevie-baby, you'll be finding out in a moment..." he said to himself and offered his most winning grin to the pale man in a raincoat standing ahead in the grey light.

"Excuse me, sir, you're blocking the road. In the way of a live police operation. Causing an obstruction. Is there any problem here, to prevent you moving your car out of our way immediately? Like now?"

"No, thank you, Chief Inspector, there is no problem. Because I've come here for you...." the stranger said quietly. Hardly moving his lips.

"Oh you have, have you? And who the devil are you?"

"No, I am not the devil. My name is Tommas van Rijn from the Statenpolitie. On secondment to Europol. This is a joint operation and I am their representative. Sent here to observe your mission. Report on its progress." He showed him a silver police badge. Obviously foreign, like a kid's toy or something out of a cracker, Steve thought to himself.

"Well, no-one told me about this....."

"No, but here I am and doing so. Now that you know, kindly permit my accompaniment."

"Oh" said Steve again, this time more weakly. "Well, in that case, welcome to the team!"

First the Italian, then that gorilla in his pinstripes from the Home Office, and now this bloody Dutchman. International collaboration was all very well but it seemed to Steve to be getting seriously out of hand these days. That what with them and the press, he had more spectators from 'interested partner agencies' coming along, inside the vans or else in convoy with them, just to rubberneck than he actually had at his disposal to do the job.

And once they all got going again, with the black Audi now travelling along at the front, Steve could realise how few minutes were left him to re-order his own thoughts. To put to one side that question of why all this high-level interest has blown-up out of nowhere over a low-level warrant job; and concentrate on envisioning in his own mind the entry and search plan he's still got operational responsibility for. Before it actually kicks-off.

A job and a plan that suddenly seems a whole lot more involved than when they'd cheerfully set off an hour or so ago, he thought.......just at that moment when - *BANG!*

A flying missile comes straight through the windscreen, making a large circular hole and throwing cubes of glass at the crew. "Jeez...." blasphemes Steve in shock, hurling himself down onto the dashboard top. "Take cover, everyone......!"

Seems he's the only one who does, sniggers coming from the back of the van.

"Chill-out, sir, it's only a stone off the road!" says Jason.

Steve could see the woman reporter trying, not too hard, to hide her laughter.

Bitch.

His nerves were on edge.

That bloody Audi. You could see it had no mudflaps. Ruddy irresponsible. Could do him under the Road Traffic Act for *'Driving Without Due Consideration For Other Road Users'*. Breach of Construction & Use. And he could imagine straight away the sort of stressful, petty, headquarters 'spat' this episode could drag Steve into. How keen Phil, the Force Fleet Manager, would be to raise a stink about the damage with Steve's immediate superiors: "*Do you know the size of it? How much a heated, laminated windscreen costs for one of these bloody vans? Plus fitting! When my department's supposed to be making the most massive efficiency savings in its entire history...?*" he would say, in that irritatingly hard-done-by tone Phil enjoyed deploying.

Suggesting that if what are supposed to be public roads are turning into little better than gravel trackways, then maybe operational commanders like Steve should be running their vans with the screen-mesh routinely down? Like they do on Westgate Road. Or if not, be willing to cough-up for the damage out of Steve's threadbare departmental budget.

What was left of it.

Unless that is, Steve thought the Audi driver would go halves on the invoice. Helped perhaps by Phil sending it off direct to Europol HQ with one of his famously sarcastic letters. An accompanying note about the merits of mudflaps addressed to a 'Partner Agency' who'd maybe even agree, '*Go Dutch*' on the cost!

This private little joke helped him steady his nerves. To concentrate on positive outcomes, not stressful situations, like he'd learnt on that big course down at Swindon.

"*Stay cool, Stevie-baby, you're still the man in charge. It's OK. Only a damaged windscreen. So move on. Get on with it. Everything will be fine. Just do the job, man, then get yourself home.*"

After all, to get home that night, was all anyone wanted.

It was coming on again to rain, but their three-vehicle convoy continued slowly up the darkling dale, over a worsening surface. That woman reporter beside him still smirking.

Bloody bitch.

Witch.

"We have together to fight the danger of a new scepticism...In every member state there are people who believe their country can survive alone in the globalised world. It is more than an illusion, it is a lie...The biggest enemy of Europe today is fear. Fear leads to egoism, egoism leads to nationalism, and nationalism leads to war."

(Herman Van Rompuy, Belgian Prime Minister 2008-09, President of the European Council 2009-2012)

- XXXI -

The rain is lashing down onto this column of marching soldiers, everyone hooded, faces wrapped in their cloaks. Looking at the ground. Wet through myself and spattered with mud, I ride up and down its length on an exhausted horse. Urging them to move faster, just to keep going. Reminding them how much is at stake when Gesoriacum is under siege and we must get more troops to the transports, reinforcements over the sea.

The stone-paved road zig-zags steeply downhill towards the distant fortress, a bevelled groove down its centre from the brake-poles of carts catching what little light is left. As if carved by a giant chisel. Beneath the dark grey walls of Portus Dubris I see the spindly masts of ships. Sails silhouetted against a brighter sea, waiting to take us away.

Smoke from the cooking fires of barrack-room and oven rises up into the rain squalls and merges with charcoal coloured clouds. Their faint promises of food and warmth an incentive to my men. When we finally enter through the double-arched gateway, there are familiar comrades' faces to greet us, fresh in from the sea. Rations from the cooks busy working rampart-side, their reward for my foot-sloggers staggering in.

Leaving the centurions to ensure shattered men are fed and watered, like a professional officer I seek nothing for myself. While they eat I go straight to the transports to speak with their captains, establish the story. Where down on the quayside I find a scene of confusion; some ships preparing to leave, others just returning. Soldiers with bloodied faces, anger in their eyes.

Seagulls milling around them, squealing and squalling so much that a *haruspex* of bird flight might say it represents to us their warning. Unwelcome omens, come fresh from Chaos.

A *trierarch* in his white tunic is crossing the dock in front of me, going from one ship to another, and I take him by the arm. Not having noticed me he is startled at my grasp, about to protest his authority when he sees my red uniform and helmet crest. Defers to my own.

"What is going on here? Who goes back?"

"My lord Triton, it is you!"

"Surely, and of which vessel are you the master?"

"Cassius Menander of the '*Aurelia*', lord. Straight in from Bononia."

"Then give me your report."

"Hell on earth, lord, and a total surprise. Daylight attacks upon Gesoriacum made by land and by sea."

"Attacks?"

"Constantius Chlorus. The junior Caesar and his men."

"He always said he'd come back...."

"Well now he truly has, and in overwhelming strength."

"Your assessment, Cassius?"

"Three legions from Germania, brought in by sea to dig a continuous line of siege dykes inside a single day. Doubtless digging more tomorrow, and then a row of stakes. Ringing our fortress and the town, sir. Gesoriacum and Bononia tied inside together."

"No chance of a break-out....?"

"No chance, my lord, not now countryside for miles around is fallen to their thrall."

"Or a break-in?"

"Even less of that. Their ships this time are wider, stronger and higher-sided, sir. Learnt from previous defeats. Capable not only of delivering a force as big as this one, straight onto beaches, but rugged enough to stay and hang about. Happy loitering offshore in what's some pretty choppy weather, beginning their naval blockade."

"Not one we can easily break?"

"Only in strength, sir, when otherwise it's suicide. Seems to me our *Classis* should be called together before we even consider that, if I may suggest. Attempted as the one coherent force - provided Carausius can organise it quick enough...."

"How long has he got?"

"Not long, my lord, not long. Already their landing ships bombard the town and harbourside. Endless showers of ballista bolts, some of them on fire. We were lucky to get out before the net closed ourselves. And from what I saw, our warships or else any ordinary traders trapped inside the port will end up sinking at anchor. That or catch fire. Pretty soon, the rate things are going...."

His face had desperation etched into it but was never a coward's, I would allow him that. A man who'd seen his daily place of station suddenly struck in broad daylight. Hit by massive military power. Feeling lucky to escape with his life from a daring surprise attack mounted by an old enemy we must show quick to counter. A knee-jerk response which, on second thoughts, ought not take the form of dribs-and-drabs. Sending over those penny-packet shipments of available soldiers I'd arrived here at Dubris intending to arrange.

No, brave Cassius was right. Caution should be the watchword and our scattered Carausian forces must first be regrouped. A personal conclusion reinforced when the Imperator and his will was among us. When this matched what he ordered.

Meaning much of his force - including my own - had to make our weary way back to Rutupiae, where a wise Augustus could assemble a bigger fleet. One comprising nearly the entire strength of his reborn *Classis Britannica*, packed out with soldiers. Now that it was our turn to mount an invasion force, as quickly as we could.

Taking nearly two weeks.

When we sailed the weather seemed set fair, Jupiter Dolichenus guaranteeing us that much. Though the auspices for victory felt harder to divine, and we must save our friends. Only upon closer arrival before Bononia could we work out their chances. A necessary assessment made that little bit the harder by an impressive screen of enemy warships rowing out to oppose us when we approach to do so.

If their show was impressive, it was only half our own and we are the Victorious British Fleet, lords of the sea.

Where Carausius was in his element on the foredeck of 'Medusa', decisive and bold. His old self altogether, issuing orders and formulating rapid messages for captains, to be sent out by voice, flag, or mirror. Directing his squadrons to form into a densely-packed 'point' of galleys whose rams and mass could punch through the oncoming enemy line like a bullock through fencing.

Break them like wattle.

Which they duly do, Imperial triremes scattering and fleeing before us in fear as we drive hard for the estuary. Aiming for Lianae.

Where sea power met its match.

Across the generous mouth of the accommodating Lianae River, between rolling dunes which my mind's-eye still haunts with parading ghosts, those phantom cohorts from the Tenth, was a brown and livid scar of solid earth.

An embankment.

We couldn't believe our eyes.

Incredible.

The sea blocked by hand of man, leaving our lads trapped inside.

In the short time it took us to assemble a rescue force, Constantius and his besieging German legions had managed to build a continuous bank of wood, earth and rubble. A mole on driven piles coming out from the sand dunes and right across the estuary. Only a narrow opening at its centre for the river to flow in and out of, admit one ship at a time. Guarded by towers, archers and catapults, then closed-off with iron chain. Imperial troops waiting on adjoining beaches, ready to turn any attempt at landing there into our amphibious abattoir.

When our 'Caius Volusenus' tried, under Tormentus her captain, it took only two shots from a stone-thrower to sink them all completely. We couldn't get in, and knew from this moment on that Gesoriacum on its hill was lost to us for ever.

No return in triumph this time.

How much things had changed.

518

"The European Commission today proposed new rules to ensure that EU countries will inform anyone suspected or accused of a criminal offence of their rights in a language they understand. Anyone arrested – or the subject of a European Arrest Warrant – will have to be informed in writing with a Letter of Rights listing their basic rights during criminal proceedings.....The proposal is essential for boosting confidence in the EU's area of justice, especially as more Europeans travel....."

(Recent public announcement, EU website)

- 32-

Why I felt so restless that night is left for you to judge. All I can say is that if I did nod off for a while, when I woke up next it was definitely the real thing. No white halogen bulbs lighting up the windows this time but first faint rays of the sun.

Venezia still asleep like the proverbial baby. Buried in a mass of tousled hair.

I check my mobile phone again: *'No Service'*. Out here? Well, what a surprise....

Leaning across to her side-table and disappointed to find the alarm clock also dead. Not even flashing "00:00" or anything like that. Knowing what that must mean.

Electric's off again.

Oh, well. Presumably she would have been right. After all, it was her house. That it would only have been *'Ed'* - Edwin the groundsman, I mean. Going out earlier before dawn. Banging the door. With one or both of Bill's shotguns like he apparently often did.

Then I remember the lights were still working then. So why no electricity now?

A reliable man, she'd said. Completely trustworthy, someone happy in his work. Gone out to sit on the hill like a sniper in ambush. Looking to cull the regiments of rabbits which come in force at first light to pockmark the Cariss's lawn. Devastate a treasured knotgarden reputedly here since the days of the Reivers.

519

It had taken a while before it clicked with me who he really was. Realised the connection.

One of the *'Nighthawk Men'*.

Not my idea of trustworthy.

No wonder it came to be said of young Ed that he was someone who felt most at ease in a half-light. Like we had now. Considering his record that might be understandable. It is written that there is more rejoicing in heaven over a sinner reconciled and if that be true, then Ed was surely their target. Reconciled is another issue, let alone his conceit of heaven, but this man was certainly a sinner.

First time I saw him working at Bill's house, leaving after my little convalescence, I clocked him at once. Couldn't believe it, but said nothing to them and kept my head down in the Range Rover while we passed. I remembered who he was, even if he wouldn't have recognised me. Not out of my suit. That I was the man who had potted him.

When I knew from the antecedent history they'd read out at the Crown Court that Edwin Ramillies Graham esquire (apparently now appointed as their general factotum and handyman, on the Stipend Howe estate) was born twenty-five years ago in West Hartlepool. The son of an unemployed restorer of historic ships. Inheriting a unique middle name and his father's ingrained bitterness over our north's industrial decline. That ex-con' Bill and Venezia so generously took pity on. Decided to give a second chance, in a shrinking selfish world where too many don't even get their first. Trusting him with a gun.

Why? What was in it for them?

Apart from an act of charity to boast about at dinner parties.

Poor old Ed. Let's say he was a person who could always be relied on to find a bit more than rabbits. Usually trouble. Including that unique case where he and I first met, despite the police cocking it up good and proper, and not for the first time. Cocked it up? Oh, yes! Harsh words, but let me explain.

By starting with poaching.

If urban car thieves and burglars are what most cops understand, take in their stride, they find country crime more tricky. A little too far outside the usual comfort zone, normal operational envelope. Muddy and dark, woody and weird. In the bad old days when a '999' call about poachers too often meant a couple of GPVs coming out from the town. General patrol vehicles resplendent in a dazzling livery of fluorescent blue-and-yellow squares. Conspicuous as a piece of battenburg cake and containing a pair of townie coppers who respond by driving slowly up a rutted track into the centre of Hangman's Wood. Headlamps ablaze. Before it even occurs to them to debus or take a closer look.

(Or maybe they daren't?)

By which time the culprits have usually hightailed out of there laughing, pheasants bagged and strung. Long before cops arrive on their scene.

No wonder it took a painstaking series of '*GameWatch*' meetings initiated between police, landowners, and gamekeepers to establish new protocols. Get an understanding. Share in some reality about what these old-fashioned poachers got up to. The serious harm they do, that fear that they cause in the countryside. Displace some of that spurious nineteenth-century romanticism about '*one for the pot*' and '*gentlemen of the night*'. Too often professional criminals on their day-off, a bit of poaching their sport. Violent, dangerous characters not averse to a farmhouse burglary en route to the copse, given half the chance.

A process and realisation aided nationally by appointing specialist Wildlife Officers to police forces. Standard practice nowadays, some very good. Knowledgeable police officers with a sympathy for nature set as go-between betwixt constabulary and country. Experts who got to know the gamekeepers and farmers then established a matrix of pre-arranged rendezvous. Places where '*plod*' can turn up quietly then be led more discreetly into the greenness. Have at least a fighting chance of catching offenders, saving some evidence.

Winning prosecutions.

This lesson in how policing learnt to deal successfully with countryside crime, its poachers, badger-baiters and hare-coursers, is useful comparator for how it arguably hasn't yet with another rural type. Creatures creeping into the countryside by night, armed with metal detectors. Gone to poach relics and treasures from the soil, steal from us our heritage. Make off with antiquities they sell on to collectors, don't declare to the state.

'Nighthawk Men'.

Men like Ed Graham, experienced in that field.

Or he was until the cops found him crossing a recently-ploughed one, out near River North Tyne. Twelve-thirty one mellow September night, dressed in army camouflage fatigues. His face and hands blacked, the earphones of his metal detector still buzzing on his head and half-a-dozen muddy Roman coins rattling in his pocket against some keys for a Nissan. Adjoining the known site of a Roman fort which, along with four similar others, was carefully marked with an 'x' inside the waterproof mapcase hung round his neck.

While the brown Nissan in question and its blowing exhaust were last heard heading away fast, away from the *locus in quo*. Back to Sunderland presumably, at the hands of an unidentified driver, his passengers unknown. Leaving Ed to face all the music alone.

In the police interview about this rather incriminating set of circumstances, as recorded on video, Ed can be viewed by the watcher bravely going *'No Comment'*. Leaving the cops to make out their case rather than dig himself another pit. Or add to those he'd already left in the field. After all, Ed was an old hand so why should he want an expensive solicitor just to tell him to decline answer? Say something so simple as that. But once Ed reached the point that he did and finally got one - which was only after the cops had kept him in for twenty-four hours then announced their application for his custody-extension, to continue their 'chat' - there was only one man who would do:

Tony *'The Pony'*.

Of all the briefs Ed could have chosen, it had to be Tony. One character to represent another. That notorious horse-loving defence solicitor from outside Chester-le-Street. A lawyer who would not move one muscle in his clients' adversarial interest until they, or else someone from their family, first went to the nearest cash dispenser and brought Tony back one thousand pounds in cash. Hidden inside a carrier bag.

The Tony so beloved of Durham criminals. Legendary for his loud suits, buck teeth, inventive defences, and unique form of address to magistrates:

"Yer Wash-ups!"

Whatever 'Their Worships', the magistates - or *'lay justices'* as we are nowadays obliged to describe them, upon the modern principle of always using two new words wherever one old one sufficed - make of that, the punters adore him. So closely does he fit their cartoon idea of a TV Boston lawyer, red braces and all; and regardless of what his peers in professional disciplinary bodies may say privately.

Ed and Tony. What a combination!

And of course it was Tony who briefed Bill in his defence, once Ed got sent up to Crown Court for trial. Clinching their holy trinity, the ultimate unholy alliance.

On my case.

Where it had been my job to make sure the indictment presented by the Crown against Ed was watertight. Its charges so thoroughly-drafted that what Ed would need to get him off was not a barrister, but a magician.

Even if there were a few little problems in our way.

Like the fact the same police so anxious about ticking the correct box on their Home Office crime-recording form (classified as "*Heritage Crime*", if you must know) lost most of our evidence. Handed it back on no more legal basis than Tony's insouciant demand of that day's duty custody-sergeant for the meek return of Ed's metal detector and earphones, his car keys and camo' suit. Just as soon as the client got bail. Leaving we of the prosecution with our only surviving Crown exhibits: namely four Roman coins and a rather grubby map.

I told you they'd cocked it up.

"Judge wants to see you...." the court clerk had told me in the corridor at Newcastle Crown Court, making a sour face. "He's not very pleased!"

That is how it always was, representing the CPS. With us, they rarely were.

"This indictment is a load of nonsense....." said the judge after he'd called us back into his chambers over the court. Me admiring that original oil painting of Tynemouth Priory at sunset mounted right above him, on the back wall. "....Codswallop."

He was a large man who sweated profusely so his wig and gown were off straightaway and lying before him on the table. Sitting there wiping his brow in the usual white, collar-studded shirt with tabs, this undress judge looked like something from a

Moliere play. His eighteenth century predecessor. If he was, this guy would be a hanging judge. Ideal stand-in for Jeffries J at the Bridgewater Combined Court Centre: R-v-Monmouth *et al.*

"Conspiracy to effect a public nuisance, your honour."

"Stuff and nonsense" said the judge, over a count of my own devising. One of which I'd been unduly proud. Bill, who was sitting alongside and also been summonsed into the judge's presence to observe this flagellation of the Crown, simply crossed a pinstriped leg and raised an eyebrow in quiet satisfaction. Wait till he told Tony.

And Tony told Ed.

At least we still had the photograph album. Even the holy trinity couldn't weasel out of digital images the police had taken of Ed on first arrest. Arrayed in all his nightime glory. Face smeared in green and black, the camouflage suit and electronic survey gear still in hand, a marked map and its motives hung around his neck. And at least we had him arraigned – the only question becoming, exactly what for? Not liking the current one, what charge would be good enough? Whether to satisfy His Honour or elicit a plea?

Theft of the coins from the field was out. Ditto any Treasure Act offence. Completely beyond question. Ed wasn't caught in the field and we couldn't prove beyond reasonable doubt that either Ed or the coins had ever come from it. As opposed to being handed him by a friend, a fellow collector weeks ago like he now claimed. Or maybe Tony told him to.

The cops who'd let half our physical evidence slip away at least had one bright idea – analysing the mud on the coins in attempt to establish a link with pits left in the field. A good try that simply didn't work. It wasn't just the coins either, because Ed and his boots were covered in mud. Some of it old, some of it new, though all we had left was on coins.

"No joy" said the mud expert. "What the trade calls 'UAS - *Unattributable Alluvial Silt.*"

'UAS': another modern acronym to conjure with. See if I couldn't work that into the next office banter round the water-cooler. What fun colleagues would have with the 'S' bit.

The coins themselves couldn't speak at all – mute issue of Diocletian, late third century. They could have come from anywhere, though it seems one of them was very rare. A

524

denarius of Carausius: *'radiate'* she called it. Common enough in the south of England, but apparently almost unheard-of on the Roman frontier. Or so our latest expert said.

"That's what makes me weep about these people. These nighthawkers, illegal metal detectorists...." the archaeologist from the Portable Antiquities Scheme we retained to identify these coins told me. A softly-spoken girl from Durham University I rather fancied, who explained the cultural background to me while we sat outside court number three. Waiting to go on and sharing a packet of mints together, as she voiced her passionate disapproval:

"Unscrupulous gangs that emerge at night onto a site, a scheduled ancient monument, then rip through all the layers. Just looking for metal. Valuable metal, treasure even. It's not only the landowners they steal this stuff from. It's all of us. Stealing our history. Dig a hole then pull it out. Leave no record of context, of what dateable level it came from. Wrecking what's left. Of course the thieves don't give a monkey's, and neither does the trade that buys it off them. So-called collectors. Barbarians! It's a tragedy all the same. Who knows what stories this coin of Carausius could have told us. And such a rare find for a frontier fort like your man was arrested on. Yet now we've no link. Nothing to locate it in the history of where we know it belongs. Nothing to show it ever had any connection with the place......suggest how it got there."

Outrageous, as she said, and why I'm so determined this time. We had to nail Ed. Use him to teach his mates a lesson. The ones who got away, might think of coming back.

Nor was Ed off the hook just because the prosecutor had a telling-off. It takes more than a kicking from a sclerotic judge to stop a terrier like me. Not when I'm such a believer in circumstantial evidence. The idea that, if there's enough of it, you still can prove a case. Persuade a jury. And in Ed's case we had plenty – the photos and location of his arrest, for example.

In archaeological, night-hawking terms, he might as well have been caught wearing a hooped jersey, black mask and beret. Carrying a brown sack marked 'SWAG'.

The unholy trinity knew this too.

Why Bill came up to me on the concourse in the foyer, and asked for a chat.

"My man might be willing to do a deal."

"Oh, yes?"

"Yes. Wondering if we could carve it. Now you know I might be willing to plead to something less. Enough for the Crown, but not to go down."

"What do you have in mind, Bill? Facing circumstantial evidence so strong...."

"But not for conspiracy, which is why the senior judge dislikes it so much. Why I'll be saying I acted alone. As the Crown knows from our Defence Statement pleading 'not-out'. No evidence of loss. And as far as exhibits go; well, you've hardly produced any, have you, Michael? I've got them all back!"

"We've got an album. A picture's worth a thousand words and I can show twenty!"

"His Honour's expecting us to come up with something else....."

"Your equipment's in the photographs, Bill. Intention in the location he's found carrying it. And don't forget the map round his neck, marked up with targets. Its cord should hang him."

"I think I could plead to 'Going Equipped for Theft'....."

"OK. And maybe the Crown could accept that. Amend the indictment."

"So I wouldn't go down?" said Bill, rhetorically.

"That's for the judge to decide, of course, but your man has no similar previous. More of a taste for violence and disqualified driving. So no, you probably won't."

"That's true, I'm not really dishonest, just easily-led. Influenced by others. With a bit of a temper. Let's give it a go. I'll just be a moment, Michael, get some client instructions."

"Taking instructions" meant Bill and Tony ganging up on Ed in the cells and telling him it was Christmas. On their advice he soon pleaded to 'Going-equipped', getting a suspended prison sentence in view of time spent on remand, while Bill and I were in the pub together by teatime. Though we didn't invite Tony.

How quickly life moves on. Now Ed was outside with a shotgun and I was in bed with Bill's wife. Hoping neither of them realised.

If Bill found out I'd seduced his wife, or maybe she'd seduced me, what would be his likely reaction? Apart from wanting to kill me. But how would he find out?

Perhaps if Ed realised I was upstairs in bed with Venezia then he might tell Bill himself, once he's returned, if only to get his own back. Bill doing the shooting bit for himself.

Though if Ed realised I was the prosecutor potting him, then he might decide to do it for him anyway. Without consulting Bill.

Suddenly, Stipend Howe didn't seem a very safe place to be.

Not that, judging by those interesting snippets of history laid out across its bathroom wall, it probably ever was.

"This project has been part funded by the
European Union
INVESTING IN
<u>*Englands**northwest***</u>

EUROPEAN REGIONAL DEVELOPMENT FUND"

(Actual wording, spacing, emphasis - and missing punctuation - from the dedication slab for a *'Roman Frontier'* pavement. As discovered on Castle Street, Carlisle, c. August 2011, when displaying names of Roman wall-forts, laid-out in wrong order)

- XXXII -

The homecoming of the *Classis* was made in sour and angry mood, tails between our legs. The irreplaceable M.Saturninus Lupus heading a roster of heroes locked inside, posted missing outside. Good men we abandon to their fates.

If they and Gesoriacum were truly gone, then our other holdings on the northern coast of Gaul stood little better chance. One by one, all of them falling within months. Cutting us off from the continent, cutting us off from trade.

If Carausius felt and showed himself more devastated than most, saying you could cut him open and find "*Gesoriacum quod nunc Bononia*" engraved upon his heart, there were already disaffected individuals within our army or the fleet, muttering how much they'd like a chance to try.

It wasn't long before some crackpot did.

The first attempt was made by a German mercenary complaining he hadn't been paid. At the time, Carausius had been making a tour of the coastal forts to check on grain supplies received in lieu of tax, the *annona*. Taking the opportunity along the way to put a bit of extra pressure on local estate owners he'd given the job of collecting it. Riding through the nearest towns, he had smiled and joked and waved to the crowds in the same old way, acknowledging their scattered cheers, but everyone knew something was missing:

Like all of Northern Gaul.

The army and his public always loved a winner, and suddenly he wasn't.

Portus Adurni was an enormous sea-fort, our giant rectangular stronghold. Guarding with its high walls and many hollow bastions that flat finger of land which overlooks Vectis Water. Ideal as a strategic naval base and for mooring ships before, though I often wondered why it never floods.

Yet like too many installations in his '*Saxon Shore*', and for all its impressive size and authentic defences, Portus Adurni was in some ways a sham. Component part in his great illusion, our stratagem of fraud.

He didn't have the troops, you see, after what we lost in Gaul. Why we had to keep on moving them around the country. Ordered those we had to set up camp inside these towering empty enclosures. Lighting lots of cooking fires and marching noisily around outside. The key thing being to give unfriendly watchers the impression they were manned, by how many speculation. Behind those inscrutable walls, inside so large a structure, it could be half a legion.

The coinage stayed good, so much better than abroad, but Allectus gave warning at our meetings of how easily it might decline. The effect of uncertainty. When people grow nervous they tend to bury money, not spend it, while the fresh metal needed to keep on making more simply wasn't coming in. The mines running out. Making the salaries of our soldiers even harder to meet, he would say soberly. No-one present need reminder.

Not that this particular embarrassment was confined to the Regulars, a corps of reducing number. Why poorly-paid mercenaries became increasing answer. The worst of all solutions, apart from all the rest.

Allectus and his Franks.

When our emperor was a webfoot barbarian, born on the Rhine delta, it made little sense to reject the place of his homeland as an alternative recruiting ground. Deny a home to tribal brothers, refugees defecting. An entire nation of marsh-people fleeing that continuous cycle of massacre being waged by Maximinanus and his Caesar Constantius along its reedy banks.

If these arrivals gave us manpower and we paid them so little, then they never meant quality. Underfed, undernourished, underdeveloped and stricken with every kind of fever they could bring out of the marsh, few of them spoke Latin and even fewer wrote. Virtually untrainable. Slung together in low-grade *Numeri*, these ad hoc military units only traceable loyalty was to the chieftains who led them. The self-important warlords whose subservience we'd bought. No wonder decent citizens in our towns feared their approach as much as any Saxon. When the two looked well-nigh indistinguishable, equally lawless.

The atmosphere that dreary day in Portus when Carausius rode in to inspect.

I had come along with him and a few members of his staff, unfortunately riding at the back after my horse picked up a stone. The *Numerus* in question had been called out on parade but even forming an orderly line proved the outer limit to their drill.

When the emperor and his party rode down the muddy path through the centre of the camp, their amateur attempts at a disciplined reception soon broke into mobs. Mixed up with members of their families, women, children and dogs. Most of the German gang crowding round him seemed perfectly friendly, in awe of his power, but there was an elemental edge of wildness to some individuals in the group which made me feel uneasy.

Why I dug my heels into my horse's flanks and tried to urge it forward, to push through the crowd, but before I could draw my sword or get any nearer a man in green had barred the emperor's way. Snatched the halter to his mount.

"When do we get that money you promise us?" he shouted, waving a fighting-axe to emphasise his enquiry. "That money or land?"

The jet-black horse Carausius used to ride in those days must have been the finest on the island. Out a Gallic crossbred-Arab imported in freer and happier times. While to look at it was a magnificent piece of horseflesh and the emperor more than its master, it was also one of the most stupid and highly strung animals that I ever encountered. My usual practice always being to give it the widest berth possible, though my normal working proximity to Carausius had on more than one occasion won me a passing kick.

The German petitioner knew none of this when he advanced on our leader with a sharp-edge in hand and dared to grab his reins. Causing the wretched horse to turn round and rear almost upright. Throwing the emperor into the crowd behind whilst delivering such a cracking blow with the forefoot to this unauthorised handler as must kill him outright. Stove in his skull. As he goes down, face bloodied and probably dead, I draw my weapon and ride forward to the centre of a scrum of barbarians forming around that point on the road surface where my father-in-law last fell.

Yelling at them in dog-latin to "Back off, you dogs, back off!"

I remember a sea of milling faces looking up at me. A few curious, most of them alarmed, but some quite definitely hostile. Several waving swords - the ones I cut down.

531

Hardly the first time in my career I'd killed men in Roman service, inside a Roman fort, but duty is duty and a *seax* needs feeding. The odd light from her garnets enough to show me that. Seeming to say something stronger to her nearer-kinsmen, too. Subdue them with a glint of russet so vivid that they soon surrender Carausius up. Shaken but not seriously hurt. The crowd pulling away from him scared, leaving two of their number dead on the floor and a third dying noisily as I dismount beside a prone Carausius.

Vault to him from the saddle.

The emperor climbs to his feet, me helping him onto my horse then turning with a snarl and a Saxon sword blade to hold back this throng of mutinous mercenaries I wish we'd never bought. They can recognise its metal and bow to my own, but here is a disastrous turn of events which could yet get worse.

The chieftain in charge calling-out for calm over all of the hubbub while the rest of our small escort forms up around Carausius, their First of Men and *princeps* to our cause. Alarm in their faces, spears pointing out. The emperor looking more shaken, more flustered, than I'd ever seen him before. Mud on his purple cloak. All he can say on leaning down towards me while I lead his mount away:

"Thanks for what you did in there, Triton. That crazy bastard could've killed me!"

These last few years have aged him, the strain of command. The loss of Diana and then Gaul, credibility crumbling with it. Grey invading ginger, new silver replacing orange, most prominent in his beard. Less sparkle in the eyes, less strength in that neck. An ageing oak in autumn, his sinews knotting and twisting like its trunk. In fear of the axe.

Their chief was fulsome in apology, bobbing and bowing, but the damage was done. We got out of Portus as fast as we could but from now on could never leave it behind. Word soon getting out, luck draining away with it.

Carausius had been attacked.

It rattled him deeply, shaken to the core, and the extra security we organised to prevent a repetition only made his sense of alienation worse. Travelling everywhere with twice as many cavalry, forcing wagons off the road. Pushing through townsfolk with the elbows of his escorts as sharp as any weapon. Enough on their own to turn cheers into jeers. Popularity into a popular resentment.

Politically and militarily, we all could read the signs: you didn't need to cut a goat open and then examine its guts. Check out the sacred chickens or watch geese fly over marshes. Things were looking bad now and everyone knew it, not just the priests.

My private response was to consider sending my mother and children away from Rutupiae. Back home to Calleva, out of harm's way. Far to the west, well away from what was becoming a dangerous frontline along the Narrow Sea. Unfortunately, my mother was having none of it, demanding they stay. Claiming her running the household would help me concentrate on my naval duties without interruption, give more support to Carausius.

A job not made any easier by a new house the emperor recently had built, his villa on the cliffs. One day's ride west from our important base at Portus Dubris, it might have been a perfect location for him, watching the Straits, but he was effectively doing the very opposite from what I wanted for my family. Moving nearer to a clear and present danger.

To quote the glassy-eyed and glib successor to our much-lamented Vitalis: Marcus Perfidius Ferox, latest centurion commanding Carausius's palace guard and monitoring admissions to his presence *"....our prince's choice of residence has created a tactical nightmare"*. Overlooking a long and curving beach below, he almost had a point. So that the house and its service-buildings' position, backing onto dense woodland, was *"...nigh-on impossible to defend."* When at night you could hear the waves breaking onto the sands far below, the wind roaring through the forest which threatens to engulf it. Building that sense of wildness in its halls I'd always detected in our little emperor's character.

Carausius, with another glimmer of his old exuberance, would have none of our objections. This was a fabulous site affording matchless panoramas and he would never give it up. End of discussion. The smell of ocean had permeated his whole life as it now did the sprawling corridors of his house and what could be more natural? Breathing in its salty vapours with relish,

533

great heaves of his chest, while he told me how he could never survive one moment longer living further inland:

"If as you say, all you care about is my wellbeing, Triton, then please stop going on about this blooming house. The sea air here, it's good for my health, believe me. And I think that I've earned it. No disrespect to your old stamping-ground, my boy, but I've had more than enough of Calleva...." he'd say with a grin. "If I stay there a moment longer, I think I'd die of boredom. Or else from respectability. Go rotten with damp!"

Sailing west from Dubris, in good visibility you could see its white-rendered walls from right across the bay. Orange roofs against the greenwood. Held in the crook of higher ground like a baby in its mother's arms. If only as safely! Visible from miles offshore, I worried that his enemies might be noting its location as readily as his loyal fleet did, but Carausius's attitude was that he always led from the front, so why not actually live there?

As ugly as he was known to be avaricious, the centurion Ferox had been transferred from Londinium and seemed to miss its streets and fleshpots. Dislike the country's dark. Lacking to my mind that innate sense of ground and natural features as a basis for defence you'd expect in an experienced infantry soldier. Was needed for a spot like this. Yet too many of the new guard had been transferred along with him, some of them Germans. Former servants of Allectus, ornaments to his counting-house. Unhappily diluting those traditional military virtues from the old British legions which I thought Vitalis and his men had once personified when they kept the palace at Calleva.

That general lack of discipline. How they slouch against the wall when you ride up. Whistling at the serving girls while they cross the yard, instead of looking outwards. Not keeping any register of visitors or patrolling far from the house. Preoccupied with pay.

Unprofessional, in short.

It was four months after we heard about the capture of our last outpost on the other side; the humiliating fall of Grannona and murder of its Moors, our brave *Mauri* ; that Allectus came to the house on the cliffs for the very first time. Until then the emperor and his *rationalis* had been content to maintain a practice of conducting their periodic liaison-meetings in the latter's palace at Londinium. On the basis this was principal city of our provinces and largest north of the Alps, it had always seemed a logical arrangement. Although personally I thought it unseemly for the emperor to be coming to him, rather than the other way around.

I wasn't there at the time but out on the '*Calliope*'. Beating up the coastline in a squally south-westerly, looking for Saxones, sniffing out the black ships. More from habit than any specific military purpose. Feeling more sick than usual too, but trying not to show it. Glad of the respite when we called in at Anderida to take on some supplies.

Where I was greeted with a curt and cryptic message passed along by signal stations.

Shorthand in semaphore to say that something was up. Beckoning us back by beacon.

It was hard work returning towards the Straits of Dubris but we realised we must. Set off against the tide anyway, using oars to speed our sails wherever possible. Eventually entering the relevant bay hours later, just as the sun was setting and a sea-fret closed in.

Seeing the fire, knowing it was the house.

The wily Callidus, my latest *trierarch*, beached '*Calliope*' gingerly but successfully in the murk and I took every armed man I could muster straight onto the cliffs. Up a vertical path that doesn't exist. Climbing and cursing in the dusk. Cutting our legs, arms and faces on invisible brambles. Forcing through bushes, hanging off trees. Slipping and sliding, one man all the way back down again in a rockfall of chalk. Followed by his shield.

By the time we emerged into the garden, a series of terraces marked out with box hedging and somewhere I knew my way around, it was pitch dark but the red glow from a burnt-out barn adjacent gave us slight illumination.

I gestured to the men with me to maintain total silence, to stay crouched down. Pointed them to where the main path led directly past the statue of Diana in the centre of his lawn to those twin folding-doors of the emperor's dining room. Today they were closed but in summer it was possible to fold them right back, so that Carausius and his guests could recline on their couches and look out across the bay.

535

There would be none of that tonight.

"In here!" I hissed.

We ran to them and one of my bigger marines smashed the doors open with one blow from his shoulder, then we burst through in a body. Swords drawn and shields held tight to the chest and face, hobnails grating on mosaic flooring. The yellow light inside from hundreds of oil lamps in the dining room almost blinding us as we crashed-in from the dark. Blinking like owls, skidding on tesserae. Each of us forced to an involuntary halt, eyes adjusting to their glare.

"You can stop right there, Triton, and tell your men to do likewise. Sheath your weapons!"

The disembodied voice of Allectus, beside a big bunch of his Franks. The *Ab Admissionibus* himself, M.Perfidius Ferox, lurking in the background nearby. A strange twist to his stance. As if they'd been waiting here especially for my lot to turn up.

I put my sword back in its scabbard and the crew of '*Calliope*' follow my example.

"Allectus, what is going on? Where is the emperor? What's happened at the barn?"

"There has been an unfortunate incident but it's over now and I've taken charge."

"Incident? Taken charge?"

Carausius was behind him, reclining on a couch.

The blood from his face and chest soaked the front of his purple tunic and pooled on the floor. Blackened and dried. If silk cushions were still supporting his head, the position of the arms was far from relaxed. Multiple scarring across his forearms showing how hard he'd fought back. As if dumb wounds could speak. Eyes closed, mouth slightly ajar, as if he only slept. His gladius on the table, broken off at the hilt.

The emperor's favourite seer in the Temple of Apollo & Diana, at its sacred grove outside the walls of Londinium, was proved right after all. An oracle uncannily correct. Carausius did not die at sea, only overlooking it. Exactly as she'd said and he'd always known. Never mentioned to us.

His assassins claiming the will of the army in their removal of a discredited leader.

A hero whose great memory I will ever respect and treasure. The father of my wife and a man good enough to take the place of my own. Killed by this creep Allectus seizing power in an independent Britannia whose doom he sealed immediately by his one single act.

"Emperor? You are not fit to…."

They had me by the arms, struggling to get free. One blow to the face, to teach me a lesson. Their traitor, Ferox, smirking on its administration. My left eye closing-up quickly.

"I know you will come around, Triton…" sighed Allectus. "Learn to obey me, maintain our defences. Because you've no choice. If Chlorus ever got across, you are one of the very first he'd have executed. You and yours, your precious little lambs. Why I know it is as much in your interests to defend a free Britannia under me, as it ever was under the late Carausius. Especially now you know we've made quite certain your delightful children are kept completely safe. Detained on my express order, my very special guests…."

"You mean hostages….."

Ferox hit me again:

"Speak when you're spoken to, and don't interrupt the new Augustus…."

Our great Carausius lying there, him saying nothing.

How his reign ended, the terror began.

*"In defence of a man's house the owner or his family may kill
a trespasser who would forcibly dispossess him of it"*

Lord Hewart in <u>R-v-Hussey</u> [1924]
Vol.18 Criminal Appeal Reports p.160

- 33-

This time, I wasn't going back to sleep.

Not wishing to disturb Venezia, I slide quietly out the side of
the duvet and down onto the floor. Fortunately the bedroom
door was already ajar, so I could sidle past and onto the landing
without its oak planks creaking or any click from the iron latch.
The '*sneck*' as northerners call it. Their whole house in silence,
a state of quiet peace.

The landing and stairs leading up to the bedroom once formed
part of the old pele tower, its interior first floor. From the landing
another, steeper and narrower staircase leads upwards onto
the crenellated roof via a heavy trapdoor.

Thick stone walls clad with one hundred millimetres of modern
insulation board. Alloy-ducted with high-tech' micro-wiring then
rough-rendered in white plaster to look as if nothing had
changed in centuries. The narrow arrow slits and glazed gun
ports which pierce them all the illumination this mezzanine
walkway inside the tower ever gets. Enough to show me an
occasional patch of dull green from the hillside outside and a
sky heavy with low cloud.

Not the signs of a promising day.

I amble slowly over its landing and into the bathroom on the
same level. Entering a world of floral pinks, papered with
shepherdesses. Her influence and taste, I imagine, inhaling her
scent. Not Bill's, though maybe the St.John Baxter print over
the bath represented his one insistence. Her one concession to
something he could like here, in a marriage I now feared to be
built on rather more in the way of compromise than this one
example.

Dashing water over my face to clear gummy eyes, both it and
the bathroom feel icily cold. Temperature dropping fast after the
cosy warmth of a bed containing Venezia. I rub my eyes again

then flick up the seat on the water closet. Another recycled piece of antique porcelain, blue and white Armitage ware, which I stand before. Whistling to myself.

I've just finished, the flush on the w.c. more like a mini-Niagara, and loitering absently in a daydream at the sink while washing my hands, when I feel a chill run across my back like a draught. Hear footsteps. Realising there is someone else in the room I turn quickly and out the corner of my eye catch sight of the retreating figure of a man. Heading for the door so quick he takes me completely by surprise.

If the image I caught before he's already outside is momentary only, I remain absolutely certain of what I saw. Would swear it on oath to any jury. Even at the Crown Court in front of that judge: '*R-v-Turnbull*' warning or no.

Of a man in rusty armour, or at least his backplate was. I never saw the front. Wearing a hat…no, an iron helmet. One of those funny, domed things with a steel central plate like a comb. The sort you see in pictures of the Spanish Armada, or their conquest of the Aztecs.

Heading for the roof?

In a flash he's gone and I rush out onto the landing after him. Put my head out the door.

Nothing.

In either direction, not up nor down the stairs. Or the ladder. He's gone.

Disappeared into thin air, leaving just the faintest whiff of leather.

And there's something else I need to tell you.

This figure had no legs.

Well hardly any. The lower part was missing though it didn't slow him down.

I can't describe how I felt but do know it was real. Nothing like this has ever happened to me in my whole life before, but I'm sure of what I saw. And what I felt too.

Terrified in fact.

What it meant, I couldn't honestly say.

A '*manifestation*' I suppose they'd call it. Of word about the house, spoken out its walls?

539

I creep nervously back across the landing, heading towards the bedroom. Notice my hands are still shaking. Helpless to stop them. In a complete state of shock.

Sidling nervously back around the door to find Venezia awake and sitting-up in bed awaiting. She takes one look at me and exclaims:

"Mikey-baby, whatever's happened? Whatever is the matter? You're white as a sheet, my darling....like someone's just seen a ghost!"

"To compel a man to subsidise with his taxes the propagation of ideas which he disbelieves and abhors is sinful and tyrannical."

(Thomas Jefferson, US President)

- XXXIII -

As if words could win him the war, Allectus kept on stamping out coins carrying more. The same old tired slogans about the *'Luck of the Augustus'*, their Virtues and their Strength. As if words were enough to see off Maximianus and Chlorus. Words and pictures.

Pictures of ships, meant as a warning.

When the reality was that all we had left from the original strength of *Classis Britannica* to intercept an invader were the nineteen or twenty vessels still operational. With more ships stamped on his coins than he could afford to send out to sea. When nearly all the lovely liburnians, our beautiful biremes, were laid-up. Including the *'Calliope'*. Sitting on stands in the winter ship-sheds of Clausentum or Dubris right through the summer.

Rotting away.

Lacking a ship and my new emperor's trust, there was little useful left me to do, whatever he might once have hoped. Deluding himself that I was the compliant type of heir. Someone who could be persuaded to agree, if only he let me out. Who would willingly fight for his adoptive father's recent killer against a worse and older murderer of his natural *pater* first. Child hostages or no.

Defending our provinces against my enemy's enemy.

When Allectus realised he was wrong and I was never made in that mould, he gave in - eventually. Releasing me anyway, now he was so short of troops that it was better to post me to the margins than waste further resources on my detention. Or assassination. My faithful crew insisting on accompanying me to wherever it is I'm sent.

At first, only to the edge of Ocean.

541

To an obscure outpost of the Saxon Shore whose garrison is never ordered back. Condemned to stand on guard there for ever. Left to its fate without hope of recall.

To Othona, that lonely fort which watches over the wide estuary of the Black River, miles from the nearest road. Where to begin with I had hated the whole place with a passion. Like a prisoner the walls of his cell.

Where what actually barred the view from its brick-lined windows was the linear flatness of that long spit of clay land on whose furthermost shore it stands. A fort constructed out of tonnes of imported stone and wood, every single piece of which our forebears in the fleet must once have brought laboriously in by sea. By hand from the holds of their ships. Shipped-in from places like Rutupiae or Regulbium to stamp this rectangular imposition of man onto an empty, tree-less wilderness beside the German Ocean.

Gradually however, I did come to terms with its eerie setting. Learn to love standing there, watching the sea at morning, sunsets at night. Appreciate the ever changing panorama opposite, away over its estuary. Enjoy the sound of wading birds, the sight of seal. The black, white and red of sandpipers.

That limitless supply of quality oysters which proved the only luxury in our place of station, apart from endless wind and rain.

Too few of us to fill the fort, too proud to let it fall.

In the summer, we rebuilt the ruined headquarters building, got the bath-house working again. Re-roofed some turrets, stockpiled more wood. Only the commander's house was left unrestored, when all I needed was a barrack room, same as my men.

And if all this constructional activity helped keep my mind off things, there always came a time when unwelcome thoughts intruded. Most often at night. Wondering about my children and the fate of my mother, where they were now. Remembering Diana and having no idea.

One day a liburnian was sent out of Dubris to offer the world an example of what by now seemed the navy's increasingly-rare attention to incursion patrolling off the coast. After nosing desultorily along the Black River for a while and finding all was quiet, it called-in at Othona to get some rest for its rowers.

Compare notes with our garrison. Where its *trierarch* proved to be a freckle-faced seaman little younger than myself.

A friendly fellow named Julius Firmicus whom I invited, along with his two navigation and rowing officers, into the newly-plastered parade-hall of our fort's repaired headquarters. Where they could witness those improvements no-one else came to inspect and receive that modest meal we laid out for their refreshment. Where we could take as much pleasure in hearing an admiration for our unique Black River oysters, fresh caught from the estuary, as any approval of remedial military works.

It was good for me, too, to get news from the outside world for a change. Hear others' perspective, renew our contacts with the Fleet. Enthusiastic professionals such as I was once, men who can report how Constantius is campaigning across the Rhine delta again. Suppressing the Menapii and wiping out Franci.

Why there were Frankish refugees streaming across into Britannia and, instead of fighting them off as raiders, they said Allectus was actively encouraging them. Recruiting more of those men I'd thought our enemy into his growing military service - under the command of one of our former colleagues, a man called Livius Gallus now the governor at Londinium.

Enlarging that new mercenary force he is forming out of murderers and thieves.

An important change in official policy which nobody had bothered to share with us out here at Othona, where in common with Constantius we kept to the old discipline of killing any Frank we found. Likewise with Saxons. A change in military approach which our visitors confidentially advised was as much disliked by ordinary citizens in the towns as it was openly reviled by *honestiories* in the country. An aristocracy reportedly muttering from the safety of their villas that instead of defending the province, Allectus was selling it down the river.

Because we had so much in common, shared in the same profession as well as the natural outlooks of our youth, these disclosures created a sympathetic atmosphere. One of mutual confidence. So much so that when they asked me directly: "And how do you do here, Triton? Living out on the very edge?" I almost broke down.

543

Admitting I was an exile of Allectus, his effective military prisoner. A loving father who had not seen his beloved children for a year or two and longed to know how they did.

"Leave it with me...." said Julius Firmicus with a concerned look on his face: "Believe me. As soon as we're back in port, Triton, I'll see what can be done."

Standing watching their liburnian, *'The Ephesus'*, floating slowly off and away from our beach, her oars testing the waves, I had expected very little from his promise. Glad only of their company, and a single kind thought.

Misjudging his resolve.

If I did, I'll admit was wrong.

Three weeks later and in the evening, a decurion and six *equites* from the first cavalry wing, Asturian horse, arrive unannounced at Othona with instructions to remove me overland. An empty mount galloping along behind them on the length of a leading rein,

The one they're intending for me.

In the morning I'm its rider. Hands tied together, blindfold tight over my eyes. As if there was any way out of Othona other than riding west over the flatness of fields. Any question where we're going. No-one talks to me or explains things further, although I know and they know. The Asturians may not be talkative men but they look after me well enough, providing food and a mouthful of soldier's wine every time we stop.

Which is fairly often.

It is a long way to go on horseback in so very little time and soon I am feeling bruised and sore. Yet when by the second morning we are galloping in through a set of city gates, I know Londinium by its noise and fuming at once. Crossing a lengthy river-bridge to clinch my identification. The smell of warm horse muck and hot food, of sewers and scent; combining with the cries of travellers and children, shouts of hawkers and workmen. Banging of hammers, rattling of carts. A heady turmoil beyond exciting for a lonely watchman just relieved from his post, if only for a day. Someone who's spent nigh-on two years of his life just looking out to sea. Counting the waves.

Riding along at the back, restrained in this way, I am an obvious other. Their captive, an outcast. A victim of sorts, offences unknown. The stinking pieces of vegetable matter or

544

worse which occasionally hit me, accompanying curses from the roadside, are their popular reward for my status. Yet if those administering these punishments have no way of divining or judging my wrong, my evil "*unto their day*" - as a man I met later would put it - it's good enough for them.

Despite this hard treatment, I cannot see anything more useful through the blindfold but remain determined to work out our route. Remember when sun falls on my face. Eventually, when I can feel it shining from my right, hear flagstones ringing under our hooves in what sounds like a confined space; the Asturian decurion orders our column to stop.

Somebody drags me off the horse and at least troubles to catch me before my face smashes into the courtyard floor. As I am pulled upright and onto my feet, then led at the double on a rope inside a building where I can hear voices echoing in corridors, sense the draughts from air currents blown in from either side. Feel the rasp of my hobnailed seaboots on what seem like the *tesserae* of a mosaic floor. An important building, in short. Prestige and probably government's.

Here in Londinium. The Governor's Palace as-was, I'm left in no doubt. Near my old office, poor *Squintgob*'s little place. Wondering where he is now: probably dead.

And no sign of Livius Gallus?

They push me into a room and I hear more commands being barked, but this time not from Asturians. They are given in a tongue I do not understand whose ring is Germanic. I am shoved onto a wooden chair where the blindfold is torn roughly from my head. Even the indoor light is an affront to my eyeballs after two days covered-over, but I cannot shield them because my hands stay tied behind my back and fastened to the chair.

When I get used to the light, my new guards are Frankish warriors. Allectus' personal bodyguard, dressed in ringmail shirts and carrying their unique fighting axes.

Why I am glad to have been able to hide my *seax* before leaving, locked in our headquarters' vaults. Knowing her hilt would have been molten red by now, gleaming like dragon's-eye. Taking out throats. While the Franks stand in each corner, leaning negligently on their spears and looking down at me with contempt. Not realising their lucky escape.

545

I take in all the detail, soaking it up mentally for use another day. Memorise their faces for the future, listing for revenge. The room itself is quite large, some sort of audience chamber, and there is a long table across its width about ten paces forward of the chair I'm tied in, four wooden stools set beyond it. All the walls are decorated with dark red squares, lined out with yellow and a series of mock marble pillars painted to look three-dimensional. A line of four, round-topped doors across the far end, any of which could be false.

I find out soon enough which are not when two of them open, and through each comes a woman dressed in the formal *stola*, pulling a child by the hand.

Lucia and Victor.

My daughter is white faced but composed, forcing a smile, but little Victor sobbing away helplessly, a rag to his mouth. Each of them held by a harridan of the emperor's household.

"Here is your father" says the taller of these harpies, a big-footed blonde with square-cut hair and red lips whose beaky nose makes her look more like a man: "Tell him how you are, and how nicely you're treated."

"Hallo, dearest *pater*, it is lovely to see you. Don't worry about us. Uncle Allectus has been very kind. Kept us quite safe. Victor is not like this normally, not with his toys...."

The woman holding Victor is tawny and shrill with a smile like a snake's, but crouches down towards him in the sort of attentive position an infant might mistake for kindness:

"Show your daddy what you have brought him, Victor, the present you want to give. So he knows you're all right..."

The sobs still come in gasps but my brave boy is fighting hard to be in possession of himself, show his father the way, and I am fighting back tears for myself. His tiny crumpled hand opens up like a flower to reveal a small chunk of greeny-brown metal.

"For Daddy..." he says "...to remind him of me!" and somehow blinks a grin through his tears, like sunshine through rain. I try and reach forward but a Frank grabs me and throws me back against the chair, so hard it almost leaves me breathless.

"I'm coming back for you, my darlings. One day, believe me...!" I roar, and then these witch-like women scurry to scoop the children up and pull them away. Out through the doors at the end of the room as if a savage lion were escaped from the arena, Franci moving in front to bar my way. One of them, a thin man with a long moustache, bends down to the floor and carefully picks the piece of metal up, then stuffs it down my tunic.

"Thank you!" I gasp to him in latin, before another of his comrades hits me.

With the blindfold back on, and on my way back out to the courtyard, I get quite a few more kicks and beatings to go with it from his other Frankish friends, but all I can feel is the weight of Victor's gift bobbing about inside my shirt. Held by my belt, leaving me happy.

Ridden back at maximum speed to Othona by the Asturians, my legs tied under the horse again. So that when they cut me off at the other end and lower me down to the floor, my body rigid with pain, their decurion kneels beside me to whisper in my ear:

"I'm very sorry, sir, if the ride back felt a bit rough, but we were only obeying orders."

"Sorry?" I say. "Sorry? But I cannot thank you men enough! Thanks to you, I am a father who has finally seen his children, and that's all that matters to me...."

My men carry me to the newly restored bath-house and deposit me in its hottest room. As the warmth gradually loosens my muscles and comforts the bruising, I roll a chunk of corroded bronze backwards and forwards in my hand.

Backwards and forwards.

A model of the forward quarters, the prow and ram, of a proper Roman bireme. An authentic depiction of the frontal part of any of my ships, the '*Calliope*' included. And stamped underneath with those evocative initials: '*CL.BR*'.

Classis Britannica.

A gift from my son.

"When this defence is raised, the prosecution has the burden of satisfying the jury so that they are sure that the defendant was not acting in self-defence. A defendant is entitled to use reasonable force to protect himself, for others for whom he is responsible and his property. (See Beckford–v-R [1988] 1 AC 130). In judging whether the defendant had only used reasonable force, the jury has to take into account all the circumstances, including the situation as the defendant honestly believes it to be at the time, when he was defending himself. It does not matter if the defendant was mistaken in his belief as long as his belief was genuine."

Judgement in <u>R-v-Martin (Tony)</u> [2003]
Queens Bench Division

Ed had grown to love this place. So different to the industrial Wearside and Teesside of his childhood and teenage years. Peerless example of a wilderness and landscapes it took multiple camping adventures across north Northumberland and the Durham dales, enforced by the youth and probation workers whose patient advice he so steadfastly rejected, to teach him to appreciate. Realise how lucky he was, as he now tells himself.

Lucky to have escaped the depressing environments those difficult years and an early career in petty crime looked set to condemn him to, forever. The town boy who'd learned how to survive on his own in the country. Integral to his ways, rejecting other people. How to make shelters and catch game; light fires and live rough. Shoot and trap. Those outdoor skills which should have made his escape from an unhappy home and background all the more complete, but only threaten to drag him the more thoroughly back. Once the *'Nighthawk Men'* in their sinister black working-gear come along, hear about him. Decide to enlist him in their nocturnal plundering of our history, mining the past.

Whether he liked it or not.

It was they who'd homed-in on him, of course. Not the other way around. Identified him as the loner who, before it closed, spent his winter afternoons in the central public library. Chose to read history books in the reference section, not *'Horseracing News'* like the dossers. His preference for paper maps over 'sat-nav' why he could navigate cross-country in a pitch dark using only the stars. Hide from pursuers in suitable ditches during the day. Eighteen months service with the TA - Territorial Army - what taught him those skills. Before they threw him out. Partly for cheek, partly for stealing kit.

"An ideal candidate for the job in hand" announced Jay-Dee, the bent antique dealer from Sedgefield who talked like a vicar and always wore a suit. Silk handkerchief in his top pocket. The fixer who organised their ring, recruited its footsoldiers. Received their finds then lied about what he sold them on for. Paying his hawkers in drugs, kicks and threats instead. Told him he was 'in'.

Wanted Ed back on heroin, to be their obedient junkie.

Why it took Ed's arrest red-handed with a metal-detector on the site of a Roman fort, wearing his stolen TA camo', to rescue him. To save him from Jay-Dee and his merry men. That and the brilliance of Tony 'The Pony' and his clever guy in the wig. What Ed, like all criminals wishing to sound big, always enjoyed referring to as *'his'* barrister.

'Mister' Bill Carriss, who knocked down a police case so strong that it looked at the time like the Prosecution were going to be able to lock Ed up for the next twenty years. Throw away the key. Came up with a brilliant deal instead. Fobbed off the CPS, ran rings round the judge. Got Ed out of jail.

Whatever people may say about Edwin Ramillies Graham, and they probably say quite a lot down in The 'Pools, much of it bad, he is loyal. A man knows who he owes.

In the case of Mister Cariss, not to mention his saintly wife 'Ness' as he was allowed to call her, this was an enormous amount. Not only had Mister Cariss dug him out of big doo-doo up at the Crown Court, but he and Mrs Cariss had decided afterwards that there was only one way to protect Ed, for the inevitable time when Jay-Dee and the *'Nighthawk Men'* came a-calling. Touring his usual Wearside haunts, looking to recruit him again. Get him back on the smack.

"Come and work for us, Ed..." they'd both suggested. "Up in the Borders, lying low. Your old gang won't find you up here. You can look after our grounds. Maintain the paintwork, mind the exterior. Keep down the pigeons, stop those flipping rabbits from digging up our lawn. Act as a gateman. Get off the habit. Don't worry, we'll pay you a basic wage and you can sleep in the stables. The old farrier's room rent-free."

The best offer he'd had in his whole life and he knew it. Ed would do anything for Bill and 'Ness', and anything for Stipend Howe. He'd never seen an old building so beautiful, its every quirky feature a source of quiet delight, while no-one had ever shown such trust or expectation in him before. Ed was determined not to let the Carisses down.

Ed worked hard. He mowed the lawns and weeded the borders. Raked the drive and pruned the roses. Gathered fallen leaves and painted the woodwork. Chopped firewood and cleaned out gutters. Removed rubbish and sorted recycling.

Cleaned the cars and fed the horses. Shot every form of vermin.

The how and why behind his developing routine of going out very early on summer mornings just before dawn, to catch the rabbits as soon as they arrived to attack the small knot garden sheltering below the stone pele tower. Ness's pride and joy. She'd told him that this exact design of lawn and the pattern of box hedging it was laid-out in could be clearly seen in old engravings of Stipend Howe dating back to the eighteenth century and beyond. Even if these were hardly likely to be the original plants, she thought the appearance of this part of the house and grounds stayed pretty much unchanged from how it would have looked back in the bad old days. Time of the Border Reivers.

"You're a Graham…" 'Ness' had once pointed out to him in her frank and lively way: "Among the most notorious of Reiving families. Cursed by the Bishop of Glasgow. Probably making you into one yourself, Ed, a product of their line. So what do you think of that for an idea? Maybe explaining quite a bit about you, don't you think? In the genes. Have you ever thought of investigating your family tree properly? Seeing if you really are descended from Reivers. And wouldn't you like to know? Because it's dead easy, Ed, looking them up on the internet….."

Ed preferred not to. Dead was how he preferred most of his relatives. After what they'd done, or not done, for him. Wrongs laid onto a son, sins of the fathers. What love he had left in him now was kept for places. For the secret places of his teenage wanderings or special ones like these. Like Stipend Howe, the refuge and safety it gave him. The peace, the dignity. That sense of purpose.

Ed thought he would willingly die to protect Bill and 'Ness' or Stipend Howe. The island of calm this house had come to represent for him in a hard world which till now had only sought to break him. His personal cathedral of Redesdale, the nearest thing for a man who'd never entered a church to recognising a sanctified place. Responding to its call as he now did from his vantage.

Ed shifting from a position of squatting on his heels to lean against a solitary silver birch. High on that shoulder of crag which rears beyond The Howe's old boundary-wall. Topped with

551

a hollow, stony crater marking the site of an ancient burial mound which gives the place its name. On that rocky outcrop which gives him such a perfect view and line of fire, straight down into the knot garden below. The vantage where he always comes to pick off rabbits in the dawn; a high-powered shotgun of Bill's taken from its locked cabinet in the kitchen and laid across camouflaged knees. Ten gauge, semi-automatic. Loaded and ready for action, another one like it hung over his back in case.

Remembering what she'd told him.

Her exciting stories about the reivers - all those Armstrongs and Elliotts, Nicols and Grahams. He liked how Mrs Cariss took time to talk to him when she was passing, the lively way she told it. Tripping away over the yard afterwards, like it didn't matter. Realising she was attractive, but never meant for him. Out of his league. Enjoying remembering later what 'Ness' had explained to him about his ancestors' long-gone world. Imagining what harsh lives they'd lived, out here in Debatable Lands. Those desperate border raiders whose usual impact on village or farmstead had bequeathed the English language their one, eponymous memorial in a single melancholy word:

'Bereaved'.

Ed's fine forebears, and the typical state of those they cruelly left behind.

All that sentimental crap in the tourist information centres about reivers. When everyone round here knew them for what they were. For what they had been - nothing romantic at all. Filthy thugs who robbed their own and their neighbours down to the ground. Reduced everyone around them to poverty and despair. Including themselves. Warlords and tribal tyrants, killers and brutes. Gangmasters and bullies.

Ed had seen enough of their modern equivalents in the back alleys and housing estates of today's north-east. Read enough in Newcastle's central library about the historic reality. And if such learning and bitter experiences combined to teach him anything at all, it was that the only way with bullies is always to stand up to them.

Punch them on the nose.

If 'Ness' and her analyses of history were right; how the Union of the Crowns followed by a robust bout of hanging and deportations together broke the power of the reivers for good; then four hundred-or-so years later Ed could think of a good few night-hawkers or Geordie drug barons who carried on their ways. A clutch of local men who were probably as dangerous. Why he was glad to be out of their scene, well out of it.

Away.

Feeling safe for the first time in his life, in a land which four centuries ago was anything but. Lucky to be paid for pottering about on his new employers' harmless country pursuits. Guarding a stone house which men once built to guard against such attackers. Appreciating the irony in it, defending a pele tower today against *nae worse* a gang of trespassers than some hungry, nibbling bunnies.

Ed chuckled at the thought and his own good fortune. Reminding himself of that classic scene in his favourite comic film. Where the fluffy white rabbit rips off the heads of some of King Arthur's knights, heroes in armour who'd dismissed it as only a bunny.

Now the security sensors had settled down and the lights gone off again, Ed could reach a more serious assessment. Judge how the visibility level stayed pretty-much dark. Think he could make out how much cloud hung around in the dale. Completely covering the rough, unmade road that leads up to Stipend Howe and the head of their valley. Why the house still seemed a grey shadow, boundaries no better than a blur.

This was another disappointingly-wet summer in the Borders and it had rained heavily overnight. Yet again. Why the dampness left behind afterwards took shape in those ghostly swathes of mist he saw rising up from the ground. Low-lying fog and a proper cloud inversion. Though he could sense the night sky growing clearer, so that once the sun rose Ed could imagine a more promising day. Capable of burning off all this water vapour now clogging their ravine. Probably quite briskly, but not yet. Not while the sun remained below the eastern skyline, below the Cheviot *massif*. Still just a golden line on its dark horizon.

No, the sun would have to ascend to the full height of those rounded, grassy humps of mountains before Ed could hope to see properly. See into Ness's beloved knot garden and catch his, her, and its greatest enemy in the open. The rabbits, once

553

they start arriving on the solar promise of another day's warmth to come.

No, not to worry.

If there was one thing country life had taught him, it was patience. So Ed wiped a film of condensation thoughtfully off the metal of his gun-barrel. Checked the shot in its chamber once more. Looked down at his feet.

Thought he heard a noise.

Definitely heard engines.

Vehicles.

Straining up the lane.

They were down below the cloud-base and it was still dark. All the same, he heard them well enough. Vans. Pulling-up and stopping somewhere nearby. Hardly surprising when there was little further they could come. When the house closed the road.

Sounds of doors slamming and low voices, like they imagined they were being quiet.

Clear as a bell.

His relaxed, cheerful mood fading in an instant to be replaced by fear.

Anxiety.

Who would come up here at a time like this?

And what the hell were they after?

Ed's answers were naturally limited to the grimmer imaginings appropriate to his world. Constructed from harsh experience, a life on the streets. He gripped the gun tighter and lay down fully-prone, embracing the ridge. Eyes searching through the murk below for any sign of movement, his steel toe-caps pointing into bracken.

Hearing feet on the road, many feet, but seeing nothing at first.

There was a flipping rabbit in the knot garden!

Ed checked the range - it was right. Bang-on. He could have blown its bloody head off.

But dare not.

'Ness' would never forgive him if the box hedge got eaten.

And he could never leave her in danger.

Then the rabbit scarpered. Something had startled it.

Ed saw the shape of a man scurrying bent-double across the lawn towards the house. Tripping over one of its low hedges and cursing. Then another guy to join him, carrying something red with him that's shaped like a tube. A bloody-big bazooka or some such equipment, how Ed guessed it. Just an infinitesimal improvement in the light to let him see their outline better. Exact way they were dressed.

Swearing to God when he did:

Men in black. Covered from head-to-toe, swarming through the mist. Ed knew then, cringed at the latent horror in his thought. The awful terror of his realisation. At being tracked to this remote spot with no hiding place left him from a people without pity.

His old marrers, the 'Nighthawk Men".

They'd found him!

Incredible.

'Ness' and her kids were alone inside that house and the 'Nighthawk Men' were coming. Gathering below, uniformly-black. Creeping through the gloom and fog. Intending to break in. Come with baseball bats and hats and God-knows-what to reclaim their own. Teach everyone within a painful lesson about never leaving the fold.

Looking for Ed.

Bill Cariss was in London on business and Ed guessed the nearest circulating police vehicle capable of an armed response to be something like forty-plus minutes away. Too slow in the fog, struggling to arrive over difficult, twisting roads. Assuming a regionalised control-room even understood his native's description of distant locations without benefit of postcode. With the Cariss's local 'Community Support Officer' safely tucked-up in bed several villages away, counting the cautions he's administered as 'sanction-detections'....

Edwin Ramillies Graham knew he'd spent his whole life running away from responsibility, always shirking duty, but for the first time ever he felt its hand on his shoulder and chose not to flinch. Because there was a woman who'd treated him with nothing but kindness asleep inside the house, two adorable children beside her. The innocent family of a good man who once stood up to fight for Ed.

Now it was Ed's turn to do likewise.

His finest hour, the moment when he finally drew a line in the sand. Stopped letting people down. Decided to stand up for what was right, for the decent people who opted to help him where so many others had passed-by on the other side. Defending Stipend Howe against mortal danger. Like those few men who kept it long-ago had stood up to the fabled Border Reiver, or lawless raiding Scot.

Ed put the gun to his shoulder and took aim at one of two sinister figures in plain view. Their crouching silhouette. Sliding his finger onto the trigger and holding his breath. Then just as he was about to squeeze, someone who shone like silver walked in through the mist. Right past the pair of them and into his sights. Upright and relaxed.

A tanned athletic-looking man in greyish cloth.

Ed hated men in suits. Whether antique dealers, probation officers, detectives or CPS, they'd always brought him grief. So who to shoot at first?

There was a wooden door at the foot of the pele tower and the men in black had been joined by this third. Ed couldn't get a decent sight on the first two of these black bastards because the man with dark hair in the silver suit was standing with his back to the crag. Between Ed and the black-uniformed creeps crouched down at the door, plotting entry.

Ed lowered the gun while he rethought what to do, and then he heard a terrible, rhythmic banging as the 'Nighthawk Men' start attacking the door. Using that red thing he'd seen them carrying earlier. Silver-suit, who he must take for the leader of this gang though he doesn't recognise him, was joined by a fourth man dressed in black. Together they stood over two similar confederates, watched them hitting the door.

"Any more of this and they'll be in...." groaned Ed to himself. Impaled on the spiked agony of a moment unlike anything known before. Torn by a range of options like no other he'd ever had to face.

"I've got to do something, make a decision. Be a man, not let them get in. Mad buggers, capable of anything. Jesus help me! And God knows, I owe it to Bill, to Ness and the kids. To act, before she comes down to open the door and they grab her...."

The merest thought of this intolerable scenario crystallised his resolve.

Ed sighed and raised the gun to his shoulder again, licking dry lips and carefully taking aim. If he chose to make such an obvious target of himself, then silver-back it must be.

Take out the head of the organisation.

The trigger slides on an oiled pivot and the gun slams backwards into Ed's shoulder, its report reverberating round the narrow valley, bouncing off the fog.

He reaches to reload.

Which one to go for next?

"Given the obligation to interpret legislation in accordance with ECHR rights, under section 3 of the Human Rights Act 1998, the courts would be required to interpret the defence that force used was not 'grossly disproportionate' in light of the State's positive obligations under Articles 2, 3 and 8 (of ECHR - European Convention on Human Rights)."

(Joint Committee on Human Rights: 18th Report 2004-05, House of Lords 111/HC551)

- XXXIV -

We got our marching orders from Othona towards the beginning of the the seventh month of the third calendar year after Carausius was murdered, and I often wondered if they represented a reaction to word getting around about my recent visit to Londinium.

Sent off to the ultimate north. Far away from a coast where Allectus thought I could still cause trouble, up to another, chillier place where I and my crew could usefully die together. Whether of cold, combat or starvation it mattered not to him, but he calculated correctly how well-trained men like us would always obey a neutral military order.

Prisoners in his service by any other name. Military exiles making our way north on foot with not a horse between us, let alone a ship. Leaving Othona reluctantly behind us, empty and unmanned. Its bleak coastline and yawning river-mouth returned to vulnerable. Unwatched. Fending for ourselves while we did so and with more chance left each of us for some deeper thinking on the way. For those private thoughts of vengeance to find themselves competing in a kitbag of trouble with our wider unit-understanding. With those tactical and strategic dangers which any competent soldier could recognise were closing-in fast on a rebel British empire. Conspire from every side.

Including the important realisation how Cousin Fergus was left as the one man in the entire miserable equation shown to honour his vow: the Painted People coming south on his order. Bringing a new war with them, opening-up our second front. Warbands and tribes arriving in a body to dash themselves to pieces against the northern frontier. Impale themselves on places we redundant marines are now ordered to defend, sent there to counter.

Suicidal attacks from a people briefly our allies down the eastern wing of that great system of entrenchments our Roman forebears built to bar their way - the whole width of this island. Formidable defences successfully serving in this noble purpose for so very long. Staying quiet under Carausius but now in total ferment.

Under siege in all sectors and calling-out for help.

To reach them and provide it involved us in a very long walk. Made along the monotonous stone highway which stretches limitless ahead. Over luxurious pasturelands full with belted cattle the property of others, over that linear route men still call their *'Great North Road'*.

Absent any sign of other military movements and precious few civilians, we passed mile after mile of it in solitary transit. Listening to the shuffling tread of our own scuffed seaboots and watching a distant line of hills slowly recede away from us, over on each side. By-passing Eboracum to its east, we found Cataractonium deserted, but that city I'd once reduced by daring we felt too ashamed to enter. So reduced by poverty we must hide from metropolitans. Begging kindness from strangers and the odd scrap from the poor, if my worn-out detachment is to keep itself from starving on the way.

Grovelling for grub.

If this tedious and humiliating slog up from the south coast and Othona took my old ship's company the best part of a fortnight, it was not till the road rose steadily from the plain and the last wayside fort, staging-post, or half-empty settlement was finally behind us that we could recognise the correct latitude. At that point where, tired, hungry and footsore, we noticed columns of smoke hanging high in the upper atmosphere. Whether from beacon-fire or enemy action we knew not. Checked our weapons over, looked coolly at each other. Thought that this would be it.

From atop the final ridge crested, views were boundless on all sides. Breathtaking panoramas. To the right shone the sea and a broad river winding into it: *Tinae Fluvius*, the 'River of Worms'. To our left the ground rose steeply west towards the centre of the country; while directly ahead the road we were following fell away into the ravine cleft by its river. Across whose narrowing width we saw a series of smaller hills rise to command its funnelled gorge. The Emperor's Wall running inexorably over the lot; right to left and east to west. A ripple of solid stone stamped onto the landscape with all the vehemence of a legionary his marching boot. Stating Rome's Might: Inviolable Will.

Beyond this Wall is no 'World's End' but further cultivated lands, albeit few proper buildings. Only the odd scattered farm to be seen today and some rising pillars of smoke. Signs of alarm, symptoms of distress?

No doubt about it. A frontier in tumult.

On the crest of this last rise we pass through a collection of metal workers' sheds and industrial structures clustered round the road. Then the highway turns sharply left and drops down via a well-engineered ramp into the gorge and its shadow. Onto its riverbank and where beside *Tinae* stand the busy wharves and yet more storage buildings. Plus a few freighters still moored at its quayside, and what appears a patrol galley set to guard them. This line of vessels my comrades insist we pause to inspect, if only from the nostalgia of exiles. Men who know themselves shut out from an honourable profession, still crave remembrance of its finer callings.

When they have covered three hundred or more miles on foot in a dozen days, with fighting sure to come, who am I to deny a loyal crew this one simple pleasure? When it may be their last. So it is in the shadow of ships we rest, enjoy the satisfactions of arrival.

Looking ahead to the crossing we're sent to defend.

Pons Aelius, the bridge of Hadrian himself, named after the late emperor's clan. Still decorated after all these years with his bronze-headed likeness, weathered and worn. Its stone pontoons and timber superstructure still the only permanent way to be had across Tinae for many miles around. Where we finally march over it with ringing tread, feeling pleasure in the sound and how the bridge flexes. Knowing these sensations herald the true end to our journey. Glad to be here at last, however that mission may end.

Reaching the river bank on the other side we follow the road as it climbs steeply up again to a small, flat mount adorned with streams tumbling down each side. Escaped from stone culverts made through the Wall itself, we find the hill these rills garland is crowned with the garrison fort of Pons Aelius itself - our final destination.

Walking straight into the *principia*, the headquarters of a part-horsed cohort nearly run out of horses, where I find myself reporting to their ex-legionary commander as if I'm his junior.

"What am I expected to do with a bunch of half-starved sea-rats like your little lot?" demands C.Felicius Simplex, the stone-

561

faced senior tribune in charge whom I knew had served with the Sixth. Probably under Bassianus?

In my salad days of scarlet cloaks and waving helmet crests, as an Imperial heir, I'd once have put him on a charge for addressing me like this. Now the world had moved on and I was little better than the leader of a warband of irregulars, so must take it on the chin.

Besides, this Simplex turned out not such a bad old stick once you got to know him, while life has taught me much distrust of men who always smile.

"Comply with the order which brought us here, grant them their place in the line. You will find they fight like demons, can climb any vertical. Cut ropes and ladders. While if you have catapults there are steady hands among them who can put a ballista bolt through a chieftain's head, at the range of half-a-mile."

"Well, that's as maybe, but you are extra mouths to feed, another draw on my granary" muttered Felicius Simplex in his kindly but ungracious way: "This is an army post, not a public bread-queue."

"Your granary will be ashes, its rations inside, if the Painted People come again and you cannot hold the line."

My best point, and he knew it.

"Oh, very well...."

How it came to be - by the third dawn following our arrival to light upon the battlements of Pons Aelius - that there stood to receive it my green-uniformed spearmen of the Fleet. Holding oval shields, embossed in relief with Neptune's Trident entwined with writhing dolphins, and standing shoulder to shoulder with their bow-legged brothers from his *Cohors Equitata*. Horsemen without horses. Standing together at a shared time of asking, knowing no relief would come. Waiting for a spring tide of blue-dyed barbarians to flow against us, break like a wave.

"How many do you think there are?" I'd asked Simplex as we stood there side-by-side. Soberly watching distant disorderly columns of enemy infantry advancing towards us over the rolling moor that lies beyond the Wall. Chanting their threats, drumming their drums; a glimmer of sunrise turning their upturned faces into copper masks of beaten hate.

"It got harder to judge, once they got to our patrols. Murdered all the scouts. The night before yesterday, we had guessed at three thousand. Today with the sunlight we may lack that intelligence - though now it looks like double...."

These forts of the Wall with their many gates were never built to withstand a siege, but for patrols and policing. Not designed for skulking inside, never the Roman way of waging war, but bequeathing instead a layout ideal for taking initiative through aggression. Opening both gates and marching outside in a body to confront and outflank disorganised enemies in the open. Destroy them with discipline and drill. When we knew that for the original plan but times had changed and perforce our tactics with them.

Defending a fort like this, we few against so many.

From an old garrison whose architecture describes an obsolete strategic confidence. Its walls so low that any tribesman getting below them with a ladder could as easily reach our walkway - not that the army of Hadrian's day allowed anyone so near. Now, just preventing this happening became the best outcome we could hope for.

The only plan we had.

Of his nominal cohort of five hundred soldiers (part-mounted) Felicius Simplex was lucky to be left with three - and no horses. The century represented by my late-arriving crew of 'Calliope' adding one extra. Enough to make me wonder why he first did quibble so.

Four hundred men then, to line his crenellated patrol-walks and stop the uninvited from joining us up there. A thin line to hold a greater one and, at this critical point on its length, all that stands between Caledonia's swarming tribes and the rest of Lower Britain. To shield the unprotected towns of *Britannia Inferior*, its houses and farms, countryside and villages. All those people they contain - whether free or enslaved, innocent or guilty - from murder, rapine and robbery.

From blue locusts on legs.

Four hundred men to prevent a breakthrough.

Not the only mortals along the Wall today envisioning this responsibility, confronting that duty. Something Simplex calmly points out to me in conversation while we wait, mentioning key emplacements by name. Lovingly reciting a string of forts from

563

memory like they were well-taught poetry, a roll-call of old girlfriends: *"Segedunum, Condercum, Vindovala, Onnum, Cilurnum. Brocolitia, Vercovicium, et Aesica... Vindolanda et al"* what he says.

Their unit titles and commanders' names rolling as easily off the tongue. Larger-than-life personalities inhabiting them: those friends, rivals, reprobates and colleagues he clearly knew well. Must trust to guard his flank.

Other forts like ours and ordinary men like us, each one facing a similar dawn. Fearful for their fate. As the semaphore flags soon tell us, beacons proclaim to those troops standing-to. With all of us lining-up to defend a whole line, the more bizarre to find the worthy C.Felicius Simplex taking time for a sermon. Aiming to lift my mood with his unexpected little homily about how fortunate we are. We, its dedicated defenders, entrusted with this important piece of rock, the fort at Pons Aelius.

Fortunate? I simply couldn't believe my ears: "Fortunate, Simplex, the gift of *Fortuna* you say? To find ourselves trapped in a hell-hole like this one, confronting certain death?"

Well, no, that wasn't fair to him because *'blessed'* is what he said, the word he actually used. And no, he didn't mean *'The Goddess'*. No common soldier's term either, I'll grant you, but *'blessed'* is how I remember the senior tribune Simplex describing it to me upon that grisly dawn. For nothing more than the judicious siting of his fort above this bridgehead. The unique layout of its walls, its ingenious defences. As if effective military architecture were the gift of a benevolent deity, not the wisdom of men.

"How lucky we are...." he'd said again.

I ask you.

It turned out I'd teamed-up with yet another follower of the reborn Nazarene. From a cult that seems nowadays to pop-up everywhere in Britain, be typical of my luck. A Christian soldier who's escaped persecution by serving on the emperor's frontier. Hiding from an empire by standing on its edge - rather like me, to be fair.

Another man uncannily at ease in the presence of death. Embracing with enthusiasm what celestial reward his *Christos* promises him after. Ascents into heaven, a life beyond death. Yet behind that sober demeanour and unsmiling seriousness,

I'd been surprised to discover a learned philosopher. Even a reckless optimism of sorts. A man to prove as careless of his own health as he surely was of ours, once enemy arrows flew. A dutiful military officer then, who was boring but brave. Oh yes, brave, I'd freely give him that. Brave *and* spiritual.

"Great is the Lord of Hosts......" said C.Felicius Simplex.

An officer who has somehow survived serving three Roman emperors and commanding numerous troops, while never of their faith. Now recommending that I join him while we await an attack on his walls, in a private prayer of thanks to his god and our joint plea for absolution. With one extra intercession for the little, wandering soul of an unknown military-surveyor. The man from long ago to whom Simplex thinks we owe our deeply dug-in safety.

Such as it was.

"See the mark of a true professional..." says Simplex. Gesturing enthusiastically at how tightly and accurately these angled defences of wall and ditch together enfold the grid of streets and barracks sheltering inside. High on his rock. This minor hilltop he's grown to love, and so skilfully surveyed that it sets him wondering if not the work of *Hadrianus* himself?

With the latter a pagan and a tyrant over whose persecutions of his cult Simplex will admit to anathema, this approval feels odd. Reviled by his biographers for a strange capacity to flit between humane ruler to his people and callous murderer of his friends, Hadrian equally notoriously believed himself to be the foremost designer of his day. That modest self-assessment which any courtier of his discounting would not survive alive. Including the then-most illustrious architect of empire, that foolish Greek who mistook the closeness of a Caesar for safety.

Like we our ditches and dykes.

Though it didn't take long to realise how this unusual tolerance C.Felicius Simplex showed, for a long-gone pagan emperor with blood on his hands, came not as committed Christian but dispassionate historian. An educated local commander who had passed long border winters in private research to further convince him how the legendary Hadrian must once have come here. Arriving by ship to plan and see for himself a start being made on his wall.

565

And if Hadrian really did, then it followed pretty inevitably to Simplex's mind, that both this fort he now had the present honour to command and that magnificent bridge it was his equal duty to defend to the death were each, and as their name suggests, personally founded by the Divine Hadrianus himself. By a god indeed. Even if not one my friend Simplex would ever recognise, let alone make an obeisance to; but someone he at least as architect could respect all the same.

Well, whoever he really was, that anonymous engineer-soldier who, one hundred and seventy years ago, chose this site and built the fort that guards the bridge which bears an emperor's name, mounted on so prominent a rounded knoll, he'd certainly done a good job.

Shaped its circuit of walls so that two sides at least lie guarded by fast-flowing streams to east and west. Each of them descending steeply-south together into a massive gorge pinched to confine *Tinae*. Drew this fort's defences so well that not all sides need ditches. Made the only possible approach for enemy attack that stern frontage his masons dovetail into their planned new frontier.

A bluff northern prospect of close-cut stone so heavily defended with deep earthworks beyond that, nigh-on two centuries later, four hundred Roman soldiers could cheerfully stand behind it. Assemble in the shelter of its massing, rearing bulk. Adjusting their sword straps and bow-strings with something approaching nonchalance, while four thousand or more of the enemy walk rapidly towards them, carrying murder in their hearts.

For Felicius Simplex and myself to await the coming battle with prosaic small-talk about a pet historical theory felt to me eccentric, verging on the comic, but at least it passed the time. Even if the wellbeing of the living was in more-pressing need of prayer, and we both could be dead in an hour, I had resolved on a generous view:

"Why not, Simplex? May a god bless whoever built this refuge. Wherever his spirit and whatever god you have in mind..." I'd said, happy to humour a fellow officer: "And, yes, maybe his soul does float somewhere in the ether beside us, even now. Watching while we his successors put that design to its ultimate test - a frontal attack by Picti!"

Though how a god had sited this fort gave not our only grounds for gratitude.

You know I have always loved catapults. Felt wonder at their power, seen what they can achieve on ships. And on that damp yellow morning at Pons Aelius, I watched a quartet of them winding-up to save a province. Saw their brass-capped headsets nodding on the turrets, shaking under tension. Crews busy feeding them tasty titbits of iron, breaking their fast. Accepting the harsh reality that, if these ferocious war machines couldn't manage the job for us, then we few lines of soldiers would only prove the backstop. A longshot at that.

One that wouldn't last long.

Province be damned! We were not fighting for the civvies, for that assassin Allectus or his tottering British empire. (The Atrebates I never considered). We were fighting for our own survival and the safety of our mates. With the extra thought in my case that I was fighting for my absent little lambs: for Lucia and Victor, wherever Allectus had moved them to by now. For my aged mother, if she lived, and the peculiar integrity of a red sandstone memorial just beyond the northgate of Rutupiae, I'd had raised-up for my wife.

"May Diana preserve us!" I breathe. Wondering if Vaballathus ever got home, or I would.

I look down at my chest and see again that strange light I recognise in its garnets. As if the seax were easing herself upwards out of the scabbard, ready for her lover without being asked. Needing to be held, wanting to be wielded.

"Here they come!" said Felicius Simplex gruffly to his trumpeter, discretely crossing himself, and then we heard their roar. Our trumpets answering back in unison, their single quavering yelp like the hunting cry of an eagle.

Now they were running at us, bare knees going and spears waving. The hairs on the back of my neck under its bronze helmet-guard standing upright at the sight. Swarming like bees over the moor, black in their mass. Recognisably Maeatae.

The fastest of them reach our ditch-lines first only to fall victim to the ankle-breaker, a subtle little slot. A clean, sharp section neatly cut into the bottom of each trench, just big enough to take a foot and recently renewed. Taking a foot by the toe in its welcoming mouth then cruelly wrenching it sideways. Where its latest victims lie, embarrassed but disabled at the bottom of the ditch. Waving their arms in helpless agony and enthusiasm like beetles in a drain. Egging their countrymen on to victory till the whole horde sweeps on and over them, avoiding their fate.

To haul itself in a body up the other, steeper side of this first ditch, before clambering onto the flat glacis beyond it we plant densely with blackthorn. Enough to slow them down, hundreds of half-naked warriors getting tangled in its impenetrable spikes. Scarring their flesh, snagging on their plaid, as they try impatiently to force a way forward through its painful cloying hedging.

Exposed to our flanking fire all the while, where our work must begin in earnest.

The blunt noses of the *ballistae* mounted on our row of northern towers lie permanently depressed, as if reluctant in the taking of life. If that's how they look, it is a false affectation. Facing slightly downwards and set to sweep the whole of this pre-arranged killing-ground, knowing its range to a spear's-length, the truth is they cannot wait. Now it is just a case for their crowding crews of winding-up these incredible engines and delivering their charge. The square-tipped iron bolt on a short wooden shank they drop into a sliding tray between twin firing arms.

That '*clack-clack-clack*' as their gunners wind them back, satisfying '*thwack*' when they go.

Flying into so dense a mass of men every missile finds a target, sometimes passing through two, but never stopping the advance. Those of our men who handle a bow now loosing at will, arrows falling onto the oncoming mob like showers of rain, but still they come on. In a world where life is cheap and here they are spending it.

To those warriors who make it, our second row of ditch and bank probably resembles an obstacle much like the first, repeating its barriers. Those fewer Maetae getting there then trying to cross what seems like another thorn-hedge fall screaming through its branches. Descend into hidden pits.

Those circular, conical manholes our engineers have covered with cut greenery to conceal a welcome crowned-off with thorns. Falling onto sharpened stakes waiting patient at its centre for their single, silent pleasure; impaling all visitors.

'*Lilia*' we Romans call them but if these planted pits less resemble flowers than an insect-eating orchid, something both varieties share in is their capacity for death. The flower of a new-made Maeatae nation now dying inside, screaming of regret. Leaving a soft pathway of victims for their scurrying kinsmen to clamber over, ease relatives' routes over thorn.

The undeserving beneficiaries of another's sacrifice found in the next wave, complacent oncomers for whom we're saving-up some more treats of their own.

Javelin and darts.

Each soldier on the battlements holds four at his disposal, so close they couldn't miss. Where the weight of all that metal when it falls on those below pins the tribesmen to each other. So tight they cannot groan. And yet still they come on, with some carrying ladders:

One of the first to be propped appears in that short stretch of rampart defended by '*Calliope*' marines and I knew what singular honour they'd take its arrival for. Savouring the short wait before a climber comes over, their enjoyment on throwing him back. Hearing his shriek.

Now there are two ladders, warriors leaping off among us, and then there are three. We try desperately to push them all backwards, away from the stonework, but the weight of too many enemies queueing aboard for ascension makes them impossible to budge.

Hand to hand combat, the hour of the *seax*.

While we fight them on the rampart walk, above us on the towers I can see the *ballistae* crews busily working away. Wearing down the tribesmen still crossing our ditches. Steadily reducing the number who can join with a brotherhood that's now vaulting our walls.

Stop us being overwhelmed?

A young warrior with whorls of blue rings tattooed around his eyes, stripes across his forehead, jumps over a dead marine I'd known for years – old Callistus - and comes directly at me. Inexperienced or untrained I know not, but he lashes out wildly.

Tries to hit me full in the face with his shield-boss then stab me with a spear. His aim so poor and reckless that when he misses me with both my *seax* sees his throat exposed, if only for a moment. Strikes it like a snake. Opening him up so quickly I never had time to think.

Going for the red.

Gargling blood and crumpling, the warrior goes down and I kick him out of the way, sending his body off the rampart into crowds fighting below. Going straight without thinking for the next man to leave this ladder, only to find myself facing what turns out to be a giant with an axe. In a foolish challenge I can immediately regret making.

Our line was broken, smoke in the fort, barbarians pouring over the wall and every man for himself. This enormous axeman holding all possible advantage over me, whether in reach, strength or power. Though as my fear of him multiplies, high on a turret there is someone else who's seen it, a friendly archer to calculate my danger.

Someone to watch over me whom I cannot name nor thank, but quickly puts an arrow in the looming axeman's back. Nails it into his vertebrae so he falls like a tree. So saving my life, until the face of yet another opponent appears right in front.

Though this one was different: a tired, baggy-eyed and jowly fellow looking too old for fighting and exhausted by the climb.

Easy meat, to be truthful.

Balding, but with faint traces of ginger like some man I knew before, although I could not think to place him. Bounding along behind him the leggy war-dog some fool among his followers has pushed up the ladder to join them. As grey and brindly as its owner, equally past-it.

I know I could have killed them both in that moment with one sharp swing from a *seax*, and maybe I should, though she felt uncanny heavy in my hand. The light gone out of her hilt, the life from her slice.

Feeling like a refusal, why I looked at him again.

Onengus son of Ferganus.

High King of Monagha and Monapia; Hound of the Venicones, Swordsman to the Maeatae. Warlord to the Painted People.

And about to get an arrow.

"Cousin Fergus!" I shout and leap forward to cover him with my shield, knocking him flat. A flighted shaft hitting Neptune's trident and quivering in its laminate, his dog leaping onto me, all in one instant.

"Cousin Fergus, it is you!" I shout out again:
"Don't you know me for Triton? As a kinsman indeed, your own Carausius' heir?"

5.1   Exercise Saxon Shore will take place from Friday 26th to
Sunday 28th June 2009 and is part of the National Counter-
Terrorist Exercise Programme. The last time Kent exercised
was in 2001, Exercise Caesar's Camp.
5.2   During the exercise both Kent and Essex police will come
together with a wide range of relevant agencies to maximise
corporate learning."

(Extract from public minutes
of the former Kent Police Authority, January 2009)

- 35 -

Aside from all the complex sonar, radar and modern
communications or navigation gear   dominating the scene,
there is also a drop-down TV monitor available on the bridge of
HMS Calliope. Set to the BBC's main satellite news-channel,
twenty-four hours.

William '*Mouse*' Cariss, barrister-at-law, is present among a
subdued group of his fellow-officers watching this monitor while
a pre-recorded announcement is screened. Shown again as a
repeat now that there's no new news forthcoming, it's the first
time that most of them have seen it. Taken last night in what
was then a packed parliamentary chamber but now stands
strangely empty, just a short way up-river from where they are
currently moored. Next to HMS Belfast, floating on the Thames.

"And I would like to convey our very deepest condolences to
the bereaved family of the carabinieri officer who was
unfortunately shot this morning, and indeed to the whole Italian
people...." the outgoing Prime Minster states on national
television. Closing what turned out to be his final Question Time
before a sudden resignation: *"Our thoughts are with them at*
this difficult time."

Among these men and women on the bridge, it is probable
most correct observers would think it reprehensible if their
words and demeanour suggest a greater sense of sympathy, of
solidarity even, for their commissioned comrade aboard.

Demonstrated for him as their friend, the householder in question, rather than this unknown foreign police officer really its victim. The individual tragically reported killed in an armed siege broken-out at Bill's home. Upon British sovereign territory, Bill's alibi unassailable.

Shot in the course of a developing media-event widely thought shocking, even by the standards of all that other toxic fallout still raining down from Brussels. On Europe's crisis and fate. A policing and public relations disaster the usual TV commentators and blogging pundits now loudly proclaim as providing the very last straw towards the toppling of a man - as they seemingly knew all along - his supporters had apparently only intended by to be an 'interim PM'.

Foresights oddly not extending to any idea of his likely successor.

And all of it resulting from this unique confrontation under Cheviot which the police spokeswoman next seen on screen can reluctantly admit to be *"viably still-ongoing, the target premises contained"*. A siege unexpectedly serving to put our man Bill, along with grainy images of his obscure period house taken from the air, at the head of whatever worldwide media remains capable of operating properly this morning. Reliable eastern outlets like *'China Star'* and *'Russia Today'* whose satellites and gizmos somehow stay safe.

In a momentary lapse, the ship's lieutenant-commander briefly puts his hand onto the politician's shoulder: "I'm really sorry about this, Bill. A terrible business. Must come as awful shock."

"Just can't believe it..." mumbles Bill back, visibly hurt by what he is watching. "My wife and kids are in there. I know it's bad about the Italian, but nobody's giving out news of my own family. Saying what's happened to them. Like no-one seems bothered...."

"We are, Bill, I promise you. We are. Look, I'll try military channels, since they're still up. Discover what's going on there now. Check that they're safe..." says the reserve captain, David Oulton OBE. A chartered surveyor in a firm of Newcastle estate agents in his day-job and former client of Bill's, today he's someone else: Calliope's *'owner'*.

So too is Bill, who's feeling hunted yet at the same time oddly-important. Like his own time has arrived. Even if a fast-fading government suddenly won't talk, whether to him or indeed anyone, but maybe the reason why Bill doesn't address the ship's master as '*sir*' but by his first name.

"So what do you plan on doing about me, David?" he asks.

"What do you mean, Bill?"

"You know it was me they were after. Me and mine. Are you going to hand us over?"

"What do you think? Who to, and on what grounds, for God's sake? No way! Though I think your little appointment in Whitehall might be off. At least till we know which way the wind at COBRA's blowing. Why Parliament is closed, what they do about the King."

The TV monitor cuts to a library still photograph of the Italian Foreign Minister, a cultured man whose self-restraint in delivery belies the fury contained in his words:

"*An outrage close to act of war! This English government - whoever's in charge of it - needs to decide what it's going to do. Where real priorities lie. Get a grip on dissent, defer to EU authority and return to the fold. Forget all this nonsense about a referendum, do its legal duty under Lisbon. Or else face international consequences - be lonely in the world.*"

"Stay on board Calliope, Bill, while things work through here" says the captain quietly. "You know that we're with you and you're safe with us. We'll keep you under wraps...."

Bill shakes his hand in silent gratitude. Outside, he could see ratings throwing off the mooring lines. He knew the minesweeper was preparing to put to sea again, readying to slip down the Thames. Next move in the crisis.

The following head and shoulders to pop up on the monitor were more familiar and this time shown live. The recently-appointed Chief Constable to England's newest police force, its "*northeastern constabulary*". Confronting reporters at press conference, a bruiser at bay.

The redoubtable Viv Mallory: folded bare arms bulging from beneath a short-sleeved white shirt under silver-braided epaulettes, evoking pink hams. Iron-grey hair to match the glint of her braid, cut back to the skull. "*Malla*" her officers affectionately dub their boss, but Bill knows her steel of old. As erstwhile combatants from the Newcastle-upon-Tyne Magistrates Court of years ago: she as sergeant-witness and he of junior counsel. Sergeant-at-law. Respecting the unflinching determination of a committed professional in a world that's come full-circle. Gone seriously mad.

Now he finds his old sparring-partner from the courtroom is senior officer in charge of an ongoing firearms operation laid around his beloved home of Stipend Howe. Their police 'Gold Commander' for the search that became a raid; the raid that escalated into a siege. Their boss making a formidable opponent for anyone holed-up there, he'd readily concede, not just the press. Though Bill is moved to wonder who on earth these mystery sharpshooters could be? If not his own dear Venezia, defending her young to the death. Asking himself who the hell else would be doing all this shooting, why it ever came to this?

A point as baffling to the assembling British press: "*Where are your officers, what good are they doing?*" the metropolitan journo's jibe rudely to Viv. Cornered as she is annoyed to find herself against an objectionable backdrop of hunting-themed wallpaper. Jammed behind a table at the far end of the *'Charles Dickens Diner'*, in this awful gastro-pub she's aghast to discover was her press officer's first choice for what's fast becoming a chaotic conference.

"*Hiding out in the heather? Pleading health & safety before a strategic withdrawal?*"

Like they've sniffed out her weakness, got wind of confusion.

Or as some of the cheekier journalists start asking: "*What the dickens is going on....?*"

Fifteen miles from the besieged house in question, frankly no-one knows. None of her senior officers among the police 'Gold Command' team recently set-up in its *'Nicholas Nickleby Suite'* who can claim to be entirely certain.

Not even their Chief, just arrived herself. Delivered headlong from this year's *'Gender Equality Conference'* in Coventry, come via M1 and A1 in a fast police car whose *'nee-naahs'* kept on blaring all the way. Or so it had seemed at the time, certainly long enough to give Viv a splitting headache. One of her secret migraines when it's the last thing she needs.

Come straight from an annual awards event which she always enjoys, feels so disappointed about leaving. As if she's letting everyone on the circuit down. Those collegiate networks of communal purpose she was successfully cultivating towards whatever future consultancies they might foster. Their promises of well-paid advice work. Saving-up for another time, for when this madness has blown-over and an imminent retirement can blossom into a portfolio of public appointments and comfy 'non-exec's.

Except that now Viv's blotted her copybook and let them all down. Friends and evangelical devisers of impeccable agenda now left casting about for a replacement. Missing a flagship speaker who's fled, leaving the whole event holed below the waterline. Her printed handouts a poor substitute for what everyone knows would have been a memorable talk on "*Investigating Intolerance*", if only given in person. Missing a legendary style sure to have delivered Viv's powerful points in that series of brilliant 'punches' no delegate ever forgets, no interviewee or suspect who faced her was ever spared.

Discovering instead more hand-to-mouth and brutal scenarios confronting her 'troops'. Crouched down in the wilderness beneath a withering fire and the scrutiny of partner agencies, some of them foreign. Banged-up by the border, bothered by governments not solely our own. God knows, a difficult enough operational situation to cope with without finding every normal means for communication currently '*down*'. Even for her, their dedicated 'Gold Commander'. And hardly Viv's personal fault either, nor how she delicately puts it "*...temporary technical issues with Command & Control...*" but still their stark reality.

Why it already feels like she's winging it. Managing by messenger, guessing the unknown. Cursing that Stevie Ryton, who never told Viv of his raid, yet three governments knew. Feeling so exposed before a corps of unsympathetic media observers busily noting things down. Intending to use every single piece of it as evidence against her, caution or no.

But Mallory and these cops of hers are hardly alone. Not when digital chaos is breaking out everywhere, all over Europe and not through solar flares. Her 'Old World' turning 'Third World'. What had been an intermittent nuisance, suddenly a major threat. Financial markets in melt-down again and nobody, not even the computer geeks, with the faintest clue how to stem it. Any idea who's behind it, apart from all the usual suspects, countries with names that end in 'a'. Like China and her PLA, Russia or Persia, to name but a few.

Meanwhile a further naval officer steps forward onto the bridge to join the group glumly watching the Chief Constable on screen. Addressing their commander directly, it's another familiar face: Alec Cadwell himself.

The accountant-turned-hotelier reporting on a successful re-provisioning exercise just completed via HMS Belfast. This huge World War Two battleship was once a museum ship, but is now a floating dormitory and feeding-station for naval crews from an impromptu fleet assembling beside her. Come down here with straightforward orders under the title of *'Exercise Saxon Shore'*. Sent to patrol along the nation's most important river much like they did a good few years ago, back in the Olympics; only to discover that everything 'the book' once took for granted has suddenly somehow changed.

"We're ready to go, sir..." Alec confirms. A long career in hotels has taught him the art of 'just-in-time' delivery. The rare intellectual satisfactions to be won from running a successful commissariat, the importance of supply: "...got everything we need for sea."

"Good work, thank you. Well, carry on, Mister Cadwell. And can you tell me, Number One, update us now on what more news there is from across the Channel?"

"A bit of a blackout, sir, but we're still waiting on Strasbourg..." responds the First Officer. "See which way they jump. Their High Representative for European External Action, Security & Defence, is expected to announce her final decision within the next half hour....."

"And what do you think that'll be?"

"That their decision's already made, sir, exactly as we feared. Consistent with what's been announced. Their stated determination to restore the one, overriding authority. Make whatever interventions are deemed necessary to restore order. And isn't that what they keep telling us, sir? The *'need to prevent anarchy across Europe'*. Discourage other cities from copying Athens, Rome or London. Put tanks in the Mall. Maintain unity and loyalty, restore confidence to the markets. Make us toe the line. Like that guy just said on the TV – *'bring us back into the fold'*. But by the time their announcement goes public I guess it'll be too late, sir. That they'll be onto us by then. Why we've already got traffic on the system reporting Orange forces in the Medway....."

"Forces? What do you mean ' *forces*'?"

"Warships, sir, frigates and infantry landing-craft."

"Frigates? That's frigging outrageous. What the hell do Orange think they're doing? Inside our territorial waters, entering a friendly country?" says their commander, fury in his eyes.

"I'm very sorry, sir, but - with respect - your view's just a bit out of date. You know Britain relinquished that level of national sovereignty long ago, and they're carrying something more powerful than armaments."

"Powerful?"

"High-level legal advice, sir. Claiming all legality rests with Europe's side for whatever they choose to do next. Quoting treaties we signed years ago but no-one remembers. Why they are saying the RRF - Europe's Rapid Reaction Force - is entitled to react immediately. Do what we think it's going to, restore their status quo. And why I suspect Orange ships sailing up the Medway will prove only the advance guard. Its first instalment, sir. Plenty more to come. Maybe from Blue, or even Red and Black. Germany, the Rhineland."

"And our small squadron here is putting out to sea, to meet with that little lot?"

"If that's what you finally decide, sir, then those would seem to be the odds. Though I'm unsure on what orders you rely. When it's feeling much like meltdown, as if each to his own. Prime Minister gone, the Scots' Self-Defence Force refusing to help, and our Home Sea Lord suddenly disappearing. Gone AWOL in a taxi and no one left who'll say."

"Kidnapped from Whitehall?"

"Quite possibly, sir, what we're starting to suspect, but no way of getting him back. Government seeming too distracted to care, visibly falling apart."

"If the top man at the navy desk has been taken-out, then the PM walks away, where does that leave us ordinary mariners? Apart from wondering what they expect from us in all this chaos. Or should we just dust down the manual, revert to 'Exercise Saxon Shore'?"

"Another staple that seems to have withered on the vine, sir. Lost any relevance. With nothing known to take its place, total silence from Admiralty. An operational and decision-making vacuum, to be frank. And when the navy's got so few ships left operational, maybe it's academic. Not unless it's NATO's last-ditch alternative in the back of your mind....?

"You mean 'Operation Gladius'?"

"Never mentioned in orders, sir, not in more recent procedure. Not for years, anyway...."

"When there aren't any to be had, then bugger bloody orders! Without any to go on, then everyone will recognise 'Gladius' for representing all we've got left. What it's got to be. If parliament only stands secondary in our nation's constitution, then chooses to be silent. When servants like us swore oaths of loyalty to the Crown, we at least know where our duty lies. Never swore likewise to a government abandoning its own. So if there's no better practical option, Number One, let's go to with a will. Pell-mell and devil take the hindmost."

"Are you absolutely sure, David, that this is really wise?" asks Bill in his first intervention.

"Yes, Bill, in defence of the realm. As our final default option and ultimate duty, I really think it is. The right course and now realising it for all that's left us: to attack, only attack!"

Bill may not be the most senior officer on this vessel but now holds a status all his own. Witness a government invitation withdrawn, by a government now withdrawing. Sensing his hour has come and that critical discussions aboard are tackling constitutional issues where he's approaching authoritative. Gaining confidence to question his erstwhile commander.

"So you are telling us, Lieutenant-Commander Oulton, that you are set on removing this flimsy barque from station and taking her off to bar the Medway? Completely alone? Expecting a plastic tub armed with one pom-pom gun and a pair of large calibre machine guns to be enough to dissuade a flotilla of fully-armed foreign warships?"

"Yes, Mister Cariss, sir. I think that's the general idea."

"And if your modest armament proves insufficient.....?"

"Why then they should realise we are left with no option. I suppose we will ram."

579

"The core element of such a fiscal union ....consists in strict and effective budgetary rules that set a binding ceiling on national borrowing........... In the event of a country not abiding by the budgetary rules, national sovereignty would be automatically transferred to the European level on a scale that can ensure compliance with the objectives.....In effect, national sovereignty would be largely retained and fiscal policy decision-making capabilities and room for manoeuvre would be preserved, as a long as a country in question complies with the limits on borrowing and debt....First, a fiscal union has to be equipped with comprehensive democratic legitimacy. It is a matter of a quantum leap. European integration would be noticeably extended, and national sovereignty and determination would be handed over."

(Extracts* from a speech made by Dr Jens Weidmann, President of the Deutsche Bundesbank, to the European Economic Forum; Mannheim-on-Rhine, 14th June 2012)

*Source: *"Everything flows..."* DB Communications dept.
www.bundesbank.de

It was much, much later, and only when order had finally been restored to the Emperor's Wall; the Maeatae and Picti reluctantly persuaded to disengage along its entire length; that a strange form of truce descended. For a short while only but, on this our north-east station, the return of a *status quo* that meant something of Rome could keep hold of her northern entrenchments. Cling on to some remnant of her former dignities, reminders of past glory.

A new northern form of Rome, one that's deliberately cut itself off from the real Rome, geographically and politically, yet still longs at heart to be part of her. Believing itself the same, wanting to recreate her ways from splendid isolation yet be spared her decline.

Pining away for something, for an idea the Mother City can no longer even attain herself. Sidelined as she and her venerable Senate are now become by our latest crop of Caesars. Left bitter and deserted by eastern men bereft of sentiment, mediocrities born of the camps. Illyrians of the plain who prefer the safer, softer pleasures of Mediolanum or Treverorum, Byzantium or Antioch, and never the Eternal City: *Romae Aeternae* herself.

We ourselves of this distant, British empire visibly failing too. Failing Carausius. Fearing already for his dream of an insular embodiment to ancient Roman values. Of restoring that Golden Age which a great man whose unworthy servants so pointlessly killed him promised we'd all come to enjoy. Leaving what poets call our *'island of usurpers'* ever more isolated. Fearful secessionists held in the weakening grip of their saviour's cowardly assassin. Hanging-on and running out of money, running out of legitimacy. Waiting in the rain for a brace of Balkan shepherds' sons to come and claim Britannia back.

More cruelly than Maeatae would.

"I'd guessed who you were, you know..." said Simplex to me privately while his men recovered twisted bodies out the *lilia* to hand back to their people. "From the day you arrived here. I recognised you from Eboracum, from my time with the legion. And that sword. From seeing you address a crowd of soldiers outside the arena there, probably only moments after

Bassianus had died. That year Carausius took power. Just a shame it took your Pictish friend so long to make the link for himself, understand what you were saying."

I grinned ruefully, nursing a dog-bite to my thigh which now looked to be going bad. Even though I say it myself, what I'd said to him there on the battlements of Pons Aelius was little short of inspired. All the while that me, Fergus, and the dog were struggling with each other. Me striving to save the king from one of our marksmen: that well-intentioned archer in a tower who'd already despatched a giant with an axe, now notched his bow for another.

The dog biting everyone.

What presence of mind I'd had in remembering his parting shot from years ago, that afternoon we rode out through the ghost-fence of his southernmost *coria* in all Pictavia; my quickness in quoting him back: *"My word. And my peoples' word. You have yourself a treaty. When you are gone, we will come south and then there will be no stopping us. We will sweep the Eagles into the sea. But, until then, you have our word."*

When a son of Carausius, albeit an adopted one, held the fort at Pons Aelius, then his line was not fully gone and the Painted People dare not, could not, break a High King's sacred word. Should not come south, no matter how many of their young men's lives had just been wasted trying to. Their gods' punishment for breach, for perjury, how his superstitious peoples took it.

Why the word had gone out from a High King standing up on the height of our ramparts, arms apart in silent command; that day they so very nearly overwhelmed us, smashing through Roman *limes*. His order to go back, to go back and wait. Be patient for revenge.

How we disengaged, that day I saved the bridgehead at Pons Aelius and our furthermost province with it. For the benefit of a murdering accountant and in memory of both my fathers; the sake of a precious family.

Wherever they were by now.

A thought to set me wondering what I could do to help them from so very far away, if only I could get chance. Knowing that if I wrote to the latest locations where Allectus might have moved my children to, the chances of any message being intercepted and read by spies, of stirring up a fresh wasp's nest of danger for them in response, were simply too high. When I did not wish to provoke Allectus again, not for my own selfish sake but theirs. Why I compromised the extent of enquiry by limiting any letter-writing to my mother. Sending it *via* my father's *collegium*, his old network of corn factors, to the two alternative addresses where I thought she still might be. To tell her where I was now, her grandchildren seen last.

"At Rutupiae, or if not, at Calleva."

As it turned out, I need not have worried about Lord Allectus himself. He soon had more important things to worry about than the custody of my darlings, or where I addressed correspondence. A point confirmed by the elderly captain of a supply ship which crawled up the river and moored alone at the quay, his crew of two nearly as old as he was. Come to collect supplies now the fighting was over, not bring them, as he brusquely explained. Silver and lead from the mines, timber and coal from the workings, and all the other basic raw materials his master was barred from obtaining elsewhere, on the continent.

In any quantity, by now.

Where once again it is traders we rely on for the first rumours of an imminent invasion.

Panic inside the walls of Londinium what he describes, as its troops were rushed to the coast on numerous false alarms. Except half of Allectus's army weren't proper soldiers anymore but paid German mercenaries. Recruited off the Rhine and billeted on the town, very much against residents' wishes. Broad-belted bully-boys, swaggering round the city with fewer regulars left to contain them, keep them in check.

A picture of growing chaos in the provincial capital and its streets to alarm me all the more. Give unwelcome thoughts to plague me, once I realise the threat to where I guessed Allectus kept my precious children. There at the heart of these ructions, held prisoner in that new wooden palace we heard Allectus was building for himself, 'protected' by nothing better than Franks.

Hostage to their father's good behaviour.

While the Picti kept to their truce and Londinium whirled in confusion, I and my men were trapped far-away here. Stuck beside Tinae with time on our hands, we helped Simplex and

583

what was left of his cohort repair the damaged defences of their fort. Adding some extra ones for luck, like the stone-throwing engines he carted in from Arbeia to supplement the bolt-firers. Deliveries of rubble to be slowly chipped-away by soldiers and some drafted-in locals into a selection of enormous stone balls, ready to lob.

In what little off-duty time Simplex allowed us, some of the men from '*Calliope*' liked to wander off down through the *vicus* and onto the quayside below to look at the ships. Sit by the river, watch them come and go. Gossip with the sailors. Bring back some news.

Where they rapidly realised that the river patrol-vessel moored among the merchantmen had not been used in ages. Its oak hull and masts faded to a light, silvery-grey, the ropework snagged and rotting. Green slime accumulating round the waterline where it hadn't moved for so long.

Something I asked Simplex about one morning in the headquarters building, while we sat together in his tiny office and he devotedly wrote his latest commander's report out in a good and stylish hand, with no knowledge or idea who would ever bother to read it.

"That derelict boat on the harbourside…"

"You mean the old patrol cutter?"

"Yes, some of my marines, those with sailing skills, have been poking round the hull. Hankering after fixing it, getting her seaworthy again. Seeing space for fifty rowers on the benches either side, imagining enough of themselves probably left to run her."

"Oh, really? It's not been used for a year or so, with no one left here knowing how."

"Would it be worth doing?"

Simplex put his pen deliberately down besides its pottery inkwell on a pile of bark noting-sheets, pushed his chair back against the office wall and slowly scratched his head:

"Mmm, it's definitely worth a thought, Triton. There were two originally, I'm told, both meant for patrolling between here and the rivermouth. The other one sank before I arrived. Mainly meant to stop Pictish raiding boats coming down the coast, I suppose, not that they're likely to get so far up-river as here. Little chance of that, not with Arbeia and Segedunum forts to

get past first. Still, if you thought she could be recommissioned, I'd have thought it useful. An extra line of defence for the bridge, if nothing else."

"Thanks. In that case, I'll get them on with starting, first thing in the morning. Gathering materials. Trees and nails and tar. A project like that should be good for their morale. Give my sailors something useful to occupy themselves with......" I promised, encouraged by his support.

Simplex smiled: "No, thank you, my friend. New forms of hard work are good for enlisted men, and thanks are due to God for granting us any focus that can keep them from sinning. Whether your men or mine. From drink or the sins of the flesh, when we're all under pressure. Everyone on a knife-edge waiting for what happens in the south, what it means for us here. Whether the Picti return. And with such uncertainty in the ranks, we officers should set a good example, Triton. Demonstrate to the slothful how honest men use their time....."

I was using mine in planning an escape, but wouldn't tell Simplex that. Not yet anyhow, not while my men of *Calliope* were throwing themselves into the restoration of this old patrol boat with a motivation and enthusiasm not seen in their tired faces for many a long month. A pleasure to witness.

"What shall we call it, sir?" a delegation asked me, pointing to the soaking hulk they'd just successfully man-hauled over rollers onto the southern bank. Ready to refit.

"What do you have in mind?"

"With your permission, sir, we'd like her as another Calliope. Remind us of the first."

So "*Calliope*" she became, as if her spirit lived once more among these tattered exiles of the *Classis*.

An important first step, because once a ship had a name, she had a soul; and once she had a soul, these mariners were magicians. Could breathe fresh life into the most aged wooden frame. Make her live again to dance across the waves.

On a voyage none of us intended.

*"It's a question of what do British people want to do? Do you
want to be an independent nation, or do you want to be a
county in Europe?"*

(John Bolton Esq. former US ambassador to UN, 2012)

- 36 -

These horses could do sixty miles a day cross-country, easily;
even over northern hills. On a good day, one hundred.

A lost breed of Galloway ponies whose DNA Bill and Venezia
once paid a fortune to a team of veterinary scientists and
specialist breeders to recover on their behalf. Extracted from
that rag-tag collection of likely nags they first identified by
surveillance and then pursued relentlessly through all the horse
fairs and travellers' camps of Britain's north-west. Commercial
laboratories waving big money and a glass jar at their owners,
all the way from Appleby to Dumfries, Aintree to Dumbarton.

Surefooted, inexhaustible and fast, these primitive ponies
resulting filled the Cariss's upland paddocks with the nearest
inheritors imaginable to legendary beasts. Horses once ferrying
armed men from the fastness of Liddesdale to terrorise the
town walls of Newcastle. Reivers come to taunt England's
Warden of the Marches, show him their limits to government's
temporal power.

Equine archaeology.

Now it was an undulating line of them which carried Venezia,
myself, and her children, high over Cheviot and briskly away
from danger. Trotting away from Stipend Howe and up out of
Redesdale into the morning mist. Out of the old English county
of Northumberland, now her *'northeast region'*; into another
country, almost another time.

Even as Edwin Ramillies Graham was setting the last of that
line of farmer's crow-scarers he'd laid on the roof. Timing them
to produce the regular series of loud 'bangs' we soon heard and
he rightly thought sufficient to keep his attackers heads-down in
the bracken.

Cowering while we fled.

586

Last man out, Ed finally caught up with us later on a faster, similar horse high in the hills beyond Kirk Yetholm. Never mentioning what he's done. Only babbling of the *'Nighthawk Men',* sweating and crying. Carrying Bill's guns and ammo'; not recognising me. On our urgent way north together, out of the jurisdiction and over the border. Riding into an independent Scotland as sure to obstruct our removal into England as we knew our homeland would be surrender us blindly into other regimes asking.

Putting our trust in contrary minds and a system of Scots law-enforcement pointedly dragging its feet. Keen after Lockerbie to remind its English counterpart of who is the boss. Giving us hope of lengthy intermissions and diversions, where our little party could quietly disappear in the meantime. Onto the next stage of its journey (a vessel for London?) before anyone else came round.

Looking to find Bill.

And the Cross being outlawed, I would swear on the CPS Policy Manual or whatever book of rules you care to name that neither Venezia Cariss nor myself, nor any of the twelve loyal local men who appeared out of the heather to join us like ghosts, held any idea then of that dreadful thing Ed did.

That an innocent man had died. Let alone a policeman, the Italian.

Fifteen horses it was that came in single-file over the tussocky grassland of Hedgehope. Fleeing as innocents how we thought it. From organised crime, if not a political persecution.

The one thought in our heads.

"The division of Europe into a number of independent states, connected however with each other by the general resemblance of religion, language and manners, is productive of the most beneficial consequences to the liberty of mankind. A modern tyrant, who should find no resistance either in his own breast, or in his people, would soon experience a gentle restraint from the example of his equals, the dread of present censure, the advice of his allies, and the apprehension of his enemies. The object of his displeasure, escaping from the narrow limits of his dominions, would easily obtain, in a happier climate, a secure refuge, a new fortune adequate to his merit, the freedom of complaint, and perhaps the means of revenge.

But the empire of the Romans filled the world, and when that empire fell into the hands of a single person, the world became a safe and dreary prison for his enemies."

('The Decline And Fall of The Roman Empire'
Edward Gibbon, 1787)

- XXXVI -

It was about nine or ten days after my men began their restoration works on *"Calliope"* that I was sitting out in the midday sunshine on a folding campaign-chair. Intending to supervise them from across the other side of the river, with another similar chair set out in front of me to take the weight off my bad leg, when I saw a small group of hooded travellers on foot come down the ramp then start to cross the Bridge of Hadrian.

Hardly an uncommon sight.

I was placed on a stone terrace slightly up from the ship-moorings, which gave me enough elevation to keep an eye on the men working opposite, but not enough to see over the bridge parapet while new arrivals crossed. Normally I would have been standing, but our unit medical officer, the *medicus castrensis*, had just changed the dressing on my leg for the first time in ages and not been impressed by what he saw. Shaking his head woefully and saying over and over:

"Dear, oh, dear! Never seen a dog-bite like it, sir, nor one less keen to heal...."

Why I was stuck there in my undress uniform like an invalid, sitting on the quayside at Pons Aelius when this latest group of wayfarers came down off the bridge and started to make their way over in a body towards me. Seeing them coming, making such a beeline for where I sat, I sighed heavily. Expecting the usual stupid questions such travellers tend to reserve for officers at ease. Like we were put there to be a source of public information, not the scourge of fighting men.

Stuck there on my throne.

A cloaked man with a thumb-stick striding boldly forwards towards me. Beside him an elderly woman, arthritis in her hips. Rolling painfully along despite it, her motion that of the old *'Minerva'* once her keel hit the beach.

Running ahead of them a small boy, about six to seven years of age.

Running with his arms outstretched, shouting my name. All the way along the riverbank he runs, with his call echoing right across the gorge and back off the banks. The men of new

Calliope high on their lashed-up scaffolding over the other side, stopping work to stand and watch, see what is going on.

Aurelius Victor, my son!

Calling out to his father.

"Daddy, Daddy...!"

I drag myself to my feet and start to hop forwards, determined to meet him halfway yet hardly feeling capable. Managing three slow steps to his every running ten. Behind him I recognise sensible, beautiful Lucia; just nine years old but the image of her mother. Gliding along after him like a self-possessed young lady. Anxious to keep an eye on the naughty little brother, keep him out of the river, but mindful of her grandmother's faltering steps coming on behind.

My mother herself, struggling painfully towards me as if she'd walked all the way here from Rutupiae. Leaning on the arm of this unknown strider with the stick.

Victor runs into my arms and I pick him up then swing him right round like I always used to: though now he's grown almost too big, too heavy for this game, and it pains me much to try. Scooping Lucia up as well, the pair of them enfolded in my arms. Priceless, beloved children I feared never to see again. More precious to me than life itself, my hostages to fortune. Escaped from the tyrant, restored to me whole.

May all the Gods be praised, perhaps even that Judaic one C.Felicius Simplex champions on the side. (Though is there anyone to tell me how a supplicant's dues to Him are paid?)

I greet my mother with a hug but she is a correct matron, impatient of demonstrated affection. Knowing well how coldly a Roman officer is expected to behave in front of his men - except only with his children, for whom the sentimentality of soldiers is notorious weakness, a wonder to behold. We cluster in a huddle, a cloud of questions and answers as tangled as our group, when I look up to recognise the walker in the hood:

"Tormentus, it is you! Not even knowing you were alive, but as glad to find you in that state today as I am for myself. But what in the name of the Unconquered Sun God are you doing strolling casually along like this with all my family? How did everyone get here?"

Their story is complex and its tellers half-starved, so we agree to retire into Pons Aelius and the comforts of its fort to discover the details, Simplex and his wife overjoyed to receive us. Pleased at the prospect of travellers' tales and glad to be offering to company the hospitality of their table.

Inside the *praetorium* it is Tormentus of the silver curls who is their narrator, the one-time master-gunner to my squadron and veteran *trierarch* from the *'Caius Volusenus'*. One of barely a dozen men who survived its total-loss, during Carausius's disastrous attempt to raise the Bononia blockade, who escaped back across, he is also the first to come up with anything like a coherent explanation. Once a few victuals are taken onboard, he's gulped down more wine.

"Your mother saw I was back in Calleva and contacted me again through a secret network linked with the *collegium*. Discharged, disabled, disgraced and distrusted former soldiers of Carausius. Men like myself. Asking if we could help. Said how much she feared for your two little lambs in the pens of Allectus. Wondered if a few old seadogs like myself could somehow work to spring them."

"A miracle you clearly wrought, Tormentus, so do not spare us how!"

The oil lamps in the room flicker from shifting air as his sleeved arm points us melodramatically south with an added shiver for emphasis, growling the name: "Those of you who knew Gesoriacum will remember their Egyptian general, Julius Asclepiodotus. Officer of its garrison, late ornament to the legion. That apostate who sold his soul to an emperor for the sake of escaping alive from a decimation of his brothers. From our Tenth Theban Legion, as the price of saving his skin. Well, I can report he has done well from his treachery and now he's here in Britain."

"Here in Britain? How in Hades has the traitor managed that?"

"Constantius as you may know has built another fleet. Bigger, stronger and better. Once Maximianus Herculius arrived from Treverorum to take command of the Rhenus it left his servant Chlorus free to run another invasion."

"Which I take it has happened?"

"Yes, and already. At least two formations sent for Britannia; one under Constantius from Bononia and the other led by Julius Asclepiodotus. The evil genius of this story, who set off in choppy seas from the Gaulish coast near Rotomagus then encountered the thick fog of Vectis Water which has turned out to be their friend. Enabled the fleet of Asclepiodotus to sneak past Allectus and what little's left of our fine *Classis*, now he'd run it down so bad - without being detected."

"That's worrying news, Tormentus. Disastrous for some. Whereabouts did they land?"

"Somewhere between Portus Anderida and Clausentum itself."

"Aiming at our fleet base?"

"Quite possibly, but they will not have found much opposition there, not in the forts. Not anymore. Not now half our ships are on stands, their crews and garrisons gone."

My mother chipped-in now, her face sagged and lined from a journey taking its toll.

"When your children were taken away from us, my dear; when you were packed off to the east like that; it left me no reason to stay in Rutupiae. Not when Allectus's men under that toad Perfidius Ferox had looted your house there. Absolutely disgraceful. Utter barbarians with no respect for private property. Leaving it barely habitable. Breaking all the furniture, defacing the walls. So not knowing what else to do, where to go, I travelled west on my own. Worried sick about the children but believing there was nothing I could do. Not yet, anyway. Heading across the province and back towards Calleva, to the one place I knew."

"Imagine a respectable lady having to travel alone through conditions like this. My own mother on foot across a field of war. Dreadful to think of what dangers you faced..." I remark, meaning it kindly like a dutiful son, but she gives me such a sparky, disapproving look. As if I've despised her ability, implied moral incapacity.

"Nonsense, I was absolutely fine, thank you my dear, and met some very nice people along the way. You'd be amazed how kind ordinary folk are. And you'll be glad to know that when I got there, I found our old home safely shuttered and intact. Well looked-after by neighbours. Could take up residence as if nothing had happened. But Calleva itself felt different, completely changed. A sense of danger I've never felt before, fear in its streets."

"Fear?"

"When word of imminent invasion came, Allectus started to bring his whole army down from Londinium. Basing it in temporary camps they built of turf outside our town, many of them full of Franks. Absolutely awful people. Billeting them in houses, seizing our food to feed them. Leaving Roman citizens to starve. The *basilica* and *forum* turned into his headquarters with military messengers on horseback to-ing and fro-ing every hour. The city walls strengthened and repaired, Everyone realising something major was going to happen, and that it was just a matter of time. Waiting in fear for when it did."

"And when was that?"

"Well, my dear, I knew things were getting critical when Allectus rode round the city in person. Making silly announcements from the back of a black stallion like that one your father-in-law, Carausius, used to ride. Maybe even the same one. The more he raved at us on horseback, the more it smacked of his growing despair. Holding up a bag of coins from the saddle and promising every able-bodied man in the area who would enlist to his colours that they could have one like that on joining, and another when Chlorus was killed....."

By this time Victor was sitting on my lap, eyes wide as he took-in some understanding of dramatic events the adults round him describe. Since I didn't yet fully understand either how some of my former mariners and an aged parent had combined in unholy alliance to free him and his sister from the tyrant's palace in London, I thought it my duty to say so.

Mother's response was pithy:

"I met a kind sailor in the street, dear. An old comrade of yours who recognised me from Rutupiae and stopped to enquire after your health. Did something rather marvellous about it later, as you can now see. The man you should really be thanking......"

"While I met a lovely widow, Lord Triton. One whose fine son I once had the privilege of serving. So that when the lady next received a letter containing news of his survival on the Wall, learnt he was still alive and wept aloud with joy, she was also moved to wonder if an old shipmate of his might be the man to help the pair of you. At least by rescuing his children....." added Tormentus, patting Lucia on the head.

"I would never doubt you for a moment, friend. So how exactly did you manage it?"

"We could feel the atmosphere behind the walls of Calleva getting more and more fraught. Tense and more fearful. By the time I persuaded your mother that now was the right moment for us to leave, we couldn't have cut it any finer. Turning out we left the city just in the nick of time."

"Where did you go?"

"Londinium!" laughed Tormentus. "Into the eye of the storm. We were heading east, to the capital of the province, while the roads were choked with soldiers and supply convoys coming in the opposite direction. Rushing down to where we'd just left."

"What about Asclepiodotus?"

"Whatever you think about the Egyptian, how ready he was to betray his Theban bretheren, you've got to admire his determination. Courage, even."

"I hear he's now Praetorian Prefect?"

"Yes, Constantius Chlorus's old job before he became the junior Caesar. So he and Maximianus, the Augustus, must think well of him. Rate him as more than capable."

"And loyal?"

"Oh yes, Triton, my friend, they've obviously got him bang to rights on that. Their first and last requirement. Who knows what grasp they've got over him. What people they hold, what secrets they know, but he's loyal all right. Suicidally-so."

"Suicidal?"

"When Asclepiodotus and his Rhineland legions land near Clausentum, first thing they do is burn all the ships."

"No going back?"

"I think that's meant to be the message. To his own men, as much as Allectus."

"Do or die!"

"Indeed, and once they've taken Clausentum then looted its Mint, captured all the stores, off they go north. Knowing that's the essential deal but feeling so much happier about it, I suspect, for all the Carausian silver now jingling in their purses."

"Heading for Calleva?"

"Yes, as you say, to the city in the woods. To the mellow walls and sheltered gardens your mother and myself, along with several thousand others, have wisely just fled - Fortuna be praised!"

"What about Chlorus?"

594

"Wandering about in the Fretum Gallicum like his steersmen forgot all they ever knew about how you find and keep to a bearing in fog. Or so we heard later. Almost like he wanted to stay out of it."

"Leave it all down to Asclepiodotus?"

"Yes, the treacherous, conniving bastard. Taking the whole responsibility, it's true."

"Tormentus, would you mind your language, please, when there are young children present!" says my mother sharply like a wife to a well-trained husband, Lucia going red.

"What happened next?" I ask, passing over this minor domestic snap.

"Allectus marches his whole force out into the rainsoaked downlands, looking for Asclepiodotus. Blundering about in the forests. Crashing through branches, wading through rivers, with not one single clue. He might be a good accountant, but a bloody-useless general....."

My mother folding her arms and glaring, the wife of Simplex squeezing her hand.

"They met?"

"Allectus's army stumbled out of the mist and out of the trees in multiple, disordered columns and units. His cavalry left behind, stuck crossing a stream. Total cock-up. Blundering wthout warning into an enormous bowl, an uphill clearing in the woods where they found the German legions of Asclepiodotus drawn up quietly before them. Waiting as if on exercise, shield-rim to shield-rim. Filling the valley with their whitened ranks."

"Allectus ran away?"

"Ha, you know the man too well, my lord Triton. Worked with him too long. His Franks at least were different, you've got to credit them for that. Fighting-mad, they charged straight at the Imperial forces with all that ferocity they're a byword for. Fought on to the death."

"But not their glorious leader?"

"No, sadly not. So much for that manly *'Virtue of The Augustus'* we saw printed on all his coins. They say he was one of the first to melt away into the forest, leaving his troops and mercenaries behind to fight. Covering his flight."

"I'm not surprised. So Allectus got away?"

"Oh, no. They found him soon enough. Covered in ash, hiding under the floor of a charcoal-burner's hut on the very edge of Spinaii Silva, pretending to be a peasant. Every dignity of office, every badge of rank thrown away. The purple tunic lost, his brown beard gone straggly and unkempt round a squared-off jaw. Just the silver coins of Carausius hidden in his shoes to prove who he really was. Confirm his one fatal weakness, worse than all the others. The man who always loved his precious metal that little bit too much. The only love which caught him out, guaranteed arrest."

"What happened when they did?"

"Gave it him to drink, like Maximianus always promised. Warming it first as they must."

"Ugh! While you were away to Londinium?"

"Yes, where things were really hotting-up. Once the battle was lost and Allectus captured, his forces just disintegrated, the army collapsing. His Franks might have been loyal, but now they had no-one left to be loyal to, only themselves. So they start streaming back to Londinium with the intention to pillage. To rape, loot and kill, then make off for the coast."

"Were there no defences?"

"The finest city-walls of any British province, a triumph of the mason's art, but no-one left to man them. No-one trained, that is…not once his levies had murdered Livius Gallus."

I turned to my mother: "This the nightmare you deliberately entered?"

"I'm afraid so, dear, but don't forget Tormentus here was with me. Plus two of his old comrades from the 'Volusenus'. All in a light mule-carriage, none planning to stay long."

"What did you do?"

Her newly-adopted *trierarch* took up the story again:

"Because Londinium now stood undefended, it made our job easier. No-one to stand in our way. All the gates left open. We made for the centre of the city immediately while everyone else seemed to be heading the other way…."

"They knew Allectus's Franks were coming, and what that would mean for anyone in their path…." put in my mother. "Especially the women."

"Yes…" said Tormentus "…why anyone well enough who had strength or money, slaves or friends to carry them, was set on escaping. By horse, litter or cart. Carrying what valuables they could. While we got into the main courtyard of the Governor's Palace completely unopposed...."

"Which was being stripped of anything of value by the people who once worked there...." added mother. "Gallus's men. His guards, servants and clerks who took no notice of us when we walked in. Too busy with their thieving and looting. Fighting over what's left."

"And where grandma' found me and my little brother sitting. Waiting under the big pillars at the top of the front steps with Victor...." announced Lucia proudly. "Just waiting for somebody to come and pick us up."

"We knew Daddy would come for us..." piped-up Victor: "Because he said he would."

"So it was just a case of waiting until he did...." intervened Lucia. "Or someone he sent. Like our lovely grandma...!" She clapped her hands together with joy at the recollection.

Remembering the relief but betraying for a moment the lonely uncertainty that must have been hers until they came. The nagging insecurity bravely never shared with the small boy who'd been her sole ward until then. The pair of them alone inside a disintegrating city.

"How did you get out?"

Tormentus looks across at my mother and makes a face:

"That's when things got interesting. We got out of the Palace alright, with Lucia and Victor holding our hands, and went back to where we'd left the mule carriage. On the main road right outside. To find my two colleagues, Aulus and Veturius, where we'd left them guarding it. Now embroiled in a scrap with two members of the palace guard. City-bred soldiers who thought our transport just the job for getting themselves and whatever they'd just robbed from premises they were guarding, out of it."

"So you lost the carriage?"

"No, my lord Triton, fortunately not. Not that time anyway; it happened later. While unfortunately for these guards, Aulus and Veturius were the wrong men to ask. The hardest men in the fleet. I remember they used to practise by chopping the guard-rail on 'Volusenus' with the sides of their hand. Improve their reflexes in sunny weather by picking flies off the deck between two fingers, like gladiators do. But the lively debate these two

597

soldiers opened with Aulus and Veturius delayed our departure quite a bit. While their request to borrow our cart was more fully declined...."

"Till the Franks arrived?"

"Not them, no, not till then. You see, from the Governor's Palace you get a really good view down to the river. Onto the Thamesis. I expect you'll remember it yourself, from what you said about working in offices near there. Panoramic, I'd call it, and the first thing we noticed - or at least once Aulus and Veturius had sorted these chancers out and we could give our attention to anything else – was a river black with ships."

"Ships?"

"The delayed fleet of Constantius. Arriving on Thamesis in the nick of time."

"Do you know, Daddy, those baddies with helmets who wanted our carriage had to beg us stop hitting them...." added Victor, tugging at the leather edging to my uniform. "Even grannie had a stick. She hit the tall one, really hard. It *was* funny!"

I smile and give him a squeeze, shifting his weight in my lap away from an unhealed wound then pressing on after eyewitness accounts of what I was realising for one of the most important events in the whole history of Britain: "So you're telling me you saw it all? That you, my very own mother, were there? Standing by the open gates of Londinium on the day when the Caesar himself, Constantius Chlorus, rides in to rescue Londinium from a fate worse than death?"

"I suppose you're right, dear, when you put it like that. How it ended up..." she responded. "You see all we were trying to do was get out. It was attempting that which brought us to the gates, and it was there at the gates we saw the conqueror coming in. Chlorus himself, arrayed in purple and gold. Entering the city in triumph, riding-in on horseback followed by his marching legions. Rank after rank. Where we saw the city fathers, priests and magistrates waiting. Grovelling in fact. Kneeling down in their togas at its entrance, giving thanks to the gods for a safe deliverance. Arms aloft in prayer."

"Yes, and a brave sight it made, I'll give him that..." agreed Tormentus. "A real Roman army for the first time in a generation. Rescuing real Roman citizens from a genuine danger. Restoring the light, the eternal light of Rome. Whatever you may think of Chlorus, my lord, or those bigger men who sent him, surely what we really need after the terror of Allectus? After his arrests, the murders, executions and persecutions. Foreign mercenaries and deserters from his retreating army rampaging all over our countryside. Peace at last."

"But never in the form Carausius imagined for us, so why in Diana's Name should you expect our lives beyond 'The Pale' to turn out any better? Let alone different..." I asked him bitterly, like they were credulous fools. Not meaning any ingratitude to three brave men and one grandmother who between them had saved my children, but tactless all the same. A tone that spoiled our conversation, cast a cloud over the future.

"Which raises the obvious question...." interjects Simplex, ever the pacifier "...of what you all plan to do next?" He looked slowly around the painted room and everyone looked troubled. The question indeed.

I can admit now that this was the last time I made a decision as a military officer, because from then on I would become a deserter. A status of outlawry adopted with no other enthusiasm than for the welfare of my own.

"I am sorry, Felicius Simplex, you have been the best of good comrades but now I must leave you, and your fort. When Constantius Chlorus has subdued the south and sends his forces up here to deal with Caledonia, I know my name will be first on their list. Why my mother, my children and myself must go into the west; you remove me from your rosters."

"I agree...." he said, reluctantly "...but what about the Painted People? When they finally realise that the heir of Carausius no longer stands on our walls?"

"Then they will come south, as Cousin Fergus always promised they would and one day they inevitably must. Whatever happens to me or however long you may serve. Though to perpetuate my impression till reinforcements arrive, whether Asclepiodotus or his master, I will leave my personal armour, uniform and crested helmet. Ready for one of your officers to wear. As long as you can make it one of the better-looking ones, if you please....."

Simplex laughed at my little joke and gripped my arm:

"If it were not for you and your marvellous marines, then we would have been overwhelmed long ago. You and your men have done more than duty demands and I for my part release you unconditionally. Willing and deservedly. Say to any man who questions you, it was the tribune to that half-cohort of Cornovii at Pons Aelius who did this thing. I, the *praepositus* Caius Felicius Simplex, late of the Sixth Victorious Legion. And the Lord God too, with His Manifold Blessings."

"And what about you, Caius my friend, what will happen to you?"

"Either the Painted People will kill me, or maybe the Caesar. One or the other. Though there are some who suspect a faithful servant of Christ concealed within his soldier's frame. A supporter or a sympathiser, but never a persecutor."

Whether Simplex was right or not about that I really cannot say, but I wouldn't have wanted to take his chances. Not with any of Maximian's men.

While my own plan was different.

Why it is that the last entries in my journal only record how I relinquished the usual arms and appurtenances of a soldier of the Fleet to dress as an ordinary, travelling tradesman. Carrying a sleeping-roll to conceal the glitter of garnets and that unique blade which owns me to this day, plus an old draw-string bag containing a set of chisels I'd kept more from sentiment than any real use, and a child's bronze model of a ship's prow, I finally set out.

Together with my family.

Holding Aurelius Victor by the one hand and his sister Lucia by the other, we begin our long trek west together. Owning nothing but ourselves and our freedom; determined to hang onto the Luck which is all we have left, last gift of Fortuna. Limping slowly along the paved stone road which the sweat of generations of legions has laid down for us below the Emperor's Wall and across this whole island.

Limited to the pedestrian pace of their father, a veteran soldier who cannot compete with their youth, let alone the arthritic-but-invincible grandmother accompanying them. Struggling slowly west at our pathetically-differing rates into a land of lowering mountains and spectacular sunsets.

Fleeing from a Caesar whose sentry I once killed, who never would forget.

600

For as long as we are in sight, I remember looking back to see Caius Felicius Simplex standing alone in farewell, high on his gate-tower. Much like Mauritius. The Christian who somehow commands pagans, the professional soldier who waits patiently beside the Sons of Mithras, to die with them on his walls when the Picti come again to Pons Aelius.

If our eagles fall.

And after a bone-breaking hug to us all, as sad as the sight of oaken-hearted Tormentus swinging down alone onto the quayside below with his seafarer's roll. Appointed by common consent and the grim approbation of what may turn out to have been the very last *vexillatio* of marines from the *Classis Britannica* to be left in existence.

Trierarch to the refurbished '*Calliope*', last element to their fleet. Waiting on permanent alert once again at its original place of station on Tinae Fluvius. Obedient and ready for the order to put to sea in their faithful service of a restored empire which has already resolved to destroy them. Or else flee to the north, try the mercy of Ferganus.

Whatever they chose, or whatever else became of those magnificent men, I truly cannot say. Only that this is the last I saw of Simplex and his soldiers, of '*Calliope*' and her crew. Their last entry in my record and may the gods have treated every one of them with honour if not kindness; however badly it ended.

More than too many I have known just like them, going on before.

"Love thyself last: cherish those hearts that hate thee. Corruption wins not more than honesty. Still in thy right hand carry gentle peace, to silence envious tongues. Be just, and fear not – let all the ends thou aim'st at be thy country's, thy God's and truth's; then if thou fall....thou fall'st a blessed martyr!"

(King Henry VIII , Act iii Scene 2: William Shakespeare)

POST SCRIPTVM

The road-gang moves slowly, as workmen always do.

All in good time, no need for rush.

The necessary tools are each to hand, correct and present in the wagon, so it is presumably just a question of what job to tackle first. How and with what weapon, using what skills. And the minimum amount of effort, of course. He knew they would all be agreed about that.

So a mile out from the city-centre, exactly, they are gathered at the roadside around the big way-marker which confirms this important distance. Down in a bit of a dip, beside the one they were told to replace. A mile-post, that's all.

All six of them, looking expectantly across at their foreman up on his wagon: awaiting the right directions and tools. Inspecting the offending item.

Their gangmaster, a man misshapen by accidents and now employed mainly to supervise. An old-stager who relishes the burden of minor responsibility and savours his power, such as it is. All the same, and to win their loyalty, he has always made it his practice first to consult with the men. Ask them their opinion on how things should go, as if they had a clue.

Even if the final decision remained with him; what he was paid by the city council for, by its *decuriones*; his habit remained a popular consideration with the men. One they generally valued, even if no-one ever agreed and he took little notice.

"Look, boss, we know why we've been sent. It's the writing what's wrong. You know, the name. What it says, not where the sign stands. That name we're not supposed to mention...." said the aged workman in plaid his nearest in seniority: "And I'm damned if I'm shifting that bloody great thing just to change 'owt as daft as that. When who reads this slavver, anyhow?"

That was how their little discussions always went. Working down their pecking order till they got to the youngest. Who should think himself lucky to be asked.

"Well, if that's what they want, their privilege. Mind, it'll take us ages, boss. Ages to move it. Longer still to find and shape another to match, drag it back down here. That's even before them words. You know, them new names they want on the front..." says the next in line, a man with one eye whose colleagues nod sagely at his concise analysis.

Sound.

He's got it in one.

"Why replace it, boss? Nobody will know if we don't. Let's not. Why don't we just take the bad words off with a broad chisel then put the right ones back over it with a thin?" said a long-standing ganger in coarse-weave tartan. Tribal and thick, not wishing to be left out.

There were widespread mutterings of approval for that as another sensible idea. Why everyone looks expectantly across at the new lad with the scarred leg whose speciality was lettering on waymarks, as if he'd obediently agree. Holding his bag of chisels.

He might well be young and recently invalided out of the army - some said navy - but just being able to read and write was enough to make him stand out in this company. Getting him more of a hearing than seniority strictly renders his due. Nonetheless, this next man pauses, scratches a full head of hair and looks briefly doubtful. More as if nervous of contradicting the wisdom of time-served elders having less, than any lack of certainty: "So you're saying we should chisel the old words off - the banned stuff - then smooth the stone after? Smooth enough to add more on top? By, that job'll take me ages: just getting it flat enough to add some fresh. And that's before even starting on any new letters. Why I've got another suggestion: couldn't the lads just dig the whole thing out quick, then put it back but upside-down? In half the time I'd spend chiselling off what's presently topside."

He could tell by their faces they didn't fancy shifting a heavy object this size and shrugged: "It's up to you. If you really don't want to try that way, then I suppose we'll be here all day!"

Which really put a cat among the peacocks.

No-one liked the sound of that, not when everyone wanted home as quick as possible. And if the gaffer hadn't considered this alternative way of tackling it before, his important supervisory position meant he needed to recover control of their meandering debate.

"So what exactly you suggesting we do, young fella'?" he asked gravely, beetling his brows and trying to convey a patient wisdom in his voice, assert his grizzled authority.

"Well, boss, your lads will know best, and bet you've done loads of these mileposts since last Kalends gone. But like I say, why don't we make it easy for ourselves? Tip this one upside-down, back in the earth? Same place where it is now, but with a fresh surface brought topside. For me to get on with knocking a few letters out on straightaway. 'Stead of the other lads chipping away all day before I can even get started?"

He had a point you know, that young stone-carver. Like him or not, and wherever he'd come from. Too clever by half for us, too good at his job, but we'll let that error go by, for today anyhow. (Tomorrow might be different).

So that was what they did.

Loads quicker. With a bit of digging and leaning with spades, grunting and groaning with crowbars, using the oxen off the municipal wagon and a tow-rope, they had the red sandstone milepost pulled out of the ground and then put back in the other way round, faster than you could say *"Imperial Succession"*. Before anyone else could notice.

Like it was a completely different object.

Gone from sight was "IMP C M AVR MAVS CARAVSIO PF INVICTO AVG" and now - once the stonecarver's finished and it's gleaming in the sun - is some fresh white paint on the engraved imperial titles of our noble lord: "FLAV(io) CONSTANTIO NOB(ilis) CAES(ar)".

Ready to greet every passing visitor coming into Luguvallium with like it was a brand-new piece. Even if the latest lettering seems a bit wavy and terse, what with all their haste and that. Almost amateurish you might say. As if the gang's new inscriber didn't really care too much for what he was writing - as if he *"couldn't be arsed..."* how the man in plaid put it.

"Best job we ever did!" grinned the gaffer - who couldn't read anyway and cared even less - as they packed up early and loaded the wagon. His ageing road gang were as pleased as he was; every one of them back in the city taverns - or home to wife and family in ramshackle bothies lining the Londinium road - before the afternoon sun was even halfway to setting.

605

And never with less trouble: or "*nae bother*" as the Carvettii people like to put it.

While those stupid clerks in the city-council's Office of Public Works - *operum publicorum* - had paid them out as if it had been a full day's work. No questions asked.

Not even quibbling about the foreman's additional claim made to the *decuriones* for his own personal expenses. For that considerable extra cost he reported being put to. For the price of a brand-new waymark in red sandstone. That blank pillar he'd apparently had to cart-in specially from a country quarry to replace their one unsuitable other.....

Sic Transit Gloria.

Either way, it was the last time anyone round here heard of that Carausius again. So far as the team-gaffer and his old gangers know, anyroad. Though all the extra cash they got that day came in more than handy, thank you very much. At least while it lasted, today's money being worth so much less nowadays than it used to.

Minimissimi.

While not so far away, near a famous temple of Venus & Mars by the western walls, the gang's newest recruit - their specialist inscriber, the mason with the gammy leg - lay quietly resting its hurt on a straw truckle in a long-house of Luguvallium. Listening to his children play outside and thinking about the day that has gone. Looking up at a ceiling woven from alder and birch and imagining how engraved letters once spelling out his old admiral's titles would be kissing the clay, given a decent burial in the earth.

Instead of erasure.

All those names for the pirate!

Saved and surviving against every odd, preserving his secret memory for another generation, whispering them into the soil like the words of a poem.

His latest victory, and maybe his greatest?

Not his last.

AUTHOR'S BACKGROUND NOTE

Word of mouth was once all people had to pass on their family and social past - either that or carving it on caves. Whatever the chosen means, its forms always betray the preoccupations and biases of their era, a selective recall.

Where the integrity of what, even nowadays, we claim to dignify as *'History'*, must rest on the fragility of parchment and paper, the private agenda of scholars. The stone that weathers, the ink that fades, the books that burn. Those incomplete records of declining resilience, sometimes still capable of speaking to us over hundreds of years, despite it. Occasionally, even over thousands.

Yet if books we nowadays discard, will we all regret one day how quickly our learning grows confined to the imprint of magnetic, digital signal, or ferric-coated, plastic disc? Hard-drive and microchip, the net-based 'cloud'.

Fragile media of little lifespan - susceptible to changes in temperature and light, the withdrawal of service, or total equipment failure. Deposits of knowledge only accessible via flimsy machines whose maximum service life of 5-10 years presents new dangers to a whole generation, across the known world. An entire society entrusting the assembly and strategic supply of whatever equipment is needed to access these records to exploited workers and alien corporations, far away in the East. To complex machines holding the key to our civilisation's existence, the only testimony we lived, yet which cannot offer-up one single page from our recent past without 240 volts direct/alternating supply. Nuclear power, coal or gas.

Switch that power off and, unlike parchment or stone, these things go silent for ever. And even without the malign interventions of STUXNET or hackers, virus and worms, that's no joke. Because, without their aid and suddenly denied access, we'll soon forget everything we ever knew, or learned.

Like a post-Roman Britain forgot within decades how to build in stone, or even make pottery. Preface to a millennium men still call the *'Dark Ages'*, one literal and figurative.

Without the memory of machines and whatever else we use to record whatever's left, it leaves us with a caste of historians, archivists, and archaeologists as backstop. The people who work away to disinter what's best not forgotten, our only living agencies for the carriage of fact. Saving a wider remembrance of what otherwise collapses into legend, is lost inside machines.

The Foreign Office threw out.

Priests to our struggle to assemble or restore something like a collective memory from what few broken fragments we can excavate from earth, or still survive in archive.

Do honour to those who've gone before.

While if Time can wear away and delete something so hard as stone; will so readily devour lives, despises digital; just think what it can do with Truth.

When all that flawed narrative which didacts call *'History'* is often little better than the successful shouting-down by victors of their unfortunate defeated.

Evident in state and corporate-controlled media whose affectations of dispassionate analysis stand riddled with social agendas paraded to suit the oligarchies owning. Political-correctness proselytised on an unwilling public, the posturings of a narrow media elite inflicted on our private thoughts. Sensationalising and moulding history to fit our contemporary cultural norms. Shoving modern ideas of *'appropriate'* into distant eras whose occupants never even recognised, let alone accepted, these conceits of our time.

Like I've doubtless done in this.

By definition, everything put into a novel is or becomes fiction. Every piece from history's record put into a novel set in the past becoming something else: historical fiction, not fact. And choose to set bits of it in a dystopian near-future characterised by an ever-increasing machine-dependency, as well as thought-control, and you might even call it science fiction. So while this book has elements of both, none of it should be mistaken for fact. Neither now nor then, not ever - like my opening disclaimer says, and from beginning to end.

Why I chose the years of Carausius, where so little of anything is certain. Like his machines of wood and sinew, all gone without a trace. No less wondrous for that.

Mausaeus Carausius: the forgotten defender of a Roman Britain, its *'Rebel-with-a-Cause'*. The first British emperor in a time of epic events and seismic upheavals for the whole island - not forgetting a continent not strictly called *'Europa'*.....

Rebel against Rome and so treated at the time as deserving in law of her ultimate sanction. Erasure from every record, deleted from history. Legally classified as a non-person. *"Ex Damnatio Memoriae"* - of condemned memory; but what a life he had while it lasted!

Witness to the clash of armies and fleets on a scale unimaginable to us now. Spectacular siegeworks, ambitious logistics, and daring naval encounters whose size and extent we may only imperfectly grasp. Glimpse the merest hints of through the cloud of centuries. His humble origins in what is now Belgium, the early years as a pilot, then his military appointments and successes, which led on to a fatal accusation. To the arrest-warrant which prefigures his declaration as Emperor in 286; Maximianus's failed expedition against him in 289; the assassination of 293. How his treacherous assassin hung on for three more years after that, until Constantius finally invades in 296 to finish Allectus off.

Inherent in all of this, an epic. The trans-european movements of ships and soldiers, continents crossed on an emperor's order. Social and political tremors against which the few slight references surviving from his time are so frustratingly general, the added elements in folk-tale so distorted. Whether about his accommodation with the Picts or defeat of Bassianus at York.

Whether robber, rogue or hero we can only guess, assuming all three. An astonishing man undoubtedly, living through astonishing times. Although, apart from the unique coinage Carausius and his lieutenant issued during their rebel regime (286-296 A.D.) and we now find in the ground, plus oblique reference in official Roman records to *'The Pirate'*, Europe's collective archive of artefacts holds almost nothing in writing to show he ever existed.

Except for one thing, found in one place:

If you travel along the A6 'London Road' to enter the southern outskirts of the great Border City of Carlisle, you pass freshly-painted 1930s semis, whose neat suburban gardens back onto open fields. Nostalgic reminders of a late 'Depression' prosperity and building boom to mark out what some imagine a kinder, truer Britain. Before another World War changed it for ever; or the banks stole all our money.

This way came the Roman first, marching along the embanked road they'd raised into their frontier city of Luguvallium. The garrison town and later a supply-base for what their own gazetteer (Antonine Itinerary) calls 'The Entrenchments' but we now know as 'Hadrian's Wall'. A well-trodden invasion route running north into Scotland, Rome's Afghanistan, its modern successor is girt with the usual impedimentia of cars and supermarkets, out-of-town shopping and light industrial units.

Though at first staying true to the course and atmosphere of that principal Roman road it started out as, where the route narrows you find characterful but shabby reminders of the Victorian 'Railway Kings' suddenly moving-in to slow progress. Obscure your way forward with brick, speak loudly of steam.

Where you must wait in your car at computer-controlled traffic lights, be surveilled by cameras. Reflecting, while CCTV lenses take from you whatever it is they want, on those first Roman legions slogging along through here. Into this city and then on towards Scotland: 'Caledonia' as it was. Crunch of marching sandals, hobnails hitting stone.

Led by their famous commander-in-chief, Gnaeus Julius Agricola, immortalised in his son-in-law's biography, a book that's still in print. Yes, even he: following the same alignments as your car does now, only on horseback at the head of an enormous conquering army, strung out over twenty miles of road. All the way back down the A6, his presence beyond peradventure, the army irresistible. Bringers of devastation and peace combined.

Stuck in your car one mile south from Carlisle city-centre and these lights still against you; Harraby Bridge on London Road might seem an unlikely place to seek any reminder of a unique emperor; of a Roman Britain's first.

Yet where the modern road descends to cross the railway-cutting, via an iron bridge, you note it dipping slightly into a modest depression, actual and visual. One that may mar it: semi-industrialised but densely-surrounded on all sides with hidden places; rich in historical associations of the foremost national importance. Almost a nodal point.

The War Memorial there on the right for instance, set behind a grille beside the road, is overlooked but not forgotten. Every year in November, fresh poppy-wreaths will appear for Remembrance Day. Local people remembering their war dead as Afghanistan brings us fresh names to honour from another fated military expedition; from a foreign policy adopted without regard to the lessons of history. Ordained by a Foreign Office newly without books.

To your left, above traffic lights which must by now seem permanently stuck on red, rises a prominent hill crowned with dated white office-blocks and car-parks used by the local health service: a place of betrayal and executions. Where defeated Jacobite rebels, abandoned by their *'Bonnie Prince'* and persuaded to surrender Carlisle Castle on a Hanoverian promise of safe-conduct, were shamefully carted-off to be hanged together in 1746, once they had.

At this same roadside, Harraby Bridge, is the original site of the discovery in 1875 of the only known stone ever to be found in Britain still bearing the name of Carausius. (RIB 2291). A milepost it was and, apart from the coinage, still the sole-surviving inscription of any description that is left anywhere in the world to testify to his existence. Or else supplement so short a list of facts reliably known about him, they would barely fill one sheet of A4.

An interested visitor can inspect this rare piece where it is now removed-to; in the Tullie House Museum & Art Gallery on Castle Street, Carlisle; and I really think you should go. Higher than a man it stands, Carausius restored to the fore once again; while Constantius and his dastardly name get their come-uppance, obscured by the museum's mount.

The carved letters picked out in white paint as they usually were in period: "IMP C M AVR MAVS CARAVSIO P F INVICTO AVG" announces its unique inscription. *'To The Emperor and Caesar Marcus Aurelius Mausaeus Carausius; The Pious and Fortunate; The Unconquered Augustus...'* what its standard abbreviations mean.

Unfortunately, those unique acronyms found on Carausius's remarkable (and rather more widely-available) metal coinage, which I rely on for a plotline in this book, are rather less clear. Not so obviously familiar. Why it took a learned Renaissance man to unlock them.

Acknowledgement, grateful thanks, and the respect of his peers must therefore be due for solving this ultimate classical crossword to the academic, archaeologist, aviator, numismatist, teacher, TV personality and writer: Guy de la Bedoyere. A combination of whose serious scholarship, detailed knowledge of Roman poetry and dazzling ingenuity enabled him first to notice – and then convincingly resolve - that hidden messaging contained in so many of Carausius's coins.

Still texting to us across the gulf of years.

De Bedoyere the first to realise how a recurring set of initials used by this British Usurper to decorate the production of his various mints in Britannia and Gaul directly matches some of the most famous lines from the Roman poet Vergil's literary repertoire. Like 'RSR': *"Redeunt Saturnia Regna"* ('The Golden Age of Saturn is Back…') or 'INPCDA': *"Iam Nova Progenies Caelo Demittur Alto"* ('…Now a New Generation is Let Down from Heaven Above').

Sequential lines with which any citizen of Empire considering themselves educated would have been instantly familiar; as once was true of Britons in the case of William Shakespeare.

LOL? IMHO, it's nothing new.

Coins carrying the sophisticated propaganda message of a real-life Rhineland river-man, upon which my whole fictional case must rest. Namely that he must have had help, some literate adviser like the young tribune 'Triton' was.

As if to show what was surely as true in the days when Allectus ran the exchequer as it remains for us today:

Money talks.

Clive Ashman   **Cumbria, August 2012**

Glossary of Roman place-names mentioned:

Abus: **Humber Estuary**, England
Arbeia: **South Shields**, Tyne & Wear, England
Augusta Treverorum: **Trier** (on River Moselle) Germany
Anderida: **Pevensey**, Sussex, England
　　　　　(full name: 'Portus Anderida' or 'Anderita')
Bodotria: **Firth of Forth**, Scotland
Bononia: **Boulogne**, northern France
　　　　　(the port, later the whole site)
Branodunum: **Brancaster**, Norfolk, England
Brocavum: **Brougham**, Cumbria, England
Calleva Atrebatum: **Silchester**, Hampshire, England
Cantiacorum: **Canterbury**, Kent, England
　　　　　(full name: 'Durovernum Cantiacorum')
Castra Exploratum: **Netherby**, Longtown, Cumbria
Cataractonium: **Catterick**, North Yorkshire, England
Clausentum: **Bitterne**, Hampshire, England
Corinium: **Cirencester**, Gloucestershire, England
Dubris: **Dover**, Kent, England
　　　　　(full name: 'Portus Dubris')
Dura Europos: **Saliyeh** (on the River Euphrates) Syria
Eboracum: **York**, England (on the River Ouse)
Fretum Gallicum: **English Channel**
Gesoriacum: **Boulogne**, northern France
　　　　　(the original fortress and fleet-base)
Garrianonum: **Burgh Castle**, Norfolk Broads, England
Grannona: **Grande**,Vosges, France
Glevum: **Gloucester**, England
Horreae Classis: **Carpow**, Perth & Kinross, Scotland
Londinium: **London**, England (on River *Thamesis*)
Luguvallium: **Carlisle**, Cumbria, England
Marcae: **Marquise** or **Marck** near Calais, France
Mediolanum: **Milan**, Italy
Moguntacium: **Mainz** (on the River Rhine) Germany
Oceanus Germanicus: the **North Sea**
Othona: '*St.Peter's-on-the-Wall*', **Bradwell-on-Sea**, Essex
Palmyra: **Tadmor**, Syria
Petuaria: **Brough-on-Humber**, East Yorkshire

Praetorio: *(An unidentified Roman base on the East Yorkshire coast, now believed lost to the sea, possibly near **Bridlington**)*

Pons Aelius:	**Newcastle-upon-Tyne**, England
Regulbium:	**Reculver**, Kent, England
Rhenus:	River **Rhine**; Germany and Holland
Roma:	**Rome**, Italy
Rotomagus:	**Rouen**, northern France
Rutupiae:	**Richborough**, Kent, England
Sorviodunum:	**Winchester**, Hampshire, England
Thamesis Fluvius:	River **Thames**, England
Tinae Fluvius:	River **Tyne**, England
Treverorum:	**Trier** on the River Moselle, Germany
	(as above – in later period referred to as: 'Treveris')
Vectis:	**Isle of Wight**, England

Overleaf:

Author's illustration of **The Arras Medallion** - found 1912:
as now displayed in *'Bibliotheque Nationale de France'*, Paris:

Obverse of a gold-finished *aureus* issued by the Trier Mint c.300 AD, showing Constantius Chlorus entering the grateful City of London in triumph on horseback; his land forces arriving from Gaul and Germania by troop-ship, in the River Thames.

Issued later to celebrate Constantius's victory, probably to men who had served in his successful 296 AD campaign:

"REDDITOR LUCIS AETERNAE:
Restorer of The Eternal Light"

CRA 2012

... Sundburg in BATO is ...
a subtle novel that provides a significant insight into what
life was like during the late Roman Empire of Constantine
by developing a slice of it into ... puzzels and some
... of adventure in a plot ... have readers ...
and the ... readers.

To find out more ... other ... of ... features, go to:
www.crawdaughter.com - "The Ransom in the Rye"

Independent reviews left by *real* readers of Clive Ashman's first novel: <u>*'MOSAIC: The Pavement That Walked'*</u>

"I enjoyed it immensely….the Roman part is very convincing and Tryton's struggle to get home after shooting down the Junkers is wonderfully vivid and exciting…utterly adrenalin-making." - **Christopher Roberts** (on back cover)

"This was the most brilliant read. It was so exciting and evocative that I got lost in the tale. I felt I knew the characters – held my breath with anxiety when something was going to befall them, hoping for a happy outcome at every page turn….Nothing dry about this book. I really hope ..(he)… writes another tale. It was magic!" - **Mary Paterson (Edinburgh)** on <u>amazon.co.uk</u>

*"If you have ever read Marguerite Youcenar's **'The Abyss'**, a classic and intensely-haunting reconstruction of daily life in sixteenth century Europe or, more immediately relevant, her **'Memoirs of Hadrian'** about the 1st and 2nd century Roman Empire, you may well consider Clive Ashman's **'MOSAIC'** a worthy companion-piece in its detailed understanding of the dilemmas confronting the magistrate of 4th century Petuaria (Brough), Marcus Januarius, who is beset by the savage and ever more effective raids of the Saxons (without sufficient weapons or troops to fend them off) and turbulent imperial politics which frequently erupt into bloody civil war."*
   *"**Clive Ashman** cleverly draws us into the human drama of this ancient story through the adrenalin-packed 1940s tale of DI Michael Tryton, widowed by a German bombing raid on Hull, whose job it is to investigate the theft of a mosaic pavement discovered in a quarry in Brantingham, once belonging to Marcus Januarius. **MOSAIC is an exceptionally powerful yet subtle novel that provides a significant insight into what life was like during the late Roman Empire of Constantine by supplying a mass of modern-day parallels, and some neat circularities in the plot. Highly recommended."***
- **Tim Hewtson** (on various websites, incl. **amazon** & <u>**thisis'ull**</u>)

To find out more, with photos of real-life locations, go to: <u>www.voredabooks.com</u> - *'The Futures In Our Past'*